Robin Matchett lives in Ontario, Canada.

In the memory of Jack McClelland.

Robin Matchett

KENNEDY'S GHOSTS

AUSTIN MACAULEY PUBLISHERS™

LONDON ∗ CAMBRIDGE ∗ NEW YORK ∗ SHARJAH

Ordering Information
Quantity sales: Special discounts are available on quantity purchases by corporations, associations, and others. For details, contact the publisher at the address below.

Publisher's Cataloging-in-Publication data
Matchett, Robin
Kennedy's Ghosts

ISBN 9781638296294 (Paperback)
ISBN 9781638296300 (Hardback)
ISBN 9781638296317 (ePub e-book)

Library of Congress Control Number: 2022915239

www.austinmacauley.com/us

First Published 2023
Austin Macauley Publishers LLC
40 Wall Street, 33rd Floor, Suite 3302
New York, NY 10005
USA

mail-usa@austinmacauley.com
+1 (646) 5125767

I would like to thank Mark Satterthwaite for his assistance in editing this novel. As well as everyone who helped with the publication at Austin Macauley Publishers has my utmost appreciation. The challenge of writing novels is a lonely and sometimes daunting task but one I have always endured through life's many uncertainties. I would like to thank those who believed in my work from early on.

Part One

The greatest enemy of truth is very often not the lie—deliberate, contrived, and dishonest—but the myth—persistent, persuasive, and unrealistic...

President John F. Kennedy

1. New York – 21 March 1960

Pigeons scattered and ascended into the overcast sky as a yellow cab pulled to the curb across from a coffee shop. A frumpily dressed woman emerged and with a nimble step crossed the street and entered the premises. At the same time, a young man wearing an old navy raincoat, avoiding the cab, hurried across the street and stepped to the sidewalk. He stopped to watch the pigeons settle on a building ledge above the fray of the street. Most of the snow from a recent storm had melted, though it was still cold and did not feel like spring.

Entering Joe's Snack Bar, the man ordered his usual fare, having lunched there regularly. Today, he sat at his place along the wall-bench at a small table with a tea and corned-beef-on-rye, while next to him, the lady from the cab made an almost manic effort to scribble something down on a piece of note-paper. She had jet black hair, wore sunglasses, and dressed like a glorified bag-lady in jeans, plaid shirt, and shabby overcoat, which was piled in a heap next to her. He glanced over, as she turned to him momentarily as if sensing some intrusion, but went back to her task, indifferent to his presence. The man ate his sandwich and sipped his tea. But something about her caught his interest. He couldn't let it go.

'Apart from lunch,' he said for no apparent reason, 'I often come here to think.'

The woman paused for a moment without looking up. She said nothing.

He went on, 'I like to observe the rush of people.'

She put down her pencil and sat back.

'I come here to escape,' she said finally.

'I know what you mean, a kind of reprieve.'

'Oh, really? I hardly think so.'

'Naturally, we all have our own views; nonetheless, at least we have a common theme.'

She sat up, took a sip of her coffee, and looked over at him. He turned to meet her look then stared straight ahead, bemused.

'The only thing we have in common is that we're sitting beside each other.'

He laughed softly, turning to look at her again, the sunglasses staring back. Something about her intrigued him. She looked vaguely familiar. She turned away.

'Are you sure?' he asked, smiling. 'I meant no disrespect. What do you write?'

'Poetry.'

'Does it help with your escape?'

'It depends.'

He remained silent, trying to understand what he saw in her.

'I'm a writer as well,' he finally said.

'What do you write?' she asked.

'Oh, this and that. I've been writing for the Trib, nothing that important really. I'm a small fry in a big sea.'

'The Trib, huh; you're still young. What do you aspire to?'

'Investigative journalism; financial stability; independence. And you?'

'Maybe we do have something in common, in part.'

'Oh?' He sipped his tea. 'What's that?'

'Need for independence, respect.'

He looked at her. 'You seem to be doing well enough, writing poetry here alone, and young too. But I sense, if you don't mind me saying so, you're hiding from something. What are you afraid of?'

The woman stifled a laugh then sighed, her manner almost teasing.

'I'm not afraid of anything,' she declared, 'except failure, mediocrity.'

He nodded his head and looked away.

'A fate worse than death.'

She laughed again, putting her hand on his for a moment but then quickly removing it.

'What's so funny about that?' he asked. 'I'm serious.'

'Listen, whatever-your-name-is, we're all in the same boat. That's why I write poetry. It's like I get to jump from the boat into some life raft and go somewhere else. It doesn't matter where.'

'George Melbo, just Mel.'

The woman extended her right hand.

'Nora.'

Melbo took her hand and they shook briefly. Her hand was delicate and soft. He felt a ring. It surprised him as he noticed quickly the large-carat diamond. He looked at her and wanted to see her eyes behind the sunglasses.

'You never answered my question, Nora.'

'What?'

'What's so funny?'

Nora laughed again.

'Because you make me laugh I guess; I don't know—a moment of lightness, a crack opens up into my dark dungeon. Thank you, Mel.'

'You're welcome. I'm only too happy to oblige. But I don't like the sound of this dungeon. Don't feel put out if I'm ready to listen.'

'Forget it.'

She grabbed her notepad from the table and stuffed it in her bag.

'I should go.'

'Can I say something?' he asked.

'Shoot.'

'That ring you're wearing looks valuable, yet you dress down—it seems a paradox. It's none of my business, of course, but perhaps if you allow me—I know I'm a complete stranger—but I can pry open a little more light into that dungeon of yours. People have said I have a good effect on them.'

Nora sighed and stared out the window of the sandwich shop.

'What are you looking for: a story? Meeting a stranger in a sandwich shop for the back pages?'

Melbo shook his head. 'No, not at all; you're an interesting stranger. Sorry to impose.'

Nora looked down and took a moment to reply. 'Forget it. Don't mind me. You seem alright.'

'I'm a stranger too.'

'You're not a complete stranger,' she said turning her head to speak to him. 'We struck a chord. *I've* been known to do that.'

'Can I venture to say that you're beautiful behind your cover? Obviously, you don't want the attention.'

Nora deadpanned. 'Are you toying with me?'

'No. Why would I? But if it makes you smile…'

'It's a mask; remember, I'm in the dungeon.'

'In what way? A smile is a smile.'

She said nothing. Melbo gave her all the time in the world.

'Nora can smile, but my twin remains in the dungeon,' she finally said.

Melbo didn't answer for a moment. It reminded him suddenly of a country song he had known. Without looking at her, he sang the chorus quietly, almost a whisper:

Where it's dark as the dungeon,
And as damp as the dew,
Where the danger is double,
And the pleasures are few,
Where the rain never falls,
And the sun never shines,
Where it's dark as the dungeon,
Way down in the mine…

She shook her head, a smile on her face.

'That was really nice,' she said. In a moment, she added, 'I'm curious; how would you know that song?'

'Merle Travis. My mother used to play him a lot—it struck a chord, I suppose. Besides, I've written up on various musical venues: Jazz, Blues, Folk, and Nashville. I know my stuff.'

Nora looked at him. She raised her sunglasses for a moment, revealing sad blue eyes. Melbo couldn't for the life of him figure out what it was about her that he recognized. She wore no make-up, but the blue eyes, the lips, nose—especially the nose—and teeth when she smiled were incredibly distinct, yet the black hair and her apparel cast a veil over his mind.

'You're wise for your age, Mel. Where did you come from?'

'I was born here, but my mother's Canadian. I grew up mainly in Montreal. I moved here to study at Columbia.'

'And your father?'

'Killed in Normandy—August '44—at Mortain.'

'I'm sorry.'

'Yeah, I was eight the last time I saw him in '42.'

'A hero.'

'They were all heroes.'

Nora stood up.

'Come on, Mel; walk with me for a bit. Do you have to be anywhere?'

'No.'

Melbo stood and helped with her overcoat. They left the café and entered the noisy streets.

*

They walked east towards the Hudson River, Nora stepping jauntily in her runners. Melbo couldn't help but feel the stirrings of libido with this strange woman, her physical being permeating the dowdy cover of her clothing, like some hidden Venusian treasure. But he followed dutifully, with the thought of Melissa, his live-in girlfriend—who was also called Mel—never far from his mind. Then it occurred to him as they were crossing FDR Drive on a pedestrian bridge—the blood even rushed to his face. *How incredibly stupid*, he thought to himself.

He had to speed-frame their entire encounter—she was obviously wearing a wig, but it was her voice that fooled him. On screen it was affected, feminine; now it was lower, serious. They were leaning on the railing watching the East River. Her use of the word 'toying' leapt to mind: she suspected that he knew all along who she was. But now looking down at the estuarine current, she was talking about existence.

'If you must know, my twin lives a glib material life. Not petty or superficial, just doing what was expected of her, trying to be serious, yet always typecast as some dumb bombshell. And you know, looking back I had a choice, but I chose—'

'Fame,' interjected Melbo.

'I was going to say "success".'

'But success wasn't all that it was meant to be, Marilyn.'

Nora didn't react and kept looking into the turbid water, a foam collecting around some garbage along the cement bank.

'I realized just as we were crossing the bridge,' he said. 'But it doesn't change anything, Nora. You have my confidence.'

Marilyn smiled. 'You really do make me smile, Mel. Okay, say I believe you. What now?'

'Nothing really. Just carry on as two strangers.'

'Hmph! Really? I don't think so.'

'I won't write about this, if you're worried.'

'Worried? No. You don't understand me.'

'Well, what then?'

'Would it help you if you did? Write about me and Nora?'

'Don't you mean Norma Jeane?'

'Well, that would have ruined it. Had you known, we wouldn't be standing here.'

'I thought perhaps you thought that I knew.'

'It crossed my mind, but I gave you the benefit of the doubt.'

'Why?'

'Because you made me laugh, Mel! And you didn't answer my question.'

'Of course, it would help. But that's beside the point.'

'The point being?' she wondered.

Melbo had to think about that. He would not write anything if she didn't want him to. But it didn't seem to worry her one way or the other. She was looking at him.

'Take off your sunglasses,' he demanded.

'Why?'

He said nothing.

She shrugged and took them off to look at him seriously before opening her eyes wide and moving her head bug-eyed back and forth as if rubbing it in his face. Then she began laughing that quintessential Marilyn expression of innocent bemusement, her eyes brimming with glee, mouth open and teeth flashing. Melbo was stunned for a moment before breaking out in unabashed laughter.

There was a palpable chemistry here which seemed to erupt a spontaneous release as they escalated into hysterics. Gradually, the discharge ebbed. They caught their breath and turned to lean again on the railing and watch the languid river. Marilyn put her sunglasses back on.

'Oh, I feel so good now!' she exclaimed, finally.

'Me too,' said Melbo. 'Nothing like a good laugh to blow away troubles.'

'A good laugh? That felt almost psychotic! My sides ache!'

For a moment a tickle in their minds seemed almost to return the hysterics.

'No more,' said Melbo, post-winded. 'My head spins.'

They stood in a comfortable silence for a minute.

'Go ahead, Mel,' she said suddenly. 'Write your piece. I want our little episode immortalized.'

'Are you sure?'

'Of course, I'm sure. I see it as a cure.'

'Like an exit from the dungeon?'

'Yes, for now,' said Marilyn, her expression calm, almost sad.

'Only if you're completely behind me on it; I won't change a thing, but no quotations. Otherwise, it will be exactly as it happened. That's my way.'

'I respect that. I won't confirm or deny,' she said, turning to him smiling again. 'Except one thing: I want our little secret to stay secret.'

'What little secret?'

Marilyn took off her sunglasses with her left hand, then with her right reached to pull Melbo from the neck and kissed him full on the lips, her mouth parting and tongue penetrating his mouth, thrashing silkily for a few moments before letting him go. She remained close to his face, her eyes searching. Melbo didn't move. His mind was frozen in a fantasy that happened to be real. Then she turned and put back on her sunglasses.

'That,' she said. 'From Norma.'

'Whoa. Now all I see is that fated script which says: your place or mine.'

Marilyn turned to him again, her head cocked one way. 'Yes, instinct is a wholesome thing. I haven't had sex in ages.'

'But Mel wouldn't approve.'

'Mel? Why not?' His speaking in the third person confused her.

'Melissa.'

'Oh!' She laughed, a bit anti-climactic.

'We live together. And I love her.'

'That's adorable. Mel and Mel. How do you keep track of each other?' she asked, almost sadly. 'I feel envy, like I just lost you.'

'Maybe it's like twins; we become one and just know.'

'Now I'm jealous.'

'Jealous? You mean to say lonely.'

'You're right, actually. I want love, enduring love, and all my love is a spectacle built on hype and power, and power is the opposite of love. Then I hurt people, or they hurt me. Miller is destroying me. Joe loved me, and I destroyed him. Tit for tat, I guess. I deserve my loneliness; I really loved Arthur but now we're just waiting for new lovers to show up and be damned.'

Melbo let that sink in. They both watched the river, just staring, not seeing.

17

'Loneliness can be a catalyst to a higher love,' he said. 'I get lonely too.'

'You're right again, dammit.' She smiled the most melancholy smile. 'I'm so spoiled.'

'Let me walk you home, Norma Jeane, if you want.'

'I don't mind.' She turned around, pulling his arm and putting hers through his.

'Where to?'

'Don't you know?'

'Why should I?'

'Oh, I could love you, Mel. You're perfect for me.'

'Because I don't know where you live?'

'Yeah. Something like that.'

'But that's no reason to love me.'

'Love moves in mysterious ways.' She was laughing again.

'You seem awfully happy to be in a dungeon.'

Her laugh turned into a giggle. 'North, my friend, 444 West 57th.'

'Ah, of course. I should know that, shouldn't I?'

'Yes, you should.' She now held his arm with both hands.

'That's a fair hike uptown,' he said, as he shook her arms loose and put his arm around her shoulder. She wrapped hers around his waist.

'You'll have to explain to Mel that Marilyn has a crush on you.'

'Mel is very understanding.'

'Don't be too sure. Women are outrageously self-centered.'

'Not Mel.'

'That's very noble of you, and I know I don't stand a chance with you, not that I would even think of it, but the better a woman makes it appear so—that's she's cool so-to-speak, all the more self-seeking she is. Women have thousands of millennia of dealing with men who have to control them. It's in our genes to make men love us and not hurt us.'

'Are you sure it's not the other way around?'

Marilyn laughed before becoming pensive. 'Perhaps that is our mystery.'

'I'll let Mel know that. I'm sure she would agree.'

Marilyn gave him a pinch on his waist.

'Ow!'

'We are ruthless, as lovers. I want to meet Mel.'

Melbo just smiled. 'That can be arranged.'

'Good, now it's settled. When I'm back in New York,' she stated.

'When's that?'

'I don't know; in the fall. I'm doing a picture or two out West this summer.'

Melbo removed his arm from her shoulder. He could see how a relationship with Marilyn would be like chasing a chameleon. She let go as well.

'What?' she asked.

'Nothing. Just wondering what it would be like being in a relationship with you.'

'Nothing? That's something. Do I detect a weakness, Mel?'

Melbo looked ahead. 'I'd be foolish not to think about it, and foolish to even consider it. What's the movie?'

She stopped walking. 'It's never foolish to consider happiness. My mistakes had other considerations.'

Melbo stopped as well. 'Happiness and love are not necessarily compatible, yet inclusive to each in a couple.'

'Exactly. You're so dammed astute!'

They continued to walk on their way.

'One's called *Misfits*, something my husband cooked up before we were married. He should've waited a few years!'

They both laughed.

'I appreciated his great skill with *The Crucible*, and *Salesman*. But depressing,' said Melbo, hesitating. 'Not really my cup of tea.'

'*Misfits* is different. Gable's on board, and Huston's directing.'

'I wouldn't want to speculate with those guys. Give it your best shot, Marilyn.'

'Oh, I will, if I can get off some meds and remember my lines!'

'Meds. I didn't know.'

'I can't seem to cope without them—some for waking and some for sleeping. I'd need someone like you to be without them.'

'And how long would that last?'

'I'd quit the movies and have kids; be a good mother. Seriously. I know what's good for me. I would drift into sweet obscurity…Norma Jean Melbo,' she said wistfully.

They both laughed again.

'I don't know if you're joking or not,' said Melbo.

'Neither do I!'

Melbo didn't respond. He knew it was all a fantasy. They walked on in a comfortable silence.

2. Flying Saucers

Late that same day, after Mel submitted his piece about his strange meeting with 'Nora' to his boss Richard 'Dick' Sinclair, he had second thoughts. Dick was delighted, and suggested something about a follow-up, perhaps a series, and all Melbo could think of was how that would betray the spirit of their meeting. George Kane Melbo, known to his few friends as Mel, was an aspiring journalist and reviewer for the New York Herald Tribune. With his long lanky looks, unkempt dark wavy hair, and sad blue eyes, one might have thought he was more artist or bohemian from the Village dressed in his unkempt flannels, unlaundered shirt, loose tie, blazer, and scuffed loafers, and indeed he did spend time there as a reviewer for the latest live music or art scene.

Oddly assuming, even amiable with a ready smile, he was not the kind that epitomized someone angling for a scoop; he earned the trust of others by being naturally friendly, and being friendly often became friendship. Born during the Depression and decidedly socialist, Melbo was an anomaly in that he worked for a decidedly right-leaning paper in the Rockefeller Republican pro-business and internationalist tradition; he had been lucky, and scored a few well-received pieces much lauded by his editor boss, and peers. His best articles, written in his simple, sharp prose and showing hints of wit without being cheeky, tended to underscore his paper's token nod to the underclass.

'So what do you think, Mel?' queried Sinclair, with his smug leer and dark penetrating eyes.

Melbo was caught in a freeze frame. His mind just jammed shut with the idea he could replicate what had happened. On one hand it might be agreeable to Marilyn to meet again, but to continue their arrangement like a serial tabloid had to be completely unrealistic. On the other hand, Norma Jeane might find some inspiration in it, not to mention her need to smile and feel good about herself.

'Melbo!' Sinclair snapped his fingers in front of him.

'I don't know, boss. I'm thinking.'

'Can't hurt to try,' he said.

'No, I suppose not.'

'Well, I'll leave it with you. With a dame like Monroe, it's a crap-shoot anyway.'

'She's not what she appears in the movies.'

'I don't doubt it,' said Sinclair, 'but that's how she comes across, and we all buy into it.'

'Therein is a tragedy.'

'Nah, she's got it made, man!'

'I'm not so sure, Dick.'

'Did you see *Some Like It Hot*?'

'Yup.'

'The girl's a miracle.'

'She did win a Golden Globe.'

Sinclair went pensive. Melbo turned to leave his office.

'We'll run it Saturday in the society column,' said Sinclair behind him. 'Oh, how about this: I have another job for you. I pulled Raymond Chester from it. He's just too cynical, stodgy—I have some personal interest in this. But you, you have the smarts for it.'

Melbo had turned and stood in the doorway. 'I'm listening.'

'I'll brief you more next week. There have been some statements from the Pentagon about these weird sightings lately around DC and elsewhere. UFOs. I think we need to look into it.'

'Unidentified Flying Objects,' said Melbo. 'I've often wondered about them; some claim that they're definitely not anything that can be explained rationally as they exhibit technology unknown to man at present; others, I gather, who haven't seen them, consider them to be illusions.'

'Amounts the same thing, doesn't it? Meaning they're real.'

'What else are we to conclude? What do you think?' wondered Melbo.

Sinclair opened the bottom drawer of his desk and took out a newspaper which he then slapped down. Melbo returned from the doorway and picked up the paper the front page of which showed a photo of numerous objects at night in formation over the Capitol, with the headlines *FLYING SAUCERS OVER WASHINGTON*.

'Washington Post, July 12, 1952.'

'Eight years ago I was with the Post,' Sinclair said earnestly, 'I happened to be outside near where I lived and saw the whole thing. These strange lights flew in formation and took off at right angles at impossible speeds, then appeared again. It didn't seem humanly possible, but I saw it. Thousands saw it.'

'How did the authorities explain it?'

'They couldn't very well say they were weather balloons, could they? There were a number of sightings that month, and jets were scrambled but couldn't get near them. I spoke to somebody in the military who told me confidentially that it was figured these disk-like ships could fly 20,000 miles an hour! And turn at right angles on a dime to go in some other direction.'

'Surreal,' said Melbo, scrutinizing the article.

'Yeah, and the government isn't talking, except to say that there are some unnatural and unusual phenomenon that can't be explained.'

'Bullshit. They probably didn't know what to say because they couldn't get near them.'

'Oh, don't kid yourself: they know something. In '47 a disk crashed near Corona, New Mexico and the Roswell Daily had the news on their front page. The news spread all over America before the military contained it claiming it was just a crashed weather balloon. But the ranchers who first responded all said otherwise before being told to shut up and had to make a retraction. Now that's news! But where are we today? Nowhere.'

'Yes, I'm aware of that; I remember my mother talking about it.'

'Good.'

'What about Project Blue Book? Who was that professor involved in it?' asked Melbo.

'Hynek. There were other projects as well before Blue Book.'

'There was that pilot who saw a formation of UFOs near Mount Rainier, Washington, which prompted the press to coin the term "flying saucers".

'Kenneth Arnold. That just preceded the Roswell Incident.'

'And Hynek? What do you think is his position on all this?'

'Well, he's obviously researching it, but my belief is that it's a double blind—an official response to the hysteria in the early fifties, but meant to put a lid on the truth and keep the public fooled.'

'Are you saying Hynek is trying to prove what the military officials want to disprove in regards to the reality of UFOs?'

'Sounds about right, but I want you to make your own inquiries without getting involved with the military.'

'And Hynek?'

'He's on a short leash, I'm afraid; best keep away from him for now.'

'I'm intrigued,' responded Melbo. 'I never really put any stock in the sightings—people see things, but what you say may have some tangible truth to it. If I were in the military, and in the loop with respect to this information, if true, I'd keep a lid on it too until I knew what the hell was going on.'

They stood quietly for a few moments contemplating the implications.

'Right,' stated Sinclair, 'It opens up a whole slew of possibilities. Take science and technology; and where the hell do these people—if they are people—come from?'

'Well, you've got my curiosity spiked.'

'Good, good, but we've got to separate the wheat from the chaff. We have a duty here to get to the bottom of it with credible sources.'

'Next week then.'

'Yeah.'

*

In the lobby of his apartment, Melbo noticed his girlfriend, Melissa DeCourt, standing at the elevator. Quietly, he approached and stood beside her for a few moments until she turned around.

'Well, aren't you the sly one,' she said.

'Hi, darling. Couldn't help myself. Your beauty had me tongue-tied.'

DeCourt smiled deliciously.

'Oh, I see. Flattery, is it? I know you better than that, Mel. Who is she?'

Melbo laughed. 'She was right. You're just too cool. And I love you too.'

When the elevator arrived, DeCourt entered quickly into the empty car and pressed 12 as the door closed behind Melbo.

DeCourt said nothing. Melbo looked at her; at twenty-one years of age, she carried herself with the poise and confidence of an older woman. She had rebelled against her family to live with him unmarried—*en flagrante*—in their eyes a mortal sin. But she had earned some begrudging respect, at least from her mother, for her unexpected success at Simon & Schuster as a junior assistant in marketing for a huge new output of educational classics including Tom Sawyer, Huckleberry Finn, Robinson Crusoe, Lorna Doone, The Three Musketeers, Ivanhoe, and others.

He loved her profile. She knew him very well and let him take it in—almost gloating in the attention. She was wearing her stylish wide collar, short-to-her-knees navy Olga coat semi-swing skirt effect with a fabric tie-belt, which made her appear slim, as she had a lovely figure. Her tight black slacks were rather risqué—a kind of personal pre-emptive sixties trend, as well as her simple black ankle boots with inside zipper and two inch heels—all a bit *chic*.

Her hair semi-long, a luscious brunette done straight, her fair skin and aquiline nose, pursed dark cherry lips, and graceful jawline gave off an air of equanimity, even softness which reminded him of some feminine mystique better suited to his imagination. She sighed and turned to Melbo, her watery blue eyes searching his. He took her in his arms and kissed her gently on the mouth.

'Needless to say, Mel, you're my best dream girl in the flesh.'

'Mmm,' she murmured, 'and you're a rascal.'

'Am I? I had a very successful day.'

'I'm dying to hear about it.'

'It was no contest, sweet.'

'I should hope so,' she said, releasing him.

'I had lunch with Marilyn Monroe, well, I should say, Nora, a noir-wigged bohemian bag lady.'

'You're kidding,' she uttered.

The elevator doors opened. DeCourt exited and Melbo followed.

'I had no idea who she was sitting beside me at Joe's.'

'Seriously?'

In their apartment, she hung up her coat.

'Yes, emphatically.'

She poured them both a glass of white wine from an open bottle in the fridge and handed him one. She leaned back against the counter taking a sip. Melbo explained the entire story to her, ending up with his conversation about aliens with Dick Sinclair.

'She wants to meet me?' she retorted, surprised. 'Forget the aliens. Sounds like she's starved for love.'

'Yes, a bit of a paradox, being the reigning goddess of love.'

'Poor woman, I feel sorry for her; I mean, she's amazing, but...'

'Who are we to judge?'

'I beg to differ; she kissed you.'

'I think it was all an act—she doesn't know what she wants.'

'You, evidently.'

'Babe, I promised to keep it a secret between us, and was quite firm with her on that; and that's the truth. The whole episode was actually quite commonplace.'

'I can think of a better choice of word, Mel. Firm?' She laughed. 'But then again you betrayed your promise with her—Marilyn—most men would have lied to their women about it.'

'I feel bad about that.'

'But not too bad.'

Melbo demurred. 'She bared her soul, Mel. She let me run with it. And wants more.'

DeCourt put her wineglass on the counter and moved to him, her eyes sparkling.

'I know that look,' said Melbo.

'I think I'd better stake my claim, George.' She puts her hand to his crotch and gently strokes his pants. 'Where is he? Where's my George?'

Melbo looked at her. 'Mel, Mel...God, you're beautiful when you look like that.'

'A little pent up, are we?'

'You could say that.'

DeCourt lowered herself to her knees, gently pushing Melbo back onto a kitchen chair.

'I think we need to blow off some steam. I'm feeling a little giddy myself.'

*

Later in bed, they laid quietly in a stupor. Melbo had his arm around DeCourt's neck with his hand lightly caressing her pert rosy-nippled breast.

'I feel like pizza,' said DeCourt, as if in a trance.

'Okay, let's order in.'

'Angelo's.'

'What do you want?'

'Oh, olives, bacon, shrimp, eggplant, peppers, mushrooms, the usual.'

'Do I get a choice?'

'No.'

'Even after your monster orgasm?'

'What about yours?' she retorted.

'A tyrannosaurus.'

DeCourt laughed. 'I'm still throbbing.'

'You pumped me dry, twice.'

'You came so hard the first time I could barely keep from choking.'

'You're a devil.'

'I am for you,' she said, matter-of-factly.

'I love you, Mel, but I want pepperoni with extra cheese.'

'You always want pepperoni with extra cheese.'

Melbo removed his hand and arm and swung out of the bed to put on his underwear. He didn't really mind her choice of pizza, but he liked to make his pitch anyway. Besides, he had a lot on his mind in spite of monster sex.

Melbo smiled and looked at her.

'Have it your way,' he said. 'But you order.'

Later, after a ravenous wolfing of pizza in their little living room watching the latest episode of *Rawhide*, they settled down to do some reading. Melbo couldn't concentrate. He had been reading Kerouac's *On the Road* on and off for a week or two. He loved the wild beatnik freedoms and semi-mythical *Americana* of hoboes and their romanticized rootless travels which led him to dream about a different life, an opening up of a poetic conception of super-nature—a place where he found utopia. Then on the other hand, the realist in him took hold in the unlikeliest of books, Blish's *A Case of Conscience* a sci-fi work that he had read recently.

He considered the book provocative but it occurred to him that a difference of space-travelling civilizations—one a utopia, and the other as Earth imposing its authority in a religious hegemony of sorts, should not end with the entire destruction of the utopian planet. It seemed to Melbo, a tragic human story, much like that of the Europeans conquering the New World. But what compelled his thinking was how we could possibly understand another civilization that was perhaps tens of thousands or millions of years ahead of us technologically?

Reflecting on his conversation with Dick Sinclair, it occurred to him that if these space-faring people had come to Earth, their elusiveness suggested that they certainly did not want to meet us since they likely anticipated a primitive response. Moreover, given that as a race we were still fighting out our terrestrial differences and were determinedly Earth-bound, we were on the whole a polluting, savage dystopic people, if Hitler and Stalin were any indication. It was as if we could go back in time to medieval Europe and be expected to be received with open arms!

These aliens, whoever they were, were likely very cautious of such an unevolved species as ours on the cusp of a potential atomic conflagration. We were dangerous! We would project our worst fears onto an alien species, as we often did in movies and books. Space invaders! Melbo considered that if these aliens came here from across the vast heavens, they had probably already visited numerous other life-giving planets and had no need to take ours, assuming that conquest was antithetical to their way of thinking.

Besides, he thought, maybe they had been coming here for a long time, millennia perhaps, curious about and wanting to observe our development. It could even be that they had something to do with us in prehistoric times when we were little more than cave people. Melbo was reminded of his friend, Ben Johnson, who studied archaeology, and used to regale him with speculations about the Sumerians having invented Adam and Eve before the ancient Hebrews. Johnson said that all indications seem to suggest that some form of hybridization happened long ago, and that our biblical forebears—now considered mythological to anyone but the orthodox—were in fact actual prototypes of present humanity—an historical fact according to many corroborating pan-world writings from antiquity.

DeCourt looked up from her own book, Tolkien's *The Return of the King* and stared at Melbo who was gazing at some place between the ceiling and the wall.

'Mel,' she said, 'having second thoughts about Marilyn?'

Melbo turned to her quizzically. 'Are you kidding? I was out in space trying to understand alien consciousness.'

DeCourt laughed. 'Jack Kerouac not up to snuff?'

'Well, it got me thinking—all work related. What if it's true? These aliens? As a serious journalist, I've to come up with some pertinent questions.'

'What makes you think they'd even stoop to answer them if you could actually interview them? The aliens.'

'You're right. The idea of an interview wouldn't likely be within their psyche.'

'I can't believe Dick wants you to investigate whatever it is he thinks he knows.'

Melbo shook his head. 'Yes, but there must be some explanation for the phenomenon.'

'If there's any truth to it and it hasn't been made public, there's got to be a good reason.'

'You mean something sinister?'

'Well, put it this way: I've never known you to come away from a story without the unequivocal truth, or at least the best take on it.'

'And you think I may be looking for trouble,' stated Melbo.

'Look, maybe someone knows something and they sure aren't telling,' said DeCourt forcefully. 'And if you go snooping around where you're not wanted … Well, I just don't like it.'

'I see it as a challenge in the spirit of our hard-won freedoms.'

'You're incorrigible.'

3. The Eyes of Liberty

On a beautiful sunny April day, seagulls shrieked over the water of Battery Park at the southern tip of Manhattan. The Statue of Liberty stood resolutely out beyond the large expanse of the Hudson River opening into the Upper Bay estuary. The ferry had docked and Melbo and DeCourt joined this crowd of New Yorkers and tourists eager to board with their children. They had never been to see the statue and thought it was as good as any time to see it. DeCourt was delighted and brought some sandwiches, fruit and a thermos of coffee. But unknown to her, Melbo had been waiting a number of weeks for a meeting with someone Dick Sinclair had proposed for him to meet, an old nameless acquaintance of his from the war years who would find him.

This fellow, Harley Greenfield, had retired from the intelligence services having come into a little money. He could not now be reached except through an answering service to which Sinclair simply left his name in order to not arouse suspicion.

Not long after, Sinclair received a postcard from St. Thomas in the Virgin Islands. Greenfield would look him up when he returned to New York. Ten days later Sinclair and his old friend caught up with each other over dinner at Sinclair's Central Park apartment. Sinclair's wife, Alecia, called Aly, came from a wealthy Virginian tobacco land-holding family near Charlottesville and cooked up a favorite buttermilk fried chicken dinner with hominy creamed grits and baked green tomatoes in a sweet red pepper sauce. Then peach pie and whipped cream washed down with vintage colonial Bourbon and afterward old time Virginian cigars for the men.

The men, now alone in the study, reminisced about their times during the war, when Sinclair was a foreign correspondent under cover as an agent for the OSS, and Greenfield was his counterpart. They laughed occasionally and toasted lost friends with due solemnity; then after another moment of levity, they fell silent, puffing contentedly on their cigars, when Sinclair put out his feelers.

'Harley, I've been meaning to ask you something; I hope it doesn't impinge on our friendship in any way. I have in my employ a young top-notch reporter who I've assigned to a most compelling task. Let me digress-'

Greenfield put up his hand. 'If this is about those Nazi scientists and intelligence wonks we whitewashed or re-settled here, well the cat's out of the bag on that. No one condemns us today for our advances in rocket technology thanks to them—Doctors Oberst and Braun at least. We're miles ahead of the Soviets in spite of Sputnik.'

'Well,' responded Sinclair, 'I know there have been enquiries and articles to that end. Still our hypocrisy as Americans when having defeated true evil then allied ourselves with some of them to justify fighting another evil, well, it still doesn't jibe with me.'

'We were *all* unprepared for the thuggery and deceit of Stalin,' concurred Greenfield. 'His totalitarianism was equally as insidious as the Nazi one we defeated.'

Sinclair crowed, 'But I'm quite proud of my war record in that regard because the war wasn't really over was it? I saw it firsthand from the rubble of Berlin in May '45; you remember I foresaw what that bastard Stalin would refuse to free Eastern Europe like he'd promised at Yalta, basically substituting his tyranny from Hitler's. But everybody was too sick of war to challenge him overtly.'

'We've known each other over twenty years, Dick, and between us we've always had that proclivity (for lack of a better word) to truth, which gave us some ballast in a duplicitous world. So before you go on don't be offended if I'm still dodging bullets. Hey, I'm all ears, and maybe I can point you in the right direction. I mean were talking about freedom of the press, right? If there's anything in this goddamned world I fight for, it's that. Hell, if everyone believed as we did, there would be no war, hot or cold, because evil would be aired for what it is before freedom got usurped as under Hitler and Stalin and the Bolshies. Law abiding decent people won't stand for thuggery, lies and manipulation. Am I wrong?'

'I suppose, as long as that doesn't preclude the conditions made ripe for manipulation, as in pre-war Germany and revolutionary Russia— impoverishment and anti-Semitism.'

'Come on, we're way beyond that. Everyone knows our standard of living

31

is coveted everywhere. America rules, man.'

'I know that, but Harley, it's up to us to keep it straight, right? Power is not known for its fidelity to integrity, or fiduciary probity for that matter. We as citizens must always be vigilant.'

'And you shall know the truth and the truth shall make you free,' quoted Greenfield.

'John: 8:32—that great motto for spooks, because it's a smokescreen.'

Greenfield eased himself back in his chair, blowing smoke towards the ceiling. Clean-shaven, at fifty-seven, his ruddy, tanned face had the look of a good-natured Rottweiler. Born of an American father and French mother, expressive blue eyes shone brightly below a shock of pepper-white hair still apparently wind-blown from the Caribbean trade-winds. His generous girth was more athletic than fat which bespoke someone living well while suggesting a kind of avuncular menace lurking below the surface. Greenfield had been the sharp point of the clandestine services: a reliable saboteur of key objectives and killer of Nazis behind the lines in '44 and '45, then as an operative against the Soviets in the early cold war, and finally an agent handler-case officer until his self-imposed retirement a few years ago.

In contrast, Sinclair, a lithe, mercurial balding man seemed almost a comical compliment. There was a Dick Tracy ambience about him, especially when he wore his hat low over his eyes on the street. His movements were quick and specific to a purpose. No one second-guessed him. Only Greenfield knew his Achilles heel: he was light-weight better suited to public life and had been turned down as a potential agent when Truman endorsed the CIA in 1947 because as a newsman his ethics were considered rather inflexible if called upon for deadly subterfuge; yet he was deemed a friendly asset in terms of news filtering, though uncalled upon.

'Dick, you're getting me all choked up here,' said Greenfield. 'Spit it out, ol' buddy.'

'Now don't laugh: I need to find some information on these flying disks—UFOs. What do you know?'

'Who's this young Turk of a reporter you mentioned?'

'George Melbo.'

'Well, tell him to tread very carefully.'

'Are you saying these phenomena are officially real?'

'I'm saying I don't know a damn thing about them, and that's God's truth.'

'Then why the warning?' asked Sinclair.

'Project Blue Book. It's the official response for the benefit of public inquiry. The government is leaving no stone unturned to protect their vested interests. It's a control operation.'

'You're kidding, right?'

'Dick, do you see me laughing? I get it: I remember you going on about it years ago when you were in Washington. You witnessed something; a lot of people saw them, and that's about the long and short of it. Leave it be.'

'Harley, you told me then there was something to it. You said a friend of a friend in tech and science came in like a ghost one day after being reassigned to look into it.'

'Yeah, yeah, but sharing classified information is something we were trained absolutely to resist, and nobody talked. You move on.'

'I'm just trying to get something to report. This is news, Harley. The public has a right to it.'

'Nobody's stopping anyone from writing about UFOs.'

'That's not my point, and you know it. From what we can gather some high-level group in the government has locked out all of our attempts to find out about it. They don't even admit that there's anything out there! We need information!'

'The question is: what is out there?' suggested Greenfield. 'Listen, I know it's frustrating. But if you're in the loop of the alien thing, who are we to judge? All you have to do is read some strange sci-fi novel and figure the truth to be something like that. How do they get here? Where are they from? Do they eat cheeseburgers?'

Sinclair smiled. 'Do you remember James Forrestal?'

'Of course.'

'He supposedly fell to his death out of a tiny bathroom window sixteen floors up in the Bethesda Naval hospital. The former Secretary of Defense? Committing suicide? His brother Henry said it was impossible; he'd never do it; he was supposed to be going home shortly; he had been kept there against his will because of 'mental exhaustion'; someone didn't want him going home; someone didn't want him talking; there was a high-up difference of opinion, and Forrestal, a highly principled man known for his judgement and decency, had obviously disagreed with someone over something; something so classified, so secret…and it certainly wasn't the atom bomb anymore.'

Greenfield blew some more smoke. 'Sure, Dick; there's something going on, and if you think they're ready to kill a Secretary of Defense, don't think they'll hesitate to come after you or your cut-out Melbo.'

'But Harley, this is America! Don't you see what's happening here? It may appear foolish of me to think there could be a cabal of individuals who are operating without any congressional or official oversight, because we the public are being shut out! It's unconstitutional! What could be so secret?'

'Two words: national security, and perhaps a whole bunch of pertinent appendages such as technology, disease, politics, and perhaps something so out of our element they must ask: are we ready for the truth about UFOs?'

'Ready or not, the sooner the better; better us than the Commies,' stated Sinclair.

'Hell, there's a cold war with the Commies; it's mean and dirty—what better leverage than the threat of superior technology.'

'Leverage yes, they're cooking up something no doubt,' nodded Sinclair.

'Meaning we're likely on the right path. You remember the Corona crash in 1947 near Roswell? Originally reported by first responders as an alien disk with bodies? The army moved in and shut it down, swore those few involved to secrecy or else, and claimed it was a weather balloon! But you and I and a lot of others know it was a cover up. Hell, it's an open secret! By now, thirteen years later they should've gleaned something from it—reverse engineered their technology if possible, and whatever else they discovered.'

'Yes, absolutely,' said Sinclair adamantly, 'but this is different, out of our depth—what does it all mean? What do they know—the aliens? Where do we fit in the big picture? I can't fathom it. As a newsman it stinks, and I aim to use my position to find out about it. Doesn't it touch you down deep? I mean, this is the most important news in the entire history of humanity! We're not alone!'

'And they seem to want to pretend it's something we don't deserve or not intelligent enough to understand,' replied Greenfield. 'I agree that, at the very least, they could've said we're not alone.'

'Exactly. It's belittling, patronizing. What right have they? What right?' Sinclair poured himself another two fingers of Bourbon.

Greenfield held out his glass. 'Then let's make a toast to Secretary Forrestal,' he said. 'And to truth!'

'To truth,' Sinclair raised his glass.

They sat there for some time contemplating the awesome implications of their assumptions.

'Dick,' said Greenfield finally, and rising from his seat, 'you know I'd always stick up for you. Let me get back to you. I'll meet your Melbo and tell him whatever I can find out. But we do it my way, okay?'

'Sure, Harley, you know the ropes.'

'I wish it were as simple as that.'

*

At half past noon, Melbo and DeCourt found a relatively isolated patch of grass opposite from the main landing docks of Liberty Island. Melbo spread the thin blanket in the sunlight between some trees near which a robin hopped along nearby poking for worms. Earlier they had climbed the stairs inside the statue that had been forged in Paris in the 19th century in commemoration of the centennial of the American Revolution. Originally designed by Frédéric Bartholdi and constructed by Gustave Eiffel, it symbolized on its crown the iconic spiked aureole of sunrays depicting the seven seas and continents as a beacon of freedom, with her arm and hand outstretched holding aloft the symbolic torch enlightening the way for seafarers and immigrants alike.

At the top they had stood silently looking out from inside the windows within the crown gazing out to New York and New Jersey all around, and the vast blue Atlantic to the south and east through the Lower Bay estuary. As if through the very eyes of Liberty herself, they looked upon the horizon, to which so many had come seeking refuge from war, persecution, and tyranny.

Even as a Canadian, at least half, and perhaps more in spirit, Melbo saw the impressive statue as an apt testament to a better world, a "Brave New World", he quoted Shakespeare. DeCourt had looked at him when he said that. He looked at her unsure whether he was being cynical or sincere in consideration of his present occupational assignment. DeCourt squeezed his hand in reassurance either way.

'You seem remote today, Mel,' said DeCourt, as they ate lunch.

'I feel remote. For two weeks I've been digging into archives of various newspapers from across the country for anything that might give me a better idea about what I'm after—some indication of what is really happening.'

'It's telling in itself.'

'Literally every article I find that reports some anomaly in the sky by numerous witnesses is debunked by the cynical tone that it's conveyed in as if the witnesses were all unreliable.'

'What would you expect?' queried DeCourt. 'Without some official cooperation—some verification, some interaction—no self-serving paper is going to endorse alien visitation no matter how obvious it is. Dick was one of thousands who saw those UFOs over Washington and he's been stymied.'

'Yeah, I know, but it tells you by the government's conspicuous silence, something big, really big is going on.'

'All one has to do is think of the implications.'

'That's all I think about.'

*

While they ate lunch, Melbo and DeCourt had been unaware of a middle-aged man accompanied by a beautiful woman who had also boarded the same ferry from Battery Park concealed in the crowd as the ferry churned across the water. He with a shock of pepper-white hair and tan with no hat, and dressed in a light casual suit and tie; and she wore her dark auburn hair neatly tied in a prim pony-tail. His larger build and her slim constitution appeared incongruous though their comfort together seemed rather unaffected as a natural couple.

Later, after disembarking the ferry, one hundred feet away behind a large tree, and gazing out to the expanse of water stood the man and the woman. Wearing sunglasses, she was cool and lithe, clad in dark brown corduroy slacks, a light gray sweater with a shoulder-slung brown leather hand-bag and tan ankle boots. People milled about the couple, who seemed as much a part of a perfect day as anyone else.

'The offer is ever-present, Hannah,' said Greenfield. 'You know there's no one else; you know I love you. Besides, I admit I'm lonely. I need a first mate.'

'Oh, Harley, but you're retired and I'm still running laps in the service. Is this why you insisted I come here with you today?'

'No, actually; I told you it was a favor for a friend. '

'All a bit mysterious,' she replied, brightening.

'Well, what better excuse to see you? You have never said no, even after Moscow.'

'I'm not saying no: and Moscow, that was at least five years ago…well, we had a whizz-bang, or two. I'm just saying I'm not ready.'

'I'm not pushing, sweet. I'm just thinking about you. It's not too late to have a family.'

'Oh, appealing to my biological clock, are you? You really are quite the knave.'

'You've always brought out the boy in me.'

Prinzenthal laughed. 'You're twenty years older than me—and what about *your* biological clock?'

'Are you saying this old goat can't get it up?'

'You're a corpulent old goat.'

'I'm not fat! Look.' He hits himself in the stomach; it's hard, not a beer-belly, protruding. 'Feel it yourself.'

Prinzenthal felt his belly, and pursed her lips. 'Not bad.'

'Everybody thickens pushing sixty,' he said, mollified. 'I'm as fit as a fiddle.'

She turned from him and looked across the water.

Greenfield had loved her since the first day he ever set eyes on her back in Berlin, 1945, but Hannah Prinzenthal was a career spy like Greenfield, and typically elusive. Even at thirty-seven, her sharp hazel eyes, high cheekbones, and creamy complexion had such a youthful yet pensive appearance, her silhouette made as if giving off an electric charge. She had a Germanic-Slav combination both demure and tempting, an exotic creature, a veritable *Lilith*. Greenfield had always liked to think that all the upheaval of revolution and civil war at the time of her conception had imbued her with a much sought-after peaceful disposition, but she was smart and tentative.

Her mother, Mrs. Lyubov Prinzenthal (née Ephrussi, Hannah's middle name), was descended in part from minor Russian aristocracy, and settled soon after the Bolshevik Revolution first in Lvov, Poland, where Hannah was born (now western Ukraine since the Second World War) then Paris. Mrs. Prinzenthal and her husband, both Jews, had fled Russia because their friends were being rounded up and disappearing at a fearful pace.

Hannah grew up speaking Yiddish, Russian, German, and some Ukrainian at home and learned Polish and French growing up in Poland and France, and English in school. Her story was ultimately tragic in that her father, Dr. David Prinzenthal, a Ukrainian diplomat, considered a paragon of the *intelligentsia*, known in wide circles of Eastern Europe, would surely have been murdered or sent to the Gulag had they stayed, when he was ironically murdered by fascists after they emigrated to France. Hannah's father was part Bessarabian German whose ancestors had emigrated to southern Ukraine and the Crimea from Alsace and Bavaria in the 18th and 19th centuries. There were even some Prussian ancestors.

With their connections, the émigrés had moved to Paris in 1929, and when Hannah was twelve in 1934, they moved finally to New York after her father's demise, triggered by his having written successfully for a socialist paper, in which he denounced extremism left and right. The world was going very dark, especially for the Jews.

In New York, Hannah Prinzenthal blossomed into a beautiful, brilliant all-American girl, and learned to speak English like an American. By the time she was eighteen and enrolled with a scholarship to Columbia University studying linguistics and history, she had been spotted by scouts from the State Department. Since there was a dire shortage of qualified translators, while completing her degree, she worked part time translating Russian, German, Polish, French and a few Ukrainian documents.

One thing led to another, and as the war raged and America became embroiled, she was upon graduation recruited immediately by the fledgling OSS. A new name and cover were bestowed on her in short order. She was sent to the American embassy in Moscow as an Assistant to the Assistant Attaché and various senior officials. Well liked, she lived and breathed her new identity as Judith Graham, an East Coast Ivy Leaguer, in whose cover story both parents were deceased.

Mrs. Prinzenthal and Hannah had previously subsisted on the Lower East Side in a tenement, until her mother had been a beneficiary of a modest inheritance from her deceased family after the war, and they moved into a three bedroom apartment with a view of Central Park. Judith Graham was rarely home, having discreetly told her mother she was doing her part for the war effort as a translator in the State Department, and after in Europe.

'So who are we to meet then, Harley?' she asked. 'The suspense is killing me.'

'A reporter who works for Dick Sinclair at the Herald Tribune.'

'Are you kidding me?'

'It's not what you think.'

'What am I supposed to think?'

'They're the young couple sitting over there behind us eating lunch.' Greenfield motioned with his head. 'We'll amble over and introduce ourselves.'

'As what? Harley and Hannah, or John and Judith?'

'The latter, of course.'

Prinzenthal shook her head. 'This has to be the most ridiculous thing you've ever conned me into doing. What on earth for?'

'Dick wants him to write an article, or articles on the UFO phenomenon—to get to the bottom of it.'

'Now I get it; you think I'm privy to some insider info about UFOs? They're as big a mystery to me as anyone! Harley, I'm going home!' Prinzenthal turned to walk away.

Greenfield said quietly, 'You once told me you slept with Jack Kennedy in Potsdam during the time of the Big Three meetings.'

Prinzenthal stopped. 'You know that wasn't a covert op, Harley; it was fifteen years ago; what's the meaning of this? Do you really think he knows something about these UFOs? I can't believe you brought me here thinking I would work your insane plan! You expect me to slither into the arms of a Presidential candidate and ask him about UFOs? Is that it? He's married!'

Greenfield just loved to look at Prinzenthal when she was mad at him. She still remained unruffled, though her eyes lasered into him. 'In a nutshell, no.'

'What then?'

'I'm not sure, though aside from my seeming misapprehensions, it was known that Kennedy was mentored by James Forrestal, the Secretary of Navy during the war, and Kennedy was a hero…I'm just saying.'

'I know what you're saying, Harley! And as I said my brief affair with Kennedy was off the books. He said nothing about aliens! He was a reporter and relatively unknown then!'

'That was then.'

'Look, I slept with a lot of men and some women—honey traps—you directed me for God's sake in most of them—but yes that was then, now I'm a consultant—I sit on committees.'

'I know. You're key player in a man's game. I got that position for you. I talked to Sulla himself. No woman had ever achieved that at your age. You're so well regarded.'

Prinzenthal placed a wind-blown strand of hair behind her ear. The diamond stud twinkled there in the sun. 'I'm not being difficult; it's just that you seem to think that this favor is some kind of game. We know precisely nothing about what your friend Dick wants. If we open up that box, we have no idea what may come out, and then your innocent little game may become something else entirely. We're not dealing with our sworn enemy here; we're talking about treason.'

'Don't get ahead of yourself, Hannah, we're not the enemy. Let's be very certain about that. And caution is the word.'

'Caution,' she uttered cynically. 'It was always me opening my legs to some fish-breath pig.'

'Nonetheless, I love you more. I owe you, dear. We *all* owe you. Look at the treasure you found. You're famous within the service to those in the know.'

'It seems so meaningless now. I'm used up.'

Greenfield held her by the arms. 'Never say that! Never! I am your knight, your champion; don't you see?'

Greenfield dropped his arms, feeling he'd over-tipped his hand. They stood silently for a full minute.

'Well, let's get it over with,' she said, finally.

'I just thought it might be a kind of interesting rendezvous, a challenge. Together we're a force. There's nothing I wouldn't do for you if you asked me.'

'Ah, a test then,' she countered smiling, 'to see if I measure up to your expectations as a potential first mate on that old yacht of yours! You better think fast old friend, I'm not buying it.'

'Come on, Hannah. I'm sure these are good young people; they know nothing of us. It'll be a breeze. Indulge me if you have to. I saved your ass a few times; the least you can do is help me here. I made a promise to Dick and you're my only hope.'

Prinzenthal lowered her head looking at the ground. 'How come you never introduced me to Dick. He was one of us.'

'You know why: he was out of the loop in Berlin, assigned elsewhere. Then he quit.'

'I know that, but still…'

Greenfield let it go, but then renewed his appeal for her feelings.

'You know,' he went on, 'I was always madly in love with you before you even knew me, besides you were off limits back then, even for me. I had no idea who you were in Berlin, only that you worked in the State Department, and I saw you speaking Russian to Stalin at one of those luncheons with Forrestal and Kennedy, the Big Three and troupes of others. You were incredible. I watched Stalin follow you with his creepy eyes around the hall. Evil bastard. I wanted to kill him.'

'Remember, he invited me to Kuntsevo, his grand hideaway dacha near Moscow.'

'I'll never forget; I was assigned as your escort.'

'Perhaps if not for Stalin we would never have met.'

'I doubt that.'

'The first thing he said to me was that I was his favorite spy.'

'Yeah, and you told him you weren't a spy.'

'He went on to tell me I was compromised, and I said I wasn't worth the trouble.'

'I know the story, Hannah.'

'I know; I'm feeling reminiscent: there I was a twenty-three-year-old alone with Uncle Joe the greatest sociopath in history. I could tell he really wanted to fuck me, and I told him off.'

'You told him off *after* he said he had a film of you and Kennedy in bed together.'

'No, after he proposed to give me the film in exchange for the opportunity to boost my career in the State Department, but I called his bluff.'

'You told him that your affair with Kennedy was consensual, and that you couldn't care less if, he, Koba, and that psycho pervert, Beria, or anybody else enjoyed it.'

'That's right; then he laughed. He laughed because he knew that I knew at that moment I had power over him; I was official. I had the whole Allied Army behind me; I had you waiting outside somewhere, and he couldn't do anything about it. In a way I made him free for a moment, free from paranoic madness. He knew I was too good for him, and he could never have me—not that I would have allowed that under any circumstance. I think in some weird way I scared him; I showed a mirror to his ugly pock-marked face, greasy moustache and dark devilish eyes...'

'Then you told him off.'

'Not gracelessly, I just said there has been enough death and destruction; it was time to let peace take hold, and to let people go home and rebuild their own countries again. I said to him—and I remember my exact words: "Hitler's fascism and your warped Bolshevik totalitarianism amount to the same thing—a crime against humanity." I said it was unkind, evil and doomed.'

'Then he showed you the door.'

'Basically, but not before giving me a small reel of film that his people took of Kennedy and me, saying it was the only copy.'

'Which had to be horseshit.'

'We were not important then. I destroyed it of course.'

'Of course.'

'I had this feeling he was actually telling the truth.'

'Well, it's never turned up again as far as I'm aware.'

'Just as well, now that Kennedy could be our next President.'

'Come on. Let's go.'

Prinzenthal sighed. 'I feel old.'

'Just think, Hannah, you may have started the Cold War.'

Prinzenthal laughed. 'You'll never let me down, Harley.'

Greenfield gently touched her arm. 'Come on; let's do this.'

Prinzenthal hesitated. 'You know, on second thought, we shouldn't use our cover names in case they get around. I'm going to use Joyce Sommers, my secret self. No one knows her.'

'You're secret self? Which one?'

'The shrinking violet one, the timid bookworm…librarian.'

'You, a librarian, shrinking violet, timid bookworm?' Greenfield looked at her evenly. 'Okay, well thanks for confiding in me, dear.'

'And you, Harley?'

'You're right of course; I'm not thinking. What shall I call myself…?'

'May I make a suggestion?' asked Prinzenthal.

'I was going to say my French *nom de guerre* Jean Hardin.'

'You always reminded me of that great character, Fielding's *Tom Jones, the foundling*. It's one of my favorite books; I studied it at Columbia.'

'A foundling, am I? *Tarry, rash wanton!*'

'That's *Oberon*, fool.'

'Precisely! How endearing, *Titania*!'

They turned and ambled over to the two Mels.

It was Melbo who first saw them approach. They had a kind of breezy swing and looked around the park like any typical couple. Holding hands they paused not fifteen feet away. DeCourt was talking about her friend Nancy who was getting engaged to a lawyer. Melbo listened but caught himself staring at this couple.

Something about them made his intuition bells chime. The man was obviously quite a bit older than the woman, yet they seemed quite natural together. The woman had a definite urbane coolness, and he a worldly charm with his deep tan. However, it didn't occur to Melbo that they were in any way connected to his meeting arranged by his boss. He assumed the meeting was with one person, a man who lived in a secret world unfamiliar to ordinary people out on a lovely Easter Saturday on Liberty Island.

'Are you listening?' quipped DeCourt. He turned to look at her, but she turned to see what had caught his attention. She saw the couple, and looked at them for a moment. 'Someone you know?' she asked.

'No, just taking in the view. You were saying about Nancy and Brandon…'

'I was saying he's always working, and Nancy feels as if she's making too great a sacrifice. She bears the burden of love…you know, waiting patiently with meals prepared not knowing if he'll make it home in time for dinner.'

'But she works too, and he's a young suit working long hours.'

'That's not the point, Mel. Why is it always up to the woman?'

'Well, perhaps he makes up for it on weekends.'

'Well, apparently he goes off and plays golf with his buddies.'

'No doubt, a career choice because his superiors probably go to the same club.'

'Precisely! So what kind of life can Nancy expect?' she asked rhetorically: 'A life of waiting for a ghost of a husband to show up and actually have a relationship as a couple, especially if they want children.'

'Surely, she must go out and see her own friends.'

'Yeah, right. They're all pregnant or have small children. She wants to keep her job and sanity.'

'If her fiancée is successful, they can get a nanny.'

'Mel, forget it,' stated DeCourt.

'Melissa, people have choices; if she doesn't like the sound of a conventional marriage, why bother and be miserable?'

'But she wants children; *I* want children.'

'Then Nancy should find someone more accommodating.'

At that moment the man who had been standing apart with the young woman was standing beside them.

'Hello,' he said, 'Sorry to intrude. I was wondering whether it would be too much of an imposition to have one of you take a photograph of my wife and me?'

DeCourt was a little taken aback by the interruption. She turned her head and glared at Greenfield, but quickly smiled and stood up. 'I'd be honored, but I must use the *Femmes*; I'm sure my friend here will oblige. Mel?'

'Oh, certainly,' said Melbo, standing as well.

DeCourt strode off towards the toilet facilities.

Greenfield handed the camera to Melbo and stood back as Prinzenthal approached.

'Hi,' said Prinzenthal, 'I hope we're not disturbing you.'

'Not at all,' said Melbo, scrutinizing the camera, a Kodak Brownie 44A. 'This is new.'

'Yeah, latest model,' said Greenfield. 'It's real easy; just aim and shoot.'

'How do you want to pose? Full body with the Statue behind?' Melbo sighted through the lens and turned to get the best angle.

'Sure, a memento of this beautiful day,' said Prinzenthal.

'Okay, ready?' said Melbo.

They smiled calmly with their arms around each other. Melbo snapped three photos in quick succession.

'There. I hope they work,' he said, handing the camera back to Greenfield, who gave it to Prinzenthal to put back in her leather bag.

'Thanks,' she said. 'A good send off to distant horizons.'

Melbo looked at her, marveling at her bemusing smile. He smiled back, expecting them to leave, but since they hesitated, he extended his hand to Greenfield, whose grip was firm but gentlemanly. 'George Melbo, glad to be of assistance on your travels.'

'Thomas Jones, and this is Joyce Sommers, my partner-in-crime.'

In turn, Prinzenthal extended her slender hand to Melbo. He took it carefully as if it were from a delicate lady, but he found a toughness there. 'Tom,' she quipped, 'You make it sound like we're naughty adulterers.'

Melbo chuckled. 'I can keep a secret.'

'We'll hold you to it,' she said.

'May I ask where you're travelling to?' asked Melbo, 'Only if you deem me worthy of your confidence, of course.'

Greenfield looked at Prinzenthal. 'Is he, darling?'

'He seems reliable enough,' she said, regarding Melbo with a raised eyebrow.

'Well, if he's prepared to sign on to nondisclosure.'

'Are you, George?' she asked.

Suddenly dumbstruck, Melbo continued to smile. In seconds, thoughts raced through his mind. This couple suddenly became a specter of unfathomable wattage. Who were they? Ordinary tourists or first responders on his quixotic search for information about extraterrestrials?

'Show me the dotted line,' replied, Melbo, collecting his wits.

'We're sailing to Dominica in a month or two,' said Greenfield. 'An emerald isle, the most beautiful of the Windwards.'

'So now that I'm in the loop, what's your rationale?' asked Melbo, looking at Greenfield, then Prinzenthal. 'Your reason for going there?'

'Aside from mountainous rainforests, hot springs and rare parrots, not much,' said Greenfield.

'I think he's asking for our credentials, dear. Forgive us the mystery, George, but we're as much in the dark as you are. So if we plan to find our enchanted isle we must tread very carefully.'

'Thank you, Dick never mentioned a couple. I'm impressed that you seem to be as interested in this subject as we are. And you can count on my discretion. Melissa will be back shortly.'

Greenfield looked around. 'Let's keep Dick out of it.'

'Take a stroll to the loo, Tom,' said Prinzenthal. 'I'll mind the missus, George.'

'You may call me Mel, Joyce,' said Melbo, and then to Greenfield: 'Shall we, then?'

4. Cold Warrior

If a bird on high flitting about those grounds looked down, it might have noticed Prinzenthal standing innocuously beside the picnic blanket with a few others here and there including children, while Melbo and Greenfield strolled away in the general direction of the public washrooms. If by some miracle, the bird were omniscient and had any inkling about the nature of this meeting of strangers, and about this woman, it would likely hover around to watch and gather the substance of the narrative. And like a god in the knowledge of all things, one can only wonder at the human propensity to deceive on one hand and the need to discover the truth on the other.

Moreover, as it occurred then to Prinzenthal, in the long stream of history, human judgement had been limited at best, because there resulted from its ineluctable purpose a dereliction of truth axiomatic with all its misgivings. In other words we are not privy to a rational or divine plan. Prinzenthal knew this from her experience in the clandestine world of international espionage. For good or ill, truth was used to manufacture distortions and outright lies to hold on to the winning side of history. She felt that at a deeper level, as we continued to emerge from our primordial stew, humanity remained engaged in an endless struggle to correct its horrific behavior.

Evolution be damned, thought Prinzenthal, *we have a long way to go, because persistent totalitarianism begets tyrannies: Communist, Nazi-like, religious or otherwise seemed never to be expunged or dismissed as the ideological hobgoblins they were.* Prinzenthal, having experienced firsthand the evils aforementioned by the murder of her father, and having knowledge of countless millions of others, saw as given in these mass histrionics the evolutionary or even divinely interventional as a journey through hell, and that enlightenment could only be attained through kindness and transparency. But being a well-tutored sceptic—or wily pragmatist—she knew kindness and transparency provided no defense against tyranny, especially the kind that suppressed these qualities for a supposed advancement of society. Prinzenthal was highly principled, and in her brief encounter with Melbo and his girlfriend, guessed that they were of similar minds. And so our bird on high swooped down nearby to hop along and commiserate.

'Hello,' said DeCourt coming up to Prinzenthal.

'*Hello,*' she said again.

Prinzenthal was shaken out of her reverie. 'Oh, pardon me; I was commiserating with the birds.'

'For the birds, are we?' joked DeCourt.

Prinzenthal laughed. 'In my life, I tend to keep a bird's-eye view; keeps me *compos mentis.*'

'I guess that means keeping it together.'

'Otherwise, an occupational hazard.'

'I'm Melissa DeCourt; I wasn't properly introduced.' She extended her hand.

'Joyce Sommers,' said Prinzenthal, taking her hand.

'And your friend, husband?'

'Tom Jones, boyfriend.'

'Tom Jones. Like the Fielding character. Pardon me,' she smirked, 'I can't help myself.'

'You're well-read; I like that in people.'

'Where are they by the way?' asked DeCourt.

'Same as you, off to the loo.'

'Shall we sit?' suggested DeCourt, sitting with legs tucked back.

'Might as well.' Prinzenthal does the same, sitting lotus.

'So the impromptu photo-shoot went well?'

'Oh, yes,' said Prinzenthal, dismissing their intrusion as a trifle, 'My dear friend is quite romantic and can't help himself.'

'Can't say I blame him; you're quite interesting. Are you from here, New York?'

'Yes, thank you, but I'm just a bureaucrat, who facilitates security for the underclasses and immigrants. I work in the Department of State.'

'As a kind of social philanthropist?' joked DeCourt.

'Not specifically, just trying to give back some of my good blessings.'

'A bleeding heart; I can respect that.'

'Let's say a freedom lover; and you, Melissa?'

'Everyone calls me Mel.'

'Well then, Mel, like your man, Mel.'

'Yeah, we're two of a kind.'

'I'll say, much like Tom and me.'

'He's older,' said DeCourt.

'Yes, well, we've known each other quite a while; and we like each other's company, but he would prefer that I'd settle down.'

'Ah, I see, like family?'

'Yup,' said Prinzenthal, intimating she wasn't quite ready.

'What does he do?'

'Aside from yachting, he's pretty much retired. For most of his life he was in international business and then with the onset of the war he fulfilled requisitions for the armed forces as liaison. Much of his work was classified, maybe still is for all I know.'

'In what specifically?'

'All *matériel* to do with parts, supplies—to keep the allies "a well-oiled machine", his words.'

'Sounds like he was an unsung hero, one of many. Did he go overseas?'

'Oh yes; Europe was his theater.'

'And you, Joyce? Were you in the war effort?'

'A little; I wish I could have done more, other than sitting on committees to organize relief efforts: helping the wounded, feeding and housing refugees in post-war chaos—I spent a year in Paris and visited parts of Belgium and the Netherlands, even Germany, where the people were starving en masse. It was horrible. I met Tom there, in Frankfurt.'

'That's a lot. Most women wouldn't go there. I admire that in you. I understand Germany was a heap of rubble.'

'That's what happens when madmen want to rule the world—Hitler and Stalin both great progenitors of true evil.'

'But Stalin was an ally during the war.'

'Of course, but afterwards he just tyrannized Eastern Europe when Hitler retreated.'

'The war isn't over for you,' suggested DeCourt.

'Not really, after what I experienced; hundreds of thousands of women raped and murdered by the Red Army, girls as young as seven and eight, old women; it was utterly savage. They weren't liberators. They justified their savagery as revenge for Nazi atrocities but it just showed their cynical contempt for life, no redeeming virtue, just Stalin's brutal regime.'

DeCourt went quiet. The terrible reality of what Prinzenthal had seen shocked her deeply. It made her realize how insulated she was. Finally, she said: 'I was just a little girl happily growing up, completely oblivious.'

'As it should have been,' went on Prinzenthal. 'But, hey, not all Red Army soldiers were bad. Some retained some humanity, and as for the German people, most had reservations of Hitler at the outset—only about thirty-three percent voted for him before he usurped the democratic process, as chaotic as it was. Certainly the Nazis planned it that way as a false flag operation with the burning of the Reichstag.

'Yet Hitler and Goebbels seduced the people with fear-stoking anti-Semitism to psychotic hysteria, and the storm troopers were their merciless agents—sick stupid animals. *Kristallnacht* was their rabid, bloody chest-thumping *abschlacten*—a dire indices what was to come. I lost family and my best friend at Auschwitz. Most German people fell blindly in line and tolerated the regime—a denial of its lurid insanity, and that meant defending themselves when war was inevitable.

'National Socialism was an utter disaster that destroyed the country they'd claimed to have saved under Hitler. They let it happen, yet, I believe in the human spirit; it transcends politics and fear; I think about those brave individuals like Sophie Scholl, the Bavarian student activist; and the Prussian Colonel Claus von Stauffenberg; and Georg Elser who both tried to assassinate Hitler, all martyred and many others who made a stand against a monstrous dictatorship. It was the same in Russia, where untold millions died under Stalin's vicious oligarchy.

'Take the *Holodomor*, the forced starvation of millions of Ukrainians; the elimination of the brightest and best of Russian society; the murder of thousands of Polish officers in the Katyn Forest and elsewhere, and the *intelligentsia* throughout Eastern Europe after the war, many sent to the Gulag slave camps of Siberia never to return; the deportations, disappearances, and darkness were the ongoing holocaust before and after the Nazi regime.'

'My God,' uttered DeCourt, 'you really have a personal involvement; I'm so sorry about your family and friend; we should all be so outraged. I feel ashamed for all humanity, that such evil exists.'

'Oh, sorry to lay it on so thick, I can get carried away when I think about it.'

'Who was your friend, if you don't mind me asking?'

'Not at all. Lizbet, my cousin.'

Prinzenthal went silent.

DeCourt gave her pause, before remarking, 'I've never heard of these people like Sophie Scholl and those horrible events, other than the death camps like Auschwitz. You know a lot about it.'

'I know enough. It has the effect that I can't let go. We must find a way to end that kind of history.'

'You're a cold warrior.'

'Maybe, but new challenges arise.'

'Such as?

'To defeat Nixon and his Republican cronies, for one.'

'I agree. I hope Kennedy wins his nomination, and is elected President.'

'That would be truly wonderful; someone from my generation.'

'What other challenges?' asked DeCourt.

'I've taken an interest in these UFOs. They've made headline news.'

'*Touché!*' exclaimed DeCourt, 'My boyfriend and I have been talking about that very thing recently. In fact, the paper he works for has asked him to do some sleuthing and write some articles as he gathers information. Unfortunately, nothing is forthcoming. In spite of credible sightings and even that supposed crash of a space ship—then retracted as a weather balloon— years ago in New Mexico, everyone is either cynical, incredulous or a servile apologist.'

'So you wouldn't want to meet some little hairless bug-eyed creatures?'

DeCourt laughed out loud. 'Joyce, you crack me up! No I don't think so!'

Prinzenthal caught the bug and laughed as well, releasing the tension. Both had to catch their breath. DeCourt looked beyond her companion and noticed Melbo and Greenfield in the distance heading their way. As she watched them, they stopped and seemed to be engaged in a profound conversation.

'Oh, goodness me,' said DeCourt, 'Our men approach, and I think saw our laughter, and are now discussing it.'

Prinzenthal turned to see them speaking intently. 'Don't mind them. Man-talk.'

'Isn't that the point? What do they say about us?'

'Does it really matter: back slapping, sexual innuendos, and conquest?'

'Not Mel; he's too cerebral.'

'And so is Tom, but just the same, they have one-track minds.'

'Men are wired that way, I guess.'

'And I suppose you and I are wired to receive them.'

'That sounds so…like programmed; aren't we better than that?'

'Some of us, even some men; don't get me wrong; Tom is one of those men.'

'Here they come.'

Prinzenthal looked up at Greenfield who now crouched near her. Melbo sat down beside DeCourt. Greenfield offered Prinzenthal his hand. 'Time to go, dear; we've overstayed our welcome.'

'Oh do stay for a bit,' said DeCourt, 'we were enjoying ourselves immensely.'

'At our expense, no doubt,' remarked Melbo, mischievously. 'I saw you both laughing.'

'Not at you, silly,' retorted DeCourt, we had a rather serious discussion about the war, then changed the subject for much needed levity.'

Greenfield helped Prinzenthal up. 'Perhaps another time,' he said, 'Joyce and I interrupted the party. Please excuse us. Mel told me of his work and I will be looking out for his syndicated column.'

'Really?' asked Prinzenthal standing above Melbo and DeCourt.

'No,' said Melbo, 'Tom's bragging about me. No such column, I'm afraid.'

'Well, nice to meet you both, Mel *et* Mel,' she replied, and looking at DeCourt, 'Maybe we can chat again sometime. Take care.'

'I would like that. Happy sailing.'

*

Sipping her glass of Sancerre, Prinzenthal glanced about the room from their table at *Le Pavillon*. She loved this exclusive French restaurant located in the Ritz Tower Hotel but rarely dined there because it was frequented by many important people including Kennedy himself. She knew Kennedy had been in Florida for a couple of days and was to begin campaigning in West Virginia. Reclusive by nature and profession, she avoided mixing with the elite for fear of compromising her cover should she encounter acquaintances better suited to more private functions.

As well, she knew that there were Russian and East Bloc spies about, especially those under deep cover as Americans, who would likely gather in such popular elegant milieus. Spying was an insidious business that could reach far into the system, as she and Greenfield knew very well from their professional experience. And now she was considering using her expertise to find out what was going on with the UFO phenomenon. Greenfield returned from making a telephone call at a nearby public booth on the street. He smiled at Prinzenthal, who looked back buttering her piece of baguette; then he took up his own wine.

'So pensive, dear,' he said, smiling, sipping.

'Not at all; I love being here. Thank you,' she said eating her bread.

'You think someone you know will appear.'

'Maybe, but that's fine. *Je suis libre.*'

'Ah, meaning: as a civilian, and/or as a friend.'

'Harley, don't.'

'Don't what?'

'Make me feel guilty for not being more romantic.'

'So you're feeling guilty?'

'Yes, a bit.'

'That's good enough for me.'

Prinzenthal laughed quietly, almost sadly.

'What makes you think you're the only man who has professed his true love for me?' she asked.

'What makes you think I care about anyone else that loves you?' quipped Greenfield.

'My happiness, perhaps.'

'Then tell me what makes you happy, and if need be I'll never bother you again.'

'You don't bother me; you make me happy in a kind of melancholy way.'

'That, my sweet, is an oxymoron.'

'Hmmph,' emitted Prinzenthal, 'You always state the obvious, as a clarification. Let's just enjoy this dinner.'

At that moment two waiters arrived with their main courses: Sole Véronique for her and Steak au Poivre for him, and side dishes of Petit-Pois and Courgette Provençale to be shared.

'Bon appetite!' said the waiters.

'Merci,' they replied, and began to eat in silence for a few minutes.

'Très bien,' said Greenfield, taking a gulp of his wine.

'Bien sûr,' as she did the same.

'May I make a supposition as to this "melancholia"?'

'I think I can guess; we've been over this before.'

'Well, then enlighten me,' he said.

'To be blunt: how I was pimped post-war.'

'Meaning I was your pimp.'

'Who else, Harley?'

'The Wise Men, naturally.'

'Listen, I don't begrudge you. You did what was expected of you; you protected me, and on one occasion killed for me, and even tried to get other girls to do that kind of work over me; but they wanted me because I always got the job done, correct?'

'I don't love you for your beauty, darling; I love you because…'

They ate in silence.

'Because, what?' she finally said.

'Because for someone so beautiful, in my opinion, you have a surprising modesty, a depth that has a kind of Zen Buddhist *s'envoyer en l'air*, a sexy innocence that makes men amorous, incapable of resisting your wiles—and like a ghost you walk right into their soul, even if they don't have one.'

Prinzenthal laughed. 'And that turns you on,' she said. 'So if I told you I feel most natural with you precisely because I don't feel romantically inclined, you'd find it upsetting. Well, hello darling, you have the real me!'

'You don't do that kind of work anymore. And I love you just as you are past and present and future.'

Prinzenthal put down her knife and fork and stared at her half-eaten sole.

Greenfield went on: 'Your work now as a special operations case officer for people who do some of the very things you were once so celebrated for within the service, and your mood now is reflective of the present situation in that I have triggered in you a reminder of the work you used to do. Let me make this clear: in no way am I asking any such thing from you. If you want out now, this will be the last time we have to talk about it.

'I brought you up to speed with this because I want you to quit and be my wife, or don't quit and still be my wife. I don't really care whether or not there's a high cabal orchestrating a program dealing with aliens outside the legitimate government; it's always been that way for us. I just think of it as a new challenge for the times, and likely our 'Wise Men' have our best interests at hand.'

Prinzenthal picked up her knife and fork and continued calmly to eat. Greenfield followed suit.

'I'd be lying to you, Harley, if I said I didn't miss the hunt. I was good at what I did back then because I loved my role. Sure I was pimped, and as a woman of taste and moral rectitude, was repulsed, but on the other hand, my dirty little secret was and still is the *voyeur*. I'm corrupted. It's an occupational hazard. Your love for me has always been my north star, my compass for righteousness, so don't go soft on me.'

It was Greenfield's turn to laugh. 'Forgive me, Hannah,' he said, still enjoying his steak. 'You were always good at keeping me at arm's length, but like a fox in the thicket you made damn sure I remained on-the-scent figuratively, and of course I did and am ready to oblige your every move.'

'Fox in the thicket, huh; I seem to recall your nose in my box on more than one occasion; you had my scent pretty much marinated on that tongue of yours, not that I didn't mind.'

'There's my girl. And the memory has ensnared me for life.'

'I must seem rather cruel.'

'Cruel?'

'To be pleasured by you that time in Paris, for instance; it was quite illuminating, then at your request my being transferred east; honestly, I had never experienced such an *apogée* if you will, then the reverse.'

'You know I had no choice; it was the op.'

'Kind of like sleeping with my pimp?'

Greenfield winced and stopped eating.

'And did you not pleasure me, rather sincerely? It was no *whizzbang*, as you are fond of saying, and it happened more than once; numerous times.'

'I admit I was in awe of you and let you into my heart, but I spurned you for fear of destroying what good I was for the service.'

'Hannah, I know that; I retreated willingly, otherwise *I* would've been putting you at risk because of us.'

'You disappeared, and I didn't see you for over a year,' she pouted.

'I…we put duty before love.'

'Nonsense. I was hurt by that, though I accepted the arrangement, because you did.'

'You were stationed in Poland.'

'Stationed,' she uttered, 'to Colonel Ryszard Sienkiewicz.'

'The closet Nationalist.'

'But a gold seam liaison in Soviet strategic behavior and personnel; I thought he was a waste of time. And a *pijana wódka*—a vodka drunk…I called him my *'napalona świnia'*—horny pig—he thought it a compliment.' She laughed.

'You were well rewarded.'

'So was he.'

'And compromised eventually.'

'Not by me.'

'No, much later—made to appear unrelated—we confirmed it was the Russians who murdered his compatriots at Katyn in '40-'41, and he got careless and was liquidated, poor bastard.'

'Well he had me many times, like a bad habit.'

'And that justified a means to an end?'

'No, just saying; I was sorry; we were actually close.'

Greenfield looked at her, and fought back his jealousy.

'Perhaps you are cruel.'

'I'm sorry, Harley; it just came out. I'm not helping, am I?'

'No, we're better than that. It makes me love you more.'

'How? I don't understand you.'

'Every time you hit me with some callous remark, I see it as a test, a way for you to earn my love.'

'Okay, if you say so. If anyone can heal me, it's you.'

Soon the waiter came and removed their plates. They ordered cognac and *glaces citron* for dessert with coffee for her and tea for Greenfield. They both dipped their spoons tentatively and finished the dessert without a word. Prinzenthal felt comfortable in the silence, wondering whether she should invite him back to her apartment. Their airing of past hurts seemed to have a positive effect, and Greenfield appeared to read her thoughts.

'*To be or not to be*,' he said, pausing to think.

'*That is the question*,' she followed.

'*Whether 'tis nobler in the mind to suffer
The slings and arrows of outrageous fortune,*'

'Or to take arms against a sea of troubles
And by opposing end them.'

'I couldn't have said it better myself,' smiled Greenfield.

They laughed and threw back their cognacs.

'Is that your way of saying you want to come home with me?' she asked, smiling beatifically.

'That goes without saying, sweet.'

'I haven't been all the way with a man for at least three or four years, maybe more.'

'Nor I.'

They both laughed again.

'Okay,' she said.

5. Stir the Beast

April 23 1960

New York Herald Tribune

Who Believes in Aliens?

By George Melbo

If it is true, and if certain insiders within a highly classified loop of government know about it, does the public have a constitutional right to hear a State-of-the-Union admission that there has been contact with an alien civilization? It's a loaded question. And as a journalist, I submit that it is a question that has no easy answer. Some might say outright: we are owed the truth in a free and transparent society.

In the name of National Security others might agree or disagree based on whether the contact made is benign or hostile. If the latter, there would have to be serious consideration because of the nature of the threat; if the former, one may think there's no harm in it: let's get to know our galactic neighbors in our friendly American way! How about a cheeseburger and a strawberry sundae, or an Elvis Presley record? How glib and ridiculous we might seem to be, even if we offered Einstein and Jesus or Bach and Charlie Parker! Or Marilyn Monroe!

In general, it should be stated at this point that there has been no hostile action taken against our nation or the world in regards to hundreds if not thousands of credible sightings of the ubiquitous UFO (Unidentified Flying Object). Just last month a teetotaler farmer in Iowa stepped out of his barn and to his amazement observed a huge disc-like object zig-zag in total silence not a couple hundred yards away over his field before coming to a stationary position above the ground then disappearing in the blink of an eye. When he told his neighbors of this sighting, they all questioned his sanity, though they had known him as sober and down-to-earth.

Obviously, then, to claim to see a UFO is an invitation to ridicule. But then there are the mass sightings such as those over Washington in July, 1952 which made headline news nation-wide. Air traffic controllers confirmed their presence on radar, as did thousands of others around the DC area—some were even sighted over the White House! It was clear that these objects defied conventional technology and what we understand of elemental nature itself; they would turn ninety degrees at impossible speeds, and even reverse direction apparently in a micro-second and continue on at incredible speed!

To our unbelieving eyes, this has to be magic. What is the secret? How do they do that? There's the rub. We haven't a clue. One must suppose that if the beings flying in these machines (or perhaps unmanned machines controlled by someone) can do that, they obviously have the technology to travel the vast distances through space to get here; and my guess is they don't take fifty light years to do so, wherever they originate, and it surely isn't Venus or Mars because of their inhospitality to life!

It defies everything we know, and we think we are so smart, having emerged this far from our primordial swamp; in fact, if these objects are real, and by logic and reputable assumption they are, these aliens are so advanced beyond our own evolutionary level (or religious creationism for that matter), we are comparatively and literally infantile in the universal scheme of things.

Let's take a step back and return to the question whether we have a constitutional right to know the truth: given the truth that they are real. Have we made contact with an alien species? It would appear that on the evidence alone we have a right to know with an emphatic Yes. *On the other hand since there has been no substantive acknowledgment from our elected government as to who or what these UFOs are (if they did they might call them* ETVs (Extraterrestrial Vehicles or Spaceships)) *but they have not been forthcoming other than President Truman once expressing that "They are not ours"!*

Well, isn't that from the horse's mouth? Or perhaps a slip of the tongue? A well-placed leak to lead us to the reality of the problem, the problem being: we don't know enough about UFOs to reveal anything. And if we did know something, we wouldn't tell you anyway because we could use the technology if available, to defeat our real enemy the Soviet Union and win the Cold War.

That brings me to the Big Daddy *of the UFO phenomenon: the Roswell Incident which took place almost thirteen years ago in June, 1947. More accurately, it took place near Corona, New Mexico, some seventy miles to the north of Roswell, the home of the 509th Bomber Group of the 8th Air Force at*

Roswell Army Air Field. According to local Ranchers there had been a thunder and lightning storm the previous evening and it was the following day that rancher Mac Brazel discovered a debris field out on the range. Before he contacted local authorities, he claimed to have found a crashed disc, partially intact with alien bodies dead or barely alive in and near the wreckage.

As the military authorities at Roswell were alerted to the bizarre crash, the story got out and was reported by the local paper, the Roswell Daily Record, and wired across the country—RAAF (Roswell Army Airfield) Captures Flying Saucer in the Roswell Region! By the time the military got up to speed and vociferously demanded the retraction of the incident, they claimed the crash had been simply that of a weather balloon, even showing a photo of a military officer, Major Marcel, holding a piece of actual weather balloon. This was sent across the nation symbolizing a kind of coup-d'état over the truth.

Ever since, the debunking of the original story has held fast as the official word on the subject. The first responders to the crash and other civilians at the base in Roswell were made to publicly declare their mistake and held to secrecy, according to anybody who followed up on the original news article. Without getting into details we might ask ourselves why someone like Mac Brazel and others would make up such a story as first ascribed. To this day any attempt by our media to delve deeper is stopped in its tracks and prohibited by our government which uses the media to claim that nothing is known.

So again, if alien visitation is real and the government has gone to great lengths to avoid making any official acknowledgment to the public, there has to be a very good reason. Think about it: if you or I were the leader of the country and were informed of this extraordinary phenomenon, what would be our best and wisest course of action? Likely, one would want to be as informed as possible in order not to alarm the public what they hadn't any idea about. That would entail a super-secret meeting of the best scientific minds and top military brass to set up a compartmentalized study group with no congressional oversight in order to keep it secret until such time we the people could be informed, if ever within the foreseeable future.

It would have to be a massive study to understand the technical, cultural, and scientific ways of these space-faring people. It is both awesome and frightening. This study group would find out what these aliens are capable of, or conversely, what our own government (those mandated with maintaining the secrecy of the study) is capable of while preserving their autonomy within *the legal parameters of government that by rights should answer to the people.*

A dangerous precedent could well be looming, with no recognized authority held accountable. This quite possibly could be the end of our innocence as a democratic nation. Perhaps someday these times will be looked back upon as the most profound turning point in the history of humanity. We are not alone!

*

Henry Arthur Lovering put down his paper—the Saturday edition of the New York Herald Tribune—and finished the last of his coffee and toast with honey. He looked pensively out on the rolling lawn of his modest Maryland home down to Chesapeake Bay where a few so-called dead-rise crab and oyster boats lingered a distance offshore. A native of New York, nicknamed 'Artie' since his undergraduate college years when he sketched burlesque caricatures in his spare time, he was an affable and courteous gentleman. Though he was unknown publicly, one couldn't miss his thick dark hair, his large brown eyes exaggerated through the lenses of his glasses, his pudgy mid-life waistline and his typically conservative suit and tie.

If he wore a pork-pie hat, one might think he was a character in his own sketch book, or a comedian on vaudeville. But that's where the entertainment stopped: he was sharp as a tack, a doctor of Political Science, a veritable workaholic, who had an almost uncanny ability to land important positions in government and with the power elite. In fact, he had been indispensable to Rockefeller and his Special Studies Project in 1956 as a 'consultant' to Eisenhower, then as director of a special 'sub-committee' of the National Security Council reporting to the president.

Although Rockefeller had left Washington that year and had since been elected as Governor of New York State in 1958, Lovering had settled in as an *éminence grise*—a kind of convenient servant of the Republican plutocracy under the radar of the press. Given the highest clearance, he enjoyed a reputation for dependability which stemmed from his war years in intelligence and his close consultation with various agencies including, arms control, research, economics, and with the Department of State during the reconstruction of Germany.

Now Monday, Lovering sat in the back seat of his ride to the White House,

60

a service provided by the White House for the duration of his job there. The article he had read on the weekend still resonated in his mind. He paid little heed to many of the reports of UFOs, but this one seemed to strike a chord in that there was an implied challenge to the system—the Constitution that is—and it made him reflect on the legality of classified issues, some of which he was directly involved in. He knew that he and some of his compatriots had entered a new era of clandestine activity which being exposed could blow off the lid of an uninformed world. Let them write what they want, he thought; better the people have a chance to express themselves, so long as they don't find out the truth. The truth, he mused: what an extraordinary concept!

In a perfect world, all humanity would accept the truth as a natural element within the continuum of our emergence; a simple benefit of our technological advances. But we are so far from perfect, and in spite of defeating Hitler and Imperial Japan, the Soviet Union had become so dangerous, nuclear Armageddon could be but a flint ready to provide the spark for our annihilation. A cold war ran deep and intense, and our new research into technologies beyond our current capabilities could someday very well provide the superiority necessary to succeed in controlling potential proliferation, or rather defending against it. We are free, he concluded, but not free enough to know the truth. And the whole truth was like a mystery we did not yet understand.

Late in the day, after numerous meetings including those with the director of the CIA and the president, Lovering received a call from Jake Whitmore, the New York magnate and owner of various newspapers and media venues.

'Put him through,' said Lovering to his secretary.

'Jake,' said Lovering. 'A pleasant surprise.'

'Artie, sorry to call during hours; I know it's not protocol and I'm the old guy, but just wanted to speak to you about a birthday party Grace is organizing May 14, two weeks Saturday in Westchester. Can you make it?'

'I wouldn't miss it. Gertie mentioned it, and asked whether we could make it.'

'Well, you know how the women are; I had to call you personally; Grace insisted.'

Lovering laughed. 'If it wasn't for my social agenda, I wouldn't be able to perform my duties. I need your party more than you know!'

'Glad to hear it. She tells me we're putting on a great spread, and inviting all sorts of people. Should be interesting.'

'I've never been disappointed, Jake.'

'Well, I'll let you go. I wouldn't want to impose on Ike's best caretaker.'

'Hey, some days I feel more of an unsung ringmaster! Politics is just plain ludicrous at times, and I'm really just a humble clerk!'

They both laughed.

'Perhaps,' said Whitmore. 'But the one who knows everything.'

'I wish. At the least, I'm behind the scenes, but can't help being drawn into all the drama. It's my job to make it easier for everyone.'

'As it should be.'

'By the way, did you read that Saturday article by the Melbo fellow?' asked Lovering.

'The alien thing? He's one of Dick Sinclair's boys. Harmless chuff.'

'Well written. The guy has some imagination.'

'Hell, Artie, Sinclair has been chomping on the bit ever since that day all those sightings happened over Washington—what, eight or so years ago. I give him free rein if it sells papers and moves minds.'

'By all means. Do people take it seriously? What if?' queried Lovering.

'What if they're real?' chortled Whitmore. 'Then our nukes oughta smarten the bastards up, and make 'em find some other world to pester.'

'You have a point. Why would they want anything to do with us? It would appear we're hell bent.'

'Well, you tell me. Is there any truth to them?' asked Whitmore.

'From what I understand we're all in the same boat—and looking for answers. They're mentioned in ancient books.'

'Is that a fact?'

'And if those stories are true, they've been here a long time.'

'What could they want with us?'

'Even if I knew the answer to that, Jake, I could never tell you,' said Lovering gravely. He then broke out in a hearty guffaw.

Whitmore responded less enthusiastically. 'I'll take your word for it, Artie. Until the party then. Glad you're on board. Bye now.' Whitmore clicked off.

*

Standing in the grand old marble lobby of the Willard Hotel in Washington, Harley Greenfield could smell what he thought was a hint of cigar in the air. Must be the ghost of General Grant he thought as Hannah Prinzenthal emerged from the elevator. Smiling, they walked out the front exit to a waiting cab. They passed the White House and merged onto Pennsylvania Avenue heading towards Washington Circle, where they continued around and kept on until Wisconsin Avenue and turned right.

'This is all a bit mysterious, Harley,' said Prinzenthal.

'Pull over here,' said Greenfield to the driver.

The driver pulled over and Greenfield gave him a few bills. Now standing on the sidewalk, Harley directed them to walk along.

'This is our chance to make a connection, dear,' he said.

'Well, I guessed as much. It's been intriguing to say the least. You bring me all the way to Washington on the train, stay at the venerated Willard in the Calvin Coolidge suite…and now this.'

Greenfield stopped. She turned to him. He said, 'You said you wanted to do this out of "a sense of curiosity" and "loyalty". Across the street and up a little is Martin's Tavern. We're going there for brunch.'

'Great, I'm starving. I was wondering why you turned down a breakfast together, especially after last night.' She reached with her arms and held Greenfield's waist. 'And I noticed you've lost some weight these last weeks.' She wrinkled her nose at him. 'So what's the big deal?'

'The big deal is this is our first op.'

'So a romantic getaway is our first op? You know me better than I thought. This *is* romantic!'

'I thought you'd like that.'

'And the connection?' she asked.

'I'm going to let you play this out as naturally as you are able.'

'Christ, Harley, you're killing me! What on earth do you have up your sleeve?'

'Oh, something exciting and a bit shocking perhaps.'

'Brunch in a tavern?'

'This isn't just any tavern; it's also a famous one.' Greenfield motioned to the green light and they crossed the street. Prinzenthal went blithely along.

They entered the tavern. The décor was old and cozy, with darkened wood booths along the segment-paned or latticed windows, a well-stocked bar, old tile ceiling, tables and old photos hanging wherever space allowed.

'Charming,' whispered Prinzenthal, looking about expecting some surprise.

A waitress came immediately and greeted them. They ordered tea and coffee, juice and Eggs Benedict, home-fries and fruit with Smithfield Ham. Prinzenthal was an irreligious Jew.

They had eaten half their breakfast when a small posse of gentlemen in suits entered the establishment and sequestered themselves at a large table in the far corner with smaller ones beside it. They all sat down. Some of them, who were obviously a security detail, sat at the small tables; from this position they kept their eyes on the entrance and on other patrons including Greenfield and Prinzenthal, but soon they shifted their attention back to the entrance.

Greenfield ignored them and continued to eat. Prinzenthal seemed slightly surprised but went back to her meal. Then both looked up a minute later when John F. Kennedy and his brother Robert walked in with another man and sat down at the big table. Greenfield went back to his brunch, but Prinzenthal was frozen in a state of shock following Kennedy as he sat down and began to talk with his brother, when he looked over and noticed her looking, her cool exterior now perfectly composed. She turned away, as everyone in the room had begun to clap. Kennedy stood up briefly saying thank you.

'A working brunch,' said Greenfield into his food. 'Don't look.'

'I'm not.'

'He's home to see his family before taking off out West. On a hunch, I assumed he'd come here for a campaign pit-stop—his favorite local place. He lives around the corner on N Street.'

'On a hunch? I know you better than that, Harley.'

'I did my research. He proposed to Jackie in this very booth.'

'Really? And is that what you propose to do with me?' she asked with an eyebrow raised.

'It had occurred to me, dear, but I wouldn't want his influence to have any bearing on us.'

'Besides pandering to his sentiments?'

'Well that goes without saying.'

'Aha! You think he'll make his rounds in this joint. I doubt he'd remember me.'

'That's what I'm curious about. It's really up to him.'

'He knew me as Judith Graham in the chaos of Berlin, 1945,' she stated. 'It feels like a century ago.'

'You were as beautiful at twenty-three as now; he'll remember. He loves women.'

'For God's sake he has a family now; Jackie's pregnant with another.'

'He made inquiries about you after your affair.'

'I didn't know that.'

'You were out of bounds then ...' Greenfield sighed. 'I didn't know until I became your handler later that year.'

'It's funny in a way. When I saw him sit down he looked over briefly; I averted my eyes so I don't know if he recognized me.'

They finished their meal and sipped their coffee and tea in a suspended silence. Then Greenfield looked at her.

She looked at him.

'What?' she said. 'Having second thoughts?'

'Yes.'

'Harley. Don't make me say no, here, now.'

'He's getting up.'

'He is?'

'He's going to the loo.'

'Oh, you had me there.'

'A bit nervous are we?' he joked.

'No, just ... a little,' she demurred, looking down.

A presence compelled Prinzenthal to look up. Jack Kennedy was standing beside the table.

'Judith?' he said. 'Judith Graham?'

Prinzenthal looked up into Kennedy's shining eyes. Everybody in the tavern was looking at them.

A few moments of interlocking eyes, and she snapped out of her shock and regained her composure.

'Senator. Senator Kennedy. This is an honor, sir.'

'Jack, please, Judith; this is a surprise. All those years ago I tried to reach you with no luck, and here you are.' Kennedy turned to Greenfield and held out his hand. 'Jack Kennedy, how do you do?'

Remaining seated he shook his hand. 'Harley Greenfield, sir. We're behind you 100%.'

'I'm happy to hear that,' he said. 'I aim to win this nomination.'

Kennedy looked back at Prinzenthal. 'I see you both like the Eggs Benedict too.'

'A delicious treat for an empty stomach,' she said.

Kennedy turned back to Greenfield. 'We last saw each other, Judith and I, among the ruins of Berlin in 1945.'

'I was there, Senator. How can one forget?'

'A war to end war, and tyranny.'

'Ah, tyranny, a cancer within any self-respecting nation.'

Kennedy observed Greenfield, nodding slowly. 'I would really like to hear your story, Harley.' And turning back to Prinzenthal, 'And yours, Judith.'

Kennedy paused, shaking his head, smiling. 'Did you know that I proposed to my future wife where you now sit?'

'I had heard,' said Greenfield. 'That's why we came here. But I didn't know it happened in this booth.'

'To propose? I'm sorry; I didn't mean to interrupt.'

'I'm glad you stopped by, Jack,' said Prinzenthal. 'Much has changed since Berlin.'

'Now that's an understatement!' exclaimed Kennedy. 'I really thought you might be dead.'

They all laughed.

'Harley,' said Kennedy, 'I would like your permission to speak to Judith after our meeting.' He quickly looked back at his table. His brother and the rest of them were all waiting for him. 'We're brainstorming the campaign trail ahead—California and West Virginia.'

'You don't need my permission, Senator; she's quite independent.'

'Judith, is that all right? Just a little time to catch up with you and your career. I need people such as you; I need your expertise.'

'I'd be delighted to help in any way, Jack. We'll be here for a little while.'

'Great. See you shortly. Nice to meet you, Harley.'

Kennedy went back to his table.

'Perfect,' said Greenfield.

'I'm going to tell him my real name.'

'Of course.'

'He's pretty sharp; he knew me right away.'

*

An hour later, Kennedy's car pulled up near the Potomac River at Georgetown Waterfront Park. Greenfield sat in the front beside the driver, with Kennedy and Prinzenthal in the back. Few people were about. Kennedy suggested a stroll by the river, which was flowing heavily from spring rains the week before. The driver and Greenfield leaned against the hood while Kennedy and Prinzenthal sauntered closer to the rushing river. Prinzenthal remained quiet as Kennedy spoke.

'What a grand day!' he said gesturing to the river and skies. 'Judith, you can't know how shocked I was seeing you there at Martin's. You were like some ghost come back to life … God, it seems like an eternity, but there we were in Potsdam … and touring the rubble in Berlin; meeting Stalin and Churchill. I was a Lieutenant then and taking it all in as part of the Forrestal delegation. Then we almost bumped into each other at one of the numerous soirées; I have to admit you just knocked me off my feet; so beautiful, adept around the bigwigs, and Stalin, actually speaking with the rogue in Russian. Then I couldn't believe my fortune when you agreed to let me take you home.'

'You flatter me, Jack.'

'Well, you flattered me! I wanted to have this conversation fifteen years ago.'

'At the time I needed some relief from the tension, and chaos. I thought you charming and sincere, and safe.'

'I really did try and find you. What happened?' he asked, seriously.

'Well, to begin I worked for OSS, now CIA, and the Cold War happened. I remained undercover for over ten years in Europe, west and east. Harley was my control for most of that time.'

'I should have guessed: two spies. And you fell in love.'

'It's a bit more complicated than that.'

'I can imagine,' Kennedy mused, watching the flowing water. 'Classified complicated.'

'I was born Hannah. Hannah Prinzenthal.'

Kennedy turned to her. 'I'm very honored, Hannah. When I become President, I will find you and Harley. Perhaps we can come up with some positive collaboration.'

'There is an old Buddhist saying: Positive thoughts make positive results.'

'I like that; you are astute. Now what are you really doing here?' Kennedy asked suddenly.

'Meeting with you, of course,' she said with a straight face.

'Let me tell you something, Hannah: I'm sure that you and Harley are good people, and I like you; but knowing what I know now about you tells me you know what I'm talking about. In fact, to a point, you have been perfectly honest with me, so I'm being perfectly honest with you. You can trust me.'

Hannah turned to the river. 'You may think this beyond the pale. And by telling you this I may get myself into a lot of trouble. I'm involved in an unauthorized project, which you now should understand is something new to me; it's treasonous if I break with my official standing to solicit classified information out of my domain on home turf. I'm putting myself at your mercy as a Senator who upholds the law of the land. We are conducting an operation to try and find out what is going on about the UFOs. Harley is doing this as a favor to a friend, Dick Sinclair, OSS himself, and an editor at the New York Tribune.'

Kennedy smiled, looking out at the water with Prinzenthal. 'A favor, huh? You have touched on one of the most deeply disturbing issues in present times. Are we alone? And if we aren't, how do we handle it? I read that article by what's his name?'

'Melbo. George Melbo.'

'His paper is decidedly Republican, and I read it occasionally to get their views. Know the enemy sort of thing.'

'Melbo is no dyed-in-the-wool Republican, I can assure you.'

'You've met him?'

'Yes.'

'The problem transcends any political affiliation. But the time is not right for me to open up on account of it.'

'Yes, I suppose you and the public who are not informed, and those that are will not give up their exclusive hold on the truth of the matter. Let's face it: it's pretty obvious extraterrestrial people have come to Earth, and these select few in the know choose not to acknowledge it publicly.'

Kennedy turned and walked along the embankment; Prinzenthal followed.

'I will say this,' said Kennedy. 'I know about them; I am informed, because Secretary Forrestal told me a long time ago. I also feel that he died as a result of his insistence on attempting to influence policy which would let the public know that at the very least these UFOs are extraterrestrial in origin—and I'd really like to know who ordered his demise. His family claimed he never took his life. He was a devout Christian and loyal American who believed in doing the right thing. I believe in doing the right thing, but so do the men who preside over the most classified matter in the history of this country. And in consideration of the threat of Communism—Soviet expansion and security—they may be right for any number of reasons. And until I'm in a position to know all there is to know about UFOs, I will keep silent.'

They walked on for several moments.

Prinzenthal finally formulated a response to such an admission. 'I could not agree more as long as you will be allowed that position. If somebody killed Forrestal for fear of his revealing the truth, what's to say in future they would keep even the president out of the loop in order to protect their control, or, rather in view of the president's plausible deniability and them acting with no congressional over-sight. What began under Truman has likely been consolidated under Eisenhower. I've heard rumors that he has not been happy with the direction of the CIA for that very scenario. I'm telling you, under the Republicans there have been some nasty policy shifts in the guise of security. It's a veritable monster. And it's up to people like us to keep it contained or fascism will rear its ugly head.'

Kennedy abruptly turned back towards the car. Then he stopped.

'Hannah.' The light in his eyes dimmed to a hard stare. 'I won't let that happen. As well, we never had this conversation, and we will keep our confidences private. I know I can trust you.'

'You can trust me on *all* accounts,' she replied, obliquely referring to their brief affair years before.

'You are a rare woman, dear, and I fear even my superior in human relationships.'

'Jack, I've had much to endure; meditation cured my fear of personal corruption—something I had to overcome; in fact, conquering fear is the pathway to knowing oneself, and happiness.'

'I wish there were more like you in politics!' he exclaimed.

'Politics is one of the basest of human struggles where people exploit weakness and strength for their advantage—not much different to espionage.'

'True, but politics proscribes debate, and policy through the democratic process.'

'Perhaps, but politics is no barometer for morality unless there is absolute freedom of media to challenge it.'

Kennedy winced then smiled. 'Well put, Hannah. You'd make a great president!'

'If you need someone on the inside to help you, Jack, know that I am available, and Harley.'

Later, outside his home, Kennedy smiled and waved after instructing the driver to take Greenfield and Prinzenthal wherever they wanted to go downtown.

6. Play the Game

One morning in early May, Dewey, the mail-room boy, pushed his metal cart up to Melbo's desk and piled at least a hundred letters on it, while the journalist talking on the phone could only shake his head in disbelief. This had been going on for over a week. As Dewey moved on, Melbo replaced the receiver with a 'Later then' and began to go through the pile selecting randomly a few letters. He passed on one then changed his mind. He picked it up noticing that there was no return address, but as he put the envelope to his nose, he detected a faint vanilla scent.

Inside he found a postcard showing a palm-lined street with the iconic Mount Lee Hollywood sign in the distance. He turned it over and read *Hi Mel! Thought you'd seen the last of me? I read your article a while ago. Did you know I'm alien? Write a movie about it...I'm your pitch...ha ha. Nora xo.* Melbo just stared at it, shaking his head. *Some strange bird, that Marilyn*, he thought.

He looked at the point of mailing on the post mark on the envelope which said *Hollywood*. He tucked the card in his inside jacket pocket, then read a number of letters, most of them congratulating him on his insightful analysis of an important subject, and some denigrating him for utter foolishness. One fellow who signed his name 'Bert' wrote: '...anybody who believes in aliens should get his head examined and you are at the top of the list—you're a national disgrace!'

The other day Melbo had followed up on another guy's claim that he had met an alien who called himself something unintelligible and was told that there were others visiting Earth and had been for thousands of years. Melbo drove to Tarrytown just north of New York to meet the fellow who would only give his name as Bill. He led him in his own car as Melbo followed in his car up in the hills to a lake in the Pocantico area near the Rockefeller estate. They parked and went to the lake down a path and walked to the location where the

71

meeting had happened. He explained he hadn't said a word about it to anyone for fear they'd call him crazy.

He said early one morning with his dog standing exactly where they were now, he saw a figure emerge from the brush a hundred feet away. The figure stopped and looked at him and words flooded into Bill's mind telling him not to be afraid. He was dressed in what appeared to be satin-like metallic-green overalls but they were tighter with no pockets. In his hand he held a device that looked like a dull metal card about three by six inches and a quarter inch thick. The dog didn't move and cowered as if he was being controlled.

The person was tall and pale—almost opalescent, with short platinum blond hair, long arms and legs. The alien introduced himself saying he was a scout on a mission to collect fresh water. When he saw the lake he landed his small craft in a field nearby in order to do some reconnaissance; when he came into view, he apologized because he was not supposed to make contact with anybody. Then he proceeded to aim his 'card' flat-sided at Bill as if taking a photo after which he appeared to use his fingers to enter some code or something. In a few moments, a small craft came over the trees and hovered over the lake in front of the alien. The craft was metallic and oblong the size of a small van. There were airplane-like windows surrounding it but they were smooth and had no frames or visible doors. Bill could see another figure in the window. No lights or propulsion system were apparent, only a barely audible hum emanated from the craft as it hovered about ten feet above the lake to suck up water without using any conduit into an aperture appearing under the craft.

Bill asked him where he came from, and he replied by again flooding words into Bill's mind, stating they used Earth as a stopover while travelling in that sector of the universe, and that they were guests of the Air Force, their main base and mothership being hidden in a bunker of the remote Nevada desert. After the aperture closed and the water stopped its ascent, the craft moved towards him and a door opened upwards at the back like a hatch. He climbed in and the door sealed as if there had been no door at all. The craft then went straight up almost instantly until it disappeared into some clouds.

Melbo asked Bill if he had any hard proof that this had actually happened, such as a photo or other witnesses reporting having seen something. Bill replied that he had inquired with the police if anything had been reported about a UFO, and they said nothing of the kind, but an officer who would not reveal his name contacted him by phone the next day. He claimed to have seen a fleeting glimpse of a strange object while he was on patrol in the same area at first light of the morning in question. Something caught the corner of his eye as he drove along. He slowed and looked in that direction when it appeared briefly again but dropped out of sight.

Stepping outside on the shoulder of the road, he listened for any sound of an airborne vehicle, because he was certain that what he had seen wasn't a bird; it was much bigger and similar in description to what Bill had described. Hearing nothing, he got back in his patrol car and drove on slowly looking over the forest where he had seen the object. He hadn't told anyone until one of his colleagues had commented facetiously about someone calling in a UFO sighting in the Pocantico forest reserve. Rather than suffer the ridicule of the others, the officer discreetly found Bill's number on the report log.

There was little likelihood of finding out who made that call to Bill supporting his experience, but Melbo detected the ring of authenticity in the occurrence. Other letters from around the country revealed sightings some of which were outlandish and nonsensical—one person described meeting aliens in an operating theatre, a 'dream' she wrote, but she swore it wasn't a dream. Aliens in metallic spacesuits with dark almond shaped eyes, big hairless heads, grayish skin, and long arms and fingers, examined her body, including her genitalia.

Though they didn't hurt her, in the morning upon waking she knew something or someone had touched her there, as it was slightly sore reminding her of a doctor one time inserting a scope into her for a hysteroscopy procedure. Melbo didn't follow up on any encounters of that sort, which seemed like dreams, but after numerous letters about 'dreams', he thought perhaps this repeated detail was no coincidence.

At present, he was more concerned about government complicity in the phenomenon. He knew that he would have to make a trip out West in order to solicit some testimony from those ranchers who were the first on site of the famed Roswell crash, which according to military authorities was actually a weather balloon. Then why the cover-up? thought Melbo. Why were the ranchers told in no uncertain terms to shut up about it? If it was indeed a weather balloon there wouldn't have been anything sensational to report in the first place. And what about the bodies? He had read for fun in a tabloid about the hearsay of a nurse at the air base that the local coroner had procured a number of children's caskets from the local funeral home. The nurse was told in the strictest terms to go home, and not return until called. The nurse or anyone at the base at the time could never be traced by the paper.

'Mel,' said Sinclair's assistant, Pearline. Melbo didn't respond. 'Mel,' she repeated. Melbo seemed to register something like a ripple in the wind. He slowly turned towards her.

'Pearline, did you say something?'

'Sinclair wants to see you.'

'Now?'

'I assume so. I walked by his door and he just told me.'

'Oh, okay, thanks.'

Dick Sinclair was as usual behind his desk covered with a number of papers, articles, memorandums, and notes. He looked up. 'Take a seat.'

Melbo placed his lanky frame in the chair opposite, placed his leg over his knee, and instantly settled as if he'd been there an hour.

'You're invited to a party,' said Sinclair.

'Whose party?'

'The boss, Whitmore. I'm invited too.'

'Should I be flattered, or am I on display?'

'Both, I think; you're article turned some heads.'

'Black tie?'

'Yup.'

'Should I invest in one, or rent?'

Sinclair laughed. 'It's likely a one-off, unless you become a Republican protégé.'

'Good career move.'

'I'll say; there are some deep pockets, Rockefeller for one.'

Melbo laughed. 'Will he be there?'

'The Governor? Good question. I'd hedge my bets on it.'

'I'll feel like a spy. Rockefeller was Eisenhower's political mentor. He'd know something I bet.'

'You have a point; but they have you now where they want you, if there is something to hide.'

'Mmm,' contemplated Melbo. 'Meaning if he may well know what's going on *vis-à-vis* our alien friends, and if he gives me some tidbit that I report—a kind of barium test—they can own me, use me—put me on their radar.'

'Perhaps, but the risk is in maintaining your independence, your integrity as a journalist.'

'The risk is my career being compromised.'

Sinclair sat back and put his feet up on his desk. He lit his pipe; the sweet smoke permeated their space. They sat in silence for half a minute. Melbo opened his mouth ready to speak.

'I'm driving,' interjected Sinclair. 'We'll pick you up. Five, Saturday.'

'Great.'

'You were about to say something.'

'Just a thought,' said Melbo, 'I should play the game and use the public domain as my insurance—turn the tables and own the public.'

'I suppose that depends on how credible you appear. On the other hand, if you come across as even a hint of a threat to some national security agenda you won't stand a chance. I know what clandestine forces can do to destroy someone's reputation. You'd become the goat.'

'Character assassination.'

'Or worse: think of Secretary Forrestal. He was no shrinking violet when it came to his sense of righteousness.'

'Forrestal committed suicide.'

'Nonsense.'

'He was murdered?'

'The only plausible explanation according to his family; he was incarcerated at Bethesda Naval Hospital involuntarily, and held incognito against his will, but died before being legally released by his family. Someone wasn't taking any chances: they knew Forrestal.'

'There was a lot of noise after that; conspiracy theories, I recall,' said Melbo. 'Some say he was an anti-Zionist, against the creation of the state of Israel.'

'True on the last bit;' continued Sinclair, 'he was hounded mercilessly, which likely caused some of his depression. Still, his family was adamant he was always sound of mind. He was tough as nails, but took great umbrage at being called anti-Zionist; he was very sympathetic to the Jews—Judaism being the foundation of his beloved Christianity, and whose people bore the brunt of Nazi atrocity. He just didn't want to provide an excuse for the Arabs to conduct perpetual war on the Jews; and he was right.

'You have to remember the Nazis enabled and trained the Arabs in Palestine and the Middle East in guerilla warfare for the stated objective exterminating every single Jew there, and everywhere. The one-time Grand Mufti of Jerusalem, Amin al-Husseini was their titular head, and a rabid racist who was the "Hitler of Palestine", having allied himself with Nazis, and having lived in Berlin for much of the war.'

'What did Forrestal want?' asked Melbo.

'As secretary of Defense, he knew that with the U. N. partitioning of Palestine into a defacto state of Israel, the American armed forces would eventually become the defacto underwriters of this new state—the American Jewish lobby was powerful—and would have to pit themselves against the Arabs who had been friends, certainly in regard to the oil industry. I think Forrestal wanted some democratic amendment to the Palestine Mandate, perhaps with Trans-Jordan; in other words a gradual one-state solution giving the Arabs some political compensation, though in fairness to the Jews, that was likely untenable because the radical Zionists like Menachem Begin, the militant Irgun leader, believed Israel to be their God-given land—all of it, and they rejected any compromise from either side.'

Melbo sighed. He hated conflict and ideological confrontation unless it was directed against murderous fundamentalists such as Nazis, Communists and their minions, in which case he believed the United Nations should have the power to cease and desist those instigators from both sides. But the reality was that the Americans were pitted globally against the Soviets, so any U.N. mandate was unrealistic.

'All the militants, Jew and Arab alike,' said Melbo. 'should have been enforced by the United Nations, to reach a peace agreement.'

'Peace,' scoffed Sinclair. 'In Palestine, never.'

'So had Forrestal lived not much would have changed.'

Sinclair reflected on that for a few moments. 'When it came to the Middle East, he didn't carry much weight; on the other hand I believe that had he lived, there might have been some revealing of the truth in regard to alien visitation; just enough to set in motion a further reckoning, especially if he was taken out *after* he spilled the proverbial beans; in fact it would have likely saved him— a revealing—the freedom of the press supersedes government sanctity; in other words they couldn't touch him if he appealed to the general public.'

'What would Thomas Jones say to all this?'

'Thomas Jones?'

'So that's not his real name?' asked Melbo pointedly.

'*That* Thomas Jones! So you connected?'

Melbo scrutinized Sinclair. 'He said he knew you in the war.'

'Listen, Mel; I quit OSS when they disbanded in September '45. Jones was a lifer; top notch operator. How did it go?'

'Oh, just fine, and we met his fiancée.'

'We?'

'Melissa and I.'

'Of course,' he said. 'I didn't know he was getting married. Did I tell you we saw him last month? I had him over for dinner. Who is she?'

'Joyce Sommers. Very smart. Beautiful and relatively young—mid thirties I'd say.'

'Damn,' uttered Sinclair. 'What does she do?'

'Something to do with State; I didn't buy it; I figure she's CIA with Jones.'

'Tom's retired; he sails a lot down in the Virgins.'

'Yeah, I gathered.'

'So what came of the meeting?'

'Just that he was doing it as a favor to you.'

'That's it?'

'He said it was treason to spy on ourselves, and information on UFOs, if they exist, was likely so compartmentalized, we'd never know, or get busted trying.'

'But?'

'But he would try on his own time to gather hearsay information and let me know. He told me not to try and find him; he would find me.'

'And the woman?' queried Sinclair.

'I could be wrong but I think she's the ace in the hole.'

'How so?'

'Melissa spent more time with her and got the impression she was multilingual—a real cold warrior. She had a dark side.'

'Not too dark I hope.'

'Nothing like that,' replied Melbo, 'just very experienced like she's seen and done things normal people can't conceive of.'

'So you think she let herself, this Joyce, be read in a way? If she's as good as you say, I don't think Melissa would have come away with all that unless Joyce had some motive.'

'Either way, she seemed light and happy; I don't take any position on it.'

'Interesting,' remarked Sinclair. 'I'll tell you this: Tom Jones had balls. The stories I've heard.'

'What did he say to you?'

'He did say he thought Forrestal was killed.'

'He did? He must know something then.'

'He told me he didn't know anything. I believed him. It was his gut impression. He would've said something had he known more.'

'I'll take your word for it.'

'See you Saturday.'

Melbo stood up.

'Right, Boss.'

7. Million-Dollar Bash

The afternoon before the party, Melissa DeCourt found herself staring into her bathroom mirror. Having bathed, and now draping a towel around her head, she looked at her face and body. In a kind of trance, she saw the parted lips, distinct nose, pale complexion, and liquid blue eyes staring back. At her young age of twenty-one, she was almost shocked at the temerity of this invitation to a Republican bastion of the power elite. She lowered her eyes to her flawless breasts and held them briefly as if they gave her some self-assurance. She then puckered her mouth to utter, 'I am who I am,' indicating she was not about to be anything but herself.

After all, her man Melbo had by a stroke of fate received this invitation, and she was going to do her part at his side. Her intuition bells were tinkling, and she felt there was an opportunity to make a great impression as a couple. She knew him well enough to know that he was almost reticent with his laid-back social graces and she was the more forward, yet that was how they got on so well; she was the parapet—his front line confederate.

Later, groomed and dressed, Melbo sat back on the sofa in his rented tuxedo and black bowtie with his legs stretched out, his black brogues polished. DeCourt stood in the center of the room with her arms up pirouetting in her deep purple ankle-length evening gown, black satin three-inch pumps, a modest pearl necklace, small diamond drop earrings and bejeweled hair clasp on one side, while on the other her thick chestnut hair was free to wave or be enveloped behind her ear. Her smart panache made her appear both chic and conservative at the same time.

'*Well?*' she intoned, doing one more turn.

Melbo couldn't take his eyes off her. 'Stunning, love; just stunning. If I didn't know you, I'd come across like a total fool just gaping at you.'

'I bet. You're just saying that.'

Melbo gaped at her.

'Oh, stop it.' She laughed, as she moved to him. He took her by the arm and planted her on his lap. She maneuvered herself raising her gown to sit full saddle.

'Don't get any ideas, Mel,' he teased.

'You're probably right; it wouldn't do to arrive with cum stains on our rentals.'

'Can you imagine? How embarrassing. They'd send us home.'

'With our tails between our legs.' She laughed. 'But what have we here?' She nestled into him. 'George has reared his head.'

'Curious fellow.'

'God, you're as hard as rock.'

She slipped down her panties and had him out in a nano-second.

'No, pull down my pants; it's safer; no spills.'

'Right.'

Five minutes later murmuring sweetly in post-coital bliss still moving still breathing, they couldn't have collapsed any deeper into each other. Another five minutes later, DeCourt turned her head from Melbo's neck and reached for a bunch of tissues which she then used to swipe clean herself and him as efficiently as a mother cat cleaning her kittens.

'I can't believe we just did that,' she purred contentedly.

'A successful operation.'

'Maybe for you, but I'll be leaking for an hour.'

And with that, she quickly removed herself from him, held her gown up, and rushed to the bathroom.

*

Mr. and Mrs. Sinclair were waiting in the front seat of their blue 1958 Olds Super 88 Fiesta Wagon parked in front of Melbo's apartment building. Both dressed elegantly, he in a dark suit with his Dick Tracy hat, and she in her black-collared beige coat and mink pillbox hat. Melbo and DeCourt climbed into the back seat with a vigor both Sinclairs couldn't help but notice. Mrs. Sinclair turned around to greet them as her husband pulled into the street.

'Hello Mrs. Sinclair,' said DeCourt. 'So nice to meet you!'

'It's Alecia, dear. Call me Aly, and it's nice to meet you too. And George.'

'It's an honor Ma'am,' said Melbo.

Sinclair drove and looked in the rear view mirror from time to time. 'Well, both of you seem well primed for the great event! A little flushed, I dare say.'

Melbo and DeCourt looked at each other. 'Can't be helped,' grinned DeCourt. 'We're still bewildered how two young Democrats have passed muster and are entering the Republican inner keep.'

Both Sinclairs laughed.

'Just don't tell anybody,' said Sinclair. 'And call me Dick.'

'Oh to be young again!' said Mrs. Sinclair. 'You're both so smart and talented. I just loved that article you wrote, George.'

'You mean the ticket to the great event. Thank you.'

'Dick is always raving about your timing or rather, good luck,' she said, as she straightened her hat.

'He's a good writer,' agreed Sinclair, though dissenting with his wife's choice of words. 'But I don't rave, dear.'

'Well, I do,' said DeCourt.

'I can easily understand why George rejected the charms of Marilyn Monroe,' remarked Mrs. Sinclair, diffidently, implying that her husband may not be of the same mettle.

'Believe me, he had no choice in the matter,' said DeCourt.

'You're a lucky man, Mel,' asserted Sinclair, regaining his good mood.

They spoke for a while about trivial matters as they went up the State Highway 9 on the east side of the Hudson River. At Sleepy Hollow they turned north-east towards Westchester, while the Headless Horseman stood in the forest shadows and watched them go.

Finally, they drove into the estate behind a limousine, with other vehicles behind. Sinclair had been there once before. Through the grand fieldstone gates, then along a heavily wooded lane they emerged into an open meadow with a small lake complimenting the mansion on a rise beyond. Limousines and cars backed up all around the large circle, but the line moved quickly. When it was their turn, a young man came to the driver's window which Sinclair rolled down.

'Here's a number and I've written your license plate on your chit. I'll take it from here, sir.' He opened his door.

'Be careful with this good friend, son,' said Sinclair, getting out.

Other young men opened the other doors, and they all stepped out. It was early evening, and the sun had made a late appearance brightening up the lawns glistening from an earlier rain. The air was so fresh it felt like a veritable Eden, only with a massive field stone mansion.

'We really should get out into the country more often,' said Melbo to DeCourt discretely breathing in deeply.

'All this fresh air might make us sex maniacs,' she replied quietly deadpan, looking about at the throng of guests slowly ascending the stone steps and approaching the open doors.

'Mel, I don't think that would make a difference with us,' said Melbo. 'Let's be normal.'

'I'm quite normal, Mel.'

A liveried servant just inside directed them to a guest book on a table where they were asked their names and checked on a list. Sinclair and his wife were behind them. A large crowd of people had already congregated in the large marble-floored entrance hall. High above the guests was suspended a massive crystal chandelier on both sides of which colonial wooden stairs led up to the upper floors and vaulted ceiling. Paintings and portraits adorned every square yard of wall. Murmuring voices were growing in decibels by the minute but levelled off as the guests slowly moved into a sunlit indoor atrium leading out onto a huge patio and garden.

Melbo and DeCourt stood for a moment like boulders in a stream as others flowed around them. They took note of a lounge and library with extensive wood paneling, and beyond that a large living area; and then they were absolutely amazed by an enormous dining room/gallery/auditorium on the other side, perhaps sixty feet by forty with three long tables all set to perfection like something one would expect in a royal palace, with wood paneling, escutcheons, old paintings, tapestries, a famous portrait of General Washington on horseback and giant rugs from some lost kingdom in Persia.

The kitchen and pantries lay no doubt beyond. Liveried servants, both men and women moved everywhere helping guests with coats and making finishing touches. In the atrium along a cloth covered table guests were eagerly lifting dozens of champagne glasses. Melbo and DeCourt took theirs, but dozens more filled almost as fast as they disappeared.

'I'll be drunk before dinner,' quipped DeCourt, taking a sip. 'Oh my God, this stuff was made in heaven, and so chilled.'

'What's the champagne?' asked Melbo of one of the waiters filling fresh glasses.

'Taittinger Brut '58,' he said, holding out the bottle. 'He bought a hundred cases.'

'Just a hundred? Must be a vintage year.'

'Yes, well, they've chilled twelve cases for this evening alone, sir. That's seventy-two bottles, just to be sure.'

'Thank you. It's good to know that when we have our return party.'

DeCourt suppressed a laugh.

'Enjoy the evening, sir.'

DeCourt steered Melbo aside from the crowded foyer into a slight recessed space with large potted ferns and a dark mahogany bench.

'What?' asked Melbo, drinking half his glass and eying more across the atrium.

'I swear I just saw Ike and Mamie.'

'Where?' Melbo looked around.

'Outside.'

They looked but a sea of dark tuxedos and sequined gowns interfered with their view.

'I think he was talking to Mr. Whitmore.'

The crowd parted momentarily before them as if by telekinesis. Governor Rockefeller emerged with Central Intelligence Director Allen Sulla and wives in tow.

'We are in the midst of the keepers of the greatest mystery known to man,' stated Melbo, finishing his champagne. 'And the Grand Viziers have made their entrance.'

'You make it sound like they're here to stay, Mel. There's an election, remember?'

'Oh, they're here to stay alright. Elected officials come and go, but not these guys, at least Sulla, or his people. I can see it just by looking at him— that smug smile with cold eyes. The guy's a devil.'

'You don't know that, Mel.'

After three champagnes in relatively quick succession, and lingering over the fourth, Melbo and DeCourt felt at ease now and stood on the perimeter of the patio. The President, Governor, Director and sycophants meanwhile huddled at the edge of the garden and seemed to be engaged in a serious summit conversation that was broken occasionally by contrived guffaws before they immersed themselves again in their discussion. Their wives stood about speaking to each other upwind from Sulla's pipe smoke which wafted Melbo's way.

'Smoke signals?' chuckled Melbo.

'He's sending a message?' prompted DeCourt, giggling with bubbly.

'If he were, we'd need a cypher clerk.'

At that very moment, as if on cue, none other than Joyce Sommers appeared on the arm of a swarthy punching-bag middle-aged man with extremely bushy eyebrows and a large nose looking like Good King Wenceslas in a frumpy black suit. Sommers was dressed in a navy gown with the identical dress shoes as DeCourt's. She also wore pearls, a deceptively simple platinum tiara, and valuable diamond earrings two inches long. They were received by a couple standing near the President and his entourage; a portly gentleman wearing large black spectacles, greeted the Good King with Joyce almost slavishly as though she were an idol.

Melbo and DeCourt could only stare in stunned silence. Thankfully people wandered back and forth across their field of vision otherwise their staring might have attracted attention—a psychometric red flag to the attentive secret service personnel. Again the crowd blocked their view.

'How on earth…' uttered DeCourt.

'Hell's bells.'

'Hell's bells is right.'

When the crowd cleared again for a few seconds Joyce Sommers was staring at them. Her expression was of subtle bemusement, but she gave no acknowledgement of familiarity, as if to say: Mind your own business. The crowd closed again.

'Mel, what was that?' said DeCourt.

'We just found our cypher. Thank God for Joyce Sommers.'

'But where's Mr. Jones?'

'Moreover, who's the dude?'

'Which one?'

'The eyebrows.'

The Good King was speaking to the owl glasses as if they knew each other well.

'Likely just a friend or colleague,' said Melbo. 'Looks familiar though.'

'What could she possibly see in him?'

'Nothing likely. We shouldn't read too much into it.'

'She's no social worker,' declared DeCourt. 'She's a sophisticate, she's too good. This woman is powerful, out of our league.'

'Is that your feminine alarm bell ringing?' inquired Melbo.

'Damn right it is.'

'Then it's good that she's on our side.'

'Are we sure about that? It scares me. Why is she here?' asked DeCourt.

'I don't know.'

'Why are we here?'

'This is an intelligence gathering mission.'

'Get off it!' retorted DeCourt, grinning and mock punching Melbo in the arm, spilling his champagne.

'Look at it this way,' said Melbo, finishing what little champagne remained in his glass, 'Joyce Sommers is way ahead of the curve.'

The crowd separated again momentarily. Joyce Sommers was now speaking to the portly gentleman, when Sulla went over to greet her with a peck on the cheek and hand on her arm. The Governor was then introduced and finally the President. Eisenhower appeared quite happy to meet her and held her hand with both of his. Clearly, she was someone he knew or had heard of and held in high respect. The Governor, as well, was obviously quite smitten judging from the look in his eyes which seemed to undress her from face to breasts to delta of Venus and down her long legs. To Melbo and DeCourt, Joyce Sommers appeared to be the *objet d'affection* by some private understanding—a veritable queen of mystery.

'Who's the pudgy guy with the glasses?' asked DeCourt.

'No idea; a bootlicker?'

'Doubt it; he's one of the boys.'

'Almost everyone here is a bootlicker, to me.'

'Tush. Should we approach Joyce?' asked DeCourt.

'She knows we're here; let it be. Give her some line.'

'She's not a fish, Mel.'

'Well, she's swimming with the sharks.'

'You're probably right considering the way she looked at us. How in hell did she know we were here?'

'She saw us somewhere in the crowd.'

'But she came in late.'

'Maybe she read the guest list.'

'The way we were shepherded through? I doubt it. There was no time.'

'There's Dick,' Melbo gestured.

Sinclair was enjoying himself immensely and with champagne glass in hand following the host, Jake Whitmore, who ushered him past the President towards the open garden where dozens of people milled about beyond the inner circle of power. Mrs. Sinclair was not to be seen and likely powdering her nose. One could hear 'Nixon' and 'Kennedy' as everybody had something to say about the primaries.

Kennedy had won West Virginia a few days earlier, and now people were beginning to predict his nomination as Democratic leader and a potentially close election race between him and Nixon the shoo-in for the Republican nomination having been Vice-President under Eisenhower, the much hailed leader and war hero. But there was change in the air. Many of the younger generation of voting age were challenging the status quo—the Republican kind.

They found Eisenhower stodgy and removed from new beginnings. Some even felt that he was losing his grasp and had caved into his powerful cabinet especially to the duo of Don Nestor Sulla, though recently deceased, and his younger brother Allen Sulla. As Secretary of State and the DCI, these two men had formed a potent symbiosis which conducted foreign policy and toppled governments in equal measure in the name of a very cold war, while democracy—or rather the people—slept at the wheel. A deep state had been spawned in which no matter who was elected there emerged an impervious substrata that answered only to themselves—a brainchild ironically to protect the hard-won freedoms of liberal democracy.

Dinner was announced. So, the murmuring mob of wealth and privilege moved like a giant caterpillar back into the mansion.

8. Smoke and Mirrors

DeCourt joined other women in a queue outside the ladies washroom near the atrium. Melbo was directed to the men's washroom in the study by the front hall or a bathroom upstairs to the left. A female servant then announced there was another bathroom upstairs on the right for the women. DeCourt quickly left the line and went to the front hall and upstairs.

On the way, she heard a barely audible voice behind her. 'Don't look. We don't know each other; tell Mel too. No names.' Holding the dark glossy banister, DeCourt went ahead casually. Ahead of her, the door opened and an elderly lady stepped out saying, 'It's all yours, dear!' As DeCourt closed the bathroom door behind her, she saw Joyce Sommers waiting next in line with a smile on her face. On her way out, she couldn't help but feel as Sommers passed by redolent of a hint of Chanel 5 that Joyce was completely in her element and appeared to be enjoying herself. Her genuine smile seemed to relieve DeCourt of her earlier fear. She told herself she needed to know this woman as if her life depended on it.

Meanwhile, Melbo went upstairs as well curious to have a look around. At the top, hallways extended in both directions for almost as far as he could see. Across the hall from the bathroom to his left, standing like a sentinel was a serious young man. An elderly man with his back to Melbo was waiting patiently at the doorway. Melbo walked up but the sentinel motioned to him to stand back. The elderly man turned. It was the President. 'Bill, you're scaring the guests,' he said light-heartedly, looking at Melbo. 'Ike,' he said, holding out his hand.

'George Melbo, sir,' said Melbo, accepting it graciously, but feeling rather intimidated by his proximity to the head of state. 'It's an honor, sir.'

'Melbo. Now where have I heard that name?' he asked himself, looking directly into Melbo's eyes. 'Mamie,' he recalled, blue eyes brightening. 'Yes, my wife thought I should read one of Whitmore's articles. You're the writer?'

'I am, sir.'

'That was quite a piece, you know; had some moxie. I like that.'

'Is there any truth in it, sir?' asked Melbo, his heart in his throat.

Eisenhower laughed politely, but held his eye contact, like the General. Other men now lined up but gave them some space at the sentinel's command.

'George, you can be sure that there's a great deal of interest; everyone wants to know.'

'It seems pretty obvious, sir. I've heard some credible accounts.'

'Fascinating, but we're in the dark; it's not up to me-'

The washroom door opened and out stepped Art Lovering.

'So you're the guy holding up the line,' joked Eisenhower.

'Mr. President.'

Lovering looked at Melbo then back at the President.

'Meet George Melbo,' said Eisenhower. 'This is Art Lovering.' They shook hands. 'Well, I'll excuse myself.' The President slipped into the bathroom.

'Nice to meet you, sir,' said Melbo.

'Likewise,' said Lovering without much cordiality, as he quickly left.

*

Dozens of servants moved with swift and steady deliberation among the three long tables. Jake Whitmore and his wife sat with the Governor and President and wives at the far end of the second table. Art Lovering and Allen Sulla with their wives sat next to them, and many other leaders of industry and institutions were seated around the room. At least fifty people sat at each table, Sinclair and his wife near the top end of the third table, Melbo and DeCourt at the bottom of the same table. DeCourt saw Joyce Sommers and King Wenceslas at the first table a third of the way down from the top facing towards the second table. But there was little time to look around, as a simple grace was offered by Whitmore after a few words of greeting to the President and all his guests.

The lobster bisque was exquisite, served with a chilled Pouilly-Fumé from the Loire. No sooner had the dishes been cleared, than pan-seared foie gras in butter and calvados with toast and cranberry compote miraculously arrived. Everyone was praising the hosts to high heaven. Talk was animated having been fueled by generous quantities of alcohol all evening, but this wasn't just alcohol, it was elixir from the vineyards of Bourbon ghosts. A lemon *glâce* came next, for the palate to digest a little before the main course.

Melbo and DeCourt marveled at the *haute couture* of the Republican Elephants. They laughed when the lady beside them said, 'Work hard and you can eat like this every day!' DeCourt was tempted to retort: And die of a heart attack! *But this was power*, thought Melbo, and he knew then that the answers to his questions addressed to Eisenhower would never be forthcoming unless he were to join them at their own game, much like a medieval church controlling the masses in a language they didn't understand.

The main course, a thick-sliced piece of beef chateaubriand with a heaping dollop of béarnaise sauce in a little side cup, crispy potatoes—*pomme rissolée*—asparagus and carrots arrived expertly on hot plates, a certain feat at such a large gathering. The wine served now was a Nuits-Saint-George Burgundy that literally diffused in the mouth lingering on the tongue, like something Aphrodite would use to enslave for life her next conquest.

'I gotta hand it to my boss, he can really kiss ass with a fundraiser like this,' said Melbo, a bit too loudly, while he finished the last of his beef and béarnaise.

'Everyone heard you, Mel,' confided DeCourt close to his ear.

'I certainly heard you,' said the lady beside him, 'but don't fret, it's not a fundraiser, it's a birthday party. But I'll tell you a little secret.' She leaned in with a surreptitious smile. 'My husband died a couple of years ago, but after retiring from the air force—a colonel—he worked for the Party of Lincoln near the top; well, he said the money flowed no matter what at fundraisers, but birthday parties were the big winners because that's where everybody got drunk and loosened their wallets! The fundraisers were always stodgy affairs.'

'I never would have guessed,' said Melbo, smiling like a Cheshire cat.

'Did you ever meet the President?' asked DeCourt.

'Oh, yes, many times, but he hardly remembered me.'

'What do you think about all the talk of UFOs?' enquired Melbo, unexpectedly.

'UFOs? You mean all those lights in Washington? I was there. I saw them.'

'Really?' said DeCourt.

'Dear, all the brass were abuzz about it. Laurence, that's my husband, told me confidentially—I suppose I can say something now—I mean he's passed on …' She fell silent, but recovered. 'Well, he said they were studying the ships, and then he winked at me. To tell you the truth I didn't believe a word of it because when he winked at me it meant he wanted you know what!'

Melbo and DeCourt were too polite to say anything. The lady thought they didn't understand her innuendo and began to laugh. 'You know … ride the flag pole? I grew up on a ranch in New Mexico, and we had our own way of saying things.'

'You're a true patriot, Mrs. …' said Melbo.

The lady smiled. 'Edna Beiderman, born Wills.'

'It's been a pleasure, Mrs. Beiderman,' added DeCourt.

'Call me Edna, for God's sake!'

'Edna!'

'That's more like it! And I don't mind telling you, my brother Garnett— he still lives on the ranch—he said he knew the ranchers back in '47 near Corona when they said space ships crashed. I'm the only person he told, not even my husband; no one knew he knew about it, and he left it at that. He said it's better you don't tell anyone, especially your husband; well, I didn't 'cause I thought it was plain crazy. They didn't get on so well anyway. Garnett was a loner, gone all native even. They all are, once you've lived on the range all your life.'

'Would he mind if I talked to him?' asked Melbo.

'Well, he'll know right away I told you about him; he might not be that happy about that. But just tell him that I said that sometimes you gotta get stuff off your chest, and these nice young folks are the new generation and really smart about all that crazy stuff. Maybe it's true for all I know.'

After a delightful *kirschwasser*-soaked Black Forest birthday cake, coffee and tea were served. Whitmore then made a short speech thanking everyone for coming to his "birthday fête" and reminding his guests to be sure to remember the party "benevolence plate" and to find so and so in the drawing room and library for pledges. Then a smiling red-faced President stood up and began singing "Happy Birthday!" Everyone followed and applauded.

Afterwards, Art Lovering, a good friend of the host, stood up to extend thanks from everybody for this magnificent spectacle and perfect feast. The wine, food, and indeed champagne deserved hearty accolades and toasts to the host and President, and even to Nixon, their candidate who was on the campaign trail.

After dinner, most of the women and a few of the men gravitated back to the atrium, while others retired to the library for brandy and cigars, pipes, or cigarettes with elegant ivory cigarette holders. Having decided against intruding on any of the groups with exclusive girdles about them, Melbo and DeCourt were perusing the shelves for interesting books, wondering if Whitmore had read any of them. Sinclair approached them pipe in hand.

'There you are my young prodigies! Well, now, what's the skinny? If you're as drunk as I am, the world wags to a black-tie circus! Did you see Ike?' he spoke more delicately, looking about. 'He's in his cups, I'd say, but who isn't?'

Mrs. Sinclair showed up in time to hear her husband's words and said, 'I *isn't*, and I'm driving.'

Melbo and DeCourt smiled, and said, 'Thank you.'

'But of course my usual sobriety always takes second place to that of the Empress of Virginia.' Sinclair puts his arm around his wife's waist. 'If not for my darling Aly, my life would be gob-smacked to knavery. She rescued me from the sins of my father who threw away a fortune before the depression!'

'He was such a sweet boy,' added Mrs. Sinclair looking at her husband, 'and wooed me in French. Little did I know how lascivious his tongue was.'

Melbo and DeCourt didn't quite know how to respond to that, but smiled innocently.

'Dear,' retorted Sinclair, 'I recall you agreed to marry me during that very subtext: don't stop!'

'See what I mean?' concurred Mrs. Sinclair unabashedly. 'I rest my case, the rogue.' But she stood by his side and let him hold her. It was obvious she loved him for that very reason. Melbo presumed she had grown up a pampered southern belle who on the surface was a paragon of etiquette and calm grace yet whose sensual appetites raged beneath the surface; she was no shrinking violet, a tribute to southern women whose legacy toughed out the privations of the Civil War.

'Men are rogues, Aly,' said DeCourt, 'but some are adorable and worth taming.'

'I couldn't agree more, dear; George reminds me of General Jeb Stuart, and he was no rogue.'

'You're too kind,' said Melbo. 'I was just thinking you are the loveliest peach of the south.'

'Oh, my, you're undermining my inbred distrust of Yankee gentlemen,' she said laughing and touched Melbo on the arm. Then taking DeCourt's hand she added, 'Melissa, you hang onto this fellow now. He's gold.'

'Well, perhaps if he wants to tie the knot.'

Jake Whitmore whisked by with a drink and cigar, then stopped and turned around, his cigar smoke swirling. He'd had several drinks, and was flying on the summit of golden triumph.

'Dick Sinclair! Have you and … Mrs. …'

'Aly,' said Mrs. Sinclair, giving him a solid peck on the cheek.

'I didn't deserve that,' he confessed, 'but I think I'll do that more often if you give me more of those!' He laughed affably. 'And who might you be?' he asked looking at DeCourt, seeming to angle for more of the same.

'Mr. Whitmore, how do you do? Melissa DeCourt.' She held out her hand.

'Ah, you're Melbo's girl,' he said taking her hand, and turning to Melbo. 'How are things, Mel?'

'Things are wonderful, sir. Thank you so much for having us.'

'Have you had a chance to meet some of the movers and shakers?'

'Well, I met briefly with the President in the bathroom line upstairs. He turned around with his outstretched hand and said: "Ike"!'

They all laughed.

'You didn't tell me that!' uttered DeCourt.

'Well it kind of stunned me at the time.'

'He arrived by helicopter earlier, and will shortly leave for his home in Gettysburg, his retreat,' Whitmore told them.

'I wondered whose helicopter that was,' said Sinclair, 'parked out back on the far lawn.'

'A new Marine HMX something or other,' returned Whitmore. 'Mamie will actually fly in it.'

'Perhaps we can see him off,' said Melbo.

'Sure thing; everyone will likely do the same.'

He spoke not a minute too soon. The President and his wife emerged from a phalanx of black suits down in the corner and walked past, stopping to shake a hand or two. Eisenhower saw Whitmore who was now waiting for him, but the President looked at Melbo and his group, smiled with a little wave and continued. Whitmore and the President disappeared into the hall and atrium. The crowd all applauded and murmured what sounded like "Goodbye", or

"Mr. President," and followed gradually behind, with the President nodding and waving to the general party.

When almost everyone was outside, and the President and Mamie, who joined him from a gaggle of women, boarded the helicopter, its motors started and blades turned to finally lift off into the moonlight. As the sound of the rotors faded in the distance, the party continued as everyone savored the fresh air which promised a second wind to the festivities.

The plan was to meet the Sinclairs out front for the drive home at eleven, so Melbo and DeCourt had an hour to fill with more observation of the rites of Republican pre-eminence. They saw Joyce Sommers traipse by at one point not giving them a bat of an eye. They realized that she was playing it safe and didn't want to draw any attention to them. Her game was high stakes with some of the most powerful men in the country, perhaps even the most powerful man, Allen Sulla, who was obviously well aware of who she was.

Melbo told DeCourt more about his short meeting with Eisenhower and what the President had tried to say about the alien issue being "not up to me." If not up to the President they wondered, who then? Only one person came to mind, and he was standing with that owl Art Lovering and a few others by a statue of Apollo: but no Apollo was Allen Sulla.

'Who's the guy with the glasses,' asked DeCourt. 'He's always around the heavies.'

'Art Lovering. I have no idea who he is, but he's obviously an insider—likely CIA by the looks of it. Thomas Jones would likely know. I don't like him; he's too coy for me.'

'You think he's dangerous?'

'They're all dangerous, except Ike maybe; I think that at this stage of the game he's been left behind.'

'I don't understand.'

'I don't think he has any control over Sulla and people like Lovering, if what he said to me has any truth.'

'Jesus, that's comforting,' said DeCourt.

'What's worse is that if it's true, these guys have created a monster that any future president could be powerless to command.'

'You mean like your defacto cabal buried within the legitimate government.'

'Yes, all in the name of national security. These guys are fighting the cold

93

war, and the cold war is a clandestine war—a war managed by mean bastards who monitor democracy like a game of chess.'

'War is war. The Soviets are the greater evil. At least that's the message Joyce went on about last month.'

'Yeah, but we've come to a new threshold that could do us more harm than good.'

'She also said in so many words that it's totalitarianism that she feared more than anything, so she may be a cold warrior but freedom is her touchstone so-to-speak.'

'Freedom is everyone's touchstone in this place,' stated Melbo. 'But it's all smoke and mirrors.'

DeCourt urged him back into the alcove with the palm plant and bench.

'Mel, you're drunk.'

'Am I, darling? Well, it makes me realize that Republican galas like these are all artifice and what's beneath is creeping fascism. Before the war and in the early years of the war in Europe they were big fans of that puppet Lindberg and political isolationism—according to Dick, they actively supported American non-entry to such an extent that President Roosevelt had them monitored like enemies by Churchill's spies. It was people like that in the State Department who sent back the German cruise ship *St. Louis* full of Jews desperately seeking asylum, which had the effect of supporting the Nazis, though Sulla actually fought for them nominally and was an interventionist when it came to Nazis and he even helped some wealthy Jews escape before the war.

'It was only after Pearl Harbor and after Hitler declared war on America that they changed their tune, but as soon as the war was won, Dick told me in confidence that Allen Sulla sought out any Nazi, even war criminals, to join him in the fight against Stalin, and gave them new identities. When Nazis were being hanged in Nuremberg, Sulla managed to save some of the lesser known such as Lieutenant General Reinhard Gehlen, the Wehrmacht Intelligence Chief for Eastern Europe, and SS General Karl Wolff, who literally got away with mass murder as Himmler's deputy and Eichmann's superior!'

'As venomous as it sounds, perhaps Sulla was just being practical, knowing the extent of Stalin's duplicity,' remarked DeCourt. 'He needed intelligence.'

'That's a fancy way of putting it,' said Melbo, irritated.

'Come on, Mel, hindsight is too easy. The Reds just took over where the Nazis left off; somebody had to do something.'

'No argument there; it's just so damned hypocritical, immoral, and these bastards are now ruling the world.'

'At least they're *our* bastards,' suggested DeCourt.

'Mel, you're supporting them?'

'Not at all, but this is America, and someday they'll get their retribution.'

Melbo sighed. 'Sorry for doubting, sweet.' Then he smiled, '*Touché.*'

At that moment King Wenceslas hesitated in front of Melbo and DeCourt. They expected him to carry on. Instead, he turned to them with a smile, 'Melbo?'

'Yes,' said Melbo holding out his hand. 'George Melbo, and my fiancée, Melissa DeCourt.'

'Edward Teller.'

'I should have known. Dr. Teller, it's an honor, sir.'

'Enchanted,' he said in Hungarian-accented English while looking at DeCourt, and shaking both of their hands. 'Someone pointed you out, George, as the author of the article, *Who Believes in Aliens?*'

'Guilty, as charged,' said Melbo.

'Most interesting. May I ask what do you believe?'

'An unequivocal *yes.*'

'So do I. One must accept that in the vastness of the universe with hundreds of billions of galaxies and trillions of stars there must be a plethora of life, and some of that life could well be millions, even a billion years ahead of us here on Earth.'

'Wow,' said DeCourt, 'we've been waiting for someone important to say that!'

'Yes, and furthermore,' he went on, 'one would have to assume that technology had been developed to enable these people to travel the staggering distances light years away from their homes.'

'And not only technology, Dr. Teller,' added Melbo, 'but the evolution of species into intelligent life forms so far beyond our relatively primitive state that we are incapable of understanding their exceptional physical abilities, except perhaps in the most basic sense: nourishment, procreation, sleep and health.'

Teller nodded his affirmation. 'So you see, in that alone is the starting point of discovery, wouldn't you say? To meet on common ground, common themes?'

'Are you saying that this is really happening?' asked DeCourt, her eyes wide with optimism.

'No,' he replied flatly. 'But you've got the right attitude.'

'Wait a minute,' said Melbo, 'There's too much evidence, and a mysterious absence of any official acknowledgement to deny that something big is going on. Take Roswell for example.'

'Roswell,' he sighed, 'that hobgoblin. I'll let you in on a little secret.' Teller moved closer to them and lowered his voice. 'You know by now that during the war I was involved with the Manhattan Project, the fanatically secret operation to build the bomb.'

'Yes,' they both said earnestly.

'I'm one of the principals of Los Alamos Laboratories in New Mexico; that's no secret as well. If aliens had indeed landed and were interested in us, there's no doubt that I and the world at large would be informed about it. We would have to accept an all new reality. But nothing of the kind has happened, just a lot of hype and screwballs coming out of the woods with fantastic stories. I for one, though, value your input, George, because you have risen above the hype and have attempted to … let's just say *intellectualize* the whole phenomenon.'

Melbo held his ground. 'But so many people, military people, people who are credible, air traffic control people, people who simply happened to see things such as the lights over Washington, which incidentally showed up on radar screens—these phenomena are real. Why disavow them? Perhaps this is evidence of our primitive condition,' contended Melbo.

'Exactly, George. Listen, don't take my word for it. Sure, I'm a scientist, but there are so many reasons no one of any authority will stand up and say: we've made contact with people from another planet! To begin with, we would not even know if they were people or something beyond our psychological capacity such that we're ill-equipped to deal with them in any rational way. Take my advice, write your articles, but don't let the whole thing get out of hand. Keep it light, entertain the theories, the possibilities; this is what's fascinating but avoid trying to expose some insidious plot within the government—it will be met with derision because no one has any idea what these UFOs are.'

'That's telling, sir, no pun intended,' said Melbo with a sly glance at DeCourt, who suppressed a laugh. 'I kind of feel like someone put you up to this, Dr. Teller, no offence,' alleged Melbo.

Teller smiled and looked up in space momentarily. 'You seem like great young folks, the future of our country. My wife Mitzi who couldn't be here tonight, has told me time and again, "Edward, you're not practicing what you preach: you're making your life more complicated!" Hey, it's been a grand evening. Take care now.' He turned to go.

'Dr. Teller?'

'Yes, Melissa,' he answered turning around.

'Who was that lovely looking woman you arrived with?'

Teller seemed momentarily stunned. 'Hannah? Nothing untoward I can assure you,' he said. 'I've known her since she was a child. Her father, David Prinzenthal, a doctor of letters, was well known in Eastern Europe, and an acquaintance of my father. We are Jews, albeit agnostic. Herr Prinzenthal was murdered we think by French fascists after her family emigrated to France in the late '20s. Hannah's an extraordinary woman, careerist in government, a polyglot—a real charmer, and I never let a chance go by to see her whenever I'm in the East, and she jumped at the opportunity to accompany me here.' He then faded into the crowd.

Melbo and DeCourt looked at each other and hugged spontaneously.

'That took some nerve, Mel,' gushed Melbo. 'Impeccable timing; you caught him off guard, but it was delivered innocently … my love.' They kissed.

DeCourt took a breath. 'I admit, it was pretty good tradecraft. Hannah would be impressed.'

'Hannah Prinzenthal, the name suits her better than Joyce Sommers.'

'Yes,' she concurred. 'Sounds like she's had quite a life; too bad about her father though.'

'No wonder she's a spy with that background. Do you think *she* put Teller up to it?' queried Melbo.

'Good question.'

'Yeah.'

'Hey,' exclaimed DeCourt suddenly,' you said something before; something about a fiancée … Well, what was that all about?'

'Yeah, right. Come here.' He gently took DeCourt by the arms and sat her down on the bench. Then he knelt. 'Mel, will you marry me?'

DeCourt stared blank-faced at Melbo with his plaintive expression. Her eyes opened wide.

'Are you serious?'

'Are you kidding?' quipped Melbo.

'Mel, I'm so shocked, my God, of course I'll marry you. Yes!'

9. When the Saints Come Marching In

'Lower,' she whispered.

Greenfield scratched lower. 'I recall reading something that Helen Keller said: "Optimism is the faith that leads to achievement",' muttered Harley Greenfield, working the bare back of Hannah Prinzenthal in her Central Park apartment bed.

Prinzenthal murmured, 'What time is it?'

'The sun's up … eight, maybe.'

'Lower, a bit more, there.'

Greenfield scratched gently, his strong hand the perfect complement to her maidenly back. He loved her lithe body, so feminine, so unassailable, forbidden.

'What does Helen Keller have to do with anything?' she purred.

'It just occurred to me that in a way, I'm deaf and blind in my love for you.'

'Well, knock yourself out, old man.'

'I'll take that as a compliment.'

She reached behind her and felt for his manhood, which stood ready at attention.

'Well, if you're so inclined …'

He slowly slid his hand over her hip and raised her leg to stroke her inner thigh for a long minute. She held onto his morning shaft pulling gently. Finally, he caressed the lips of her plum as she guided him inside like a cob spun in butter, then drumming her cherry ever so gently, he induced sweet cries that would be the envy of Venus. Over and over and over they synced perfectly until finally, in an indeterminable time, they both burst into paroxysms so profound she milked him, both shuddering almost violently. Flooding her with his hot cream, they released in unison a moan so deep that the walls of her bedroom seemed to vibrate in their ears. For minutes afterwards, they moved until their gasps quietened as if to sleep.

Forty minutes later, washed, dressed, and sipping coffee at the kitchen table, they hardly spoke, as if some Rubicon had been crossed from which there would be no return. Prinzenthal was particularly silent, almost morose, as if something had changed within her—some instinctual shift that allowed her to feel love. She put her hands to her womb as if there was another reason for it. It was Saturday a week after the Republican gala birthday party.

'Hannah,' said Greenfield. 'are you okay?'

'No, I'm not okay.'

'That was the most beautiful…' He didn't finish his sentence. He knew their amity lay somewhere between the expiation of love and her rejection of it. But he thought he should at least half say it.

'Fuck you, Harley!' she exploded. Her face was wrenched in emotional turmoil, eyes angry like two shiny emeralds in red-rimmed purgatory. 'I'm crazy! I'm probably pregnant! I'm ovulating!'

'I love you too.'

'That … that … What was that? What we did this morning? I've never felt like that before! It blew my fucking circuits!'

'It was the same for me.'

'Did God decide to personally get us off! You know? I don't even believe in God! It wasn't normal! How am I supposed to do my job after that?'

'You said you had the weekend off.'

The way he delivered that, she abruptly stopped her rant and almost laughed. Greenfield could turn a supernova into a trifle.

'I'm never off!' she exhorted.

Greenfield let it go at that. He'd never seen her so worked up on account of their relationship. Ostensibly, she had lost her control, her cool, and bottomed out in the realization she was human after all. The stress of her walking the tight rope for so many years had formed in effect a crystal like a perfect manifestation of experience now shattered. Greenfield had had his own crisis when they had gone their separate ways years before. She couldn't have cared less then, so immersed was she in the secret world. He had eventually retired because he knew he couldn't be with her. But now was different. That morning as she said was like a divine intervention—a Leda and the Swan event without the rape which changed everything.

'We'll get over it,' he said.

'Not if I'm pregnant.'

'How can you know that?'

'I just know!'

'Okay,' he said evenly.

'I let it happen. That's the problem.' She was thinking now, calming. 'With you I allowed myself to be in love … and then …'

Greenfield looked at her. She looked up at him, eyes searching.

'Yes,' he said.

'That happened … we connected like … like God or whatever.'

'Why can't we just let it be like that?'

'Because it can't just be like that.'

'This is not an op, Hannah.'

'Don't belittle me.'

'Never.'

'You said we're meeting with the Mels today,' she said suddenly changing the subject.

'This evening.'

'Where?'

'A place of his choosing—don't know yet.'

'Playing spy, are they?' She smiled and raised an eyebrow.

'Just as well.'

'Now that eyes are on him.'

'I'm rather curious to know how it went for them at the party,' said Greenfield.

'They behaved, as far as I could tell.'

'Did you behave?'

'You know me.'

'You mentioned you switched a place-name, why?'

'Oh, for fun.'

'Come on, darling.'

'Whitmore graciously submitted a guest list to the secret service because of the President, and we got a copy.'

'And?'

'On a whim I noticed that a widow, Edna Beiderman (née Wills) in her brief profile grew up on a ranch in New Mexico near Roswell, so I thought …'

'Ah, very Prinzenthal.' He smiled.

She looked back at him her eyes almost pleading, her demons not quite placated but tamed for the time being.

'I want this baby, for Lizbet.'

'Okay, dear.'

*

Saturday, May 21 1960
New York Herald Tribune
The Saints Come Marching In
By George Melbo

Last weekend I was invited to the birthday party of the owner of the New York Herald Tribune. There must have been between one hundred and fifty and two hundred people, and what a gala event it was, attended by President Eisenhower, Governor Rockefeller, military brass in civilian attire, and many of the country's Republican élite, including Allen Sulla, our top spy. I can only assume that as a young relatively unknown journalist in Jake Whitmore's employ, I was honored with his invitation for having written an article last month about UFOs, an article that seemed to get the attention of numerous citizens and officials alike.

In fact, a few people sought me out in that Westchester mansion to applaud my gumption for having written it at all. Well, I must give credit where credit is due. If it weren't for my immediate boss, my editor who also attended the party, I would have likely never undertaken the task. But here I am. Some of the readers might now rightly ask whether I used this glorious opportunity to grab the bull by the horns and ask our leaders what on earth is happening in the skies! I even thought, naïvely perhaps, that that was the reason I was invited, namely, to ask the question: What do you know? Because if they don't know, nobody does. Well, being a humble civilian and feeling a little overwhelmed by all the spectacle of wealth and power, I submitted meekly to the commanding presence of the many dignitaries and even their wives!

Nonetheless, fueled by the great vintages of famed vintners, I had the good fortune of shaking the President's hand near the bathroom. I was much comforted by his modest introduction as "Ike" and even summoned enough nerve to ask him after he acknowledged that he had been urged at "Mamie's" request to read my article: "Is there any truth in it, sir?"

And he replied: "George, you can be sure there's a lot of interest; we all want to know," *before the bathroom door opened and he darted in, thus avoiding any more pesky questions from me. I have to hand it to Ike: he's truly a paragon of steady control in a dangerous and tumultuous time with murderous Soviet hegemony in the East, wars ending and beginning a perpetual threat of nuclear war, a sluggish economy, and now UFOs. I'm surprised more leaders aren't jumping out of windows like poor Secretary Forrestal a decade ago, though I've heard rumors that the jury's still out on that.*

Taking a step back from their grave responsibility of managing this great country and as a leader of the Western World, the public should be thankful for the tremendous sacrifices being made by our over-worked leaders, the armed forces, and civilians alike. We must trust in their judgement whether to acknowledge or not the extraordinary events such as UFO sightings, or ruthless decisions made in the name of National Security that we never hear about, because certainly as in war, dark doings are anathema to the utopia of our aspirant forefathers who wrote the Declaration of Independence and Constitution. No one wants to be held accountable against that backdrop of our heritage notwithstanding our shameful record in areas such as racial disparity and the consummate evils of ignorance.

During the course of the delightful evening, after a most sumptuous dinner, a man I did not recognize introduced himself to me and my fiancée. We went on to have a most agreeable conversation about UFOs and aliens. Observations were made such as that there are billions of galaxies and trillions of stars, so statistically speaking there has to be some vast proliferation of life out there! And some of these life forms no doubt must have developed like ours, but perhaps are millions of years ahead of us. They would be evolved beyond our understanding, perhaps a thousand fold, which makes us almost next of kin to our distant ancestors: cave people!

We're a lot closer to them than to so-called people even a hundred thousand years ahead of us on the evolutionary curve. But let's not upset the creationists! That bible hasn't been written yet! This interesting and immensely knowledgeable man I spoke with was Dr. Edward Teller, one of our leading scientists, who presides over Los Alamos Laboratories, working on our technological future even as we speak. But he rejected the notion of UFOs in spite of all the evidence. Well, I was relieved because he urged me on to write about it, and, in a manner of speaking, to enlighten people with the possibilities. "Intellectualize the phenomenon," he said, and I add: because the future is here and now.

Upon reflection, as I write this piece about the grand birthday party at which Republicans could celebrate with some pride their grand dominion over national and world affairs under our heroic President Dwight Eisenhower, I can't help but feel that as a member of the new generation a certain decline is perhaps in store for the party due to the capricious nature of politics. But something else struck me as I observed in general with both professional and personal interest: there seems to be a prevailing confidence in the power élite that has instilled so completely their brand of government in the public consciousness that, barring their incumbent champion Richard Nixon winning the election—given he will be nominated to lead the party which seems likely— nothing is going to change.

The President's government has on the whole managed our country effectively enough that our populace have all but embraced our supremacy as a nation and although there is likely much to be desired in terms of social and racial progress by both Republican and Democrats alike. However, although much to be admired, there may be a sinister stratagem in respect to our champions of freedom. This could be the result of the ineluctable imperative to fight the evils of the world with equal force. So, UFO believers or not, emancipators, establishment doyens, law makers, and civilians rich and poor, be advised that our freedoms are not some veneer of policy and subscription given to some emblematic stamp; no, we must be vigilant and uphold our democracy against complacency and inevitable atrophy.

Now is the time for the saints to come marching in, and for us to take the baton from the hands of our tired warriors who have fought and vanquished horrific tyrannies. We must continue to defend democracy no matter the succeeding party and fight for the soul of the nation! Only then will the promise of our freedom be guaranteed. Cheers!

*

That late afternoon, Greenfield took alone the subway down to Greenwich Village. As arranged with Melbo when they first met, a message could be left in the name of Thomas Jones at an answering service, typical in its day. Melbo had told him to meet them at the Minetta Tavern around seven pm and had reserved a private booth in this old bohemian landmark central once to the notorious nineteenth and early twentieth century neighborhood. The tavern was situated near the original Minetta Creek and where the early Dutch settlers farmed and later to 'Little Africa' where freed slaves made their homes. It had seen better days having somewhat exhausted by 1960 the iconic currency of artistic, beatnik or notorious patrons; however, its simple fare was decent and premises clean, if in need of a refurbishing.

Greenfield had taken every precaution to ensure that no one had followed him. And he would make sure that no one was following Melbo and DeCourt when they arrived. Only then would he send for Prinzenthal by taxi and make sure of the all clear. He wasn't going to take any chances. Meanwhile, he would read the paper sitting by the window of a lowly pub down the street. After having read Melbo's curious column on the extravaganza last weekend, he put down the paper and watched the street. He surmised that Melbo had written a kind of parable that on the surface appeared to appease the Republican status quo in their triumph as a party.

Even his cavalier comments about UFOs were smart and topical; it would likely dissuade any deep state insider from labelling Melbo as a threat to their secrecy. Moreover, Melbo had ingratiated himself honorably to the party leadership and secured himself a place, if tenuously, as a kind of young coxcomb—a court fool, immune to the heavy hitters bent on squashing the mice. Unfortunately the mice had a predisposition for cheese—bait. Greenfield knew personally these people in Sulla and his minions. He knew they would gleefully welcome Melbo into their camp only to use him and then eat him alive like the proverbial cat.

He had no doubt that Melbo had made a deep impression the previous month with his first article and that Melbo had been fêted on account of it. He presumed that media magnate Jake Whitmore, as a confidante of the Sulla brothers—though Don, the elder brother had died—had been prompted to invite him. But it also occurred to Greenfield that Melbo already knew this, hence the placating second article. Melbo was no fool and courageously kept to his task at hand by revealing ever so sagaciously the true meaning of his parable—*there is an on-going concealment of the government's complicity in suppressing information about an alien presence here on earth.*

For instance, Teller had been the perfect foil—someone who would have to be in the know, stating a categorical "no" there are no aliens and spaceships, regardless of thousands having seen the phantoms of the sky. Then Eisenhower deferred his questionable affirmation as being oblivious or alluding as such. This in itself was an irony if there ever was one. And finally Melbo's deposition on freedom, and the party's defense of it, which made Greenfield's stomach turn aware of the insidious ways in which so many people had been skewered and destroyed by the HUAC (Un-American Activities Committee) under the amoral McCarthy and his queer side-kick Cohn, Nixon, and pit bull Scott McLeod.

The hypocrisy was frightening. The Republicans' authority was usurped under the auspices of these mendacious scumbags who gutted the State Department of its best and brightest, including George F. Kennan, apparently with Secretary Don Nestor Sulla's blind approval. Then they took on the CIA, and even the army, before self-destructing thanks finally to Allen Sulla and Eisenhower. Yet Melbo with his free pass, courtesy of his unique position, spiked the truth by calling on the saints to free us from an unconscionable regime! It was pure genius, all predicated on the brutal reality of cold warriors and political expediency. Greenfield knew he had underestimated Melbo, and that worried him.

Prinzenthal arrived as planned a block away, and stepped out of the yellow cab. Greenfield met her and they walked towards the Minetta. She was still under a shadow of solemnity and said nothing, but looked good in her bohemian garb of black harem pants slightly embroidered with a cream loose shirt and short denim jacket. Her hair was tied back casually and strapped over her shoulder a simple leather hand bag matching her casual ankle boots.

'You always wear the perfect outfit, dear,' said Greenfield.

Prinzenthal walked along.

'Is there anything you'd like to say about our meeting here?' he asked.

Prinzenthal stopped walking.

'I'm sorry,' she said. 'You know what a bitch I am, the real me. This is the real me. I'm not wearing some cover for an op. These are the clothes I like.'

'I'm not complaining.'

'This morning,' she went on ignoring his remark, 'was so very beautiful. It just really got me down deep. All these emotions came pouring out, after … it's my life now, you know. I haven't been happy lately. I don't like things at work anymore.'

Greenfield listened carefully. He always knew there was more with Prinzenthal.

'I went to that party last weekend with Edward only because of you and Melbo and this stupid op. I hated being there. I hate the whole fucking Republican establishment. They fawn over me like I'm some Dionysian call girl. Sulla kissed me, as he always does—I can feel his snake charming conceit slithering around looking for some chink in my feminine armor. He knows he'll never get what he wants and it drives him mad. He makes my hair bristle.'

'I suspected as much.'

'I'm a Henry Wallace democrat; and he was turfed out for being too pacifist. The country's going to shit with those assholes. Why did Franklin have to die so soon?' she asked rhetorically.

'I feel the same as you, darling.'

They arrived at the Minetta. Melbo and DeCourt both stood up smiling to greet them at their table before all sat down. DeCourt was wearing beige pants and a mauve cashmere sweater looking as bohemian as Prinzenthal.

'You look marvelous, Joyce,' she said. 'It's great to see you.'

'Likewise.'

A waitress took their orders for drinks and supplied menus.

'Great article,' said Greenfield to Melbo.

'Thanks.'

'I liked the subterfuge. But don't worry, your secret's safe with me.'

'What subterfuge?' quipped Melbo back.

They all laughed.

'Was it that obvious?' asked Melbo.

'Yes and no, to me at least.'

Melbo looked at Prinzenthal who smiled. 'I haven't read it yet, George,' she said.

'That's reassuring.'

They all laughed again.

'I have to know something, Joyce,' queried DeCourt, suddenly.

'Go for it.'

'We were rather surprised—to put it mildly—to see you there; and even more surprised that you wanted us to remain anonymous to each other. I never realized you were so-'

'Well-connected?'

'Yes-'

'I did it for your protection, and mine. You see I work for the CIA. There's no reason at this point that you shouldn't know that. If I had spoken to you without a formal introduction and you knew me, it would have blown our little cover. You don't mess with those people.'

'The President seemed charming enough,' said Melbo.

'Ike has little control over the government, especially now.' she said. 'He lets them do what they do, because he generally agrees with them.'

Greenfield explained, 'Under Eisenhower the levers of power were somewhat reassigned to the Department of State and the CIA. As well, Eisenhower became a figurehead to the corporate leadership; it was a perfect setup—a sea-change, if you will, orchestrated by the Sulla brothers who presided over a military-industrial hegemony of sorts.'

Melbo and DeCourt said nothing for a moment; however, DeCourt wasn't finished yet with Prinzenthal.

'Joyce, that may well be true, but I need to know if you asked Dr. Teller to speak with us?'

'No, I didn't realize that he spoke with you. What did he say?' she asked, impassively.

'How would he know who we were then?'

'Any number of people could have known who you were. Certainly Whitmore, who by the way asked to see me for what I haven't a clue.'

Ignoring the reference to Whitmore, DeCourt forged on: 'Teller said he had known you when you were young. It was a bit cheeky of me, but I hope you don't mind that I asked him who the woman was—you of course—that we saw with him speaking to the President and Governor.'

'I see,' said Prinzenthal, smiling. 'Well, I suppose that means he introduced the real me—*alors, il ne peut pas être aidé*—then, it can't be helped.'

The waitress brought their drinks. They took a moment to look at the menus, and ordered. The waitress left.

'Sorry, I just wanted you to know,' said DeCourt.

'You must still call me Joyce,' she said, 'but I'm not upset you know my real name.'

'It's for the best,' said Greenfield. 'So let's have a toast! To the real us!'

'And to the aliens!' declared Melbo.

They all drank.

'If we are being so candid,' added Prinzenthal, 'I need to clarify a few things just so you know where I stand; bear with me. In spite of my misgivings about this … op, as it were—Tom here convinced me it was in the national interest, though I advised him we would be putting ourselves at risk; anyway, I did seem to make an impression on the Governor, and he, as you may be aware, was asked by Eisenhower early in his administration to reorganize the executive branch, and given top clearance.

'I know that within the capacity of my occupation—Tom can confirm this—some very interesting changes were made in regards to the President's oversight of the clandestine services. Specifically, his plausible deniability when it came to nefarious activities carried out by the company, so he was by and large held to be unaccountable; which also, I should add, put the onus on the company to have a fail-safe contingency as pro forma.

'Let me illustrate: Governor Rockefeller and his ilk like Whitmore are as thick as thieves with the Sulla brothers, well Allen at least; Don died last year. The Sulla brothers having attained their long coveted reign at State and Central Intelligence were not going to stop there; they wanted absolute power over heaven and earth, and they got it—a very dangerous precedent, thanks to Rockefeller. We operate outside the legal parameters of government, true; but under this regime the service had taken on a whole new dimension—their ideology is as rampant as Soviet, Nazi, or otherwise, and transparency is not something they are in accord with unless it's the illusion of such for appearance's sake.

'In effect, they embarked on a mission not only to roll back Communism—which in itself is in our best interest, though to do it so viciously that they became a defacto fascist state within the state, while America slept—but as well they covertly promulgated an undeclared imperial design. They toppled decent democratically elected moderate leaders in Mossadegh of Iran and Árbenz of Guatemala, Lumumba of Congo, engaged in despicable doings with Trujillo in the Dominican Republic, and other places and propagandized Communist imperialism to the world when, in fact, they were working on world domination themselves, or hegemony.

'Thousands of innocent people were slaughtered as a result of this and continue to be. The outfit employed hard core criminally accountable Nazis to operate in the European theatre, some of whom murdered tens of thousands of Jews and others, and continued to permit psychological and medical experimentation on humans as guinea pigs, all under the auspices of American security. Also, they were quite serious about using American nuclear superiority to force the Soviets out of Eastern Europe or anywhere. It should be said that Eisenhower, although he was complicit in these activities, still had control of that looming scenario and fortunately refrained from acting on it.

'Okay, so you get the big picture. Now, after Tom got me involved here, it reminded me of a conversation I once had at least ten years ago with Admiral Hillenkoetter, the first director of the CIA. He invited me for lunch after a successful year in Europe—'49-'50. I liked him; he was an honorable and decent human being and respected me as a human being. He even apologized for the kind of work I was known for. "Hannah," he said, "if you could know the reality behind the reality in this secret world from my vantage point. You deal with the practical object of an operation, as odious as it must be at times. I deal with the constantly shifting sands of political and clandestine intrigue—it's a goddamned nightmare. There is a cabal of right-wing people, powerful people, who are not even part of the CIA at present, but who still have such great influence in the media and corporate affairs that I would fear for this country if they ever got into power."

'Well,' went on Prinzenthal presently, 'we know these very people have been running the country for eight years now. The Admiral then said, and this is what is pertinent to us, "Somehow this cabal," he said, "specifically one person who has been part of the intelligence apparatus since before, during and after the war, still carries on as if he is in charge, when he was never actually the top guy, but is so well-connected and disarmingly friendly he always gets what he wants! But he is utterly unscrupulous, evil, and a danger to the democratic process. This man knows about—and I don't know how, because as I said he's supposed to be out of the loop at present—the most classified program there is, and I'm not talking about the bomb—which is old news."

'He then apologized for running on and venting. I asked him quite naïvely not really thinking how brazen it was at the time, "You mean the Roswell weather balloon thing?" He then looked at me seriously before breaking out in a smile, "I don't think you're qualified for that kind of expertise, Hannah. Believe me, you don't want to know." Then we both laughed. You can read into that whatever you want.'

'It had to do with aliens,' said Melbo, 'assuming I understand your drift.'

'That's the first time I've heard that story, Joyce,' said Greenfield. 'We can assume the Roswell incident was an open secret among the insiders. Certainly, Sulla would have been pulling all his strings for information—calling in debts or using blackmail until after the election and he was back in the service, if he ever really left. The man's impervious and we have to stay away from him.'

'He makes my skin crawl whenever I'm around him,' stressed Prinzenthal. 'As infrequently as we meet, he always displays that salacious familiarity and bonhomie, but behind that twinkle in his eyes there is the dead soul of a quintessential devil—his eyes give nothing away yet I can see through them, and I get the feeling that he knows I can, like some warlock. Even Hoover, the wily autocrat, when he tried to control Sulla by threatening to expose his numerous sexual liaisons, crawled back into his cave when Sulla had a short film reel sent to him of Clyde Tolson, his personal aide, performing fellatio on him, and vice-versa.'

'My God!' exclaimed DeCourt, 'I had no idea our supposed revered leaders were so horrid, tyrannical!'

'I gather, an exposé of these guys wouldn't get much traction in the press,' noted Melbo. 'They control the news, as it is.'

'Don't even think about it: you'd be setting yourself up for a lifetime of public disgrace or be accused of committing a crime you didn't commit,' said Greenfield. 'They destroy people who get in their way, even kill people and make it look like suicide or an accident. That's the nature of the beast they've created.'

'I'm getting a healthy understanding of the world you two have been living in,' said DeCourt, a little unhinged.

'During the war, and after, we could be proud of our work,' stated Prinzenthal.

'Now they frighten everyone by using their influence in the media to justify their brand of nationalism,' said Melbo. 'I would like to change that.'

'And be accused of being soft on Communism?' asked Greenfield. 'Keep your head down for the time being. If Kennedy gets elected, then you could help launch a new era of politics, if he can control the CIA.'

'You seem a little skeptical, Tom,' said DeCourt.

'I know these people. They won't give up power so easily.'

'By the way, Joyce,' said DeCourt, 'You were saying something about Whitmore?'

'He just said he wants to see me.'

'He does? Why?'

'I assume he knows about my work at the agency, and thought I could be of use. He didn't specify.'

Greenfield chuckled. 'A private luncheon, I imagine.'

'Will you go?' asked DeCourt.

'I don't know; it depends on what I can get in return. I wouldn't expect much.'

'You mean information on UFOs, if he knows anything; but that might give you away, wouldn't it?' wondered DeCourt.

'That depends on how fine a thread has been sewn,' said Greenfield. 'Joyce is a genius with embroidery.'

'Don't flatter me, Tom; you're liable to raise the Titanic,' avowed Prinzenthal, eying him seriously.

'I would never think of it, dear. Whitmore has no idea what he's got himself into.'

'Thank you. I can manage.'

Melbo and DeCourt assumed that little tiff was best ignored.

'I have a question,' said Melbo, deflecting.

'Shoot,' said Greenfield.

'Have you heard of the guy, Art Lovering?'

'Yeah, he's one of the backroom boys. I worked with him in Europe after the war. He's in the White House now, a kind of *éminence grise*; he's like a compulsive concierge, pandering to all the henchmen of the President—I don't know what his exact position is—assistant something or other. He was Rockefeller's *aide-de-camp*-advisor and was likely the hands-on renovator of the executive branch knowing his background in political science. You met him?'

'Just to shake his hand. He didn't have much to say.'

'I'd put money on him telling Teller to talk to you,' said Greenfield. 'He was Teller's connection to the White House.'

The waitress brought the first plates of soups and salads. They began to eat with a much needed respite from the dialogues of the underworld.

'*Bon appetit!*' said Melbo.

*

After their meal they sipped coffee and tea. Melbo looked at Greenfield hoping for some kind of advice. He felt that he had discovered enough about government sinister agendas, albeit circumstantially, to challenge the status quo, but lacked the power to carry it off. He needed some leverage, a media baron or party kingpin. Greenfield seemed to sense his dilemma.

'You've had your food; now for your thoughts,' said Greenfield.

'I doubt I can make a difference, Tom, or anyone can for that matter unless someone takes a stand and denounces the government.'

'And lose your job,' said DeCourt. 'People are getting the message with your articles. Don't push it.'

'She has a point,' said Prinzenthal to Greenfield. 'It's either go all the way from here and face the consequences, or toe the line with the fascist bastards.'

'I have a lead out West,' said Melbo, ignoring her short rant. 'A woman who sat beside us at the gala dinner—Edna Beiderman—spoke of growing up in New Mexico near Roswell. She claimed her brother, Garnett Wills, who manages her family ranch knows something about what happened back in '47.'

'Good,' said Greenfield, 'gather all the info you can; there's no hurry. In fact I'd wait until a new administration has been elected—hopefully Kennedy, in which case I think we could get you that leverage.'

'When will you go West,' asked Prinzenthal.

'Not sure, maybe in a month or two. I'll take a holiday.' He looked at DeCourt. 'Would you like to go to New Mexico on our honeymoon, Mel?'

'Really? Why not?'

'I didn't realize you were engaged!' exclaimed Prinzenthal.

'He proposed at Whitmore's party,' glowed DeCourt.

'Right after speaking with Edward Teller,' said Melbo.

'Wonderful.' Greenfield smiled in approval.

'When are you two sailing to Dominica, or was that a cover story?' asked DeCourt.

Prinzenthal and Greenfield looked at each other.

'Perhaps in a month or two,' answered Prinzenthal. 'We're not all cover, you know; this old goat has a way with me. My life is just a bit complicated.'

'No argument there,' agreed Greenfield.

10. Deviled Eggs

Art Lovering reclined on the sofa in the Oval Office. President Eisenhower sat behind his desk. Their business concluded, Lovering posed a question: 'Sir, I meant to ask you before: What do you think about that Herald Tribune writer Melbo? Did you read his latest piece about Whitmore's party?'

'Funny you ask, Art. Mamie raved about him and insisted I read it. A lot of gossip I thought. I don't remember saying much to him.'

'I get the impression he's paying lip service to our administration to ingratiate himself and gain access to classified information.'

'What of it? I could say the same for myself when it comes to the aliens. Sulla has shut me out, as you and Rockefeller had prearranged in your executive retrofit.'

'For precisely a situation like this: plausible deniability.'

'I went too far in that directive, Art. I've said it before and I'll say it again: it sets a dangerous precedent whereby the president can be made subordinate to Central Intelligence. Its reach has inveigled itself everywhere, and with little oversight. Hell, even the Joint Intelligence Committee is stymied.'

'We're all loyal to you, sir.'

'And what about the next guy? They could pull an Árbenz on him, or worse, and we'd be none the wiser.'

'This is America, sir.'

'Damn right it is, Art. Listen, you're a good man, and I trust the people around me will always do the right thing; and if they don't, they should have to answer for it.'

*

In early June, Prinzenthal received a telephone call from an aide of Jake Whitmore. She was told to meet him in the early evening at his suite on Fifth

Avenue. She had definite, mixed feelings about meeting with him, and only did so out of curiosity, thinking it must have something to do with Melbo, Whitmore being his boss. She got out of the cab and stood for a while on the street beside the building as people hurried by. It occurred to her that in spite of Melbo's reasonable articles he did not pass muster with someone guarding the gates of the inner sanctum of intrigue; and who was in a position to take a closer look at him.

There was an excruciating irony if that were the case and they chose her to investigate Melbo. Greenfield had already chortled at the predicament. But it made the situation all the more delightful for her as a special operative knowing that, if she were seen to befriend Melbo there would be no better cover for their actual friendship. Yet if it got out that she already knew him and didn't speak up, well, the game was up and all her credibility and career would be forfeited. It even seemed like a double irony in that she felt a bit paranoid as if she were behind the Iron Curtain.

Has it come to this? she feared. All her private reservations about the service that she had given her life to now arose and blistered to the surface of her soul. After this, she thought, she would leave the outfit and have a baby with Greenfield, that embryo already engendered deep in her womb, intensifying her acute desire for self-preservation.

Whitmore's classic art deco building was designed to his specifications when it was erected in 1934. It housed his business conglomerate and numerous tenants. Prinzenthal stepped into the lobby and informed a Louis Armstrong look-a-like concierge that she was to meet Mr. Whitmore. From his engaging smile she got the impression that her visit evoked some subliminal "Hello Dolly" response, though not inappropriately given, that Whitmore likely had all sorts of people ushered in at all hours. The concierge directed her to the private elevator for the exclusive use of the penthouse occupant, using a key.

The Whitmore Group's extensive holdings in real estate, international finance and media were worth hundreds of millions if not more. But unlike the Rockefellers, Whitmore preferred to operate *sub rosa* with as little publicity as possible, and politics treated as anathema to be avoided at all costs, were left only to his newspapers, though they were decidedly Republican. He was a man known privately for his anti-Roosevelt, anti-New Deal politics, for his close association with the vast clique of Sulla brothers' acolytes many of whom littered the State Department, and high finance.

Generally anti-Semitic, their waspish influence certainly prompted the bureaucratic resistance within Roosevelt's government by not allowing more Jewish refugees from Nazi Germany into America before the war. The plight of the German passenger ship *St. Louis* turned away during the summer of 1939 with over nine hundred Jewish immigrants on board exemplified the tragedy. Roosevelt himself with an election looming the following year was fighting a populous ideology of American isolationism, and remained neutral, though he was personally outraged when an anti-immigration congress thwarted his plan to bring a couple of hundred thousand refugees into America and other countries.

He was desperate to win re-election for the good of the country and it was acute political shrewdness that led him ultimately to victory. Prinzenthal knew very well the insidious nature of the conservative establishment, be it Republican or Democrat. It was Wild Bill Donovan, the chief of the OSS who authorized the Judith Graham cover in the State Department in the last years of the war, which she fit into perfectly like an entitled Ivy League wasp. No doubt, somehow Jake Whitmore knew something of her exploits.

She stepped out of the gold and mirrored elevator into a hallway of paneled wood and mirrors. She supposed his wife, himself, or both of them liked to see themselves in some narcissistic fantasy; but the effect was neither claustrophobic nor unpleasant. When Whitmore opened the door dressed in a red and black housecoat, slacks and slippers, she put on her best Mona Lisa smile.

'Miss Hannah, thank you for coming,' he said, blithely, extending his hand.

She shook it. He turned and bade her enter the front hall.

'Anything for America, sir.'

'Call me Jake, please. And yes, our exceptional nationalism has its obligations.'

Immediately Prinzenthal wanted to reply: *Does that imply any number of crimes, including the overthrow of democracy in Iran and Guatemala, the tolerance of a brutal and murderous ally in Trujillo, and the collection of heinous Jew-massacring Nazis in our European intelligence apparatus? Is that your idea of benevolent America?* But she simply said, 'We strive to do better, Jake.'

Whitmore paused for a moment, sizing her up with a silly grin on his face.

He took in her plain Egyptian blue dress with simple ivory trim, short honeydew cardigan sweater opened to reveal a silver Star-of-David necklace and her low-healed black shoes with ankle strap. Prinzenthal watched his eyes go quickly up and down while she was still projecting the Giaconda smile. A moment passed and he seemed to shake himself out of whatever fantasy that he had been experiencing privately. To him she seemed perfect and glowing, and it showed in her creamy complexion, shining hazel eyes, and loose luscious auburn hair. She wore no earrings.

'Hannah, permit me to say you are captivating, glowing.'

'Thank you,' she said, ignoring the thought of her pregnancy—though he hadn't a clue—and looked beyond him at the interior, which appeared ornately art deco with heavy light-beige drapes, dark cherry walls, and expensive furniture.

'I apologize that my wife is not here. We are alone, but believe me as such, the circumstances are determinedly a call to duty, shall we say.'

'I assumed as much,' she said, looking into his eyes, her expression unchanged. He was about Greenfield's age, perhaps a few years older. He was smooth-shaven for the evening and had a shiny face from which his sharp brown eyes radiated an inquisitive intelligence. Tall, with a medium build he stood erect with a powerful frame topped by a full head of short, gray hair.

'Well, please, come in.' He motioned for her to proceed before him through the parlor, and into the living area in the corner of which was a small bar.

'I'm told I make an excellent Manhattan. May I offer you one?'

'Please.'

She walked to the floor-to-ceiling window and looked down onto Washington Square Park. 'You're quite the downtowner,' she commented.

'I'm a businessman in New York and eschew the uptown social scene. My home is Westchester.'

'Well, you certainly know how to throw a party.'

'It was a birthday party-cum-Republican-gala for the cause; I am a media baron, they say.'

'I was lucky to have attended; it was a very interesting and spectacular event, and I was most honored to meet the President.'

Prinzenthal walked slowly to the bar. Whitmore had all his ingredients arrayed on the counter.

'I use only Canadian Club rye, two and half ounces, and Turkish cherry liqueur instead of vermouth, though at two thirds of an ounce, then the Angostura Bitters and cherry garnish.'

'Perhaps you should call it the Whitmore.'

He laughed. 'That would be vainglorious, cheating.'

'Do you think someone would challenge you on that?'

'That's not the point.'

'For a media baron you are modest, then?'

'Modest? No, I've been lucky in life. I inherited a fortune when I was a young and foolish socialite. Jake the Rake some used to call me; I've been improving myself ever since.'

'And how would you grade yourself now?' she asked, her expression still unchanged.

'Unhappy, tired, hopeful, undaunted.'

'That's quite an admission.'

'Life's too short to hide from the truth.'

'Let's drink to that.'

Whitmore mixed the ingredients in ice, strained them into two chilled gold-rimmed cocktail glasses, and then added two freshly pitted cherries skewered on gold sword picks.

'Voilà,' he said, giving her one.

'Merci.'

'Puis-je offrir un toast à la santé à la vérité?' he said.

'Certainement.'

He held up his glass. 'And to an America we can be proud of.'

'Of course,' she said touching his glass, and taking a sip, 'Mmm, lovely. You're right, it's the best Manhattan.' Prinzenthal smiled graciously.

Eating their cherries, he motioned for them to sit on the plush sofas. Once seated facing one another they relaxed and sipped again. Prinzenthal put her drink on the side table.

'Jake, without meaning to sound impatient, perhaps you should tell me why I've been invited here. We met at your great party, but I don't recall any indication this was going to happen-'

'Hannah, forgive me. Naturally, I was coming to that, and I don't want you to think I have any ulterior motive because of my influence and so-called "power". I don't use people that way. I'm married to a wonderful woman, who has given me children, now grown up, and I will not change anything.'

'But you are unhappy.' She immediately regretted saying that, but it just came out. Her talents seemed to have needed some flexing and as an operative she knew what to do.

'I've been married for thirty-five years. Love has run its course, if you will, and there comes to mind that one is trapped in a cage of one's own making. Our culture is the likely fault. Divorce is treated as a crime and doesn't account for nature, which would suggest happiness is unnatural.'

'Interesting. I'm the opposite. I've never been married, and I've been mostly happy in the thrill of the profession, until recently when I realized nature was calling on me to … settle down.'

'And you are entering unfamiliar waters so-to-speak?'

'My work, as I presume you know—I wouldn't be here otherwise—has over the last twenty years been prolonged by war and treachery, sometimes leaving me not knowing if I would survive. I had to have faith in people who may or may not be trusted because of a constant turnover of personnel through no fault of their own—it's a monstrous business. I've been lucky too.'

He did not respond immediately, but looked at her. She took another sip of her drink.

'You're so calm,' he finally said. 'Is that your professionalism, or just the way you are?'

She laughed. 'You make it sound as if underneath this "calm" exterior there lurks a conniving player.'

'Is that a job description?' he suggested, raising an eyebrow.

'I neither confirm nor deny, Jake,' she said raising her eyebrow in return.

They both laughed.

'Oh, I almost forgot,' he said getting up. 'I'll be back in a sec.' He quickly left the living room and walked through elegant double doors into the dining room. A few moments later he returned with a large tray of finger vegetables with dip and deviled eggs. He placed the tray on the glass-topped coffee table between them. 'Help yourself, please.'

'Did you prepare this, Jake?' she said, taking a devilled egg and putting all of it in her mouth.

'I did, actually. Devilled eggs are one of the few things I like to prepare. I use homemade mayonnaise with olive oil, lemon and mustard, and eggs and paprika of course.'

After a few moments, she said, 'A man with unusual talents. It's delicious!'

'When I was young I had an idea to be a chef.'

'But other distractions seemed to get in your way?' She took another devilled egg.

'When you're born with money it can cloud best intentions.'

'Which were?'

'To live a humble life.'

'A humble life,' she repeated, looking about the room, but pausing at the food tray.

'I know it sounds ridiculous,' he went on, 'When I was twenty-four I pretended to be a bohemian in Paris for a year until my father died suddenly of a heart attack. I came home and soon took over the business. It was the experience that counted. It gave me perspective.'

'Am I hearing a slight socialist in there?' She scooped up some dip with a carrot stick.

'Socialist, no, compassionate citizen, yes; a Teddy Roosevelt Republican. People need to make their own way and not be dependent on the government. If someone like me has been fortunate enough to inherit and then amass even greater wealth, then it's his obligation to give something back to society, not the government's. I support numerous charities that underwrite missions for the indigent—orphans, single pregnant women, immigrants, the sick. I loan money to help people get on with their lives.'

'That's very commendable, Jake. I was an immigrant, a Jewish one, in 1934.'

'And you're commendable. You've given back in your own way as much as I, probably more.'

'Why am I here, Jake?' Prinzenthal took her third devilled egg.

'Yes, well, to the point,' he said, slightly discomfited. 'Listen, I need to get something off my chest. I'm not one of those anti-Semitic believers in the Protocols of the Elders of Zion bullshit. I'm ashamed of what happened before the war when Americans like me didn't pay attention to the plight of the Jews looking for a new home. I'm ashamed of so many things, but we won the war and destroyed Nazi Germany. And now we must destroy Soviet Russia.'

'No argument there.'

'You're here because I was asked to try to persuade you to do some domestic moonlighting for me, because certain authorities don't have a legal mandate to spy on their own people.'

'That never stopped them before. But what about the FBI?' she asked.

'The FBI is run by Hoover, and they don't want him involved for reasons I don't understand.'

'Hoover would make a mountain out of a molehill, and use it against the CIA, his nemesis, aside from the Commies. He also hates Jews.'

'Personally,' he said, 'I think he's long served out any usefulness.'

'For what it's worth they made a wise choice going to you, if it's of any consolation.'

'Hannah, they want you to find out and report to me about one of my employees. He was at my party. They asked, or rather told me to invite him, which I was quite happy to do so.'

'And who might this employee be? And why are they so concerned about him?'

'George Melbo.'

'George Melbo. Is that supposed to ring a bell? Never heard of him.' Her intuitions had been right.

'He's become a bit of a sensation for writing about the taboo subject of UFOs.'

'What of it? They've been in the news often enough. Do you know anything about them?'

'Me? I know next to nothing, but I can tell you it's obvious there's something to it if they want me to ask you to spy on this guy.'

'What did he write that's so provocative, then?'

'They never explained anything to me. His articles have been well-received. He questions the government's secrecy about UFOs, gives his opinion that the people need-to-know, and describes certain credible sightings. I find it fascinating myself.'

'I don't really understand. He's a journalist. What can he possibly know? It's all speculation.'

'True, but they think he's some kind of threat.'

Prinzenthal took another sip of her drink.

'Don't you find this a bit xenophobic?' she asked.

'I agree, but these people have something to fear.'

'These people? I work with these people, yet no one has said anything.'

'Well, they want it off the books I guess, a safety net. I don't know. They just asked me to talk to you.'

'*Who* asked you, Jake?' She looked at him attentively.

'Does it matter?'

'We're all on the same side! I feel I'm being kept in the dark!'

'Okay, just say nothing to anybody. I was told not to name names.'

'I can't promise anything unless I know who asked you, Jake. I'm stepping out of my legal parameters here.'

'Arthur Lovering.'

'I met him at your party.'

'He's close to Edward Teller, Rockefeller and even Eisenhower. Edward Teller knew your mother, right?'

'My father was an elder acquaintance of his in Europe when he was a young émigré; they were part of a group of moderate Jews who kept in touch— scientists, professors, and businessmen. And yes, he knew my mother.'

'I'm sorry about your mother. I was told she passed away a few years ago.'

'Yes, she suffered a stroke, became an invalid and she didn't last much longer. She wanted to die to be with David, my father; she's with him now in Père Lachaise, Paris.'

'I'm sorry.'

'Thanks.'

'I hope you don't mind me asking, but do you have any family or someone close?' he asked.

'I'm close with a retired colleague. We're thinking of marriage; I'm the one dragging my feet.'

'It's none of my business really, but will he be involved if you decide to take on this job?'

'Harley knows the business and respects my place. He was my case officer after the war well into the Eisenhower administration. We've remained close on and off over the years. He retired a few years ago and we parted ways, but now we're back together.'

'An enviable romance,' declared Whitmore.

'I was thinking about retiring myself.'

'And start a family?'

'Maybe.'

They both ate more vegetables and eggs.

'A refill?' he suggested lifting his empty glass.

'No thanks, I'm fine.' She took another sip.

'They asked me something.'

'Oh? What's that?'

'At the party Dr. Teller spoke with Melbo and his girlfriend at some length. Did he mention anything to you about him?'

Prinzenthal ate another devilled egg, giving herself a moment to think. It occurred to her that this could be a trick question. She remembered that Teller had indeed mentioned Mel and Mel. What if Teller himself had been asked by Lovering if he had mentioned Melbo to her? She remembered having had quite a few drinks at that party, but she now stayed with her intuition.

'No, nothing, as far as I can remember; after all, Jake, you wined and dined us so indulgently ...'

'Yes, we did, didn't we?'

'It was a masterpiece!' she exclaimed. 'The champagne flowed like an eternal fount; everyone was tipsy before dinner!'

They laughed.

'That's the secret behind a successful event. Champagne makes everyone happy.'

'The bubbles.'

'So how would you approach Mr. Melbo?' he asked suddenly.

'First do some homework. Find out who he is. Find out where he lives. Find out where he goes, what he does, then arrange a little 'serendipitous' meeting—see how he reacts, whether he's open to further contact, and measure his loyalty to his girlfriend, if he has one. I might have to entice him with some information.'

'Such as?'

'Edward Teller, perhaps, or some cut out.'

'Cut out?' he queried.

'Someone to represent me as a credible source, or foil.'

'I see.'

'Someone to share information with him; in other words angle for his sources,' she said.

'Yes, good, very good; but what if he doesn't play your game?'

'There are a number of ways to coax information from people. The best is involuntarily, either by like-mindedness in a cause, or a love relationship, or even through retribution when the innocent target is set up by circumstances that make him or her determined to redress some perceived injustice. The worst kinds of spin are blackmail and punishment, which can lead to violence and worse. It all depends on the kind of person you're dealing with. Some are impervious to manipulation, while some are experts at manipulation with an agenda of their own. I've seen all types.'

'Have you seen death?'

Prinzenthal took another devilled egg, and held it as Hamlet held Yorick's skull.

'Death. I've seen death.'

'Care to elaborate? You intrigue me. You seem so innocent.'

'Innocence. An excellent ruse. Even better if you are actually innocent at heart.'

'Have you ever killed anyone?'

Prinzenthal ate the egg. She wanted an end to this inquisition.

'Have I shot or stabbed anyone? If that's what you're asking, no. Others do that.'

'But people have died as a result of your actions?'

'People die no matter what. Espionage is not for the faint of heart.'

'I guess one would have to look at the big picture.'

Prinzenthal stood up. Whitmore stood too.

'The big picture is sometimes an illusion,' she went on, 'Things are done that degrade our humanity on all sides. For me it's about someone like Melbo being able to write freely about UFOs, or politics, or whatever, and not fear some dark totalitarian force taking that freedom away in the name of whatever ideology is prevalent at any time.'

'Yes, as long as freedom is not a byword for subversion.'

'Spoken like a true Republican.'

'You're a Democrat, I take it. I have many Democrat friends, some of whom were at my party.'

'Democrat or Republican, Jake, it shouldn't make any difference when it comes to human kindness and social justice. I've been in the trenches of the Cold War. Believe me when I say I know the difference between freedom and tyranny, and the merchants of ideology are experts in obfuscating the reality one way or another to get what they want. Both sides are guilty as hell; that's the nature of war. But I'm the first to recognize that peace and freedom come at an almost intolerable cost.'

'You're a remarkable woman, Hannah. Come, I'll show you out.'

They walked back to the front hall, where they shook hands again, Whitmore holding her hand in both of his. Then he opened the door for her and they entered the main hall, where she pressed the button for the elevator and waited as the doors quietly opened.

'Thank you for the devilled eggs, Jake.' She smiled. 'And for the best Manhattan ever.'

'Here are my private numbers, both here and in Westchester. Let me know when you know anything.'

She took his card as she stepped into the elevator.

'Don't expect much,' she said. 'From the sound of it, you should be praising this Melbo to the skies; but I'll read his articles first. It will take me a few weeks to get this off the ground.'

'I do praise him, and I think this is all for nothing, but I have to do what they ask me to do.'

'Good night.'

The elevator door closed.

11. Moonlighting

George Melbo, in his customary non-pressed attire and loose tie, sauntered down the street musing about the sea-change of affairs regarding his new-found notoriety with some high-level person in the Eisenhower administration. He felt no anxiety or fear, just the satisfaction that through his few articles about aliens and the government, he had succeeded in getting someone's attention. Moreover, he had the backing of his editor, Dick Sinclair, and supreme boss, Jake Whitmore, a paragon of the right wing community, not to mention the general public who seemed to be hankering for more of his views. He presumed this was progress, although these new currents had elevated his former relative anonymity into something rather more celebrated.

Harley Greenfield had explained to him that he should be under no illusion: both his and Melissa's lives would be monitored discreetly, and he should perhaps be prepared for some overt interference. This could come in the form of a belligerent right-wing attack either in the press, or even on the street. The idea was that he should watch his step! Melbo's rejoinder to that was that obviously they were covering up something quite extraordinary. The question was whether or not their antipathy was justified, or some hard core right wing paranoia, a result of the ice-cold war. Certainly the architects of this policy came under the aegis of the Sulla brothers, and their myriads of acolytes including heavy-hitters Nixon and Hoover.

And now as he approached his favorite place, Joe's Sandwich Bar, he was to encounter a stranger, Hannah Prinzenthal, who—as planned—would start up a friendship with an unassuming reporter for the Herald Tribune. He sat down at his usual place his back to the wall with the windows to his right. He had brought along a paper to read. A review he had written about Bill Evans, the jazz pianist, was in that day's edition in the entertainment section. Evans was just a few years older than Melbo and they seemed to get on well even beyond their mutual interest in the music.

Melbo and DeCourt went to see him and his trio at the Jazz Gallery exalting in his languid fluidity that Miles Davis once described as "quiet fire" and like "crystal notes cascading down some clear waterfall". Melbo spoke with him for a while over a drink, as he had met him before when reviewing Davis, and had given his trio a rave review.

Twenty minutes later, Prinzenthal entered the Sandwich Bar, ordered a coffee and donut, then sat down at the table beside Melbo, in the same place that Nora had occupied two and half months earlier.

They sat quietly ignoring each other for five minutes while Prinzenthal ate her chocolate-glazed donut. She was dressed somewhat casually in slate blue slacks, a cream-colored low-cut collar shirt with semi-long sleeves to mid-forearm, and light brown ankle boots. Her style always fit the occasion with uncanny precision. Sipping her coffee and gazing dreamily out the window, she accidently spilled a little when she put the mug back down. 'Oops,' she said, looking around for a napkin.

Melbo offered his own napkin. She quickly swiped up the spill and smiled. 'How clumsy of me. Thanks.'

'No worries, I won't tell anybody,' said Melbo.

Prinzenthal laughed slightly. 'I'm a little distraught at present.'

'Sounds like a generic New Yorker.'

'Am I that obvious? Then guilty as charged,' she said.

'On the contrary: I see it as a credit.'

'Why's that?'

'For one, as I'm not a native here, I appreciate the hard knocks one must take in a hard town, so anyone who shows a little sensitivity is high in my books.'

'That's kind of you. Where are you from?'

'I was actually born here, but grew up in Canada.'

'So in fact you're native after all.'

'Technically speaking, I suppose, but I couldn't feel farther from the truth.'

Melbo refilled his tea from the small steel pot.

'The truth,' stated Prinzenthal, 'is always a matter of perspective.'

'Isn't that the problem with the world? We should all have a built-in truth meter so everyone knows who is telling the truth.'

'What an odd thing to say, but I like it, Mel.'

'You're welcome, Joyce.'

They tried to avoid each other's eyes, but managed a quick sly glance.

'Well, isn't this a fine feather?' said Melbo.

'Indeed, we are well covered, but shouldn't we perhaps make some formal gesture of introduction, don't you think? For the sake of appearances in case of some wily tail? Tom's begged off to keep it clean.'

'George Melbo.' He lifted his right hand from his side. Prinzenthal reached over and took it.

'Joyce Sommers.'

'Now we can go on a first date with impunity.'

'Well, then, aren't you going to ask for my number?'

'I'm not so sure; it may seem awkward given that I'm engaged to be married.'

'Congrats! Then we'll have to settle for a professional lunch. I'm a government worker with access to classified information,' Prinzenthal offered, opening their faux interview with tantalizing details.

Melbo faced her. 'Really?' He replied, maintaining his composure. 'I work for the Herald Tribune.'

'Melbo…name rings a bell. Didn't you write about UFOs?'

'Jackpot.'

'I know for a fact that they're real,' she smirked, clearly enjoying herself.

'My next headline: *Government Insider Says UFOs Are Real!*'

'You're serious?' Prinzenthal stifled a laugh.

'Of course.'

'Shouldn't you check my credentials?' she joked.

'Done.'

'You're putting me in a tight spot.'

'Let's make them squirm, don't you think?'

'I'll tell them it didn't come from me.'

'That's fine.'

'Then from who?'

'I think you'll have to work for that information, Joyce.'

Prinzenthal looked at him impassively before she gave way to laughter.

'Mel, I'm beginning to like you too much.'

'That's the idea isn't it?'

'Well, yes, but you've turned the tables on me.'

'Have I?'

'Perhaps not. They're setting you up through me after all.'

'Precisely. So I need to hold my ground, for your sake as well as mine.'

'Okay. Let's do it your way then.'

*

Melissa DeCourt stirred her tea. She and Melbo had just finished a quiet meal at the Roosevelt Grill, a restaurant they visited occasionally. It served decent American food and was reasonably priced.

'Mel,' she said, 'you haven't told me anything about your article for tomorrow. In fact, you've been rather coy since your meeting with Joyce last week. Is there anything I should know?'

Melbo looked up from his tea. 'I've been doing a lot of thinking, Mel.'

'I'm listening.'

'I'm going to need your intuitive wisdom in this.'

'Go on.'

'Joyce is supposed to report back to Whitmore what I'm doing, who I'm using as sources, and what is the material, the stuff, the information. I told her I would tell her exactly what I've found out so she would be only reporting on my progress. Meanwhile, she's going to try and arrange a meeting with Dr. Teller and tell him what they have asked her to do about me, and use him as a sounding board for whether my information is at all genuine before she lets Whitmore in on it. Sound reasonable?'

'I guess so. But doesn't that depend on Teller being honest, and he was decidedly dishonest with us at the party last month.'

'Right, so that puts Joyce in a delicate position. If she's a good enough spy, she can use her charms to get the truth out of Teller and this would let us know if my sources are reliable.'

'She would be playing a double game—a double agent.'

'Yes, and I have just the ace up my sleeve.'

'Tell me,' she asked, searching his eyes.

'It would be safe to tell you here but not at home; you realize we may be bugged, and our phone tapped.'

'We were fairly warned.' She paused. 'Ah, that's why you've been distant! How silly of me.'

'Everything has changed, but we have been apprised of it, so we have to control it by telling the truth, and by letting Joyce report the truth. The public will then get the truth, and we will be protected as innocent purveyors of truth.' Melbo let that sink in. 'However,' he went on, 'that doesn't mean we won't be demonized by a ruthless press—even my boss may be asked to fire me on some trumped up charge, and make me a pariah to the world. Tom Jones said as much.'

'How can we fight back if that happens?' DeCourt asked, concerned.

'Blame Art Lovering. Publicly accuse him.'

'But they can lie and get away with it with the full backing of the government!' declared DeCourt.

'True but the ball is in their court. The public would see that the government is overplaying their hand for the very big reason they have something to hide. Otherwise why would they pick on me?'

'Makes sense, but still, they might just kill you if they're capable of such evil.'

'Let's just hope a new administration will be elected, and send Eisenhower, Sulla and their cronies into the dustbin of history.'

They sipped their tea. The waitress brought their bill.

'So what's this ace you mentioned?' asked DeCourt.

Speaking lower, Melbo told her: 'You know, I have received all kinds of mail, mostly positive, some hateful, and some from people who have claimed to have actually seen or experienced a UFO event. The day before I met Joyce at Joe's Sandwich I was at my desk at work going through the mail ...'

*

A man in a hat and gray civilian clothes stood on the New York City Hall steps in City Hall Park and gazed up at the New York Herald Tribune Building across the street on the old Printing House Square, now Park Row and Nassau and Spruce streets. A historical gem, the red brick building was eighteen stories high with a clock tower and was known to have the first 'sky scraper' elevator. He then walked toward the Jacob Mould water fountain and sat down in a shady grove of trees to watch the pedestrians and sightseers.

Eleven stories up, Melbo, was sorting through his mail which had been accumulating. About a hundred unopened letters were piled on his desk. Another hundred or so were opened and neatly piled to his left. One letter which he had received last week he now pulled from his locked drawer and kept in front of him. The letter revealed that an unnamed army sergeant had been for over ten years a leader of a retrieval unit in the Foreign Technology Division and would be willing to speak to Melbo at noon sharp that appointed day by the Jacob Mould water fountain in City Hall Park.

Melbo looked at his watch, put the letter back in the drawer, and locked it. Greenfield had warned him to make sure he wasn't being followed, and to case this mysterious sergeant as well. The cue was a phone call for him to reception at 11:50 a.m. from Thomas Jones saying they could meet at 3 p.m. This would mean that the coast was clear; however, if the message was that Thomas Jones couldn't meet him, there was a problem. Once on the street Melbo was to walk towards the City Hall and around the long way for a stroll towards the fountain. In a phone booth on Broadway Greenfield would be appearing to make a call, and, if he was seen to be speaking, it signaled a green light, otherwise Melbo should abort the plan.

Melbo thought it all a bit silly, but having received the message from reception in the affirmative he dutifully followed the plan. As Melbo passed the phone booth, he noticed Jones speaking into the receiver and looking at him; then Melbo walked into the park towards the fountain.

When he saw a man sitting alone on the bench under the trees, he went over and sat at the other end of the bench. The man with a hat low on his brow simply said, 'Afternoon.'

'George Melbo at your service,' said Melbo.

'Phil Clifford.' This was all the man said.

'Is there somewhere we can talk, a little less public?' asked Melbo.

'I'll leave and go to that Irish pub on Beekman. Follow in five minutes.' He then got up and left.

Melbo knew the pub but hadn't been there for some time.

The man was at the back in a booth facing the door. Melbo sat down opposite him and took a good swig of the beer that was waiting for him.

'I'm sorry for all the trouble, Mr. Melbo,' the man said, nursing his own beer, 'but what I am about to say to you is classified, in fact it's the very highest kind of classified.'

'How do I know you're not some plant for disinformation?' queried Melbo. 'To set me up for a fall?'

'It goes without saying that I'm no plant, Melbo. I'll tell you this, it really doesn't matter what I tell you because there is no way you can get the military to acknowledge anything I say. Besides, the risk of my telling and your writing about it will send red flags all over the place specifically to the unit I used to serve. They'll be all over us like flies on shit, and at the same time publicly carry on as if nothing had happened. They don't want anyone to know if they're pissed, which might lead some to think they're hiding something.'

'That's all fine, but I need some more evidence of who you are, or at least some inside scoop to see if they really will be 'flies on shit' as you say. That would be an acknowledgment of sorts, would it not?'

'Let's just ease into this carefully, Melbo. I believe the public has a right to know that aliens—or as I like to think, people from other worlds—have been visiting our blue primitive planet for a very long time. I first worked with General MacArthur in his brainchild Interplanetary Phenomena Research Unit back in 1943 in a minor capacity. He was very intrigued about UFOs, as there had been many sightings before and during the war. He took it upon himself to collate the available material and find out about this phenomenon. When MacArthur fell out with Roosevelt and then Truman and subsequently fell out of the loop of their inside intelligence, his unit was sidelined—usurped—by a committee called MJ-12 after the Roswell Crash. This Majestic-12 consisting of numerous high ranking military and civilian leaders in science and technology was chaired by Admiral Hillenkoetter of the CIA, and everybody involved answered to President Truman. Do I have your attention now?'

'Unequivocally.'

'This group presided over the study of every aspect of what these space-faring people represented, technologically, biologically, culturally, historically, politically, you name it. You can imagine the shock among our leaders when they had the living proof of extraterrestrial visitation—to see with their own eyes these strange looking creatures … It just blew them out of the water of their preconceived notion of reality.'

Melbo took another gulp of his beer.

'Furthermore,' went on Clifford, 'I hitched a ride with the committee as an adjutant to General Montague who was on the committee. As I said, I was in on just about every aspect of the operation. I won't say much more because there are definite security issues with the potential windfall of new technology, and it must be kept secret from our enemies. I will say that this technology is utterly incredible.

'Our scientists have reverse-engineered many new fantastic discoveries such as optic fiber circuitry, microchip circuitry, light indestructible metal, smart metal that can transmit light and circuitry, engines that generate antimatter producing electromagnetic gravity waves … therein lies the secret of space travel—using substratum space to shorten and connect vast distances—by accessing the zero-point field; this very flexible massless substratum allows a craft to move in a mass-free manner. It's a frequency-shift to the other side of the light barrier, in effect manipulating the 'rigidity' of linear space, enabling travel at many many times the speed of light. I'm telling you it's all real.'

'It sounds real. Incredible! But it's incomprehensible to me. Where do these aliens come from?' asked Melbo.

'The Roswell aliens come from about forty light years from Earth, but they claim they're part of a loose confederation of thousands of star systems, the oldest races having progressed to date for hundreds of millions of years as space travelers. It defies belief. The broken space vehicles in our possession are only scout craft. We're told that some species have ships hundreds of miles in length and ten miles wide, but most of these so-called mother ships are only a mile or two in diameter.'

'Only. What is their belief system?'

'It's science based, as they know how life originates, but they still question the origins of the elements themselves, and ironically in the nothingness of space they count 'god' as we term it a valid denominator. What is, *is*, and no one knows why or how the universe exists. Call it god if you want, and just fill in the void with whatever we want to believe.'

'No one's going to believe me if I reveal any of this,' said Melbo soberly.

'That's what I'm talking about. Unless the elected government is given this closely guarded information and tells everyone, no one will believe anything you or I or anybody else says.'

'So unless the President makes an announcement that extraterrestrials are among us we'll all remain lunatics for calling it out.'

'Yeah, that's about it,' said Clifford.

'Do you know Edward Teller?' asked Melbo.

'Not personally.'

'Is he in on it?'

'He's part of a team of scientists that are directly involved with alien technology and more. The general told me he was attending a meeting with the scientists and a gray alien sat in on it!'

Melbo shook his head. 'I hope you're not fucking with me.'

'Why should I? Some of the top people think it should be revealed, at least that there are aliens coming here, and that the universe is full of intelligent life! Statistically it's obvious, so anybody who remains unconvinced is just the same as flat Earth believers hundreds of years ago.'

'Who thinks it should be revealed?'

'Forrestal was for it, but he's dead. Hillenkoetter for another, others. But there is a hard core group in the military and intelligences services who are dead set against any public acknowledgement.'

'Sulla, Eisenhower?'

'You know what I'm talking about.'

'Yes,' concurred Melbo, 'it's evident they're holding sway; from what I understand from now on they want to deny even the President clearance in order to justify plausible deniability. It's dangerous.'

'Look, I've said my piece, but don't stop. If enough people want the truth someone has to feed it to them, and let the chips fall where they may.' Sergeant Clifford stood up.

'How can I reach you?' asked Melbo.

'Forget it, and destroy the letter, I insist. If they found out about that and about you trying to find me I'm a dead man. Take care.' And he was gone.

*

June 18 1960

The New York Herald Tribune

Government Insider Says UFOs Are Real

By George Melbo

For a few weeks now, I have carried around with me a ponderous weight of insider knowledge of government complicity in the cover-up of their UFO activities. Let me begin by saying we must move beyond the 'UFO' syndrome; they are no longer Unidentified Flying Objects but in actual fact ETVs (Extraterrestrial Vehicles). And they have been visiting Earth for thousands of years.

To my readers: when I was directed by my editor to write these articles, I undertook with a sense of awe and caution to question their reality and if so our right to know in a free and open society. Now I come to the Rubicon: do I cross that stream that once long ago demarked the demilitarization zone approaching ancient Rome, or do I bring my power and cross it so that the people can be informed of the truth? If this parallel is fitting, then I have, like Caesar, committed a terrible act of provocation, not only to the secret government, but to the security of the United States. I am no Caesar, let's be clear; he brought his army as he feared for his survival in a corrupt system, though perhaps similarly, I should fear for mine.

Some might decry my arrogance if that were true and others might laud my courage in bringing to light a mystery that we deserve rightfully to be enlightened about. Many readers have written me, the lion's share in the positive about ETVs either from personal experience, hearsay from credible people, or philosophical and mathematical certainty that life exists throughout the universe in all stages of development, ours being at the lower end, embryonic in comparison to the much higher end of the spectrum where apparently species live hundreds of millions of years ahead of us.

Even the most intelligent among us are hardly equipped to deal with that kind of disparity. From a religious or evolutionary point of view our understanding of this is well beyond the range of our perceptions. How can we bridge countless versions of reality beyond our present actuality? We are far closer to our distant ancestors roaming new frontiers having emerged from their caves. It is with a profound sorrow that I write this article because it tells us of our almost pitiable state. We're far from perfect not only from our destructive terrestrial issues—world war, ecological myopia, political suicide, and nuclear proliferation—but because we strive for ideological supremacy like the blind in a hostile environment, facing death at every turn.

It becomes a wholly existential argument better examined by philosophers, or the creative writing departments of colleges or science fiction novelists. But here we have it: a very credible person that I am not at liberty to expose because that person has committed high treason by revealing to me, a journalist for the free press, the most classified secrets they've sworn to defend.

Others, of course, have derided and tried to debunk me at every opportunity. And I have no doubt that this harassment will only intensify. I feel persecuted as were so many members of different religions or scientific communities in history or even in the present time if one considers how

135

Einstein himself was ridiculed by the old guard for his Theory of Relativity which set a new threshold for our understanding of the elemental universe; his Nobel Prize was awarded twenty years late! These debunkers are themselves elemental in the universal scheme of things.

Dark and Light abound in eternity, whether government initiated or not! I want you to know that I am on the side of light, and just a simple messenger of information of truths. If not me, then someone else will come forward; and if they fail, there will always be someone willing to tell the truth in spite of all official oppositions. I write here directly to the wizards of the high cabal of government policy. Have no fear! I am not the enemy! I'm a reporter to whom the constitution granted the right and privilege to speak freely.

Some of you might argue: prove it, as if my use of the word 'truth' is nothing more than a tool for sensationalism or political hearsay. If that's the case, then all I ask of you is to do some homework. Read some of the books and scour the papers for information on sightings and follow up on the individuals involved and see for yourself if they are credible. People have to get their heads out of the sand on this if they want to know more, because the government, including the military will not be forthcoming with any deeper insights other than the usual dismissiveness, and that goes for the media as well.

We may ask: why should they be forthcoming? If they have our best interests at heart, they likely think that the reverse-engineering of alien technology far in advance of ours will surely lead us to victory in the Cold War. But in a zero sum game this technology will eventually be made public in ten or thirty years from now, and even our enemies will have it. I'm talking about computers the size of a packet of cigarettes that send wireless messages around the Earth and beyond; precision global co-ordination; the generation of anti-matter and machine produced gravitational waves with which we can manipulate space through its substratum into short distances in order to transit the vast reaches of space in a short time; the molecular breakdown of the human genome which will lead to disease-free long lives.

We will make a significant leap in our progress as a race, and I mean the human race. But all comes to naught if we can't galvanize our leaders to make our world safe, just and healthy. This journey for humanity begins every day. It is forward looking, and not fixated on the past. Imagine yourself as an alien: visiting our planet would have to be an utterly frightening experience. We're the dangerous and hostile ones! No wonder these ETVs are so elusive.

Do not presume to think that my revelations here are the product of some foolish naivety by a man whose thinking is both dangerous and destabilizing. Of course the world is dangerous and we must remain vigilant about the enemies of freedom. Our superior military is the shield of the West and any technological improvement must be seen as necessary to win the Cold War. However, the enemies of freedom also have vested interests, and from their point of view, they are purveyors of 'freedom', though they are ideologically opposed to us. But we stand for individual rights whereas the other side is for servile subjugation to the state; ours is for human dignity, theirs is for tyranny, though it should be said our system has at times succumbed to the same evils as our enemies in the assassination of perceived enemies and in other nefarious deeds. But we all have to learn to live peacefully and withdraw from the threat of policies that threaten a potentially life-terminating nuclear holocaust.

Perhaps these prescient aliens from these seemingly impossibly advanced civilizations out there in space recognize our dilemma and seek in some way to protect us from ourselves. Perhaps our space neighbors know that our primitive atomic systems are a threat to the entire universe—potentially disturbing some natural subspace striatum unknown to us! It is my hope that the military and scientific committee in charge of this alien phenomenon do communicate with these aliens in order to understand our predicament. Is it possible that, to some degree at the least, we must all be part of this process? How more binding in the interests of peace and harmony on Earth could that be?

Most certainly, if these alien spacefarers had evil designs for us, they would have made their move centuries ago before the nuclear age, unless they have all the time in world—millennia—possibly to implement an agenda to hybridize us as we do ourselves among our own races. But that's another article. To date their forbearance shows patience and compassion. Let's not disappoint them. Let's show them that we deserve the right to self-determination.

12. Hannah and Lizbet

Across Nantucket Sound, a beautiful warm sea-breeze carried them peacefully towards Martha's Vineyard on a hot day in late June. Greenfield gave the tiller to Prinzenthal while he sat back, silently half-gazing at the receding distant shoreline of West Yarmouth on Cape Cod, and the chiming of the rigging gently lulled them even deeper into their repose. Once out in the middle of Nantucket Sound, the couple watched the land disappear in the haze of heat. Occasionally, a sailboat, or cabin cruiser could be seen in the distance.

They had driven up from New York the day before to stay at his family's old pastel blue and white cottage on the lee side of a spit of land near Lewis Bay, where the family moored their sailboat, a twenty-eight foot single masted yacht—*Becky,* named after his mother—this a recently refurbished vintage 1932 pilot cutter of teak and oak, was similar to his own down in the Virgins but twenty years older. It had a galley and could comfortably sleep four on overnights, making it perfect for the area. Greenfield told Prinzenthal about his summers there as a boy and young man, where he learned to sail, and then taught it later.

Prinzenthal had never met Peggy Sackett, his younger sister, who with her husband and family had kept the place up and let him use it for seasonal visits. Technically, they used to own it together after their mother died, but Greenfield had rarely used the place since before the war and his career in the clandestine services; he had told her it was hers as long as he could visit from time to time until eventually she had bought him out for a modest sum a few years ago. Still, they kept up the same arrangement.

Prinzenthal and Greenfield enjoyed the surf, sun and breeze and little was said. She had told him a few days previously that she was definitely pregnant. He was so dumbstruck with happiness that tears came to his eyes. She teased him mercilessly, suggesting he was going soft on her. Then she let him know that if it was a boy his name would be David Prinzenthal Greenfield after her father, and if a girl, Elizabeth (Lizbet) Ephrussi Greenfield named after her best friend and cousin on her mother's side who died at Auschwitz during the war—her mother was born Lyubov Ephrussi.

Hannah and Lizbet were born the same year in Lvov, Poland and together the families went to France, but the wealthier Ephrussis stayed in France, when the Prinzenthals emigrated to New York. Lizbet had spent the summers of 1936 and 1937 with Hannah in both New York and a camp in Maine and an entire year in 1938 with her before returning to France in 1939. She intended to return to New York but never made it. The entire family was wiped out by the Nazis. Prinzenthal never fully accepted her cousin's death, believing such a beautiful spirit lived eternally. Greenfield acquiesced unequivocally to her naming their child.

Greenfield did not like the turn of events in regard to Melbo and his provocation of the government with the latest article. Moreover, it put Prinzenthal in a difficult position when asked, or rather assigned, to act as a cut-out to spy on Melbo under Jake Whitmore, his boss. However ironic it was in that her superiors did not know Greenfield and Prinzenthal's prior acquaintance with Melbo, they both knew they had little advantage with any other covert action the CIA might have undertaken against Melbo. But Greenfield worried that if there was any leak of their personal involvement and deception they could be held accountable with severe consequences.

Prinzenthal, as usual, felt no such trepidation; she thrived on such subterfuge by reminding Greenfield that Whitmore was under her spell. She had reported to Whitmore twice on her progress with Melbo, informing him of having first struck up a friendship with the journalist, then as part of a couple with Greenfield starting a friendship with Melbo and Melissa DeCourt.

Naturally, she had said to him that they got on famously, and though she informed Whitmore, Melbo would never reveal his source for the 'Insider' article, in her view he was quite innocent in his pursuit of the truth like any journalist on the scent of a story. She opined that most people took his revelations with a grain of salt; and to attempt to silence him by any means would instantly transform his innocence into something far more likely to reflect badly on the government. So best leave Melbo alone, she argued.

Greenfield was upset because in his opinion she was being naïve. He knew what the bastards would do if they took action: they would set up either a patsy, or a whistleblower, to destroy Melbo, thus forcing him either to let an innocent person be arraigned for treason, or to publicly denounce their ploy as fraudulent. Either way it would create a scandal and impinge on Melbo's integrity as a defacto spokesperson for the people against the secret government. Prinzenthal argued they would be stupid to do that and create a scandal. But that was the point countered Greenfield: scandals were the tools of the trade when they distracted from the truth. The public would then be doing the CIA a service by obfuscating everything in the confusion of conspiracy.

'Did you know the Kennedys in Hyannis Port?' asked Prinzenthal suddenly.

Greenfield stirred from his sunny somnolence and looked at her, amazed at how she presented herself like a native Cape Codder. She held the tiller as a seasoned sailor would, though it was her first time since being a teenager at camp. Barefooted and braless, she was wearing only sunglasses, an open shirt and magenta shorts.

'No,' he said. 'I remember them, the kids, when they were young—Joe, Jack and the girls.'

'What were they like?' she wondered.

'Oh, they seemed happy, active, quite a brood. Of course back then they were unknown unlike today.'

'Will Jack visit this summer?'

'I would think so for a while at least. He bought his own place I gather.'

'Can you arrange a meeting?' she asked.

'You mean like last time, on a hunch?'

'Whatever, you know.'

'I don't know. If he wins the nomination he'll be surrounded by people and preoccupied with meetings.'

'We need to meet.'

'Why? He said he would be in touch.'

'Unlikely. We need to apprise him of our work, to remind him that we know about stuff.'

'Go on,' urged Greenfield, curiously.

'I was thinking about retiring from the service.'

'And you think Kennedy will get you a job?'

'*Us* a job. He needs *us*.'

'If you quit now they might get suspicious.'

'Why?'

'Especially if you end up working for Kennedy.'

'*Us*, remember.'

'Maybe, but still.'

'Not if I tell them I'm pregnant.'

The breeze blew strands of hair about her face. She didn't bother with them and smiled showing her lovely teeth.

'Well, then, we can disappear for a while, down south, Dominica.'

'This could be our test run. Am I an able sea-mate?'

'More than able—*mère de la mer*.'

'Lizbet loved sailing,' she said.

'And we are sailing in her spirit.'

'Yes we are.'

'Did I tell you my sailboat is called *Hannah*?'

'No.'

'Perhaps we should call her *Hannah & Lizbet*.'

'Yes, I'd like that.'

'Done. I'll make the call.'

'Where exactly is your boat in the Virgins?'

'St. Croix, Green Cay.'

A gull shrieked as it passed overhead; looking up Prinzenthal began to cry.

'I think I could live like this for a while, Lizbet,' she said smiling through her tears.

13. New Mexico

Melbo and DeCourt emerged from the faux-adobe Stardust Motel just outside Corona, New Mexico. It was almost noon. Needing something to eat, they drove in their rented 1956 red Ford F100 downtown where they went to the same diner they had eaten the previous evening—Billy's. They were hungry, after what had turned out to be the real honeymoon sleep-in—making love and sleeping, then making love and more sleeping throughout the night and ending with more love-making. Annie, the friendly middle-aged waitress, brought four plates, two in each hand. Now before them were two plates of Huevos Rancheros—eggs sunny side with black beans, bacon, salsa, avocado and corn tortillas; the other plates had each a stack of buckwheat pancakes with agave syrup and whipped cream. A jug of water and orange juice accompanied them.

'Oh my god,' said DeCourt, digging into her pancakes first.

'Amen,' uttered Melbo, wolfing the huevos down without preamble.

Within fifteen minutes almost all their breakfast had disappeared and they sat silently gazing at each other and their plates, sipping on water. Annie returned with pot of steaming hot coffee.

'You look like you earned that,' she said, beaming ear to ear. 'Coffee?'

'You could say that,' said DeCourt. 'Yes, please.'

'We're on our honeymoon,' stated Melbo, proudly.

'Mel!'

'What? We're legal.'

'Men,' she said, looking at Annie. 'Sorry, my husband likes to advertise…our happiness.'

'Hell, Ma'am, I'd be hog-tied to feel what you feel. Congratulations!'

Annie poured coffee into their cups.

'Thank you,' said DeCourt, 'it's just a little embarrassing the way it sounded.'

'Are you kidding? What else would you do in this desert on a honeymoon?'

Melbo laughed. 'See, darling; these folks are real down-to-earth.'

Annie laughed. 'You got yerself a real bronco here, sweetheart; a bit lean, but the best always are.'

'Not after this breakfast-brunch, whatever,' said DeCourt, rubbing her tummy.

'Do you by any chance know a Garnett Wills?' asked Melbo, off the cuff.

'Mr. Wills, sure thing; his place is down near White Oaks. Why do you ask?'

'We met his sister, Edna Beiderman, and wanted to pay our respects.'

'Never met her.'

'She was married to an Air Force colonel and lives in Washington.'

'That where you're from?'

'No, New York,' said Melbo. 'We flew into Albuquerque from Denver.'

'How do you get to his ranch?' asked DeCourt.

'I've never been to his place, but I know approximately where it is. It's called Pine Bluff.'

Annie told them where to turn off Highway 54 South through the White Oak range. His ranch was northeast of Ancho Peak about 40 miles from there. She said there was a short-cut through Ancho but it was best to take the highway to White Oaks instead of the back roads because they could get lost.

They found their way easily enough as a sign, although shot up, still announced White Oaks, now a ghost town known to have been populated in the nineteenth century because gold had been discovered in the local Jicarilla Mountains. It was beautiful and desolate as expected, but the physical reality of that desolation struck them particularly hard being city dwellers.

'No wonder Edna moved away so young,' said DeCourt.

'They're some tough weather-beaten bunch of ranchers out here, no doubt. I mean look at the distances to any store or anything else.'

'Fiercely independent, I'd say.'

They continued northeast on AO40 marveling at the hills and mountains of pine forest and oak shrub. To the east the pine thinned out and before long the road forked and they took the right to AO39. A few miles down, a weather-beaten sign on which was written Pine Bluff Ranch led them to turn left or north along a pine ridge for a couple of miles, and there they found the horse ranch—a beautiful stone house with surrounding veranda and garden and sheds, a horse training ring, barns and stables.

They cautiously approached and parked beside a navy Chevy 1950 pickup truck. Nearby was a large open garage with a pristine white or cream 1958 Lincoln Continental Mark III inside, and an old green Chevy pickup that looked in good shape for about a 1920s model due to the dry conditions.

They got out of their truck and stood looking at the ranch. Behind them to the west the Pine Bluff rose up about three hundred feet. An old cabin could be seen up there as well as a windmill, and a horse, saddled and tied to a fence. A slight breeze turned the vanes of the windmill slowly. Another small building, an open hut that looked to contain about a 2000 gallon water tank, was situated beside the cabin in the trees.

'Seems like a paradise,' said Melbo, 'for a rancher.'

'If you want to live like a hermit,' replied DeCourt.

A woman came out of the house and walked towards them. They walked towards her.

'Hello!' called out Melbo. 'We're looking for Mr. Wills.'

The woman approaching was not unfriendly but cautious. 'He's out on his horse.'

Melbo looked up the bluff and she followed his direction.

'Up there?'

'May I ask what your business is?'

'My name is George Melbo, and this is my wife Melissa.'

'How do you do?' said DeCourt holding out her hand. 'It's a pleasure to meet you.'

The middle-aged woman was brown-skinned, had large, brown eyes and wore her grayish-black hair tied back, revealing a small turquoise necklace. Weathered jeans and an unremarkable buttoned blue shirt, and what looked like Mexican huaraches on her feet completed her casual outfit. She shook DeCourt's hand.

'Maria Cortez.'

'We're friends, or acquaintances rather of Mrs. Edna Beiderman,' continued Melbo. 'We're on our honeymoon, and well, we thought that since we're in the area—she suggested actually, that we drop by and say hello.'

'This ranch is *so* beautiful,' crooned DeCourt. 'What a wonderful life you must lead here.'

Maria looked at them with a half-smile. 'We get by.'

'Mrs. Beiderman never mentioned you, Maria,' said Melbo.

'She's not that native friendly,' she replied.

'Oh, well, that's not right,' remarked DeCourt.

'Wrong or right, I'm Apache,' Maria responded without rancor and keeping the same half-smile. 'Edy's not enamored of the Apache—they murdered some ancestors—but Garnett says she's not racist, just old-fashioned, and doesn't approve of me living here out of wedlock.'

'Well, we haven't been exactly kosher—for lack of a better word—ourselves—we lived together for a while before tying the knot,' declared DeCourt.

'We'd rather have loose ends,' said Maria, 'to weave as we please. And it's worked for twenty-five years, or more.'

'I'm sure we would've done the same out here.'

'Can I offer you some water, or snack while you wait for Garnett?' she asked.

'Some water, thanks,' they both said in unison, and laughed.

*

Sitting on the veranda each holding a glass of water, Melbo and DeCourt looked east across the scrubby desert. The house was situated a couple of hundred feet higher above the plains. A few miles away the dust from a car moving along the road rose up and dissipated. Maria was inside the ranch house.

'Somewhere out there,' said Melbo, 'an alien craft crash-landed thirteen years ago almost to the day.'

'I wonder. Do you think Maria knows anything about it?' asked DeCourt.

'No doubt in my mind.'

'Yeah, she's smart. I bet she knew something the minute he came back.'

Something caught the corner of Melbo's eye. A horse and rider were coming up the road. The rider approaching was obviously Garnett Wills; he still rode tall and firm in the saddle, even though he must have been well into his seventies. Deep-tanned, white-haired and three-day whiskered he stepped down from his muscular bay gelding and tied it to the fence nearby. Dressed in similar attire to Maria, but with a cream-colored Stetson and dark brown well-worn cowboy boots, he climbed the stairs of the veranda. Unsmiling, he stood before them. Melbo stood up and introduced himself extending his hand, just as Maria came back outside. Garnett shook his hand.

'Pick up some strays, honey?'

'Edna sent them.'

'Edy? What for?' He looked at both Melbo and DeCourt in the eye, sizing them up. DeCourt was now standing beside her husband.

'To visit you,' uttered DeCourt, courageously in face of what seemed to be his stern disposition.

'Is she alright?' he asked.

'Oh, yes,' spoke up Melbo. 'Quite a character. We met at Jake Whitmore's birthday party.'

'Whitmore? That wind-bag's nothing more than a pretentious sycophant.'

'The president attended as well as-'

'The whole god-damned rotten establishment,' finished Garnett.

'That about sums it up.'

'If I were you I wouldn't go within a mile of those pricks.'

'I was asked to join the party in a professional capacity,' said Melbo, somewhat amused at Garnett's churlish behavior.

'And what would that be?'

'I'm a journalist, and my wife works in publishing. We're actually on our honeymoon-'

'Honeymoon? Why didn't you say so?' He broke out into a smile showing white teeth.

Garnett pulled up a chair, sat, and filled a third glass with water from the jug. They were all seated now. Maria went back inside.

'Welcome to Pine Bluff, folks.' He drank down the whole glass, then filled it again, but put it on the table.

They spoke of their travels, and the big Republican bash. He was interested in Edna's health.

'She kept up with the best of us,' said Melbo. 'Gotta hand it to Whitmore, he served the best champagne, and wine, booze, you name it.'

'Hell, she could drink me under the table.' Garnett laughed. 'Well, she had ten years on me when I started drinkin' beer 'n whiskey at eighteen. And didn't stop much until sweet Maria showed up one day with her boy lookin' for work; I'd put out an ad in the Roswell Daily. Long ago my wife had left me with my daughters. She died last year. Cancer.'

'Sorry,' said DeCourt.

'Sorry for what? She was seventy-four, two years younger than me. Smoked like a chimney. Met her when we were kids at the rodeo; God, could she ride, pretty as a picture; lived a great life—remarried some ranger. We were fine until my drinking got the better of me. Never laid a hand on her, mind. My kids come by with their families once a year, sometimes twice. Maria's son, Ricky, has family too, and brings the whole Apache tribe.'

He laughed heartily. Maria came out carrying some sliced carrots in ice water, and ham and cheese sandwiches.

'Don't believe it,' said Maria. 'He has five kids and eight grandchildren.'

'And they all come together,' said Garnet.

'You love it.'

'Damn right, I do; I call it Moctezuma's revenge. That bastard Cortez is rollin' in his grave knowing his descendants are native in his name! That's what you call God's justice!'

'Are you really one of the Conquistador's descendants, Maria?' asked DeCourt.

'There's a family story passed down through the ages. Cortez raped an Aztec princess. And her baby survived. One of his descendants went with missionaries to Santa Fe where he eventually married a Jicarilla Apache convert, so the story goes—there are some other tribes mixed in and Spanish, and white. The name survived.'

'I'll be damned,' said Melbo. 'We're in the presence of royalty.'

Maria laughed for the first time.

'And she lords it over me!' exclaimed Garnett. 'I'm forever grateful.' He took her hand.

The afternoon wore on. Garnett and Maria loved their company. Garnett took his horse, Jack, to the stables and Melbo went with him. Out back there were numerous paddocks with about thirty horses divided equally among them.

'You look after all this by yourselves?' asked Melbo.

'I've got some helpers, a young couple, horse people, you know.'

'But not today.'

'That other house back there has all the amenities; they live there; they went to town—Roswell; she's pregnant; due in a month.'

'You'll be a hand short.'

'Maria and one of her friends help out.'

Garnett talked about his horses. He didn't break them in anymore, he told Melbo, but would ride a green horse out in the desert for a day or two sometimes—staying overnight in a few shacks with small yards built here and there way out beyond the immediate horizon. He claimed a horse and its rider needed to bond properly, and only by spending that kind of time in the saddle would the rider break them in properly. The two men stood by the fence and watched the horses feed at a trough of hay.

'Garnett, I don't really know how to ask this,' said Melbo.

Silence.

'So I'll say it straight.' He took a breath. 'Edna mentioned you were out in the desert the night of the storm back in late June '47.'

'My papa used to say it ain't desert. We call it the sage. Desert is like Sahara or Gobi.'

'Okay, sage.'

'I figured this might come up someday. I swore Edna off it. I didn't want trouble.'

'So you were there. You know what I'm talking about.'

'Why did she tell you?'

'I recall she said her husband had passed. Said you weren't too chummy.'

'You can say that again; he was some arrogant piece of work—had his head so far up his ass, thought he'd found his true calling eating his shit. But you didn't answer my question. Why did she tell you about that?'

'We were talking about the lights over Washington back in 1952. It was headline news then. She was a little tipsy, and just told us.'

'I told her never tell anybody.'

'I swear to God it won't go past here.'

Silence.

'Frank must've been too old to fly in the war,' stated Melbo, thinking to prompt Garnett.

'He fought in the first war, as a pilot; in the second war he ran a training base in Texas, and other places. He was in on the Trinity Project, you know the A-bomb.'

'And ended up in Washington.'

Silence. Melbo could feel his agitation. He had to get it off his chest.

'I told Edna what happened that Thanksgiving when she happened to visit with Rosie, my niece, and her grown-up kids, but I told her in the strongest terms never to tell a soul, especially Frank, because all the others who were involved were tagged no matter what they did or where they went. The government, that is the military and secret services, were just paranoid, beyond the pale. People even disappeared. But no one knew I was there.'

Melbo let that sink in. 'No one knew you were there. How's that?'

'I was out on the sage with a young horse, that one in fact,' indicating his horse, 'about twenty miles almost due east from here. I was going to turn around and head northwest to a cabin I preferred where there was hay and supplies. But the storm clouds gathered quickly so I went a bit farther east to an old unused shack and corral to hunker down for the night. I quickly unsaddled the horse under the shed roof at the side of the shack, watered and fed him some rolled oats I had, then closed the gate so he was well-secured for the night ...'

... The thunder rolled in from all around, it seemed. The day, though darkened, had turned to night. Garnett, having slept restlessly awoke and was lying on the cot under his blanket listening to the wind howl and moan throughout the old shack. The thin glass panes rattled in two small windows. Flash lightening lit up intermittently the structure and the sage all around. Garnett sat up and looked out to see for brief moments the sage illuminated as if it were high noon. A massive bolt of lightning smashed the ground not a hundred yards from his window facing south. The horse began to neigh fearfully. Another crack of thunder followed a shaft of lightning on the other side, and another.

Garnett swung his feet around and put on his boots. He stood up and was about to open the door outside to the shed when another ear-shattering bolt struck not twenty feet outside the north window, lighting up the sky yet again. He saw something in that fractious second—bluish and purplish lights on an object that disappeared as fast as the black night closed in. Turning instinctively to the south window, he saw for a micro-second the same lights evaporate in the sudden cloudburst of torrential rain.

It was odd, he thought, as he hadn't heard any engines in that proximity. The horse went silent as if it too had sensed some unusual event. Then after some moments came a boom of impact aside from lightning. The distant sky became incandescent briefly even in the rain, then nothing. After a few more flashes of lightning in the distance, the receding thunder gave away to the deafening roar of rain hitting the steel roof. Garnett opened the shed door and went to his horse.

'Easy boy,' he called out. 'We're okay now, Jack. Did you hear that? I think somebody crashed. We better go and see when the rain subsides.'

In the last shards of lightening he saw the water barrel in the shed overflow with the rain from the roof gutter on the facia. 'Well, Jack, at least we won't go thirsty.'

Within a half hour, the rain subsided to a light drizzle. Garnett got up from his cot with his boots still on and saddled Jack. He filled his canteen and waterproof bag with fresh rain water then opened the gate and led out his horse. He pulled himself up onto the saddle and headed southeast in the pitch dark.

They walked like that for an hour and found nothing. The rain had stopped. He looked all around and listened. He saw nothing and heard nothing. Strange, he thought out loud, 'I could've sworn that whatever it was had crash-landed around here somewhere, Jack. We've covered at least three miles.' Garnett urged the horse on. He knew dawn was yet a few hours away. That plane, he surmised, must've been going a lot faster. He presumed that there would likely be no chance of any survivors. They carried on in the blackness, Jack picking his way among the dips and hillocks, brush and rocks.

Then something caught Garnett's eye to the left. Whatever it was instantly vanished—a faint bluish light. He turned around and back-tracked. There it was again in the distance. Some obstacle must have blocked it; he bee-lined straight for it. Twenty-five minutes later he came across some debris, pieces of metal, an aluminum-like material scattered all about. Continuing his search, he finally came to the source of light.

It was the weirdest fuselage he'd ever seen. Jack became somewhat nervous and hesitated to move forward. Garnett got off him and led him away, up and around a knoll out of sight. He staked the ground and tethered him. 'Easy fellow, I've got to see if anybody survived.' Then he took his canteen and walked back to the wreck. The bluish light seemed to emanate from the metal hull itself; there was a gaping hole on the one side, and the light was actually coming from inside. The shape was roundish and about thirty feet in diameter.

Must be some prototype, he thought. Where were the pilots? He touched the metal hull, and recoiled. It was freezing, even in the humidity and heat. Moving closer, he stepped inside the hull. He saw a console but no levers or *gauges, buttons or knobs. What is this? The pilot seats were small like for a child and were formed out of the hull as a mold. He looked deeper inside…he quickly darted back outside. Shock pierced his mind and body. Kids? In space suits? He composed himself, and looked again.*

There were five of them, three inert, one moving uncomfortably, and the other sitting up staring at him with large, dark, almond-shaped eyes. He was dressed in a skin-tight greenish-blue suit, had no ears, or hair, and had a tiny mouth. The creature raised his hand, showing only four fingers, long and whitish. 'Geesh!' said Garnett. The creature seemed to cower at his voice, and Garnett sensed great fear. His mind was invaded by thoughts of great despair and cries for help, but there was no voice.

In Garnett's mind, he knew this was not humanly possible, yet he felt these terrible emotions, which were as human as anything he had ever felt. In his confusion, his horseman's sense kicked in so he approached cautiously with his water canteen held in front towards the alien creature-boy. 'Water,' he said. 'Have no fear; I won't hurt you.' The alien stared at him with those intense eyes. Garnett could feel something infuse his brain.

The alien messaged that there had been an accident; we were being followed by one of yours; we were on a scouting mission in our small craft; we easily evaded the jet, but found ourselves in the electric storm and were hit; our people are in a mothership behind your moon; my fellows are dead except…unintelligible… Then he took the water and gave some to his wounded friend, before drinking a little himself.

Garnett felt devastated. Something in him broke and tears began to well up. The predicament of these people was too much to bear. He had no fear of them anymore, as they were like children. His mind was befuddled with the realization that they were from somewhere out in space, marooned on a hostile planet. Questions arose. He just stared at the alien, who gazed back. He could see that he was wounded, as well. There was some purplish liquid that seeped from a tear in his side. Some gasping emitted from the severely wounded other alien. He shuddered and went still. The living alien put his hand on his friend.

Garnett said, 'Let me take them outside and cover them.' The alien didn't respond. Garnett then went and picked up one of the dead aliens—he was light, only about fifty pounds, and took him outside. After, all four were laid in a row. The remaining alien came out with a grayish synthetic blanket and both he and Garnett covered the bodies. The alien sat with his friends. Garnett sat facing him. *'What can I do to help?' he said.*

There was no response. The alien lay down, obviously in pain. Garnett was stricken with helplessness. He knew the authorities would eventually find the wreck. Likely by now they were aware that a UFO had been seen and chased by scrambled jets from the air force base in Roswell. There were other ranches in the area; he knew them. Should he report it? He couldn't very well take the alien with him for medical attention. The alien seemed to sense Garnett's dilemma. Don't worry, it telepathed: they will come for us. You may go. So, Garnett figured they had already sent for help. But he stayed.

'Where are you from?' he ventured. 'What is your fuel? I don't smell any. How do you travel in space?' But the alien seemed not able or willing to translate this information. They sat there for over an hour. As dawn approached, a slight sign of daylight appeared in the east where low cloud cover eventually gave way to a line of pink sky. Garnett stood up to scan the sage. He saw the lights of a vehicle crawling along at least a couple of miles away. He knew he had to make a decision. What difference could he make after others had discovered this phenomenon? he asked himself.

It was like the world of Frank would descend on them, and he would be shunted off to some room on some base and be damned for life having seen what he saw there. He knew they would never reveal to the public what had happened. He made his choice: he had to leave now or risk being seen on his horse in the vicinity if helicopters or planes began searching around the sage. He said goodbye to the alien, took out the bivouac stake, mounted his horse, and in a canter headed west for home.

'I never told Edna the whole story,' said Garnett.

'I can see why. But why tell me?' asked Melbo.

'You're a journalist, and a decent sort. I can read people. If any good can come of this, you're the one who can do it. Just keep me out of it.'

'I give you my word.'

'Can you make a difference?' asked Garnett, taking off his hat and looking at him sternly.

Melbo stood quietly for a few moments. The horses moved restlessly in the paddock.

'I'm not so sure,' he finally said. 'I've been writing articles for my paper about this very phenomenon, and people are interested, and want the truth, and there's a lot of it out there—people who have experienced a bit of what you experienced, but the 'pricks' as you say in government, the secret government have another agenda that takes priority over opening up about it to the public.'

'Do you think a change of government, say this Kennedy gets elected, will change anything?'

'Again, I'm not sure. Under Eisenhower, they have created a deep state power with its tentacles imbedded into the system—the CIA and the war machine. All because the threat to the freedom-loving world in the West is palpable, and they have taken it head-on fighting fire with fire. Nevertheless they consider any technological windfall from alien spacecraft as manna from heaven. I don't even know that if Kennedy were elected he would be briefed on this, so deep is the secret, which ironically is out in the open!

'They neither confirm nor deny to protect the secret programs; so the legal apparatus of government has no oversight, and the President cannot be held liable for something he is uninformed about. The secret arm of government has effectively taken over. These are uncharted waters for this country, all to do with protecting our freedoms, but perhaps destroying them in the process.'

'Goddamn,' uttered Garnett. 'How fucked up is that? The people at least have a right to know, and the government should come clean! They're corrupt!'

'There are many who think so too, but sticking your neck out too far is dangerous. Look at what they did to all those people involved in this Roswell incident. No one is immune to their reach, even the president, I fear.'

There was a holler from the main house. It was DeCourt.

'Looks like you're invited for dinner, George.'

'Friends call me Mel.'

153

14. Spooks

About fifty miles northwest of Washington on the Maryland side of the Potomac River ten miles east of Harper's Ferry, a modest group of influential guests gathered at the family estate of the wife of a senior member of the intelligence services. Aubrey and Honey Woods hosted every few years this summer fête for friends and family. All the top intelligence people were invited, as Mr. Woods was one of them and had been Harley Greenfield's younger colleague when he was still employed by the agency. Attendees included Art Lovering and Allen Sulla and wives, as well as Greenfield and Prinzenthal to their surprise, this being their last stop before going down to the Caribbean for a few weeks. It happened to be the same day that Melbo and DeCourt were visiting Pine Bluff Ranch.

The Woods' estate was called Swan Cottage, or the "Cottage" and was situated on a high point of land with views to the Potomac and valley. Apparently Potomac translated as 'river of swans'. Fields and forests created a lovely mosaic of bucolic countryside. Mrs. Wood's parents were still alive then, but they were elderly and moved discreetly about the house and porch. Numerous children, including young Nevin James, thirteen, and his older sister, Carolyn, cousins and others swarmed like rogue bees here and there to the delight of all, except perhaps a few stodgy career officers.

Greenfield and Prinzenthal arrived late having flown into Washington earlier that day. They both had reservations about going but thought it best to keep abreast of the political concerns of the intelligence business—social venues were often a barometer of intrigue. Greenfield, specifically, having retired from the service, didn't want to appear too interested, and let the revelers open up among friends. Prinzenthal on the other hand, rose up to the occasion in her best form, all bonhomie with a decidedly subtle sophistry.

Naturally, she stood out among the women, as a newcomer from the underclass in that she had been invited to this party for the first time. Her appearance at the request of Woods himself, from Sulla, given her notoriety as a *femme fatale,* smiled a kind of acquiescence upon seeing her. Never doubted was Sulla's perspicacity in all things personal, political or otherwise. Appearances for him were always calculated, deliberate and even carefully prepared; he carried himself with an air of social grace and authority, but some, including his wife, Clover, said that he was the Great White Shark relentlessly cruising the depths of both domestic and American foreign policy with the cold animus of his ocean ally.

During the war, he was the OSS chief in Switzerland, its neutrality a hotbed of intrigue being surrounded by the Nazi war machine ever-threatening, ever mindful of Swiss banking convenience, Sulla's powerbroker, like an unassailable castle of the Alps. According to his sister he had had over a hundred mistresses. Greenfield had known him for many years before his ascension to Director. He didn't trust him as far as he could throw him. He had known good people that Sulla had thrown to the wolves and thought he believed himself above reproach. All through the Roosevelt years and beyond he knew Sulla to be the smooth operator for the ever-spinning Republican right-wing which coveted attaining unprecedented power.

Now that he was in power, behind the very pinnacle, he was the perfect broker, often seen, charming, and untouchable. Greenfield hated him because his control was so effective it didn't seem to matter whether he was working for the government or not; his influence knew no bounds. Such was the secret imperium created by him and his older brother Don Nestor, the Secretary of State, during the Eisenhower years.

This was a delightful way for everybody to spend a sunny summer afternoon, thought Greenfield, with his extra minty Mojito in hand served from an iced punch bowl. The mood was naturally jovial and plain fun, especially with the children's laughter—boys and girls, the peels and shrieks of delight. Some kids attacked the croquet grounds with a feral vigor; others took turns on a big swing on the branch of an ancient tree down in the corner of the extensive lawn. There was also tennis for the adults who preferred to separate themselves from the children. He watched Hannah mingle among the women, spending some length of time with Penny Poirot Beyer the estranged wife of Ford Beyer, the war hero, and high-ranking officer of the company. Perhaps she came with the kids, he thought, as they all knew each other. What would it be like with his own kid, he mused? Would Hannah insist on them attending these parties? Perhaps, if she was still working.

'Are you feeling your age, Harley, with all these kids?' said Art Lovering, from behind.

Greenfield turned and shook Lovering's outstretched hand.

'No, Artie, in fact I'm just getting started,' he retorted happily.

'I envy you, retired, boating in the Caribbean, and now with Hannah on your arm.'

'Well, the old flame in me just doesn't seem to run out of fuel.'

They laughed.

'Good for you!' exclaimed Lovering. 'I know you were close back in the day; what brought you two together again?'

Greenfield could sense Lovering's feelers probing; he was very cagey for a government clerk.

'Well, in all honesty, and I'm quite sure about this, I never fell out of love with her, and only kept my distance these last few years because she wished it so.'

'She changed her mind about ol' Harley?' he said, egging him on.

'Not quite, she claims she always loved me, by default, only work came between us. You know the business.'

'So she called you up? Come on, you're killing me!'

'Hannah never calls; you know how coy she is. I called her, and we went out for old time's sake.'

'And she missed you so much she professed her love for you?' he asked, his eyes looking at him behind a smirk.

Greenfield knew this was more than a friendly chat. Lovering was fishing and by deduction, he suspected that there was some deeper interest in them. He had known Lovering in post-war Germany; they had little to do with each other back then and almost nothing since. The professional spy in Greenfield was no match for a bumbling bureaucrat.

'Artie, do you really want to hear the juicy details?'

'Oh, I didn't mean to pry. It's just that with all what's going on now, the timing's a bit …'

'There's no timing in love, real love, Art. I'm moving on in age; Hannah is approaching limits of child-bearing age; not that that was any reason to get together-'

'But it helped.' Lovering just couldn't get anything right. He began

156

searching around for someone else to nose in on.

'No in fact, Hannah is a perennial loner, like me. Our trade seems to have converted normal social behavior into something less reasonable. I seduced her, or she seduced me, I can't tell which; anyway, we both decided we can't live without each other.'

'So what's the plan? She's still working the last I heard.'

'She's taking a few weeks off. We're on our way to the Virgins where my boat is waiting, then taking a leisurely sail to Dominica and back. By the way, what did you mean by what's going on?'

'Oh, nothing really, the election, you know, there's always something.'

'There's always an election, but this'll be a tight one. I predict a Nixon-Kennedy battle—a new order attempting to dislodge the old.'

'On the face of it, perhaps, but Americans are generally conservative; communism scares people into remaining that way, decidedly conservative. Oh, look, more hors d'oeuvres.'

Before Greenfield could reply Lovering bailed as one of the wives passed by with a tray from which he took a bite-sized olive-melon-prosciutto spiked with a toothpick. 'Oldest trick in the book,' whispered Greenfield to himself watching Lovering side up to Sulla and Ford Beyer. Project fear; and if that doesn't work, supply it. He could see them observing Beyer's ex-wife and Prinzenthal. He knew Sulla had a soft spot for Hannah. Well, at least he equated "soft" for wanting to sleep with her. Shut up, he told himself, don't even think about it. He knew she was capable of extracting anything she wanted from anybody, including Sulla. But it wasn't worth getting killed for it if things went south. These were dangerous men.

Prinzenthal and Penny Poirot Beyer seemed quite involved in a conversation. Hannah looked in Greenfield's direction and smiled. Penny looked as well, sizing him up, not unpleasantly. The two women also noticed Penny's ex-husband and Sulla as inscrutable as ever, and could tell that their eyes were all over Prinzenthal.

'You're rather brave showing up,' said Prinzenthal. 'Your husband seems none too pleased.'

'I wouldn't have come but the kids insisted,' Penny replied. 'Honey Woods gave me a call, saying she hadn't seen me in ages.'

'And Ford?'

'Well, he had no say in the matter.'

They both laughed.

'With you here,' she added, 'he seems distracted. Believe me, I'm quite grateful.'

'I'm happy to be of service.'

They laughed again. Prinzenthal didn't know Penny Poirot but liked her verve and keen intelligence. She was beautiful in a gregarious way with artistic flair, an hourglass figure and social grace. It was a pity her marriage had broken down, not an uncommon problem in the intelligence family. Prinzenthal presumed that her charm among the movers and shakers was rather more diverse as ingratiating which led to some conflict with her husband in that she was too independent, a Democrat and supported Kennedy. Not ideal for the principled Ford Beyer.

'The way they look at you,' continued Penny, 'I know that look. They're in awe of you. I'm not asking for an explanation, but if I were to hazard a guess, you're a secret weapon. Am I wrong?'

'They're looking at you too.'

'The difference being they take umbrage with me.'

'Only because you're a new kind of woman.'

'And you're not?'

'They trust me to fight their battles.'

'I knew it.'

'But not for long.'

'Our powers over men are the aphrodisiac of youth—young flesh.'

'And over women.'

'My, my, Hannah, you are a weapon.'

'I spent over ten years undercover in Europe, east and west.'

'Oh my God, in my wildest dreams I thought of myself doing that, but I'm not cut out for it at all. In fact, I'm downright transparent, and best suited to home fires. You must be a polyglot. How many languages do you speak?'

'Oh, five fluently, and bits of others.'

'You still seem modest. How old are you?'

'Just thirty-eight on the fourth of July.'

'God, you look twenty-eight.'

'No older than you look.'

'I wish; I'm thirty-nine, going on forty in October, but feeling fifty after three kids.'

'You got out and now you're free,' declared Prinzenthal. 'I envy that.'

'Well, I could use a little more sex.'

'The kind that makes you blush.'

They laughed yet again.

Allen Sulla broke away from his group and slithered up to Prinzenthal.

'Hello Hannah, I better get my kiss before I miss the chance,' he announced beaming behind his steel-gray eyes, as he pecked her cheek. 'And Penny,' he added, turning to kiss her cheek as well. But no sooner had he finished his greeting, he steered Prinzenthal away, saying, 'Pardon me, Penny, I need to borrow her for a couple of minutes.'

'Al, I know better than to stand in your way,' said Penny, unapologetically.

'You were always the model wife, my dear.'

'I *was*; that's true.'

Sulla led Prinzenthal across the sloping lawn.

'Hannah, I'm happy to see you here. I've wanted to have a chat with you for some time now.'

'I'm always available to you, sir.'

'Yes, well, it's these lovely summer fêtes that can allow the kind of casual or rather more light-hearted discourse than does the office.'

A couple of young girls raced past them, summer dresses flapping, green-kneed and red-cheeked.

'No doubt about that.'

They both laughed.

'I'm pleased with your progress on *Backslide*; not only are the commies compromised in France, Benelux, but so are their connections in New York. Good work.'

'My father, David, guides me from heaven, Mr. Sulla.'

'Indeed he must.'

Sulla stopped near the edge of the forested ravine. 'We have always counted on you and your loyalty. Your post-war work in Europe is the talk of the trade manuals. Our windfall from that still shines like gold in the intelligence vault. But now we're entering a new phase, if-you-will, a transition from post-war to pre-emptive cold war. Our position is strong thanks to Eisenhower, and a hard-headed administration.'

'That would be you, sir.'

'Hannah,' he said smiling, 'you've got my number. But do you have what it takes to follow through in another administration, say a Kennedy one?'

'I-'

'Hear me out,' he continued. 'The world is but a flint-spark away from cold war to hot war; the Soviets continue to pervade the world with its doctrine and back it up both surreptitiously and overtly, as you are well aware, and they don't hesitate to embolden any weak new-liberated national movement with arms and overt political control. We've created a backstop, a counter-movement unpopular as it is, but effective, as in Guatemala, Congo and Iran. There is no compromise with Bolshevism. You know this. I need your continued support, Hannah; you're a star in our world.'

Prinzenthal remained pensive. It was a trait that Greenfield knew well, which usually meant she was uncomfortable. 'I don't allow myself to be flattered by my successes through three administrations,' she remarked, 'if they can be called that. Human suffering doesn't flatter easily. And I have suffered. Yes, I have fought for freedom in the grand gesture, in the bedrooms and salons of the corrupt, ignorant, sick, and boorish, and survived to tell the tale. I'm a pawn, sir, a pawn turned into a queen. If I may, a queen pointed in wherever direction I'm needed like a weathervane. But now I'm needed here at home. And the weathervane has jammed in one direction. See that man over there. You know him well, at least as an operative, and my former case officer years ago ...'

Sulla looked and saw Greenfield now speaking with Penny Poirot Beyer and Honey Woods.

'Harley,' he said.

'And the father of the tiny bub growing in my tummy.' Prinzenthal rubbed her womb.

Sulla was the kind of man who rarely showed any emotion, but for a split second his eyes opened wide and revealed something like shock, or betrayal— betrayal because in his mind he held Prinzenthal in the highest veneration like a vestal virgin for whom no real love interest was possible; in other words a sacrilege. If he was the High Priest, she was sacrosanct.

'H-Harley?' he stuttered. 'That old dog...' He couldn't get his head around that—a reaction to the splinters of jealousy, envy, burning and crashing, ricocheting in his brain.

Prinzenthal went in for the kill. 'I've always been madly in love with him, and tortured him on account of it, which resulted in his quitting the service to boot. You see, I've been a bad girl, but I aim to be a good mother.'

'A good mother,' he said like a robot. He finally collected himself. 'I'm thrilled for you, Hannah. It comes as a surprise, knowing your … ah, temperament. I never knew that Harley-'

'The best lover I've ever had,' she added, twisting the knife, 'we just melt together. I don't really get it. Almost makes me believe in God, or some such thing.'

'You're making a clean break then?' he asked, feebly.

'Sir, I'm good for desk work, even that *Moonlight* case.'

'*Moonlight?*'

'Yes, you know the cut-out job with Jake Whitmore, about Melbo the journalist?'

'Oh yes, of course, the sci-fi writer.'

Prinzenthal suspected he hadn't a clue what the case was about.

'How's that going?' he asked.

'Well, I've connected with the subject, and started up a friendship. He's quite monogamous and is on his honeymoon as I understand it. I don't really know why I was asked to case him; he's a writer in the opinion column of the Herald, and he helps sell papers according to Mr. Whitmore.'

'Does Jake approve of his opinions?'

'I think he rather enjoys them for entertainment value, but someone—I assumed you—asked him to check Melbo out.'

'And you. Why you? I'm not up on that file.'

'I asked him the same question while knocking back his famous Manhattans.'

Laughing through his teeth, he said, 'I've had a few myself.'

'To answer your question, one of your people obviously thought I was up for the task. Thank you for your faith in me.'

'Hannah, thank you for your four-square update … And keep in touch. And keep up the good work.' With that Sulla disengaged and sauntered over to Lovering and Woods who were amidst a gaggle of women.

*

Nevin James was a bit of a loner with intense blue eyes graced with short, dark brown hair, who if someone had known, resembled a younger Mercury in

Botticelli's *Primavera*, though perhaps without the winged feet, red robe, sword and wand reaching up to chase away the clouds, though not for want of trying. At the back end of thirteen years of age, he was no longer a keen reader of Franklin Dixon's *Hardy Boys* series and had ascended to Ian Fleming's James Bond series of which he was reading *From Russia With Love.*

But today, he had no book to read. He liked to look at the old photographs that covered the walls in his grandparent's house. He would explore the study with its smells of old leather and pipe tobacco. There were files in the drawers and letters with strange stamps from strange places. No one took notice of him as he snooped around harmlessly. He had grown up around this rarefied air of important government officials, and now knew they were spies, his father and Uncle Aubrey among them, and was told to be on his best behavior during these gatherings with them dressed in their light summer suits with drinks and tobacco. Some of the girls about his age, even his older sister, as there were no boys his age, would try to coax him out to play. He would go along for a while but would soon wander off. They thought him rather odd.

A path led down from the edge of the lawn into a forest and down to a field. From there he could walk across the field to another forest and railroad tracks, and then across a footbridge over the Chesapeake and Ohio Canal built in the 1830s parallel to the Potomac to haul coal. He liked to watch the river from some rocks. There were gentle rapids, pools and eddies, and little islands of greenery. He loved the sound of the water surging and gurgling and moving relentlessly like a colossal dark silken tapestry. He would imagine how the armies in the Civil War would cross the river at various fords allowing the safe passage of horses, gun carriages, caissons and men.

After some time in his dream state, he would walk back and up the forested ridge toward the house, and in a cave hidden in a shelf of rock in the forest just beneath one extremity of the lawn, he would sometimes sit and ponder the natural world around him.

On this particular occasion, as he sat in his private retreat, he heard voices coming his way and settling just above him.

'…I don't blame her,' said a voice that sounded like Uncle Aubrey's.

'We can't jump at every opinion questioning our policy,' said another.

'Al, I just wanted to be sure, you know; cover a potential leak,' said the third voice.

'Potential leak? They flew over D.C.; they crashed in the desert; they've been seen everywhere! People aren't stupid. Melbo's not stupid.'

'Let's wait and see the outcome of the election,' said the first voice.

That *is* Uncle Aubrey, Nevin thought to himself.

'And what then if Kennedy wins?'

'Artie,' said the second voice, 'Kennedy has no clue how to run the country; and it's likely he won't even get the chance.'

'Even if he were elected, we should do our best to see that he has the best people working for him, you specifically, Al.'

'By all means.'

They all laughed.

'And Melbo?' asked Uncle Aubrey.

'Melbo be damned. Forget him.'

'Then Greenfield?'

'He's retired.'

'Old spies never retire.'

'Well then tap him and see. I can tell you one thing: he's got a lot on his plate at present.'

'How's that?'

'Hannah's pregnant with his child.'

'Prinzenthal? Are you sure? I thought she liked girls.'

'No Art, she's as straight as they come; her work in Europe was work, full stop. She wants a family; she just told me.'

'Should she proceed then?'

'She said she would but thinks that there's nothing there to warrant it. Jake claimed he sells papers. Fair enough, but…'

'But what?'

'Greenfield's a dyed-in-the-wool Democrat, like Roosevelt was his daddy, and Truman his big brother.'

'So you're saying Prinzenthal may not be completely … honest here.'

'She's never let us down.'

'Then what?'

'Artie, thanks for your concern, but let Aubrey handle it. In future, come to me first.'

'Right, you know I was just fishing. So much hinges on Majestic.'

'Fishing, indeed. We have more fish to fry, my friend.'

'I'll get on it,' said Uncle Aubrey.

'I need a refill.'

They ambled away their voices fading. Nevin hadn't a clue what they were talking about, but he never forgot Melbo. Who was Melbo? And Majestic? All so very strange and secretive, yet it thrilled him.

*

While Nevin was reclining under the shelf of rock at the far end of the lawn, Greenfield and Prinzenthal were once again together just beyond a gaggle of spooks and wives who by now were well lubricated with drink and food. Both were feeling their stay had outworn its purpose, which was simply to make an entrance together and let someone know their general state of affairs. The idea was that they were small-time players in a big player field, and Prinzenthal's pregnancy would signal a further withdrawal from any attention.

Greenfield had tried to dissuade her from revealing her pregnancy until it was unavoidable, but Prinzenthal being still ensconced in the secret services felt some admission was obligatory if she wanted to be in control and dictate the terms of her departure. Prinzenthal felt a great relief in making that sudden admission to Sulla. And let the chips fall where they may; she knew she'd be gone soon.

Nevin James appeared coming through the woods near them and walked by. His father William stepped out from the immediate gathering to meet him. William James worked in the FBI and secretly liaised with the CIA, and was as well a member of the prestigious Alibi Club in Washington, where his father had been a senior member.

'Where have you been?' asked James of his son—and overheard by Greenfield and Prinzenthal.

'Nowhere,' said Nevin.

James looked up and saw Greenfield and Prinzenthal. He smiled at them.

'I guess it can't be helped given the paternity,' he said to them.

'It's said the fruit doesn't fall far from the tree,' remarked Greenfield.

James laughed and Nevin seized the opportunity to leave.

'Bill James.' He introduced himself, extending his hand.

'Harley Greenfield.' He shook James' hand. 'And my fiancée Hannah Prinzenthal.'

164

'How do you do?' She smiled gorgeously.

'It's a pleasure. Have we met? You're familiar. I'm obliged not to ask, but I presume you're in the service.'

'Well, I'm retired,' said Greenfield.

'And I'm pregnant,' said Prinzenthal.

'Well, I'll be. I should have known that; I'm counter-intelligence, FBI.'

They all laughed.

'I think we can be done with due diligence,' continued James. 'I'm the host's brother-in-law. Honey is my wife's elder sister by fourteen years.'

'And the young fellow?' asked Prinzenthal.

'Nevin, my son. He's a good lad, if a little furtive.'

'Well, he's among kin, isn't he?' she added.

'No doubt about that.'

'An uncanny resemblance.'

'Now I remember,' declared James.

'What's that?' asked Greenfield.

'Jedburgh. You were one of the team leaders?' queried James.

'You were a Jedburgh?'

'Midi Pyrenées and Languedoc-Rousillion.'

'Île de France and Centre-Val-de-Loire,' stated Greenfield.

'My God! You must be Jean Hardin!'

'Not too loud,' said Greenfield, smiling. 'I'm still on a Nazi hit list.'

'I don't doubt it. You had a reputation for killing the psychos. I always wondered what happened to you.'

'He was my handler after Potsdam,' said Prinzenthal. 'I was in the State Department then.'

'You're not Judith Graham?'

'Not anymore; burned too many bridges.'

'I'll be damned … you both fell off the earth after the war. I'm truly honored.'

'From one Jedburgh to another: see ya on the other side,' said Greenfield.

'I still get nightmares.'

'Hannah cured me of that.'

'Then he knocked me up,' she said, wryly.

They all laughed.

'What do you think of Kennedy?' asked Prinzenthal suddenly.

'Well, being a Republican, not much; however I'm moderately Republican unlike some of the gang, and if I was convinced Kennedy offered a hardline towards communism, I could stomach his refreshing or new political take. And you?'

'I like him,' she answered. He's just a few years older than me. America has to evolve from the old guard.'

'He's close to our age yes, but that doesn't make up for the wisdom of our elders,' he surmised.

'It depends who he would keep in his cabinet,' said Greenfield. 'A blend of young and old.'

'That might work,' said James. 'But I'm inclined to think we're not quite ready for him. He's too inexperienced and progressive for the complex issues facing the country.'

'They say that about every new boy,' replied Greenfield.

'I did vote for FDR, because he had called it right—the imminent war,' remarked James.

'So, Bill, you disdained the isolationism during the beginning of the war in Europe?' asked Prinzenthal.

'Initially I towed the party line,' he said, 'but became a quick convert when I saw what was happening in Germany, forcing out droves of Jews and other resistors of the evil that was fomenting. Hitler unleashed hell on earth; it had to be stopped. Need I remind you, Kennedy's father was pro-Germany, or rather, appeasement, at the time; a damn fool he was, and embarrassed the hell out of Roosevelt.'

'The sins of the fathers,' said Greenfield. 'Jack, though, in his defense, is not his father, who had close ties to the Irish, who considered Germany an ally during the first war.'

'I grant you that.'

'The same could be said of the pre-war Republicans.'

'But now I think the cold war has made devils of us all.'

*

On the way back to Washington, Greenfield and Prinzenthal drove in silence, steeped in the atmosphere of the afternoon fête. By the time they arrived at the Willard, where they were staying, Prinzenthal had one of her prescient flashes.

'Harley, do you really think Kennedy—if he is nominated and wins the election—should keep some of the old guard, as a non-partisan gesture? I don't. He should clean out the stables. I don't think any of the "gang", as Bill James succinctly described them, would allow Kennedy any latitude to change things from the way they are. I could really feel their arrogance today; of all of them with the exception perhaps of James. They think they own America, and all who govern in it.'

'You're probably right, but politics has a nasty way of interfering with one's better judgement.'

'Politics be damned. Kennedy has no idea who and what he's dealing with here.'

'I don't know about that; but his humanitarian nature may not give it the significance it deserves.'

'We have to speak with him,' said Prinzenthal.

'I agree, but how? Kennedy lives in a fish bowl. We have to remain neutral, discreet. We can't be seen to be running our own domestic spy operation, because that's what this gang would deduce, if they haven't already.'

'Perhaps Melbo can get a private audience,' she said. 'A professional pass.'

'And we would use him as our messenger?'

'I'll throw it past Whitmore.'

'Yes, dear, but we should keep things in perspective: if we position ourselves with Melbo as our cut-out we'll take on a decidedly political operation. We were never political, always intelligence based. And we've more or less succeeded in what our original plan wanted us to do: find out about aliens and the cover-up, which is now beyond doubt.'

'I've yet to debrief Melbo,' she said. 'He's gone to New Mexico.'

'And he's got a pass to the Democratic Convention.'

'That too.'

'So if we are seen to be working for Kennedy, we'll be seen to have thrown in our lot with the enemy.'

'It's shaping up that way, isn't it?'

15. The New Frontier

A man in a brown linen suit stood smoking his non-filter Lucky Strike cigarette by an upper exit, watching thousands of people mill about in the new Los Angeles Memorial Sports Arena. Kennedy had just won the nomination. Delegates brandished signs and placards, hats and ribbons in the hot stifling air; the crowd sounded like the roar of surf crashing on the coastal beaches not so far away. Pinned onto the smoker's lapel a press name-tag for the Miami Herald identified him as Eduardo Sanchez.

Gimlet-eyed, with a cynical smile that looked as if it never left his face—judging from the bird's feet imprinted at the corner of his eyes—he gave the impression that he was a bagman for the seedy side of politics. Certainly his appearance did not corroborate his credentials. He was of medium build and tanned with slick black hair. Throwing down his cigarette and smudging it with the toe of his two-tone Thom McAn brown and white wing-tip shoes, he walked down the aisle towards what looked like a press encampment. Among his colleagues, Sanchez moved within hearing distance of Melbo, who was standing by a railing in conversation with Raymond Chester, his senior Tribune colleague.

Sanchez didn't know either of them; in fact he wasn't even a reporter himself; he had procured fake credentials just to play the part. In spite of that, it was Melbo he wanted to talk with. His nefarious boss, Earl Bunting, had simply given him Melbo's description to make contact and relay for whatever it was worth some salacious gossip about Kennedy and Johnson. The puppet-masters of spin thought it would be prudent to sow confusion among the gullible at the convention. Sanchez had no idea whether it was true, and it wasn't his place to ask.

He heard Chester speak in his raspy voice.

'It seems Symington's got it all but wrapped,' he said.

'I'll do my piece on their ticket,' returned Melbo. 'Senators Kennedy and

Symington—A Match Made in Heaven.'

'Has a ring to it, but it's not for certain. What about Johnson? He carries Texas and the conservative south.'

'There's something a bit odd about him not collecting more support with all his experience as Senate Whip.'

'Yeah, I know the bastard; it's almost as if he knew he'd never get the nomination, so why bother.'

'Just as well; he doesn't exactly inspire trust with all the skeletons in his closet.'

'He's as ruthless as they get, but he knows how to get things done.'

'Personally, Ray, I think he's a blight on the party.'

They both fell silent. Then Chester turned to go.

'I should head back to the pressroom, and finish my piece; I'm overdue wiring it in to make the deadline.'

'Thanks for the help, Ray.'

'Just remember, do me a favor and leave out any crap about aliens. It'll debase our integrity here. This is politics.'

'Will do.'

Melbo watched Chester disappear into the crowd.

'Are you the guy that's scarin' the shit out of all the housewives with hearsay of green men?' asked Sanchez.

Melbo turned to see this grinning dandy. His first thought was to ignore him, but, on second thought he wanted to hear what he had to say. It was his job after all. He took note of his name tag.

'I don't believe we've met, Mr. Sanchez,' said Melbo, without extending his hand.

'By George, it's about time then.' He held out his hand. Melbo took it as if it were covered in excrement.

'So tell me something: make it worth my while.' Melbo looked him in the eye.

'How much money ya got?'

Melbo laughed. 'You've got to be kidding.'

'No joke, but I'll do ya a favor.'

'Not interested.'

'Really? I don't think so, if you knew what I have to say.'

'Where'd they find you? Washed up from Cuba?'

'You're a smart kid. It's a fact.'

'And just like that you show up in Los Angeles.'

'I was an officer in Batista's militia. Escaped from Cuba when I had the chance.'

'So who do you really work for now?'

'I can't tell you that; I'd blow my cover.'

'You're already blown, friend.'

'Okay, okay, listen.' He put his face near Melbo's ear. Melbo could smell his cheap cologne mixed with body odor. 'I'm an informant with the FBI. This is my first gig. Don't go hard on me.'

'You work for Hoover? What possible explanation can you come up with for being here? Has there been a crime? Some candidate working for the mob? What's the deal?'

'No deal. Let me tell you something.'

'What now?'

'Johnson and Hoover have each other's back.'

'Is this the rumor running down the halls of the FBI?'

'Not just rumors. Johnson will be VP. Guaranteed,' he declared.

'Johnson's spent; the Kennedys hate him; they know he's a crook. Everyone knows he plays dirty; look at the way he tried to wrangle the nomination from Kennedy, citing his father's wartime foibles, such as his recommendation to appease Hitler, and his own failure to vote for censuring McCarthy when at the time Kennedy was lying in a hospital, in Miami of all places, critically ill—besides, Senator Symington's the better man with all his experience: Secretary of the Airforce, a member of the Armed Forces Committee, and Foreign Relations; he's honest, an intellectual and being almost twenty years Kennedy's elder adds a ballast to Kennedy's relative inexperience. And the Kennedys have indicated he's their best bet.'

'What if I told you Johnson has evidence of Kennedy's extramarital liaisons with some women?'

'I'd say you were full of shit.'

'Like you said, Johnson's a crook. And you don't think he'd expose Kennedy as a Lothario?'

'Kennedy'd call his bluff.'

'And risk the election? No way, José. With Johnson his election as President is almost certain.'

'Even if it was true, Johnson wouldn't scuttle his own party.'

'Who's kidding who? Johnson couldn't care less. He's the king of the Senate. That won't change; he's got more clout there than as VP, which is largely ceremonial.'

Melbo turned away and looked at the crowd around him. Something was gnawing in the back of his mind. The little truth gnome was tunneling in his brain. He had a sense of something truly sinister. What if Kennedy had been with some women? What if Hoover had dirt on him? Maybe this creepy Cuban was on the money. He'd heard the rumors too, that Johnson was a pathological liar, and power mad to boot; he'd stolen a senate seat in the 1948 election in Texas; he'd been allegedly connected to insidious crimes, including embezzlement and murder. What did he have to lose? Nothing, except the Vice-Presidency. No, he ruminated. It was a double-blind.

Of course, Johnson wanted the Vice-Presidency, more than anything because it'd get him inside the White House and ultimately the Presidency itself, which he coveted above all else. So that's all he really cared about: the Presidency, not his own nomination; he knew he hadn't stood a chance there, but as VP—that's how he'd make it. Melbo realized Johnson mustn't get near the White House.

'Maybe you have something,' said Melbo. 'Why are you telling me this?'

'Somebody's got to tell it like it is. Who better than you?'

'Why not Raymond Chester, my colleague? He's the senior political writer on the election.'

'I woulda talked with him, but you were available; besides, he's not too smart.'

'Well, thanks; I'll let him know that.'

'Wouldn't do any good.'

'If you knew what's good for you, you'd crawl back into the hole where you belong.' With that Melbo made a fast exit from the arena.

Sanchez kept that smile on his face only this time it was genuine.

Melbo found Chester in the pressroom about to leave and wire his article on Kennedy's nomination that day as the Democratic presidential candidate.

'Ray,' Melbo said with emphasis, 'are you going with Symington as running mate?'

'I thought we understood each other, Mel. Hey, you look like you've seen a ghost.'

171

'Some guy just told me Johnson's threatened Kennedy with leaking smut on him—some extramarital affair—in order to twist his arm into making him his running mate.'

Chester began to laugh. 'And you swallowed the bait? I've heard Johnson's had more mistresses you can count on your fingers, and even has a kid somewhere.'

'Just the same; the guy's evil.'

'Who? Johnson or this guy who happened to tell you this?'

'Both.'

'Look, Johnson's got support in Texas and the South, but nowhere else. You saw the debate; Johnson's politics are anathema to Kennedy's.'

'He's got a lot more votes for the nomination than Symington did,' said Melbo.

'Yeah, well, but running mates are chosen for more than votes. Symington's a Southerner too. Remember how Johnson voted against desegregation.'

'Precisely, the South isn't ready for Kennedy. It's a dilemma: either lose the election or make a pact with the devil to win it,' stated Melbo.

'I've been in this business too long to fall for that. Kennedy's an angel compared to that polecat Johnson, and people know it.'

'Sure thing but just the same it stinks.'

'Politics, my young friend. Break a leg. You write opinion columns; leave the hard news to me.'

Chester walked away with papers in hand. Melbo looked at the typewriter and sat down.

*

July 13, 1960
The New York Herald Tribune
Kennedy: The New Frontier
By George Melbo

Hallelujah! Change is coming! It appears that John F. Kennedy with his running mate Senator Stuart Symington is set to turn the American Presidency Democratic again! The momentum is in his favor. I think the nation is tired of a hawkish, oligarchic Republican regime. Certainly, members of the younger generation of voting age have propelled Kennedy, or the idea of Kennedy to popular acclaim, as he is one of ours.

Now, I can hear my publisher—a good Republican—swearing under his breath, careful George, opinions matter, this is my paper! Yes, sir, it is, but I was hired to express my views, and thank you for the privilege. I think we can both agree that America is a bastion of freedom and our duty is to exercise our inalienable right to protect that very concept by our actions. Of course, Nixon may win the election and carry the torch of the old guard. We all want to defend our freedoms, and our military has been a sentinel to protect us from tyranny abroad. But there is also an enemy among us.

For instance, the government got the message finally that McCarthy himself was un-American and publicly denounced him and his ilk for fear-mongering and worse, but not before he had made their point—Communism is a creeping menace. And that it is: an immoral ideology devoid of human kindness. And in that respect we witnessed in Senator McCarthy's actions what approached the show trials of Stalin or Nazi judge Roland Freisler.

How easy was it for some to get caught up in his evil diatribe; the Republican Party let free speech take its course in an ignoble way before they eventually did the right thing and put a lid on his hate. We can excuse their tardiness in confronting and ending McCarthy's witch-hunt because we also have being fighting wars, both hot and cold, against that nemesis of freedom, the Soviet Union, whose gulags and systemic mass murders under Stalin were challenged by our great freedom fighters Eisenhower and his warriors. And we should all be sincerely grateful that their steady hand at the tiller of our nation has since spared us from the trauma of war.

We may have some serious complaints with their heavy-handedness in Iran, Congo, Guatemala, Haiti, and other places but such issues are explained away and smoothed over by a believing public. We're Americans and proud of it. However, in an election year we must air our differences.

But now, we can see the future, what Kennedy has called the New Frontier. *A fresh face, they say, a wise man beyond his years; someone versed in war, indeed a hero; someone versed in the disparities and hypocrisies of modern America, rich and poor, black and white. Yes, he comes from a privileged background; though some disdain his Catholicism, he touts secularism; and he has that youthful, even glamorous air that some may think detracts from serious leadership; but whatever else he is, he is brave and smart and open-*

minded.

He instills hope for a better, kinder world. He has compassion for the common working man and woman. All this is evident in his speeches on the nomination trail and actions as a Congressman and Senator. He writes about courage in others and has won a Pulitzer for his acclaimed Profiles in Courage. *This man is the paradigm for courage. Even diehard Republicans begrudgingly allow him that. The power of words, his words, have rung true with anybody who has listened.*

His appeal lies not in just in the persuasiveness of his rhetoric, but in his commitment to confront certain unpleasant truths facing our nation today: the issue of civil rights, need for healthcare, jobs for troubled sectors of the economy, urban overcrowding, poor schools and a whole host of other problems eroding the dignity of the average American. We must be proud of our accomplishments, challenge ourselves, and believe in our great potential.

Okay, I know this is all fine to proclaim in an election season. But no matter whether Democratic or Republican, we all want what is best for us as Americans. The challenge of course is to go forward with conviction, to serve the highest ideals of the constitution. We must not let incendiary prejudices and partisan corruption hold sway in the name of nationalism or cold war operations. Too often individual ambition and arrogance have led to illegal actions. Evil has begotten evil throughout the long history of humanity, but if we are to shine a light for the future, whether we elect Kennedy or Nixon as our leader, we must work together to achieve this.

We need leaders who offer transparency and justice in a non-partisan way if we are to eliminate the darkness that threatens us even invoked in the name of freedom. We deserve the best in ourselves and in our leaders. If in God we trust, let it be our conscience that drives progress. Are you listening? Our future depends on it.

*

No sooner had Melbo's article appeared in the following morning's Herald Tribune than a metaphorical sonic boom reverberated across the airwaves. Kennedy reneged on Symington and it was announced from the newsroom of the Biltmore Hotel late on the afternoon of 14 July that Lyndon B. Johnson would be his running mate. Both Raymond Chester and George Melbo, along with every other newsman, had been blind-sided. The more cynical of them assumed the decision had been based solely on the pragmatism of numbers and pressure from right-wing Democrats.

Kennedy won almost 53% of the votes and Johnson came second with almost 27%, while Symington placed a distant third with only 5.6%. Melbo felt first shock, then anger then terrible depression, not so much the result, but because of his inability to act on his inner voice telling that what Sanchez had said must have been true. Melbo felt he had sold himself out to ideological wishful thinking and thereby done a disservice to his paper and readership. The idea that a Kennedy-Symington ticket would somehow purge us of the darkness covering the political landscape and would produce a new sunny landscape was naïve at best and downright foolish at worst. He cursed himself for not acting on his knowledge; he could've had the scoop of a lifetime.

Even Chester said as much but with a sarcastic quip: 'Kennedy's no different than any politician. How could we know?'

Melbo refrained from answering but he wanted to say: 'Kennedy just ruined his presidency and lost a measure of credibility; and by the way, we did know!' Instead, he just slumped in his chair in the pressroom and agonized in silence. Furthermore, that evening, Dick Sinclair left a message that he was to submit nothing more on the election—"from on high"—he added, as rather more a commiseration, showing he understood Melbo's dilemma and by way of saying he disagreed with his superiors, namely Jake Whitmore.

In other words, Melbo was not allowed to redeem himself. He had been caught in a trap of his own making and they pounced on him. But Chester had that opportunity to report on the new ticket of Kennedy-Johnson. His earlier article was a typical hodgepodge of conventional news and half-baked formulations of political gibberish. His follow-up would certainly be no different, but he had chosen the safe way as endorsed by his boss and the sitting government.

Melbo took a taxi from the convention to join DeCourt at the Chateau Marmont in Hollywood. For the last few days he had been up at all hours covering the convention, and had barely seen his new wife. She would be in bed when he arrived late, and he often left early, though now he planned to stay all the next day, before taking her to hear Kennedy's acceptance speech in the evening. They had chosen the Chateau because DeCourt didn't want to be near the convention center, or the Biltmore; and besides, she said they were on their honeymoon. Although it cost more than Melbo was allowed on budget, they saw no reason to leave, having booked well in advance a simple bedroom with a view. She would spend her days reading and indulging herself at the pool and around the grounds, going for walks, even spending one hot afternoon at the beach in Malibu.

After a breakfast of eggs Benedict, and a small pitcher of fresh-squeezed orange juice for two, they sat and read the papers with their tea and coffee. When the waiter came to clear their plates, he informed Melbo of a message at the desk. Later, Melbo picked up this message in a simple envelope with his name on it and then joined DeCourt at the elevator, and as they stepped in he opened it thinking it was from his boss. When they reached their floor DeCourt asked, 'Well? More bad news?'

'No actually, it's from Nora. She's in town and wants to meet me … us.'

'Really? That's interesting. Let me see it.'

Melbo handed it to her and she read it aloud.

Dear Mr. and Mrs. Melbo,

Congratulations on your wedding! I'm so happy for you! Let's celebrate. Great article! Call me at …

Nora

'How did she know?' wondered DeCourt.

'I don't know. Perhaps she called the office.'

'At least she's a fan,' said DeCourt.

'That takes the cake,' he answered, and they both laughed.

'You see, Mel? She's your excuse to get back at Whitmore.'

'Politically? I've been censored.'

'Don't be so hard on yourself. Use her as a foil and get your opinion heard.'

'We'll see; everything's changed.'

'No kidding. Carpe Diem.'

'Seize the day,' said Melbo. 'Right.'

He took DeCourt by the hand and led her to the bed.

*

Dressed casually in summer wear, DeCourt, in a light blue skirt and beige blouse, and Melbo, in shirt and shorts, sat hand in hand in a taxi cruising along the Pacific Coast Highway. It was two in the afternoon when they were dropped off at an address on a rocky bluff near Dume Cove on Malibu Beach. Melbo opened the gate which was unlocked, and they followed the driveway down around under a verdant panoply of semi-tropical cypress and bougainvillea. The bungalow style house nestled perfectly on the bluff surrounded by a lawn and picket fence enclosing numerous imported Italian Stone pines displaying their unique inflorescence. Built of stone and smooth pinkish stucco above the windows, and mostly stone on the windward side, it seemed a little out of place as if it should have been in a fairy tale.

A shiny two-tone baby-blue and white 1956 two-door convertible Chevrolet Bel Air was parked beside the building. They knocked but no one answered, so they wandered around to the front where they could see through intermittent shrubs, grasses and Stone pines, the blue expanse of ocean. Standing on the patio they could hear the surf and immediately experience the soothing effect of its murmuring at least fifty feet below.

'Wow,' uttered DeCourt.

'I could live here,' responded Melbo. He thought of their dingy little apartment in New York.

'She doesn't own this place, does she?'

'I don't think so; she said it's "borrowed". She just said she'd meet us here.'

Minutes went by, so they sat down on the simple patio chairs. The distinctive ocean smell of the soft sea breeze in their nostrils and the feel of it on their skin made them feel wonderfully relieved of the tensions of the past few days, though they had certainly found pleasant relief earlier that day. It seemed like a fantasy their honeymoon was undergoing extraordinary alternations, from aliens in the desert to Kennedy's triumph and perceived sell out, and now Marilyn Monroe in an enchanted Malibu villa.

'I've been reading up on Monroe,' said DeCourt, 'in magazines and articles.'

'Does she inspire you?' asked Melbo, almost sarcastically.

'Yes and no, but I have more respect for her, as a woman.'

'She's no dumb bombshell, that's for sure.'

'No, and she gets a bad rap.'

'The price for success in a man's world.'

'Now who's being cynical?' she retorted.

'I was merely making a point, for women in general.'

'She stood up against the studio for better scripts, roles. And started her own production company.'

'Like a modern-day Mary Pickford,' said Melbo, 'our home-grown Canadian girl. You know she began United Artists with Chaplin and Fairbanks, and I think D.W. Griffiths.'

'Yeah, she was awesome. But I'm thinking more political. Marilyn's rather outspoken.'

'She's a left-leaning Democrat. I don't buy into her Castro accolades.'

'I don't think she's communist at all; she admires his intellect, his education, and supported the overthrow of the Batista regime and its corruption—fascism and the mob.'

'Fulgencio Batista, the old boss, and now Fidel Castro the new boss, same corruption, fascism, torture.'

'Mel! You know what I mean, at least something was done. If America had been more accommodating, perhaps Castro wouldn't have had to ally himself with the Soviets. Now look at the situation.'

Melbo let her have the moment. There was no point in arguing. Even if Castro had intended a moderate socialism like Árbenz in Guatemala, the Eisenhower administration would never brook it. He presumed they were probably planning an invasion even as he and DeCourt spoke.

'I support her stance on nuclear weapons,' stated Melbo.

'Exactly, dear, the woman is principled.'

'She's also tormented.'

'Who wouldn't be as a Made in America sex goddess with men licking their chops and drooling like dogs,' declared DeCourt.

'She has power and should use it; all women should for that matter.'

'Women are castigated no matter what they do.'

'Not long ago it used to be called female hysteria.'

'Jesus, Mel, you're full of laughs; more like male hysteria.'

Hearing someone laughing, they turned to see Marilyn Monroe in a racy red polka-dotted bathing suit, still dripping wet with a towel in her hand and sand on her feet. She began to dry her hair.

'Let's be honest, Mel One and Mel Two, female hysteria is a well-earned epithet. So give a girl a vibrator and a few amphetamines: problem solved,' said Norma Jeane in her typical soft screen voice. 'As for a man, it's a success just to have that bimbo on his arm.'

The moment and her voice were ridiculously perfect. They all laughed.

'You should be careful in the ocean with that bikini, Nora,' said Melbo standing up to greet Marilyn, 'the sharks are known to like red spots.'

'That ought to make a splash for you, Mel: *Shark eats Marilyn Monroe!*'

How absurd it all was. They laughed hysterically.

Marilyn gave Melbo a hug and kiss, her wet top leaving a slight water mark on his shirt. DeCourt then held out her hand, but Marilyn took it and hugged her as well.

'Sorry,' apologized Marilyn, 'in this heat I couldn't help myself. I had to dive in for a cool little refresher. I'm so happy to see you both, my secret, well, not-so-secret friends. After the article, you know.'

'I feel honored to meet you,' said DeCourt beaming.

'Believe me the honor's mine; you're the woman who snatched Melbo here. I'm just a worn out floozy who can't remember her lines anymore. Give me a minute and I'll get the champagne.'

She darted into the house and emerged with a bottle of Veuve Cliquot in a bucket of ice and three flutes. Melbo took the bottle and popped the cork. Marilyn smiled gleefully, as he poured the golden bubbles.

'I want you to know,' remarked Marilyn, 'although I'm thinking of buying a house out here, this place is a rather private hideaway for me. An anonymous friend in the industry lets me use it when they're not here. I borrowed the car as well. Isn't it amazing? The old movie royalty used to come here—during the twenties and thirties, when Malibu was more like an exotic club, hardly developed.'

'We were actually wondering about that, and mentioned Mary Pickford and her entourage,' said DeCourt. 'We're living a dream.'

'To tell you the truth, Mel, I feel the same as you. I grew up an orphan living in and out of foster homes and prayed for some seeming off-world life just like this. I've never really adjusted, which is the root of my problems; anyway, my whole being yearned for it as in a dream. Marilyn became that dream, but it's not me, the real me. When I met your husband back in March I was my old self, my refuge, albeit depressive. Even here, although it's still a refuge for Marilyn, it's my dream come true. It makes me happy alone, but I wanted to share it with you.'

'Well, then, cheers,' said Melbo, 'to Mary Pickford and Nora!'

'Cheers!'

They settled into their chairs and looked forward to a pleasant afternoon. Marilyn went on about her recent movie and affair with Yves Montand, the French actor and singer. After opening a second bottle of champagne, she asked about their recent marriage and honeymoon. They told her about their trip to New Mexico, and without mentioning names as per the anonymous owner of her villa, relayed the incredible story of the crashed disk out on the sage plains near Roswell, New Mexico. Marilyn was utterly riveted to the tale, her eyes opened wide, lips parted.

'So it's true! It's really true! I knew it! And why shouldn't it be? We're here on Earth after all; it could be anywhere in the universe! Once you know, it makes complete sense! We're part of a much greater whole living universe! People should be enlightened about this. The government should at least let us know that we are not alone! It's not fair they keep it to themselves.'

'I've been told that the very few who support non-disclosure think it's best to leave it ultra-secret for security reasons, never to be let loose by insiders,' said Melbo, adding 'too many people have seen them flying in their phenomenal ships—hence, we are all aware of their oxymoronic "open secret".'

'Security? Nonsense,' retorted Marilyn. 'If aliens wanted to destroy us, they could in a heartbeat, right? But they don't because they are far more advanced than we are, technologically and spiritually, so they wouldn't even consider it. We're still like primitive savages to them, and they probably pity us; most likely they'll leave us alone until we're more stable, and ready for them. Hell, they probably don't even have weapons.'

'Maybe some of us are ready now,' offered DeCourt.

Melbo smiled at Marilyn. 'You should be an emissary, Nora,' he suggested.

'I'd do it. If I can sing for the army, I can do it for the aliens.'

They all laughed as if it was an obvious thing.

'Suggest it to Kennedy if he's elected,' said DeCourt.

'Oh, wouldn't that be swell? *I aim to serve, Mr. President!* I've never met him, though I did see him once at a ball in New York in '57; there were at least a thousand people. I was with Arthur, and he was with Jackie.'

'I'm serious. You could be the Ambassador of Space!' exclaimed DeCourt.

'Oh, thanks, for most people that would define the meaning of airhead,' she said.

Again they laughed at the inanity of it all—perhaps it was the bubbly, or rational people attempting to make sense of an irrational world.

'Oh, I almost forgot,' said Marilyn, after their levity subsided, 'I bought some canapés at a local shop.'

She went into the house and returned with three little boxes, which she opened on the table. One contained puff pastry with smoked salmon and crème fraiche. Another had little bruschettas, and the third, cherry cheesecake bites.

'We can't thank you enough,' said DeCourt, eating. 'I feel so …'

'Special,' said Melbo.

'Yes,' concurred DeCourt.

'It's the least I can do. Your husband is truly great in my book. I mean, he writes about things we should all be so lucky to know about. Even your last article, Mel, about the Democratic Convention; you knew exactly what needed to be done, and you said it. I think Kennedy was a fool to allow that cracker Johnson on his ticket.'

'Thanks,' said Melbo, 'but the owner of the Trib has banned me from writing anymore political articles. So now it's just you and the aliens.'

'What a scoop!' exclaimed Marilyn. 'Well, you can write that I believe in you!'

'No worries, I'll hold my own. My editor, Dick Sinclair, believes fervently in my voice to deliver the truth.'

'And the readers,' added DeCourt.

'It's like show business,' said Marilyn. 'If it sells, you own the audience; keep them happy and informed, you can't go wrong.'

Their merriment continued well into the afternoon, and two more bottles of bubbly. Marilyn, like a kid on a picnic even led the way down the little path to the secluded beach where they swam. It was a blast as they frolicked in the surf with no one about. Afterwards, she returned the two honeymooners to the Chateau, and its wide-eyed guests and staff.

16. Shark Eats Marilyn Monroe!

Dick Sinclair had been working overtime during and since the Democratic Convention. He'd been reprimanded by Jake Whitmore for his support of Melbo's opinion in last week's article about the Kennedy-Symington ticket that had never happened. He was told "we don't do opinion equals speculation equals lobbying equals proselytizing" and Sinclair defended the article as nothing new in the tradition of the paper, as both parties were well represented. Nothing of the sort was the retort, and Sinclair had wisely backed down. He knew Whitmore well enough, and he realized that he wouldn't have taken that stand without some encouragement or even threat from his invisible peers.

However, Sinclair did point out that Melbo sold papers and that it was against the commercial instincts of any paper to interfere with good stories, and well-written stories at that. What kind of message were they sending to the public? he argued. The New York Times had written in an opinion column that Melbo "was a breath of fresh air", but that the conservative Tribune had "knocked him down a peg" for his views. Whitmore had contended that Melbo for all his eloquence was a charlatan and needed some "downsizing". The message was clear. Melbo had stirred the beast in American culture, and the people were going to be treated to his bloodletting if he didn't back off the political brinkmanship.

Sinclair knew Melbo better and realized that they both shared a deep commitment to change. Their success was a double-edged sword: to continue in the same direction meant imminent termination of employment, but to back off meant they were engaging in a professional sellout. What irked him most was that they were reporting what people were eager to hear, namely, an insider's view and to deny them was antithetical to the American expectations of journalism. Herein was a hypocrisy inconsistent with their values, and sooner or later there would be a reckoning.

Upon Melbo's return, there was a cooling off. Another article about

Marilyn Monroe was in the works, and the usual trade of musical reviews and social events about town needed his attention. Melbo was his usual self, if subdued from the highs of a wonderful honeymoon. Sinclair had yet to broach the subject of his New Mexican sojourn. He felt there was something brewing beneath the surface. The Democratic convention had taken its toll and he thought it best to wait for the resolution of that particular episode. Who was this Eduardo Sanchez he had mentioned?

Melbo alluded to some adventure in the sage near Roswell but would not clarify. Sinclair didn't want to appear nosey about the nature of these adventures as it seemed inappropriate to inquire about their honeymoon. Even before Melbo left, there was some undisclosed shadow over his usual candor. Besides, at present, there was enough traffic on the wires about the Republican convention in Chicago; Nixon had it all wrapped up with his Vice-Presidential nominee Henry Cabot Lodge of Massachusetts.

The election campaign of 1960 was underway and the Tribune's own Raymond Chester was dutifully reporting the surging Republican tide; and Kennedy's "new boy" epithet was getting negative traction except for Johnson's hold on Texas and the South. The likely defining public debate between the candidates was way off at the end of September. News of UFOs and Marilyn Monroe now took a back seat to the sweeping events of political fortune. The ramifications of the election victory in November would speak for itself. Perhaps Whitmore would make a concession allowing Melbo a chance to join the political debate if Kennedy won.

Sinclair expected this to happen because the last time he spoke with Jake Whitmore, his boss had complained about the interference from his peers that he was too soft on rabble-rousers like Melbo. He had even gone so far as to tell them he didn't really "give a rat's ass" about Melbo's politics or articles, as he thought he was "fair and square" with the temper of the times. All Whitmore needed was to show solidarity with the Republican cause and save face.

*

By the end of July Greenfield and Prinzenthal had sailed in the newly christened *Hannah-Lizbet* under near perfect conditions enjoying mostly gentle trade winds, blue skies, with occasional cloudy skies and warm sun-showers. His eleven meter yacht, the relatively new, steel-hulled, teak-finished

German-built Abeking-Rasmussen Asgard had all the modern comforts. They had charted a course from St. Croix to St. Martin, Saint Barthélemy, St. Kitts, Nevis, Antigua, Montserrat, Guadeloupe and Dominica, then back the same way and were now a day out of St. Croix on their return journey.

Other than Prinzenthal's queasy stomach at times, or morning sickness, she had been a hardened sailor who never complained; she loved it, in fact, and felt that the little bud in her womb was the reincarnation of her childhood friend Lizbet. Greenfield was so happy he couldn't believe it and kept quiet, fearing some mistake. In their minds, the promised romance of evenings—when they moored in enchanted bays to enjoy rainbows; when they felt the soft fragrant breezes surrounding them while they cooked their fresh fish or langouste; and responded to the silent swells of the ocean compelling their naked bodies to join in an ecstatic consummation of this divine chorale—had them all but entranced as if it were a dream that would not end.

Their timing had been ideal; soon the stormy season would begin, or rather the risk of it. The unfurled sails, ocean spray and accompanying dolphins at times filled their spirits with rapture and their beautiful boat seemed to glide through the swells as if on a god-sent mission.

Prinzenthal was at the wheel when she saw land on the horizon.

'Land Ho!' she called out.

The wind had picked up and they were tacking along at a good clip. Greenfield emerged from below to have a look.

'It's almost sad,' he said. 'I don't want it to end.'

'Happiness is measured by circumstances. We have to get back.'

'I prefer being off the radar.'

'And I; yet I don't think we warrant any kind of attention.'

Greenfield didn't respond. He didn't want to feel negative. The world he knew was fraught with peril. He watched the land become more distinct as they approached the shore. In a few hours they would dock at the marina, cleanup, gather their belongings, and take a taxi to Christiansted, where they were booked into a hotel. Tomorrow they would fly to New York and reenter that hazardous world of intrigue to which they were so habituated. How foreign that all seemed while they were here in this paradise, and now his dear love was as inured to it as he was.

'I could use a juicy steak,' said Prinzenthal. 'My little chick needs some iron.'

'What if it's a puppy?'

Prinzenthal laughed. 'Because it has wings!'

Greenfield smiled and began to trim the mainsail. 'Well, let's see how fast she can fly!'

*

July 23, 1960

The New York Herald Tribune

Shark Eats Marilyn Monroe!

By George Melbo

Catchy headline, right? Well, Norma Jeane suggested it during a champagne-bubbly afternoon at Malibu in a secluded cottage overlooking the blue Pacific. I had suggested she stay out of the water in her red polka dot bikini for fear of attracting those sinister creatures of the deep. Her reaction to this caution was figurative and genuine, if hilarious, yet my idea was that it served as a metaphor for her life in show business as a sensitive artist. My wife and I were quite honored and delighted to be her guests, especially that it capped off our honeymoon, and because we all got on like kids at camp without a care in the world.

Perhaps that is the unique thing about 'Nora', as we called her; she really is the most natural friend. She claimed she never felt better in a kind of reprieve from the grueling schedule of film production. She had recently completed Let's Make Love *with Yves Montand and Tony Randall, written in part by her husband Arthur Miller, from whom she claimed to be happily separated. And now another movie called* Misfits, also *written by her husband with whom she starred with Clark Gable and Montgomery Clift and directed by John Huston, was to begin production shortly in Nevada. What a life!*

Well, if the truth were known (she says) it's not all what it's made up to be. The thing is that in spite of comedies, Marilyn is actually a serious girl, a sometime poet who eschews the limelight. She unabashedly offered her views on many topics, including Kennedy, Nixon and the election. We even touched on UFOs and joked that she would make an excellent emissary if there was ever to be some meeting with these elusive aliens.

But first, we spoke of the Kennedy-Johnson ticket and how I had mistakenly assumed Kennedy would choose Symington as his running mate. I apologize

185

for making that embarrassing assumption. I had actually been given a tip that Johnson would in fact be chosen. Nora commiserated with me because she thought Symington was the better man. Her view was quite simply that Kennedy needed to clean out the hubris in the system which had been ossified by a Republican administration bent on resisting any change. We were both in agreement that Johnson, although his power base is in Texas and the South, was not sufficiently liberal and not to be trusted.

As for Nixon, well, we all know what he represents: the same old! Now, that's not so bad in itself with a General at the helm having given us almost a decade of peace, but the levers of government have been overhauled to suit the incumbent party with a decidedly disquieting agenda—the militarization of our industrial engines. Certainly the Cold War has something to do with that, as do our newfound world power and responsibility to protect our freedoms.

Nora says, and she gave me permission to say this, we need to change the way the government does business around the world. The social underclasses are in need of better living conditions, education and healthcare. These are elementary matters for everyone: black, white, indigenous and all races. The generation of wealth comes not without responsibility; it is a privilege that must be embraced by Western nations, to open our minds to the benefits of prosperity for others.

Politics aside (and let me tell you my superiors insisted that I refrain from that subject after the convention), under the influence of Nora's golden bubbles, we became rather animated in our discussion about the veracity of witnesses' accounts concerning alleged UFO sightings. For months now, I have been gathering information from excellent sources, and those readers who have followed this adventure of mine will be pleased to know there is a big picture. Let me explain:

On our honeymoon in New Mexico, my wife and I spent some time in the Roswell area and poked about the community in search of witnesses to the "weather balloon" that crashed in late June 1947 out on the sage. Strangely, people were reticent about the subject and seemed to wonder why there was all this fuss about a weather balloon? But that was not the fuss. It was rather more sinister. People were afraid to talk and anyone involved in the sighting and recovery back then of the so-called "weather balloon" were held accountable and sworn to secrecy by serious men in suits and military officers who gave the official stamp to this highly sensitive recovery operation.

We spoke to someone who was there on the sage before the U.S. government hegemon descended like a dark cloud on the scene. Simply stated, there was no weather balloon. A disk-shaped spacecraft of extraterrestrial origin crashed and the bodies of several small slim aliens with large dark almond-shaped-eyes lay dead beside one that was still clinging to life. It was learned that they were from a star system many light-years from Earth, and that they were members of a training team in a scout craft conducting a reconnaissance mission, their huge mothership parked on the dark side of our moon.

The conclusion arrived at through this investigation is that we are a primitive species in a remote star system of a vast galaxy among billions of other galaxies in an endless universe full of life from primeval to advanced intelligent civilizations with hundreds of millions years of galactic traveling experience. Now is the time to stop and think, and think hard, that, if this being true makes us very special indeed. They see us as a new potential member in a huge confederation of intelligent species; in other words, they care for us.

But at our present level of evolution, we are very dangerous and considered hostiles. They were deathly afraid of us; this was told to the brave first responder when he offered them water and comfort and covered their dead. They carried no weapons; they had no evil design on us; they were observing us on a mission to a hostile planet by being constantly shot at. Apparently, we have been observed for hundreds of thousands of years, and even tampered with genetically back in a more primitive state, just to hasten our development. Are we to believe that Adam and Eve are our ancient biblical ancestors? Perhaps, through word of mouth, in ancient Sumerian tradition (where Adam and Eve were first configured) this tale came down to us from actual prototypes of our modern human, hybridized long ago by an alien species. How does that grab you? What is your reaction to that? Horror? Disbelief? Laughable nonsense? Enlightenment?

No wonder the authorities have shut down any approach to the truth. Are we ready for the truth? For the most part, it's an unequivocal No, so let's either challenge their wisdom by electing someone who might enlighten us, or pretend that we're alone in the universe. This is the big picture. And a shark did not eat Marilyn Monroe, though not for want of trying! Careful Nora, sharks come in many forms!

Earl Bunting was the kind of man you'd never notice in a group of people, or even if you walked by him standing alone on the street. He was of an average build, in his early fifties six feet tall slightly balding at the temples gray-dirty blonde-haired and carried himself almost affably. There was no smile, nor frown, just a kind of average generic person who happened to land in the CIA as a special operator and did what he was told. Originally he had worked for the Meyer Lansky Mafia organization as a bouncer, but soon joined the OSS during the war like many others who qualified through their possession of a number of particular talents. His talent was as a confidence man for disinformation, and sometimes was called upon to make people disappear.

Just after the war he was sent to Italy to fight the Communists, but during the war, his fluency in Spanish enabled him to put his talents to use in Central and South America where he was hired as a consultant for the Rockefellers in Standard Oil affiliates and third party deals that saw oil channeled through to Germany. This was facilitated by neutral countries whose connections with Standard Oil saw huge inflows of income to their economies through the company. This was rationalized by the super-charged American economy underwriting the massive war effort. So what if by association, a few shiploads of oil made it to the Nazis, they reasoned, if overall the balance was far to our advantage? The irony was that the fuel supplied the navies and air forces and armies on both sides of the conflict.

A cynic might maintain that the global economy mattered more than humanity. Earl Bunting was just such a cynic. In the fifties, he had worked undercover in Cuba and anywhere in Latin America that needed his expertise. He was one of the key players in the Árbenz take-down in Guatemala that saw a right-wing military junta usurp power. He was the point of the sword in the CIA's clandestine military agenda.

Since the Cuban Revolution that saw Castro overthrow the Batista regime, its American corporations and Mafia high-rolling crooks, Bunting had been relegated to domestic concerns, to train a militia for an invasion to retake the island, which ultimately became known as the *Bay of Pigs* fiasco. That day in July he was in Washington waiting in the ante-room of Aubrey Wood's office in the old CIA office on E street. The new Langley headquarters was under construction and wouldn't be occupied for a couple of years. He was finally ushered in by an assistant who then immediately left. Inside the spartan office, giving little indication of the kind of individual who worked there other than perhaps a ghost, sat Mr. Woods and William James of the FBI.

'Earl, take a seat.'

Bunting sat down saying nothing.

'Have you met William James?'

'Earl Bunting. How do you do,' he said.

'Fine, thanks,' replied James.

'We have a lot on the go here so I'll get to the point,' said Woods. 'Where's your Cuban fellow? The one who was out West at the convention; he did some good work there.'

'Sanchez? He's in Louisiana.'

'I want you to find him or someone else to trace this fellow Melbo's path in New Mexico early this month, and to find out who spoke with him about the weather balloon incident; you know that event back in '47.'

'Right, and if he's found?'

'We need to make an impression, a permanent impression. Those folks can't interfere with national security.'

'Over a weather balloon?'

'There's a lot more at stake than a weather balloon.'

'So, just take him out,' he said deadpan, compliantly.

'It's a small sacrifice for civilization,' added James, who, given his special status as liaison, felt he best support Woods, his brother-in-law, though morally repulsed by it.

Bunting looked at him.

'Do you read the New York Herald Tribune?' asked James.

'I read that article about the convention. Is this about Melbo again? Why not take him out.'

'No, people will read into that it's an inside job,' said Woods.

'Read the article,' said James. 'You'll understand.'

'What day?'

'Last Friday.'

'That was last week.'

'You'll find a copy on the rack out there.' James motioned with his thumb.

'You can count on me,' said Bunting as he got up to leave.

After he had gone, James grimaced.

'I know what you're thinking,' said Woods.

'You mean like we're the bad guys?'

'Just as in war there's collateral damage, and this is war.'

'Yeah, but I'm a law man; and some innocent person just doesn't make an easy victim in the interest of national security.'

'Innocent? Don't go soft on me, Bill; it doesn't matter how many innocents were slaughtered in the war; we fought and continue to fight for freedom, and if it's any consolation it doesn't sit well with me either.'

'I know, I know. Let's just never forget who we are, and become so numbed to the cause that we lose our conscience.'

'Nobody's that innocent in this kind of war.'

*

Melbo's New York apartment on the Upper East Side was located not far from a large natural pond in the middle of picturesque Central Park, where in the heat of early August many people escaped the noise of the city and enjoyed walking, sitting, lying down or boating. There were a few rock formations one of which stood out. There Melbo sat in his usual unpressed work attire on a ledge as if in meditation. Before long a slim woman, Hannah Prinzenthal, quickly left the path and clambered over the rocks to sit beside him. Grinning, she looked out over the water, as Melbo turned to her.

'You're looking pleased, and tanned, Joyce. Does the sun follow you everywhere?'

'I could say the same for you, Mel. How's the missus? And I think you can call me Hannah.'

Prinzenthal was dressed in a short light blue summer skirt and beige blouse and white runners. Her hair was loosely tied in a ponytail.

'She's well and happy too.'

'Lovely spot here. Do you come here often?' she asked, looking at him and squinting from the glare.

'Once in a while.'

'I live not far away on the west side,' she confessed.

'With a view of the park?'

'Yes, a corner flat on the fifth floor at Seventy-Fourth and Central Park West.'

'Nice. How's Harley?'

'Great. He's moved in actually, after our romantic sailing trip to Dominica from St. Croix and back.'

'Am I missing something?'

'Well, we're engaged. We think it best for the baby if we're hitched.'

'Really? Wonderful! You do glow! So it's not just the sunshine: there's new life incubating within!'

Prinzenthal remained quiet. Melbo sensed her unusual temperament, like a dominatrix who has found religion.

'Don't go poetic on me, Mel. The egg was fertilized; ol' Harley cocksure at that; he rather did me I hate to admit, but I'm not telling secrets of the skin trade.'

'We do have a good cover story.' He looked across the pond. 'My lips are sealed.'

'I actually knew the very moment two months ago.'

'You honor us by your blunt appraisal, Hannah.'

'Hey, friend, I'm all here, but they're expecting more from me. They want a debriefing.'

'Ah, the hitch-pin.'

'And there's quite a load riding on it. Were you careful coming here?'

'As far as I can tell.'

'Harley's covering me, and likely someone's covering all of us.'

'Can they be that paranoid?'

'Our 'friendship' is manufactured on account of it.'

Melbo pulled out of a bag a Reuben sandwich from Joe's. 'Hungry?' he asked.

'I seem to be.'

She made him smile. He gave her half of the sandwich, which they ate quietly; then he offered her a tea in a paper cup with a napkin and he had another cup for himself.

'How thoughtful,' she remarked.

'The least I could do.'

In a concise summary, Melbo related to Prinzenthal everything that had happened to them out West. He mentioned his paper, and the Trib's decision to curb his political opinions, but he declared that he would continue to write in the vein that he had originally been hired for in his reviews and cultural comments, including the successful run on the UFO phenomenon.

'Garnett Wills, brother of Edna Beiderman. Who would've guessed?' she said rhetorically. 'You can thank me for that. When we vetted Whitmore's ball, I put her beside you, knowing she was from New Mexico.'

'I'll be damned.'

'Don't thank me yet, but rest assured I will not say a word about it. That would sink you, and me. I can't emphasize how serious it is. It's one thing to hypothesize, and quite another to tell the world the truth.'

'I told the truth.'

'You told a story that people read but will likely reject later, to carry on blind; blindness being safe under the aegis of truth.'

'Truth is a rare thing, isn't it, in our present state of evolution?'

'Rather more like a dangerous thing. But don't worry; I'll explain that your information gathered from some nameless cowboy is old news, and that nobody takes it seriously.'

'Kind of defeats the purpose.'

'That's yet to be seen. We want you to interview Kennedy, and I'm going to instruct Whitmore to make it happen.'

'That's a little presumptuous, isn't it?'

'Perhaps, but I'm also going to resign my position at the CIA, at least the field work. Maybe after a few years of devoted motherhood, I might seek something else.'

'Will we, you and I, and our spouses, ever be able to be friends without the CIA breathing down our necks?'

'Mel, not in the foreseeable future, at least not until Kennedy wins; and only when he has consolidated the services. There is a darkness there now; Harley is very worried about it.'

'All the more reason to let the media do its best to reveal it,' stated Melbo.

'The media is owned by people to do as they're told. Only criminal exposure of the high and mighty can make a difference. But I tell you, they're so well insulated by Hoover and others in the government community, it's doubtful that any of them could be indicted. Witnesses will be compromised, might even disappear. It's a shame it's come to this, and that's why I'm quitting.'

'I don't fear them.'

'Don't play the martyr for these people.'

'Who's playing the martyr?'

'A man with a target on his back who thinks we live in an attractive sanctuary of freedom.'

'That's something Mel would say.'

'Mel is very smart.'

Part Two

I'd like to tell the public about the UFO situation, but my hands are tied.

John F. Kennedy
To Bill Holden, steward on Air Force One, while flying over Germany

17. Dark Mettle

Eduardo Sanchez had been given a list of people: ranchers, local news reporters, and military personnel in the Roswell area of New Mexico where he had driven from Albuquerque. With his friendly banter, toothy charm and fake FBI identification handy, he was received by everyone cordially. Asked whether they knew the journalist George Melbo and his wife—a photo of the unsuspecting couple taken in Los Angeles was passed around—he was met with blank stares and indifferent denials. He knew better than to push any of them, as the community members had preferred to be left alone than risk some exposure in the local paper.

Only as a last resort would he go public to trace the Melbo's time spent there. Sanchez always found a way. And find it he did initially back in Albuquerque at the car rental affiliate of a local auto dealer. He was told by an affable fellow wearing a large, white Stetson that they had rented a red pickup truck; actually it was a used vehicle for sale, but served their purpose.

The dealer, Ambrose Clanton, recalled that they were tourists "lookin' fer aliens", and that more people were showing up convinced they were somewhere in the vicinity. He had no idea where the Melbos had gone, but he did say the "big event" happened out on the plains somewhere near the Foster ranch about half way between Corona and Roswell.

On his way to Roswell, Sanchez thought he would visit the ranch. Driving through the endless sagebrush desert, he came around to thinking that he realized there was little chance that he could make someone disappear without his being implicated after his inquiries. What was Bunting thinking he wondered, to make a sacrificial lamb out of him, an expendable illegal? Making it look like an accident was a non-starter. When he found the Foster ranch, he spoke to some ranch hands who they directed him on to Roswell where an old hand, Zane Madill, witness of the debris field, lived.

When the ranch hands told him that Madill wouldn't talk about the episode because the government had come down pretty hard on him and even had him incarcerated for a while back in '47, Sanchez figured that he was on the wrong trail and decided to head back to Corona closer to where the incident had happened. Once there, he asked around whether Melbo and wife had stayed there, pretending he was investigating a fraudulent insurance claim. At the Stardust Motel, he struck gold when he found out they had spent a couple of nights there and had eaten at Billy's Diner.

At the diner, the Melbos were remembered; however, no one could give him any clue as to where they had gone. The only waitress, Annie, who had spoken with them and knew that they were looking for Garnett Wills and the Pine Bluff Ranch, didn't trust Sanchez. His Mexican accent was off and she could sense a menacing agenda behind his superficial affability. She felt that the Melbos were good people and in no way could be involved in the scam Sanchez suggested. All she said was that they had gone south as far as she could tell. Sanchez, a confidence man, and as cagey as a fox, sensed she knew more and put on his serious face.

'If you know something, miss, and don't tell me, you will be indicted as an accessory to their crimes.'

'Listen, Mr. Sanchez, I'm a waitress, not a mind-reader. They were on their honeymoon, but it doesn't take a lot of thought to know what was on their minds! They were in love! Why in hell would you think otherwise?'

'This is a matter of national security, princesa.'

'Are you challenging my patriotism, amigo?

Some patrons of the diner turned their heads at her raised voice. Billy the Kid, the owner and cook, stepped out of the kitchen.

'What's the problem, Annie?'

'This … guy is asking questions I have no answer to.'

'Can I help you, sir?' asked Billy.

'This employee of yours is being impertinent to an officer of the law; I'm trying to find out where this couple by the name of Melbo went after staying here in Corona.'

'I remember them. I heard they went to Los Angeles.'

'Los Angeles,' repeated Sanchez in exasperation. 'I know they went to Los Angeles; I want to know where they went the day they left here.'

'Annie,' said Billy, turning to the waitress, 'didn't you say something about him being a reporter or something?' He turned back to Sanchez. 'You know his name; you're the FBI. Why don't you find out the paper he works for and go ask him yourself?'

'Don't tell me how to run my investigation, Mr. Billy is it?'

'Then don't harass my waitress, sir.'

Sanchez looked hard at them both. He knew he was reaching for straws. There was silence in the restaurant as the tension hung in the air. Sanchez suddenly broke out in a big toothy smile.

'Hey, alright, I'll head south then. Thanks for the tip,' he uttered looking at Annie.

'Will that be all?' asked Annie.

'The bill if you don't mind,' he said looking at Billy. 'Nice place, Billy. You any relation to Billy the Kid?'

'If I was, you'd likely be starin' down my Colt six-shooter, bud.'

'Be careful who you point your pistol at, friend.'

'Careful was not what he was known for, friendo.'

'Yeah, yeah, you got me.' Sanchez put up his hands.

'Then best be on your way.' Billy the Kid turned on his heels and went back into the kitchen.

Outside, Sanchez got into his rented blue Ford sedan and sat there contemplating what to do when he noticed the other waitress out back smoking a cigarette. He started the car and slowly drove up close to the woman and stopped. He reached over and opened the passenger window.

'Hey there, I'm looking for some ranches south of here. Happen to know any? I'm in the insurance business.'

The waitress, Julia, a stocky woman in her early twenties just stared at him.

Sanchez pulled out his wallet and waved an Andrew Jackson at her. She looked at it with interest, checked to make sure no one was watching then took it.

'Don't say anything, but I distinctly heard that those folks from New York who were here a while ago were asking about the Wills ranch, Pine Bluff it's called.'

'Now why couldn't I get that from Annie?'

'Annie don't trust Mexicans.'

'Well you tell her I'm Cuban.' He then ripped out of there.

*

As he was tearing down the highway, Sanchez realized he was leaving himself wide open to prosecution for murder if he went through with his task. He also knew he would be left in the cold if he got caught, and his superiors would deny any connection with him; furthermore it would be easy to simply have him 'taken out' to seal the deal of his 'lone' attack on the unsuspecting rancher. What to do? He thought. He didn't approve of the assignment but he had agreed to it because his fast track American citizenship was contingent on him working for them. After stopping at a gas station to get directions to the Pine Bluff ranch, which were sketchy at best, pointing east through Ancho over the mountain range—somewhere near Jicarilla, the old guy said—Sanchez came up with a plan, which was no plan at all in fact. He'd simply introduce himself to the rancher and state the situation as it stood, then he would warn him that if he kept his mouth shut, he would tell his superiors nothing about him. He would tell them he had had no success in finding the rancher who had spoken to Melbo, and that it would backfire if he were to arbitrarily kill an innocent person, the whole idea being ruthless and reckless; he would say he didn't inform on Bastita for nothing, and as sure in hell didn't ask for Castro, at least what he turned out to be, another dictator.

Sanchez was for social justice like Kennedy; but Sanchez was also for Sanchez, and of course Inés Ruiz his second cousin whom he loved back in Cuba, and to whom he had sworn he would get her out and marry her. She was waiting impatiently. How could he have her if he was a murderer? His superiors said they would get her out if he worked for them, but he knew in his heart he could never live with himself, and Inés would know somehow—she saw through him, and would never accept him. He would not accept himself, in the name of God, even if he was faithless.

After another hour of driving around haplessly, he came across the quaint beat up Pine Bluff ranch sign. He stopped and looked at it; the image appeared of the girl Inès standing before him. She wasn't happy. He knew then and there what to do. He ripped out of there.

*

Prinzenthal was once again sitting with Jake Whitmore the media baron in his deco lounge. She nursed slowly her Manhattan and put it on the side table. Just one, she told herself, but they were so good. Whitmore stared at her, and she let him; she would break away from his gaze and look about the room, then go back to it.

'I'm not the Mona Lisa, Jake.'

'Well, you should be.'

'Leonardo was a bit before my time.'

'I've been told you're a legend.'

'Legends have a way of being big disappointments in real life.'

'Why is that?'

'Because they are antithetical to truth; the truth no one wants to hear.'

Whitmore looked away and took a good swallow of his drink.

'Isn't that why you were hired?' he finally said.

'I was hired to perform a task, not tell the truth as I see it.'

'We all have our truths—a very circumspect answer.'

'Spoken like a true insider.'

'I wish ... If that were true you and I would not be having this conversation.'

'It's not my place to question the Wise Owls of my profession. The fact of the matter is you were chosen, and I was chosen to augur the fate of a newsman.'

'I don't think it's up to us, Hannah. They have something to protect—something I don't actually know the extent of—and Melbo seems to be a bee in their bonnet.'

'How does the government ask the owner of a respectable paper to spy on one of his own star journalists? Melbo is what we Americans deem to be the best kind of patriot—someone who unerringly stands up for the principles of freedom; someone so guileless, so intelligent, that he makes it easy for us to understand the deeper implications of our times.'

'I suppose national security. I could ask the same of you.'

Prinzenthal sighed and took another sip of her drink.

'I've met him twice; he's happily married now, and a little upset with the way things turned out after the convention. He said he made a mistake by predicting Symington as Kennedy's running mate. He was upset because he had been tipped off by some Cuban exile—a cut-out I presume from the intelligence services—that Johnson was to be his running mate.'

'So he didn't trust this informant. So what?'

'He thinks you told his boss Sinclair to have him back off politics, when he was simply writing an opinion.'

'What if I did? Believe me, I preferred Symington over that hustler Johnson, but I'm a Republican, a Teddy Roosevelt progressive one. Look, it was a mild rebuke, okay? I think Melbo's great! But I was doing him a favor; your Wise Owls, as you say, are concerned about him; not for his political opinions but about him stirring up the idea that aliens are coming to Earth and that the government is somehow involved with them on account of a bogus crash in the desert out West. But, heck, it sells papers, and there are some circumstances that, well … need to be clarified—like this Roswell thing.'

'Why is the government so concerned? If they knew it's bogus, why don't they just drop it? On the other hand if somebody like Melbo stirs up the public they could simply ignore him, but the government doesn't because I own a respectable paper, as you say—thank you; I'm proud of it.'

'He told me that all the ranchers who were around at that time weren't talking. But it was because they weren't talking that they interested him. One of them—Brazel I think—had been incarcerated, and there was some nurse who disappeared, and then the coroner asked for the delivery of children's caskets, presumably for the little alien bodies … I admit I read about that in the National Enquirer!'

They both laughed.

'But seriously,' she went on, 'someone spoke to Melbo, likely someone close to the first responders to the accident. Melbo would never make anything up; you know him; he's as honest as the day is long. The point is that these ranchers took this thing very seriously, and they took the government's position very seriously as well.'

'My point entirely.'

Yes, well, you can tell your control that Melbo is harmless, as far as I can see. The problem is not with Melbo, but with the government: they should make some reasonable gesture to the public; the fact is that their denials of knowing anything is wearing thin. And if they go after someone like Melbo, it'll just make it worse.'

'I think you're right.'

They sat in silence for a while. Prinzenthal let her words sink in; she felt she had made enough of an impression for Whitmore to report back that there was nothing to worry about. His employee was a good man, and he wouldn't tolerate anything but that kind of character, as a matter of honor.

'I have a favor to ask of you, Jake,' said Prinzenthal.

'What's that?'

'I think to reduce the effect of these vile accusations of your star writer, you might well help defuse the situation by seeking some alternate narrative about him; set him on some more tangible course rather than scaring them about alien agendas.'

'What do you have in mind?'

'It's not really my place to peddle my own feelings about this; you've been a gracious host and a kind gentleman … but here goes: let Melbo interview Kennedy. You own a Republican paper, but you're a purveyor of news first and foremost. What better way to have Kennedy answer to the Republican view than by asking someone much younger than the old guard and even working for a Republican paper to challenge him? Both of them are intellectuals, and appeal to a wide range of American values. If he pulled it off, Melbo would not be so troublesome to the government, but rather more down to earth, on the level, don't you think?'

'A novel idea,' he mused. 'But hardly something Kennedy or his advisors would endorse; they'd be more inclined to find some well-heeled politico suitable to their party line.'

'I beg to differ. Kennedy is a maverick. He might just take a chance to show how strong he is, to show the public how reasonable he is … Well?'

'And fall flat on his face?' He laughed. 'But the debates with Nixon are coming up in a month or two.'

'The interview should be a low-key affair—a *tête à tête*, so-to-speak, just a cozy chat.'

'I don't know. Perhaps. I'll pass it on to Dick Sinclair and see what he thinks.'

'Just a thought. It might be the thing to smooth over the ruffled feathers of Wise Owls.'

They laughed again and finished off their drinks.

'Another?' he asked.

'No thanks, Jake; I need to go.'

'Why?'

She leaned closer to him, as if in confidence.

'Can you keep a secret?' She smiled.

'Yes,' he smiled back.

'I'm pregnant.'

Whitmore wasn't sure whether to congratulate her or commiserate with her.

'Oh, is it against the rules?' he asked, dumbfounded. 'Not part of the mission?'

'Yes.'

'What will you do?'

'Get married, I guess.'

'Perhaps it's none of my business, but may I ask who the father is?'

'He's my old control, no longer in the company—we've always had a soft spot for each other.'

'I suppose that's putting it mildly.'

'We like to sail together.'

'Sounds romantic.'

'I don't know what overcame me.'

'Do your superiors know?'

'Yes.'

'How did they take it?'

'The jury's still out; I'll likely take some time off.'

'Of course.'

'Mother Nature, you know.'

'Right.'

She got up to leave.

'I'll find my way out. Thanks for the drink, Jake. You're the best.'

'Well, come again if you hear anything.'

He stood up to see her to the door.

'There's really nothing to worry about,' she said.

They approached the private elevator.

'All the best.'

She gave him a peck on the cheek and stepped into the elevator. The doors closed. Whitmore looked like he had just been dumped.

18. Alphabet City

The plan had been set in motion just the day before Prinzenthal met Whitmore. Although previously they had agreed to get married in a playful teasing— Prinzenthal was more accommodating in that regard—Greenfield made a more formal proposal when they got back to New York. He called her at the office and asked her to meet him at the King Cole Bar in the St. Regis Hotel under the pretense of an idea, which he didn't reveal. 'Can't it wait?' she said.

'It's too important,' was his reply.

She knew better than to press him on the phone. Late that afternoon, she entered the St. Regis, the old iconic hotel built by John Jacob Astor, who went down with the Titanic almost a decade after his magnificent hotel opened. Greenfield loved the ambience there under the grand mural of Olde King Cole by Max Parrish and knew one of the waiters who remembered him from before the war years when he worked there as hotel security for a time. At present, like many of the grand old hotels of the first half of the century it had lost its glamour and was to be sold to a foreigner.

Years ago, just after the war, he had asked Prinzenthal to meet him there, but she stood him up. Undeterred, he asked again before they were headed back to Europe, and that time she showed up, even on time. It was then that Greenfield gave himself away by saying he wasn't sure if he could work with her again—this was well after Potsdam—and she answered that he damn well had to! She said she didn't trust anyone else. Encouraged, Greenfield revealed that his feelings for her went beyond the call of duty and it would affect and perhaps endanger them.

He never forgot the look in her eyes: they opened wide and stared at him; they were serious, almost feral. Nothing was said for what seemed like a minute. Then she began to laugh almost hysterically; she put her hand on his shoulder and leaned into him. Harley, Harley, she repeated. This became their little secret. She put her hand on his cheek and kissed him lovingly on the lips, forcing her tongue into his mouth; then abruptly she stopped to say that duty outranked love but love had the moral high ground. He knew she had been stirred; he also knew she was a turbulent ocean away from returning his love. And she told him: 'I'm corrupted, Harley; you can't have me; no one can that way; I'm doing God's work!' Yet, he knew she didn't believe in God.

He never forgot that response which encapsulated perfectly who she was, a strange dichotomy of personas, an incredible irony of parts. He had realized then that he would work with her; he would die for her.

She entered the lounge, and seeing him at the bar, she smiled and approached. Ned the waiter came by and asked if they wanted a table, pointing to the empty one in the corner. Both agreed.

'I'm in the mood for that famous Bloody Mary,' she said.

'And you, Harley? Another?'

'Sure, Ned; make it a double.'

Ned went away.

'What's the matter, dear?' she asked once the waiter had left.

'A man's prerogative: to be fortified.'

Smiling, Prinzenthal picked up his Canadian Club with one half-melted ice cube, and downed it crunching on the ice.

'Now there,' she announced, 'we're equally fortified. What's the big secret?'

'We're going to celebrate Lizbet's birthday on August the second—Tuesday.'

'Okay, great. Is that it?'

'No, we're going to the city hall.'

'Why the city hall?' she asked.

'We're going to meet the Melbos there.'

'I thought you felt we shouldn't meet them again; too risky.'

'Yes, but love has the moral high ground; we're doing God's work.'

'You never believed in God.'

'True, like you, but I think we can make an exception in our case. Remember long ago? We sat over there,' he said indicating. Greenfield, grinning ear to ear.

'Oh! So that's it! You want to get married on Tuesday! I should've guessed; I'm really losing it!'

'Yes, Hannah, on Lizbet's birthday!'

'She'd be happy for me,' she said evenly.

Ned brought the drinks and placed them on the table.

'She'd be delighted, honey bee!' exclaimed Greenfield.

Prinzenthal broke into a smile. 'Yes, alright, why not?'

'If you want, we can have a church service later.'

'I'm Jewish, Mr. Greenfield.'

'A synagogue, then.'

'You don't mind?'

'Of course not.'

'Who do you want to invite?' she asked.

'My sister and family; perhaps others: Dick and Aly.'

'Edward Teller is about the closest to family I have.'

'Would he come?'

'Yes.'

'You seem certain.'

'I want to bring him into our little *la coterie.*'

'Dear, that's wishful thinking; he works with Lovering.'

'Exactly, he's like family and protective.'

'Still.'

'When I was young and we had just arrived here my mother took me to Bialystoker synagogue in the East Village, near where we lived—I always called it by its other name Alphabet City, or even Lizbet City when she was here; this was our city. Anyway, the *shul* was rather orthodox, but I always liked the simple field-stone building and its interior and I used to dream on the balcony with the women and Lizbet that I would marry in that place. I loved the colors and *aron kodesh*—that's the Holy Ark—its mystery—and the frescoes and stained glass—so intricate, beautiful. I didn't care about the *shachah*—worship, just the atmosphere.

'Edward Teller went there too once, and came back to our place for tea and cookies. Believe me I think he'll try and make it for me. He always had a thing for me; when I was a girl, he awakened in me the idea of power over men; it was innocent and instinctive, and of course he was a perfect gentleman. But I knew he would visit because of me.'

'Does he know what you've been doing all these years?'

'Not completely; he thinks I worked in the State Department *sub rosa*, but I will tell him.'

'Then we shall make the arrangements.'

'Thank you, Harley; it's so wonderful that you care for me.'

'You know I love you, Hannah.'

'I know. And although it pains me—my silly neuroses—I love you too.'

*

Earl Bunting happened to be in New York on the Tuesday of the planned marriage at city hall. He was at the office where Prinzenthal worked. They were acquaintances at best as they had collaborated occasionally in years gone by. Prinzenthal disliked his venal personality, and conveniently ignored him. He knew of her exploits and figured she was a bit like him; but he kept his distance, knowing how much of a sacred cow she was to his superiors. Greenfield had worked with him as well and despised him for his amorality, yet he knew he was an effective weapon in the business. Thugs like him had become more necessary of late; that was one reason Greenfield had had enough of the service.

Bunting left the building and positioned himself near a magazine stand reading a paper. He kept one eye on the entrance and fifteen minutes later out walked Prinzenthal. He quietly moved out of sight as she scanned the area and turned away. She flagged a cab, and Bunting did the same, telling the cabbie to follow the other from a distance. Shortly after, she got out at the city hall and walked towards it. She knew Greenfield was somewhere in the park watching them as they congregated. He would enter last after assuring himself all was clear. Bunting, however, got out of his cab well ahead of Prinzenthal's and he concealed himself behind some trees from where he watched her enter the city hall.

Then he saw Melbo crossing at the lights and following in the same direction as Prinzenthal. Other people went in as well, one of whom was DeCourt, but Bunting didn't know her; nor did he know the arrangement made by his superiors about Prinzenthal and Melbo. He decided to go around the long way up to the city hall from the other side. Then he cased the area to see if there were any lookouts. Seeing none he moved with a small sparse crowd towards the steps. Greenfield had done the same thing coming up behind. To his shock he recognized Bunting.

'Now what could Earl Bunting want in the city hall?' said Greenfield, stepping in beside him.

Bunting swung around like a wily cat.

'Harley, fancy meeting you here. Paying off some parking tickets?'

'I could ask the same of you, Bunting.'

They stopped at the top of the steps.

'Ask away, old man.'

'The last I heard, you were in Washington, so let's skip the pleasantries. Why are you following Hannah?'

'Hannah? I was following Melbo. Seems you let the cat out of the bag, Harley.'

'Don't get cute, asshole. Mind your own business.'

'Well, in case you need your memory jogged, this *is* my business.'

Greenfield knew he was stung. He had to make an impression.

'Listen, we're getting married. Can you please get lost.'

'Married? To that hustler? Christ, I thought she was damaged goods. Must be desperate.'

Greenfield slammed his fist below his solar plexus so fast Bunting crumpled like a rag doll, but stood up reflexively like an inflated balloon, though winded.

Face to face Greenfield said calmly, 'There's no need to follow her, jackass. Your superiors already know.'

'Okay, then why the sucker punch?' Bunting, wheezed.

'Because you insulted my fiancée, a human being far above your pathetic excuse for one.'

'I could've said a lot worse.'

'Then I would've put you out of your misery. Now fuck off!'

Greenfield left him there.

'Fuck you, Greenfield! I owe you one.'

*

The civil ceremony went very well with a woman officiating. Greenfield and Prinzenthal were elated when they were declared husband and wife. Prinzenthal shed all her armor and even took the initiative to kiss Greenfield rapturously for some euphoric ten seconds gushes and all. The Melbos stood back beaming delightedly. Any indication of the confrontation with Bunting was erased from Greenfield's mind as he put the rolled certificate into the inside pocket of his linen blazer.

Hand in hand, they exited the building and squeezed into a taxi. Bunting, true to his nature still lurked in the background but gaped at them in their unmistakable happiness. Seeing Melbo and his woman just as glad compelled him to concede that these folks seemed to be as tight as a pod of dolphins. Without a moment to lose he flagged another taxi and had it follow the other now a dozen cars ahead.

'Mr. and Mrs. Greenfield?' inquired DeCourt, who sat beside them in the back, while Melbo rode in the front passenger seat, 'how are we to celebrate? I mean with all the subterfuge of this rendezvous, we never knew what was in store for us.'

'On a need to know basis we're to have a special early dinner at the St. Regis hotel,' said Greenfield. 'It's been arranged by my friend Ned, who works there. We have a booth in the King Cole Bar.'

'The scene of our first date,' chipped in Prinzenthal. 'I really wasn't expecting that, you know; I tortured him for years on account of it.'

'When was that?' asked Melbo.

'After the war; I was shocked that he loved me and because he knew all my dirty secrets, and I had no private life. It was like: Harley get your head examined!'

They all had a laugh.

'She stood me up the first time,' said Greenfield.

'He became my case officer, and expected benefits.'

'Did he get any?' wondered DeCourt aloud.

'That's classified,' said Greenfield.

Their laughter was infectious. Even the cabbie was laughing.

Later, ensconced in their booth in the St. Regis they toasted with tall flutes filled with Dom Perignon '45 to commemorate their personal trajectory from that time. Smoked salmon and puff pastries stuffed with Chesapeake crab were presented, accompanied by a flinty-aromatic Sancerre Pouilly-Fumé '56. Greenfield spoke of a Frenchman he knew in the resistance from the same Loire region, Alphonse Bechet, who started a vineyard after the war. Bechet used to call Greenfield the 'satyr' as in some local iteration of Sancerre, the beast being an ancient mascot in Roman times, the area was always known for its bucolic atmosphere.

'You never told me that,' said Prinzenthal.

'When I was there, we used to eat large quantities of chèvre ... Ste. Maure de Touraine with bread and *jambon de pays* all downed with numerous bottles of the local vin blanc much like this we're drinking here.'

'We've never been to Europe,' said DeCourt. 'I envy you both, being so imbued with culture.'

'Don't feel that way, Mel,' said Prinzenthal, in their defense. 'We were thrust into the maelstrom. When you go someday you will get to experience the best of that world, not the horrors and depravity that we witnessed.'

'We are honored you brought us along here,' said Melbo, raising his glass. 'I'd like to propose a toast to the bride and groom!'

They all clink glasses.

'The honor is ours nonetheless,' replied Greenfield, after they imbibed large mouthfuls. 'You've been a tremendous morale booster for us in a tired world. The notion that we can do something positive comes from your inspiration. Our experience, if you will, is a perfect match, don't you think?'

'We just like you as friends, Harley,' replied DeCourt. 'You know, all this government xenophobia about aliens is disconcerting to say the least.'

At that moment, Greenfield noticed Earl Bunting at the far end of the bar, smirking at him. He showed no outward indication that he had seen anything.

'Certainly,' said Greenfield, 'there's a degree of harassment that they can deploy; and when one's tolerance is at its tipping point, the law can provide some protection if there are sufficient grounds for indictment against innocent citizens. But let's not dwell on these things now. Excuse me, I need to visit the men's room.'

Greenfield was sitting at the outside of the booth so he quickly removed himself. Prinzenthal watched him go. She saw Bunting, and like Greenfield, made no acknowledgement.

'It seems Harley's bladder has got the best of him,' remarked Prinzenthal with amusement. 'I suppose in bed at his age I'll have to get used to his numerous nocturnal visits to the loo.'

'Don't exclude yourself,' laughed Melbo, 'given your condition!'

'God, you're right; I almost forgot,' agreed Prinzenthal, putting her hand to her womb, 'I can be such a bitch; poor Harley!'

'Hannah,' countered DeCourt, 'if I may say, if you're a bitch then womankind must be positively loathsome—I've never known anyone whose heart is more impassioned to love and faithfulness.'

'Yes, I agree,' said Melbo. 'By all appearances your natural toughness is a mask for the champion of bleeding hearts.'

'Well put, honey,' agreed DeCourt.

'Oh my God, my cover's blown!' exclaimed Prinzenthal loudly enough for Bunting to turn his head and look right at her. She looked back but gave him the Giaconda Smile. Bunting turned away quickly, retreating into his insipid ego.

Almost immediately, Ned approached Bunting with a heavyset fellow in a three-piece dark gray suit. Words were spoken, and the heavyset man touched the elbow of Bunting, who suddenly scoffed at him to let go, but stood up, finished his drink, and was escorted from the bar, without more ado. Neither Melbo nor DeCourt reacted, so seamless was his removal.

They were laughing when Greenfield returned.

'We were having fun at your expense, dear,' said Prinzenthal, brimming with mirth.

'Doesn't surprise me; that's the back story of our romance.' He smiled as he slid back into his place.

'You're a testament to man's tolerance of a woman's wiles,' she added, her eyes gleaming.

'I love you too, smarty pants.'

*

The very next day Prinzenthal tendered her resignation to the CIA, citing marriage and personal reasons. When her superiors in Washington received the news, and later, after receiving Bunting's account, they still gave her the benefit of the doubt, even in view of the insinuating report that they were "up to something"—after all, she had been a highly respected asset, and had openly revealed her circumstances to Sulla, the month before. Any camaraderie between her and the Melbos was seen as a well-placed exit strategy, considering her clandestine matter with Whitmore, known only to the Wise Owls, and certainly not to Bunting and his ilk. So it appeared Prinzenthal had a free pass to the rest of her life.

Even Lovering's suspicions were laid to rest when Whitmore insisted all was aboveboard and nothing came of her careful debriefing of Melbo. And when Sanchez confirmed that there had been no collusion of any consequence with ranchers, and the one rancher in question had disappeared, the operation was dropped. This led Aubrey Woods to conclude that if any threat to their secret programs was real, it was no different from all the public apocrypha of alien visitation in general.

But it did give him comfort that if Melbo had in fact received some verifiable account of the Roswell incident and was protecting his source, the journalist himself could be exploited by the government to discredit the truth as he would definitely never reveal his source. A smear campaign to tarnish Melbo's impeccable reputation could very well be as effective a deterrent than something more sinister. Even more so if he could be used as a lure to discover, when under that pressure, to whom he would turn and what he would do, which might perhaps lead to some unforeseen windfall. All in all, he felt their position was as secure as could be.

Dick Sinclair was unaware of all the machinations concealed beneath the ongoing popular column penned by Melbo. Not an inkling did he have when Whitmore made one of his rare appearances on the floor of the newsroom. Sinclair, working at his desk when Whitmore gave a light knock, looked up; his eyes opened wide and he put down his pipe and stood up with his hand extended in an enthusiastic greeting.

'I'm not here to impose, Dick; was just in the neighborhood.'

'Not at all, sir. We're always happy to see you; in fact, we have cause to celebrate, as you are likely aware: circulation has increased almost twenty percent these last four or five months.'

'Yes, I know and am well pleased. How do you account for it from your side? If anyone, you've got a finger on the pulse of the people.'

'Please, Mr. Whitmore, have a seat,' said Sinclair indicating the seat just to the side of his desk and returning to his own chair.

'Yes, well, obviously the election has something to do with it,' continued Sinclair, 'and this particular election, I might add. A Kennedy-Nixon contest will go down in the history books, I'll wager.'

'Indeed, and who are you wagering on, Dick?'

Sinclair was momentarily taken aback by the unexpected question, almost an ambush, but he kept a straight face and answered without missing a beat.

'Nixon, by a hair,' he stated unequivocally. 'Experience over pretender; Nixon is a fighter, a man experienced in the corridors of power; and Kennedy, a parvenu, an upstart who would flatter the public with fancy speeches.'

'He does that, doesn't he? But I think there's more to him; he's captured his generation, and the next.'

'True, but I've taken that into account. The party of Lincoln will prevail. We've had peace and growing prosperity; surely that counts for something.'

'I've seen my party lose too many times under Roosevelt to hazard any sure thing. In fact, after the McCarthy inquisition—in spite of their best intentions—has backfired; this will impact the swing vote.'

'McCarthy was a thug, and a thorn in the body politic; Christ, he went after anybody who voted Democrat.'

'I rarely intervene in the newsroom, Dick, but I have an idea.'

'Yes,' prompted Sinclair.

'How about we use one of our younger reporters and set up an interview with Kennedy. Hear me out: people are tired of the old guard; they want fresh blood. My sources tell me we need to appeal to the younger generation or we lose this election, even by a hair, as you say. When I asked you about the increased circulation, some of that surely is the consequence of George Melbo's articles, is it not? What better man to represent our paper and the Republican cause?'

'Sir, we have always prided ourselves on our impartiality, not to say that our opinions lean to the right.'

'Of course, of course, but nevertheless, if we could rally behind our star writer who has taken us great strides forward in our quest for answers to the mysteries of the universe, and politics.'

Sinclair sat quietly for a moment contemplating the rather strange request from the owner of the paper. A month ago he had been asked through an associate to curb Melbo's political aspirations.

'So Melbo's back on the front page?'

'Was he ever off? Where is he, by the way? I'd like to meet with him.'

Sinclair picked up his interphone. 'Is Melbo in the office, Pearline?'

Silence.

'Could you get him for me? Thanks.' He put back the receiver. 'He'll be here shortly.'

A few minutes later Melbo appeared at the door.

'Mel, glad you're around,' said Sinclair. 'Come on in. You've met Jake Whitmore. He's asked to see you.'

Melbo shook his hand.

'Hardly a day goes by I don't think about that gala birthday bash, sir,' said Melbo.

'Oh, there'll be more. Please have a seat,' said Whitmore.

Melbo sat in the remaining chair.

'How's your lovely fiancée?' he asked.

'We're married now, sir.'

'Congratulations! What a fine couple you make.'

'Thank you.'

'She's in publishing isn't she?'

'Yes, she is.'

'Well, if she ever needs a change tell her to contact me. I'd be glad to place her in one of our houses.'

'That's very kind of you, sir.'

'Call me Jake, Mel.'

'Alright, Jake.'

'Let's get down to business, shall we? Mel, Dick and I have been discussing your first rate column. I have asked him to consider arranging an interview between Kennedy and yourself, the intention being to get a younger man's opinion on the Kennedy agenda for our paper. Would you be interested?'

'I don't think there's a newsman anywhere who wouldn't jump at that opportunity in a heartbeat!'

'Great. There's someone I know, a woman, who has recently retired from the clandestine services. I've been told she has an inside track to the Kennedy campaign. It may be possible through her influence to get you that exclusive.'

'I'm all ears, Jake. Does this woman have a name?'

'Let's just say that for the time being we leave her anonymous; she'd prefer it that way.'

'Okay, whatever you say.'

Melbo was of a mind to reveal his relationship with Prinzenthal, believing his innocent part as an unwitting informant could do him no harm. Besides, he thought it almost obvious he should know this woman when Whitmore had in effect just now revealed her to him. The question was how did Whitmore know Prinzenthal had some back channel to Kennedy? Nothing in his relationship with Prinzenthal could allow him to know that she had an inside connection with Kennedy, or could allow Whitmore to know this either: most likely, she had worked her magic on him, in which case, it would be best to just let the events carry themselves.

'How will we get through to Kennedy then?' asked Sinclair.

'She'll make contact, then I'll leave it up to you guys,' said Whitmore, standing. 'My suggestion is that Melbo makes a stab at it. Eh Mel?'

'Sure, Jake; I'll just waltz into his camp and announce myself.'

They all laughed.

'You'll have to make it worth his while. Good luck.'

With that Whitmore left the office.

'Do you know something I should know?' wondered Sinclair aloud.

'I think I know who this anonymous woman is,' said Melbo.

'Who?'

'Were you introduced to her at the million dollar bash? She came with Edward Teller.'

'No, actually, but I couldn't help but notice her. She was rather gorgeous, alluring, wasn't she?'

'I think she was with the State Department in Berlin and Moscow in '45, '46.'

'Really? How do you know that?'

'She just married Harley Greenfield aka Thomas Jones and is pregnant with his child.'

'Holy Mother Mary! You mean Joyce Sommers?'

'That's not her real name.'

'How do you know all this?'

'Melissa and I were invited as witnesses to their marriage at the city hall last Tuesday.'

'Jesus, Mel, why didn't you tell me?'

'You know Harley. He's very good at what he does. And he's determined to look out for us. You were the one who put this in motion. All hush-hush and we have to keep it that way.'

'Yes, of course, but I had no idea about this. Who is she?'

'Hannah Prinzenthal. He was her case officer for about ten years from the forties and fifties.'

'And how does she know Whitmore?'

'I don't really know. But we can assume the intelligence community put her up to it.'

'Damn.'

'Damn is right, and we're been swept along by a rip tide in this.'

'Well, I must say she appears to be playing it both ways. Can you trust her?'

'Oh yeah, it's just the other side I'm worried about.'

'The CIA.'

'Yeah, and Greenfield doesn't like his old bosses. Thinks they're not much better than fascists.'

'Thanks for bringing me in, Mel. You've been under a lot more pressure than I was aware of.'

'It just kind of happened, Dick. No problem.'

'Do you know how to get to Kennedy?'

'No, but Harley does. He's always got something up his sleeve, and I think Hannah has something to do with it.'

'You mean she knows Kennedy?'

'I don't know, but it wouldn't surprise me. She's someone with more skeletons in her closet than I can even begin to fathom. You should've seen Sulla and even Eisenhower and the governor fawn over her at Whitmore's.'

'I didn't notice. A veritable Mata Hari?'

'But she's on our side, Dick; remember that. Harley loves her with a ferocity I've never seen.'

'Very well, but can they deliver an interview with Kennedy?'

'Let me work on that.'

'He never once said anything about her,' stated Sinclair whimsically.

'Don't feel put out. They're spies, remember?'

'I was in the OSS during the war—disinformation; that's how I know Harley.'

'Did you work with him?'

'Indirectly. The first time I met him briefly a year before the attack on Pearl when we were working for Herbert Yardley the signals chief here in New York, then a bunch of us were being briefed by an army liaison about a year before D-Day; Harley was tapped to give information because he'd been in France working with the Resistance; I was asked to disseminate information through the press and radio about an imminent invasion: none of us at that time knew where it would take place.'

'What happened to him?' asked Melbo.

'I assume he went back to France. The next time we saw each other was at Frankfurt during the close of the war. General Headquarters was set up there. I was assigned to various staging areas for POWs in Germany and reported back from them to the OSS in the hunt for ranking Nazis. Harley ended up in Berlin, then Moscow. When OSS was disbanded, I came home and got a job with the Washington Post. Harley remained incognito until I saw him in '47 and invited him to my wedding in Charlottesville, Virginia. He attended but told me then he was heading back to Europe. And I've seen him barely half a dozen times since before this year.'

'And no mention of Hannah?'

'None, whatsoever. But that's the business. She must have been some high-wire spy.'

They fell silent.

'Good, then,' said Sinclair, ending the conversation.

Melbo stood up to leave. 'I'll keep you posted.'

19. Topping the Bill

During the sultry, humid mid-summer days of August, a potpourri of activity had forced Greenfield and Prinzenthal out of their pleasant lethargy. New York was a steam bath. A million air conditioners and electric fans were on full blast in a futile attempt to cool apartments, houses, offices, and public buildings. Greenfield and Prinzenthal visited the rabbi at Bialystoker who told them he wouldn't perform the ceremony because Greenfield was an agnostic. But he did say another rabbi might help if they intended to raise their children Jewish.

This rabbi, Jacob Elfman, would be leaving for Israel later that month though, so they had to marry soon, very soon. Prinzenthal called Teller to announce the good news, and to invite him to the ceremony. Could he make it by Thursday? Today was Sunday. Yes he could. So it was confirmed. Teller and his wife, Mitzi, with Dick and Alecia Sinclair, the Melbos, and a smattering of others including Greenfield's sister and family, and Melbo's old university friend Ben Johnson were the only guests.

The ceremony went as planned with the most abbreviated ritual religiously possible. All the men wore *kippahs*—the traditional skull caps of the faith. The *bedeken* veiling of the bride was particularly touching. Prinzenthal wore a French cream-colored bridal gown with a traditional round headpiece of lace and florets. So stunning was she, Greenfield was beside himself in blessedness as he noticed her eyes fervid and fixed on him. Then, under the simple white four-posted *chuppah* and intricate woven cloth canopy which had been smuggled out of Europe before the war, they stood before the rabbi and were married in both Yiddish and English.

The breaking of the glass underfoot was performed with great aplomb, and was accompanied by everyone in unison proclaiming '*Mazel Tov!*' This rite was symbolic of the destruction of the temple in Jerusalem by Titus and the Romans; and of a certain rebuilding; but, more so, it was symbolic of the reunion of their souls. It was believed that their souls were joined at birth, then were separated, and now rejoined as one soul. Greenfield lifted Prinzenthal's veil and they kissed for some moments then stopped and smiled looking into each other's eyes. The *kabbalat panim,* or signing, followed and received the *ketubah,* their marriage contract, written in Aramaic under God in heaven indivisible.

Whisked away to a nearby reception venue in a new chauffeur-driven open-top white Cadillac followed by everyone, including the rabbi and his wife, the bride and groom seemed charmed like two blushing sophomores. They were not used to that kind of attention, but reveled in their audacity. The rabbi introduced them as man and wife, and then the band—a local quartet of stand-up bass, drums, clarinet and violin—struck up the *horah* which Greenfield and Prinzenthal were obliged to begin dancing, with the few others joining in, so that by the end, the dancers were almost in a flying circle.

The band tempo increased from slow to very fast that by the end all were almost maniacally trying to keep the rhythm. They abandoned the raising of the bride and groom in chairs because there were simply not enough strong arms to do the lifting. Champagne flowed and a simple kosher dinner of clam chowder, a slow-cooked beef rib-roast, rosettes of potatoes, various vegetables, and rum cake and vanilla ice cream for dessert proceeded happily with delightful speeches from Melbo, Greenfield, Teller, and Prinzenthal.

Melbo stated that Prinzenthal had come in from the cold to the warmth of a New York heat wave, and that would most likely extend into their sunny Cape Cod honeymoon on the family yacht! Greenfield spoke of his long courtship, saying if she hadn't said yes he would be courting her memory into the afterlife! Teller spoke of Hannah's parents, who in their daughter's early years witnessed her intelligence attest in her extraordinary abilities, and must now be so proud of her as they look down from on high this day.

Prinzenthal was remarkably thankful, claiming Harley all but gave her the confidence she needed to perform her work. She finished by joking that her reputed intransigence had been a 'test' for Harley, and that marriage was not a reward, but a lifelong adventure during which she hoped they would always remain true to the spirit of love. Finally she toasted her parents and Lizbet.

The next day, a lunch buffet was presented in the Versailles Room of the St. Regis Hotel, where Greenfield and Prinzenthal had spent their night in the 'Bridal Suite' with a view of Central Park. Edward Teller left that morning for the West, leaving Prinzenthal disappointed not only that he couldn't attend the lunch buffet, but also that on the previous evening, when they had had a chance to talk, he had carefully avoided any discussion of his work. Teller could sense Prinzenthal's interest in the subtle way she approached the subject by referencing Melbo's 'wonderful' articles, and by her noting that Teller had spoken to Melbo and his fiancée at Whitmore's bash months earlier.

Teller dismissed the articles with a wave of his hand, calling them grist for the mill of human curiosity and then diverted the conversation to their sailing in the Caribbean. But Teller was a cagey fellow. Even when Melbo tried to engage him, he begged off with a laugh: 'Mr. Melbo, you're the last person I should be seen with; they'll think I'm the germ that unleashed doomsday! But for Harley and Hannah, I was never here!' Their conversation went on to politics with a clear signal to maintain Teller's anonymity; he would never risk his position and responsibility in matters of national security, especially as he was in deep with the CIA science and technology division, which had oversight of the vast desert mountainous regions of Nevada ubiquitously known as Area 51, but was actually much more, working with both very compartmentalized elements of the Air, Army and Navy military and with some civilian aerospace affiliates.

However, by Teller's evasion, Prinzenthal knew very well he was the proverbial goldmine. When she was young back in her early years in New York, Teller would visit, and she remembered him being eager to share with her, at least literally, the nature of his work as she showed intelligence and curiosity about subjects beyond her years. They had a kind of secret relationship with science being the foundation of a deeper friendship. Now there was an empty void. At the close of the evening, as he departed—having given Prinzenthal a kiss and hug from him and his wife—Teller said to her quickly that he had to head back West on urgent business; but he wondered if, in his stead, the following day, an old acquaintance who had fallen on hard times could attend the bridal couple's luncheon for which he had insisted on "topping the bill" in his absence. Prinzenthal agreed, of course, but afterwards thought it strange and forgot to ask the fellow's name.

A sumptuous buffet awaited them in the Versailles Room (very modest in size for its name), far more than enough for the dozen or more people who showed up, including the Melbos. After light conversation—a muted continuation of the previous evening's celebrations—everyone helped themselves to smoked salmon roulades, lobster and tomato salad, Caesar salad, chicken thighs cooked in white wine with olives, tarragon and thyme, spiced beef brisket, a lemon-garlic olive oil pasta, pomme frites, various vegetables, white and red wines, and for dessert cherry cheesecake, apple crisp, and chocolate mousse. As the last few guests filled their plates, a gray-haired man dressed in an old rumpled suit, frayed white shirt and a tie that looked like some relic from the turn of the century Ivy League, sidled up quietly to heap his plate with all that was offered. He then went and sat at an unoccupied table behind the others and ate undisturbed, averting his eyes from anyone looking on, including Greenfield and Prinzenthal.

He had the sad look of a poet who had missed his queue in a soup kitchen, and being of a benign nature could not or would not fight for his rightful place. His innocuous appearance at the table while everyone was in full feed didn't lend itself to introductions. Prinzenthal was amused by the situation knowing full well Teller had left her or them a wedding gift. Just what it was remained a mystery. Melbo didn't seem to care one way or the other and presumed he was some old friend so let him be.

DeCourt in jest was the only one who offered an explanation saying the guy was a crasher, and a rather bohemian one at that, though whose benign appearance was incompatible with the scorn of such an accusation. To Greenfield, who hadn't been informed by his new wife, and still bolstered after last night's pleasures, this unexpected guest appeared harmless enough, even perhaps adding a funny flourish to the momentous occasion. After all, there was enough food for more than a dozen like him. Little did Greenfield know this fellow was as rare as a virgin birth.

Greenfield beat Prinzenthal to the punch, so-to-speak, as he got up from his table with cherry cheesecake and chocolate mousse in his sights, but steered himself in the stranger's direction on impulse. Prinzenthal watched him, wondering whether she should intervene, aware of his penchant for cutting to the chase, but giving him the benefit of the doubt as to what he had in mind.

'How do you do?' said Greenfield, without extending his hand, fearing to impose on the fellow's obvious indulgence in what Versailles had to offer. 'Harley Greenfield, the newly anointed groom.'

The man barely noticed him, and continued to eat as if he were deaf and dumb to his surroundings. Finally after an agonizingly endless moment, which impelled Greenfield to the edge of indignation, the man replied in a quiet voice that carried not only sophistication, but some desperate charm laying claim to a lost and found Ancient Mariner.

'Please extend to the host, whoever it is my most grateful appreciation. I do apologize if my presence here has caused any trouble, sir, most happy sir— my sincere congratulations. And please tell the chef he saved my life, as I was subsisting on boiled navy beans. I feel like a man resurrected to the heavens of earthly delight, without the wife of course—well, I mean no offense.'

With the last word, the man looked up at Greenfield with green watery eyes that first awakened sympathy; but held by the man's eye contact, Greenfield saw something far more cryptic. He wondered if he was a junkie as he certainly didn't appear to be an alcoholic, drinking only water with averted eyes.

'None taken, Mister....'

'Leverton, Keith Leverton.'

'Should I know you, Keith?' asked Greenfield, intrigued.

'Well I can't say for sure, Harley, but I did get an invitation, from whom I know not, but I came nevertheless, and most gratefully.'

'Now don't get me wrong here, Keith, we're happy that you came, but what was exactly said, and by whom? Have you any idea? You see we're ... let's say recently retired from a kind of esoteric business, and wouldn't want to draw any undue attention to our private gathering. Do you get my drift?'

Leverton offered a sudden smile from which emerged a beatific laugh so quiet with his head nodding and bobbing up and sideways. Greenfield thought he was out of his mind.

'Then I'm terribly sorry but it appears that I'm your fatted calf,' he said returning to his lamentable self.

'You mean an offering to God?' queried Greenfield a little confused.

'In a manner of speaking.'

'Can you be a little more specific, Keith? God hasn't spoken to me yet.'

'Well, he spoke to me.'

Prinzenthal came to Greenfield's side. 'Hello. I'm the bride, Hannah.'

'Hello,' said Leverton, casting his eyes on her and then looking down having seen forbidden fruit.

'Thank you,' he said, briefly looking at her again.

'Did Edward call you?' she asked quickly.

'Edward? The only Edward I know ratted on an old friend of mine.'

'Ratted for what?' she asked.

'For the clearance of Bob.'

'Bob?'

'A visionary who saw beyond science and politics.'

'Oppenheimer?' wondered Prinzenthal, connecting the dots of the riddle. Teller had mentioned to her a few years back that when subpoenaed, he had been wrongly accused of selling short Robert Oppenheimer the 'father of the bomb' during the hearings about the latter's Communist associations. He had believed Oppenheimer to be innocent, more like a renaissance figure involved in everything, but the case against him in that climate of fear was a *fait accompli*. 'Bob' was decidedly against the proliferation of nuclear weapons, along with Einstein and a host of others.

For all his gifts as a scientist and astrophysicist, notably his theories about gravitational pull and the collapse of stars into black holes, he was above all opaquely spiritual and an expert in ancient Indian philosophy as written in the Bhagavad Gita and other texts.

'Who called you?' asked Greenfield.

'I asked the same thing. He wouldn't say.'

'Did he have an accent?' urged Prinzenthal.

'Like a foreigner? No.'

'It doesn't matter; it could be anyone,' she responded. 'The fact remains you are here at someone's request.'

'Keith Leverton, at your service, ma'am.'

'What do you do, Keith?'

'Hah! At present I'm unemployed, and live in the Village busking at times in cafés playing jazz blues guitar…the rest is classified,' he said mischievously.

'How do you know Oppenheimer?'

'Did know; we were friends at Stanford before the war.'

'As colleagues?'

'You could say we were colleagues, of a sort; of course that is precisely why we were friends; we believed that science and spirituality meet at some place in this great container we call the universe. As a doctor in advanced psychology, I was an astronaut of the mind—everything out there, is in here.' He tapped his head. 'We fell out or lost touch because his security clearances didn't account for my kind of astronaut, rather more terrestrial issues—total war—but he did encourage me to seek some work in the military during and after the war in what began as clinical with some experimental applications—

trauma related issues, but progressed to something more unparalleled.'

'So what happened?'

'I quit a few years back. I didn't like what was going on. But I'm under oath to hold my peace, and that is exactly the cause of my own problems. Now, if you'll excuse me, I'd like to get some dessert, and be on my way.'

He stood up. He was rather tall with a kind of forward leaning head that almost gave him a Gary Cooper impression but even more stressed than the actor looked in *High Noon*. His eyes were quite revealing, as if they had seen the face of God and were forever glazed.

Prinzenthal gave Greenfield a look that said leave him to me. Greenfield joined the others saying a Mr. Leverton had joined the party, apparently by misadventure. Everyone thought it was quite funny.

'What did I tell you?' quipped DeCourt.

Melbo observed Prinzenthal sitting across from Leverton and suspected there was more to him that met the notorious eye.

'Don't worry about the others,' she said, while Leverton dug into his apple crisp with a spoon.

'I stopped worrying about anything the day I found God.'

'For a psychologist that's saying something.'

'I don't see myself as a psychologist.'

'What then?'

He wouldn't look at her, as if it pained him.

'A beatnik,' he finally said.

'Okay, then: if you were a psychologist what would you say to an answer like that?'

He continued eating, seeming to ignore her.

'Keith.'

He finished eating and put down his spoon, gazing into his plate.

'I would say a cover for some undisclosed intrigue—in other words don't go where angels fear to tread!'

'Keith, look at me.'

Slowly he looked up at her, seemingly transfixed by some monstrous apparition.

'I'm the angel who came in from the cold,' she said. 'Believe me when I say I have tread fear.'

'You don't know what you're saying,' he said, standing up.

'How can we reach you?' she asked simply.

'Why on earth would you do that?'

'I want to introduce you to somebody, but this isn't the time or place.'

'Listen, I'm very grateful for the invitation, but this ends here.' He walked out of the Versailles Room back to oblivion. Prinzenthal followed him.

In the hall she called after him. 'He reviews gigs in the village.'

Leverton paused and turned around.

'And who might that be?'

'George Melbo.'

'Never heard of him.'

'He works for the Trib; he's back there.'

'I never read it.'

'He's syndicated now.'

'I like my anonymity. It's safe and sound. I manage by subbing at various colleges 'cause music don't pay.'

'We like our anonymity too. If you don't mind me saying, I think you could use some friends, the kind that respect our kind.'

He paused dramatically, not moving a muscle, just staring into space.

'I'm off their radar and want to keep it that way,' he said at last.

'No one knows you're here, Keith.'

'I don't trust Teller.'

'Edward is an old family friend from long before the war in Europe. He would have done nothing to compromise me, or you; in fact, I think he was making some kind of amends for what went down with 'Bob'. His work was far too important and likely some *political* compromises were made. He's not your enemy, Keith, nor Bob's for that matter.'

*

Melbo was familiar with most of the old beatnik haunts of the Village. While at university he spent most of his free time there, and at times even sat in with them in some of the cafés and jazz joints habituated by the likes of Ginsberg, Kerouac, Burroughs and others. Melbo was immediately interested in their culture and observed their sometimes insane antics, though when as a student he kept to himself and remained dutiful to his studies. He found their spontaneous prose and poetry fascinating in the moment as a rebellion or counterculture and accepted it as such, though in a critical sense he thought it much like de Kooning and Pollock in that their abstract paintings were milestones to the times.

He also realized that the artistic thread through which these artists progressed had a long past going back to the *Années Folles*—Paris in the 1920s—and Baudelaire and Rimbaud in the nineteenth century. Little did he realize what was on the horizon with the 1960s and 1970s and how it would go mainstream psychedelically and be manifested in the ubiquitous sex, drugs and rock 'n roll of the hippie generation, not to mention the anti-war crusade and the revolution of the mind which itself foundered in narcissism and burnout. The extreme liberality of these movements served to fuel the contempt of conservatists and the hatred of racists.

They met in Washington Square as planned facing the arch. Melbo arrived first and Leverton sauntered by ten minutes later. He stopped and pretended to tie his shoelace on the bench saying quietly to meet him at the Café Wha? then strode off across the park.

Later, seated at the back of the café, Leverton had a coffee in front of him. Melbo ordered a tea.

'The other day I read some of your articles in the library, Mr. Melbo. I like your style, but it wouldn't do for me to have you review me; first of all because I'm not good enough as a guitar player, and second because any connection to you would guarantee my likely liquidation.' He laughed, his head doing that bobbing motion.

'Everyone calls me Mel. My sources are ironclad and cloaked in the syntax of the hypothetical.'

'Alright Mel, and you can call me Mike, Mike Roberts, just so the chance of your residual proximity doesn't wash off on me.'

'Sure, Mike. I'm happy to oblige, and appreciate that you're meeting with me. Hannah said you were one of us; "ready to make a difference" I think she said.'

Leverton stared at Melbo for some moments in his usual manner.

'Make a difference, huh; well, I've got news for you; they've got this thing so locked up it'll be a hundred years before they come clean, if ever; in fact there's nothing I can say or you can write that will make any difference.'

'Why?'

'Listen, for over five years I've been happily living my life around here, hangin' with the best of them—Charlie Parker, Miles Davis, Wynton Kelly, Paul Chambers, Billie Holiday and Coleman Hawkins—not that I would gig with them professionally but we're better than acquaintances putting my classified persona deep down in a cave at the bottom of my soul, and jazz found me a way back into the light. I can handle that. I'm well out-fitted that way. Let's say I feel enlightened. But my enlightenment is most everyone's worst nightmare. I have a working knowledge of the *big* picture, Mel, past, present and future.

'No one would believe it even if the president made a State of the Union address about it; they'd all think he was nuts, unless they—the people from out there'—he swept his hand in the air—'came around to endorse him! Our ignorance is skepticism. People are convinced in disbelief. And truth's not going to happen for a long long time.'

'Why is that?'

'Why? Do I have to spell it out? You've come to that conclusion yourself in some of your articles. They're tens of thousands, and some hundreds of thousands, and others hundreds of millions of years ahead of us. We're too ignorant, narrow-minded to even conceive of a basis on which to communicate with them, or understand their significance; we're still wrapped up in a primitive ego. They are very cognizant of our evolutionary timeline—they had something to do with it tens of thousands of years ago, when some of them hybridized us, then cut us loose.

'Believe me, it's true and it's staring us in the face as per Adam and Eve, the original Sumerian prototypes which became the biblical ones. Some mythologies have their inception in truth. That's what I was told; evidently the aliens knew that much about us. How would the authorities bring that to the world?'

'Tell the truth.'

'That's what *I* said.'

'And?'

'Truth is just another illusion to skeptical minds.'

'Can I use that line?'

'Yeah, sure, as long as you heard it from Mike Roberts.'

'I wouldn't even go that far. So tell me more.'

Leverton took a sip of his coffee.

'Fast forward to the present: our blind fate was to obtain crashed disks—

various shuttle craft and living aliens. Believe me, they want nothing to do with us; we're perilous, violent and at war with ourselves. Now that doesn't mean that a few of us can't rationalize our behavior as opposed to theirs; so because of my military expertise in clinical and paranormal study, I was assigned to study, interpret, and research psychologically a live alien for three years in a bunker deep beneath the desert surface. And, consequently, all I wanted to do was set him free! And get him out of that hellhole.'

'Jesus Christ.'

'Hardly,' he responded, barely suppressing this attempt at biblical humor. 'I called him Raphael, after one of the archangels. His real name was unintelligible, like trying to sound off strange radio frequencies. But he didn't really need to speak; he could communicate telepathically, which took some getting used to. When he'd look at you with those big bug eyes they kind of latched onto your brain and paralyzed you, not to harm or control, but to link up which we are pathetically not equipped to do, and so they had the effect of scrubbing down every synaptic fiber with Mr. Clean leaving us dazed and confused.

'Apparently, his species evolved from a cetacean species like dolphins which could use their brains to stun prey. All members of Raphael's species are bipedal like all intelligent humanoids, and have long arms and fingers necessary for their dexterity in building and creating things. He was super skinny and around five feet tall and weighed about fifty pounds. His skin was smooth but tough with almost a whitish-grayish translucent quality if healthy, and more yellowish if not. He claimed to be relatively young at about a hundred of our years. He had no hair, protruding ears or nose, but had nostrils and could hear through highly developed auditory orifices, even underwater.

'As for sexual orientation, there were no visible organs, all were internal. Males would dispense a pollen-like substance and females would absorb it, all ecstatic but best in water, though they could procreate in dry conditions. He breathed our air but needed extra oxygen. He needed proximity to water and green vegetables and seaweeds for nourishment. He did like various protein sources such as krill and small fish, such as smelts. He would not eat land-based meats like chicken or red meats, which were too rich and made him sick. They eliminated liquid waste by excreting it in water, but they could also do it in air; however, the air would give off an ammonia-like smell, so water was best, for obvious reasons.

'As for solids, they were a thicker liquid, which were excreted through an anus; again, water was best. You see, on their planet, water is their main conditional necessity, a bit like us, for hydration, showers and bathing, but much more so, obviously. They were somewhat chameleon-like and by adapting his vocal chords he learned English very quickly.'

Melbo's tea arrived. He stirred in a cube of sugar and cream, which helped offset the shock reverberating through his mind.

'I can't believe we found you,' said Melbo, cautiously. 'I have so many questions...'

'Sure, I know, but first let me tell you something: the kind of people who are in charge of all this are the problem; they represent our worst instincts. Actually, I think they wish it never happened, but since it's real they just want to use the technology to their advantage. They miss the whole point of this amazing crossroad in human history—our chance at truth, our chance at godliness, our chance at turning our pitiful past into an informed, tolerant, sensible future, but these leaders of ours just exemplify our nativist and xenophobic mentality. And they've been told! By Raphael! And others!

'The people in charge can't get their heads around the superiority of these aliens. Do they carry weapons? No. Have they ever in history attacked us in some grab for our planet, like we do in our terrestrial wars? No. These aliens are far beyond our primitive projecting of our fear onto them. We think they are ultimately like us, but they're most emphatically not; they fear us!

'In my final analysis and report, I made it very clear that we should let him go, but also that we should reveal to the world what had happened, and explain the universe as we had learned from them, and our own revised history. This is what Raphael recommended! The cat was out of the bag, so we should attempt to make that leap in our best interests as the human race. Well, the people in charge didn't like my recommendation one bit, as you can imagine. They want to possess all this knowledge for the most selfish reasons. They think of themselves as superior because we are human; their unbelievable stupidity on an emotional level surpasses every rational and judicious ounce of our intelligence. It's an oxymoron, the irony of which confounds all reason! Then they fired me.'

Melbo didn't respond, just sipped his tea. Leverton did the same with his coffee. Melbo liked him, and had the grace to let what he'd been told hang calmly in the air as if they were talking about the Olympics in Rome, but inside he was a cauldron of anxiety. He could feel Leverton's uncanny loneliness, and how he seemed to compartmentalize it like an episode of the *Twilight Zone*.

'Where was he from, this Raphael?' asked Melbo, finally.

'In our description, Zeta Reticula, about forty light years from here.'

'What did he say about himself, his "people"?'

'They don't really talk about themselves. They function like a cohesive unit. Everyone is trained from youth to a general field of use, technically speaking. He was an average person whose domain was aeronautics—a flying engineer would be the closest description. They really didn't have pilots because their ships were driven automatically as if they had brains of their own. In fact, they could communicate with the ship's control telepathically. You see, a specific 'job' if you will, was punched into their computer system—a system we are trying to understand by reverse engineering components of the recovered vehicles.

'All aspects are being rigorously studied, mine being their so-called 'human' element, which was a misnomer from the start. They're devoid of humanity—passion, art, politics, romance—they function on a completely different plane. But that does not make them evil; they are actually rather benign and have no animus towards us. I would say they have an understanding of our primitive behavior but don't qualify it as such—we just are who we are and intend to leave us be, almost as if all is equal in the universe—we are all made of each other in various forms in various timelines. They're interested in our DNA—deoxyribonucleic acid—the genetic coding of all life. It wasn't Raphael's specialty but he said aside from technology it was the driving 'science' of all advanced species.

'DNA is used to enhance, fuse, cure, blend, and hybridize all life. One reason why they were here was simply to take samples of our DNA in order to help them. They have some genetic weaknesses from millennia of artificial breeding, and need to reverse it. Our young human DNA is highly regarded by the Grays—Raphael's species. He claims they are very much a subservient species to the really old ones. There are thousands of species that we group loosely as Reptiles and Nordics, the Grays falling under the Reptile grouping who are more passive-aggressive, some of whom are way beyond our reckoning. The Nordics, so-called, because some of them look very human and have been more sympathetic to our problems on earth at our present stage of development, are the ones who implemented various hybridizations around earth ages ago.

'They consist of various species: black, white, and even bluish and act as protectors for us against the Reptiles, who seek our alignment with them in the future, but nonetheless, both groups contain us for our hostility, nuclear weapons being the enemy of all things, as are fossil fuels.

'The Reptiles are truly incredible. The name can be misleading and attests our human fear factor, as they are not crocodiles, and are ostensibly some of the most advanced species in the universe. Some of the oldest species can actually make themselves look like us by transforming their physiology like chameleons; they reconstitute DNA any way they want using antimatter nanotechnology beyond our understanding. They can go back and forth in time. They play God with impunity. Forgive me, I think they don't just play God; they use the idea of God because they see no answers to it, even at their level.

'Apparently, there are energy fields out there in the universe that have withstood multiple universes over trillions of years. These energy fields, I'm told, seem to be supernaturally intelligent and shut down everything near them like a massive electromagnetic pulse, and unless the transgressor shows some submission or benevolence, it won't be released. If this wasn't the source of some godliness in the universe, then there is none. Perhaps the good in humanity or anywhere is some distant resonance of these very forces.

'Strange but true, according to Raphael. Therefore, it is incumbent on us to seek out these things such as manipulating DNA like so many of the advance species who can live for hundreds of our years, and some even thousands, as incredible as it sounds.'

'I think "incredible" is a bit of an understatement.'

'Believe me it took some getting used to,' he said, with his elbow on the table and thumb and forefinger to the bridge of his nose. He sighed and remained like that for a few moments before continuing. 'I really needed to unload some of this stuff.' Then Leverton paused for at least a quarter minute. Melbo thought he was about to change his mind, but he suddenly started up again. 'It took me almost two years to help Raphael find a way to transfer his way of thinking so I could even understand him. I'll never forget the day in late 1953, December 29…'

*

Earl Bunting took it upon himself to wiretap the Melbos' apartment with the latest equipment he had at his disposal. He stayed away from Prinzenthal's place near Central Park for the time being as a professional courtesy knowing she had quit and that his immediate boss, Aubrey Woods, had let that mission slip away with her being gone and pregnant. Besides, there were so many other Cold War operations all over the world such as the Berlin theater, Vietnam, the Gary Powers debacle, and the CIA-planned invasion of Cuba, in the last of which he had an important part with Eduardo Sanchez, his wily cut-out and point man.

Anyway, the bosses had everyone running in every direction, so he could easily manage a sideshow. Bunting figured there was more to Greenfield and Prinzenthal's new friendship with the Melbos as newlyweds. When he had been seen, just as he had planned it, in the King Cole lounge after his altercation with Greenfield outside the city hall before their rather hasty marriage, it suddenly dawned on him there had to have been some very deft tradecraft in all their familiarity—a double blind whereby Prinzenthal had used her cover with the mission with Melbo as a mask for something deeper within their relationship.

Naturally of a suspicious mind, and a certain unacknowledged jealously of Greenfield's relationship with Prinzenthal, Bunting was quite prepared to go rogue on account of it; after all that was his specialty. He didn't really care what they were up to; he just wanted the satisfaction of seeing them fail at whatever it was. And if perchance he was proved right, his superiors would reward him—one man gathers what another man spills. To what purpose he knew not, but Hannah Prinzenthal loomed large in his twisted mind.

Phil Garvey, a mentor to Bunting, had used him in one of a number of cut-outs since the end of the war in dirty operations. Some of them were dead, others retired, all serious bastards. Anyone who worked for Garvey was not what anyone would call a decent human being, or if he was he wouldn't last long. They were killers who inhabited the underworld of drugs, crime, and political corruption, some of it necessary to undermine the Communists. Garvey was well-used by his superiors the likes of Sulla and Woods as the sharp point of the spear in Cold War intrigues.

For the most part, the underworld appreciated Garvey because he had the deep pockets of the government behind him, and rarely did an operation fail in its financial obligations. For most of the players when Garvey called in his agents, there was little hesitation because he delivered. If some player did not do his part he or she was tempting the devil, and the devil is the epitome of patience. One of these fellows was Gerald Osbourne, who as a known confidence man had murdered a mobster in Milan on his own volition, was an important informant for the company and rival to Osbourne's burgeoning business ventures.

At fifty, he was a few years younger than Bunting, and, loquacious and swarthy, spoke Italian like a native, born of an Italian immigrant mother in the Bronx. Osbourne was known by his nickname 'Johnny Goodnight' because he sent off his victims quietly, the Italian mobster being one with his throat cut. The 'Johnny' came from his European prostitution business begun during and after the war in Italy where he worked for the fledgling CIA, and muscled in on the lucrative market of soldiers in need of some tender loving care. This extended to France and Germany in the years ahead.

When years later, the company found out that Johnny had killed their informant, it was leaked to the Italians that he was responsible. Johnny hightailed it back to New York, living under another name, Joe di Lucca. It was Bunting who helped di Lucca escape from Italy and obtain a new identity. Now di Lucca did the occasional job for Bunting and monitored the wiretap of Melbo's apartment.

There was little forthcoming information other than some rather plenteous sexual activity. They were a happy couple and spoke mainly of work, living or family related topics. To the Melbos' credit, nary a mention of Greenfield and Prinzenthal was apparent, other than some references to their wedding and the possibility of taking some holidays up in Cape Cod. On the face of it, they were like any couple who wanted to get away from the city in August. The Melbos, of course, had been cautioned by Greenfield never to talk about their mission at home in case there were some bugs planted. They were told that Greenfield could do a professional sweep of the apartment, but that in itself would raise a red flag, so it would be best to just carry on as usual. Privately, they even flattered themselves: if there were bugs, their sexual proclivities became somewhat conspicuously accentuated.

One day, they did not come home, or the next day or those following. Di Lucca called Bunting and reported as much saying they had gone on holidays, likely to Cape Cod.

'Where in Cape Cod?' asked Bunting.

'Never said,' replied di Lucca.

'Come on, Johnny; give me something.'

'How the fuck should I know? They didn't say, ever.'

'Why Cape Cod?'

'You could ask twenty thousand people the same thing, Earl.'

'Yeah, but there's gotta be a reason.'

'Beats me.'

'And Greenfield? What about him?'

'What about him? Does he have a place there?'

'I'm asking you.'

'I know nothin' about Greenfield.'

'Maybe you should take a few days and go up there.'

'Cape Cod? You're shittin' me. I wouldn't have a clue.'

'I'd go myself but I'm up to my ears here in New Orleans.'

'If you're payin' I don't mind a few days away, but where in Cape Cod? They could be anywhere?'

'Start with Hyannis Port.'

'Why there?' asked Di Lucca.

'The Kennedys have a place there.'

'So you think Melbo was invited up for the weekend?' He laughed.

'Just have a looksee.'

'These people have something on you, Earl?'

'Just doin' my job. Take one of your girls along so you'll fit in like a regular guy.'

'If you say so.'

'Joe, don't sound so goddamned unwilling.'

'Alright, alright, I have a bird, Cherry; she's willing.' He smirked.

'Okay.'

'I almost forgot.'

'Yeah?'

'I followed him the other day.'

'Who?'

'Melbo.'

'And?'

235

'He met up with some guy in the village. Tried to make it seem like they didn't know each other; real amateurs.'

'What happened?'

'Nothing. They spent at least an hour over coffee at the Café Wha?'

'Who was this guy he met?'

'Looked like some local Village guy. A friend likely, but the way they met and split and met again didn't seem right, so I went in and had a coffee as near as I could.'

'All I got was his name, Mike something. A wiry fellow, kinda worried, down and out sort, older, about sixty.'

'Did you get a photo?'

'After, I did. I know where he lives.'

'Good. Send me the photo.'

'In Washington?'

'Yeah.'

20. Monomoy

The oppressive humidity lifted overnight with the wind shifting to the north. Everyone slept like logs. In the morning, they gathered on the veranda for a light breakfast of toast and fruit, juice and coffee. Lewis Bay stretched out before them. The yacht *Becky* was moored at least a hundred feet off the beach, the clanking of its rigging barely heard in a light breeze. Greenfield's sister, Peggy Sackett, and her family had gone North on an annual trip to Campobello Island in New Brunswick, where Franklin Roosevelt used to spend his summers growing up.

It had been arranged at the wedding that Greenfield could use the cottage that week. Prior to that, he had also been in touch with someone he knew at the marina in Hyannis; he was inquiring about the whereabouts of Kennedy, who for obvious reasons hadn't been around, but the local vibe was that he was coming soon for a few days, as the *Victura*, his beloved sailboat, a sloop given to him on his fifteenth birthday, was being serviced.

'Today's the day,' announced Greenfield.

'For what?' asked DeCourt.

'To go sailing, of course.'

'I thought you meant something else,' she replied.

'Have you ever sailed, Melissa?' asked Greenfield with a big smile.

'No,' said DeCourt, 'unless you count camp dinghies with one little sail.'

'Then you've sailed; size doesn't matter.'

Prinzenthal laughed. 'Don't be too sure, Harley.'

'Tut tut, honeybee; in terms of the basics, one size fits all contingencies.'

'Really?' DeCourt wondered.

'For our purposes, yes; you'll love it.'

'Where will we go?' she asked.

'We could head for Cape Poge, then east to Monomoy Point, all within the Sound.'

'Sounds fantastic.'

'We can picnic there, too.'

'Aye aye, skipper. When do we set sail?' quipped Melbo.

The plan was to embark by mid-morning. Prinzenthal and DeCourt went shopping, while Melbo and Greenfield went out to the *Becky* in the little outboard dinghy to make sure all was ship-shape. Greenfield started the motor and checked the rigging, the pump and did some general maintenance; then they took the yacht for a spin to the nearest jetty that sold gasoline and topped it up, and filled up the fresh water as well. After, Greenfield went to a telephone booth and made a call.

On the way back Greenfield explained to Melbo what he had been doing since the day before, when he and DeCourt had arrived.

'It seems our ship is coming in, Mel.'

'How so?'

'I spoke with Dick, your boss, about you possibly meeting Kennedy— under the public radar. He's already been in touch with one of Kennedy's staff, who on my initiative, was to slip Kennedy a sealed note bearing your name and Judith Graham's: you're both on holiday sailing in Cape Cod.'

'And did he get a response?'

'No.'

'So what now?'

'But he didn't say no either.'

'So you want to just happen to meet up with him sailing?'

'That's the idea.'

'What's the point if he doesn't want to meet with me?'

'The fact that we're in Cape Cod leaves it open I think.'

'Seems a bit far-fetched.'

'Let me put it this way: he and Judith Graham have a past—long since passed, mind you—Berlin 1945. When we spoke a few months back, he was quite intrigued with the idea of seeing her again, as an insider. She'll be your ticket.'

'Does Hannah know what's going on?'

'Only the big picture. Otherwise, her surprise won't be genuine.'

'I admit I'm rather flattered by all this.'

'Yeah, well, sometimes we have to give fate a little push, you know.'

'What if he's with his family? Jackie's pregnant.'

'We'll just do the best we can.'

'You have no idea where he'll be or even if he goes sailing.'

'Someone will radio me when he leaves Hyannis Port.'

'How do you know he'll go sailing?'

'He's a sailor; I just found out he's here. Today is a perfect day for sailing. I'm almost certain he will go out...politics be damned, today.'

'Well there's always tomorrow.'

'Yes, but today is the day. I would even hazard a guess he's expecting us out there.'

'Won't he have security?'

'Perhaps, but once he knows it's us nearby, he'll wave them off.'

'This is quite the spin, Harley. You really are an old pro.'

*

The day was indeed perfect. By noon the temperature had reached almost eighty degrees and getting warmer; a decent breeze came up and a cerulean sky mirrored in the sparkling blue sea. They sailed with the wind, towing the little dinghy towards the lighthouse at Cape Poge. Greenfield had given the wheel to DeCourt, who now beamed under the brilliant sun. About halfway to the lighthouse, the radio on an open channel stuttered to life, and the voice of a garrulous sea-dog voice proclaimed that these were the best sailing conditions in Nantucket Sound all summer. Then closed with a rather odd addendum: 'Ship ahoy! Monomoy!'

'Who is that?' called out DeCourt above the wind surf.

'That, my dear, is Nate Jenkins!' exclaimed Greenfield. 'He's an old friend who taught me how to sail as a boy. We used to call him "Spike" because in his flask he'd spike Coca Cola with rum, mostly rum.'

'Does he always do that?'

'Spike his rum?'

'No, the message?'

'Not as a rule, but I asked him to say "Ship Ahoy!" if JFK was heading out in the *Victura*, his sloop. So let's go ready-about and try to locate him.'

'He said Monomoy, too,'

'I think he meant that he was heading toward Monomoy, a giant sandbar.'

'What if a lot of other boats are around?'

'If all goes well, he'll know what to do.'

DeCourt went about and turned the yacht around so they were heading northeast tacking against the wind. Greenfield pulled from a drawer an old spyglass—an antique monocular telescope like something Admiral Farragut would've used and scanned the horizon. Numerous boats were heading in every direction.

'Still too far away,' said Greenfield. 'Steer for that land you can see to the east in the distance. If they're heading there we'll cross their wake at some point.'

An hour later Greenfield called out: 'I think I see it. That sloop really moves. There's a launch keeping its distance behind her.'

'Must be the muscle,' offered Melbo. 'How do we approach him without attracting undue attention?'

'We'll come in parallel about a quarter mile away, and let him approach us, and head for the south point; it'll be calm there.'

Another hour went by before they came within a quarter mile south of the sloop. Prinzenthal took the helm. By then Greenfield had confirmed it was Kennedy with Jackie and another couple, all wearing sunglasses; no children were on board. Kennedy's boat headed closer, as Greenfield had predicted, and the launch came between them. Greenfield could see Kennedy gesturing with his arm for them to back off, and they did just that to the previous position. Before long they were slipping through the waves side by side no more than a hundred feet apart.

DeCourt took the helm again for a few minutes while Greenfield and Prinzenthal also wearing sunglasses stood up on the foredeck and waved happily arm in arm giving them a good look. Kennedy and his guests waved back. Eventually the two boats reached the lee side of the south point of Monomoy, where the wind died down to a slight breeze. Close to shore the boats came along side each other facing north with their sails luffing gently in irons.

Greenfield pulled out a six-foot boat-hook and the man aboard Kennedy's boat grabbed it, pulling the boats together. Prinzenthal came up beside Greenfield. Kennedy stood up next to the man with one foot on the gunnel. Melbo dropped the anchor and secured it on a cleat.

'Hello Senator,' said Greenfield, extending his hand. 'Harley Greenfield. What a coincidence. I saw you from a distance with the old spyglass and thought it right to at least say hello.'

'Harley, of course; and thank you.' Kennedy turned to Jackie and his guests. 'My wife, Jackie, and Reed and Sally Burton, an old school chum of mine, who's helping a little with the election.'

'Pleased to meet you,' said Greenfield, shaking Reed Burton's hand. 'May I introduce my wife Hannah, and our friends George and Melissa Melbo.'

Greetings were exchanged without them shaking hands because of the gap between the boats.

'So you tied the knot?' Kennedy smiled, looking at Prinzenthal.

'Finally, after a fifteen year engagement,' returned Prinzenthal, 'In New York last week. We thought of inviting you, but knew you were rather busy.'

There were laughs all around.

'If I had known I would have made an effort to alter my schedule!' joked Kennedy before turning to Jackie, and his guests. 'Harley and Hannah worked in the State Department,' he informed them, 'I first met them in Berlin at the Potsdam conference, 1945. I couldn't believe my ears when I heard Hannah speaking Russian to Stalin. These are real American heroes, Cold War veterans.'

'Well, that's all behind us now; we're expecting a new addition to our conjugal union.' Prinzenthal said, putting her hand to her womb.

'How wonderful,' said Jackie, graciously. 'How far along are you?'

'Oh, about two months.'

'I'm six months,' she said, holding her tummy.

'I'm very happy for you both. The baby will come just after Jack wins the election.'

They all laughed again.

'That baby will be the deciding factor,' said Burton.

'And Jackie,' agreed Sally Burton.

'Let's not jump to conclusions,' added Jackie.

'Are you the George Melbo who writes for the New York Trib?' asked Burton.

'Guilty,' stated Melbo.

'Well let me tell you how interesting your views are. You write with great conviction. Eh, Jack?'

'That he does. They really spurred my interest on a personal level; I know a few things myself. I could use someone like you on my team, George, but then I'd have to field a lot of awkward questions about what's going on in our skies. I don't think it's the right time, in an election year, to bring that kind of controversy into the public forum.'

'Well, count me a supporter, Senator,' replied Melbo, 'in spite of my affiliation with the Trib. And I would certainly defer to your judgement in the political arena, with few exceptions.'

'Don't tell me that, George, and you can call me Jack here; I read the one about the convention; I got a lot of flak for that, but first and foremost I aim to win this election and, though I'd prefer to have Symington, Lyndon does own the south. Nixon is one formidable opponent with a huge following in the hinterlands, America's gut. However, I'll say this and I've said it enough times; it's on people like you that the success of our future depends.'

'Thank you, Jack; I appreciate your candor.'

'Believe me, I wish I could've had Symington; he's a much better man than Lyndon, but there are some things we can't have if we are to stay the course to victory. I considered it a small sacrifice for the greater good.'

'Jack,' interposed Greenfield carefully, 'we've imposed on you this glorious day. With no further ado would you mind a short briefing in private so we could then get back to what we love most?'

Kennedy turned to Jackie. 'Give me a half hour; it's important we do this now; it wouldn't happen otherwise.' Then he turned to Greenfield. 'Harley, what do you have in mind?'

'Let's take the dinghy to the shore. George will accompany us. Hannah and Melissa will stay.'

'Fine, though Reed here might feel a little intimidated with four gorgeous women.'

'Hey, don't worry about me; Sally has my back.'

'We'll look after him,' said Jackie. 'Do you want some refreshments?'

'We'll take our cooler,' Greenfield answered.

With that Kennedy stepped into the *Becky*. Melbo pulled in the dinghy, and they all got in with the cooler. Greenfield started up the little fifteen horsepower Evinrude, and they drove the hundred yards to shore, where they beached it. Melbo jumped out with Kennedy in bare feet and shorts and they both pulled the boat onto the beach with the motor locked in the tilt position.

Melbo couldn't have felt more exhilarated, being there with Kennedy and his modest, easy-going manner. Here was the hero of the PT 109 battle, crash and rescue like one of the boys on a beach. Here was the most famous man in America, the great orator and hope for the future; a man blessed with social charm and poise, with an almost reckless charisma, ready to take on the massive conglomerate that was America in which deep state right wing agendas were entrenched. But he was born to it, backed by fabulous wealth and intelligence.

They sat down below a grassy dune. Greenfield opened the cooler. In it packed with ice were six bottles of Heineken and three large bottles of water.

'What'll it be guys?' said Greenfield.

All three took a Heineken.

'I really shouldn't,' said Kennedy, 'but it's so beautiful today…you only live once! Cheers!'

They all clinked their bottles.

'I used to come here as a kid sometimes,' said Kennedy. 'Did you know there used to be fishing settlements here long ago—just back there was one called Whitewash by Powder Hole, a decent harbor. It had two hundred people, a tavern and school, but it was abandoned after a hurricane just before the civil war.'

'I'd heard that,' said Greenfield. Like you, I spent my summers here as a kid. My sister, Peggy Sackett, has the cottage now.'

'How old are you, Harley? Fifty?'

'Fifty-seven. Born in Hartford.'

'Damn, you're a young fifty-seven.'

'I have to be with that wife of mine; she's insatiable.'

They had a good laugh.

'We're all lucky to have good women in our lives. Jackie's like my rock and North Star, my true mate; she has impeccable judgement. I'm not as good as she is.'

'Hannah's always been the only one for me, or bust.'

'From the sounds of it, you two have been through a lot.'

'I still get nightmares.'

'Indulge me, Harley. What was the worst?'

Greenfield sighed, looking out to the boats. He could see Hannah laughing.

'There were at least three incidents that were razor's edge. The worst? One time in East Berlin about ten years ago one of her contacts—a military liaison between the East Germans and Soviets—named Kapitän Gunter Brass—was compromised by the East Germans without her knowing—he hadn't identified her because he apparently had fallen in love with her—she was unaware of the situation and we had no way of contacting her. Fortunately, we found out through another channel that they were onto him. It was a race between the Stasi and me to get to her first. I was in West Berlin as her handler. She had previously given us an address where she and Brass would meet. I found them in bed. I killed him. We made it out of there not two minutes before the Stasi arrived.'

'Jesus. How'd you kill him?'

'I strangled him.'

'What was Hannah doing?'

'Lying there naked.'

'God, what a sight.'

'"God" is right; she gave him a perfect send-off.'

'She did? As you strangled him?'

'I told her the Stasi knew about them.'

'What happened?'

'She didn't know what else to do but hold him to her with her legs; he didn't resist so much, having just got off. Lucky for him I guess. Not a bad way to go, considering what they would've done to him.'

'That's some story. In a way we'd all like to be so lucky.'

'Well, at least in the timing, yet she didn't forgive me for at least a year, even after I saved her life.'

'She's a rare woman; no doubt about it. And what of your wife, George?'

'I can't say she's as rare as Hannah, but she's equally my loving wife. She works in publishing.'

'Mine did as well, briefly before we were married.'

There followed a silence during which they took swigs of their beer.

'Senator, if I may,' said Greenfield. 'Since we last spoke, we've been working to find out as much as we can about the deep state of our elected government. Unavoidably, George here became a kind of canary, as he uncovered brilliantly what has been going on with UFOs, all instigated by his editor, Dick Sinclair, who actually witnessed the July 1952 mass sightings over Washington. He couldn't get his head around the phenomenal technology of these UFOs and the lack of response from our government.'

'Right. Let's get to it. What do you know?'

Greenfield paused for a moment.

'I'm just going to spell it out in plain language. Within the present legitimate government, there is a cabal of senior people who are not subject to any oversight, even by the president. They are in the intelligence community, the military and some are civilians with science and other backgrounds. This group was set up originally by Truman to deal with the crash and retrieval of alien disks, as you are aware. Then Eisenhower excused himself of this group of his executive authority for political and legislative reasons—primarily plausible deniability because of the nature of its extremely sensitive research, especially in light of public interest and the continued sightings of these so-called UFOs.

'Over the years, by default this group has gained unprecedented power, exclusively dominated by a select Republican elite. The excuse for this draconian power grab is National Security and the Cold War. Now Mel here has written his articles on the subject and has attracted some attention, both positive and negative, as you can imagine. Some very credible people have secretly come forward and revealed themselves to him, the most recent one being a psychologist who spent three years in a deep bunker in the desert studying a live alien in the custody of the working group, sometimes called Majestic-12.

'He and the alien apparently became friends and over the years he learned about alien civilizations and their technology. This psychologist pleaded with his superiors to release the alien, and to reveal in a graduated way to the general public—humanity—that we are not alone by a long shot. He was fired.'

'And you interviewed this man?' asked Kennedy, turning to Melbo.

'Yes, sir.'

'And he's who he says he is?'

'Without a doubt.'

'So why are you the canary? What happened to make you think you are?'

'They started spying on me, sir. Harley knows these people, and Hannah was approached to inform on me. This was before they knew of any connection between Hannah and me. To us it was a bit of a joke, but we went through the motions. She 'befriended' me in a sandwich shop.'

'But they know now.'

'Yes, of course; we attended Harley and Hannah's wedding.'

Greenfield added, 'Logistically, they "created" our friendship. So far, we are free and clear of any deceit in their view. And of course, Mel here is a well-respected investigative journalist who works for Jake Whitmore's paper. Last May, he was even invited to Whitmore's grandiose birthday party that all the bigwigs attended, including the president.'

'But not Nixon.'

'No,' said Melbo. 'Though Hannah attended.'

'Really? And not you, Harley?' inquired Kennedy.

'No, I was out of the picture then. Hannah is much beloved by the intelligence community. She went to the event with Dr. Teller, an old family friend, and was introduced to the president.'

'Teller worked with Oppenheimer.'

'He did.'

'You've managed very well, Harley, but why this urgency? I know what I'm up against with that group. If I become president I can change all that.'

'If I may, Jack,' said Greenfield, 'if you become president, you must wipe clean the entire old administration, including Hoover and Sulla. They have become entrenched, and you will have no control over what they're really up to. Ruthless people are involved here. I decided to quit on account of them; so did Hannah, just last week.'

'Come now, that goes against my democratic instincts. If both parties don't work together, our purpose is lost.'

'It may already be lost, sir,' said Melbo. 'By using this alien excuse in a manner of speaking, they've usurped the power of the presidency. If a strong president wants to change things and the group feels a threat to their agenda, they could take him out; they'd be untouchable because no one knows what is going on. They'd be like a satellite government beyond the legal oversight— an invisible hand. It's a dangerous precedent.'

'He's right, Jack,' stressed Greenfield.

'Duly noted, fellows, but I don't buy it. We're all Americans here, with our best interests at heart. Sure, the Republicans are a bunch of dinosaurs. Lincoln would roll in his grave if he knew what his party had become. But I have to believe in the goodness of our intentions. If I get into power, I will address these issues. I will find out all there is to know, and I could use help, from all of you.'

Kennedy stood up, downed the remainder of his beer, and put the bottle back in the cooler.

'If you don't mind I think I'll swim back; I could use the exercise. Thanks for the beer!' With that he dove into the surf. All Greenfield and Melbo could do was look on.

*

Gerald Osbourne aka Johnny Goodnight aka Joe di Lucca sat on a beach near the Hyannis Port Yacht Club. With him was Cherry aka Rose McCann, a pretty nineteen year old girl from the Bronx with a pale complexion and black hair. She sat under a rented beach umbrella wearing a black bikini, while di Lucca scanned the bay with binoculars. They had been there all day since mid-morning, in time to see Kennedy head out in the *Victura*. Di Lucca searched for other boats of any kind, trying to identify any of the occupants as Melbo and his wife. It seemed like a futile task, and as the day wore on, Cherry was getting increasingly impatient.

'Come on, Joey,' she complained, pouting, 'if you've seen one boat you've seen them all. Let's go get a drink or something.'

'Help yourself, Cherry, I'll stay here. These boats interest me; I'm thinkin' of making an investment.'

'What for? You a sailor boy?'

'Yeah, why not?'

'I don't know how to swim, for one.'

'You can learn.'

'You gonna teach me?'

'Sure.'

He put down the binoculars and turned to her, his favorite young tart. They had driven up the night before in his black Corvette convertible, one of three cars he owned, and luckily found a cheap motel room in Hyannis, when no one showed up to claim the reservation. Over a few drinks at a local pub, they ate fish and chips then back in their room fucked themselves silly. In the morning, they fucked some more, before enjoying the motel breakfast of sunny-side eggs and bacon, toast and coffee. Di Lucca figured a paid holiday shouldn't be a total waste of time, and Cherry, suffering from delusions of marriage, was game.

'Listen,' he said, 'tonight we'll find a nice steakhouse and live it up. What do ya say?'

'I say okay.'

She got up. 'I'm going for a walk.'

Di Lucca picked up the binoculars again to focus on a sailboat coming in from the distance. It was the *Victura,* with the launch a few hundred yards behind.

'Maybe I'll join you, Cherry love.'

He stood up with the binoculars around his neck, and taking her hand, headed towards the club docks, where he noticed the *Victura* being moored farther down, along the private beach of the Joseph Kennedy family property. The launch, meanwhile, was being moored at the club docks. The older men aboard were obviously security; some of the crew were boat hands and quite young. Di Lucca approached one who had just finished tying up.

'Is that Jack Kennedy over there?' he asked, presenting himself like a gawking tourist, with Cherry hanging on to his arm.

'Yes, it is,' replied the youth, 'taking a break from the campaign trail.'

'That's a real nice sloop. Where did they sail?'

'Out to Monomoy then across to Martha's Vineyard.'

'That's a fair distance. He must do that in good time.'

'Oh, it's fast alright; would've been faster if he hadn't stopped at Monomoy.'

'Something the matter?'

'Nah, just met up with some friends.'

'In a sailboat?' he inquired casually.

'Yeah. A real nice pilot cutter about thirty feet. *Becky* it was called. Mr. Kennedy, he knows a lot of people around here. Some say this is ground zero for his election race.'

The boy smiled at them.

'Be sure to vote for him; he's the right man at the right time.'

'I'm looking at sailboats myself. Thinking of buying one,' said di Lucca, seizing the opportunity to get information. 'Would you know anything about these friends or their sailboat?'

'Don't know 'em. I could make enquiries for you. I'm Jimmy, the son of the harbormaster.' He held out his hand.

'Joe,' said Di Lucca, 'and this here's my daughter, Rosie.'

'Hi Jimmy,' purred Cherry, shaking his hand, too.

Jimmy looked at her and melted; she couldn't have been much older than him.

'My dad's in there.' He pointed to the building behind them. 'He knows everybody.'

'That's awfully kind of you, Jim,' Cherry said. 'Can a girl get a drink in there?'

'Sure can, I'm a member.'

Jim bounded ahead, and they followed him leisurely.

'Why'd you call me your daughter, Joe?'

'Because I wanna milk this guy for information about boats.'

'So what!'

'Listen, I'll throw a few bills your way for doing me a favor, see? Go to Jimmy, and take a hike. Give him a blowjob or something. I need to do some business.'

'And I thought this was a romantic getaway.' She pouted.

'It is darling, and you're my cherry pie, don't forget it. I'll make it up to you.'

'Oh, fine then!' She hurried after Jimmy.

21. The Mission

The William James family lived on O Street in Georgetown, Washington. They were Episcopalians who had a relatively liberal involvement in spiritual well-being. After the revolution a number of the Anglican Americans became Episcopalian—a kind of mixed Protestant-Catholic congregation. Traditionally, however, and fundamental to the James family's values, their children took their Sunday lessons at the local church, a two hundred year-old red-brick edifice nearby. Every Sunday, William James attended services, a much needed personal restorative to his senior position as a counterintelligence agent with the FBI, and unofficial liaison to the CIA; his much older brother-in-law was Aubrey Woods, one of the operational chiefs of the company.

Nevin, William's adolescent son, had been going reluctantly to the Sunday school for a number of years. Increasingly, though, he began to question the entire approach to his 'studies' and the longer he went, the more sophisticated his responses became. It dawned on him that perhaps he was meant to be a "truth-seeker" and he rejected the blind obedience to religious doctrine. "Isn't that what Jesus was? A rebel?" he'd ask his teacher, Elton Purdy, a rotund junior deacon, who would begin to ignore him because of his disruptions in the class. Or, "Jesus had a body like any of us, so was he a man or God?"

The deacon explained that Jesus ascended to heaven to sit with God, and we must listen to his sermons and learn from his example, as he was a teacher. "But is it true, or just wishful thinking?" returned Nevin. And so the argument would go round and round.

A wavy-haired brunette about Nevin's age named Mary McBride, known as Mollie to her family and close friends, was of similar inclination. Sometimes during break they would hide in the basement behind an old piano and some chairs and skip class. She said giggling that when she asked her mother what happened if Jesus had to pee, her mother scolded her for asking. But being stubborn she told her mother he didn't have a "dink" like her daddy, and her mother said of course he did, but that his water was pure. Even more cheekily, Mollie tried to get Nevin to show his "dink" to her. Nevin refused, but when she suggested she show her "mouse", he would have to show his "dink". So they did and laughed as they gazed at each other. Later, she let him touch her there, and he became erect and then she touched him. Embarrassed at how silly and naughty it all was, they didn't see each other for a while.

In his own mind, Nevin felt a new empowerment. Mollie had given him something by her curiosity. It impelled him to be more overtly curious, too, since he had overheard Uncle Aubrey speaking about secret things. The very nature of Nevin's secret world bloomed into a sort of mantra for knowledge. He realized at his young age that the world was full of mystery, and he wanted to discover its secrets. No more *Hardy Boys*. He told Mollie he wanted to be a secret agent. She said she wanted to be one, too. They even kissed to seal the deal, and petted each other more vigorously. She let him feel her little breasts but she became so aroused that she stopped and said if they continue, they would have a baby, even though it was unlikely at their age since she had yet barely begun menstruating.

In an agitated state, Nevin knew enough to say that couldn't happen because he hadn't put his "dink" in her "mouse"; this mollified her, and she let him touch her gently for some extended length of time before she cried out and then instinctively did the same for him with her hand. Enjoying their moment of ecstatic temptation, they did not see or hear the deacon who, happening to pass by, heard unusual gasps and then craning his neck around the piano, witnessed to his horror their feverish *prova sessuale*. Stunned for a moment, his eyes fixed on these young teenagers' *atto flagrante*, he quickly and quietly removed himself, too embarrassed or shocked to interfere under God's roof.

At home that night, reeling between guilt and love, Nevin moped around the house, the reverberations of their intimacy recycling in his mind. His father had been called away for an emergency meeting, and to appease his beating brain, Nevin ventured into his father's study where no one, not even his mother was supposed to go. His sister and mother were watching *Bonanza* and *What's My Line?* and the door to the study had been left unlocked probably due to the hurried departure of his father.

He sat at the desk and opened the drawers, but found little of interest. One drawer was locked. He looked for a key by rummaging in the other drawers, careful to keep the contents in the same order. He looked around the study;

there were a few items on tables and shelves. He picked them up to look underneath or inside, but he still found nothing. Then he went to the bookshelves. Nothing seemed out of the ordinary, until he noticed a new book *The Craft of Intelligence* by Allen Sulla protruding more than the others. He pulled the book out, opened the clean-paper-jacketed cover, and turned the crisp new pages. On the first page he read a note signed by Sulla himself: *To William James, We're in good hands! Allen Sulla.* He read for a while, but got bored. Then, as he was replacing the book, he noticed a small key at the back in the space.

The key fit the lock on the drawer. Excitedly, Nevin opened it, and to his surprise found a notebook among letters and mementos. In the notebook he found handwritten pieces of paper with scribbles and notations that went back to his father's university days, and war years. There were several photos of friends, men and women together. Nevin, slightly astonished, looked to the door and listened for anyone. It seemed his dad had an active life, or did have outside his work.

Under the notebook was a folder, which he took out and opened. He went through numerous newspaper clippings quickly, most of them being short reportages of strange things seen in the sky—UFOs. One was a front page cover story and photo in the Washington Herald from July, 1952. He read it utterly fascinated by the seriousness and implications of the phenomena. Then he found a series of articles from the present year all written by George Melbo in the New York Herald Tribune. *Melbo.* He remembered the name from eavesdropping at Uncle Aubrey's. He quickly read them, and came to the last one dated just a week before.

August 20, 1960
The New York Herald Tribune
Special Feature—Alien Logic
By George Melbo

Indulge me, dear reader, I want to thank you for your continuing faith (or curiosity) in my assignment here as a writer of stupendous developments. Whether political, cultural, or indeed miraculous, I am bound to you as the other half of the public whole, a relationship best described as the freedom of the press! Now I beg of you neither to commend nor to acclaim my work, ascribing it to any renown or infamy, because quite simply I am a reporter, who seeks only to convey the results of my investigations because I was given the task by my superiors. Please leave it at that.

However, the story goes on and new revelations have occurred and been received with a growing notoriety. Strangers will write to me, or contact me, with extraordinary tales of mysteries which they purport to have witnessed. How do I determine whether these accounts are true? How do I know they are all credible sources? The very nature of the paranormal and reporting of it leaves me wide open to ridicule and to charges of indulging in reckless conjecture. Therefore, I can only submit to the provenance of my honor as a kind of last refuge. Amen.

This refuge of provenance is in effect the protection of my sources; and I can tell you they are ironclad. Nothing I have written is wildly personal fiction or exaggeration. For instance, if we include ourselves amongst those who profess a belief in some higher knowledge, we are simply following in a long history of human experience. The presentations in Sumerian texts of Adam and Eve as the true prototypes of humankind: the Roman ideal of Pax Romana, that is the concept of the civilizing of the so-called barbarian hordes, which provided the empire with the justification for conquering or else being conquered; the precepts of Christianity based on one Judean's exemplary life and teachings, displayed in his struggle to reform his faith in the name of God the Father; and the long trajectory of philosophical and scientific enlightenment from ancient to present times—undoubtedly, all of these suggested pieces of human narrative, and many more, are generally recognized as attempts to document our upward movement across the millennia, culminating in our present dominance.

It is easy for us to feel superior in light of this ascent of Man (or Woman— my wife had something to say about that!). Our emergence from the primordial soup is a fact. Our intelligence is a fact, judging by our progress since the Stone Age, though some might argue about that! Let's allow God to be the judge, given our perception of Him as a Supreme Being—a euphemism, if I may, offered as an explanation for the greatest mystery: life in the universe! Because nothing is above the concept of God (or wondrous numinosity) whether you believe in it or not: why are we here? This question is what leads to the premise of Alien Logic.

Let me tell a story. I will describe my understanding of alien logic with a hypothetical situation. But can we agree from the outset that a hypothetical situation might well be another term for the truth? If yes, read on; if no, humor yourselves with the notion of your own superiority because you work hard, pay your taxes (or not), are self-made (or not), and subscribe to moral convention like all good philistines (or not)—the salt of the earth, but likely with a few peccadillos (kept to yourself)! We are a forgiving group, if you meet the rigorous and social standards of our place in time (or not). And you know what? Responsible people—insiders in government—are in charge, who as the ubiquitous non-believers of aliens, now have to believe what their eyes have seen, and moreover must protect the public from what must remain in their view non-believed!

So, here's the hypothetical circumstance: in a bunker under the desert somewhere out west an alien has been removed from a crashed 'flying saucer'. This small, wiry, hairless, alien with dark, almond-shaped eyes, dressed in loose-fitting inmate cottons and slippers—let's call him Bobbo—has for years been living in a windowless room with a cot, desk, running water—shower and bath—kitchenette and a shelf holding a chess set, playing cards, Monopoly, Scrabble, Backgammon, multifarious scientific technical manuals, as well as coffee-table books of photography showing Paris, Germany before the wars, the illustrated British Empire, Asia and America, an atlas and a box of magazines including, National Geographic, Look and Life, and funnily the children's book, The Cat in the Hat!

Bobbo has been systematically examined by various doctors—medical and others, including a psychologist and psychiatrist. The general consensus of these doctors is that Bobbo is humanoid with a working anatomy (albeit different) and brain, but that's as far as it goes, because his mind is not at all like ours. His perception is considered dysfunctional because we have no way to measure his intelligence by reference to ours. His feelings are inexplicable to us because he didn't seem to have any feelings at all. Nor does he react to any of our attempts to elicit a response through painful procedures, such as anal and oral biopsies, a bone marrow and spinal tap. In other words he appears incapable of any empathy for human sentiment in idea or realization—in other words, an automaton astronaut.

One doctor didn't see it that way. At night he would take Bobbo up to the surface and star-gaze. He attempted to teach him English with little success, until one day during a meeting between Bobbo and a committee of important men who sat behind a viewing window as if the alien were a violent criminal *about to be executed. The doctor, on Bobbo's side, began to report on his efforts to understand who Bobbo was, where he came from, and what he knew of Earth and the universe. To the doctor's surprise, after twenty months of relative silence, Bobbo began to speak in a clear staccato English, easily understood.*

He explained that he was an ordinary engineer-technician from Zeta Reticula (in our lingo). He understood that he was of exceptional interest to them and proceeded to communicate what he knew of the universe. His 'people' were part of a loose confederation of advanced species numbering in the thousands, some of which were hundreds of millions of years old. Their species was still young, with problems concerning sterility, and needed primitive human DNA to reverse some of these problems.

In the universe, this was done on the principle of sharing of resources to enhance life everywhere, life being precious and fragile in the hostile environment of space. Despite the disparity between highly advanced and primitive species, there is a general understanding that all species are cherished as one. It's true that some species are dangerous, especially those with primitive agendas who discover interstellar space travel; these are isolated until they reform their militant tendencies—we would likely be such a species.

For the benefit of the committee of men, Bobbo even explained using his own rudimentary equations to describe the existential meaning of God. He said no life form is above the mystery of life: x=all life is equal; y=all life is forfeit to change; z=God in birth and death; xyz=life as manipulated through natural evolution (y) and then genetically manufactured in longer life, health, compassion and love (z); xyz-squared=conscience sublimated in the search for God (or its euphemism for the nameless—my words). Bobbo went on to say that humans were lucky to have such a bountiful planet and that they had been hybridized over twenty thousand years ago creating the prototypes depicted in our mythologies; this, he pointed out, was typical of all emerging species.

No harm from exospecies will be forthcoming; only the eventual welcoming into the galactic community. Now he just wanted to go home. Now we would have a whole new understanding if we should accept some of the information or logic that has been bequeathed to us through Bobbo, who suggested that we inform all the people of our planet.

Does this hypothetical situation ring true? Your guess is as good as mine.

Alien logic is really just the concept to deliver spiritual and scientific enlightenment for the well-being of all life in the universe. Can we measure up?

*

Nevin lay in bed. He was exhausted but unable to sleep. That day had been seminal in more ways that he could understand. He had to look up a few words appearing in Melbo's articles, but he absorbed the basic essence of all he was reporting—the main point that it was true, and it was being kept from the public, and likely he, himself, knew some of the people who were doing it, Uncle Aubrey being one. No wonder they were talking about Melbo: they saw him as a threat to their control. It frightened him, a bit like how Mollie had frightened him with her persuasive desire to please him. But that had changed.

Now he wanted her again. He wanted to tell her to find Melbo's articles in the library and read them so they could discuss them together. Then they could do more of the same that brought them such amazing pleasure. He was beginning to drift when the door to his room opened and the light was turned on. He opened his eyes and saw his father and mother standing there, having shut the door behind them. They were not coming in happily to say good night, which at that hour was unlikely anyway.

'Nevin!' exclaimed his father. 'Wake up!'

Nevin raised himself on his elbow.

'What?' said Nevin.

'I just came back from the church after speaking with Deacon Purdy.'

Nevin didn't know what to think only that he had been missing classes.

'You've been expelled from Sunday School.'

'Oh.'

'Oh? Is that all? I just had to tell your mother that you and a girl were seen by the pastor doing some lewd and carnal activity in the basement!' James came to the bed, and picked Nevin up by the shoulders and shook him like a rag doll. 'How could you? You're a beast! A pervert!' His enraged face glared just inches from his own.

'Nevin, is this true?' asked Muriel, his mother, tearfully.

'We were kissing!' said Nevin, defensively, not understanding how it was possible they had been seen.

'Kissing?' James smacked him across the face. 'That's not what Mr. Purdy saw!'

'What did he see?' asked Nevin, his face smarting.

'What did he see? I can barely bring myself to say it in front of your mother! He saw you forcing this girl to…God, I can't say it.' James backed off, deflated. His mother then went to Nevin.

'What happened, Nevin?' she asked. 'Did you hurt this girl? Who is she?'

'No! Of course not! I love her!' he blurted out.

'You're only thirteen!' declared his father. 'You know nothing about love! You committed a crime against everything we have tried to raise you with!'

'Well, you made me! Is that a crime?' retorted Nevin. 'And I'm almost fourteen!'

'How dare you!' His father smacked him again.

'William,' said Nevin's mother, 'that was unnecessary.'

'Like hell it was. He's turned into a monster. Who's the girl? The deacon wouldn't say.'

'Why should I tell? You want to beat her, too?'

'I want you to apologize to her parents for what you did to her!'

'I won't!'

'Yes, you will!'

'No! Besides if the deacon didn't tell you who she was, it's none of your business!'

James raised his hand again, but Muriel stopped him.

'William, we need to deal with this in a calm and thoughtful manner.'

James stormed out of the room. Nevin got back into bed and pulled the covers over his head.

Muriel sat down. 'Nevin, your father is ashamed because he has high hopes for you.'

'You're hypocrites,' said Nevin under the sheet.

'No, dear, love is fine when you're married.'

'Leave me alone.'

'Alright. Let's try and learn something from this terrible shock. As your mother, I can only imagine your confusion with sexual matters. Just know that I'm willing to speak to you about it, if you want.'

'No. Go away.'

Sighing, his mother stayed for a moment, then got up and left the room, closing the door gently behind her.

The next morning, nothing was said as if nothing had happened. Nevin's father went to work and Nevin's mother went out with his sister, Carolyn. It seemed as if the whole episode had been proverbially swept under the rug.

*

At the beginning of September, Earl Bunting was back in Washington. He went to his little office, not much bigger than a windowless utility room. The desk and chair and gray metal set drawers were all that the room could fit. On his desk lay a few letters and one small package from Joe di Lucca. Opening the package, he found a number of photos: some were of Melbo and a man in his fifties or sixties tying his shoelace on a New York park bench, and another showed the man about to enter an apartment building in the Village.

Other photos showed a yacht near Hyannis, and a zoom photo showing Greenfield, Prinzenthal, Melbo and his wife, Melissa. Some notes explained that the yacht, as well as the family cottage in West Yarmouth, was owned by Greenfield's sister, Peggy Sackett. The yacht returned an hour after the Kennedy boat had returned. Bunting put the package in his desk, leaving out the one photo of the man entering the apartment, which, the note revealed was on Bleeker Street. He had an important meeting with Woods at the top of the hour and needed to prepare for a grilling on the plans for *Mongoose* and the invasion of Cuba.

Bunting was the hands-on liaison with the military and found himself pressured for more intelligence. He had sent Eduardo Sanchez to Cuba undercover to scout out various places around the coast to land an invasion force comprised of Cubans and mercenaries. A number of sites were considered, one of which was *Bahía de Cochinos*, or Bay of Pigs.

After some discussion about the Cuban operation, Bunting took the photo and pushed it across Woods' desk.

'Any idea who this might be?' he asked his boss.

Woods picked it up and looked at it.

'Can't say off hand. What's the relevance of this?'

'He met with Melbo in the Village.'

'I thought you were to drop that.'

'I did, but a guy I know who does some work for me on occasion did some overtime, and just sent me that. Just thought you should know.'

'Well, thanks Earl, I'll pin it up on my most wanted list.'

'Called himself Mike; that's all I heard, but it was obvious they were in some deep parley.'

'You think he's a source?'

'I suppose he is, maybe, unless they were talking politics or something.'

'Leave it with me; I'll have somebody from resources look into it.'

Bunting exited.

Woods left the photo on his desk on top of other papers. That afternoon, Sulla dropped by Woods' office to discuss a certain matter. When the assistant informed him that Woods was in the men's room, Sulla made small talk and then he noticed the photo. At first, he just looked without thinking, but having looked at it again, he excused the assistant, and picked it up just as Woods returned.

'Where did you get this?' Sulla showed Woods the photograph.

'That? Bunting dropped it off; said one of his people took it.'

'Do you know who it is?'

'No, I was going to find out.'

'You won't find anything.'

'What makes you so sure?'

'He's Majestic.'

'Majestic? Art mentioned that name at my summer party.'

'Yes, and he shouldn't have. But it seems we have a leak.'

'A leak? This guy met with Melbo and went by the name Mike.'

'Melbo?'

'They spent an hour in a café, before my guy followed him home.'

'His name's not Mike. It's Keith Leverton, a doctor of paranormal psychology.'

'Never heard of him; well, he doesn't look like a doctor; rather more like one of those beatniks.'

'Now you know. He worked for three years with one of the captured aliens.'

Woods let that sink in. 'Damn.'

'Did you read Melbo's last article?' asked Sulla.

'No-'

'I thought it was all hyperbole, the way he dressed up his assertions. But now I know he's getting it from ground zero.'

'I see.'

'Leverton always kept to himself; he knew the consequences.'

'Melbo drew him out,' said Woods.

'He didn't seem like the kind of guy who would just go out in the cold like that. He's been off the radar for a number of years, considered a minimal risk.'

'Someone encouraged him?'

'I don't know. Melbo could have got to him with those articles; he seems to have taken up this bohemian lifestyle.'

'We can bring him in, this Leverton; William James can help us there.'

'No, we'll create a legend; make Leverton a crackpot and destroy Melbo's credibility, who writes fiction passing it off as news.'

'I'll get right on it.'

'And Bunting? He seems to be the man of the hour.'

'He's got a lot on his plate, but he knows people. I'll speak with him.'

'This is a priority on a need-to-know. Whatever you do Majestic is to remain unmentioned and known to you only; no one else, nobody. Majestic will win us the Cold War, Aubrey; it's an extensive mission to reverse-engineer alien technology with incredible applications for the military such as laser guidance systems and computer technology generations beyond our present capabilities. It must be defended at all costs. Do I make myself clear?'

'You can count on me, sir.'

'And we never had this conversation.' Then Sulla walked out. Even Aubrey Woods was overawed by what had just transpired. He realized his own position, as powerful as it was, was nothing as compared to the depth and scope of that wielded by his boss, who almost scared him, but for one thing, his patriotism; otherwise, his power was lethal. America had to win the Cold War.

*

On the twenty-ninth of September, Nevin James turned 14. He was in his first year of high school at Bidwell and took to his studies with enthusiasm and he played soccer and participated in numerous extracurricular activities, such as the film club and the debating team. He heard no more of his summer trouble from either his parents or anyone else, which he found curious, but he didn't follow up on it, fearing more admonishment. Mollie attended the same school but seemed to pretend they didn't know each other and kept to her friends.

One day he tried to ask her if something was wrong, and explained that he had been expelled from the Sunday classes. She replied that she had been expelled as well for missing classes, but she gave no indication of any other trouble. On another occasion, while waiting for class, he quickly said to her that they had to talk. She barely acknowledged him, but told him in passing to meet her after school. When he found her with a couple of her girlfriends, she led him aside after saying goodbye to her friends and they walked down the street towards Wisconsin Avenue, where they took the bus south a mile or so back home. She lived in Burlieth-Hillandale just north of Georgetown.

Nevin was happy sitting with her. She was cool, rosy-cheeked, and seemed more mature than in the past. She was still a girl but was becoming quite a pretty young woman with that thick brown hair in a ponytail and a slim body that had filled out. When he took her hand, she didn't seem to mind.

'Why have you been so distant towards me, Mollie?'

'I didn't want to draw attention to us. People talk, you know, if they see us together.'

'What will you tell your friends?'

'Nothing, only that we know each other from Sunday School.'

'I got into a lot of trouble that night. My father was called to the church. The deacon had seen us together.'

She looked at him aghast.

'He did? When?'

'When we didn't show up for class again, he went looking and saw us behind the piano.'

'Are you kidding? When we were ...'

'I'm not kidding; we were too ... to hear him. My father was ready to kill me and demanded to know who you were. Mr. Purdy hadn't told him.'

'He said nothing to my mother when she was asked to see him, only that I was not allowed to go back to Sunday school until I took it seriously.'

Nevin reflected on that. 'He was too embarrassed to tell your mother.'

'My mother would have had kittens if she'd been told what we did.'

'I told my parents we just kissed.'

Mollie laughed. 'And you didn't tell them it was me?'

'Of course not.'

'Thanks.'

'We should get together sometime.'

'We're together now,' she said, teasing.

'I mean *together*; I can't stop thinking about how beautiful that was.'

Mollie looked at him.

'I don't know.'

'We can just do something like go to a movie.'

'My parents wouldn't let me unless I was with my friends.'

'We can figure out a way. We're spies, right?'

Mollie giggled as she had done in the church.

'Maybe.'

'By the way,' he said, 'you should read all the articles written by this guy named Melbo, George Melbo. He writes for the New York Tribune.'

'Why?'

'He writes about aliens, real aliens, the ones the government know about and won't tell anybody.'

'Do you believe they're real?' she asked.

'They're as real as you and me; and I can prove it. One time I heard these real spies mention Melbo's name like they were frustrated about him.'

'What spies?'

'My dad works in the FBI.'

'He does? Cool.'

'And at family gatherings there were others who are very important people in the CIA. Believe me, it's true; but you can never talk about this to anyone. Promise me.'

'Okay, I promise.'

'I know what we can do.'

'What?'

'Let's go to the library. The newspapers are archived there as public documents. You can read them and understand what I'm talking about.'

'You're so interesting, Nevin; you're a real spy.'

Nevin was rather pleased with himself; he imagined his first agent in Mollie.

'If you ever tell anybody about this we could be in serious trouble.'

'I won't tell anybody; I never said a word to anyone about … you know.'

'Okay, let's be smart about this; we'll figure out ways to meet and when.'

'Like with secret messages?'

'Yeah, I read once about this code—you take out every third, seventh and tenth letter on each line of a paragraph—here I'll show you.'

Nevin took out a piece of paper and wrote quickly a simple paragraph that specifically had the designated letters placed. When he took them out and put them together it read: I LOVE YOU.

Mollie looked at it without saying anything.

'It's easy, right?' said Nevin.

'Are you just saying that or do you mean it?'

'I mean it.'

Mollie leaned over and kissed him on the cheek. Nevin turned to her and kissed her on the lips.

Mollie got off the bus on the next stop. Nevin kept going with his mind full of Mollie.

*

In mid-October, Keith Leverton was found dead in his Village apartment. His friend and neighbor, a woman artist known professionally as Naomi—her friends called her Mimi—hadn't seen him for days and after repeated attempts to contact him got the superintendent to open the flat. Leverton was hanging by a rope on a makeshift gibbet—a hook newly screwed into a beam below the plaster of the living room ceiling, leading authorities to conclude that his hanging was premeditated. He had been dead for a week.

The investigating detective, Kyle Merrell, could find no sign of struggle or foul play and wrote it up as a suicide. There was no note, no drugs, no evidence of alcoholic distemper, but just the appearance of a well-ordered universe. Though the coroner concluded that his death was by suffocation and the neck marks were commensurate with hanging, Leverton's few friends disagreed.

Keith, they said, was a psychologically sound and generally happy individual. Granted he was a loner, who had no family, just an ex-wife from before the war, and no children, he still seemed well-adjusted in a quirky way. He was respected like a medicine man by the Village tribe of misanthropes, who saw him as both an enigmatic and venerable character. By all appearances Keith died without much fuss which was likely his way of accepting the inevitable, given his deep philosophical bent.

Perhaps his last thoughts were of Raphael the alien in that their demise was a kind of sacrifice for the truth, the truth manifesting a sinister cachet of human folly. As the last stars of asphyxiation faded inexorably into nothingness, Keith Leverton must have welcomed the release of his soul bearing his message of deliverance, ghosted to heaven.

22. The Whole Bouquet

John Fitzgerald Kennedy won a substantial election victory on November 8, 1960 in Electoral College votes, but only marginally so in the popular vote. A wave of relief and cautious hope spread among the liberal regions and enclaves across the country of both the urban East and West coast and traditionally Democratic South. The remaining demographics were generally Republican which disdained, as a matter of principle, everything Kennedy represented. Political slogans such as 'the new frontier' aside, a deep distrust of change and shift to the left were tantamount to treason in some of the more conservative factions and territory such as Texas, though Lyndon Johnson helped carry the state as a good ol' boy. Yet, however successful the election was, it coincided with the very depths of the Cold War, and the bureaucratic apparatus remained as it was, guided by the invisible hands of their overlords whose reach extended far and wide.

Greenfield and Melbo had done their utmost to influence Kennedy, but they were at worst ignored, at best listened to. By the New Year, Kennedy had formed his government, seeking to achieve some parity of ideology—keep some of the cold warriors to fight the fight and appease the right—and place the best and brightest of his generation close to him in cabinet. In fairness, he played his cards well for all appearances, but as his presidency evolved, it gave the dissenting forces within some latitude to shape their designs inimical to his.

As new leadership is often molded by trial and error, Kennedy came to realize that there were forces he could not control deeply imbedded in the culture of government. As a result, for instance, the Bay of Pigs fiasco and his refusal to let the military save the day for the mercenary army created by the CIA set the tone for the remainder of his presidency to change the way he did business with the enemy, some of whom were within. Some might say he was 'flying by the seat of his pants', others would say he was 'hogtied' by an entrenched system on perpetual war footing, one of its architects being Allen

Sulla.

And for that, and other things, Kennedy fired him which set in motion a catastrophic contention of power under the aegis of national security. And when he was stymied from participating in any briefing on the most classified programs, some of which he knew about, and others (specifically the Majestic committee) of which he knew nothing, Kennedy had reached his limits, and determined "to splinter the CIA into a thousand pieces and scatter it in the wind". Privately, he regretted his naivety and arrogance whenever he recalled what Greenfield and Melbo had told him about the CIA being a power unto itself.

In the New Year, Inauguration Day came and went. Greenfield and Prinzenthal were living in the Virgins at least until the birth of their baby, and were out of the picture. Melbo, on the other hand, had been fighting an insidious battle to defend his integrity. The shock of Leverton's death and the seriousness of the situation struck home with the authorities. Greenfield was convinced it was murder.

Melbo felt terrible guilt and remorse and had been in a funk ever since. He had written an article, a tremendous panegyric celebrating the election victory of Kennedy. Both he and Sinclair were then castigated by Jake Whitmore for being too partisan when they should have been commiserating more with the Republican cause. Whitmore may not have been a fan of Nixon, but nevertheless, he believed he was better for America. But Melbo could ride that out because his following was at an all-time high and the paper competed with the best of them.

But well before Election Day, Whitmore complained there had been no article forthcoming about the "interview" that had supposedly taken place. The excuse was that Kennedy had abruptly ended the meeting and had swum back to his boat! This fostered some acrimony, placing the blame squarely on Melbo. Then the election turned the disapproval even more.

In December, a small article appeared in a New York tabloid, claiming Melbo and the recently deceased Leverton had been acquaintances and pointedly suggested he had been a source for Melbo. It went on to describe Leverton as the village fool who aligned himself with the local scene as a doyen of the macabre. The gist of it seemed to catch: and at first in New York then in other cities all across the country; competing newspapers decried the sensationalism of phony journalism with Melbo being in the vanguard.

Abusive epithets against his very professionalism were thrown around indiscriminately: "pseudo-science" and "scam" and even "fear-mongering and corruption" were like body-blows devised to destroy his reputation.

No matter what he wrote in defense of his relative oeuvre, the damage became irreparable, even to the point that his reviews of the arts, of which he displayed his original strengths, were circumspect. And by the time of Kennedy's inauguration, he had become a pariah to the establishment press.

Sinclair stood valiantly by him, and even Whitmore to a point could see that an orchestrated assault on Melbo was an assault on him and his media interests. But there came the tipping point when he had to cut his losses. Both Sinclair and Melbo were fired. It was a sad day for the free world, a day that passed silently, without a mention. The world moved on with the New Frontier almost as if sleep-walking into a black hole. All its players, both of the new-fangled "Camelot" of Kennedy's time and the venal underwriters of its extinction, were like a choreographed Shakespearian tragedy in the making. In Melbo's mind he saw his kind of quorum of hope—a filibuster of dire warnings—against the dark forces within go up in smoke, but how easy it was for those forces to do what they pleased to further their agendas.

Even Kennedy at the helm of the most powerful country in the world was unable to see and combat what was deployed against him. This was an unprecedented tyranny crafted to the times. Melbo appealed to the White House to help him in any modest way but his appeal went unanswered no doubt because he had become a political liability.

Almost a year to the day after all this started, two unrelated things happened that would change the lives of those concerned. One: at about 4 a.m. on March 13, 1961 a baby girl was born in Christiansted, St. Croix, in the Virgin Islands. Greenfield had purchased a delightful three bedroom green-gray-roofed bungalow up in the hills above the town, with a great view of the sea. It had a small pool, a reddish tiled patio and a garage for their little 1956 dark green Renault 4CV convertible that Greenfield purchased used when they went back to St. Croix in early September. They had lived on the boat while they house-hunted, and moved in by the end of the month, after quickly furnishing the place with modest necessities.

And two: Melbo received in the mail a package of letters forwarded to him from the Tribune. He went through the letters, mostly expressing sympathy to his plight. One was different, though: in a somewhat undeveloped level of penmanship, but revealing an unusual level of expression, the young writer invited him to speak to a grade nine class at Bidmore High in Washington whenever it was convenient. This fellow, Nevin James, hinted he was "very cognizant" of Melbo's predicament and had "inside knowledge" of the situation. How on earth could a boy of fourteen or fifteen know anything about "his situation" wondered Melbo? That evening he gave the letter to DeCourt who laughed.

'You have nothing to lose, dear,' she grinned.

'You're right,' he joked, 'my humiliation has now entered a new phase; I can look up to a kid!'

They both laughed.

'Well, don't take it too hard. It seems this kid is onto something.'

'What, so I can get laughed at by the whole class?'

They laughed again. Melbo then felt a wave of anguish.

'Who's kidding who?' he said. 'I couldn't even get into teacher's college.'

'Now don't go there again; martyrs make bad bedfellows.'

'I'm no martyr; I'm just a goat.'

'But I'm in love with this goat.' DeCourt came up behind Melbo who was sitting at the table and held him and kissed his unshaven cheek.

'I feel more ghost than goat.'

'You just have to get back to work. Why don't you think about that offer from the Post and Mail?'

'A tabloid? It'll just confirm what they say about me.'

'We need the money, Mel. All this will go away soon enough.'

'They'll never let up on me; it's too easy for them; a word here a word there; I have to rethink my life, my career.'

'Does that include us?'

'Of course, but what if I want to move back to Canada?'

'You have to clear your name first, then I'd go anywhere with you.'

'How, Mel? How?' he moaned.

Before she could answer the black rotary wall phone rang loudly. She picked up the receiver on the third ring. 'Hello?'

Silence.

'Harley!' she exclaimed. 'You're timing is impeccable. I was just asked by my poor husband here for an answer to his dilemma. How are you and Hannah?'

More silence.

'Oh my God! That's so wonderful! Amazing!' She turned to Melbo. 'Hannah gave birth to a baby girl!' And back to Greenfield: 'We're absolutely thrilled, Harley!' Back to Melbo: 'Mother and babe doing splendidly! Lizbet Ephrussi Greenfield! What a lovely name!'

On it went. Greenfield insisted they come down for a visit soon, perhaps around Easter in early April or whenever they could. It was left open as they could barely afford it, given Melbo's ill-fortune, though this went unmentioned. Greenfield knew that he was out of work, ostensibly out of a career, and said they could count on them to help in any way they could. He left it vague because of the risk of a tapped line though it was no longer so. The serendipity of the occasion even answered Melbo's dilemma. He decided to take the position at the Post and Mail (he called it the Ghost and Mail) just long enough to defend his name in spite of the taint of tabloid news. He had little choice. But he still had a voice and felt unrestrained in his new position as a 'celebrity' journalist. And the first thing on his mind was to resurrect Keith Leverton and his own good name.

*

Nevin James was called to the school office where he was informed that George Melbo had agreed to speak to his class. The principal, however, found out about this arrangement and decided that the whole school and parents should hear him speak. Surprised, after school, an early day, Nevin told Mollie on the bus what had happened. She was excited about the development.

'I can't believe it!' she exclaimed. 'How a simple letter can lead to this: in front of the whole school!'

'To tell the truth, I'm feeling a little queasy about it,' replied Nevin. 'I mean, we're exposed now; I'll have to make some kind of introduction in front of the school; before it was just the classroom.'

'You know, I never thought it would happen.'

'Me too, in a way; I hope I don't get into trouble with my dad; if he finds out he may think I was snooping in his desk and discovered his secret file on Mr. Melbo, or something.'

'I'll stand up for you!'

'Great, but all that will do is make him suspicious about you being the girl

I was with when we were seen … He doesn't know, and that really bugs him being who he is in the FBI.'

She giggled, 'That was then; now we're going steady, don't you think? There's nothing wrong with that.'

'I guess you're right, but we haven't done anything since except kiss.'

'Nev, it scared me, being seen; I told you.'

'I know but we're in high school now, and I get so horny thinking about you.'

'Nevin!'

But they both laughed.

'My mother would lock me in my room if she knew,' she giggled. 'She's such a prude; I think that's why my father left.'

'When did you last see him?'

'Last Christmas; he works in California now; he lives in San Bernardino.'

'Doing what?'

'Something to do with aerospace engineering.'

'Really? Was he in the war?'

'Yes, he flew a plane in the Navy on an aircraft carrier.'

'Wow, cool.'

'Yeah, but he's more of a business man now for companies like Grumman and Northrop. Mom said he was connected to the navy in acquisitions or something.'

'Does he talk about it?'

'No, never; he's kinda strange. I don't think he cares about me. Mom says he sees other women. They're gonna divorce.'

'I'm sorry. And your mom? Does she see anybody?'

'Are you kidding? She's too religious.'

'Have you been with anybody besides me, Moll?'

Mollie looked at him and wrinkled her nose.

'And if I did? What then?'

'I don't know; I'm just asking.'

'Would it bother you?'

'That depends.'

'On what?'

'Well, maybe I'd be jealous.'

Mollie giggled. 'Don't be. Okay, some boy showed me his dink, last summer.'

'Who?'

'I don't know. It was at a church thing; at a club.'

'What did he do?'

'He wanted to show me something, so I followed him into the bathroom and he showed me his dink.'

'That's all?'

'Nevin, it's embarrassing; he was older.'

'How much older?'

'I don't know; maybe fifteen, sixteen; he had more hair down there.'

'What did you do?'

'I went to the door, and he stopped me. He said you can't go unless you show me yours.'

'And did you?'

'Not at first, but then I just wanted out of there, so I pulled down my panties and lifted my dress.'

'Then what?'

'He asked if he could touch me there.'

'What did you say?'

'I said nothing; I was scared. Then he said it would feel good, and he just touched me there for a bit.'

'Then what?'

'I was shocked of course, but he was gentle and after a bit it did feel good.'

'Now I'm jealous.'

'Well, we're telling the truth aren't we? You wanted to know!'

'Of course, but you know how I feel about you, but I'm glad we're having this out. Did you touch him?'

'I wasn't going to but he took my hand and put it on him. I couldn't believe what I was seeing; it paralyzed me; it was like big—hard.'

'Then what?'

'He told me to pull it so it would feel good.'

'What happened?'

'I did for a bit, and after a while he like groaned—you know, very quickly like—I had no idea at the time what it was—on my hand; then he was resting and I pulled my panties up and ran out. That's it.'

Nevin felt terrible pangs of despair, but he took her hand and held it. She gripped his in return.

'I'm sorry, Nevin; it just happened; I was so stupid.'

'No, Mollie, you were innocent; it was something you had little control of. Doesn't it happen to everyone?'

'Maybe, but what about us? We did the same thing.'

'We're different.'

'How?' she asked.

'You were showing me love, weren't you?'

'Truly, I don't know; I was just like—I liked you, why not?'

'You knew what you were doing because of him.'

'Not really; I just—just wanted to be close.'

'I want to be close now,' said Nevin.

'All this talk is making me feel that way too.'

'Where can we go?'

'Let's go to my place; it's early; my mom won't be home until later.'

'Okay.'

They both fell silent. As for young teenagers the concept of love was purely hormonal, which raged within each of them. Nevin's voice had begun to break and sounded like an awkward *vibrato* with an occasional squeak. Mollie was blooming like a red rose. Their relative loneliness found a perfect companion in the other.

'I'm on a pill,' she suddenly announced.

'A pill?' responded Nevin.

'You know, *the* pill.'

'Like that new birth control pill?'

'Yeah, my doctor prescribed it for me last fall, when my period was so bad, I missed school.'

'Really? What happened?'

'I bled so heavily—the first time; well, the second time it was worse, and I could barely get out of bed—so the doctor gave me a prescription which has worked like a charm.'

'So you can't get pregnant.'

'Well, yeah. I'm not supposed to tell anybody.'

'So why are you telling me?'

'Because we don't keep secrets from each other.'

'Of course, but—'

'But what? Don't you want to do it?'

Nevin remained quiet for a moment. 'I never expected to, but yes, of course I do. I want to do it with you, only you.'

'Okay then.'

At Mollie's house, a gray-brick set back more than the other homes on the street, they walked to the back door. A tabby cat greeted them and quickly ran into the bushes. Silently, they entered and climbed the short stairs into the kitchen. They put their school bags on the kitchen table, and without a word, Mollie led him up the back stairs to her room at the top of the stairs. As they were about to close the door, they heard something—a kind of weeping cry coming from down the hall.

Mollie put her finger to her lips. They looked at each other completely perplexed. Mollie, keeping her finger to her mouth, then looked into the hall. The sound was coming from the end of the hall from her mother's room. She tip-toed towards the sound, with Nevin following. The door was slightly ajar as they both approached and both looked in. What they saw would forever remain etched on their memory. Deborah McBride and a man were naked on the bed in full coitus, her legs wrapped around him, and his arms around her and hands gripping her bottom both as one body in a frenzied climax gyrating like an unstoppable locomotive.

Mrs. McBride uttered a final '*Oh my God!*'—part moan part cry. The man groaned as if it came from the depths of the earth, and slowly the locomotive eased back still rocking. In Mollie's shock, she accidently knocked the door with her foot as she was about to back away. The door opened a few more inches and the surprised couple on the bed immediately jerked their heads in its direction. Mollie and her mother looked directly at each other for a microsecond. The man staring at Nevin was his father.

Both Mollie and Nevin ran like their lives depended on it, down the stairs, Nevin grabbing his school satchel, and out the door. In panic, they ran down the street to the bus stop and waited for the bus.

'Where will we go?' cried Mollie.

'The library?'

'Yes, anywhere.'

They looked back down the street frantically expecting their parents to come after them. They didn't really speak until the bus came. They got on then realized that they were going in the wrong direction.

'We can go to this coffee shop I know,' said Nevin.

'Okay,' said Mollie, nervously.

In the coffee shop on Wisconsin with hot chocolates purchased by Mollie because Nevin had no money, they finally settled down. They just stared at each other, as if concussed in some strange new world, the world of adultery and hypocrisy, terror and deceit, but ultimately in this case, love.

'Let's face it,' said Nevin, 'they're no different than us.'

'How can you say that? They're liars.'

'Of course they are, but they're putting their love for each other above everything normal.'

Mollie thought about that. 'Maybe,' she said, using her favorite word, adding, 'Unless it's just sex.'

Nevin had a grin on his face. 'You know, Moll, we can use this to our advantage.'

'My mother will kill me.'

'Why? For coming home early? It's not your fault.'

'With you.'

'So what!' Nevin thought for a few moments. 'We're working on a speech together which is true; besides, she wouldn't dare risk your saying anything; she'll want to make sure I don't say anything either.'

'They'll put two and two together if your father tells my mom about you … and me.'

'I hadn't thought about that; no wonder I didn't hear any more about it.'

'What will your father do?'

'I think he'd like to kill me too.'

'Seriously?'

'No, my mother would have something to say about that; I'll make sure he understands that I'll blow the whistle on his affair if he so much as lays a hand on me.'

'I just can't believe what we saw. They were like wild animals,' she said. 'We could do that!'

Nevin laughed then they laughed harder until it became hysterical. They tried to suppress it unsuccessfully, which made it worse until it hurt.

'Oh my God!' Mollie gasped for breath. That made them laugh again, remembering her mother's use of that expression *in extremis*.

As it turned out, nothing really came of the incident, likely because of its sensitivity for both parents and children. Both William James and Deborah McBride were probably so mortified at having been discovered that they pretended nothing had happened. Mrs. McBride did say to Mollie that she hadn't expected her home so early and hoped they could respect each other's privacy, hers being a single mother with "needs".

Mollie replied that she understood only as long as the feeling was truly mutual. It was left at that. Nevin could tell that his father was truly distressed when he asked him into his study, where he said he was sorry but that "men" kept confidences to themselves. Nevin replied only as long as "we" respect each other, and his father would promise never to hit him again. His father appeared relieved that his son understood his pitiful situation; then he swore that he would never again raise a hand to the boy. Nevin smiled as he left the room, having successfully recruited his father to his advantage.

*

By the middle of April, Melbo was able to get away from New York and visit Bidwell High School as long as he could wire an assignment from the Virgins. DeCourt accompanied him because after his speaking engagement, they were flying to St. Croix for a week. They flew into Washington and stayed at the Willard on Pennsylvania Avenue, where they got a bargain because Greenfield knew the manager. The Willard had seen better days, but still impressed guests with its stature and history; the problem was that the local area had been in decline, and literally gone to seed.

The following day they took a taxi to the school for the event. Just after lunch everyone congregated in the auditorium, a wood-paneled hall with fixed benches sloped slightly down to the stage. Melbo, with DeCourt, presented himself at the office and the principal ushered them through the school and backstage. DeCourt excused herself with a kiss and found a seat in the auditorium. Melbo found a chair backstage and sat there contemplating his situation.

Schools made him nervous given his rebellious youth and he never for a moment ever expected to speak at one. But this was different: he felt it imperative to use every opportunity to redress the injustice done to him and Leverton, specifically Leverton, who in all likelihood had been murdered. They could have murdered Melbo as well, but that would have raised a public outcry in that his growing stature and message could well have pointed to dark diabolic elements of government subterfuge. People were not convinced, however, and believed in the beneficence of good government and gave the benefit of doubt.

Melbo mused that he had been lucky, and perhaps they had better uses for him, such as the target of a smear campaign which would be of greater benefit to their cause. Nevertheless, death was a card that could still be played; this gave him all the more reason to take the stage; there was a kind of morbid pride in his mission. He could not bear to reveal these thoughts to Melissa, who was anxious at best. His fear had turned to courage in the name of his dead father who had died fighting tyranny on Hill 314 above Mortain surrounded by an SS Panzer division. The Nazi counter-attack was held off by seven hundred gallant men of 120th infantry regiment, of whom almost half were killed. His father George Sr. known as "Willy" (from his middle name William) had defended his position to the last, letting the wounded be removed to safer ground. He and two others took a direct mortar round after they had killed at least a dozen enemy troops.

Nevin and Mollie stood aside among older students and staff. They noticed the lanky wavy-haired fellow in the rumpled gray suit and navy tie sitting alone. Hesitant to approach him, not having been introduced and unsure of who he was, though it appeared obvious, they held back. He looked their way, his expression thoughtful: blue eyes, straight nose, pursed mouth, and friendly smooth face which could've been transferred across time from a Roman bust of a philosopher. Nevin approached him.

'Nevin James, I presume,' said Melbo, his hand outstretched.

'Yes, sir,' said Nevin politely extending his hand.

'Call me Mel, Nevin; we're both truth-seekers, are we not?'

Mollie moved up to Nevin like a whisper.

'I'm Mollie,' she spoke up. 'We're both happy you came. We wrote the letter together.'

Melbo smiled at them, seeing a flicker of their obvious connection in that they were a team. 'Mollie,' he said, shaking her hand, 'What made you decide to write to me?'

Mollie looked at Nevin. 'He did,' she said. 'He read all your articles; then encouraged me to read them too.'

'Nevin,' said Melbo, 'you mentioned some "inside knowledge" perhaps you should tell me about it before I stand up in front of the school.'

Nevin looked around to see who was near. Melbo followed his field of vision.

'Is it classified?' asked Melbo, amused.

Nevin leaned in closer. Mollie did as well.

'My father works for the FBI, and I searched his desk one day and found your articles.'

'Did he ever mention me?' continued Melbo.

'No, never, but I heard your name mentioned at my uncle's place last summer; I heard a private conversation, and they didn't know I was there.'

'Who mentioned my name?'

'I'm not sure exactly, but my uncle was one of the people speaking. They work for the government.'

'Who's your uncle, Nevin?'

'Uncle Aubrey. My dad's married to Aunt Honey's younger sister.'

'Uncle Aubrey? Never heard of him.'

'Woods is his last name.'

'What does he do?'

'I think he's in the CIA. I know the director of the CIA was at the party.'

'Allen Sulla?'

'Yes, that's right. I think he was one of the guests speaking with my Uncle, and another guy named Art.'

'Art Lovering?'

'I didn't catch his name.'

'So that's why you wrote me the letter?'

'Yes.'

'What did they say about me?'

'Not much only that they felt worried about something; they mentioned Majestic too.'

'Majestic.'

'What's Majestic?' asked Mollie.

'I believe it's a classified program,' said Melbo, 'but whatever you do don't mention it to anyone; it's very serious; very serious indeed.'

Mollie and Nevin looked at each other, satisfied.

'We won't,' said Mollie. 'We're spies.'

'I can see that,' said Melbo.

Principal Oatway entered backstage and went straight to Melbo.

'It's time. Everyone's assembled.' Then looking at Nevin: 'Perhaps you should introduce Mr. Melbo, since you started this whole thing.'

'Yes, sir.'

'Is Mollie part of this?' asked the principal.

'Yes she is.'

'Well, let me introduce the two of you to begin with.'

The principal walked to the curtain and slipped around it.

The student body was loud and effusive; everyone seemed to be excited. A few parents sat with teachers in the audience, consisting mostly students. The principal raised his arms to lower the noise, and then he spoke into the microphone: 'Please be quiet! We would like to begin! Students! Thank you!' Everyone stopped talking. 'Thank you! We are gathered here today to hear our guest speaker, who has been invited by two of our freshman students. Our guest, Mr. Melbo is a reporter, now with the New York Post & Mail; we are privileged to hear him speak about the mysteries of the unknown! But before he comes on stage, let's hear some applause for Nevin James and Mary McBride who will say a few words of introduction.' The principal stepped aside and Nevin and Mollie came onto the stage from the side, where Melbo remained unseen. From the podium they looked out at the crowd, who stared back in anticipation.

'Hello everyone,' Nevin waved then looked at his principal, 'Thank you, Mr. Oatway.' Then back at the crowd: 'Mollie and I would like to say a few words about Mr. Melbo, who so graciously has come all the way from New York at our invitation. To begin with, he has made a great impression on me, and Mollie. His articles were written when he was with the New York Herald Tribune, and kind of woke up in me a new understanding of the big picture of this little earth in a vast universe full of billions of stars.

'What if all Mr. Melbo has informed us of is true? What will our future be like? What if our government doesn't want us to know about aliens coming here? It seems to me that the recent events which have brought about his enquiries are perhaps the most important events in the history of man. Mollie?'

'Yes, Nevin, and thank you for encouraging me to read those articles!' Laughter from the audience. 'Otherwise I think I would still be worrying about being a girl in a man's world!' More laughter. 'Maybe, I still am! Anyway, let's give a great welcome to Mr. George Melbo!' They both stood aside and looked to stage right.

Melbo sauntered onto the stage and shook hands with both teenagers and Principal Oatway, before they exited. Melbo stood at the podium with his hands holding the lectern, and looked around the audience. The clapping stopped. Melbo looked at his notes, then looked up and began speaking slowly, delivered in a steady clear voice.

'Students, ladies and gentlemen, Principal Oatway, and especially Nevin and Mollie, thank you for having me here! It's an honor. And I hope that what I say today will inspire you to think positively about our place in the universe, so we may do good things here on Earth. Such grand platitudes! Well, I'm an optimist! But I think we need to clean up our own backyard before we can be welcomed by alien visitors out there!' He swept his arm across in front of him.

'The challenge will be for present and future generations to find ways to end war, poverty, pollution, overpopulation, starvation and intolerance. This is what I've learned through my investigations. No one out there will help us achieve those goals; we must succeed all by ourselves. Perhaps that is obvious, self-evident, but what is most interesting, and I can attest to the truth of this, is that we now know we are not alone! These beings from other worlds have lived in this universe for a very, very long time, millions upon millions of years for some species; during this time they succeeded far beyond overcoming terrestrial issues much like those we face here on Earth today, before leaving the worlds of their emergence and primordial past.

'We could be on the cusp of this great journey—a thousand year cusp or longer because we have now the means and capability to move forward with the advance of science, and yes, with the fortuitous windfall of alien technology which is apparently being reverse-engineered even as we speak. So, perhaps we will make leaps and bounds in the years ahead when this technology becomes publicly known and available.

'I am no optimist without foundation. Because of my work, numerous people have come forward—some of them whistleblowers, people active in the secret world of classified programs—and have shown me their credentials. And believe me, I separate the wheat from the chaff, so to speak, and I'm confident that my sources are reliable. When I look out at you, I can anticipate a thousand questions. You want proof, answers, and corroboration from authorities. Well, I can only place trust in my own experience; there will be no such official corroboration forthcoming. Such information is tightly controlled by certain people in our government who are not necessarily bound to any legal imperative for disclosure.

'No, because the very nature of our freedom-loving democratic institutions are no match against totalitarian regimes which seek to destroy us, so we are told we have to create powerful forces to fight these tyrannies, perhaps losing our innocence in the process. Let me clarify: we have survived a world war that was spawned of an ideological war; this active, hot war has been followed in its turn by the present so-called cold war, which has justified all kinds of nefarious intrigues to win the war. And if alien technology can help our side win that war, our masters of war will do whatever it takes to make sure that we alone are in a way its progenitors.

'Some of us may not agree with that but fear drives most of our strategy. Yes, fear, fear of an apocalyptic loss of our freedoms and way of life; and in a larger sense, fear of the unknown, fear of extraterrestrials—aliens—that so many of us believe cannot be trusted although they have never interfered in probably their last fifty thousand years of visiting Earth since when we were rough cave-dwellers and such, and through whose interbreeding with our distant ancestors, may have hastened our development. Fear drives power, our military-industrial might.

'Let me leave that concept as food for thought; I don't want to challenge conventional belief or religious sentiment, but I do believe that all of what I've just said is true because there's a direct link between alien visits and our remote ancestors whose mythologies provide tantalizing, vivid images of aliens and their spacecraft—any emerging species could be subject to similar events and processes at this stage of their evolution. We are not alone.

'But don't take my word for it; we all have our own journeys to follow; I'm here to move minds with the results of my investigation; I've been punished for it, demoted in effect, and censured, because I've gotten too close to the truth. I believe in the truth. I know one hundred percent these things have happened and continue to happen. And I also know that when someone publicly exposes these issues and attempts to reveal the truth, he is deemed extremely dangerous to certain government officials promoting these supposedly national agendas and puts his own life in danger. No one is immune!

'The fate of the nation takes all precedence, and is in the hands of people who are not subject to judicial oversight; in fact these people have been entrusted by political leaders to do what it takes to protect us, even if they contravene the laws in order to do just that! An oxymoron if there ever was one! Nothing new there, you might think!

'Great Caesar himself assumed the role of dictator to sort out horrendous deficiencies in the old republican system, but he was assassinated before he could correct them. Any takers?' Laughter from many students; he noticed his wife in the second row smiling warily at him. 'Yes, but we all want to believe in the goodness of our system, which is dependent on the men and women who serve as its stewards. Not that many women yet! A pity! Their influence could yet mitigate power and male dominance, or aggression.' He winked at his wife.

'We human beings need to unite to make the changes necessary—and that means all religions and cultures—because some day we will be one homogeneous species like the aliens who continue to visit here—all races together. We are just beginning to see the universe for what it is: a giant life force in itself. Wherever and whenever conditions are appropriate, there is life. We know this from visits of numerous species far in advance of our species. Yet these visitors don't see us as ignorant worthless savages—they see the universe as a vast inclusive community, in which we are all concerned for each other's welfare, even though we occupy different positions in evolutionary time, or are just timeless.

'From whatever we are today, we will eventually evolve into what our visitors are far beyond us in this constantly shifting universe of life and death. God, if you will, is in the mix, an ever-present force that no intelligence can remove; we exist, or we do not. I believe that our destiny is to be out there some day, and forever. Thank you.'

Tremendous applause erupted. Everyone in the auditorium stood up, including William James sitting at the back. His arrival went unnoticed by Nevin. He seemed quite moved by Melbo's speech.

'Any questions?' asked Melbo. He pointed at a student with his hand up, 'Yes!' Numerous others were vying for attention. Melbo answered them all to the best of his ability.

Most of them were about aliens and how they were dangerous. Melbo calmly responded that if it was us going to some new planet where intelligent life at our present level existed would we not expect some fear and distrust? Still, he pointed out the idea of dangerous aliens has clouded the general consciousness in so far as we have projected our own hostile responses on those who would come to this world. Some students wanted to know how they could possibly come here at all, given the distances in light years, and thought it ridiculous anyone could fly that fast. Melbo replied that we don't understand space as they do; apparently, they 'bent' space to fold back on itself thus shortening the distance, and he gave the example of how gravity waves bend as they do around the sun enabling one to see behind it.

He went on to say that the aliens created their own artificial gravity waves by generating antimatter, an idea which had everyone completely puzzled. One person, a science teacher, stood up to denounce Melbo, telling him he was doing a disservice to students who took science seriously, and he assailed Melbo with contemptuous remarks such as "proselytizing", "communist propaganda" and "science fiction". Melbo told him he was like many who had attacked him, as was their right in a free country. Nevin told him later that the teacher in question was a "real prick" who went out of his way to demean and put down anyone who didn't subscribe to his "high standard", a hypocrite of laughable magnitude.

Melbo and DeCourt mingled among the students with Nevin and Mollie hovering. Nevin gave a piece of paper to Melbo explaining how he could use his coded system if he wanted to communicate. Melbo put it in his pocket.

'Burn it after you read it,' said Nevin, seriously.

'Okay,' said Melbo, amused.

Eventually they found their way to the front of the school, where in the driveway, Nevin saw his father leaning against his car. William James approached his son.

'Well done, Nevin!' he said proudly. 'And Mary! You two were really great. I had no idea how outstanding you both were.'

'Dad,' said Nevin sheepishly. 'I ... didn't expect to see you here.'

'Hello, Mr. James,' said Mollie blushing.

'I found out from your mother, Nevin. The school called to say you'd be speaking. She had an appointment and couldn't come so I came instead, and I'm glad I did.'

Melbo and DeCourt stood nearby. Nevin was momentarily dumbfounded.

'George and Melissa,' said Melbo, smiling.

'William James.' They all shook hands.

'You have one smart son,' remarked Melbo.

'He is that and more. Can I offer you a lift?' asked James.

Melbo and DeCourt looked at each other.

'Why not?' said Melbo.

Nevin spoke up. 'We have more school, Mr. Melbo. Thanks for coming.'

'It was my pleasure. I hope they won't be too hard on you for having me speak,' he joked.

'It would still be worth it.'

'Take care, and you too Mollie.'

DeCourt gave Mollie a quick hug. 'Thanks for inviting him.'

'See you later,' said James to Nevin, on the way to his car.

Melbo and DeCourt got into the black Chevy sedan, Melbo sat in the front with James, and they drove off.

Nevin and Mollie watched them go.

'What was he doing here?' asked Mollie.

'I don't know, but he seemed okay with it.'

'Yeah, but—'

'Likely he just wanted to meet him; if not for Dad I wouldn't have read those articles.'

'Maybe, but he *is* FBI.'

'Somehow I don't think he means any harm; he wouldn't have presented himself like that in front of us otherwise, knowing our secret about him and your mom.'

'Well, I'm glad he didn't bring her!'

They laughed as they went back inside the school.

23. The Eye of the Needle

You have such a great kid!' DeCourt was addressing James from the back seat. 'And that Mollie; she's so smart.'

'She is that,' replied James, smiling, 'and thanks.'

'Your son mentioned you work for the FBI,' said Melbo. 'Are you here today in an official capacity?'

'No, not at all; I wanted to hear what you had to say. I've read your articles. No one knows I was at the school; and no one knows from my end you're even here, if you're worried.'

'The FBI?' said DeCourt, more severely, 'That adds a new dimension to this little *autour*.'

'Hey, I'm here purely for personal reasons; I'm not going to report anything, if you're worried. The subject of alien visitation interests me profoundly; and if it makes you feel any better, I'll let you in on a little secret— I work in counter-espionage. Just between you and me, seriously. In fact, I'd be willing to help you in any way at all, if possible.'

Melbo and DeCourt looked at each other.

'Listen,' James went on, 'Nevin found those articles in the locked drawer of my desk in my locked study; he doesn't know that I know that. I locked them there because I didn't want anyone to know that I'm a supporter of your investigations. You see, I'm part of the system that wants to keep a lid on all of it. Like you said in your speech—bang on—elements of the secret government do have a very big interest in this phenomenon. I don't know anything about these so-called classified programs; you know way more about it than I do, but the public exposure of these things has them worried, to say the least.

'In my profession, they can do exactly what has happened to you: debunk and destroy your credibility. You can take it to the bank, and if that doesn't work, believe me they will do whatever it takes to protect their mission. This is a highly classified strategic objective to create absolute supremacy over our enemies. But you know all that. So please, I wouldn't be admitting all this to you if I wished to make trouble for you.'

'Thank you for your candid appraisal of my situation, but how can you help me?' asked Melbo.

James drove on deep in thought before answering.

'I haven't thought it through to know how best to approach this so that I can keep my anonymity, and give you the heads up, if or when necessary. I work as liaison to the CIA—yes there are cross-channels; in my case, they came easily because of my family connections which have run deep in the culture of intelligence. I worked for the OSS during the war as a young recruit. My present position came as a favor from Hoover, who knew my father and knew of my hardline battles along with de Gaulle and the Nationalists against the French Communists during and after the war. I earned my spurs, in spite of de Gaulle being a pompous snob, and Hoover, a god-damned queer—pardon me, ma'am.'

'Really?' said DeCourt, 'you're pardoned.'

'Thanks, I'm sorry, but I have an irreverent side, though I'm religious, and a sinner—an occupational hazard.'

'So, Mr. James, is this confession an expiation for something?' asked DeCourt delicately.

'Yes, and no. You can call me Bill. I'm doing my job keeping America safe; and you two are the kind of people who make this country worth fighting for.'

'I do believe we have a found a new friend, dear,' noted DeCourt to her husband.

'What's your position on President Kennedy, Bill?' inquired Melbo.

'Huh, well, I'm a dyed-in-the-wool Republican, but I do accept him as our President. We'll see what he's made of next week.'

'Next week?'

'Yeah.'

'Something big gonna happen?'

'Today's Friday the fourteenth, right? Well, next week you'll find out. Just keep it under your hats.'

'We're going to the Virgins tomorrow,' said DeCourt. 'Should we cancel?'

'The Virgins? Sounds great, go; but you may not hear for a day or so.

Relax, enjoy yourselves.'

'That was the idea,' she said.

'Whereabouts in the Virgins?' he asked.

'St. Croix.'

'First time?'

'Yes, friends of ours have a house, and they've just had a baby.'

'Wonderful.'

'Harley has a yacht and we hope to do some sailing.'

'Harley?'

'Yes.'

'And Hannah?'

'Yes. You know them?' asked DeCourt, surprised.

'That was a wild guess, total coincidence.'

'Really?' said DeCourt.

'Hey, Harley Greenfield is someone I have the greatest respect for; he's a hero in my books. I knew him in the war; he was my commander of sorts, though I met him only once; the way the operations worked, at least. He's quite a bit older than you folks.'

'It's a long story,' said Melbo.

'Hannah had a baby girl last month,' said DeCourt, quietly changing the topic of conversation.

'I'm happy for them. She's a legend, you know.'

'We know,' said DeCourt.

'Both retired now,' said Melbo. 'Well deserved.'

'I thought they were dead, until I saw them last summer at my sister-in-law's summer party; I didn't even know their real names. I called him Jean, and I saw that she was Judith Graham, worked in State.' He laughed. 'I met her once back in France; we were on the same plane heading back here; it was in September, 1945, what a knockout. I was married though, with a kid, my daughter Carolyn; she's sixteen now. Can you believe it?'

'Time is a chameleon,' said Melbo, curiously.

'Never thought of it that way.'

'Did you know Keith Leverton?'

'Leverton, no, can't say I have. Who's he?'

'He died last year; used to work with Majestic.'

'Majestic? How did he die?'

'Officially suicide, but we think he was murdered.'

'Why?'

'We think he was photographed with me by someone unknown to us. He told me he had worked for Majestic a few years back. He was a source for me.'

'I'm sorry.'

They turned onto Pennsylvania Avenue. The Willard was a few blocks ahead.

'You can let us off here,' said Melbo.

'Sure.' James pulled over.

'Who would do such a thing?' asked DeCourt.

'Listen, I hate to say it but there are rotten people who will do that sort of thing, people who are convinced they are doing a service for this country. I can't stand it but I'm not in a position to stop it.'

'Who *is*?' asked Melbo.

'Take a guess. Anybody who has the power to be untouchable—and you've said it before—actually believes it's the right thing to do. I'll tell you this: most people just want to get on with their lives in this country; do what it takes to succeed at something, so as long as this country can return the favor of protecting our freedom and prosperity. So if some official is taken out in Central America, or wherever, most people couldn't care less as long as they can still play golf, go to the movies, sleep without worry. To these people all is well.'

'Is Aubrey Woods one of those untouchables?'

'Christ, Melbo, he's my brother-in-law. I'm not going to rat on him.'

'What about Allen Sulla?'

'Sulla is a titan. I think you can rest assured he is exactly what he is. No one knows him really well, probably including his wife; he's positively remote but he's a loquacious bastard, a shark in a dark sea. Hoover tried to get leverage on him—well, Hoover just about self-destructed.'

'We heard something about that.'

'So you know what I mean.'

'And the president?' queried Melbo. 'He's a titan as well; perhaps there's a chance they'll find amity in the battle for the soul of America.'

'Well, I sure as hell hope so, because if it comes down to a brawl … I don't know. Our real enemy is Soviet.'

'Kennedy can dismiss him.'

'I'm not a betting man, but I'd wager Kennedy wouldn't leave Sulla unchecked. That's a fight that this country cannot allow.'

'What are you saying?'

'I'm saying Kennedy would be wise to keep him where he is until Sulla dies a natural death.'

'Or?'

'Kennedy has no idea who he's dealing with.'

'I don't think you give him enough credit.'

'Alright, could be. But you get my drift.'

'I get it.'

'I'm not sure you do. It's like the eye of the needle parable—a seemingly impossible supposition that a camel must pass through the eye of a needle before a rich or powerful man can enter the kingdom of God—it's a metaphor.'

'Meaning what?'

'You may find this a bit idiosyncratic, but knowing the people I know, it kind of makes sense to me. You know "In God We Trust"? Eisenhower declared it as a national motto in '56; it had its origins in secret societies which likely influenced its choice. When I was undercover in France in 1944 during the war, I once spent a few days hidden in a secret cellar of a barn, evading Nazis. There was this wise old Jew, Isaac, who had been living there with his granddaughter for some time.

'We spoke at length about religion. He said that when he was a boy, he was told that 'the rich man' proverb of the so-called New Testament was actually mentioned in some ancient Hebraic texts—'prophetic' was the word he used— a 'man of power' even a powerful priest of—say a rival faction; well, the camel was actually the glyph for the Aramaic third letter, *gimel*, depicting a hump, which also represented a level of rank in their ancient hierarchy; and if that person graduated to a higher level, the *qoph*, a letter depicting the eye of the needle, it was a simple metaphor for succession, the camel passed through the eye of the needle and the powerful man could claim entry into the kingdom of God.

'Well, one can then see its significance in its present incarnation: the high priest of the intelligence world who succeeded would find any justification in God's name to carry out His divine plan. And if we accept that Kennedy is the 'king' of sorts, the people's ruler, he would be outranked according to ancient doctrine by the high priest who would be considered the supreme authority in spiritual matters, the earthly representative of God.'

'You actually believe that?' asked Melbo.

'As an historical anecdote, yes; but as a bureaucratic model of sorts no, yet the essence of some entitlement in it can't help but stick. I know these people. I grew up with them, just like my son is now.'

'It's like a cult,' offered DeCourt.

'Yes, exactly, and it runs through the very soul of the constitution written by our founding fathers. No one is above the law, except God.'

'Come on, Bill!' laughed Melbo. 'One would think you live under the auspices of a Masonic creed!'

'And justice for all; they were honorable men.'

'When such policy comes to the aliens then, it's out of hand. Perhaps Kennedy should take this to the people—bring it down from the mountain—and take the place of the High Priest.'

'Good luck with that, George!' James laughed, as they got out of the car.

'I think you know how to reach us. Through that son of yours.'

'I'll take your word for it.'

*

The Eastern Air Lines DC-6B four prop landed at the Henry E. Rohlson International Airport in St. Croix in the late afternoon after a short stop in Miami. Exiting the plane, the Melbos walked down the mobile stairway breathing in the warm air. Earlier in the day, there had been showers and the humidity still remained heavy. They were collecting their two small bags when Greenfield, sporting a light green linen shirt and khaki shorts with runners and socks appeared tanned and beaming like a young man. After a hug and kiss for DeCourt and solid handshake with pats on the back for Melbo, they got into the green Renault with the top down.

'I have to hand it to you, Harley; you've got it all figured out,' said Melbo. 'The scented air, warm sea breeze, young wife, baby girl. What more could you want?'

'Absolutely nothing,' he laughed. 'After crawling through hell to get here, I find heaven just as it should be, and Hannah agrees!'

'We're so thrilled to be here!' cried out DeCourt uncharacteristically.

'I thought you might approve!' exclaimed Harley.

'And mother and babe? How are they?' she asked eagerly.

'Couldn't be better; Lizzy's healthy and growing by the minute! Mom is the dairy queen—her words!'

They all laughed in perfect joy.

'Hannah must be the best mother,' continued DeCourt.

'You know,' agreed Harley, 'it's as if everything in her life, and that's saying something, had led up to this most natural and loving thing, her motherhood.'

'That *is* saying something,' agreed DeCourt. 'Quite a flipside from the cold warrior!'

'So it's Lizzy, is it?' said Melbo.

'I call her Lizzy; she calls her Lizbet.'

'What do we call her?'

'What you will!'

Soon they arrived at the house. Prinzenthal greeted them like long lost family, she was so happy; she had trimmed her hair leaving it shorter, above her shoulders and was tanned. Wearing a loose cream blouse and similar cotton pants, and barefooted sans bra, she was ready to feed at any moment. They all gushed over the baby, who looked up with her bright blue-green eyes, which seemed the only visible sign of Harley in her; otherwise, she took on her mother's looks, though Prinzenthal insisted she was a good mix.

The following day, Greenfield and Melbo drove over to Green Cay to check on his yacht, the *Hannah & Lizbet*. They took it out for a short sail around the island in a soft breeze. All was ship-shape and ready for their longer trip to St. Thomas the next day. Melbo related the peculiar events of the previous days in Washington, and in some detail he let it be known that William James seemed like a good man, if a little odd with his Masonic ideas, though if he really was a member of a lodge, he was not being particularly loyal.

Greenfield was amused by the whole episode. Recalling his brief chat with James the previous summer and his brief meeting with the boy, he then connected the dots upon hearing that the boy eavesdropped on senior officials in the garden; he remembered clearly that Sulla, Lovering and Woods had had a little parlay down in the corner by the ledge and presumed the boy by chance had been directly beneath them.

'This Nevin has the makings of a spy it seems.' Greenfield grinned.

'And his girlfriend, Mollie—Mary McBride—they were very close.'

'And they're only fourteen—precocious.'

'I couldn't help but get the feeling that Bill James was a touch intimidated by them.'

'Because his son rummaged through his desk?'

'No, he didn't seem to mind that, or if he did something held him back.'

'Like he's using his son to get to us?'

'Well that obviously; but no, something else.'

'Whatever it is; it's working.' Greenfield laughed.

'Yeah, I guess.'

The yacht sliced through the surf; dolphins leaped and dove alongside them. Greenfield and Melbo watched the spectacle for some time.

'I was contacted by the White House,' disclosed Greenfield out of the blue.

'By whom?'

'Someone who works for the Chief-of-Staff.'

'Doing what?'

'Kennedy's looking for someone to consult with the Assistant National Security Advisor, me evidently.'

'That's encouraging, isn't it?'

'One would think so, but I'm familiar with the nature of this business. It operates on a need-to-know access to classified material; the intelligence services are very selective who they impart information to. If the national security issues are in the news, the public sphere, they will reveal what needs to be divulged, say in a state of war. This is my experience, anyway. Otherwise they remain quite secretive, which makes them more effective obviously when they're in the field.

'The problem is that intelligence chiefs like Woods and Angleton can get carried away with their own agendas. It was quite common to keep certain people out of the loop because they feared the executive branch might inadvertently leak classified info if it were found out. What concerns me is that I couldn't be effective in situations involving Kennedy pitting himself against the CIA because in such confrontations, I would fall in on his side, and thus, as I said I'd be kept out of the loop. Only by being on the inside of the intelligence services could I be of any use as a liaison to Kennedy.'

'And you're finished with it,' said Melbo.

'Indeed I am and love it,' conceded Greenfield.

'But you could still advise, just because of your experience.'

'Yes, and I'm considering it. I mentioned you.'

'Me? They ignored me.'

'They would of course. To hire a discredited reporter would only serve to endorse much of what you have investigated.'

'So what did they say?'

'Not much. I told them I would need an assistant.'

Melbo laughed. 'An assistant to the assistant to the assistant, and probably a few more.'

'They didn't balk at the idea. I said I needed someone to do research, off the books.'

'We may be able to use someone on the inside,' suggested Melbo. 'William James is an insider.'

'My very thought. Even if he's playing it both ways, our position is still strong.'

'How do you mean?' asked Melbo.

'We have leverage. You know his kid.'

'I'm not so sure I like the sound of that.'

'No, don't misunderstand me; it doesn't matter what the kid gives us if he's not aware what he's giving us; it's all gotta be very quiet, *sub rosa*; you see, we'll feed something back to his dad and there's no way he'd ever implicate his son, or the girl.'

'He'd protect them, as we would,' said Melbo.

'Precisely, a perfect foil or cover. No one would suspect the kids if they were passing along information; they think it's a game they're qualified to play.'

'But it isn't.'

'No. Still, they take it very seriously from the sounds of it.'

'Yes, they do.'

'I could be way off here, but I don't think these kids are as innocent as they seem.'

'How so?' wondered Melbo

'Any kid who brings in his girlfriend, if that's what she is, who he's likely trying to impress, and goes to all the trouble of educating her about your articles and his secrets, is rather driven, cagey, even cunning. But we know it shouldn't matter because they're just kids, still they're—'

'*Entitled* kids,' stressed Melbo.

'Yes, but, *underestimated.*'

'I suppose, but does it matter?' Melbo thought about this. 'We'd be culpable no matter whether we use minors or not.'

'Perhaps, but they'll never be caught if their father's involved; he'd blame us, or himself first.'

'And we'd be working in the national interest,' added Melbo, more convinced.

'Therefore, as long as James is onside with us and is willing to divulge classified material through his kid, no one's the wiser.'

*

At the same time in the afternoon that Greenfield and Melbo were sailing around St. Croix, William James was sitting in his study in a high-backed chair reading numerous briefs and some magazines. After a while he stood up and paced for a bit, trying to work through some difficult problem. Then he went to the door and called Nevin, who was watching television. Nevin came upstairs and stood at the open door of James' study.

'Come in, Nevin.'

Nevin entered and stopped. His father was leaning against his desk.

'Please take a seat, son.'

Nevin sat in a low sofa chair. 'What's up, dad?'

'I just want to say how proud I am of your initiative at school to bring Mr. Melbo down to speak last Friday. That showed courage, given your age and interest in the subject of alien visitation. And Mollie too; she takes after her parents, who are both superb people.'

'What's this about, dad?'

'I don't want to rain on your parade, son; in fact, I want to apologize for my behavior after meeting with Deacon Purdy; I just lost my temper, when I should've been more … understanding. Not to say it was right—you're thing with Mollie—I assume it was her; we're all guilty of wrongs, but as teenagers your curiosity about sexual matters is quite natural. What I'm trying to say is be careful; you're very young and smart; I wouldn't want you to get into any kind of trouble. At her age girls can get pregnant.'

'Dad, we don't do that, yet.'

'I'm relieved to hear it, and I urge you in the strongest terms to delay it until you're older.'

'Don't worry, after seeing you and Mrs. McBride—well, it kind of shocked us.'

'Damn it, I'm so upset about that, we were just as shocked; I have no excuse; we love each other, always have, but I married your mom because I got her pregnant during the war. We were young and reckless, and I was going overseas; and Deborah was seeing other guys. I'm truly sorry you had to see that.'

'It's okay, dad. I won't tell mom.'

'I'm counting on you, Nevin; it would ruin us as a family. My relations with Deborah Godfrey go back to high school. She met John McBride after we graduated. The world was in disarray, infernal war with Hitler and Nazi Germany and Japan. She found out about me and your mom who was barely seventeen, and I twenty-one. That's just how things were.'

'I have something to confess too, since we're being on the level.'

'What's that?'

'I found the key to your drawer and opened it. That's how I discovered George Melbo.'

James nodded his head in acknowledgement. 'I'm glad we're both on the same page.'

They actually laughed.

'There's more,' said Nevin. 'Mr. Melbo and I have agreed to communicate.'

'How?'

'By letter.'

'What will you communicate?'

'I said I would let him know if I found out about aliens, or anything.'

'From me?'

'Or from anyone.'

'Now listen to me: you can't do that; at least not in the way you're going about it.'

'We have a code.' Nevin explained to his father about the letters.

'Alright, but I think you should confide in me whatever you're thinking about communicating.'

'Will you help us?'

'As long as it's safe.'

'We're just students interested in aliens. What's the harm in it?'

'People might read Melbo's mail.'

'Really? Even still they wouldn't find anything.'

'Likely not, but if they found out who you are, it might implicate me.'

'I sent the letter to his paper.'

'One time is fine; I'm just thinking that in future you should use a cut-out, another person at an address no one is aware of, and letters should be sent from a box somewhere else, not from our local post office.'

'Like who?'

'Perhaps his wife at work.'

'Mrs. Melbo? I don't know where she works.'

'I'll find out.'

'Okay. Why are you doing this?' Nevin asked, skeptically.

'I feel a need to protect you; there are some really dark forces at work in this business.'

'Mollie and I aren't breaking any laws.'

'Not yet, but if you get caught with classified material—well—'

'Well what?'

'Look, this is my area of expertise and I don't like this situation about you and Mollie spying—as harmless as it appears—at all, it's wrong; but since you … you know, we're both wrong, but that's not going to change, is it? You wouldn't give up Mollie, and I can't give up her mom. So let's be smart and keep it simple; maybe we can make a difference. Someone needs to know the truth about the real world.'

'But not our truth, right?'

'You can say that again.'

'It's kinda hypocritical isn't it?'

'You're learning fast, Nevin; there're bigger fish to fry.'

*

The *Hannah & Lizbet* tacked effortlessly with the dinghy in tow in an easy trade wind towards St. John, the Virgin Island, the landmass of which was mostly National Park. The fifty mile or so trip would take the better part of the day, but that didn't stop Greenfield from laying down a fishing line with a live ballyhoo attached to a large hook and spoon weighted to send it deep. The rod was secured in the boat and, as they approached the banks off St. John, the rod bent suddenly, to everyone's delight. With DeCourt at the wheel, Greenfield reeled in their prize with consummate skill, a three foot wahoo, its bluish iridescence glittering in the sun as it was netted by Melbo and pulled aboard.

'Dinner!' exclaimed Greenfield gleefully.

He then gutted and fileted the fish, threw overboard the remains except for some to be used for the lobster traps, and put the meat on ice in a tray of a refrigerated cooler. Both DeCourt and Melbo marveled at his skill making quick work of the fish. Prinzenthal emerged from the cabin holding little Lizbet awake and fed.

'Isn't daddy wonderful?' she cooed to Lizbet as Greenfield flushed out any remains of fish from the deck with a bucket of seawater.

'She seems to take to the sea,' commented DeCourt, smiling. 'We haven't heard a peep.'

'Nothing like a gentle sea to keep her asleep.'

'Oh, look, her eyes are open wide!' gushed DeCourt. 'May I hold her?'

Melbo took the wheel, and DeCourt held the baby, who stared back at her passively.

'Such a beauty,' she smiled. 'Those eyes melt me!'

They all hovered over the star attraction as St. John appeared on the far horizon.

Greenfield weighed anchor in a small, deserted cove near the National Park. No one else was around. He explained that he could drop a few small lobster traps attached to little floating buoys and rope; these traps he proceeded to bring out from the small forward hold by the engine, then putting pieces of the wahoo in the traps he lowered them into at least forty feet of water. They lifted the anchor slightly and put in all three traps about fifty feet apart.

'I was successful here before,' said Greenfield. 'I caught a five-pounder—best langouste I ever ate.'

'How did you cook it, Harley?' asked DeCourt.

'On the beach over a fire on a camp grill, then I melted butter and herbs. We can do the same with the fish this evening.'

'We'll camp on the beach for the night,' offered Melbo; 'to give you some space on the boat with the baby.'

'There's no need,' said Harley. 'There's the extra berth.'

'Oh, Harley, let them camp,' insisted Prinzenthal. 'I think they have more than star-gazing in mind.'

They all laughed.

'We don't mind,' said Melbo.

'I think under the circumstances perhaps you could use the tent.' Greenfield smiled knowingly.

'Not in the open under the stars?' suggested Prinzenthal, mischievously.

'Mel snores,' replied DeCourt. 'We wouldn't want to keep you awake; it might carry across the surf.'

'The only thing carrying across the surf would be your banshee howls, my love,' retorted Melbo.

'Oh really?'

'The neighbors at home always complain by knocking on the wall.'

'That's an outrageous lie, George Melbo. Don't listen to him.'

'Okay, it happened once.'

'You're tempting the fates, husband.'

Greenfield and Prinzenthal were laughing so hard the baby began to cry.

Later they all climbed into the dinghy, fitted with oars and folded sail, and stowed all their camp equipment and coolers. Melbo and DeCourt each pulling an oar, drove them onto the sand about a hundred yards from the moored yacht. Onshore, they set up the tent and a large open canopy as protection from the intense sun near the wild semi-tropical flora above the tide line. The land radiated heat and sweet scents, and they could hear the incessant sound of exotic birds. A few lizards darted about. Once they were organized, everyone except Prinzenthal and the baby went snorkeling towards an old coral reef farther along the beach. Greenfield came back sooner so Prinzenthal could get some snorkeling in herself.

That evening they built a fire and grilled the fish marinated in lemon and herbs accompanied with fried potatoes and butter with some sautéed *callaloo*—generic name for various pigweeds in the Caribbean—in peppers and green onions. They ate their delectable meal around the fire with a chilled Bordeaux sauvignon blanc. It was certainly a meal to remember. DeCourt set up her camera for automatic pictures and quickly nestled in beside Melbo to take several pictures showing all of them, even Lizbet. Afterwards Greenfield brought out an unopened pack of hand-rolled Bolívar Royal Corona cigars and cognac. Both he and Melbo lit up. DeCourt took a hit off Melbo's cigar and managed quite well.

'Take one, Mel, if you're so inclined,' quipped Greenfield.

'Just testing,' said DeCourt. 'I wondered what all of the fuss was about—a man thing.'

'It goes well with cognac,' he said. He poured her a couple fingers in a glass.

'Thanks,' she said, taking it and another hit on the cigar from her husband. 'If you're gonna smell of cigar, dear, I might as well too if we're gonna sleep together.'

'That's my woman,' said Melbo, putting his arm around her.

After much merriment and some discussion about Cuba, Melbo rowed Greenfield and his family back to the yacht, then back again to the beach.

Next morning, they were all cooking again—eggs and bacon served with bread and mangos, bananas and avocados. They had a five gallon tank of water from which they made tea and coffee.

Then, leaving their camp they sailed the *Hannah & Lizbet* to Coral Bay, a small town over an hour away, where they replenished their water supply and bought newspapers, sundry items and fresh vegetables. After a lunch of conch sold on the dock, they returned to their little paradise.

'A fiasco,' said Greenfield, commenting on the contents of the newspaper.

They were now apprised of the disastrous *Bahía de Cochinos* invasion of Cuba by mercenaries, Cuban exiles, and others.

'Bay of Pigs,' said Melbo, 'Just as Bill James had alluded to something big. He likely thought the military would follow through.'

'Kennedy backed down; it was in all probability a CIA operation, and there're going to be some really pissed off people,' said Greenfield.

'Are you intimating that the intention of Sulla was to pressure Kennedy into a war in Cuba?'

'Likely, but you have to wonder why Kennedy went along with it in the first place.'

'To appease the hardliners,' suggested Melbo.

'Or let it play out and see how successful it was. No doubt it's been in the works since the previous administration.'

'It'll be a showdown,' stated Melbo, 'between Kennedy and Sulla. Who's in charge? Who conducts foreign policy?'

'Sounds like Jack is in deep trouble now,' added Prinzenthal. 'Sulla and the old guard will be sharpening their knives.'

'He knew what had to be done,' said Greenfield. 'He made a choice to show them who's the boss; the logistics for a protracted war, a guerilla war was more than they could chew without a major invasion involving all the armed forces; a war that would be seen as reprehensible, exorbitant.'

'It's unfortunate for the men who lost their lives,' said DeCourt. 'The survivors will want revenge for being left without help. That's surely why they signed up in the first place with the promise of support.'

'Kennedy should've nixed it at the outset,' said Melbo.

'Too late now.'

'It's not even a hundred days in the White House for him,' said Greenfield. 'Baptism of fire.'

When they arrived back at their cove they pulled up the lobster traps and found four lobsters in varying sizes. That evening they cooked them on the camp grill and Prinzenthal made a mushroom-vegetable fried rice. For dessert they ate the coconut, pineapple, guava, and mango tarts they had purchased that day.

After dinner, sitting again by the fire and puffing his cigar, Greenfield announced he was going to take the offer from the White House on the condition that Melbo could be used incognito as an analyst in New York. He and his family would return the following week; then he would find a place to rent in Washington. But for the time being their little paradise held sway with the sound of the gentle surf in their ears. The next day after pancakes with agave syrup and fruit they packed up and turned the *Hannah & Lizbet* once again towards St. Croix. A decent breeze came up, hurrying them along to the future coming on like a riptide.

24. Nora

Melbo and DeCourt were eating supper when there was a light knock on their door. Melbo stood up from the small dining table and went to the door and opened it. Standing in the hallway, dressed in her bag lady outfit—jeans, runners and old raincoat with sunglasses—and her black hair wig covered by a simple bandana was Nora.

'Mel,' she said, 'Thank God you're here.'

'Come in,' he said quickly, and shut the door.

They hugged briefly, DeCourt as well. There was an urgency in Nora's manner.

'Sorry to come unannounced. I really needed some refuge; it's been an intense few days.'

Marilyn took off her sunglasses revealing the sad eyes of her archetypal twin.

'News was abuzz with you in town,' said DeCourt. 'We heard about Madison Square Gardens.'

'I hope that's all you heard.'

Melbo took her raincoat and hung it up. 'Please sit down. Are you hungry?'

'I hadn't thought about it, Mel, but I am a little.'

'Melissa's made some fried chicken with potatoes and veg.'

'If it's not too much trouble.'

'Are you kidding?' he said as he pulled up a chair while DeCourt fetched a plate and wineglass, which Melbo filled.

Marilyn sat knock-kneed on the edge of the chair, with her hands together and head bowed like a penitent.

'I'm so sorry I've been out of touch,' she said looking down at her plate, 'Off the top, life has been, let's say, unlovely. I've come to realize I'm not a creative being in my best estimation of it; in fact, I'm rather lazy and indolent and ride the magic carpet of fame and notoriety as a deceit.' Looking up at

DeCourt, then at Melbo, she continued: 'Just the very imposition of my presence here and this pitiful confession is a perfect example of my pathetic life.'

'I disagree,' said DeCourt sympathetically. 'By the looks of it, you're suffering from lack of sleep.'

Marilyn looked at her and smiled. 'You're probably right, Mel.'

'Mel is always right, Norma Jeane,' stated Melbo. 'The lioness is the oracle of the constellation Leo; what she is actually saying is that, in spite of your self-pity you are the most magnanimous and enlightened of women.' To his wife he then said with mock formality. 'Should we not conjure up the spirit of Malibu here in rainy New York?'

'Indeed,' replied DeCourt, picking up on his gesture, 'Let's toast one of the happiest days in our lives.'

'How could I forget?' said Marilyn, picking up her glass of Sauterne. 'I love you both. It's like my internal compass sleep-walked me here, darting out of the back door of my building after being holed up for two days in some existential void. To Malibu!'

They all clinked their glasses and drank.

'Mmm, so delicious,' purred Marilyn, putting down her glass. 'A Bordeaux?'

'Yes,' said DeCourt, 'one of my favorites.'

'She's quite the wino,' said Melbo, beginning to eat again.

'How have you two, been?' asked Marilyn, cutting into her chicken leg. 'You know I think of you often, and thanks for your birthday card last year, and Christmas; sorry I've been negligent.'

'We're fine,' said DeCourt. 'Very fine; no worries. Mel's been very busy writing weekly columns for the Post, and also does some research and consulting with someone attached to the White House, unofficial I might add.'

'Oh, really?' Marilyn brightened. 'Impressive; that's quite a turnaround from a year ago; I recall you were let go from the Trib—likely getting too close to the truth for those Republican dinosaurs after Jack was elected.'

'It's been an interesting year,' responded Melbo. 'I actually feel like I'm getting through now to where it counts.'

'Do you mean you have the attention of the President?'

'Well, not his personally, but others.'

'Well, not meaning to pry, but you have my strictest confidence; and in turn I will tell you I spent the night with the President after his birthday celebration—early birthday that is, last Saturday night.'

They ate in silence for a moment, her disclosure hanging in the air.

'I didn't *sleep* with him, though he seemed to want it; I couldn't let myself because of Jackie; we talked actually, rather intimately about many things, troubling things. It was a night of confidences; it was like we bared our souls to each other, a very cerebral and insightful *tête à tête*. It left me exhausted, depressed.'

'We saw the news clips of you singing 'Happy Birthday',' said DeCourt. 'You were wonderful.'

'Thanks, but was I *nervous*. I was late because I had a panic attack, and had to take a few pills, which seemed to have had the desired effect.'

'It was perfect, Norma, very cool and fun loving at the same time,' chimed in Melbo.

'Thanks, Mel.' She smiled. 'I can always count on you to lift my spirits. Does he have that effect on you, Mel?' she asked DeCourt.

'We're very different creatures with the same nickname.' She laughed. 'A friend of mine at work did our astrology, and apparently we're quite compatible.'

'When's your birthday and year?'

'August 13th, 1938.'

'And Mel?'

'March 4th, 1934.'

'Pisces and Leo, interesting.'

'Why?' asked Melbo.

'The fish and lion…I don't know, I suppose what seems unlikely on the surface in astrology can be deceiving.'

'I was told we have good planets in synastry and composite,' said DeCourt, defensively.

'Good for sex, anyway,' teased Melbo.

'Mel!' exclaimed DeCourt defiantly.

'Whatever it is,' observed Marilyn laughing, 'you have an amazing relationship. It makes me envious.'

'Don't be,' advised DeCourt. 'He may be smart and literary, but like men in general he can at times be rather indifferent to my needs.'

'Tell me about it,' said Marilyn reflectively. 'It's the story of my life.'

'What Mrs. Melbo is really saying,' said Melbo, 'is that she wants a baby, and I want to wait another year, or two.'

'What a charming dilemma,' said Marilyn, 'to have or have not a baby!'

'I keep threatening to stop taking the pill,' answered DeCourt, simpering.

'You're what, twenty-three?' stated Marilyn, 'What's a year or two?'

'I suppose,' she answered, backing down. Then looking at Melbo with a mischievous look in her eyes, she added, 'But, my dear, when that time comes, look out for a woman unheeded!'

'Does that mean I'm a lucky guy?' quipped Melbo.

'You're damn right it does!'

They all laughed and thus defused the matrimonial tiff.

When they had finished dinner, Melbo announced suddenly that he wanted to go downtown to review Bill Evans, the jazz pianist who was to perform new material at the Vanguard. Marilyn sparkled in anticipation, relieved of her earlier funk, and DeCourt would not challenge this spontaneous suggestion for the world, even if she did have to get up early. Marilyn's presence offered some famous undercover deployment, and DeCourt was determined to find out what the actress and Kennedy had talked about.

She knew her husband would not broach the subject, given his personal disposition; however, they were both involved in a clandestine arrangement whereby she had become the conduit named Diva for coded letters arriving at work containing sensitive information from Nevin James and his father, Bill. It was a strange situation, and on the surface innocent enough; yet this contact was crucial to Melbo's work with Greenfield, who had the ear of the President. And now, Marilyn had an inside account.

DeCourt knew her husband thought the same thing but in his inimitable way, he would let it play out guilelessly. Was it not in the interest of national security she wondered: little me as the living breathing agent transmitting intelligence? Certainly Hannah would agree, as long as she didn't have to sleep with anybody.

*

They found the perfect table somewhat dark at the back along the center bench out of the general view. Marilyn kept her sunglasses on, though where they sat she would have likely gone unrecognized. She pulled out a pack of

L&M filter cigarettes, and excusing herself lit one. The old black waiter approached and smiled.

'Mr. Mel, sir, and the Missus, nice to see you again.'

'And you, Buzz. How's it going?'

'Oh, you know, every day just fine.' He smiled.

'This is Nora, our dear friend.'

'Hello,' said Marilyn.

'Ma'am.'

'Is Bill here yet?' asked Melbo.

'Not yet. Chuck's here, and Paul.'

'When he arrives, let him know I'm here, would you?'

'Sure, Mel. What'll it be ladies?'

'Do you have any Calvados?' asked Marilyn.

'Yes, I believe so, Ma'am.'

Looking at DeCourt, Marilyn said, 'Trust me on this.'

'Okay.'

To Buzz: 'Then make it two champagnes in a wine glass, each mixed with a shot of Calvados and a squirt of grenadine and cherry garnish.'

'And an iced gimlet for me,' said Mel.

'You got it,' replied the waiter, turning to leave.

'If I recall, in Malibu we drank the champagne neat,' said DeCourt smiling.

'Yes, well, and had we added that to it, I don't think we would have walked out of there,' Marilyn said, laughing.

'It seems so long ago now; so much has happened; Kennedy's election; Mel's new work, the Berlin Wall-'

'It's been well over a year, babe, with the Post,' cited Melbo.

'I know what you mean, Mel,' Marilyn said to DeCourt. 'Time has slipped away like a ghost. I have no idea where it all goes; life has no meaning anymore.'

'Maybe you just need to get back to work,' suggested DeCourt.

'I'd like to if I could handle it; apparently I'm not so easy to work with.'

'Don't say that, Norma,' remarked Melbo. 'I thought *Misfits* was one of your very best; your character Roslyn, came across as an absolute natural, ahead of her time.'

'Some say I killed Clark; I drove him to it,' she lamented. 'He dropped dead not long after.'

'That's hardly your fault. He had a heart condition.'

'It doesn't change how I feel; it's like I'm a demon who draws out all these awful reactions in people.'

'You're no demon,' stated DeCourt. 'You're an angel, and it's the men's fault if they trip over you.'

'I agree,' said Melbo. 'It's a man's world, but change is going to come; we're on the cusp of something big. People need change more than ever, and Kennedy's the man who will lead us there.'

'You know,' said Marilyn, 'that's exactly what I told Jack. I said that he's a much needed jolt to the system.'

'And how did he respond?' asked DeCourt.

'He told me confidentially—and I trust you to keep it that way—that he's up against a real monster. Even after he fired Sulla last November, nothing's really changed. He realizes that the CIA is necessary with its tentacles in everything, but that it's precisely an "oxymoron", his word, in that the nature of the business is uncontrollable by the executive branch; so whatever he does or commands the system carries on relentlessly, with or without him.'

'It depends on good men,' said Melbo.

'In the big bad world the good men are few and far between; it's about power and power corrupts.'

'We have laws,' said DeCourt. 'A separate judicial institution based on the constitution.'

'Oh yes, by all appearances, but nonetheless flawed; and depending on what part of the country or how much money you have, its meaningless. Look at the South, the lynchings—Jack is so appalled at the violence and behavior of whole groups of people; there's no justice; the courts are corrupt, they're so infused with racial bias. Even here in New York or California.'

'Freedom is a concept that goes both ways, for good and bad.'

'True, and the final defense is the press, a free press,' said Melbo.

'I mentioned you,' said Marilyn. 'I said you were punished for telling the truth.'

'What did he say?'

'He said you are young and naïve, a bit like he was, and that though he has the highest regard for your talent, in the brutal landscape of politics we all must tread very carefully around the vested interests of the country and how it manages itself. He said change must ultimately come from each and every one of us with the will to differentiate between right and wrong and able to see the way forward.'

'What else did he say?'

Buzz appeared with his tray of drinks and deftly walked through the growing crowd before he gracefully lowered it to place each drink on the table.

'Bill arrived, Mr. Melbo.'

'Thanks, Buzz.'

Taking a decent sip from her drink, Marilyn seemed to settle into a grand mood.

'I knew it was the right thing to do and show up at your place.'

A few notes from the piano rose above the crowd, whose noise lowered markedly before the bass and drums kicked in smoothly like the fitting of an old slipper. Once underway the music held the murmuring crowd in check, but gradually people resumed their conversations discreetly as the jazz club fell into its natural rhythm.

'I just love it,' Marilyn continued, 'the atmosphere, the music; it feels like it's made for me.'

'He's known for that,' commented Melbo. 'He captures melancholy and hopelessness but with a sunny effervescence like running water over stones in a brook.'

'Yes, I hear that. What's his story?'

'A prodigy really; he worked with Miles Davis for a time, and others; has his own following now. It's been a tough time for him; his bassist Scott LaFaro was killed last year in an auto accident. They had had a great run here and in the recording studio. Chuck Israels, the bassist up there replaced him; and he's a catch; he worked with Coleman Porter, Benny Goodman and even Billie Holliday, but Scott and Bill really connected stylistically.'

'I hope he plays *My Foolish Heart*,' said DeCourt.

'I know that,' said Marilyn, 'It was nominated by the academy for best song a while back.'

'Yes, but what else did Jack say?' asked DeCourt. 'We were interrupted. This drink is amazing by the way.'

'Isn't it? Once some rogue got me into bed with these during my early pictures.'

'Well, it's not for me to say, but perhaps he can be forgiven for it, it's such a great spritzer.'

'I call it Marilyn's Folly.'

They all laughed effusively. At the end of the song, Marilyn lit up another cigarette, just as the music started up again.

'Jack's ahead of his time,' she said, blowing smoke up to the ceiling. 'He told me about women's rights and how the courts are systemically entrenched against them; he told me about the Soviet threat and that in a zero sum game their bombs were just as destructive as ours—and he recommends *détente* but the prevailing opinion is "might is right"; he told me about UFOs and said he is being denied any debriefing as if they don't exist, but he has known about them since the Truman administration; he is completely exasperated by the intransigence on all levels.

'He even told me about his marriage—how much he loves his wife, but has failed her in a kind of male dominated conceit in which unbridled manhood is a compulsion at odds with his obligations to fidelity. He considers his greatest sin to be vanity and believes that if there is a God he will someday have to pay the piper. I told him his qualities far outweigh his weaknesses. He's a human being after all like any other, but his heart is in the right place.'

'What more did he say about UFOs?' asked DeCourt.

'You know, he didn't give specifics, but admitted they are real and that the world has a right to know the truth … though he said nothing about how he could change anything. In spite of that, I think he feels the situation is in good hands and doesn't want to tamper with it. I suggested he take it to the people—open up that box and let it out like what you did, Mel. As President his word would carry a ton of credibility; it might follow that others would then open up without fear of retribution.'

'And?' urged Melbo.

'He said it was a political decision, but that national security trumped his instincts on it.'

'That's it?'

'Well we had a laugh when I suggested he make me his running mate in the next election.'

'And what was his response?' urged DeCourt, laughing.

'He said first he'd have to dump that hustler Johnson and then convince the party I was the Second Coming!'

Melbo grinned. 'You would be if he then came down the mountain with news of alien spaceships in the government's possession and named you as emissary to our galactic neighbors!'

They all laughed again at the absurdity of it all.

'It's not so preposterous as you might think,' giggled Marilyn. 'He said that once he'd consolidated his presidency in the next election, it might be worth a reckoning. I got the distinct impression it was something he had considered in order to return the CIA to his control.'

'He said that?' asked DeCourt.

'No, but he did say that Sulla is still pulling strings, and it irks him to no end.'

'What about the new director, McCone?' wondered Melbo, who knew already that Kennedy had been informed by Greenfield about Sulla through himself by way of Nevin and his father, the father, Bill, having attended meetings at Sulla's home in Georgetown with a number of his Masonic buddies, the topic of conversation being "that fucking Kennedy"!

'He thinks McCone a decent fellow and friend who he can more or less trust, but is no match for the cunning of Sulla and his latent loyalties within the service.'

'He should've fired Hoover instead,' declared Melbo, 'and kept Sulla close at hand: you know, keep your enemies close.' Melbo wanted to say Kennedy had been warned for that very reason and Kennedy needed someone there on his side. Although Hoover was the law, he was no friend of the President. Greenfield had failed to persuade him through his immediate boss, Marty Cayton, the assistant to McGeorge Bundy, the National Security advisor, or even later when he had a chance to speak with the President himself. He told Melbo that he believed Hoover had some dirt on Kennedy and Kennedy wasn't about to risk his moral high ground with his supporters by firing him. Greenfield had revealed to Kennedy that Sulla had some serious smut on Hoover, but likely Sulla would never have helped him anyway, certainly not after being dumped last November. As a result Kennedy was vulnerable with two powerful enemies, even with his brother as Attorney-General.

'Another drink, Melissa?' asked Marilyn.

'One more, then I must get home; I have an early start tomorrow.'

'Mel?'

'The same.'

They listened to Bill Evans and his trio, and ordered more drinks. At the end of the set, Evans, a tall lanky man dressed formally like a professor with dark-framed glasses and combed-back hair made his way to their table and pulled a spare chair from the next table. He was introduced to Nora, and seemed to be quite captivated by her mystique.

'How do you do,' he said. 'Have we met?'

'No,' she lied, 'but I attended one of your shows when you were with Miles and Trane a few years back.' In fact, she'd met him when she was with Arthur Miller.

'Not here then,' he said.

'No, at the Café Bohemia.'

'In '58. You look familiar.' The shades, her wig and disguise worked their magic.

'Everybody says that, Bill.'

'I'm not everybody, but I'll take your word for it.'

'Superb set,' said Melbo. 'Really new.'

'That was the idea: people complained I'd gone white or something.'

Marilyn said, 'You are white.'

'Sure Nora, but I've a black soul.'

'Well, you sure dress like it.' He wore a black suit and tie with a white shirt.

'Thanks, well, I hate to confuse anybody.'

'Not with that playing; you move me.'

'Thanks, but I'm not much of a ladies' man, so Ellaine says.'

'You could've fooled me the way your fingers do the talking.'

Evans laughed, and they all followed, as Buzz brought a drink for Bill.

'Could you play *My Foolish Heart*?' asked Marilyn.

'I don't do requests, but I'll consider it. Actually, I might do one that's better in my own estimation something called *In Love in Vain*—it's on the menu.'

When he played it in the next set, DeCourt and Marilyn seemed to swoon at the way he hunched over the piano as if he was ready to crawl into it. In the third set he played the song that Marilyn had requested, and then, at the end of the set, Melbo prepared to take them home because Marilyn was getting too inebriated, but not like a drunk, just stoned. Evans came by as they reached the exit.

'It's just midnight, Mel; you seem to have the situation in hand,' he said, staring at Marilyn, tottering slightly under a light near the exit.

'My wife has an early start.'

'Which one?' he joked.

'Well, Melissa, actually.'

'Good to see you.' Evans smiled, shaking Melbo's hand. 'Thanks for coming, and you, Melissa.'

'Great show, Bill; we'll see you again soon,' said Melbo, steering Marilyn, with DeCourt's assistance.

'Oh, thanks,' said Marilyn to Bill. 'I really do love that song.'

'My pleasure,' he said, and a moment later, 'Marilyn.'

She turned her head flashing that iconic smile.

25. Spook Central

Mollie dropped the penny into the small wide-mouth Mason jar. It was almost half full, each penny representing another bout of sexual intercourse between Nevin and her. On the weekend after her sixteenth birthday in November, they were trying to do it sixteen times. There wasn't much else to do that rainy day. Her mother was away in Florida out in the Keys with her 'girlfriends', but they both knew she was really with Nevin's father, who was away on government 'business' at the same time.

The Eleventh penny dropped as daylight began to fade, and they had had a late start mid-morning; and that was after their passionate activity of the night before. Nevin was played out and had by then needed an hour or so to recoup his stamina. At their age, of course, this was quite possible. They had ice water, potato chips and chocolate bars to help them; it was a marathon so some preparation was expected. Mollie took it upon herself to be the coach doing all sorts of wild and kinky things to stir her great love to get back in the saddle. She would even entice him with their world record-setting pace as the most continual sex ever for the age of sixteen, or any age.

Years later, she would boast that she and Nevin were the true progenitors of the sexual revolution. The Pill of course was their Providential Potion, which put them on par with God. In a few years' time they would add Hashish, LSD and Magic Mushrooms to their Divine Service, all to the sound track of the general psychedelia of the times. Mollie would be the one to go away to Stanford in California and turn into a *deadhead* following the Grateful Dead band on their quest for immortality. Nevin was less pious deciding to attend Yale, where he eventually obtained a law degree.

They never married, Mollie having taken up the Mission of Free Love, and Nevin the Vows of Chastity. But all that was on a foggy horizon and for the time being number Twelve was the only thing of importance. And then Thirteen, Fourteen, Fifteen, and… well, on the stroke of midnight, after a desperate final ten-minute sprint to the finish line, Sixteen. They both passed out from exhaustion having outdone the proverbial rabbits.

On Sunday afternoon, Nevin, well-rested, went home. To his surprise, his father arrived that evening in time for dinner. Over dinner, his mother, Muriel, asked pointed questions about his father's work. She noted that he had a slight tan and remarked sarcastically that the FBI looked after their own by sending them South for recreational duties. Bill replied that it was true he went south but the seriousness of his work would not allow him to say anymore. To everyone's shock, she stormed out of the room, grabbed her car keys and left the house.

'Don't you care about mom?' asked Carolyn, upset. 'You could've followed her out.'

Nevin looked at his father, who said nothing and continued to eat.

'Well?' entreated Carolyn.

'Your mother and I will patch things up.'

'Mom is unhappy, Dad. You never give her any affection; in fact, you ignore her.'

'I'm sorry.'

'You're sorry. What's that supposed to mean?'

'It means,' injected Nevin, 'that Dad is stressed.'

'So what?' she exclaimed. 'I'm stressed, everybody's stressed, but as a family we can help each other!'

'You're right, Carolyn,' said James. 'I'm a negligent husband and father.'

'Well then, what are you going to do about it?' she asked.

'I will speak to your mother and do the right thing.'

The right thing of course was to end the marriage because he loved Mrs. McBride, or rather, Deborah Godfrey, but that's not what he had in mind. When Muriel returned from driving around, he went to her and kissed her in front of the kids watching *Bonanza*, then led her away to the bedroom. Carolyn had a knowing smile on her face. Nevin wondered if she was still a virgin but thought it best not to ask. He wondered what the family would think if they knew what he'd been doing all weekend, all year, and in between.

Then it occurred to him that his father treated his family like an intelligence operation, with his own son as cut-out. He considered that if the family imploded his father's cover would be blown. Stable marriages made stable careers, especially in the clandestine services, or at least marriages with no red flags did what might otherwise draw attention to instability. Nevin devised Rule Number One: appearances were everything; and Rule Number Two: appearances were everything.

He hadn't thought through Rule Number Three that appearances were everything, even for obvious reasons, but were also misleading in that what was assumed to be conventionally normal was anything but, like a double blind. For instance, he couldn't know that Hoover kept tabs on his occupationally sensitive agents even if they had the reputation for being hard-core anti-Communist fighters. This was especially true of William James, as he was Hoover's special liaison with the CIA; not in an official capacity, but because of his connections.

James kept Hoover informed with monthly reports about various groups and operations around the world, including local Cuban exile groups and their nemesis in pro-Castro or appeasement socialists, of whom Hoover felt certain Kennedy was sympathetic, at least from the Socialist point of view. James had used the CIA's Eduardo Sanchez on occasion through Aubrey, his brother-in-law; this had gotten the attention of Hoover, because unknown to James at the time, Sanchez had originally been one of Hoover's informants chosen from refugees after the revolution.

Sanchez was prepared to do almost anything to get his girlfriend, Inèz Ruiz, who waited patiently in Havana, stateside. Recalled to Washington by Earl Bunting, Sanchez was a reluctant agent for being bounced around between Bunting and James. He had been given the task of bagman for an op about which no one had any information. In the typical agency mode of compartmentalized access, he alone was given the names of people to be paid off with certain sums of cash released through off-shore companies controlled by the CIA; each of those payees in turn had their own job to do. While in Washington, Sanchez had been told over the phone by an anonymous agent at the request of Hoover, who directed him to case the James' residence.

Sanchez complained that he was needed elsewhere but did as he was told because of Inèz, and Hoover was not one to cross. After watching the house for a few days, Sanchez figured the best time to go in was on an early afternoon when everyone was away. The mother went to a women's group at the house of a prominent congressman's wife for what he didn't know why, played golf one day, and had a cooking class another day, but she was always home by four in the afternoon. Usually, the kids were home from school at about the same time.

Dressed undercover as a workman for a plumbing company, Sanchez parked on the street and went in the back door with his tool kit. After having a quick look around the main floor, he went upstairs and looked in the bedrooms. The one room with a locked door he quickly opened with his lock-pick and closed the door quietly behind him. Stealthily rifling through the drawers of the desk and opening the locked drawer, he found nothing of questionable significance. Sanchez had figured he would find nothing as James was to his mind a solid asset incapable of any deceit against his masters.

James was a decent boss who sympathized with Sanchez's dilemma with Inèz; and once even told Sanchez that he would make sure that she would be smuggled out of Cuba on one of their missions. Sanchez had wanted her out the year before when he was sent to Cuba to help with reconnaissance before the Bay of Pigs, but it was deemed too risky at the time; at least he had been able to spend a week with her under the name Antonio Nuñez, but that was almost two years ago.

In the locked drawer, Sanchez also found James' personal folder of photos and mementos of his youth and later, including the newspaper articles by George Melbo. He didn't think they were of any importance, but snapped a few photos to show he had been thorough in his search. One photo of James with an unknown woman was taken recently in the South; they were smiling, standing barefoot, arm in arm, wearing shorts and loose shirts on a breezy beach with palm trees; in the distance stood a barely identifiable bar-shack called *Dan's Paradise.*

Sanchez presumed there was some work-related explanation, perhaps an affair. Then he noticed another old, black and white photograph, taken when James was young with the same woman as a girl. On the desk a family photo showed his wife and children, but the wife was not the woman in the photo. Could it be a family relation? he wondered. But, if so, why was it hidden in this secret stash of personal items?

A sudden idea flashed through Sanchez's mind: he would use this information to undertake a little op of his own. He would present James with his photos of him and his friend—a likely lover—and in exchange for not revealing what he knew to Hoover, he could get James to bring Inèz to America pronto. Additionally, he would present the photos as a favor to reveal Hoover's paranoid surveillance scheme to James.

314

Just as Sanchez was about to leave James' study, he heard voices of people climbing the stairs. He looked at his watch; it was only 2:45 p.m.

'*Mierda!*' he cursed under his breath. He stood behind the door and waited until the voices faded into a room down the hall and the door was shut.

Los niños, he thought, slightly relieved. Slowly, he opened the study door and peeked down the hall. He could hear muffled speaking and hurried movements. Quietly, he padded along the carpeted hallway and put his ear to the door behind which he could hear the sound of a bed being bounced as if someone was playing on it. Then he lowered himself to look through the keyhole and understood. Through the narrow slot of the keyhole, he saw a naked teenage girl lying with her legs spread as the boy threw off his socks and jumped on the bed. Without seeing their faces, Sanchez in a mix of shock and amusement watched the girl reach for the boy's erect penis and guide him in.

'I'm so fucking horny,' she gasped. 'It's been three days!'

'Mollie,' muttered, the boy, 'Mollie, I love you so much; I'm gonna pump you full!'

They began to copulate aggressively, kissing and moaning with urgency. Sanchez could hardly believe what he was seeing. He thought of Inèz and what it would be like, having not seen each other for so long, let alone three days. He couldn't imagine these teenagers lasting long in their intensity, so he waited patiently, knowing there was little risk of being seen. And sure enough, a few minutes later they both seemed to explode in spectacular cries of passionate release. Obviously, they were unconcerned about anyone showing up at the house, having likely planned it that way. *Pequeños demonios*—little devils, figured Sanchez. After a few minutes, they decoupled and lay there side by side looking at the ceiling.

'God,' she said, 'you pumped me good.'

'Give me a few minutes; there's more where that came from.'

'Oh, Nevin, you're my Apollo, my hero, my spy, my everything … I love you!' she cooed.

They kissed and held each other.

After, she asked, 'Anything new from Diva?'

'I haven't checked the box, but nothing for a while.'

'I think the Missile Crisis put a damper on things.'

'Yeah, fucking Castro just had to let the Russians in. What a maniac.'

'He doesn't care about people,' she said.

'Kennedy saved our asses. Dad said the hardliners wanted all-out war, said it was winnable.'

'It makes you realize how precarious the world is; I mean had it been … I don't want to think about it.'

'No doubt we would've been little piles of ashes scattered in the wind.'

'I would've wanted to be together right here doing it and coming at the moment of …'

She burrowed her head into Nevin's chest.

'We're here; that's all that matters,' he said, caressing her back.

'I'm relieved but I wish the aliens could have interfered to prevent a possible extinction event.'

'Yeah, you'd think they'd be more concerned about us.'

'I don't know. Maybe it's the planet they're interested in and couldn't care less if we self-destruct.'

'Yeah, you're probably right, except we're destroying the planet too.'

'So why don't they do anything?'

'Why bother? Humans are too stupid.'

'You and I aren't. They should make us king and queen of Earth.'

'Hey, Queen Mollie, you're making me horny again.' Nevin smiled.

'Oh, forsooth! The king is horny! His desire is my command!'

Mollie moved on top and lowered herself down his body.

Sanchez had seen and heard enough so he carefully backed away, went quietly down the stairs, and left the house.

*

That evening on Q Street, about half a dozen blocks away from the James' residence, a group of men associated with the intelligence community were gathered. Some were retired, others still active, and a few were elected officials; they were all members of a secretive society called the Ghosts, which was now convened in the home of Allen Sulla, their leader, and the ex-Director of the CIA, who had been fired the year before and asked to resign. Because the Ghosts had members in the higher echelons of the intelligence community, industry and government their loyalties remained solidly behind their leader as if nothing had changed.

There was a new director, of course, John McCone, yet the status quo under their previous director had not altogether changed because many of the programs and operations continued on seamlessly. Therefore, this meeting could be described as a debriefing since Sulla had been at the helm of the CIA for so long—the longest of anyone before or since—and the Ghosts had no compunction about seeking the wisdom of this grand old master of the spy world. Aubrey Woods became his general link to the agency as a prominent Ghost, and William James, a Ghost as well, was his close cohort.

When it came to making a decision for some clandestine undertaking, a tactical nod or subtle hint was all that was needed to proceed. This showed that the germinal source of this kind of protocol held little liability for its owner or indeed for its henchmen as the same tactical process trickled down through the ranks. At the lower end a job was a job sometimes with no acknowledged case officer other than a cut-out at his command, using a dead-drop or coded phone message. Only when the final objective of the operation was made clear did those agents have any clue about what they were doing.

At that point, hired professionals with no connection whatsoever to the chain of command did their business, rendering any blow-back to the unidentified source, almost negligible. However, a risky high-stakes operation might bring about other consequences such as political and judicial fallout, and often required the creation of a miasma of confusion; any attempt, then, to investigate such an operation as a criminal act would be confounded by a manufactured plethora of scenarios designed to obfuscate the truth, a truth with no apparent foundation.

In this case, there was a necessary fixing of witnesses who provided insight into any number of cracks in the cover story which then needed a scapegoat, one that could be as opaque as a Communist plot, or an unsuspecting individual. Here it was imperative to have highly placed people on the Ghosts' side in control of the investigative instruments of law to steer the evidence away from their complicity. It was an insidious and evil business.

William James was nursing a bourbon and ice by the door of the sunroom when Senator Rushford Endicott with his ever-present brandy disengaged himself from Sulla, Woods and a couple of others. James said hello as the Senator walked past.

'Hello,' said the senator, stopping and turning to him. 'Feeling left out?' he joked as an afterthought.

'Not at all, Senator,' replied James. 'The times weigh heavy and I'm just taking a pause.'

'FBI, right?'

'Yep.'

'So what does Hoover have to say about all this?'

'I'm quite sure, whatever it is, he's in agreement.'

'Can you be more specific? ... It's James, right?'

'Bill James. He's not quite up to speed yet, sir.'

'Call me Rush, Bill.'

'Rush, I don't think anyone is prepared to do anything that might tarnish the integrity of our electoral system, Hoover included.'

'Where do you stand then? At present, Kennedy will be re-elected hands down.'

'He's not my choice for president, but the people have spoken otherwise.'

'If you had the power to change that, what would you do?'

'I'd take it to the people, I suppose; let them decide.'

'What if the people can't be trusted?' asked Senator Endicott.

'It may be a weakness in the democratic process, but all the more reason for the people to know the truth and make an informed decision.'

'The truth. What is the truth?'

'Whatever you're alluding to that Kennedy is unfit for office.'

'He's a god-damned disgrace and yet has the majority dancing to his tune; and a few young women, including a wife or two.'

'They'll just have to ride him out then. The people won't stand for a cheat.'

'I don't think the country can afford it. The oilmen are up in arms; the brass thinks he's a chicken-shit; he's a Socialist, for crying out loud. What else is there to know about him? He needs to be gone.'

'How would you propose to do that, Senator?'

'I don't propose anything; but if I had the ways and means I'd take him out. End of problem.'

'I believe I've heard of that method before. Stalin was rather fond of it.'

Senator Endicott finished off his brandy.

'Stalin was a Commie psychopath, Bill. We're Americans looking out for America's best interests.'

'Of course, but making a martyr of Kennedy would in the long run just consolidate whatever it is that you don't like what's happening with him alive.'

'How so?'

'For one the youth of today wouldn't stand for it; they'd probably start a revolution to end war.'

'Nonsense. What makes you say that?'

'They want a better world, a kinder world; they look at this world more rationally. What would you do if you were brought up with the threat of nuclear annihilation? Hide under your desk in school, as if that would provide any chance of survival?'

'I'd damn well make sure we'd be on the winning side.'

'That's the problem; there'd be no winning side in their estimation, and in mine.'

'What else then?'

'There should be disclosure about the aliens; at least, that we're not alone.'

'The aliens? What the hell's got into you, Bill?'

'Isn't that what some of us are so concerned about? That Kennedy wants to share the alien technology with the world?'

Senator Endicott swiftly guided James into the living room away from the others.

'Listen here, Bill, it may be okay to speak about that here in this house to me, but you can be assured that very situation is well in hand and Kennedy has no say in it. I didn't realize you were in the loop on that; it's the Gordian Knot of security; no one talks about it.'

'Well, Kennedy does know about it, and Sulla knows he knows, whether he's in the loop or not.'

'So you'd think he'd use it like an ace up his sleeve and take it to the people for political leverage?'

'Why not, given the nature of the man? He'd use that or anything to get a few more votes.'

'Bastard.' The Senator turned and lifted his empty tumbler. 'Come on, let's get a refill.'

At the mahogany sideboard they were refilling their glasses, when Art Lovering arrived. He was helped out of his trench coat by Clover Sulla, greeting her with a kiss, then came straight to the bar.

'Rushford! Good to see you! I need something fast to warm me up; it's damp and cold out there.'

Both the Senator and James greeted him, as he poured himself a three-finger scotch.

'How're the wife and kids?' he asked the Senator.

'Kids? Hell, Artie, Gordon's started his own oil company in the Caribbean; even does a little moonlighting for the agency—Sulla's protégé, war hero n'all; Cuban exiles n'such. Handy labor I understand.'

'Sounds like your understudy, old man.'

'He comes around the office sometimes,' said Bill. 'We grab lunch occasionally.'

'Cooking up a storm,' said the Senator.

They have a hearty laugh.

'I just flew in from Boston,' said Lovering. 'I have to say I've missed Washington and the three-ring circus!'

'Are you finding academia a bit too tame, Artie?' asked the Senator.

'Well, I don't notice the gray hairs.' He laughed. 'I've even managed to write a book, almost finished.'

'About what?' asked James.

'I call it *Security in the Nuclear Age*,' he replied. 'Jake Whitmore has agreed to have it published under one of his imprints, not sure which yet.'

'When will it be finished?'

'After the recent Cuban Missile fiasco I've had to amend it.'

'What's your view on Kennedy's handling of it?'

'As a diplomat, he at least saved us from another war; but if there was ever a right moment to invade Cuba, in a contained war and a moral one, he failed as a Commander-in-Chief. The Soviets wouldn't have risked Armageddon over Cuba. We could have bombed those missile sites into oblivion and taken over that island before the year was out in a full-scale assault. They saw Kennedy as weak; they never would have put missiles there under Eisenhower.'

'Good point,' said Senator Endicott. 'Kennedy's destroying this country top to bottom; he's risking our very power base in the free world. He seems to think that giving them parity is a reasonable defense strategy, but all he's done is hand them political legitimacy or an alternative to our beleaguered freedoms, which portends disaster.'

'Kennedy's not going anywhere,' predicted James. 'Most people feel that he succeeded in averting a world war.'

'That's why we must make sure he doesn't get re-elected,' said Lovering. 'If the people don't understand what's happening here, well then, someone has to go about it differently. That's all I have to say on the matter.'

'It boils down to a crisis of conscience,' remarked James.

'As Republicans we didn't have any qualms about going to war against our own people under Lincoln,' said Senator Endicott.

'Who's talking war? We missed the perfect opportunity like I said,' reiterated Lovering.

'You know what I'm talking about, Artie,' said James. 'The unthinkable.'

'Put it this way,' added Lovering, 'his presidency hangs in the balance. We're not monsters, we're patriots; and if he thinks he can wrest control of our putative interests—the kind that could win us the Cold War—he becomes a casualty, not an advocate.'

'And these interests wouldn't have anything to do with flying saucers, right?' asked James, smiling.

'Flying saucers? I wish it did. He'd be laughed out of Washington!'

They all chuckled, and took a gulp of their drinks.

'Now that would be unthinkable,' said the Senator finally.

'Precisely, and to use Aubrey's favorite axiom—none the wiser,' stressed Lovering.

'In God We Trust,' said James, shaking his head.

'Amen.'

26. Swamp Lilies

Hannah Prinzenthal carefully lowered the navy blue four-wheeled perambulator down the stairs of their old narrow Olive Street townhouse. On this beautiful spring day in Washington D.C. they were going to the park nearby, then shopping at the local grocery store. Lizbet, a two-year-old toddler, remained at the top of the stairs holding onto the railing until her mother helped her down and put her in the pram.

For over two years now, Prinzenthal had been transformed from a worldly agent of the secret services into a doting mother. She couldn't have been happier, though long days at home with her daughter sometimes made her a little edgy. She was an ardent reader of news and novels whenever she had the time, and they would go to the Georgetown library on a regular basis. She had become friends with some other mothers at the park, but their relative youth and inexperience couldn't hold her attention for very long. She kept a private post office box in the name of Joyce Sommers, as per their arrangement with Melissa DeCourt, known as Diva, who passed on information received from Bill James using his son Nevin's coded system.

It seemed a rather roundabout way to receive intelligence from James in Washington sent to Melbo in New York, then back to Prinzenthal and Greenfield in Washington, but both James and Greenfield felt it was best that way, far off any suspicion. Then something changed when James let them know through Nevin and Diva that his son would no longer be involved; James was very worried about being caught as Hoover had had him investigated.

As a rule, Hoover did this with everyone in sensitive positions, yet nonetheless it rattled James for undisclosed reasons. And Greenfield sensed there was something more ominous going on, because the last productive information from James was an intimation of a conspiracy against Kennedy, but nothing more. When Kennedy had been informed of this, and having no proof, he laughed it off in his cavalier way to say that the Republicans were running scared because they knew they were losing the battle for the hearts and minds of Americans. In his last message, James said that he was trying to get more information, and that he wouldn't communicate until he did.

That was four months ago. They all knew that any way forward had to come through Kennedy, whether it concerned some opening up about the aliens or numerous policy directives that had yet to bear fruit, namely civil rights, social security, healthcare and other liberal agendas. As for Greenfield, his expertise lay in the field of the Cold War, and the building of the Berlin Wall the past year had created a new face to the monster reshaped from the old. He thought that it stated the obvious in that if the Soviets and their East German proxies were so afraid of freedom why would they create an edifice that had the effect of advertising to the world their very xenophobia?

It certainly demarked the differences in political brinkmanship, and offered Kennedy a wonderful opportunity to denounce Communism and show his enemies at home and abroad his position against them. A few months later, of course, he made his famous Berlin speech in sight of the wall, stating to the world his outrage: '*Ich bin ein Berliner!*'

Prinzenthal in her own peculiar wisdom expressed to her husband the death knell of Communism, though perhaps a few decades prematurely. But not to miss any opportunity to further her career, she asked him to speak to Kennedy—given an appropriate moment—about a position in the State Department appropriate to her skill set as a linguist and diplomat, albeit an unconventional one, to put it mildly. Kennedy was only too happy to help out and had Secretary Dean Rusk find her a place in the European Bureau in Washington. Ostensibly, she was still listed in personnel as Judith Graham, who had retired years before, but was now resurrected as Hannah Prinzenthal. Only those in senior positions knew her true story as an OSS officer during the war years, and subsequently with the CIA.

That morning she set out with her darling Lizbet who talked incessantly in her toddler talk and gleefully looked about sitting up with her little legs and feet in the open foot space of the little compartment—the trapdoor having been removed for her from the bed of the carriage. The sun dazzled and birds sang as if heralding a most auspicious day. It began with a letter from Diva, which Prinzenthal picked up at the Post Office and placed unopened under the mat of the carriage bed.

At the tot park, she let Lizbet play on the various climbers and a small hand-driven merry-go-round with another girl her age and nanny, who watched them carefully. Lizbet loved the merry-go-round, but she was too small to spin it alone, so the nanny put them on and turned it around slowly to their joyful shrieks.

Meanwhile, Prinzenthal read the letter and easily deciphered the code within it. It was from Nevin. *i am sorry dad has been compromised dont write take care all being monitored.* She put the letter away and watched the children from her bench while she looked around for any suspicious characters; there were none she could see. She felt that the FBI—the likely authority having compromised James—could not have penetrated them that far, but didn't for a minute assume they hadn't; it seemed Nevin had taken a chance in sending the letter.

She needed to find out what was going on. William James was the only one who could enlighten them, but it appeared that meeting with him would be a risky venture. Has it come to this? she wondered. There had to be a way forward; she would discuss it with her husband.

On the way to the grocery store, she walked past a woman in sunglasses. When the woman hesitated and stopped, Prinzenthal recognized her as one of the guests, whom she had befriended almost three years ago at the Woods' summer party. The name suddenly clicked: Penny Poirot Beyer. 'Penny?' she said.

'Yes, I knew it was you,' she replied, forgetting Hannah's name.

'Hannah Greenfield.'

'You're married now?'

'Yes, that August, the month after we met.'

'I seem to recall you had that glow about you.'

'Indeed, I was pregnant.'

They laughed and gave each other a brief hug.

'And such a little beauty!' she gushed, looking at Hannah's daughter.

'Lizbet.'

'Oh my, I always wanted a girl, but I suppose I'll get girlfriends of my boys instead.'

They laughed again.

'I'll forego the 'How are you?' You look just brilliant,' said Poirot.

'And you as well,' replied Prinzenthal.

'If I recall correctly, you're a New Yorker, my birth city.'

'Yes, well, now I'm the dutiful wife of a civil servant.'

'Harley's your husband. I remember. I'm just sorry we've never followed up on our meeting at the Swan Cottage fête a few years ago. I haven't been back; I wasn't invited.' She laughed. 'I think my ex-husband saw to it.'

'Us as well; but here we are.'

'Do you live nearby?'

'Yes, on Olive Street. We're just heading to the store.'

'Will you be home in an hour? I'd love to drop by if it's alright.'

'Certainly, I'm a little short of friends here, but I suppose I've always been a loner.'

'Have you taken a leave of absence from the company?'

'Actually, I've officially retired from it, but I'm looking for something less adventurous because of my little honey bee.' She stroked Lizbet's head.

An hour later Poirot and Prinzenthal were drinking tea on her small backyard patio, while Lizbet was having a nap inside. Conversation had come around to Greenfield's present occupation and how their connection to Kennedy had helped him, though Prinzenthal said nothing of her own part in it. Poirot hadn't known about any of it but admitted she had known Kennedy since school in the thirties when her circle of friends mixed with his.

'Back then Jack and some of us had the typical persona of entitlement for the new generation,' she went on, 'We were a pretty hard core clique. I say that because many of us had radical ideas about social justice—the depression and all—at least within my circle of friends. He was a bit older of course, three years, yet I could never get any sense of his political stance other than his being a Democrat. I think he was more interested in girls.'

They had another good laugh.

'I was too oblivious of boys,' said Prinzenthal. 'Growing up in the tenements of the lower eastside gave me a healthy pass on entitlement. But I admit the boys were not oblivious to me.'

'I can see that,' smiled Poirot, lighting a cigarette.

'Nevertheless, I worked really hard; I wanted to show my new country— and I had lived in two others before, Poland and France—how grateful I was to be here. My father had been murdered by fascists in Paris in 1929 for his social views, and a Jew. He was such a wonderful man; he hated the racist extremism tearing through Europe at the time. His death so destroyed me; I think it set me on a fatalist course that I've only recovered from since marriage, with Harley's support and undying love. I'd always felt unworthy of him, and treated him badly at times, but it seems motherhood has cured me.'

'Hannah, your journey,' stressed Poirot, with some awe, 'must have been extraordinary. Sometime I would love to hear about your escapades in the trenches of the Cold War. I'm so sorry it had come at such a personal cost, to lose your father like that at a young age.'

'I had no choice but to grow up in a big hurry; we had so little money, just ourselves, my mother and I and a few supportive relatives.'

The conversation went on in that vein until Prinzenthal mentioned her having just received a letter from the State Department before Poirot arrived. She had been informed she was to meet the following week for an interview with some senior officials.

'This *is* an auspicious day!' exclaimed Poirot, impressed. 'Someone must be pulling for you. What exactly is your husband doing?'

'Harley is working as a special consultant to the National Security Adviser, his assistant actually, but it was Jack Kennedy who got him the job, and he has helped me too.'

'How do you know Jack?' asked Poirot.

'I was with the State Department during the war, and after. I attended the Potsdam conference in a minor role, and met Jack there. We had a very brief affair. Then I didn't see him until three years ago by chance here in Washington with Harley. And then that summer Harley and I saw him sailing his family yacht in Nantucket Sound near Monomoy with friends. I met Jackie then as well.'

'And you never saw him in all those intervening years since Berlin?'

'No. Harley, who was my control, claimed that he had once tried to find me, but I was unavailable for obvious reasons, being undercover behind the Iron Curtain. Jack told me that time we had met a few years ago that he'd actually thought I was dead.'

They both laughed.

'My oh my.' Poirot smiled, knowingly. 'That was before he went into politics.'

'Yes, I gather; I was only twenty-three at the time; I hadn't a clue who he was; just some navy reporter war hero who seemed to be attached to the Forrestal entourage.' She shook her head at the memory.

'That's just too funny, and now he's the President.'

'He was a gentleman, and I never expected to see him again.'

Poirot turned quiet as if there was something she was considering to say. She took a sip of her tea, looked at Prinzenthal and lit another cigarette.

'I need to tell you something, Hannah,' she said exhaling smoke, 'I know I can trust you. Jack and I are quite close. In fact, we've been seeing each other whenever the opportunity comes up.'

Prinzenthal said nothing. The first thing that entered her mind was how incredibly stupid they both were then she thought that Jack must be half crazy under pressure and Penny Poirot Beyer must be the antidote, or something like that.

'And Jackie?' asked Prinzenthal, evenly. 'Is she aware of this affair?'

'One never knows with Jackie, at least in public. She's a rock, I admit, and puts the Presidency above any personal misgivings about her husband. I'm more like his confidante, someone he can use to ease his mind from a world of trouble. It just so happens that we are intimate—a key component of our relationship; but also I offer him insight into his mental outlook, if you will; I act as a sounding board of his perceived mastery of his position—we really click. We have similar social sensibilities and political ambitions, mine not being public of course. I know it's a dangerous game we're playing but we believe it's not completely unfeasible. We happen to take great joy in each other, whatever the risks.'

Prinzenthal showed no surprise and drank her tea.

'I'm going to be frank with you, Penny, and I'm not judging your personal motivations, but believe me when I say you should end this affair. I know about high stakes relationships: that's my forte. Once they've served their purpose, it's imperative you move on, slip away; or you will crash and burn and take the president down with you. My husband is privy to some very sensitive information regarding some personal threat against him and has disclosed this to Jack through the proper channels.

'His response was that every president has had conspiracies revealed against them, like it's a job description; and if there's nothing specific to report about some rumored conspiracy, his position is to carry on like a soldier in the face of adversity. Very brave, yes, but foolish. My intuition tells me—and I'm usually right in this—something very bad is being hatched by his enemies to destroy him. Your relationship with him could be the sort of exposure they would dearly love to exploit, or worse.'

'You're probably right,' she replied, 'at least out of respect for Jackie, but he needs me. Jackie doesn't give him what he needs right now. I think of it as a duty. Have you heard of LSD?' she asked, suddenly.

'Yes,' said Prinzenthal, 'the experimental drug. I know it's been used as an interrogation tool, an enabler like a truth serum, though I've had nothing to do with it.'

'I know Tim Leary, the Harvard psychologist, a keen advocate for its use. Jack and I tried it; it's quite legal apparently, and available, if you know where you can get it.'

'In the White House?'

'No, at a house I made available for us.'

'So I'm guessing you discovered the truth about something.' Prinzenthal smiled.

'The truth?' she laughed. 'It goes way beyond the truth. I can't begin to describe what we experienced. It was like God gave us a personal tour of everything. We saw the world in all its infinite beauty, and its darkness. We knew exactly how it all fits as if all was implicit—how simple life seemed—yet not. For a few hours we were the embodiment of perfection. We made love that was so intensely intimate we couldn't stop looking at each other. Eye to eye we saw eternity. I don't know why I'm telling you this; I just had to tell you because I've told no one. There's something about you I trust completely. You know Jack too …'

She lit another cigarette.

'I appreciate your candor, Penny; it goes without saying, but it's not about me,' remarked Prinzenthal, 'the experience awakened something in both you and Jack. I can understand that. I've had something similar happen to me, though not from drugs, but from love, deep abiding love, something I had been denied, or denied in myself for a long time.'

'Yes,' she said, automatically, as if in a trance, 'we can all achieve that kind of consciousness. After, he talked about the world, the government, people, even Jackie. His mind just seemed to spill out as if so much had been pent up for so long. We talked through most of the night.'

Prinzenthal went silent as she felt there was little more to say. She looked up at the sun cascading its munificence through the green leaves of an old tree.

'He mentioned aliens,' Penny went on. 'He said certain individuals would not brief him about them, so he found out about them by going around these people to others—he mentioned a Colonel at Wright-Patterson Air Force base. It really upset him that as president he couldn't be briefed because the previous government had set it up that way to prohibit a president's need-to-know inquiries; it goes to show what bureaucratic resistance can do. Eventually, he found out there were about half a dozen different alien species who had visited Earth, and probably a lot more they didn't know of. He revealed that Eisenhower had even met some aliens at Edwards Air Force Base in the California desert in '54.

'Apparently, he was given a demonstration of their anti-gravity propulsion technology by generating gravity waves that can manipulate space which I'm told bends, stretches and contracts like rubber. Jack was really upset that he'd been denied that information about that kind of meeting, and he swore he would regain control over it, even if he had to take it to the people.'

'I've heard similar stories too,' said Prinzenthal. 'I believed them. I'd advise you not to tell anyone about that; it's dangerous knowledge because those individuals who want it kept secret are more concerned about the Cold War, and they take National Security very seriously as they should, but so seriously that even a sitting president could find himself perhaps threatened as a risk when it comes to the aliens.'

'Hannah,' replied Penny, puffing nervously on her ever-present cigarette, 'I know I shouldn't be shooting off about all this—I mean we hardly know each other—yet I feel a real bond with you like you're kin with me and Jack and the Service and need to tell someone. Who better than you? And don't think I don't know what the Secret Services are all about—my ex-husband is right in there with the senior people. It's like the multi-headed hydra, and as you know, only a few know what the other heads are doing.'

'Actually, I met him on a couple of occasions. He seemed like a decent fellow, smart, studious.'

'I think Ford was always more faithful to himself and his career. We grew apart after the death of our son several years ago.'

'I heard about that. I'm so very sorry.'

'One never really gets over that kind of shock.'

'I know.'

'We have some common ground.'

'So you became an artist,' said Prinzenthal, changing the subject not wanting to disagree.

'I think I was always an artist. You should visit me sometime at my studio.'
'I'd be delighted.'

*

Sanchez sat in the corner table of a coffee shop near the Washington Naval Yards. Outside, the sky was overcast and threatened rain. At least five months had gone by since he had met with James and confronted him with the situation with Hoover. James at the time seemed unruffled and repeated his willingness to bring Inèz to America, but it would take time and had to be in concert with some operation there.

Since the Missile Crisis last year, things had settled down, though James was privy to various plots to assassinate Castro. Sanchez had decided against bringing up James' relationship with the other woman, and the strange conversation he had overheard between his son and his girlfriend, specifically, the offhand mentioning of 'Diva' and a postbox.

It didn't occur to him that it involved anything more than kids playing games, or something to do with school. Yet, he had a nagging suspicion from their sexual familiarity that there was more to these youngsters than appeared. Regardless, Sanchez was impatient, and James was late. He felt it was now or never to act on his own behalf or he would lose whatever he had as leverage.

Five minutes later, James arrived and, taking off his raincoat and hat, sat down opposite Sanchez.

'Sorry, Eduardo.'

'You're here, boss, that's all that matters.'

'Listen, it's been just crazy these last months. How are you?'

'Crazy too, man,' he said smiling.

The waitress came by and took his order of coffee and sandwich.

'But I've got good news, finally.'

'That's the song I've been waiting to hear.'

'But not without something more I need from you.'

'I thought as much. Well, tell me the good news first.'

'You're going back to Cuba and will bring your girl back with you when you return.'

'Okay,' said Sanchez cautiously.

'I persuaded someone you're the best man for the job.'

'What job?'

'You're gonna run the small team who will assassinate Castro.'

'What do you mean "run the team"?'

'You'll be in charge of the mission.'

'Me? I can't get near that bastard.'

'That's been taken care of. You're just the logistical support.'

'It sounds very risky.'

'I want you out before it happens.'

'How will it happen?'

'Poison.'

'That means you will need someone on the inside.'

'Your job will be to get the ingredient to the individual who's prepared to dose Castro's drink.'

'Sounds like a suicide mission.'

'The poison has a delay of up to two hours depending on whether food has been eaten.'

'Time for him to escape.'

'Who said it was a he?' said James.

'A woman?'

'You're not going to like this: Inèz Ruiz has agreed to do this. She's been working with the CIA, and at their instigation found a job in the government kitchen. She's even served Castro on a few occasions.'

Sanchez just shook his head; he was livid. 'You bastards, you're using her because she wants to come to the States to be with me. I refuse to help you unless you find someone else.'

'I had nothing to do with it, Eduardo. And you're right, it's shameless, but that's what they do.'

'But you can do something! I know you can!'

'My position is tenuous as it is; your going for me was the condition that she would do it; you don't know the half of it. I'm doing this for you whether you like it or not. They didn't want you to go anywhere near her, but I convinced them.'

'I don't believe you.'

'Listen to me,' asserted James. 'They don't give a rat's ass about her, or you bringing her here for that matter. This is your one good chance, but you have to trust me. Once she's done her part in poisoning his drink and food, she'll leave the building and go straight to you. You're not to use the smugglers we've been using; you're going to take a bus to Baracoa on the eastern coast where an older man, Juan Luis Matus, will meet you and take you to his fishing village called Lupa de Esperanza. Then at night, he'll take you at least fifteen nautical miles out to sea towards Haiti; there'll be another boat to pick you up at specific co-ordinates.'

'Why different? Pedro's got me in and out before, *no hay problemas.*'

'Not this time. No one knows about this other asset who I've known since before the revolution; he owes me because I saved his ass when he got caught up in a drug running operation. He's old now but reliable because we're friends.'

'Are you implying the agency is setting us up to take the blame if Castro dies?'

'I don't know that, but it wouldn't surprise me, and I don't want to take that chance.'

'Jesus. When will this happen?

'In two weeks.'

'If we make it out alive … There's nothing I won't do for you, boss.

'If Castro dies, there's nothing any of us wouldn't do for you.'

'Don't count on it; the guy's like a cat with the luck of the Irish.'

Even James had to chuckle at the comical phrasing.

'Before I forget,' said James, pulling an envelope from the inside pocket of his jacket,' here's some Cuban pesos, American dollars and two permanent American working visas for both you and Inèz. I had to pull some serious strings for that. By the way you'll be dropped off in San Juan, Puerto Rico: from there you can fly back here, or Miami. You'll likely be red-flagged, and detained with Cuban passports back-dated, but I'll speak with Customs to call me and make sure you're let through; or better yet, I'll meet you myself.'

Sanchez stared at the documents with their photos and official stamps, and a wad of money.

'Thanks, you won't regret this, boss.'

'Don't thank me yet. You'll be briefed tomorrow by Earl Bunting about the mission. Use your normal protocol to reach him. You should be in Cuba by week's end. Just remember, you'll likely be followed in Havana so you have to lose your tail before you get on a bus with Inèz.'

'I'll arrange it.'

'One more thing.'

'What's that?'

'When you're back here with Inèz, I have another job for you.'

'Doing what?'

'You're going to spy for me. I know you've been doing work for Bunting; I'll need to know everything he has instructed you to do. I will want copies of any transactions, whether it is banking, transit, photos, names, anything. Do you follow?'

'Sure, boss. He's had me running all over the place: New Orleans, mostly; Dallas once.'

'Names, I need names.'

'I was a bagman. I delivered money, and received messages.'

'Who from? How much?'

'I wasn't given names, just places to meet. I gave one guy ten thousand dollars, and another guy seven thousand dollars. I got the impression they were working the same job from different angles. I spent some time in a club—the 500 Club—I knew from Mongoose days, where various people in the trade used to congregate. I recognized one of the guys I gave money to with some people, one of them I knew to be Clay Bertrand, a local asset, and this lawyer guy with him … Anders, Dean Anders. Also, I know that General Cabell's brother Earl, the mayor of Dallas was there. And a bunch of others I didn't know.'

'Good, anything else?'

'Bunting introduced me to some guy at Langley a month or so ago, Phil something…'

'Phil Garvey?'

'Yeah, you know him?'

'Only from hearsay,' said James, 'he's a guy Bunting seemed to look up to, like a mentor—close ties with French and Italian mafia, who helped him shut down the Communists in Marseilles, Italy and other places. So what about him?'

'He and the General seemed close. One time, this other guy, Braydie Farnes, came by and they had a meeting in Cabell's office. Bunting told me later that day that he felt something big was in the air. Now I presume it was about this operation you've got me hooked into.'

'Farnes. He runs the domestic operations, and steers clear of the FBI,

333

according to Woods.'

'Sí, sí, un maldito coño.'

They laugh.

'So you think this is the big deal?' asked Sanchez.

'Perhaps, but I think it's something else—something to do with your work in New Orleans. The Castro thing may be a cover or blind, but an op nevertheless. That's tradecraft, to create many scenarios, covering the one that is the main objective. Accountability is everything; that is, being unaccountable.'

'Right, so what do you think? Is Farnes involved?'

'I don't know. That's why I need you.'

'I'm your man, boss.'

Part Three

Those who fail miserably can achieve greatly.

John F. Kennedy

27. Good Samaritan

Three weeks earlier when Melissa DeCourt had gone to check the *Diva* post box near where she worked, she was surprised to find two letters; one was written in the hand of Nevin, and the other written by someone else. At home, she opened Nevin's letter first and read that he would no longer be writing because his father had been compromised. She quickly opened the other letter. It was from William James. It wasn't coded.

Dear George and Melissa,

Pardon me from breaking protocol with this letter. I am in urgent need of some assistance from you to get this message to our mutual friend. It may be advisable for you, George, to come as well to Washington, as soon as possible. I can't begin to explain how important this is.

Sincerely,
Bill

DeCourt just stared at the letter. 'What on earth!' she wondered. At home that evening, she and Melbo, at her request, went to a diner nearby, where she informed him of the developments concerning Nevin and his father. Melbo said little in response, only that he should go to Washington and that they should not use 'Diva' anymore in case someone was onto them. This came on top of a difficult year.

The death of Marilyn out West the previous August allegedly from an overdose of barbiturates combined with alcohol had hit them both particularly hard. They weren't that close to her; months would often go by without any communication, yet there was a bond between them, which, in their brief interludes as companions, gave them reason to think they had a positive influence on her. Anyhow, for this reason they believed that there was a deeper darker explanation for her untimely death. It was rumored through a friend and reported in a tabloid that Marilyn had been planning to have a press conference in which to reveal national secrets about aliens.

If this was the case, someone must have been monitoring her phones or house and knew about it. Without a personal investigation, Melbo couldn't bring himself to write about her, though he had received an offer from the Sunday Post, a periodical, to commemorate her. As well, his work with Greenfield and the White House put him in a delicate position. An article was brewing in him, but he was not yet ready to write it until he felt informed and safe to do so.

He believed that her life had unfulfilled her true calling—that of a new kind of woman—one who would lead a new generation of women to equality and respect, never having been realized. Yet her early death elevated her to a mythical status and immortalized her, not so much for her stardom, but for her martyrdom and beauty as a *cause célèbre*, hounded by the public her entire career.

When Melbo returned from work the next day, he packed a bag and was about to book a flight to Washington that evening. DeCourt was unhappy about the situation as she felt left out but understood that something was obviously very wrong, the significance of which they could only guess.

'Honey,' she said, 'perhaps you should wait to hear from Harley. We'll send him Nevin's letter, so he and Hannah know there's trouble. Let's be patient here; we're in the dark. Let's not get all stressed out. We could make a mistake.'

Melbo stood there in the bedroom immersed in thought. 'Fools rush in,' he murmured to himself. 'Maybe you're right, darling. If we're being monitored, which is not implausible, Harley will know what to do.'

'Good, then that's settled. Put your bag away.'

Melbo did as he was told, but didn't unpack it.

'We should wait for Harley's weekly call at work, quid pro quo. Better still, perhaps I can leave a message on his answering service.'

'Yeah, tell him something urgent requires his presence here.'

At DeCourt's request, he made the call from a payphone: then they carried on as if nothing had happened.

Tuesday morning, the next week, Greenfield watched Melbo walk by head down on his way to work in a group of pedestrians near his apartment building.

Leaving a message the day before at Melbo's office from Tom Jones, they were to meet at Joe's Sandwich Bar at eight-thirty the following morning. Greenfield had arrived a half hour early outside at Melbo's apartment building. On a whim, he took with him his camera, which was just small enough to fit into his jacket pocket.

He knew his young friend left for work at about eight, so he thought he would case the area as a precaution, given the serious nature of his visit, and take a few photos. For a while he stood inside the front door of an apartment building just across and down the street. His caution seemed to pay off when he noticed a man walk past twice and then a third time, always looking to the entrance of Melbo's building. This man, wearing a gray suit and hat, blended in with the morning crowd of suits and hats, but Greenfield's trained eye caught him looking into other apartment entrances, especially those where individuals had stopped to light a smoke or appeared to be waiting for something or someone.

Greenfield quickly retreated into the recesses of the vestibule of his building when this man began looking along his side of the street. This man had hood written all over him by his slick appearance and cool, calculating demeanor. He was a pro, the kind that Greenfield had seen the likes of before, and he quickly sized up the situation; then he pulled out his camera and took a few photos in quick succession. Putting the camera back in his pocket, he realized that he had to take him down somehow and find out who he was without revealing himself. Figuring this hood was packing a gun or knife, probably both, he had to be very careful to blindside him and hit him so hard so there was no chance for retaliation.

Greenfield didn't like it at all. He thought of other ways, such as calling the police in the name of national security on a trumped up charge, but there wasn't any time. A few buildings down from Melbo's building, an alley led to an old underground carpark, dating from before the Great War. Greenfield exited his building and walked purposefully down the street from Melbo's building parallel to the man, who was walking just ahead in the same direction on the other side of the street. It was now or never, and avoiding the oncoming traffic, Greenfield crossed the street diagonally and like a charging linebacker tackled the unsuspecting hood, both hats flying into the alley as he knocked him flat onto the ground. No one noticed except a man and a woman just behind on the sidewalk.

Once down on the ground, before the man could react, Greenfield smashed the man's head onto the pavement with a sickening crack, rendering him unconscious. Kneeling, he turned and holding up his official-looking White House Security pass, told the gaping bystanders: 'FBI! Move along!' As if stunned, they hesitated, but when Greenfield yelled, 'Now!' they moved off.

Quickly, Greenfield checked the man's pockets and, as he had expected, found a stiletto in his jacket and a holstered gun on his chest. From an inside pocket, he removed the man's wallet containing a wad of money—at least five hundred dollars in big and small denominations—which he scattered around the inert body. Also, he found a driver's license, with the name of Joe di Lucca and an address in the Bronx. Further examination of the remaining contents of the wallet revealed a few cards with the names of escort agencies and Club Europa, all of which suggested that he was probably a pimp.

Having noted the address and a telephone number on the card, he hurriedly picked up a bunch of large bills, to make it appear to Mr. di Lucca—who now stirred from his pounding—that he'd been robbed. Then putting the cards back, Greenfield dropped the wallet onto di Lucca's jacket flap, grabbed his hat, stood up, and peered around the corner. He fell in with the pedestrians walking by, who looked indifferently at the prostrate man in the alley, bloodied and apparently alive, likely a drunk.

Greenfield hailed a cab, and circled the block a few times. He noticed di Lucca, with his hat on, now standing and gathering himself with a handkerchief to his forehead. A woman had stopped to see if he was alright, but di Lucca pushed her aside and walked away. Greenfield had no idea what the man was actually doing there, but he did seem to be following Melbo; he could've been there for any number of reasons. Greenfield knew he had done the right thing, and until he followed up and fully identified di Lucca, he would not be satisfied. There was something about him: Earl Bunting was written all over him.

Meanwhile, Melbo sipped his tea at Joe's Sandwich Bar, waiting impatiently for Greenfield. Twenty minutes late Greenfield showed up, looking exerted and unusually anxious. He sat down, as Melbo signaled the waitress to bring over a pot of coffee. She turned over the mug at his place setting and filled it. Thanking her, Greenfield asked her for a glass of water, before stirring in a cube of sugar and cream.

'Harley.'

'Something came up,' he said. 'I had no choice but to find out who he was.'

'A tail?'

'Likely. He was walking back and forth in front of your building—a pro. I was lucky he didn't see me.'

'What happened?'

'I'm not entirely sure but I think he was following you; that's when I decided to take him out.'

'In front of all the people?'

'Yeah, it was a risk I had to take.'

'Was I in any danger?'

'I don't know yet. If he turns out to be one of Earl Bunting's hoods, we have to take precautions. There's no way around this. The only person who can help us here is Bill James.'

'Who's Earl Bunting?'

'A company flunky; a real piece of work.'

The waitress brought the glass of water.

'Thanks,' said Greenfield, taking a mouthful.

'So did you identify this tail?'

'I tackled him into an alley, and knocked him out. I rifled through his pockets. He had a stiletto and a .38 Smith & Wesson in a shoulder holster with a silencer adapter. This guy's a killer.'

'Shit on a bun.'

'Yeah, I could've killed him, but that would've created more trouble because I was seen. I flashed my credentials and told them I was FBI and to move on.'

'Did you find the silencer?'

'No, listen, I knew he was bad, and just wanted to identify him; his license read Joe di Lucca from the Bronx, I took a few large bills from him to make it look like a robbery, so he wouldn't think it was anything else.'

'Damn, Harley; you could've saved my life.'

'We have to take control, Mel.'

For a moment they sipped their tea and coffee.

'But why would he follow me?' asked Melbo. 'He would've likely known where I worked.'

'Yes, but if he was Bunting's cut-out, he could've been following you for another reason—maybe he thought you were meeting a source.'

'I never thought of that. Maybe he followed me when I met Keith.'

'Just what I was thinking. And if that's the case this guy's probably off the books, and works for Bunting as an independent.'

'How will you know for sure?'

'Let *me* worry about that. This is what I do.'

'So Harley, it's a good thing you showed up when you did.'

'I met with Bill. He came to me actually.'

'Are these events connected? Do you think they're onto us?'

'Not officially. They know nothing of Diva or Nevin. Bill thinks Bunting is running a sideshow, and Woods is giving him the rope. Why, I can only guess: to cloud or obfuscate other operations that Bunting is involved in—and that is actually why I'm here—or if this di Lucca was involved in Keith's death. There must have been a photograph that was passed around identifying Leverton as your source. Only the very top people, and perhaps only Sulla himself, would have known about him, so it was probably decided to terminate him and cover up the leak. Di Lucca was not carrying a camera.'

'Jeesh. Which makes *me* expendable, too.'

'We can't take any chances, but I think you're insulated by your public persona.'

'It didn't help Marilyn. What do you suggest we do?'

'We'll get to that, but first I need to explain the reason I'm here. Bill needs some help with an operation—off the books.'

'It seems like everything is off the books.'

'It is and it isn't, to varying degrees; this is definitely off the books. He wants me to pick up someone with my yacht off the coast of Cuba in a week. He says it's critical to his investigation of some very suspicious activities involving the company possibly in a plot to assassinate Kennedy. The man we're picking up works for both Bill James and the CIA. He's just a pawn but's in the thick of it.'

'God damn. Are you serious?'

'Mel, I'm sad to say it's true. I'm sorry it's come to this, but I need your help. I want you to accompany me. I need a first mate, and I don't trust anybody else.'

'But I can't leave Melissa with this di Lucca hanging around.'

'No, you must both come with me to Washington. Until this operation is done, I'll have some secret service recruits watching Hannah and my house around the clock. Then we can figure out what to do next.'

'God, I can see how these things get complicated when something's set in motion, and nobody knows what's actually going on.'

'Something like that. When there's an objective, nothing else matters as long as the objective is reached. It's a brutal business.'

'Bill's FBI. Why doesn't he shut it down himself? And alert Hoover?' asked Melbo.

'There's no proof, yet. And I can't imagine Hoover going out of his way to do anything to stop some plot against Kennedy. Besides, Bill would just be putting himself in harm's way. And then what?'

'Go public. That's what *I* would do. Then Hoover would be forced to act.'

'I agree, but only if we had proof—people who would testify—otherwise we'd be crying wolf, and I've already done that. Almost every day someone threatens the President.'

*

Exactly forty-eight hours later, Greenfield and Melbo were out at sea heading west from St. Croix towards Puerto Rico in the *Hannah & Lizbet*. They sailed at a good clip in a stiff breeze expecting to make the coast in a long day or more, after which they would sail around the island and head for the Dominican Republic and Haiti. Greenfield estimated it would take three to four days and nights to position themselves at the prearranged coordinates well off the coast of Cuba. The forecast called for much of the same weather with sun and cloud and slight chance of thundershowers.

With water and provisions for two weeks if necessary, they were in a good mood away from troubles, but as the horizon was dark in spirit, there was little levity. Their understanding was that this 'package' to be picked up and delivered, was the key to what Bill James felt would lead to the proof needed to implicate the conspirators in a deadly plot. Before he and Melbo had left for St. Croix, Greenfield had met James to find out all he could about di Lucca; and whether Bunting was involved with him.

James said he hoped to have something for him when they returned. All they could do now was to deliver this 'package'. James didn't reveal the name of the person, fearing that if something went wrong, it was best there was little information with which to incriminate them, other than their proximity to Haiti sailing on a 'holiday'. Besides, there was supposed to be a friendly coast guard ship on patrol in the area that could intervene if necessary, courtesy of an asset of James.

In Washington, DeCourt was happy to spend time with her great friend, Hannah. Over the last couple of years, they had become close and confided in each other, having spent a number of holidays together with their husbands and having visited each other. When her publishing house received a telex from Greenfield at the National Security desk of the White House, indicating that her presence was needed for a couple of weeks in Washington for an undisclosed reason, DeCourt had been excused from the office, though she did have some assignments to work on during her absence.

Questions were asked, of course, but she said her husband was doing some research that required her assistance in the name of that general moniker 'national security'. Both she and Prinzenthal were nonetheless feeling nervous about being watched day and night, though they had come to like the retired secret service special agent, 'Jimbo', a wartime acquaintance of Greenfield, along with two other young recruits brought in by the retired man.

Greenfield had also reminded Hannah to keep her gun handy, just in case. She knew how to use one, but had never needed to in her career as a field agent. The two women spent their days with Lizbet, shopping and visiting various sites such as the Smithsonian Institute and the Washington Monument, as well as making a few visits to the art studio of Penny Poirot, who once invited them to the prestigious Cosmos Club for a ladies' luncheon.

Prinzenthal had begun working at the State Department in the consular section, specifically in the European sphere. This included the processing of refugees from the East, technically as a 'Foreign Service Specialist' in an advisory role because of her past affiliation with the intelligence services. Within a few months, she had been given an opening position in the State Department's Bureau of Intelligence and Research carrying her new title with her, which was more to her liking, given her experience. She had a babysitter who came to the house, another mother she had befriended.

During the days while Prinzenthal was at work, DeCourt settled into a routine in their study, to carry on her own assignment involving the acquisitions of rights to an extended series of children's books, and a couple of table books. She spent half her day on the phone, long distance, the expense of which was covered by Greenfield's work allowance; he had been compensated under these extraordinary circumstances, though it was frowned upon by his immediate boss Marty Cayton, who'd been told by his boss the National Security advisor, McGeorge Bundy, that their budget was exceeding its limits.

"Mac" Bundy didn't approve of Greenfield, or his paranoia about assassination plots, but he deferred to the President. A decade younger than Greenfield, and well connected politically, he'd been decorated for his intelligence work in the OSS during the war, when Greenfield went largely unsung. Bundy's family were tight with the Eastern Republican Establishment and close to Henry Stimson, the Secretary of War under Roosevelt, although he was a moderate Democrat.

One afternoon during the week of Greenfield's sailing, a blue Ford sedan cruised slowly past his house. Jimbo, the retired officer sitting in his parked car down the street, took note of it and the license plate, as he did for every vehicle that moved down the relatively quiet street. The occupant of the sedan was none other than Earl Bunting, who the week before had received a call from Joe di Lucca, telling him he'd been assaulted, knocked out and robbed by an unknown assailant in an alley near Melbo's apartment.

The fact that he'd been robbed in broad daylight on a relatively busy street, to Bunting, had the ring of desperation; but it looked suspicious. Besides, how would the mugger know that di Lucca had money? Something didn't add up: di Lucca was a wise guy, a cagey tough, but hardly a known figure of wealth. Such people don't usually get mugged in alleys in broad daylight, and a thief would be expected to choose a more vulnerable target.

Possibly somebody had a score to settle with him, but di Lucca wasn't the kind of person to allow anyone a chance for vengeance—he was skilled at making people disappear; besides, for just a couple hundred bucks, that explanation didn't wash. Bunting knew that in his shady world someone had taken out di Lucca for another reason entirely; this someone didn't likely know who di Lucca was, but had seen him follow Melbo, and then acted on impulse. There was only one person with that kind of perspicacity associated with Melbo: Harley Greenfield. But Greenfield lived presently in Washington, and that is why last week when Bunting first found out where Greenfield lived, Bunting had parked early one morning down the street to watch his house.

At eight o'clock, Greenfield emerged from the house and drove away, Bunting tailing from a distance; to Bunting's surprise, Greenfield went straight to the office building next to the White House, known at the time to house the National Security advisor and staff, where he now presumably worked. It was a worrisome development. Bunting needed to find out if Greenfield had been in New York earlier that week; and got his answer when he saw Prinzenthal and Melbo walking the perambulator to the park the day after he had followed Greenfield.

Bunting figured Greenfield must have been visiting Melbo in New York, and being extra cautious about something—something telling in itself—had cased the street looking for anything suspicious, and noticed di Lucca going back and forth a few times. My, my, thought Bunting: that Harley was good, really good, and it meant something very important had transpired in order for Greenfield to take out di Lucca on a hunch and squirrel away Melbo to Washington under his protection. Inadvertently, di Lucca had set off the alarm bells for both Greenfield and Bunting. But for what?

Greenfield had likely identified di Lucca, but that wouldn't tell him anything because he likely didn't know who di Lucca really was, namely: Gerald Osbourne aka Johnny Goodnight, or did he? He couldn't take that chance. Now, days later, Greenfield had disappeared again, and there was no Melbo either.

Jimbo referred to his notes, but he knew that this same blue sedan with Virginia license plates had driven by on numerous occasions; and he didn't like the look of the driver. He decided he would call a friend of his in the Secret Service who worked in the District of Columbia with access to local and statewide vehicular registrations to help identify the vehicle and driver.

Meanwhile, Bunting felt he had no choice but to report to his boss all that had happened recently. His greatest fear was that there was a leak somewhere up the chain of command, though it was not his place to act on it. The Castro operation was his priority, yet he had the feeling there was another mission in the works by a number of curious circumstances, specifically in New Orleans, one of his territorial zones. But he knew in the company the right hand didn't generally know what the left hand was doing; it was rather more a multi-armed Kali where so many arms were playing, that only the very top chiefs had any idea what was truly going on.

Bunting presumed that pawns like him were cut loose to facilitate these objectives themselves, without questioning the job, unless a glaring problem arose that might disrupt the outcome or worse, and create a public furor, in which case such dispensable people like him were left out in the cold and disowned. Bunting would do anything to prevent that.

28. Big Tuna

Juan Luis Matus was the sort of humble fisherman of whom appearances were misleading. A soft spoken man, he had lived most of his life in Lupa de Esperanza, about thirty miles south of Baracoa on the east coast of Cuba. A good fisherman, known in the community as reliable and decent, he was also a notorious smuggler, who in the past had used his profession as a cover for running arms and drugs.

Before the Dominican dictator, Trujillo's assassination, Juan had sold guns for his regime to Cuba, and before that he had been involved with illegal contraband as far back as the nineteen-thirties. Now, as he was just a fisherman who often fished for yellowfin tuna at night, it was quite normal to see him prepare his thirty-five foot diesel-powered Purse Seiner, rigged for longline trolling. His boat was named the *Atún Grande.*

In Baracoa, waiting in his old Plymouth pickup truck, Juan kept a lookout for the couple he was to take to sea. They were to wait on the corner where El Jeffe's cantina was located. The bus had arrived, and people spilled out with their cheap burlap sacks and wooden cages holding chickens and rabbits. Numerous couples and families disappeared into the crowded street. One couple, carrying only a typical shoulder bag, looked around and made their way to El Jeffe's, where they sat down trying to appear inconspicuous. Juan waved a boy over and giving him money, pointed at the couple and told him to tell them to come to the truck. Sanchez and a slight, pretty woman were soon squeezed into the single passenger seat, and Juan immediately drove off, having checked his rearview mirror for any suspicious characters.

'*Señor Juan Luis Matus, supongo?*' asked Sanchez.

'*Sí, sí, todo bien?*'

Sanchez explained that they had escaped undetected from Havana, introduced Inèz as his fiancée, but she said little and appeared frightened by the whole ordeal. Less than an hour later they reached the village of Lupa de

Esperanza as the sun was setting. Juan drove up to the dock, and, as soon as they hurried aboard the *Atún Grande*, he started the engine. Within a half hour, night had enveloped them and the lights of the village disappeared below the horizon. The choppy sea made Inèz feel sick and forced her to take refuge with a bucket below deck.

Juan, meanwhile, baited the hooks on the longlines setting them deep to lure the bigger fish, and for an hour they continued east to rendezvous with a mystery boat. Juan knew better than to ask questions and Sanchez just stared ahead into the blackness, feeling relieved at least to be away from Castro's Cuba. He'd already paid Juan with ten crisp Ben Franklins.

According to Inèz's later account, everything had gone as planned with one exception: Fidel Castro did not show up, which was somewhat typical of the dictator. Inèz then made sure that the poisoned food and drinks were disposed of and quickly left the building. During her bus ride home, she was joined by Sanchez at a later stop, and they got off together at the next stop; a taxi then took them to another bus station across the city, where they boarded a local bus to the outskirts of Havana; they then took another taxi to a town nearby to board the main bus to Las Tunas; and the next day completed the final leg to Baracoa.

If they had been followed—and Sanchez had made sure they were not—it was unlikely the tail alone could have kept up with all the changes. Bunting's plan was for Sanchez alone, without Inèz, to head in the opposite direction west to the same village at which he had arrived in Cuba. Pedro would smuggle him out, and Inèz would come out later, which Sanchez knew would never happen. Thank God for Bill James was all he could think about.

Another couple hours went by with no boat in sight. Though, Juan didn't show any worry; it seemed he had done this so often he wouldn't bother worrying about something he didn't know the answer to; all he could do was steer his boat around the coordinates he had been given. Heading into the wind, he decided to pull in the longlines to see if he had caught any fish in that part of the ocean. The winch groaned to life and pulled in the longlines. He unhooked a couple of small yellowfin tuna and wahoos, then winched again and brought in a few more, including a sixty pound yellowfin. Then a huge bluefin jumped out of the water with a lure in its mouth, and dove deep before being pulled back in; it fought for all it was worth, but no large fish could pull away from the winch. The bluefin must have weighed at least five hundred pounds, a rarity in those waters.

Soon, the big tuna was lying on the deck, expiring with a final convulsion of flapping. Juan was pleased as it would fetch good money, and pointed out that bluefins were known to breed in the Caribbean, but spent most of their lives out in the deep, open ocean. He gutted all the fish except one and put them on ice in the hold before hosing down the deck. After midnight, a faint light could be seen to the east on the horizon, appearing and disappearing in the sea swells, but coming ever closer to the lights of the fishing vessel.

Eventually, as the *Hannah & Lizbet* came alongside with an unshaven Greenfield at the wheel, Juan threw over the *Atún Grande's* gunnel a couple of tires attached to ropes to serve as bumpers. In the dim light and rough water, Melbo, unshaven as well, used the long boat-hook to bring the boats together. Sanchez had already brought Inèz from below and now helped her into the yacht with Melbo receiving her, then he too jumped aboard unaided, when Juan, without a word, lobbed a twenty-pound yellowfin after him, waved and steered his boat away.

Still feeling seasick, Inèz was settled in a berth with a bowl. Greenfield at the helm, headed east. Sanchez, introduced himself and Inèz, and thanked him and Melbo, shaking the hands of these scruffy sea dogs. Greenfield used his pseudonym, Thomas Jones.

'Feel free to get some rest,' said Greenfield. 'There'll be no stopping until we reach Puerto Rico.'

'Thank you. Yes, I will later,' he replied.

'Mel, could you take the helm for a bit? I'd like to fillet that yellowfin.'

Melbo took the wheel and in the dim light of the console turned to Sanchez.

'So we meet again. You surprise me, Señor Sanchez.'

'Please call me, Eduardo.'

'Sure. Can I ask what you're doing here, Eduardo?'

'Bill James arranged to get Inèz out.'

'And you just happened to be in Cuba? Come now, the last time we met, almost three years ago in Los Angeles, you were clearly some kind of confidence man. How did you know Kennedy would go for Johnson?'

'It was all the talk among the people in my business.'

'But why did you come to me, Señor Eduardo? Who sent you?'

'Listen, Mel, a lot of things have changed since then. For one, I was working for Hoover as an informant, and other various people in the company.

That particular time, I was sent west to watch you; see who you met and what you did. The time I approached you was my own decision. I didn't care what you did on your honeymoon. May I ask why you didn't take my advice about Johnson?'

'Honestly, I was blinded by my own arrogance and presumptions. I thought that you were playing me for a fool. I was wrong.'

'No hard feelings, man.'

'None intended.' Melbo looked ahead into the gloom as the yacht crashed into wave after wave.

'You're a newsman,' said Sanchez. 'What are you doing here?'

'Just helping out Tomás, who's doing a favor for Bill James; it seems he's placed a high priority on your safety and your girl.'

'This is a mighty great favor, and I'm indebted to you both.'

'I think we both know there's a much bigger picture in which you're some mysterious player.'

'I don't know what that is, Mel, but rest assured I will do what I can to help Bill, who alluded to it as well.'

'Can you be a little more specific?'

Sanchez paused to think. 'I suppose it can't be helped now. I was sent to Cuba to facilitate an assassination attempt on Fidel. They tricked Inèz into serving poisoned food and drink at a government cafeteria he frequented and was supposed to be at that day, where she worked, but he never showed. It was a failure. I was supposed to return the same way I came in, but Bill organized this instead, so I could bring her out, otherwise, who knows what would have happened. Bill thought they were setting her up to get killed after the assassination, to make the killing of Fidel seem like a homegrown operation. I could've been killed too.'

'Leave nothing to implicate the Americans.'

'You know how it works,' said Sanchez, bitterly. 'The FBI first pressed me into service with the promise of letting Inèz come to me in the States. Then the CIA found in me a good agent—Bill had something to do with that. But I've no regrets; he got us working visas.'

'I'm happy for you, but they will want to know who helped you get those.'

Sanchez smiled. 'I'll tell them J. Edgar Hoover.'

After Greenfield had cleaned the fish and iced the filets, he relieved Melbo from the helm and told him and Sanchez to get a few hours of sleep before

Melbo took it over again. Greenfield remained at the helm for four lonely hours, until the first hint of dawn, when he awoke Melbo to take over while he could get some sleep himself.

'Mel,' said Greenfield, at the wheel when Melbo emerged from below, 'I haven't had so much fun in a long time!'

'I'll say, Tomás, but last night was a bit nerve-wracking. I don't know how you found them in that darkness, and rough seas.'

'The compass, ol' mate! And Polaris, the North Star! You remember that last starry night I got the direction. As long as they were due east from Lupa, and we held to that latitude, I knew we'd see 'em.'

'I just about cried when we saw their lights.'

'Surprised me too; I thought we'd have to wait 'till morning.'

'How far along are we?'

'Oh, we've been doing about seven knots: probably fifty miles. If we can keep this up, we'll be in San Juan two days from now.'

'We've been lucky with the wind. I didn't realize how far it was.'

'It's been a challenge alright. Just keep the compass at about 100 degrees east; Tortuga should come up starboard anytime. Keep well at sea to the north, and eventually the Dominican will show itself. I'll be up by then. When our guests are up, engage the steering. Get them eggs and bacon, toast and coffee. Tonight, we'll cook that fish.'

'Aye, Aye, skipper.'

Greenfield went below. The sea had settled into less choppy swells, but the wind still offered a decent rate of speed and the *Hannah & Lizbet's* sails pulled a tight beam reach. Melbo kept his eye on the compass and the thin sliver of pink cutting across the skyline.

*

A few days after that weekend, Prinzenthal and DeCourt had just returned home from the park with Lizbet, who had insisted she walk along with them until her mother put her back into the stroller. With their husbands gone for at least ten days, they had settled into an easy routine of work and leisure, both minding the adorable Lizbet. Jimbo, their kindly watchman during the day, and Ken and Dave, his young charges at night, all became acquainted with the women, who seemed to revere them as family whenever they invited them in for tea, coffee and sandwiches at reasonable hours.

A couple of days before, Jimbo had relayed to Prinzenthal that a stranger in a blue Ford sedan was also watching the house and that he had tried to identify the vehicle, but the registration was in the name of Samuel Hollinger, who upon further scrutiny didn't appear to exist. Jimbo presumed he was a company man, which worried him. Prinzenthal took it all in calmly, realizing that somebody had alerted the CIA about her husband and Melbo, who had definitely, she concluded, been followed that time in New York.

As her husband insisted, she kept in her purse her Beretta 950 pocket pistol with an eight cartridge magazine. The gun had been a gift from Greenfield almost ten years ago after she had had a close call with a KGB agent, named Anatoly Zahkarov, whom she had befriended during her posting as Judith Graham for the last time in the American embassy in Moscow.

Zahkarov, posing as an anti-Communist libertine, had tried to infiltrate a network of Russian artists, intellectuals and even scientists, who were mostly subversives working against the Soviet system by willingly giving away anything that might compromise Soviet tyranny. As his lover, she discovered his deception, and dumped him rather callously after one last fuck. Later, in a fit of rage, he then attempted to kill her by holding her underwater in a bathtub. The flat that she used for this liaison had been bugged by the CIA, and Greenfield, who was monitoring it from next door, came rushing to her rescue. He didn't kill Zahkarov, but knocked him senseless with a brick supporting some makeshift bookshelves.

When he recovered consciousness, he was given an ultimatum: either die or spy for them. He chose to spy, of course, but didn't last long though he had given up some insider gossip pertaining to Beria, the death of Stalin and the Politburo. Later, being a faithful Soviet agent, he foolishly told his superiors what he had done; and, on the order of Beria, who took over the leadership briefly after Stalin died, was sent to the Lubyanka where he was tortured and shot for treason. Beria's turn came soon after.

Prinzenthal remembered everything. Instead of thanking Greenfield for saving her life, she just opened her legs in the bathtub while he stood there, and continued to wash herself as if nothing had happened. She told him that Zahkarov would not have killed her because she was too important to him; he had just wanted to control her. But the operation had been completely successful and he was of no more use. She knew what he was like, and said as much to Greenfield. They soon departed Moscow for good.

Now in the kitchen, as she prepared dinner, her instincts prompted her to think that the agency was up to something truly nefarious. She kept asking herself, *Why bother with us?* That man, Earl Bunting, she recalled seeing in the St. Regis bar a few years ago, had been following them then and seemed to have had some kind of unrelenting fixation on her and Greenfield, as well as on the Melbos. Then the incident with her husband, having recently accosted this Joe di Lucca—a likely Bunting cut-out—tipped the scales of the agency's paranoia. In her experience, this sort of behavior meant only one thing: they were hunting down a leak which could somehow implicate them in an operation.

The Castro plot had to have been in part a blind or a set up to make it appear that Castro would want to get revenge on the Americans. Could some rogue element in the company be so audacious and evil as to actually consider assassinating Kennedy? Would Sulla in his iniquitous way, actually have approved this and set it in motion, with a word or a nod to one of his lieutenants? If so, his role was over, but the multifarious wheelhouse of the agency rogues were let loose.

She knew the kind of go-to persons who would be considered a safe bet to carry out such a task. Her understanding of the Nazi and Soviet hierarchies was well-founded; these evil regimes were magnets to the uglies that crawled out of the woodwork to do their murderous deeds. She knew that her own agency had used these types to fight the Soviet menace, and now it appeared that they were being used to take down President Kennedy, the very person who wished to eradicate their kind. What had Kennedy done to make them feel he was a threat that had to be taken out? Certainly, one was his challenging the company apparatus built under Sulla, but Sulla was no longer the head, or was he a kind of *éminence grise* using his loyal soldiers to carry out a mission in what he thought to be an emergency in the name of national security? It was insane.

Kennedy must have unwittingly done something that set this whole catastrophic process in motion. Aside from the Bay of Pigs, and relative power contentions, the only thing that came to her mind was the issue of the aliens. Perhaps Kennedy, in order to take back control of the CIA, had threatened to go public with the most classified program in the country's history, surpassing that of the Manhattan project during the war.

Well, the Manhattan project had served its purpose to produce the A-bomb, but the alien one had yet to bear fruit. And to what purpose? Perhaps it was as simple as an ideological impasse between the Republican cold warriors, who had to forego their absolute power under Eisenhower in a time of extreme Cold War tension, and the new-fangled Camelot of Kennedy's White House, which was ironic as "Camelot" was a derogatory term originating among the military brass to signify Kennedy's weakness in comparison to their strength. Then she reminded herself to pick up the developed photos of di Lucca that her husband had taken in New York.

Prinzenthal also considered that Bill James was that leak; and, obviously, the company—if her whole theory was true—was desperate to find out who it was. This put Greenfield and she in their sights, because whoever her husband had to rescue from Cuba, must know something about what was going on, or at least have access to the very thugs who were carrying out this insidious agenda. The whole scenario was ramping up to be a ticking timebomb.

The phone rang in the kitchen, jarring Prinzenthal out of her concentration. She picked it up hurriedly.

'Thank God, Harley!' she said, as calmly as she could. 'You were gone for ages, it seemed.'

They spoke of his great 'fishing' expedition, on which he had caught a big tuna. They were still in St. Croix, but would be flying home and arriving very late that evening. Elated, Prinzenthal put the phone back on its hook, and went to tell DeCourt the good news. Lizbet awoke from her nap as if she too had received the message.

29. Phil Garvey

'What's going on, Phil?' Bunting asked his old boss from his European sojourn after the war. 'I mean, what's the big picture here?'

'Big picture? Hell, Earl, there ain't no big picture; it's just the same picture as it's always been: fuck the Communists. What makes you say that?'

'Don't pull your classified rank and file on me, ol' buddy; I've been in this game long enough to know something's goin' on: payoffs, verbal messages. And why bring you out of retirement? The last I heard they retired you because of your drinking, with respect.'

'With respect, then lay off the inquisition. What does it matter to you, anyway?'

They were sitting in the cafeteria of the new agency building surrounded by forest near Langley, Virginia, just south-west of Washington. Garvey had appeared in Bunting's new, windowed office that morning. His once good looks were now rather bloated and he looked older than his sixty-one years: gray hair, a rotund but once athletic constitution, a face that made enemies by looking at him, with his bulging dark eyes and surly smile, something almost Dickensian; nonetheless, he was regarded as an effective and able leader. Thirty years ago he'd been a well-known strike buster with the FBI, one of Hoover's boys ruthlessly targeting leaders who had a habit of turning up dead through some unfortunate accident.

At the outbreak of the war, his reputation earned him a quick recruitment in the OSS to lead a European intelligence operation, beginning in North Africa and then through Sicily and Italy. At first, he worked with all anti-Nazi partisans; then, as the Nazis were pushed back into Germany and Austria, he turned on the Communist partisans who were filling the vacuum of tyranny left by the Nazis. As well, he became Sulla's main operator to smuggle Nazis out of Germany after the war, the focus then being to fight the Soviets. He could be very reasonable if there was cooperation from his charges; otherwise, the alternative was Earl Bunting and his favorite killer, Gerald Osbourne.

'Have I ever been disloyal?' replied Bunting.

'That's the point, Earl. You know how it is in this business; you don't want to know.'

'So there is a big picture.'

Garvey was smiling. Bunting knew that smile. Someone usually ended up in the Promised Land when he smiled like that.

'So tell me again about this Sanchez,' said Garvey. 'Do you trust him?'

'He's been reliable, yes, until he decided not to follow orders after the failed attempt on Castro.'

'Not unusual in the field,' remarked Garvey. 'He got spooked: figured he'd been fingered to take the rap for Castro. Isn't that so?'

'I argued against it, but Woods over-ruled me.'

'Woods doesn't do anything without someone pulling his strings.' Garvey pondered for a moment. 'Obviously, Sanchez was getting too smart for his own good. You mentioned a woman. There's always a woman to twist a man's allegiance. Where is he now?'

'Miami. Somehow they got in with working visas. He called in yesterday and told me he brought her here on his own initiative because nobody cared— he claimed someone he knew in Cuba helped him. But the visas are legit; I very much doubt he obtained them in Cuba. I contacted Miami customs, and they were interrogated briefly. Someone from the FBI called customs, a man, saying they were both agents; the customs official wouldn't say who called; must've been Bill James.'

'You said Sanchez was Hoover's snoop.'

'Yeah.'

'Interesting—just whooshed in with legit papers, two illegals. My, my, why would someone do that?'

'So you think he's no longer reliable?' Bunting asked.

'I didn't say that; he may well be reliable, but for someone else, just another angle of the same picture. I'm gonna tell you something: I'm on board here to procure some killers, some very cagey ones, the Sicilian kind. As for the target, I've no idea, and probably won't until near the end. These guys will be tipped off once they arrive at their destination, which is yet unknown, where they'll be in charge of their own reconnaissance and exit plan, likely with the help of local assets who would be informed at the same time.

357

'I know this much: special rifles are being reconstructed to be taken apart into three segments, for quick assembly and disassembly. You know the drill. We took out countless people in Europe, perhaps not with guns like that; but this is different, an obviously public event, which means a hard target. I've warned against it; there're simply too many variables and witnesses for us to cover up something like that. And do you know what Woods said?'

'No idea.'

'We control the investigation. The confusion is our cover, a patsy. Just like that.'

'Jesus, that's pretty fuckin' audacious.'

'So tell me again: who else knows Sanchez besides Woods and yourself?'

'I told you: Hoover and Bill James, who's Woods' brother-in-law; they're all in the same league and club.'

'Hoover's not in the same league; he came up from the street. What do you know about James?'

'Not much. OSS in the war. He's a family man like most of them. It was through him that originally loaned us Sanchez. I gather Hoover had something to do with that.'

'So Sanchez is being kicked around like a football. It must have been the FBI that fast-tracked those visas for Sanchez and his girl. Though, somehow I don't see Hoover doing that, unless he's using Sanchez.'

'My very opinion,' stated Bunting. 'Could Sanchez be the one being groomed as a patsy?'

'If I know Hoover,' replied Garvey, 'he wouldn't get involved like that. For the greater good, he would always cover up our misdeeds, an accessory after the fact.'

'Perhaps,' said Bunting, 'but that doesn't mean anything if they're all in on it; there're any number of others, such as Cabell or Angleton who could be dealing with that.'

'I'll say one thing,' observed Garvey, 'Woods is keeping this very tight to his chest, even with me; must be big.'

'Any educated guess as to who the target is?'

'Like I said, I don't know, nor do I want to know.'

'I know you better than that, Phil. You've got to know if you're bringin' in the Sicilians. I'll tell you what I hear from the Cuban exiles, and a lot of others, especially in Texas: Kennedy's a closet Commie.'

'Then you don't know me well enough, Bunting. Keep your trap shut.'

'Okay, okay. It's just that if this operation is going to be successful—it's obviously of the utmost importance to the security of this great nation—I just know there are some people who are on to us, and nobody seems to think it's a problem.'

'Who are you talking about?'

'Harley Greenfield, for one; and a reporter, George Melbo, whose wife has been staying with Greenfield's wife here in Washington while their husbands have been away for ten days. It had to have been Greenfield who ambushed Osbourne in New York when he was tailing Melbo. It was Melbo who led him previously to another source of his about classified agendas involving aliens.'

'Aliens? What the fuck are you talking about?'

'Don't ask me. Ask Woods.'

'And you think Greenfield and Melbo are involved by helping Sanchez?' asked Garvey, concerned.

'He owns a yacht in St. Croix; Osbourne told me. I made some calls and found out he went fishing during the time Sanchez was in Cuba.'

Garvey looked at Bunting. The smile reappeared.

'I met him once. Greenfield. And his squeeze, Prinzenthal. She's one wily bitch. You say she's working in the State Department again, courtesy of Kennedy?'

'No doubt about it. They knew each other somehow. Woods told me Sulla has had a hard on for her ever since he first met her in Potsdam '45; and she was seen with Kennedy there. She went on to do some great work for us when Sulla took over the agency in '53. Greenfield was her handler—more like a personal guard dog. Woods told me Sulla had him invite them to his summer party a few years back. She quit the service and married Greenfield; has a kid now.'

'How sweet. How do you know all this?'

'Osbourne told me. He worked a prostitution ring in Germany. He was in Potsdam, and got himself a VIP pass as a courier for OSS. Shit, the stories. The guy was everywhere.'

'I'll say. He went AWOL on me in Italy. I thought he got what he had coming from the Italian mafia—Johnny Goodnight's curtain call. Now you tell me he lives in New York.'

'Yeah, I kinda helped him out of a jam back then.'

'He's turned out to be useful again.'

'I know talent when I see it.'

'Yeah, you've always been overlooked, Earl.'

'Put in a good word for me, Phil.'

'So you think Greenfield's the problem. He's got the President's ear, and if he's on to us, the President could fuck us up.'

'Nothing's happened. Greenfield can't know squat shit.'

'Don't kid yourself. Greenfield's like a patient lion waiting in the shadows; he'll wait and wait until he's sure, then he'll pounce with extreme prejudice. He leaves little to chance. Look how he took out Osbourne; he didn't even know him, and Osbourne's one street-smart hustler—Johnny Goodnight.' Garvey laughed.

'Should we take him out?'

'Greenfield, nah, leave him be—as a professional courtesy; we partnered at times post war. We should start lower down. These Melbos oughta suffice for now. Get Osbourne here. What does he call himself now?'

'Joe di Lucca.'

'Name suits him; he was always a wop.'

'And Sanchez?'

'I'd like to see that spic. Tell him to get back here.'

*

Two days later, Sanchez was sitting in Bunting's new office. He was relaxed and smiling like a Cheshire cat, showing a new gold incisor.

'What are you so pleased about, Sanchez? The last I heard Castro's still ranting.'

'What do you think, boss? Inèz and me got married yesterday. We were going to take a honeymoon, until you called.'

'I'm all sentimental. Where?'

'Miami. We found a nice house near a park in Little Havana. Then we were going to go to the Keys for a few days.'

'I don't give a goddamn where you go! What happened in Cuba?'

'Fidel never showed. That's not our fault. We did everything as planned.'

'Like fuck you did! You slipped away with your little Chiquita!'

Sanchez shrugged. 'What did you expect, Señor Bunting? No one cares about us, so I made a decision to bring her out.'

'In ten minutes we have a meeting with Woods and Garvey. I need answers now! You appear back in Miami with two work visas, bonafides from the State Department passport office; you buy a house; you have a new gold fucking tooth!'

'Señor Boss, don't be angry, sir. I can easily explain. Before the revolution, Inèz's family had some money. They stashed almost ten thousand American dollars, but didn't dare use it after the revolution. Last time I went down, I smuggled it out and put it in a bank. I told Hoover's people when I was recruited that I wouldn't work for them unless I was given a guarantee that I could bring Inèz here. My contact in the FBI is Bill James. He was told, so he said, that I would be given that guarantee; and he told me he would personally make sure it was in the works. All I had to do was get all our identification papers from Cuba and new photos. So I did, and he did as he had promised.'

'Then why go AWOL?'

'We were afraid she would not be allowed if I got out of Cuba with Pedro. I was afraid that we were being used as goats, to be sacrificed to that fucker, Red Beard, you know, Piñiero, of the *Dirección General de Inteligencia*. Many of my friends were tortured and murdered by those bastards.'

'How did you get out?'

'I know people, Boss. Then the Coast Guard picked us up and took us to Puerto Rico, where we caught a flight to Miami.'

'The Coast Guard? Who arranged that?'

'Bill James, of course.'

'You're playing a dangerous game here, Sanchez.'

'Damn right, boss. Sanchez is everybody's favorite goat.'

'Just what do you do for James?'

'Same as you. We're on the same side, no?'

'What do you think about Kennedy?'

'Kennedy? That sonofabitch killed friends of mine, when he didn't show up with his army at *Bahía de Cochinos*. He's one gringo … You know.'

'No I don't know. What?'

'Boss, I've just been given legal status in America. I'm not gonna suggest someone should whack the bastard, right?'

'No, you shouldn't. You're a clever little prick.'

'Walk a mile in my shoes, Señor.'

Five minutes later, Bunting and Sanchez were seated in a conference room with Phil Garvey and Aubrey Woods. Bunting briefed them generally about what Sanchez had told him, emphasizing Bill James' participation in Sanchez's obtaining working visas. Woods didn't say a word.

'So, Eduardo,' said Garvey, 'let me clarify: you escaped with James' help, yet you tell us you deviated from the original plan on your own initiative. It seems to me a contradiction. Either you did it by yourself, or you planned it from the get-go with James. I might add that Earl here was your case officer, not James.'

'I carried out my task, sir. And I brought back my fiancée, who is now my wife. And you know that I work for the FBI as well; in effect, they loaned me to you.' Sanchez looked at Woods. 'Mr. James has always watched my back. I trusted him.'

'And the visas?'

'Hoover had originally promised me them, when I was first interviewed for this job.'

'But you never actually spoke to Hoover.'

'No, but Bill James was acting on his direct orders, or so I was told; promises were made to me and never kept for four years, until now, thanks to Mr. James.'

'Did James request anything in return for this act of good will?' asked Garvey.

'Do you mean did he fulfill his promise in the expectation of more work from me? Well, yes, I suppose. I told him I was very grateful, and that he redeemed my belief in America to do the right thing for Cubans. And yes, I said if there was anything I could do for him, I would be obliged, just as I have done all along.' He looked across at the stony faces of Woods, Garvey and Bunting. 'What's wrong with that? We're all on the same side here, hombres! We're fighting Commies, are we not?'

Aubrey Woods finally spoke: 'Thank you, Mr. Sanchez. We've always counted on your professionalism, and you've shown us how capable you are. We realize that you've been put into a difficult position serving two masters, the CIA and the FBI. Now more than ever, the Cold War being what it is, we must all be seen to be working together for a just cause.

'For instance, Mr. James has been privy to some of the agency's closely held secrets, and he in turn has been most helpful in securing cooperation

362

between the services for operations inside America. I hope that we can continue to count on you in this unique relationship. You're free to go, and we'll be in touch. And, by the way: congratulations on your marriage and the successful removal of your wife from Cuba.'

After Sanchez left, Woods and his henchmen sat silently for a few moments. Garvey was shaking his head.

'That's one cagey spic,' he said. 'Personally, I think he's James' man, and can't be trusted, which leads me to conclude James can't be trusted.'

'You're insinuating that my brother-in-law is a traitor, Phil,' said Woods, suspiciously.

'I'm just saying that the operation has a liability here when we don't know what the other hand is doing. Hell, I know Hoover, and he sure as hell keeps his boys in line, no exceptions. He may not be aware of our progress, but I'd put money on him having informants out there and knowing something is going on. James is his counter-espionage guy who likely briefs him regularly about us and whoever he's running, like Sanchez.'

'Are you suggesting we bug James, or Hoover, to take back total control?' asked Woods.

'Given the gravity of this operation, we can't take any chances.'

'And when this operation is concluded, it won't matter because Hoover and Johnson, for that matter, are going to be in control. We must tread carefully here: we don't want to be on the receiving end of that liability if it becomes convenient for them to implicate a few scapegoats.'

'We have a scapegoat, Aubrey.'

'Yes, well, like you say, if Sanchez is any indicator, scapegoats can't be trusted to act in accordance with best laid plans; you know how things go: people in the field are in control of their own actions, and do things beyond our control. You know how it is.'

'Damn right I do; that's why I need one hundred percent dedication to me when I conduct an operation of this magnitude.'

'If I may,' interjected Bunting.

Woods and Garvey turned their heads.

'We have a cure for this malady: Joe di Lucca, our very own resurrected Gerald Osbourne. We can put him onto James, just to see how patriotic he is. Also, what about Greenfield? And Melbo? Something stinks about them.'

'Bunting, we've got a handle on them,' declared Garvey, curtly. 'Mind your place.'

'What kind of handle?' asked Woods.

'You don't want to know.'

'Well, I'm asking.'

'They're loose ends we can ill afford, Aubrey. Melbo is my preferred quarry. Bunting says he's working for Greenfield, and accompanied him 'fishing' these last weeks in St. Croix, at the same time Sanchez was in Cuba. That's too much of a coincidence for me, given the circumstances.'

'Are you're saying they're working with Bill?'

'Damn right I am.'

Woods shook his head disbelieving, yet there was a despondency revealed in this, as if he'd been betrayed.

Raising his head, Woods responded. 'So you think by eliminating Melbo, it will stop the leaking if such a thing were possible?'

'It will send a message to Greenfield, or even James, if he's involved, that they better heed their little voices if they want to survive. I was hoping I wouldn't have to read the riot act to you, sir, but if we don't act now, this operation will be found out. Greenfield was the best there is back in the day, and he's decidedly not in our camp anymore. He's a killer if he has to be, and he's a Kennedy man, and he's on the scent of us. I know it in my gut.'

'Have you considered what would happen if these people all died? There'd be a shit storm.'

'Dwarfed by the big hurricane.'

Woods sat quietly, unable to respond. He knew his brother-in-law had to be the lynchpin in any scenario involving Greenfield and Melbo, if they were indeed in contact, somehow. 'Don't do anything hasty,' he finally said, 'I need proof. If you find the proof, do what needs to be done. I don't want to hear about it; it's too close to home.'

Woods abruptly stood up and left the room. Garvey turned to Bunting.

'If you ever go over my head again, you little fuckin' weasel, I'm gonna shoot you myself.'

'Jesus, Phil, relax.'

'Relax? I'm called out of retirement to conduct the biggest event of the century, and we're being monitored?'

30. Beyond the Pale

Unshaven and bedraggled, Greenfield and Melbo arrived home in Washington to the immense relief of their wives, but there was only a brief time for celebration. If anything, their return created a higher sense of urgency that didn't go unnoticed by Prinzenthal during their husband's absence and she hadn't been completely open about her worries with DeCourt, who for her part was eager to get back to New York. In bed that night, after what she liked to term a *whizbang*, to release her pent-up tension, and to provide Harley a sure-fire shot to sleep, Prinzenthal came right to the point.

Staring at her husband, who was rapidly shutting down with a Lethian fatigue, she cupped his balls and squeezed them just enough to get his attention. She explained to him Jimbo's and her concerns about Bunting's regular visits to their street at all hours. Something was very bothersome about all this, and her inner voice was ringing off the hook. Greenfield, fighting his hypersomnia, made a grand effort to allay her fears for the night.

'It was a necessary risk, darling. Of course, they're onto us. I've factored all of this into a plan.' His eyes began closing.

She squeezed him again.

'Easy, love, give me the benefit of age; I'll explain in the morning.'

She was smiling now as she squeezed harder.

'Hey, that hurts!' he exclaimed, alert.

'Balls,' she purred, 'are what God gave women to squeeze. You will tell me now or regret it.'

'Okay, dear, okay, I've been sleep-deprived for days. Ken and Dave are out there now. We're in good hands. Tomorrow I'll brief my bosses about what happened in Cuba, as well as the CIA surveillance of our house, and about what has happened to my personal assistant, Mel, who was followed by a hood named di Lucca: a Bunting cutout. Prognosis: the Melbos should move to Canada under an assumed name. You and I need to stay and prevent a potential assassination.'

'Di Lucca. I know who he is.'

'What? How?'

'I had those photos developed. The ones you took in New York.'

Greenfield was awake and open-eyed.

'And?'

'He's older obviously, but just as slick. I met him in Frankfurt once, and I saw him in Berlin just before I met you. Gerald Osbourne.'

'Johnny Goodnight? I thought he'd been killed.'

'Yup. Deceased, according to records; I looked him up. Supposedly murdered in Milan, whacked by the Mob, revenge for a boss. The story went that his body was thrown to the pigs. '

'Johnny Prosciutto.'

'Ha Ha. Very funny. He hit on me in Frankfurt waiting for a contact outside a makeshift pub surrounded by rubble. He thought I was local, because I was wearing civilian clothes. I played along with him as "Hedwig", who didn't understand English. Then he tried Italian, and I pretended to know a smattering, so I let him buy me a beer. Eventually, my German contact showed up, a minor assistant to Adenauer. I had been asked to liaise with them by General Gerald Templer, as a favor from the State Department. It was the strangest thing. Anyway, I left the creep gawking at me, thanked him for the beer, and spoke German to this assistant, Herr Gunther; then, when some American MPs showed up, Osbourne made a quick exit.'

'And Berlin?'

'Potsdam. I was helping as translator for a couple of senior American officials in the State Department conversing with a group of Russians, and I noticed this guy nearby staring at me. What do you know? This same Osbourne. I had just met Kennedy at the same function. Osbourne came up to me later and winked, saying "Hedwig". Before I could reply, Kennedy took me by the arm and introduced me to Secretary Forrestal. Osbourne remained on the periphery, listening to me speak English. I think I winked at him. That's the last I saw of him.'

'He was Phil Garvey's boy. Bunting ran him. Bunting probably facilitated his return to America and had his death faked. They were pals, obviously.'

'What will you do, Harley? He's dangerous.'

'First things first. Sleep.'

'Okay, darling.' She released his balls with a gentle caress and a kiss on his lips. Harley rolled over and was soon snoring. Prinzenthal listened to him for a while before nodding off, thinking she had almost missed the snoring as it receded in her sleep.

In the morning everyone sat at the kitchen table for breakfast while Prinzenthal fed Lizbet Pablum oatmeal in a high chair. Greenfield looked at Melbo and DeCourt who were sipping tea and coffee enjoying their eggs, toast and honey. Lizbet kept trying to take the spoon from her mother and finally succeeded, which distracted Greenfield when she fed herself, spilling half of it.

'That's my girl,' he said. 'Just like her mom.'

'Thanks, Harley,' quipped Prinzenthal, to laughter all around.

'I meant it being in control, sweetheart,' he said. 'You know: take charge.'

'That's fine, I'm still happy you're back to look after us,' she said, kissing his smooth shaven cheek, 'and your funny ways.'

Greenfield addressed the Melbos: 'That's Hannah's way of saying: be careful, Harley, you can be in control, but I'm still the boss.'

Again everyone laughed, even Lizbet imitating them.

After breakfast, Greenfield suggested they take their coffee and tea and sit in the yard. Prinzenthal put Lizbet in the crib with some dolls and toys and left the back door open so the infant could see them.

Greenfield's mood became somber.

'I've got bad news, Mel,' he began. 'Hannah found out who that guy was following you in New York. His name is Gerald Osbourne. He supposedly died after the war in Italy. He also went by the nickname, Johnny Goodnight, among his colleagues because he was a particularly skilled killer, and was used by the agency to kill Communists, and others. I had nothing to do with him, nor did Hannah, although she had met him briefly by chance in Germany before I knew her. He was known to be a very convincing individual, both as a gentleman and as a tough guy, whatever the occasion required—a superb poseur. Anyway, he became a marked man in Italy when he ran afoul of the mafia, and the company, before he went rogue. Well, one day he simply vanished, and it was revealed by sources he'd been whacked by the mafia. Good riddance.'

'And this very same man was following Mel!' cried DeCourt.

'Yes,' went on Greenfield as calmly as he could, 'but resurrected, as Joe di Lucca. Someone, and we know who, had smuggled him out of Europe with a new name and passport. Joe di Lucca was undoubtedly the thug who murdered Keith Leverton. This means they are going to kill you, me and anybody else who could threaten them. I'm not talking about aliens anymore; that may have been a trigger-point; but sinister forces within the service are using these really rotten people to carry out their agenda.'

'To what purpose?' asked DeCourt.

'We think there's a plot to assassinate the President, though we have no proof, yet.'

'Haven't you alerted the President and Secret Service?'

'Yes, of course, but it fell on deaf ears, because there're always threats against the President, and I had nothing conclusive except hearsay from right wing elements: Texas oilmen, Cuban exiles, and assorted others, such as the mob. Most of these groups have been vocal privately about Kennedy being a traitor. We live in a very diverse country, in both thought and culture. All one has to do is study our history to understand that. The Gettysburg centennial is coming up in a few weeks. That hellish bloodbath was only a hundred years ago and hard feelings still exist. Blacks are being lynched. Violence is endemic. Enlightenment is the anomaly. It's our cure in the long run, though not now. I know how this works.'

'What do you have in mind?' asked Melbo.

'You have to leave the country, both of you. Change your name. Go to Canada. Otherwise you will be killed if you remain here. You're on their hit list, and so am I.'

DeCourt was speechless, in shock.

Melbo seemed quite calm. 'And what will you do?' he asked.

'I'm going to kill them first.'

'We can help you!' exclaimed DeCourt.

'No.' Prinzenthal spoke more seriously than they had ever heard her before. 'Harley's right. You must go to Canada. We'll fix you up with new identities.'

'You can't stay here, Hannah!' declared DeCourt.

'I'm going to leave too. I'll get a transfer somewhere, Paris maybe. I know the Ambassador, Chip Bohlen. He was one of my superiors in Moscow.'

'Paris? I want to go to Paris,' exclaimed DeCourt.

'We can't be together, Mel. I'm so sorry about all this, but we know what's best. We love you as our dear friends. Please trust us.'

'When all this blows over,' said Greenfield, 'you can come back.'

'You're just saying that,' said DeCourt, pouting. 'You know that will never happen. Everything changes.'

'We can meet in St. Croix,' said Prinzenthal, halfheartedly. 'Or Paris, later.'

'Think of a new name,' said Greenfield, standing up. 'I'll make all the arrangements, security, passports, everything. Don't leave the house.' Then he was gone through the side gate.

Melbo stood up and hugged DeCourt, who was sitting there stunned.

'Just call me Sadie,' she said morosely, 'Sadie Sadlands.'

'Then meet William Kane, darling. Everybody calls me Will, or Willy, like my dad.'

'Very funny.'

'Yeah, I write books.'

'Oh, really? Never heard of 'em.'

'Wanna be my literary agent?'

'Stop it, Mel.'

'We'll start a family.'

DeCourt said nothing, as two tears rolled from her eyes.

*

In the weeks ahead, time seemed to stand still. The tension in the air became like a phony interlude; there were no more pass-bys from Bunting or sightings of di Lucca, whose photograph was passed around among Jimbo and his crew. For the duration, until new passports had been produced through Greenfield's clandestine contacts, it was almost as if a period of grace had been bestowed upon them in order to allow some movement on his part. Greenfield was at his wits end to get a handle on Bunting and di Lucca, but they were either out of the picture, or invisible. He desperately needed to speak with Bill James, as the only link to what could possibly be going on, but he thought it best to wait, fearful of exposing himself as a result of the Cuban operation. James would likely be feeling the same pressure and would have contacted him somehow if he were able. Something had to give.

Meanwhile, the Melbos moved back to New York, minded carefully by Ken Helmsley, Jimbo's young recruit. They were in the process of quitting their jobs, packing up and moving to Montreal with their new identities, William and Sadie Kane. Ken would help them settle in a new place, and would report back once the dust had settled removing any danger.

Prinzenthal had worked her magic with the State Department after contacting Ambassador Bohlen, who was thrilled to have his old "young" friend and legend—albeit that was secret—come on board during his tenure in Paris, and he created a position for her as 'special' consul. Greenfield had no say in the matter, but Prinzenthal wasn't leaving until after her birthday on the fourth of July. He had met with the Secret Service and explained their tenuous situation with the alleged rogue operative, Earl Bunting, who, when he was summoned by the Director of the CIA, John McCone, at the request of the White House, was reportedly on a leave of absence, and unlikely to return for health reasons—cancer—but in a deposition miraculously submitted, Bunting had accused Greenfield of assault a few years ago.

McCone, unaware of any operation, or conspiracy, was nonplussed, to say the least that his agency was being used to conduct such incredulous deployment, boiled it down to bad blood between a retired employee and lesser operative, and summarily dropped the matter. McCone considered himself a protective "uncle" to Kennedy, and Kennedy had hired him in kind to replace Sulla. So again Greenfield was stymied, the consequence being that he was reprimanded by his immediate boss for using government resources irresponsibly, and told he should desist from making any further inquiries into his "alumna". Undeterred, Greenfield took the bull by the horns and made a visit to the FBI, with a request to see Bill James; if James was being monitored, it would not likely be within the building itself, it being considered inviolate.

He was taking a chance, but he felt he had nothing to lose, though he used his old credentials as John Hardin, which he had kept current. To his surprise, after a short wait on a third floor bench, he was conducted into James' office, by an assistant, who then promptly removed himself, shutting the door behind him.

'John Hardin. This is a surprise,' said James, standing, looking a bit weathered with some gray hair appearing at the sides. 'Coffee, tea?'

'No thanks, Bill.'

'Please,' he said, indicating a chair.

They both sat down.

'Under the circumstances,' he continued, 'your coming here is no small thing.'

'I do believe we understand each other.'

'Yes, the cat's out of the bag, but you're relatively safe here. They watch me from outside, though I can't be sure whether someone's on the inside. Hoover keeps tabs on us all, but for reasons unrelated to our present dilemma.'

'Do we need to take a stroll?'

'No, I'm the one who usually does the bugging around here—we caught an East German mole a year ago and routinely scan the office. Trouble with the trade, as you would know, Harley.'

'Yes, indeed.' He paused before asking: 'Bill, what happened?'

'In a nutshell, Phil Garvey. Officially retired, unofficially involved.'

'Garvey. That maniac murdered—had murdered—more people than I can count.'

'What's happened is that my one good source, Sanchez, is compromised. I took a chance getting him out of Cuba with his woman, and I'm glad I did for his sake. And I'm most grateful for your tremendous help. All went swimmingly for you, I presume?'

'Yes, yes, a bit strenuous, and rough seas at times, but successful.'

'Thank you, but to the point: Garvey and Bunting convinced my brother-in-law, Aubrey, that I was their leak. I suppose you know what that means.'

'Jesus, Bill. What can I do?'

'For one thing, keep Nevin well out of it.'

'Of course. My first priority is protection of all our loved ones. I sent the Melbos to Canada. Hannah is taking a position in the embassy in Paris. Nevin, well, he's been out of the picture for months now. How did he take it?'

'I couldn't actually get a definitive reading on him either way; he just accepted it. I did tell him it's not about aliens anymore, at least overtly.'

'And he didn't ask why?'

'No, he just said that he knew I was under a lot of pressure, and he didn't want to add any more. He's very much involved with his studies, and girlfriend, Mollie. He wants to go to Yale.'

'By the sounds of it he's matured a lot.'

'He's a tall young man now.' James smiled.

'Sanchez told me about being sent by Hoover to surveil your home.'

'Yeah, he told me too.'

'He said he was interrupted by Nevin and his girlfriend. They came home

371

early, and I hate to say it, but I think you should know that they went right at it in his bedroom.'

'Oh, so he told you about that.'

'Yes.'

'Doesn't surprise me,' admitted James. 'Her mother told me Mollie's been on the pill for a couple of years now. For menstrual hemorrhaging.'

'Her mother?'

'I've known her since we were kids—Deborah Godfrey—and always loved her; we've been involved now for years. During the war, everything went sideways. We were seeing others. I got Muriel Doddart pregnant when she was only sixteen; I was twenty. I had to marry her.'

'Honey Woods' baby sister?'

'Yep. And I love her, only half as much. I put family and career before divorce and remarriage.'

'Jesus, Bill, you're walking a tightrope.'

'Until now. The game's up.' He laughed, almost sadly.

'And Nevin knows.'

'How'd you guess?' asked James.

'Intuition. Must be a chip off the ol' block, my friend. And Aubrey? Does he know?'

'I never told him, but he probably knows.'

'From surveillance?'

'I asked him to protect my family if anything happened to me.'

'God. And Deborah, does she know?'

'She insisted I tell him. She wants to be free, with me.'

'And you agreed.'

'No. I said not until I was finished with an operation of national importance, to put it mildly.'

'But the cat was already out of the bag.'

'Yep.'

'So do you think Aubrey told his wife?'

'I doubt it.'

'Who's Mollie's father?'

'Commander John McBride. Flew planes on a carrier in the war; was in some major engagements, including Midway and Leyte. They're divorced now. He still works closely with the Navy and now the Airforce as a civilian in procurement; works partly out of Edwards, and lives in San Bernardino. Mollie's been out a few times.'

'He must've found out about you and Deborah.'

'He knew all along; well, after the war at least. He got her pregnant too, before they were married.'

'What does Hoover know?' asked Greenfield.

'About me? Not a lot.'

'And the event?'

'Nothing. But they, the old guard, Sulla et al, all know they can count on him. He's tight with Johnson, too; they all think alike: crocodiles. It'll be a bonafide coup d'état, Harley. It's happening and we both know it—at the very least, we suspect it—yet there's nothing we can do. It's like something preordained, and could happen anywhere, anytime. No proof, no knowledge.'

'That's the way it works in black ops: nobody knows much of anything until almost the day it happens.'

'And then in the following chaos a coverup is orchestrated by the very people in charge of discovering the truth.'

'Not if I can help it.'

'What do you propose?'

'Prevent it somehow, then take it to the people.'

'Melbo?'

'Who else? Then if it happens, the public will know that it was a coup d'état and demand justice or the sky will fall.'

'Watch your back, Harley; the sky will fall anyway.'

'Believe me, I'm careful. Tell me about Woods. What happened?'

'Woods is a puppet, like one of those Elizabethan pictograms that show's his image coddled by a hand that appears from a cloud or a curtain. I don't think he really has a clue who he is. The irony is telling: here I'm the one who's being cast as the bad guy, emotionally dishonest, while he's the one who's most morally corrupt, yet representing a stable marriage and appearing to be a stalwart of the status quo, doing their bidding.'

James leaned back in his chair and pulled out a cigarette, offering one to Greenfield, who declined making excuses: saying he'd quit when he retired from the service, adding that Hannah could not stand smoke in a confined space, and he knew that if he wanted her, smoking would be non-negotiable. Besides, he felt so much healthier.

I've been trying to quit,' said James, 'along with Debbie. We're down to six cigarettes a day, next week, five, and so on. Muriel doesn't smoke, and while at home, I smoke only in my study, with a window open.'

'I understand Woods was a desk junkie during the war,' said Greenfield, keeping the thread of their dialogue. 'I didn't know him at all back then. It was only in the last years of my service I knew of him; he was involved on the periphery of a couple of operations I ran, as my superior, but he never interfered. He was like a politico and just watched from the sidelines, before taking the credit.'

'His theatre was the Pacific during the war, from Hawaii with his family. Postwar, he lived in Japan for a while, alone, while his wife and kids remained there; they visited him once during the summer.'

'I see.'

'When Eisenhower was elected, Sulla had him take over the Southern European desk: Greece, Italy, the Balkans.'

'With Garvey,' said Greenfield.

'Garvey remained in Europe of course, and Aubrey stayed in Washington, and probably didn't know half of what was going on.'

'Now, Garvey's back.'

'Either that or he's just visiting,' remarked James.

'Just the kind of thing he's good at, visiting; then he'll disappear, but leaving all his goons waiting in the shadows autonomously. Impossible to detect.'

'Did Sanchez say anything to you?' asked James.

'Nothing about Garvey. He mentioned some people of interest from New Orleans and Texas.'

'Such as?'

'Oh, a bunch of them you know already: Clay Bertrand, Guy Banister, David Ferrie, a fellow named Lee Oswald, Earl Cabell, Ed Clark. He didn't know much about them other than they received money from Sanchez. However, he made it clear that Oswald, Cabell and Clark were just people he'd heard about; they hadn't received money from Sanchez. Clark is a lawyer out of Austin for a lot of powerful Texans, including Johnson—some say his mentor—and Cabell is the mayor of Dallas. Personally, I feel that they're part of the so-called "Texas mafia". I'm told it's always been that way in Texas. He didn't know much about Oswald, a self-proclaimed Communist, other than that he was an employee of some kind for Banister, which didn't make sense because he said Banister's a rightwing fascist, if there ever was one.'

'Lee Harvey Oswald,' said James. 'He's actually an informant of ours; an unreliable one, or rather inconsistent. I don't put a lot of stock in him, and I never met him; Sanchez got to him for me. He lived in Russia, has a Russian wife. I tried to find out about him discreetly through my contacts with the agency, but came up empty handed. Someone I know in the State Department claimed he was a "blind", someone "allowed" to emigrate to the Soviet Union as a sleeper, because when he returned, having defected and given up his citizenship, there was no big deal, no red flag; he just basically waltzed back in. Someone had to have been pulling strings. Sanchez said he wanted to go to Cuba.'

'Interesting. Where does he live now?'

'He was in Dallas, then New Orleans the last I heard. Sanchez said he was all over the place, a perennial misfit who hated fascists, and couldn't hold down a job.'

'Did you ask your brother-in-law about him?

'I did, but he'd never heard of him.'

'Sanchez told me—with the exception of Oswald—these people were all anti-Kennedy, some virulently.'

'In that part of the world, it's the norm, Harley.'

'We shouldn't overlook that part of the country as a setting for some attempt on Kennedy's life.'

'Not at all,' said James leaning forward on his desk, 'but remember, we're getting threats all the time; from the mob mainly. People like Santo Trafficante, Sam Giancana and especially Carlos Marcello, who has a pathological hatred of the Kennedys, because he felt he'd been betrayed by him and Robert; and with the agency's close contacts there and in Europe, what better foil for murder?'

'We live in dangerous times, Bill.'

*

Nevin and Mollie were lying together prostrate on top of his bed, fully dressed, listening to music on the old family RCA Victor portable record player. Both parents were home: his dad in his study and mom preparing dinner with Carolyn. Uncle Aubrey and Aunt Honey had been invited for dinner to celebrate Carolyn's election as a Student Fellow at Vassar College—a ranking leadership role after completing her freshman year, majoring in bio-medical sciences.

When the Woods arrived, Carolyn went upstairs to tell Nevin and her father. Knocking on Nevin's door and not hearing a response, she entered his room and, closing the door behind her, looked at them both listening intently to the loud music of a new British band called the Beatles. Everyone they knew was ecstatic about them, including her friends at Vassar that spring, when their hits were first being played on the radio. She preferred female singers such as Connie Francis, Sarah Vaughan, and recently Lesley Gore; but she caught the bug with the Beatles like every teenager, though she was a far cry from the screaming mania that would inflame the younger girls.

Nevin and Mollie looked up to see her smiling and gently moving to the song *Please Please Me*, from the album of the same name, released early that spring in Britain; Nevin had obtained a copy from a friend who had been over there and brought back a couple of copies, so impressed was he. Mollie got off the bed and began dancing and shaking to the others' delight.

At sixteen, Mollie had really come into herself as a young woman; she was confident and grew in looks a bit like a mix of young Hedy Lamarr and Grace Slick with a whole lot of Mollie. After a few more songs, Carolyn announced that their aunt and uncle had arrived, and they were to join them downstairs, as Mollie too, had been invited to dinner. Carolyn and Mollie had become unlikely friends over the last few years, but not so close that Carolyn knew their inner secrets. She did, however, know that they were sleeping together, as she had found them once in bed when her parents were out.

After, Mollie confided to her that she was on the pill for medical reasons and saw no reason to abstain from sexual pleasures with Nevin. This shocked Carolyn who, being a virgin at the time, felt intimidated by their promiscuity, but she never said a word to either of her parents. And later that year, she revealed to Mollie she 'did everything' with a 'boy'—the son of one of her mother's friends—but that it ended because he had joined the air force and eventually was tragically killed in Vietnam.

As Carolyn opened the door to get her father, Uncle Aubrey was curiously standing there for what had seemed like some moments. With a smile on his face, he greeted his niece and nephew as they filed out.

'Was that the Beatles?' he asked amused. 'I couldn't help but listen.'

'Yes, uncle,' said Carolyn.

'What outrageous popcorn. What will become of your generation?'

'Well, we'll probably grow up and have babies,' she said laughing.

Woods laughed too.

'We listen to all kinds of music, Uncle Aubrey,' said Nevin. 'Even your Lawrence Welk.'

'I'm a Benny Goodman fan.'

'So am I.'

'Hello Mollie,' said Woods, ignoring Nevin's apparent cockiness.

'Hi, Mr. Woods,' she replied. 'How's life in the spy world?'

'Oh, and I was going to ask: what kind of music do you like?'

They all laughed.

'Motown bands like the Miracles. And the Beatles, of course.'

'I'll get your dad,' he said to Carolyn, dismissively. 'See you all downstairs.'

Woods watched them go for a moment, then turned and went down the hall to his brother-in-law's study, knocking lightly before opening the door. James welcomed him in with a hello and smile.

'Are you a Beatles fan, Aubrey?' he asked, suddenly.

'What's the world coming too?' replied Woods, smiling.

'Youth today have a real need to express themselves. Our generation had better accommodate them.'

'Our generation paid the piper, Bill, with many lives.'

'Indeed, our lot was a hard one.'

Aubrey settled in the sofa chair in the corner.

'Dinner in ten, I was told,' said Woods.

'Then I guess we should get to the matter.'

'Bill, what on earth is going on? I have operatives chomping at the bit to take down some prying civilians. You know who.'

'Perhaps these civilians are concerned patriotic civilians.'

'It leads back to you, Bill. Are you a concerned patriotic citizen?'

'I am, Aubrey. Like you, though of different mettle.'

'Christ, man, I can't be responsible for this!'

'Why not?'

'It's a foregone conclusion! And it's the poor fuckers like me who bear the brunt of it!'

'Whatever you do, don't hurt them: Melbo and Greenfield.'

'Is this the deal? You come clean and they go their merry way? You know it doesn't work like that.'

'At least call off your thugs for a few weeks. They haven't any idea what's going on. They may suspect something, but Greenfield's no fool; he's the best there is.'

'Bill, I need to know what happened. I suspect it all began when that son of yours invited Melbo to speak at his school a few years ago, right?'

'I had nothing to do with that.'

'Perhaps, but you attended and made the connection.'

'I went for purely personal reasons. Aren't you a little bit interested in the alien phenomena?' he asked, smiling.

'Not the hogwash Melbo spins.'

James sat back in his desk chair and lit a cigarette, blowing his first puff at the ceiling.

'I'm going to tell you something,' he began, inhaling more smoke, 'and you're going to listen. You're not my boss, you're my brother-in-law. We work for the United States government, which under the Constitution have an obligation to do the right thing given its encomiums of liberal democracy and enlightenment. Where did it go wrong in this present imbroglio? What can possibly justify the actions of a few zealous men who have an axe to grind with Kennedy? It's a goddamned sacrilege!

'For many years, I believed as they did. Our war-weary minds had to turn to the task of defeating yet another insane ideological autocracy: Soviet Communism, a morally corrupt, murderous, Stalinist monster. Stalin's long gone, but his shadow remains and the system he managed—that of a psychopathic paranoid—still carries on. It has brought us to the brink of human annihilation. Had it not been for Kennedy, can you believe we'd still be sitting here? Had General LeMay or Admiral Radford had their way in the crisis last year, there'd be an irradiated crater where Washington once existed, and unspeakable suffering here and around the world.

'We've got to change, Aubrey. And that's not letting down our guard. But to take out a symptom of the future in a man with Kennedy's qualifications would be a terrible disaster and burden on this great nation. Sure, he's a flawed man, but no different than any of us. It's not too late to stop this runaway train.

You have the power to derail it, Aubrey, and stop these rogue misfits from doing their worst.'

'You've got it all wrong, Bill. I have no beef with Kennedy. He did the right thing, even if no one wants to admit it. The problem is political, or rather could be political. And I'm not a politician; I'm an intelligence bureaucrat.'

'That doesn't make sense. This has nothing to do with politics. Simply put, you're saying you're not at liberty to tell me anything.'

'I'll tell you this: there's a bigger picture than we realize and we must make sure we're on the winning side. Kennedy, you, me, or anybody, doesn't matter unless we see it through.'

'The big *It!* Tell me about the big *It*, Aubrey.'

'I'll leave it up to you to make your own deductions. You've been doing pretty well on your own.'

'But it's not good enough! No matter what I do, there's a spotlight on it!'

The tension in the air seemed thick as cement. Both men knew each side was helplessly ineffectual to stop the wicked situation unfolding with pathogenic magnitude. It appeared that whoever had set this big event in motion was sourced in some dark biblical-like revelation. And to cure the disease someone or other had to die.

'Does Hoover know your mind on this?' asked Woods, shifting in a chair.

'I was called into his office, and he asked me about Sanchez. I told him exactly what I did.'

'What was his reaction?'

'He reprimanded me, but let it go on the condition I keep him personally informed about what Sanchez finds out about his dealings with your people.'

'That's it?'

'Hoover's not stupid. He knows something big is happening on his turf; he knows the mob and seems to have effected a rapprochement with them because they're anti-Communist; well, he's always been that way with the commensurate ideology. Actually, he's just another paranoid control freak. If it's not Communism, it's Malcolm X and Black Power, homophobia—what a hypocrite in that—and liberal Democrats. He's an anachronism who belongs back in the days of Bonnie and Clyde.'

Woods said nothing, as if he wasn't listening. He seemed to be preoccupied with the dilemma his brother-in-law presented to him. He felt no guilt or remorse, just the ramifications of Bill's wrongheadedness; then he looked at him, and Bill looked back.

'You've been followed,' said Woods.

'I know.'

'You know?'

'I expected as much.'

'Yet you still went to her.'

'How long have you known?' asked James.

'Not long. I was surprised, but not that surprised. I can see how Nevin finds the same attraction in Mollie.'

'Yeah, well, you know what they say: like father like son.'

'I haven't told Honey.'

'You can tell her.'

'And Muriel?'

'I'll ask for a divorce, soon.'

'Bill, I'm sorry.'

'I'm not. Just let me break it to her.'

'Agreed.'

They remained silent for half a minute, each within his own swirling thoughts.

'We're not like Russia,' said Woods, suddenly.

'Funny you say that.'

'Why?'

'Because it's not true. In one way we are like them: we're just too proud to admit we're capable of anything so evil.'

'That's ridiculous.'

'Is it? Don't hurt my family, or Greenfield and Melbo, or Sanchez for that matter.'

'I would never do that, Bill. Hell, you should know me better than that.'

'Yes I do. You're weak when it comes to authority.'

'And you're not?'

'I'm prepared to make personal sacrifices.'

'So am I.'

James stood up, smiling. 'Okay, Aubrey; let's call it a draw.' He walked to the door and opened it. 'I don't know about you, but I smell Muriel's famous pot roast.'

'Now that's more like it,' said Woods, smiling and standing up. 'I'm famished.'

31. God On Our Side

In the weeks following Ken Helmsley's departure from Montreal, the Melbos felt rather shell-shocked. They had little fear of being discovered because they considered themselves now remote from their previous lives. Why would anyone even bother? But they felt as if they were on another planet, even though Melbo had grown up in this city.

At first, they had rented a furnished apartment by the month off Atwater Street, having put their furniture and other possessions in storage. They didn't want to impose upon his mother, Wendy Melbo, who now lived in a grand old apartment building, Gleneagles, for fear of her home being watched, and they didn't even contact her for a month. When they did finally and explained to her what had happened, she insisted on helping them find a place of their own. The family cottage had been sold the previous year, and she gave them more than the equivalent of the proceeds which wasn't much but enough for a decent down payment for a modest old fieldstone house in Westmount near Mont Royal, which greatly lifted DeCourt's spirits and awakened her latent nesting instincts.

Melbo didn't have trouble finding work at the Montreal Star with his credentials as George Melbo, but he made an arrangement with the management to be known and published under his 'sobriquet' William Kane, and eventually Sadie Kane found work with Reader's Digest Canada in advertising. Gradually, they adopted a new life, made new friends and their past receded. The relative excitement of their previous life now transformed into the kind of normality most people just accepted. Yet, somewhat haunted by the specter of aliens and sinister objectives of the power elite south of the border, they never felt quite at ease.

Back in Washington, Greenfield maintained his vigilance with the help of Jimbo, Dave and Ken, who divided around the clock the day's protective surveillance. Both he and Prinzenthal were relieved that the Melbos were safe in Montreal. DeCourt had given to them the key for the Diva mailbox at the New York post office. At convenient times he would retrieve its mail, which was usually empty.

Meanwhile, he helped prepare Kennedy's trip to Europe and particularly to Berlin, but he himself would remain in Washington. On the twenty-sixth of June, Kennedy made his famous 'Ich bin ein Berliner' speech to the huge crowds and great accolades at the Brandenburg Gate, facing east, overlooking the recently built wall. As well, through his office, Greenfield received word from his superiors that President Kennedy after meeting with Vice-President Johnson and Governor Connally of Texas earlier in June in El Paso on a quick stopover had arranged a date for an extended trip to Texas in November.

Kennedy was keen to do some fundraising for the upcoming election next year and improve on his narrow victory there in the previous election. The Secret Services in charge of the President's security had been on a heightened alert, so Greenfield felt that extra measures should be put in place wherever he went. His main concern was the President's prerogative of using open convertible limos so that the people could see him, which was the usual arrangement with previous Presidents, if the weather permitted. The time had come he felt for this reckless folly to end, specifically in the circumstances but traditions die hard, and Kennedy was determined to be seen as a man of the people.

Having been dumped by the CIA, and because James had been uncovered as a leak, Sanchez quit associating with the FBI and now worked in Real Estate with his wife in Miami. There was a lucrative market for Cuban exiles and émigrés getting their feet on the ground in this district; and he was certainly under no obligation to work for the government, as he now had permanent status, and in a few years he and Inèz would become naturalized U.S. citizens.

Greenfield, though, had other ideas: for one, he knew Bill James was in trouble with his brother-in-law, because Garvey and his band of thugs would take it upon themselves to clean up the mess of his 'betrayal'; and for another, Sanchez was still a potential asset as he knew all the various players in the field around New Orleans and Dallas, having been a bagman, supplying money in a paperless trail to a bunch of corrupt rightwing individuals who he could identify. Greenfield would have to convince Sanchez that he still had an obligation to his adoptive country.

Furthermore, it appeared Woods had followed through as James' brother-in-law, who had insisted on his compliance with family concerns, leaving the Greenfields and Melbos alone, as well as Sanchez. The security Greenfield had put in place for his home and family had almost become unnecessary as no one suspicious, and certainly neither Bunting nor di Lucca had been around. All appeared normal as it had when they first moved there. Yet Greenfield didn't trust the present situation for a second. Woods had little control over Garvey and his dark priorities.

Once Garvey had set some plan in motion, he would go back to his cave and let the plan carry itself to finality. All Garvey needed now was a time and place to focus on. And soon, in the months ahead, there would be a public acknowledgement of Kennedy's itinerary in Texas, if they hadn't already found out.

Greenfield found it necessary to make a visit to Miami. Having obtained an address from James, he flew down, rented a car at the airport, and drove into Little Havana where he found the Sanchezes' yellow bungalow with a terra cotta roof. For a while, he parked and observed the quiet street making sure there was nothing suspicious before knocking on the door which Inèz opened with a smile.

'*Señor Tomás! Qué sorpressa!* What makes you here?' She asked, speaking both Spanish and broken English.

'Hello, Inèz, I was in Miami, and thought I'd see how you've settled in. Bill James told me about your new home. *Una casa tan Hermosa,*' he added, complimenting her house. In the garden he could smell freshly cut lawn mixed with the fragrance of bougainvillea blossoms.

'*Gracias. Tanto ha pasado estos meses. Por favor entra.* Eduardo come soon. He shows a house. *Como está, Señor Mel?*' She stood aside from the threshold to let him in.

'Oh, he's just fine,' said Greenfield, entering the house.

'*Bueno.*'

Inèz led him into the kitchen where she was preparing supper. She was wearing a simple red and white floral dress with sandals and had tied her black hair in a ponytail, emphasizing her lean frame and pretty face, which now beamed with a happiness that had been absent during their sea voyage six weeks earlier.

'*Por favor tome asiento,*' she said indicating a chair. 'I hope you stay for dinner. I cook a *vaca frita con frijoles negros. Quieres una bebida?*'

'*Agua helada y lima estarían bien gracias,*' replied Greenfield. 'And yes, dinner would be great, if Eduardo comes.'

'He happy to see you, Tomás.'

'I'm not so sure about that; there's some unfinished business.'

'*Negocio importante?*'

'Yes, and I will need Eduardo's help.'

'*Te estamos muy agradecidos por ayudarnos,* and we like to help, *pero estoy preocupado ...* I worry about the people Eduardo worked in CIA.'

'I am too.'

She gave him a glass of ice water and lime.

'*Gracias.*'

She spoke of their new life in Little Havana, and in half an hour Sanchez pulled up the driveway in a red and white red-top '61 Plymouth Fury. Entering the house, he called out, '*Inèz, Rodríguez compró la casa!*' expressing the successful sale of a house. When he entered the kitchen he was surprised to see Greenfield. '*Tomás.* This is an honor, sir.' Then he went to his wife and kissed her. Inèz explained quickly why Greenfield was there. Sanchez nodded and motioned to their visitor to follow him.

Outside, they sat under a simple green awning covering the small patio, beyond which lay a modest garden containing more bougainvillea. Soon Inèz set the table and then brought out a pitcher of mojitos with glasses accompanied by *pasta de camerones y queso bocaditos,* little bite-sized shrimp and cheese pastry hors d'oeuvres, which she said were homemade from family recipes. Sanchez poured them both amber rum mojitos.

'*Deliciosa,*' said Greenfield eating a *bocadito,* and taking a sip of his mojito.

'Made with Santiago de Cuba 12 year,' said Sanchez, sipping his as well. 'Someone I know smuggled in a dozen cases, and I got one. It reminds me most of Cuba, and my choice for mojitos.'

'Here's to Cuba,' said Greenfield, raising his glass and adding, 'without Castro and the mob.'

'*Beberé por eso!*'

'*Aclamaciones!*'

After the three of them had eaten a lovely supper and reminisced about their multi-day sea voyage and their Cuban escapade, Greenfield and Sanchez were left alone drinking coffee. Greenfield asked Sanchez if he would go with him to New Orleans to look up some of those characters he had met. Sanchez was adamant that it would be like signing his death warrant.

'Tomás, I am done with them, *lo comprendez?* If someone there reports my presence, I'm a dead man.'

'I had to ask, Eduardo. I need to go there and find out more about these people and you know what they look like.'

'They are *loco*, my friend. That Ferrie: guy's a thief, a queer who likes young boys; he's connected to the mob; even flies for them.'

'He's a pilot.'

'Yeah, he was involved with the Civil Air Patrol, but was fired or something, because of immoral behavior.'

'And Banister?'

'Detective Banister, a real prick, a fascist in my book; he was some kind of special investigator from Chicago.'

'What was he doing in New Orleans?'

'He ran an anti-Castro movement with Ferrie, and the Cuban Democratic Revolutionary Front; at least they worked out of the same office building. He didn't seem to have any official status, kinda like a rogue operative. Maybe his bosses just let him loose. He'd been with the FBI for some time, and it got around that he was involved with the take down of John Dillinger, the gangster.'

'Did you actually speak with these people?'

'Not in any official capacity; they didn't know who I was working for, but I posed as an anti-Castro exile, and that was all the credentials I needed. A bunch of us used to go to this club—the 500 club—and a bar, called Cosimo's, and other places like Felix's Oysters. Ferrie was close to this fellow Clay Bertrand, both queer. Oswald told me they were into all kinds of sado-machismo with whips and bondage.'

'So you spoke with Oswald?'

'Yeah, he was always around when I was there; said he was a runner for this "Dutz" guy, a bookie, who worked for Carlo Marcello. He was strange, Oswald; somebody said he could speak Russian and had a Russian wife.'

'And yet he was a runner for a bookie?'

'Yeah, he had a mysterious past, no question about it, but was tight-lipped and volatile. I heard he was an anti-fascist, and tried to kill a general known for his extremist views.' Then he paused to think. 'I remember now, Edwin

Walker.'

'Yes, I've read about him. He considered Roosevelt and Truman to be Communists, even Eisenhower; the guy's delusional, a John Birch Society member.'

'That may be, Tomás, but if Oswald did shoot this general, why was he working for Banister, another fascist?'

'Good question. Sounds like some kind of operation. Who was in overall charge?'

'General Lansdale. The main base of operations was here in Miami.'

'Edward Lansdale. He was air force, known for psychological warfare.'

'I don't know any of that. I was not part of that group. '

'Someone trusted you with all that money. Who did you leave the money with?'

'Nobody. It was a dead drop, but I waited nearby to see who would pick it up. Turned out it was a woman; I followed her to a law office. Drew Anders. He was a regular at the club too, and knew everybody. I figured he was a lawyer for the mob.'

'Who told you to put the money there, in this dead drop?'

'I made a call, and a guy answered and told me what to do.'

'And you have no idea who it was?'

'No, nobody I recognized.'

'But the money was for Ferrie and Bertrand?' asked Greenfield.

'Yes.'

'Tell me about Bertrand.'

'He was a high roller; Banister kissed his ass.'

'What's his business?'

'International Trade of some kind. I heard he was a decorated army major in the war.'

'Interesting.'

'And well-connected.'

'It all rings of the agency. But for what?' asked Greenfield to himself.

'Bertram is extremely anti-Castro; he helped with the funding of the local branch of the so-called "Mongoose" operation last year, which was shut down by the FBI on orders from Kennedy.'

'But what the hell were they doing? You'd think they knew that it was doomed without a major military invasion by the U.S.'

'I don't know. I think they're running their own mission. Crime boss Marcello had apparently invested in it as well, for future benefits, entitlements.'

'Could be a blind,' suggested Greenfield. 'My theory is that they're involved in a plot to kill Kennedy as local facilitators. Bill James told me Oswald had said they were all virulent Kennedy-haters.'

'That's true, but there are many in the anti-Castro community who feel the same.'

'And you, Eduardo?'

'I thought maybe Kennedy would follow through with an invasion at *Bahía de Cochones,* and I was disappointed that he didn't. I told my handlers at the agency that I hated Kennedy, but to tell you the truth, I never had those extreme feelings. I think he's both wise and smart. A war with Cuba would've killed many thousands of innocent people. I couldn't abide that even if they would've won. My Inèz was there and could've been at risk.'

'I believe you're right. Instead of a war, there should've been some limited rapprochement with Castro, which of course was reprehensible to the Republican hardliners, and to corporations like United Fruit, and the Mob of course, who owned substantial holdings.'

'I worked for the Batista government; I hated them as much as I hate Castro now for turning the country into a totalitarian state allied with the Russians. Because of the Cold War, there are no compromises. Kennedy is the—how do you say? *Anatema?*'

'Anathema.'

'Yeah. Damned if he did something to help Cuba and damned if he didn't.'

'And all he's done is put a target on his back. But there's more to it than that.'

'How so?' asked Sanchez.

'There are some deep political divisions at the highest levels. On one side you have the rightwing old guard who feel that after losing power to Kennedy, it's incumbent with them to try to preserve the stewardship of state over and above the current administration. Sure, that's obvious for any opposition party, but what isn't, is how far they will go to defend this country against what they deem to be a threat to their agendas; and with Kennedy being so strong, they believe he will capitulate our country's power and make *détente* with the Soviets. In effect, the right-wingers perceive that any compromise is a defeat, and the likelihood of Kennedy being reelected gives them reason to want to take him out.'

Sanchez nodded. 'I'll tell you something: back in 1960, Bunting had me go to New Mexico and track down a rancher in order to kill him; Bill James was there when Woods gave Bunting the job, so he could verify it. However, I could not go through with it; I found the ranch eventually near the Jicarilla Mountain range; it was so remote, I decided then and there to stop that job, so I told Bunting on my return that the rancher had died, and I never mentioned the name Wills. They thought it was someone else anyway, and he couldn't be found.

'Just the same, I couldn't understand why they would want me to do this. It got me thinking that it had to be something to do with those supposed UFO crashes, and this rancher, Garnett Wills, who shouldn't have seen what he allegedly did see. The thing of it is this: the crashes were supposed to be weather balloons, so why all the bother with a rancher? Maybe there really is something to the UFOs. Maybe that if true, and the CIA are involved with these aliens, they fear anyone knowing about them because they have some global advantage to exploit from them. Maybe Kennedy would use this knowledge, this power, and take it away from the CIA.'

Greenfield said, 'It was Mel who found Wills and later wrote in one of his articles what happened, but from another corroborating source, Keith Leverton, a psychologist who had worked for the CIA in a bunker deep in the desert. Shortly after, he was found dead, an apparent suicide.'

'*Jesucristo.*' Sanchez crossed himself.

'And you're absolutely right; the real reasons they want Kennedy dead are much bigger, all the more reason for them to obfuscate any liability on their behalf with anti-Castro plots and organized crime vendettas. This leads me to conclude that the people put in charge of such a heinous crime need a patsy, a scapegoat, to protect themselves and take the fall. Bill James thought that you were being setup by taking the fall, but since Cuba, they've got their sights on someone else, one of those guys in New Orleans perhaps.'

'I got out in the nick of time,' said Sanchez, recovering with a smile.

'Be careful. Do you have a gun?'

'I take it with me everywhere.'

'Good. Watch your back; they might not be through with you yet.'

'*Señor Tomás*, don't worry about me. If you go to New Orleans, worry

389

about yourself.'

*

Back in Washington, Greenfield thought he should do some more research before going to New Orleans or Dallas. He asked Hannah to do some hunting through archives at State for any information about Lee Oswald, David Ferrie and Clay Bertrand. As well, he needed to make another visit to Bill James.

'Honey, do you know anybody at the agency who might know something about American expatriates moving to Russia?'

'You know those kinds of files are kept by department heads, Harley.'

They were sitting at the kitchen table as she was feeding Lizbet between them.

'There's no way I could find out about Oswald at the agency,' she continued, 'unless I knew who was specifically in charge, and happened to be a close associate of mine. And if this Oswald is who I think he is—a kind of ghost who comes and goes without much scrutiny—he'd be very classified. From the sounds of it, he's being pawned as a legend; either that or he's under contract, in which case he's actively involved in an operational plan, which I doubt from what you say about the guy being unstable.'

'I've been out of the game for too long; there's no one I can talk to.'

'Harley, keep away from them,' she said, worried.

Greenfield again drove to the FBI building, but was told James was not available. When asked where he was, the man at the front desk said James was on leave for personal reasons. Greenfield figured that the shit had hit the proverbial fan for him personally and decided to leave him be for a few days to sort out his family crisis. That evening at home Prinzenthal told her husband that she hadn't been able to find any record of Oswald anywhere, nor of Clay Bertrand, though Ferrie had a passport under his own name, and was known to have flown planes for Carlos Marcello; the others, she and Greenfield concluded, had either been erased from the files or had used aliases. Frustrated by his inability to move forward in his investigation, Greenfield decided to go about it differently.

He had known numerous people in the agency during his long years with them, some dating back to before the war when he had been a security official with the so-called 'cypher bureau' under Herbert Yardley. Before that, in his twenties, Greenfield had worked with the railroad, trained as a telegrapher, then was fired for accountancy in a small illegal booze operation during Prohibition. He resurrected himself as a railway security 'bull', until he took kickbacks for turning a blind eye to any spirits peddlers; escaping fortuitously from the law, he found himself more suited to life in the big city of New York, first as a bouncer, then as a watchman in the St. Regis Hotel, then later as a security agent under Yardley, where his knowledge of French came in handy.

Greenfield's mother, Rebeque Fortin, was French having come to the US as a teenaged *au pair*, who spoke no English. Within a year she'd been impregnated by her widower employer; who, at least, honorably, married her, though he was almost forty years her senior, and after Harley subsequently he sired Harley's sister, Marguerite—called Peggy—a couple of years later. Greenfield's father, another Herbert—called "Herbie" by his friends—had been a minor shareholder in the Connecticut Southern Railroad; he died of a heart attack while recovering from the infamous Spanish Flu after being quarantined, when Harley and Peggy were just eighteen and fifteen years old.

Greenfield rummaged through all of these memories. Herbert Yardley had had a falling out with the services so he was no longer involved, but Greenfield remembered another fellow, one he had resisted considering, because they had had an issue about ten years before when Sulla took over the agency. Brayden Farnes was a new handler for some agents in Eastern Europe, who, as it was found out much later, had been betrayed by Kim Philby, the British MI-6 mole in charge of Eastern Europe for the Brits, and subsequently his agents were murdered by the MVD, predecessor to the KGB.

Farnes, ten years younger than Greenfield, had received some intelligence that implicated him, which turned out again much later to be pure disinformation fed back into the mill through Philby to wreak havoc with the Americans. Farnes, for his troubles, dug a hole for himself when he then accused Judith Graham of being a double agent, which didn't go over well at all with his superiors. Greenfield, trying to be reasonable, had attempted to talk some sense into him—no hard feelings, and this is the business—a kind of pep talk—but Farnes had been shipped off to the Philippines and Vietnam. He had just returned at about the time Harley retired from the service to take a position that included the Caribbean and Central America, along with Cuba, under Richard Bissell, who then took over Domestic Operations.

When Bissell was fired along with Sulla, Farnes presumably had taken over Domestic Operations, as he was well liked by Cabell and the hardliners. Greenfield had never set foot in the new agency headquarters at Langley, Virginia, and thought he'd get at least a brief tour of the modern premises.

Approaching it through a forest, Greenfield's first impression of the building was of a colossal Howard Johnson's Hotel, with a portico that looked like the wing of a B-52 bomber. When compared to the old offices off C Street in downtown Washington, this structure made one think the CIA had been definitely chartered as a growth industry. The designers, whose plans Sulla had approved as Director, certainly had sunlight in mind, an idea that could have been considered as contradictory to secrecy's expected environment of clandestine shadows for there must have been a thousand windows set closely around all the five or six floors.

Once through security, as a guest, he was escorted up to the fourth floor, where he waited in an ante-room. Half an hour later, Farnes welcomed him into his office, shaking his hand.

'Well, I'll be, if it isn't ol' Harley. What in God's name are you doing here?'

'Just thought I should check out the new digs, Brayden. And when I heard you were back in town, I thought you might need another pep talk.'

Farnes laughed uproariously. Greenfield just smiled.

'You were one crafty bastard, I admit,' said Farnes, composing himself. 'I was rather green, wasn't I? No pun intended.' He laughed again.

'Not a bad pun, I'm flattered.'

'Well, you would be, old man. And I'm flattered you've come by, though I know this isn't a social call.'

'No, I'm here in an official capacity, actually. I work at the White House as an analyst for Mac Bundy, or rather I'm one of his assistants who's connected to the DOD.'

'Is that right? I've heard rumors that the DOD is none too pleased that they're supposed to be taking over some of our clandestine ops.'

'I think you're right, Brayden; the agency has a habit of conducting their own operations untethered to the politicos, and the military were better at taking orders.'

'It's always been that way, and you know it.'

'Yes,' agreed Greenfield, 'and I'm not unsympathetic, unless someone or other has been using the agency to further personal allegiances by taking down the present occupant of our most cherished and esteemed executive branch of government.'

'Jesus, Harley, I'd forgotten how you never beat about the bush; perhaps your artlessness was why you were never promoted like some of your contemporaries.'

'My artlessness could have been a damn good foil. I always read the tea leaves and didn't lose my people.'

'Ouch, but I'll give you credit where credit is due: you could always count on Harley. Nowadays, though, dependability is more of a high wire act, which, by the way, is political. Partisan lines are entrenched and niceties a sham.'

'And what side are you on, Brayden?' asked Greenfield, pointedly.

'That's classified, old man.' He laughed.

'You're a barrel of laughs. But I'm serious. Since when does tradecraft include the possible murder of our own president? There're a bunch of misfits playing at some very treasonous business down in New Orleans. Are you in any way involved with them?'

Farnes looked at Greenfield, shaking his head.

'Greenfield, you've really lost it, haven't you? I haven't the foggiest idea what the fuck you're talking about. What misfits?'

'David Ferrie, for one. I know he's a company man, and a liaison with Marcello and others in the mob. How about Clay Bertrand? Guy Banister, or Lee Harvey Oswald?'

'I know of Ferrie; he's a goddamned embarrassment. What's he been up to?'

'I've been told he's a handler for Cubans and others; works with a John Bircher, this Banister, ex-FBI and Bertrand, who must be using an alias. All to do with Mongoose.'

'Mongoose is based in Miami, for your information. And it's being shut down by your hero in the White House. He made a deal with Khrushchev, as I understand it. No invasion. No missiles. Wake up, old man.'

'Kennedy may not be that popular among some of you, but there is such a thing in this hallowed democracy of ours called the chain of command, and he's the best shot we have at defusing a nuclear holocaust and perhaps creating a worldwide Pax Americana in the bargain. There *is* the bigger picture that some of you with your petty hates and evil plots can't begin to fathom. It's out there!' Greenfield waved his arm in the air. 'But I'm here, Farnes, to wake you up!'

'The big picture, huh? Well, perhaps your patriotism comes into question when the most powerful country in the world bows to a bunch of Commie thugs on account of your hallowed leader; and by the way, I do take orders through the chain of command.'

'No doubt about that, but not Kennedy's. Let me give you some advice, like I did back in '53: if you think that a coup d'état can work in this country, you're sorely mistaken. Help me, Brayden; we're both Americans trying to do the right thing here. The gray areas between good and evil are our stock in trade, but not this. Someone or other, likely from the top of the deep-seated anti-Kennedy old guard, has set in motion the most heinous conspiracy in the history of our country. I know you know if you're worth your salt in this business. Now help me, for God's sake!'

'Jesus, I'm all broke up, old man. Where do you get your information? From that canny bitch Prinzenthal you used to handle? I still think she's a plant.'

Greenfield stood up but kept his cool.

'You're a piece of shit, Farnes, like Bunting and his ilk. She's my wife, and works in the State Department. She's got more devotion and patriot faith in the ideals of this country in her baby toe, than all of you pricks combined.'

'It's always a matter of perspective, isn't it? But my compliments on your marriage. Some of the boys thought she was quite the catch: well-lubed in honeytraps and they even envied you with a front row view.'

'You're the big man, Farnes,' said Greenfield, barely holding back his burning anger. 'What can you possibly gain from all this malignancy, but a ticket to hell?'

'As opposed to heaven? The greater good, old man.'

'The greater good begins in here,' remarked Greenfield, with his hand on his heart.

'Jesus, Greenfield, did you become a Jehovah's Witness in retirement, or is that a requirement for working in that White House?'

'You could use a little religion there, man. I'll be sure to send around Bill James. Maybe he can get through to that sick heart of yours.'

'Bill James? You know James?'

'Sure.'

'You don't know?'

'Know what?'

'He was found yesterday, dead—a murder-suicide, I gather. A woman was found dead with him. His lover, apparently, Deborah McBride.'

The color washed from Greenfield's face. He was speechless.

'I guess you didn't know,' continued Farnes. 'Well, put it this way: he'll have some explaining to do with God, if, as you presumed, he was on God's side.'

'There was no news,' uttered Greenfield.

'Kept under wraps, I understand; Hoover's orders until the facts are ascertained.'

Greenfield turned abruptly, walked like a zombie from the office, down to his car, and drove straight home, his mind a maelstrom of grief, anger, and loss.

32. Thunder and Lightning

The day Nevin, Mollie, and two friends went camping near Swan Cottage was not just memorable for its humidity and heat. Mollie had borrowed her mother's 1959 Black Buick Riviera with whitewall tires and the incredible fins, now iconic in automotive lore. Nevin drove it, as Mollie had just received her learner's permit. Once out of town, he stopped and she took the wheel, feeling more confident. That weekend had been planned in advance shortly after their last exams for the year, and he had obtained permission from his mother and grandparents to use the property, which extended to the Potomac River.

The 'Cottage' had been in his mother's family for generations, originally secured through marriage by an ancestor, Gillian Griffiths, at the time of the revolution, when her husband, Floyd, of Welsh descent, was killed at Yorktown. Much of the original property had been sold much later after the Civil War, but one hundred and thirty acres still remained on title, mostly forest and meadow, with only about fifty acres of worked land leased to a farmer.

During the Civil War, a lookout was placed down the ridge seven hundred yards from the house, and was manned by a small company of Union soldiers. Not a trace of their encampment had survived, though when Nevin was eleven, he had made some small discoveries when he dug up bits of kit, such as discarded bottles, satchel buckles, and unused minié balls buried near where the lookout log edifice had apparently stood.

The story goes that when General Lee invaded the north, on both occasions Confederate scouts were seen in the vicinity because there was a decent ford by which to cross the Potomac just up river. It was used by a detachment of cavalry in September, 1862, during the retreat from Antietam, or Sharpsburg, as the Rebels had called the notoriously bloody battle.

Mollie parked the car at Swan Cottage, and when Nevin had paid his respects to his grandparents, they took their gear and box cooler and followed the path towards the river, and crossed the railroad tracks, where soon the hot air was already less intense. Crossing the footbridge over the Grand Old Ditch—the Chesapeake and Ohio Canal, which had been designated a National Park, they set up camp in a natural clearing familiar to Nevin where a little brook emptied into the Potomac.

No sooner had they pitched their tents than Nevin and Mollie stripped off their clothes and jumped gleefully into the cool water. Their friends, John and Lucy, were somewhat aghast as Nevin and Mollie had no inhibition about their nudity but seeing them frolicking happily like ducks in the water pooling among the rocks, they didn't hesitate long in the stifling heat. Soon, they were undressed too and swimming just as enraptured—a *fête de nu*. They languished for the whole day there, alternately swimming and drinking preblended strawberry daiquiris brought by John, snacking on peanuts and fresh strawberries, and then taking a siesta when each teenaged couple retired to their hot tents for hot sex, then more swimming at which time Lucy announced tremulously in the spirit of the free bachannalia, 'We just lost our virginity!'

And that called for another daiquiri. For dinner, they prepared yam fritters in corn oil and a dozen blue crabs in the fire. Nevin showed them how to put a flat rock over the fire and place the crabs on it where they fried. Once the crabs were cooked, they shared two pairs of pliers to break open the shellfish before sprinkling them with lemon.

John brought his guitar out and sang some songs around the campfire that evening, including Dylan's *Blowin' in the Wind,* which Lucy and Mollie sang and they all joined in the chorus. By nightfall rumblings could be heard approaching from the distance. The air was thick with ionic tension, and before long the wind picked up spraying sparks from the fire around them, then came the rain drops, and finally a deluge accompanied by ear-shattering thunder and lightning.

The storm came on so fast they barely had time to make it into their tents to wait it out. The thunder and lightning crashed incessantly around their campsite making them feel as if they were in the midst of a bombardment at Bastogne during the Battle of the Bulge. It went on for at least twenty minutes but seemed like an eternity, so fearful was it. Finally, the thunder and lightning moved off, leaving torrential rain pounding their tents, until a steady shower settled well into the night.

The morning brought sunshine and high pressure that had purged away the humidity, but the ground was soaked as was their camping gear and the firewood they had collected. John had been a Boy Scout and suggested they get a saw and axe so they could cut down a small dead tree into blocks to split for a supply of dry wood. Nevin and John left the girls at the campsite to hike back to his grandparent's house and fetch what was needed.

After a quick hello and talk of the storm, the boys found what they needed and made it back within the hour. By mid-morning, they had finished their breakfast of scrambled eggs and ham with tea, and the sun was quickly drying the land. As it was going to be a glorious clear day in the mid-eighties, Nevin suggested that they take a hike up to the ford where some of the Confederate cavalry had once crossed a hundred years before. When they got there, the water was too high to cross safely, so they had a swim instead in their shorts this time as there were some families and fishermen in the area.

In the afternoon, they spent half of their time in their tents and only emerged to swim now and again and then to prepare a spaghetti dinner. The gratitude they felt being in nature and away from parental authority gave them a sense of freedom for being left to their own devices. They supposed if their parents had suspected the kind of sexual liberation they engaged full-fledgedly—the girls and boys were entrusted to sleep in separate tents given the norms of the day—they would have been seriously busted.

The grandparents, when asked by Muriel over the phone the first day, said they were the most responsible and well-behaved young people and not to worry; besides, the girls had said they had their own tent. Little did the grandparents know that the sexual revolution was being hatched as they spoke, *un nouveau monde.*

*

Muriel James drove her car to a Saturday gathering of friends at the Washington Golf and Country Club just across the river in Arlington, Virginia. Bill had yet to confess his long-standing infidelity, simply saying he'd be busy for the day and night on a classified operation, and as soon as she left, he took off and parked near Deborah McBride's house, knowing she had loaned her car to Mollie for the weekend. They spent the day together, discussing their plans and making love. She cooked him dinner which they ate in front of the television watching *The Twilight Zone.*

When the storm hit, they went back to bed, leaving the dishes on the living room table. Up to that moment, James had been in a kind of paralysis, going through the motions of work and responsibility to family in disillusionment. He told Deborah everything about his job and the threat to the presidency, all that was eating away at his soul. He told her about his brother-in-law and how he knew about their long affair. They prayed together that soon all would be settled, they would marry and he would find other work, perhaps in more conventional law enforcement.

On Sunday, they planned to go to church separately as usual then he would tell Muriel at home that he was leaving her, and pack a bag and move in with Deborah. Once this decision had been made, much of the stress of recent weeks dissipated with the tremendous unleashing of thunder and lightning. The violence of the storm seemed, almost in their minds, to be God's judgement for good or ill, but nevertheless a releasing of relentless personal pain borne of guilt and failure.

Coupled like two spoons, he held her as they slowly copulated. He could feel her orgasm as he reached climax himself, her body milking him so profoundly in concert with a deafening crack of thunder simultaneous with the lightning, he felt like the bolt entered his ecstatic brain and knew no more— and in a split second, neither did she.

Standing over the two dead lovers, Gerald Osbourne, aka Joe di Lucca, and more poignantly, Johnny Goodnight, held the gun, James' new service revolver—a nickel-plated Smith and Wesson .357 19-5 Magnum with a four inch barrel—and looked down as a flash of lightning eerily illuminated the now inert couple in and out of darkness. He carefully wiped clean the gun for prints and put it in James' right hand. He was expressionless, a phantom, but mumbled something about his *pièce de résistance*—at what he thought of as an almost enviable end to life.

Then, being careful to not leave a trace of his presence behind, slipped through the back door into the subsiding storm, grabbed the umbrella he had left outside in a dark corner, and walked a couple of blocks to where he had parked his car.

*

Mollie arrived home with Nevin because she couldn't drive alone with her learner's permit after dropping off his camp gear at his house. They kissed goodbye and he walked away with a wave and a smile to take public transit back home. Inside her house, she called her mother. Receiving no answer, she went upstairs to her own room and changed into some clean clothing before making a sandwich in the kitchen and turning on the television as a bulletin appeared showing footage of Kennedy's speech in Berlin.

Noticing the dirty dishes on the table likely left from the previous evening was unlike her mother, a fastidious homemaker. Curious suddenly about the whereabouts of her mother, she went back upstairs and looked in her bedroom. Briefly staring at the two of them bundled in bed, and apparently asleep, she sighed, quietly closed the door, and went back downstairs.

An half hour later, it seemed odd to her that they were sleeping so late in the day, but she presumed they had been to church and had come back separately and ended up in bed, which had happened before. She went upstairs again and opened the door to her mom's room. They hadn't moved a muscle.

'Mom,' she called out.

Somewhat alarmed, she approached the bed and looking down saw blood darkened from desiccation, the gun in James' hand, a hole in the side of his head, and one in the back of her mother's. Alarm instantly turned into a convulsion of trauma. She couldn't move: such was her complete and consummate shock. Simultaneously, she fainted with a thump to the floor. Eventually coming around, she crawled frantically around the bed out of the room, and then staggered down the stairs. Staring madly about her searching desperately for the phone that was on the wall where it had always been, she at last took it and dialed the operator. Nothing came from Mollie's mouth until she began screaming hysterically into the receiver.

The police arrived within ten minutes. Mollie was sitting on the sofa in a catatonic state, the television still on with an episode of *Hazel* playing. A policeman turned it off. Within half an hour, the FBI arrived; by this time, Mollie had been taken to the hospital and sedated, her father had been called, and he was on his way the next flight east. At just after eight p.m., two FBI agents walked up to the James' residence, where Carolyn answered the door and was surprised to see their identification credentials shown, let them in. Nevin was upstairs reading when he heard his mother cry in an outburst of anguish he would never forget.

Rushing down the stairs, he saw Carolyn and his mother embracing, sobbing pitifully, and the two morose agents standing back in commiseration.

Upon seeing Nevin, one of the agents took him aside and briefly explained what had happened. Nevin, in a sudden fit of manic distress, screaming '*Mollie!*' lunged for the door, but the detective grabbed him by the arm. Nevin resisted with all his strength and was manhandled into the hallway, and told in no uncertain terms he was not to leave the house, but must stay with his mother and sister. Nevin cried that Mollie needed him, but to no avail.

The detective, realizing suddenly the family dynamic, told him that the girl was no longer at home, was sedated and in good care under professionals with her father on his way. Defeated for the time being, all Nevin could do was join his mother and sister, who now sitting silently reached for him as if he offered some form of therapy to assuage the emotional impact of their father's and husband's death. Nevin hugged his sister then sat beside his mother, who wrapped her arm around him.

Before long, the detectives began asking questions, to which Muriel's answers were helplessly insufficient to explain how her husband could have done such a thing; he'd always been the man in charge, a believer in family values, putting duty before prurient behavior. Nevin was outspoken in his denial of his father taking their lives. He admitted that he had known of their affair for over two years, and the pressure he'd been under at work, though he hadn't any idea what his father had been involved in. Muriel remained stunned and incognizant of what was being revealed.

The other agent, meanwhile, had gone upstairs to find James' locked study. Muriel then provided him with a key and he went in. Searching through James' desk for any clue to the tragedy, he came to the locked bottom drawer and asked for the key. Muriel was unresponsive, but Nevin said it was behind a book on the shelf. He explained that his father had trusted him because they had shared an interest in UFOs. The agent opened the drawer and went through it, finding nothing of any glaring importance, including the numerous articles by George Melbo.

Nonetheless, he filled a cardboard box with everything in the desk. By then, Aubrey and Honey Woods had arrived—Carolyn having called—both grief-stricken and concerned for the James' family welfare; Honey, Muriel and Carolyn wept together, while Woods found Nevin upstairs and told him that his father was one of the greatest men of his generation, and that whatever had happened was not the action of the man he knew. Nevin replied that he must use his resources to find out the truth, saying again and again his father would never have killed Mrs. McBride, or himself, because he knew them to be deeply in love.

Woods kept nodding sadly and put his hand on Nevin's shoulder, dismayed at his nephew's intimate knowledge of his father, but Nevin shook off his hand and said some dark force had taken the lives of his father, and that of his girlfriend's mother. Woods didn't contradict him with the heretofore evidence of murder-suicide, though he promised to leave "no stone unturned" in the quest for justice if any evidence contradictory to the seemingly obvious facts were to be found.

Nevin then turned and went to his room. He needed desperately to speak with Mollie and Melbo, the only people he felt he could trust. He would write a coded letter to Diva.

*

Three days later, the news broke on the second page of the Post and on the front page of the Herald in the usual ignominious way: *FBI Agent in Murder Suicide* and *G-Man Kills Self and Mistress*. The blunt verdict reverberated among the Washington elite. Bill James had been one of their own, and, after the shock settled down, he was soon forsaken as someone who had evidently lost his mind. The funeral held in his local Episcopalian church, was attended by many dignitaries of the intelligence community.

Nevin was stone-faced during the entire service and reception and going through the motions in a protracted state of shock. Mollie didn't attend; he hadn't seen her, nor did she call. Her mother's funeral was held the following day in the same church. Nevin wanted to attend, but under the circumstances his mother insisted he forgo it and not see Mollie until such time that there could be a reasonable reconciliation. His instinct inclined him otherwise, though the notion of self-doubt crept into his confused mind.

Perhaps she blamed him, or perhaps her father had forbidden any contact; these and any number of scenarios flitted in his brain. He let it be for now, though he did call her only to find no one answering; he let the phone ring for five minutes in the hope that if she were there, she would know it was him calling from the depths of despair.

His soul had caved; he felt it in his face, a horrid tingling where the pain emerged from deep within and tried to get out but couldn't. He reeled in mental torment as he lay face down on his bed, tears streaming into his pillow. Pain filled everything. His mind was erased. Carolyn came and sat by him with her hand on his shoulder, but no words came. His mother came as well, and seemed strongest of all, saying she still loved his father and forgave him. She couldn't believe he had done what he did, but she had resigned herself to the facts. Nevin turned toward her and sat up.

'Dad was murdered, Mom. It had something to do with what he was working on. It was a professional hit, probably hired out by some mobster. I will never accept his killing Mrs. McBride and himself. It's impossible!'

'Even if you're right, how could it be proven?' she asked, dejectedly.

'I don't know!'

Nevin got up and went downstairs.

*

In the weeks that followed, Nevin heard through his mother from Aunt Honey, who presumably had been told by Uncle Aubrey, that John McBride had taken Mollie out West to his new recently purchased home in Pasadena near Rosemont Avenue, where she would live. Her mother's remains were cremated and taken West as well. Needless to say, Mollie had suffered a terrible shock having found the bodies. She'd been treated for trauma akin to what soldiers can suffer in war.

But after a month, Nevin received a telephone call from her. By her subdued tone, it was obvious things would never be the same again, but she apologized for not calling sooner and didn't want him to think he'd been in any way to blame for his father's actions. Nevin tried to convince her that they'd been murdered, and she was open to that possibility but said it didn't matter because they were gone and nothing could bring them back. She explained that she had come through a nervous breakdown, and that, in her process of recovery, she had told her doctor and father all about her and Nevin.

Her father was not open at that time to any renewal of their relations and thought it best they be terminated for good, or at least for a few years until this episode of her life was long past, if ever. She was in no frame of mind to resist her father's wishes and thought it best for them to go their separate ways for the time being. She told Nevin she would always love him but that any memory of their love now seemed to be fatally poisoned. He reminded her that they were young, not yet seventeen, and that they had had a relationship the envy of older people, citing their lovemaking and genuine friendship. She agreed but reiterated her previous position, adding that long distant phone calls were very expensive, this one being allowed, and that though writing was fine, after their intensity of love, it couldn't possibly measure up.

Nevin was at a loss to provide any adequate response, only offering the wishful ideas of a visit perhaps later in the summer, or the possibility that they could go to the same university in another year. Mollie just absorbed these attempts to keep their flame alive, neither resisting, nor encouraging. He hung up after he promised to call her in the days ahead. When he did, her father answered, and kindly extended his condolences for the loss of his father, and said he understood how close he and Mollie had been, but for the continuing recovery of his daughter, he insisted Nevin cease any idea of getting together with her.

Afterwards, Nevin felt as if he'd been designated as the son of the man who killed Mollie's mother, the stigma of which could never be removed. Falling again into a depression, he decided not to call again. 'What will be, will be,' he realized, which gave him some pathetic hope of redemption. *Que sera sera.*

33. Happy Birthday, Dear Hannah

For several days, Greenfield, in a funk, stayed home from work. He knew there was little he could do to assist the investigation of Bill James' and Deborah McBride's deaths, if indeed there was any real investigation in view of the circumstances. In brief, James, a well-qualified and respected federal agent, had apparently by all indications discharged his service revolver into his lover and then himself during sexual intercourse at the moment of climax, or in the immediate aftermath. She was filled with his semen, and showed not a whit of reaction to any violence; in fact, it was quite the opposite, her death expression was one of complete bliss, as was his.

It just didn't make any sense, though powder residues were commensurate with close contact with the weapon, and bullets fired from the weapon were definitely his, as ballistics had proved. After the murder-suicide was reported to the public, there was little impetus for officials to try to seek an alternative explanation.

When he returned to his office in the Old Executive building next door to the White House, Greenfield had asked his much younger superior, Marty Cayton—Mac Bundy's protégé deputy from Harvard—to obtain the initial report from the FBI on the understanding that James had been working on some very classified projects, and that there should be some follow-up in regards to national security. Greenfield had lost his key connection to the mysterious activities in New Orleans with no photos or protocol for meeting anyone there, because Sanchez had flatly refused to have anything more to do with either the CIA or FBI having been shamelessly used by them, and held ransom with the threat of being turfed out of the country, or charged with illegal entry, or set up as a patsy, not to mention the denial for four years of his one condition for working for them, his ardent request to bring over his fiancée, Inèz Ruiz.

Subsequently, Cayton felt compelled to include his elder underling, Greenfield, in a small think-tank committee to prepare a brief for the president in regards to the Diệm regime of South Vietnam; he figured Greenfield had better uses than banging his head against the wall on account of the murder-suicide of a like-minded colleague and his lover. Greenfield dutifully put his efforts into the new task assigned to him, but considered it more of a distraction to his more urgent need to pursue his suspicions of a presumed attempt on the life of the president.

He was given a twenty-page document provided by the CIA and a copy of a recent reel of footage showing in color the entire self-immolation of a Boddhisatva Buddhist monk in the middle of a main street in Saigon. The document gave a brief history of Vietnam, and described how the various tribes of a generally peaceful culture degenerated into warring factions, stemming back centuries when the Nguyễn lords ruled the South, and Trinh lords ruled the North. Names and politics changed but the same basic factions were still in power.

Greenfield quickly realized that the old guard and military hawks were making the case for Vietnam as being a victim of global Communist aggression by the Chinese, who were to the Vietnamese traditional enemies, and by the Soviets who supplied ordinance. To Greenfield, the problem lay in the cultural dynamic of nationalist ambitions: Ho Chi Minh, himself, a one-time ally of the Americans during the war with the Japanese, was actually a moderate and disdained the implanted extremism of Communist ideology.

Both North and South were guilty of murderous rampages on their own people. It was easy to see that anyone with imperialist colonial ambitions in Vietnam was now to be met with a renewed fanatical antipathy, beginning with the ousting of the French after the disastrous battle of Điện Biên Phủ, then surely the Chinese, the Soviets, and finally the Americans would all be unwelcome. What Greenfield predicted was that any war in Vietnam was a no-win situation; in fact such military activity would be a quagmire, that half way around the world would use up and expend America's blood for what the CIA deemed a necessary vehicle for continued American supremacy and power, ultimately serving only the economic war machine at home.

Greenfield watched in utter horror and incredulity the monk, Thich Quàng Đức, dousing himself with fuel, igniting then burning himself to death into a darkened crisp; his absolute discipline and apparent calmness during this self-immolation, as he maintained the lotus posture during what must have been an unimaginable agony, was staggering. This very act symbolized in gruesome detail the underlying suffering of the soul of Vietnam, a peaceable, agrarian people foisted onto the world stage of global Cold War politics and their refusal to be a part of it. Greenfield clearly believed that had these people been left alone to resolve their own civil differences, the Cold War would have passed on without them, and that the decision to wage prolonged war would only bring out the most virulent extremes on each side, as the country had already endured.

However, when he presented his beliefs to his immediate superiors, his views went soundly unheeded, Mac Bundy taking a militant approach more in line with the hawks. Though, Kennedy himself, when apprised later of Greenfield's view—Cayton mentioned it as an alternative, Greenfield being absent from that meeting—took the idea of non-intervention rather more seriously, his having already decided that America would not invade Cuba, to the deep-seated chagrin of the old guard. In a few months' time he would actually enact a National Security Action Memorandum to bring back home from Vietnam a thousand troops by Christmas.

The image of the burning monk remained with Greenfield for days; it seemed to kindle in him a greater urgency to renew his mission to continue James' and his own perceived foreknowledge of Kennedy's demise.

This second wind brought him out of the funk. Sitting in the backyard after supper that evening he had just opened up about his feelings to Prinzenthal.

'And you really think you can make a difference by going to New Orleans?' she replied. 'Harley, there comes a time when you have to put your faith in your fellow man. You are not responsible for something that may or may not happen. What about us? Lizbet?'

Greenfield didn't answer immediately. He looked tired and was in no mood to challenge Hannah's position.

Prinzenthal continued, 'If there's anyone in this insane world I believe in, dear, it's you. I know how helpless we are against forces that answer to no one. I know you were super frustrated that you couldn't at least pay your respects and go to Bill James' funeral for fear of casting light on us in front of the whole bunch of them. Some of them probably knew exactly what happened, yet they can go and pretend to be shocked and saddened in public! We're nothing but the conscience of the downhearted, the powerless, the disenfranchised and those deprived of truth.

'Oh yes, there is a truth at the center of all this: a truth too large for those hypocrites to surrender. All for what? A backroom pat on the back? Another corporate deal to fortify the military complex? Well done! We know they're blind! It's we who are the eyes of the world! We see the star-spangled truth, Harley, and like the forefathers of this nation: Jefferson, Washington, Franklin and Lincoln, we would deliver it to the people! It's really not that complicated.'

'I know, darling, but it doesn't change anything.'

'Precisely.'

'But I can't stop what I'm doing.'

'But a bullet can.'

Prinzenthal rose from her garden chair and hugged her husband from behind.

'You will come with us to Paris in a week,' she declared. 'Next Thursday is my birthday, and I've never seen the Fourth of July fireworks at the National Mall. We're going as a family, and that's final.'

'Okay,' he said, submissively. 'I'll let them know once we're settled in Paris.'

'Damn right.'

'But before I do I'll make one more foray into this mess, then let this place go and join you in Paris.'

Prinzenthal sighed and released him. 'On one condition.'

'Okay.'

'You keep Jimbo and crew with you until you're on that plane.'

'Oui, bien sûr, mon amour.'

*

Six days later—the following Thursday, the Fourth of July and Prinzenthal's forty-first birthday—looked to be a gorgeous sunny day reaching a high in the eighties. That year she was unusually particular about her birthday, though normally she shied from any celebration at all. In the morning she insisted on buckwheat, oat, and wheat flour crêpes mixed with eggs, buttermilk, nutmeg, cinnamon, and apple butter, cooked with gobs of butter and eaten with warmed honey, or real maple syrup—a new-world addition for her. When she was growing up, these crêpes—*krepes*—were her favorite thing: she and cousin Lizbet would make them together using the original recipe from their Ephrussi grandmother.

Greenfield did a commendable job with them, having insisted she get what her heart desired. They had planned a day trip to Mount Vernon, George Washington's birthplace and estate, and packed a lunch. The pram had to be tied down with rope when put into their '61 aqua blue-green Ford Fairlane, as the trunk wouldn't close. Jimbo and his crew were given the day off, so both Greenfield in beige shorts and light green shirt, light socks and runners, and Prinzenthal wearing light blue, cropped linen pants and lavender blouse with a natural woven straw hat and tan ankle-strap sandals, packed their guns just in case.

To an observer, they would appear to be a normal family, but decidedly they were not a normal family. Though it was a public holiday, Mount Vernon seemed an unlikely place to make any attempt on their lives; however, the likely murder of James gave them no feeling of safety anywhere. Their lives were an open book now; this was a new experience for both of them. It was the price they were paying for helping out Dick Sinclair over three years ago. As they were backing out of their narrow driveway, it occurred to Greenfield that he should contact Sinclair before he moved to Paris, as he might know some people in New Orleans, or Dallas.

The drive to the Mount Vernon parking lot took just under an hour. They put Lizbet, looking about excitedly, into the pram, and their picnic basket fit nicely in the under-cage, and off they went to tour the house and grounds, which took the better part of two hours. The location and position of the mansion was breathtaking with the lawns gently sloping down to the wide Potomac. One could imagine the long history of the place and its once thriving enterprise to manage such a vast property of five thousand acres, a veritable fiefdom.

The mansion itself was simple yet elegant having been extended a number of times during Washington's long residency there. Yes, he owned well over a hundred and forty slaves, of whom he took good care of the families. He had trained both men and women from a young age in many skills and vocations and kept together as families, even taking in orphans, without which such a large operation would likely have been unsustainable, as well doubled with the equal addition of slaves owned by his wife, Martha.

However, he was of an uneasy mind about the institution itself, and left directions in his will for the emancipation of the slaves upon his death. Obviously, the very tenets of the Declaration of Rights of this brave New

Republic that he presided over as its first president were at odds with the culture of slavery, and this must have weighed heavily on him. Prinzenthal commented that had he lived at the time of the Civil War, one might wonder what side he would have supported being a landowner of the South. Greenfield suggested that judging history is easy in hindsight, and that one is subject to one's era, which Washington seems to have had an enlightened, though foreboding view of the dilemma; fortunately he did not have to fight that battle.

Carrying Lizbet and letting her walk at times, they explored the mansion: the New Room, a large parlor for entertaining with high ceilings and large windows letting in streams of light; the central passage, stairs and beautiful woodwork, furniture, Washington's study, and numerous other rooms, including the 18th century kitchen and cellars; and even the cupola atop the garret where Martha Washington slept after her husband had died in their bedroom; and, of course, the original dining room and its impressively large round table.

All of the rooms had fireplaces, and were adorned with numerous paintings—both portraits and landscapes—heirlooms and books. The many outbuildings around the mansion showed what a community it was: the blacksmith shop, grist mill and distillery; various farm buildings, paddocks, gardens, orchards and slave quarters, and wharf. Lizbet had by then endured enough of the tour and wanted to play; they naturally conceded and let her run around the expansive lawns and gardens, while they took some photos of her and the mansion.

Since picnicking was prohibited in the Mansion area, they decided to look for other recreational grounds nearby with toilet facilities and water; and, soon, on the edge of a meadow leading to a marsh and the Potomac, they were setting up in the shade of a tree. A hand water pump was situated centrally and the outhouses, out of view, were located on a path which skirted a ravine and the marsh. Lizbet napped after they finished their lunch of cucumber, tomato and homemade mayonnaise sandwiches fixed on the spot, accompanied with French compté cheese and fruit, and a potato salad with dill and chives.

There were few people near and Greenfield dozed after mixing a little vodka with iced lemonade from the cooler. Prinzenthal sat back against the tree and scanned the area—the trees and grounds, people and children. Occasionally, some kids came by, usually fetching a ball or a little brother, and an elderly couple strolled past. She noticed a young woman approaching other picnickers and appeared to ask for a light as she then lit up a cigarette. Shortly after, the family then packed up and left and twenty minutes later, this same woman approached Prinzenthal who was by then sitting up.

'Hi,' said the woman with a cigarette between her fingers, 'sorry to disturb you, but do you have a light? My lighter ran out of fluid.'

'Don't smoke,' said Prinzenthal coolly.

Greenfield, hearing the voice, stirred and looked up. The slim, pale-skinned woman had her black hair tied in a ponytail and she wore a pink sleeveless button down dress with a fancy white hat and chic runners. She seemed a bit racy for a picnic, but he didn't make much of it.

'Damn, my boyfriend took off and is taking his time.'

'There are others over there,' said Prinzenthal, pointing to people in the distance.

'Yeah, I feel kinda stupid going up to everyone.'

'You're a New Yorker,' said Greenfield. 'The native lingo.'

'You got me.' She laughed. 'We're from the Bronx.'

'A fair hike from here.'

'Yeah, my man, you know, he's on assignment in DC; brought me along for the hell of it. Always the same: "can't do without you, baby", but won't tie the knot.'

'Then turn the screws,' said Prinzenthal, smiling.

'Oh, I have, believe me, it doesn't work with him.'

'A pretty girl like you can do better.'

'Yeah, I guess.'

'Do you work for a living?' asked Prinzenthal, curiously.

'Me? I used to dance. Just wanna start a family. I'm Rosie, but everyone calls me Cherry.'

'Where's your picnic basket, Cherry? Are you thirsty?'

'He just took off with it, leaving me. He'll be back soon. I'm a bit thirsty, though.'

Prinzenthal poured her a cup of chilled lemonade and handed it to her.

'Thanks, you're so nice. Where are you from?'

'Washington.'

'Yeah, kinda figured.'

'Did you visit the estate?' asked Prinzenthal.

'Mount Vernon? We drove in but it seemed a bit crowded, so we thought to come back later.'

'I see. Well, it's worth the visit. The mansion's spectacular in a modest way. I think Washington was quite a practical man, unostentatious, always working dutifully for his people; it's probably what killed him, out in that inclement weather when he should've been warming by the fire.'

'Dear,' said Greenfield, as Lizbet awoke in the pram, 'I think it's time we moved on.'

'Alright,' she replied, standing up. 'But first, I need to use the privy.'

Prinzenthal started down the path with her handbag.

'She's so great,' said Cherry. 'What's her name?'

'Joyce. I'm Tom, her husband.'

'Nice to meet you both.'

Lizbet sat up with her hands on the edge of the pram.

'She's sooo cute.'

'That she is.' Greenfield lifted her out of the pram and let her stand there for a moment as she looked at the stranger warily, recognizing that she wasn't her Mom.

'What's her name?'

'Lizzy.'

About a hundred yards away, Prinzenthal found the outhouses in a shaded area at the edge of the ravine. No sooner had she touched the door handle, than a man in a light suit and hat appeared in the distance, coming from the opposite direction. Instinctively, feeling vulnerable, Prinzenthal opened the door and pulled out her gun. The man passed, then stopped and turned around. Prinzenthal stood there holding the gun behind her. Looking at the man, who smiled back, she recognized Gerald Osbourne.

'My, my, if it isn't Heddy the spy. Fancy meeting you here of all places. Is that a coincidence or what?'

'I'd say hardly a coincidence.'

'You coulda fooled me, just like in Frankfurt.'

'Joe di Lucca? I doubt it.'

He began to move his hand to his inside pocket. 'They say it's your birthday, Hannah. I wouldn't miss it for the world.'

'Now that we've got the introductions out of the way, would you mind keeping your hand well away from that inside holster?' She quickly brought her gun out from behind and aimed it at his head, then chest. 'One move and its Goodnight Johnny.'

'Damn, Heddy; you really know how to give me a hard-on. I'm not gonna kill you. Hell, I just wanna fuck you, but I know that would be unwise, knowing your expertise, wouldn't it?'

'On the count of three, I'm going to kill you unless you remove very slowly the firearm under your jacket and gently place it on the ground. One ... two ...'

Di Lucca reached into his inside holster and took out his gun with his finger and thumb, then he placed it on the ground beside him.

'You wouldn't kill an unarmed man, Hannah.'

'Now move away back down the path from where you came.'

Di Lucca did as he was told walking backward, facing her. He began to sing:

'*Happy Birthday, Dear Hannah; Happy Birthday to You! Happy BIRTHDAY, Dear HanNAH! Happy Birthday to YOU!*' On the last word, he stopped walking backward and turned around taking a few steps, suddenly darting down into the trees and shrubs of the ravine. Losing sight of him, Prinzenthal almost pulled the trigger, but hesitated, fearing that a gunshot might alert someone to call the authorities; otherwise, she could claim self-defense if he was armed.

'Shit!'

A moment later, there was a thud as if someone had hit a tree. Prinzenthal heard a grunt and the sound of someone retching or choking. She followed the sound down the ravine for about a hundred feet and in the brush, growing thicker as it neared the marsh, she saw somebody in a green shirt struggling with someone. Approaching cautiously, she could see that it was her husband beside the now lifeless body of Gerald Osbourne-Joe di Lucca-Johnny Goodnight. With her gun still pointed in front of her she called out: 'Harley? Thank God!'

He was sweating and winded. 'I just had to go after you, when I saw from a distance a man approach the outhouse, so I ran into the trees and around in case there was trouble, as I didn't have my gun. Below the latrines I saw you point your gun, and I knew then it must be di Lucca. When he took off down into the ravine I surprised him and tripped him, sending him headfirst into a tree.' Greenfield removed the string that he had used to strangle Osbourne, a piece of the same string he had used earlier to tie down the trunk. He stood up and looked at the dead man, whose eyes were bulged and tongue protracted.

'And Lizbet?' asked Prinzenthal.

'I left her with Cherry. I had no choice. She's fine.'

'What will you do with the body?'

'I'll weigh it down in the marsh. You should go back to Lizzy.'

Prinzenthal turned and went back up to the outhouse to quickly relieve herself. There, she saw Osbourne's gun and decided to take it back down the ravine. Without a word, Greenfield stopped dragging the body towards the marsh, and took the gun from her and stuffed it back in Osbourne's holster.

Prinzenthal hurried back to Lizbet, and was grateful to find Cherry playing with her.

'Thanks, Cherry.'

'Tom was answering the call to nature, and left Lizzy with me!' said Cherry, gleefully.

'Sorry I took so long. Yes, he showed up. It's my birthday. Well …'

'Congratulations.' She smiled, adding slyly, 'A birthday tryst?'

They both laughed, Prinzenthal more from relief after the shock of what happened.

'There was no one around,' stated Prinzenthal, flushed keeping up the pretense.

'I love doing it in nature,' said Cherry, whimsically.

'When the sun is hot.'

'Yeah, it's so intense.'

Prinzenthal had a drink of lemonade, and poured Cherry and Lizbet cups as well. Twenty minutes went by before Greenfield returned red-faced and wet.

'Looks like your husband's the worse for the wear,' remarked Cherry with a mischievous smile.

'I went all the way down to the Potomac to cool off,' he said as an explanation, not realizing what was so funny.

'And you didn't come back to get us?' complained Prinzenthal.

'Well, I thought—'

'It's settled then; let's take Lizzy in the pram down to the river.'

They packed up and walked down the path past the outhouses. Cherry went along because her boyfriend had yet to return.

'What could've happened to him?' she wondered aloud, looking back.

'We can offer you a lift if you want,' said Prinzenthal.

'Maybe I will. He doesn't deserve me—the things I do for him.'

'It's up to you. We're going back to Washington to watch the fireworks this evening.'

'If he's not back before you leave, screw him; I'll take that ride, thanks.'

'Fine.'

*

After a quick splash in the river, they drove Cherry back to Washington since her boyfriend still hadn't returned. It dawned on both Prinzenthal and Greenfield that perhaps di Lucca was her boyfriend in spite of the age difference. They were both from the Bronx, though it seemed she was oblivious to his secret agenda and was likely with him for purely recreational reasons. Cherry opened up and said that her boyfriend was a "tough guy" who owned a "joint called Club Europa". They were astounded, to say the least, having just murdered him, though they felt that any sadness his girlfriend might feel had she known of his untimely death, would be mitigated by the fact that she was now permanently free from him.

She seemed to be not a bad girl, in fact, charming, but just a bit gullible and naïve, a girl whose coquettish and even innocent good looks had landed her in a bad relationship with an evil man. When Prinzenthal intimated to her that Rosie was such a lovely name and that she should use it, she shrugged and said Cherry was originally her stage name, but she didn't do *that* anymore. "*That*", thought Prinzenthal, being obviously what di Lucca had her doing, made her feel a twinge of familiarity with her own life, though antipodal in context to Cherry's.

With Cherry's directions, they arrived at this cheap motel in Southeast Washington, and Greenfield escorted her to the door in order to have a look-see. In her room, she exclaimed brightly that she still had her boyfriend's bag, full of cash stashed in a false bottom, and there was no way he would desert her without taking his money. Greenfield gave her some sound advice: take the money and run. She was better off without this hood who had left her stranded like that. She replied that she would wait for a day or two—he had disappeared on other occasions too—then go home; she revealed she had only turned twenty-two early last month, and promised Greenfield that she would make something of herself.

Later, Greenfield called Jimbo from a pay phone, and told him urgently to meet them at his house. Jimbo arrived soon after, and was surprised at the Greenfields' pleasant mood. Greenfield took him aside and when he revealed to him what had happened, Jimbo was upset that he had let them down by not being there. 'Now, Jimbo,' said Greenfield, 'it couldn't be helped, but we need you to do something.' Jimbo replied, 'Anything.' Greenfield gave him a set of car keys that he had found on di Lucca, and told him where to find and destroy the car identified by Cherry as a 1962 two-door black Impala somewhere parked in a lot near their picnic location. Jimbo knew the area, having done his early training as a marine back in 1918 at Quantico, east of Mount Vernon and he eagerly set off. Prinzenthal, meanwhile had changed her mind about watching the fireworks: 'We've had quite enough for one day,' she announced to Greenfield.

*

The day after Rose McCann was dropped off at the Star Motel, she was disturbed from a nap by a loud knocking on her door. Thinking Joe di Lucca had finally returned—but forgetting he had a key—she opened the door and was confronted by a middle-aged man dressed in a beige linen suit with a matching hat and well-worn brown brogues. He had the look of some of di Lucca's tough friends: pale half-dead brown eyes, set in a flaccid clean-shaven face beneath a crew-cut of grayish hair. Without introduction, he forced his way into the room.

'Where's Joe,' he demanded, looking around.

'He's not here. Who the fuck are you?'

He ignored her question, and in a menacing voice, growled, 'Now I'll ask nicely one more time. Where is he?'

'How should I know? He took off on me, yesterday.'

Earl Bunting looked her up and down, as if he was scrutinizing a piece of meat.

'I can see why he liked to have you around, Cherry.'

'I'm not Cherry anymore. I'm Rosie.'

'Well, you're a fucking Cherry to me. Why did he leave you?'

'My lighter was out of fluid when we went on a picnic. He took off to find some matches, and never came back. I'm here waiting for him, obviously. Who are you?'

'His boss.'

'Your name.'

'Where did you go on this picnic?'

'Joe never said he had a boss.'

'Listen up, Cherry: you either tell me what I want to know, or I'm gonna mess up that pretty face of yours. He was supposed to contact me yesterday, and didn't. In our business that's unusual. Now tell me exactly where you went and what happened!'

He pushed her onto the bed and stood over her.

'I told you! We went on a picnic; it was near Mount Vernon. He took off and never came back! It's happened before, but this time I was stranded with no money, no lighter, nothing.'

'Why did you go on a picnic?'

'He said that morning we were going for a drive. First, we went downtown and drove around a bit. I said we should buy some snacks or something. I was hungry. So we did—a couple of sandwiches, and apples. Then we drove to Mount Vernon, but he didn't want to go in—said it was too crowded.'

'And?'

'We waited in the car.'

'For how long?'

'Too long. I said I needed to get some air and use the ladies' room. He said come right back.'

'Go on.'

'Well, I went, then came back, and we sat some more. Finally, we left and went to this picnic area a mile or so away. And he left me there.'

'How did you get back here?'

'I waited around for hours, bumming lights off people. Some even shared their lunch. I got a ride with a family.'

Bunting shook his head.

'Joe's the smartest man I know.'

'Yeah, maybe he fucked up.'

'It's not like him to fuck up.'

'So what's the big deal? Maybe he did fuck up. Haven't you ever fucked up?'

'Let me see his stuff.'

417

Rosie showed him the small suitcase. Bunting rummaged through it.

'Where's the money?' he demanded.

'He had it with him,' she lied.

'Don't fuck with me, Cherry.'

'What? If I took his money, why would I stay here waiting for him?'

He looked down at her with lust in his eyes. She immediately rolled off of the bed and stood there.

'Don't even think about it,' she remarked. 'Boss, or not, Joe would have your balls for a Mexican windshield ornament.'

He hesitated, knowing di Lucca's reputation for revenge, then smiled.

'Have it your way, Cherry, but if something's happened to him and you're not telling me everything, somebody's gotta answer for it. I'll be back tomorrow.'

Bunting then left the motel room without closing the door. Later that day, Rosie McCann hopped on a train back to the Bronx with the suitcase and money.

34. Aubrey Woods

During the hot, sultry summer months following Bill James' death, his brother-in-law, Aubrey Woods, went through a severe crisis of conscience. He had had nothing to do with James' death, in fact he specifically told Phil Garvey to lay off any monitoring of his family. But he knew that he was powerless to stop Garvey and Bunting from carrying out their agendas, as they also worked for Farnes, who had been a black ops manager for Sulla in the old days. Farnes still considered Sulla his boss and Woods had seen them together chatting amiably at his summer party a month ago at Swan Cottage.

There had been no doubt in his mind that their domestic operation was going ahead as planned. Woods had been put in an awkward position because of James, and, in the usual company way was sidelined when someone was compromised. He still ran operations but had little more to do with what he had started with the Leverton situation a few years before when Sulla was still the director. Following the general consensus of hardline insiders, he was self-righteously convinced that Kennedy was a national security risk and something had to be done about it.

His justification was a deep-seated patriotism, though he was quite relieved at not being involved of late, and would do nothing to impede or undermine the obvious implications of a coup d'état. The carry-through and ultimate action to facilitate such an event was something else again. He felt quite inadequate to the task, better left to the Garveys and Buntings of this world and comforted himself in the mantra: I see nothing, hear nothing and know nothing. However, when he saw his nephew, Nevin James, as recently as at Swan Cottage that summer, he felt himself slip into a quagmire of shame and self-doubt.

Nevin not only looked like his father, he had the same uncanny ability to see into the heart of matters, and was courageous like him too. Woods had always envied James' war experiences in occupied France. At the cottage,

Nevin barely spoke, though numerous guests extended their condolences again. When Woods himself tried to make conversation, Nevin left him dumbfounded by something he said: 'I'll never be a Ghost. Dying is like being born: either way, you don't remember a thing.'

'You're your father's son alright, Nevin,' he replied. 'You know, he was a reluctant Ghost.'

'I'm nobody's Ghost now. I'm like Saint Francis living barefoot in a cave.'

'Come now: think of your mother and sister, and Mollie. We have all suffered a most tragic mishap. Forgive them.'

'Mishap? There's nothing to forgive. They loved each other. They were murdered, and you must know it, even if you had nothing to do with it.'

Nevin turned and walked away. Woods watched him disappear into the trees at the far end of the lawn. There was no way of convincing Nevin, because he knew the truth, and knew that his uncle knew, no matter how sincere his own personal grief was. Uncle Aubrey would always be the enemy, when Nevin felt his uncle should have filled the void of what his father had been.

Some news of domestic operations reached Woods' ears through Bunting, who'd been in a funk ever since his lethal sidekick, di Lucca, had disappeared a few months back. Some thought he had simply vanished like Osbourne had done in 1949, only to emerge a decade later as di Lucca. And this time, who knew when he might reappear? But Woods clearly thought Bunting was right that di Lucca had been killed. Though, by whom no one knew; it could have been a mafia hit. God knows, thought Woods, he likely deserved it.

Bunting grumbled to him that Greenfield was the most probable suspect, because di Lucca had been tailing him, and was looking for an opportunity to pull another seamless wet job. Woods' response was there was no such thing as "seamless", and that the burden of sin was implicit with di Lucca. Bunting looked at him as if he had lost his mind, and said that in this business the means were not for the squeamish, but the ends were for the country, and non-negotiable. Besides, he added, di Lucca's disappearance was seamless.

Bunting had followed the Greenfield lead but came up empty-handed. There was no one who could verify Greenfield's whereabouts that day. He had put so much faith in di Lucca, it was never even considered. Besides, Greenfield would have spent Independence Day with his wife—whose birthday he knew it to be as well—and child; hardly a time to murder someone of di Lucca's skill set, even if he could actually find him.

Cherry was the only one who had been with di Lucca that day, but it seemed that di Lucca had dumped her for a very good reason. And that reason could only have been Greenfield; therefore, he must have been at Mount Vernon with his family. In the following days, Bunting had scoured the region looking for di Lucca's black Impala, but could not find a trace of it. He even found Cherry again in New York, but when asked if she had seen a couple with a kid looking like Greenfield and Prinzenthal, she was adamant that no one like that was there, and everyone had kids.

He asked who drove her back to Washington. She replied Joyce and Tom. What kind of car did they drive? She didn't know, only that it was blue, or green, like half the cars out there. Anyway, it hardly mattered because Prinzenthal had taken a posting at the American embassy in Paris and Greenfield had accompanied her, though he had since returned to fulfill his duties for the Kennedy administration with the National Security team.

*

Nevin James refused to celebrate his seventeenth birthday, though a week later agreed to a Columbus Day long weekend celebration for everyone the following Saturday, October the Twelfth. Muriel and Carolyn had prepared his favorite meal, duck confit, the traditional way steamed then seared in a pan on high heat, until crispy on the outside and tender on the inside. They had gone out and specially procured three large quartered ducks and a small tub of duck fat.

When Nevin was twelve years old, his family went out and dined at a French restaurant to celebrate New Year's Eve; Nevin ordered duck confit that turned out to be very delicious, so he decided it was the greatest thing he had ever eaten. But it wasn't the duck confit now that raised his spirits. The previous weekend, he had received a short note in the same post box that they had used during his and Mollie's spy days. Decoded, all it said was to meet at Martin's Tavern after school Thursday.

Nevin was overjoyed because he thought that Melbo had finally received his note sent months before, just after his father had died. Having taken so long, he had begun to think the Diva post box was defunct. And now there was a shred of hope he had a friend who would understand his terrible ordeal. He counted on it as if he had been thrown a life vest after falling overboard at sea.

421

Sitting with his back to the wall at a table for two at the far end of Martin's Tavern, Nevin sipped on an iced fresh lime and soda water with a couple of sugar cubes. He sat there for over half an hour waiting for someone he presumed to be George Melbo. But when a black man in a smart gray suit, white shirt and black tie approached his table and smiled, to the obvious curiosity of a few patrons in the tavern—DC was generally desegregated, but many were still implacable racists—and said, 'May I?' Nevin didn't answer, so unexpected was this man. Waiting for a moment, the man pulled out the chair and sat down. Very black, with large lips and nose, he was tall, slim, athletic, with piercing brown eyes that looked right into you; his general manner and close-cropped hair gave him a distinctive military vibe.

Finally, Nevin said, 'Sorry, I was expecting someone else.'

'I assume that would be Mr. Melbo.'

'Yes, where is he?'

'Mel is unavailable, Nevin. His location is classified for his protection.'

'Oh, I didn't realize. Things got that bad, huh?'

'More as a precaution.'

'Then who sent you, and who are you?'

'Dave Washington. I work for the Secret Service—a trainee actually.'

'The Secret Service? Forgive my ignorance, but I didn't know they hired blacks. I've never seen any around the president.'

'Get to the quick, huh?' Washington laughed.

'Truthfully, I'm reassured,' replied Nevin. 'I didn't mean to be … ignorant.'

'I don't think you're ignorant at all; rather more the opposite. That's why I'm here.'

Nevin looked around the tavern and noticed a few people staring.

'Well, thanks, but you know how it is. I'm not one of those.' He indicated the stares with a nod of his head.

Without looking, Washington responded, 'If we're being frank, I certainly know how it is. There's only one token "nigger" on duty in the service for the president and White House. Abraham Bolden. And believe me, some of his colleagues still think he's only a "nigger" working for a "nigger lover".'

'I'm sorry.'

'Why are you reassured, then?'

'That change is in the air.'

'The struggle continues.'

'And I love the blues,' said Nevin seriously.

Washington broke out into a hearty laugh. 'Which ones?'

'One time in our correspondence, Mel suggested I listen to a variety of music. I bought some John Lee Hooker: *Hobo Blues* and *Boogie Chillen* and recently *Boom Boom*. I like B.B. King, Willie Dixon's *Hoochie Coochie Man* recorded by Muddy Waters, some others like Leadbelly and Blind Willie McTell.'

'I'm a Frank Sinatra fan. Elvis. Sam Cooke. Sarah Vaughan. Motown too. Marvin Gaye. Funk Brothers.'

'Cool. How about the Beatles and Bob Dylan?'

'Can't say I've caught the bug, yet. Don't know Dylan.'

'New York folk scene. Writes protest songs like about Medgar Evers.'

'That right?'

'Yeah. It inspired me to join the march in August. I heard Martin Luther King speak at the Lincoln Memorial.'

'I have a dream?'

'Yeah, after I went up to him and shook his hand.'

'You're some kid. How old are you?'

'Seventeen.'

'I was real sorry about your pop.'

'Do you know anything about it?'

'Me? No, just that he was one solid guy, and the last kind of guy you'd think that'd do what he allegedly did. Personally, I don't buy it. I'm black. I know the system from my side, and that same evil doesn't only apply to blacks. Listen, Nevin, I was told to come here and pay my respects for Melbo and his friends, who for reasons can't meet you.'

'What friends?'

'My boss, for one: he's trying to find out what happened. All I know is that he's very concerned about national security, and threats from within the system. With the Cold War, there're some serious differences of opinion of how to go about fighting it, especially in view of nuclear brinkmanship. Everything relates to that.'

'What about the aliens?'

'I was told you might ask about that. I don't know anything about aliens, but I believe that where there's smoke, there's fire; and there's been a lot of smoke in regards to them. I've read Melbo's articles. They're true accounts in my humble estimation.'

'Who's your boss?'

'He would have liked to meet you himself. He became a close friend of your father in the last year or so, but the situation is too dangerous for him to risk being seen with you. He's thinking of your safety first and foremost.'

'I see. Well, tell him I appreciate his discretion, but I want to meet with him as soon as possible. I might be able to help with his investigations.'

'He also said you'd probably say that. I can pass that on.'

'Please do. I can meet wherever he'd like. No one will know. My father taught me well. Tell him.'

'Sure thing.'

'Where are you from Mr. Washington?'

'Right here.'

'I'm curious about your family history.'

'You're quite the sleuth, aren't you? A true son.'

'Well?'

'I've been told my ancestors were slaves owned by Washington himself and were freed when he died.'

'By word of mouth?'

'I think so. My name's not uncommon among black people, so I can't say with any absolute certainty that it's true. But that's what has passed down from my grandparents.'

'Thanks for telling me.'

Washington stood up.

'Take care, Nevin.'

'You too.'

Nevin watched him leave. A few patrons followed Washington out with their eyes.

*

On an overcast Friday after the Columbus Day weekend, Nevin was on the bus heading home from school. He missed Mollie terribly, though by then his anxiety had eased from the excruciating months following his father's and her mother's deaths. She had written him a letter in September wishing him a happy birthday, telling him about her new school and a few new friends she had made. The tone of the letter was distant, almost as if she was a different person; there was no mention of their intimacy or their parent's deaths, just words about her new life and her hope that he was "finding himself", as she had. Her passion had been derailed permanently it seemed. She mentioned her new spirituality after attending church, which gave her "solace and a possibility of atonement for youthful mistakes".

Nevin had nothing to say to her after that as he still burned for her love which had obviously been extinguished in her. Yet, he wrote back a short note to say that he was happy that she had found some peace of mind and he would never forget their beautiful love, which had become like a cruel martyrdom, not just for them but their parents. She didn't write back, which he felt was in effect the last word—a deep resonant silence—but nonetheless in his estimation, knowing Mollie, it was a deferment. It would be six years before they would see each other again by coincidence under extraordinary circumstances in August, 1969 at the legendary Woodstock Music and Art Fair in White Lake, upstate New York.

A man sat beside Nevin after the first stop, but actually he had just moved from the back of the bus to the front. Nevin was looking out the window, and hardly noticed him. Only when the man said, 'Looks like rain,' did Nevin turn and look at him. Dressed in a casual light blue suit, he was old, hatless, perhaps late fifties or sixty, but clean-shaven with a healthy athletic build and a generous head of salt and pepper hair kept loosely, at least it appeared that way by its waviness. Smiling, the man was looking at him with expressive blue-green eyes.

'The name's John. I became close to your father in the last year of his life, or at least as close as our professions permitted.'

Nevin's eyes opened wide.

'Don't worry, I'm Dave's boss.'

'How did you know my dad?' asked Nevin, staring.

'We had mutual concerns. As well, we knew of each other in the war.'

'He spoke to me once of a Jean Hardin, someone he looked up to in France. Are you him?'

'I was one of the leaders of the OSS behind enemy lines, yes.'

'The Nazi-hunter, I know.'

'Let's not dwell on the distant past; we have more pressing matters at

425

present.'

'Can you help me find the killers of my father?'

'Perhaps we can help each other.'

'How?'

'We can't talk here. I'm going to get off at this next stop. I'll meet you at your stop in my car, an aqua Ford Fairlane. Don't walk down your street; continue down Wisconsin and I'll pick you up. Are you okay with that?'

'Yeah.'

Nevin did as directed, and shortly after, when the car stopped, he quickly got in the front passenger seat. They drove towards the Potomac River.

'What happened to George Melbo and Melissa,' asked Nevin.

'They're safe and sound, and give you their sincere condolences. Like Dave said, it's best if their whereabouts are unknown, not that I don't trust you, but as a rule in this business ignorance is bliss.'

A few moments went by. Nevin was feeling very emotional as if Greenfield's comfortable presence was a catalyst to it. There was something reassuring about him and that his father had surely confided in him.

'Mr. Hardin, I can't thank you enough for thinking about me. I've been really down. I lost my father and my girlfriend, my girlfriend's mother ... I was so depressed ...' Suddenly, Nevin couldn't hold back tears. They seemed to come as if released through an opened floodgate. He tried stoically to suppress them, and began to tremble slightly in his efforts, barely emitting a sound. Greenfield looked over at the poor stricken fellow, who at such a young age had had to shoulder so much pain and confusion. He hadn't thought that there was likely no one else with whom Nevin could feel free to unburden himself.

As a father now himself, deeply moved, Greenfield realized that this outpouring of grief had been triggered by him being there for the boy who desperately needed someone to talk to. Dave Washington had done a great job by introducing his connection to the boy's father—someone who was now was on Nevin's side and understood the family dynamic. He put his hand on Nevin's shoulder.

'Let it out, son; it takes guts to be human in a world of pain. I admire your courage and know that your father, wherever he is, is so proud of you.'

'It's all my fault!' sobbed Nevin. 'Had I not tried to be a spy like him, he might still be alive! It was a game to me! I killed him, and Mollie's mom!

Mollie hates me now! I loved her! I loved my dad!'

'Nevin,' said Greenfield carefully, letting his thoughts merge, hardly knowing what to say to his profound sensitivity and guilt, 'Nevin, your father was working on a very dangerous mission. You had absolutely nothing to do with their deaths. You must not blame yourself. I'm going to tell you something—only because you need to know this, and as a spy you must keep it strictly confidential. Can I trust you? Will you trust me?'

Nevin began to calm down; he nodded affirmatively, wiping his eyes with the sleeves of his shirt. Greenfield took away his hand.

'Okay, first I need to hear from you that you understand there was nothing you did or could have done to prevent what happened. Your father would have wanted me to insist on this, one hundred percent. Secondly, collateral damage can have relentless repercussions that can unhinge the very best of us. We must be strong to be able to continue the fight against such monstrous acts which fly in the face of everything we stand for to make a difference in this crazy world.

'I'm talking about this country and a moral obligation to preserve our God-given freedoms. The trouble is, some people think there're other considerations that must supersede these moral obligations, in the name of national security, and it makes monsters of the most seemingly dutiful of persons. War does that. I've killed with my bare hands, and would do it again under the same circumstances.

'But I'm not a monster. Those people had it coming. And some day the same may happen to me, hopefully not, but rather in a warm bed surrounded by my family. We all have it coming one way or another. The point is: we must be true to our moral instincts—we have to do the right thing in the name of love for this thing called humanity in spite of all the evil and injustice. Do I have your agreement?'

'One hundred percent.'

'Good, and you're not in any way responsible for the tragic events of last June?'

'Yes, I see I couldn't have known. It wasn't my fault.'

'And the loss of Mollie was not your fault, nor hers. She has suffered equally as you have.'

'Yes, she's trying her best in her own way to move forward.'

'Okay, we're good?' Greenfield made a fist with his left hand and held it over to Nevin, who smiled finally and made a fist to bunt Greenfield's.

'What were you going to tell me, Mr. Hardin?'

'The person who murdered your father and Deborah McBride is dead.'

'How do you know?'

'I need you to trust me that it's a done deal.'

'Okay. I just hope that whatever happened to him he really suffered and knew what was coming.'

'Believe me, it was his worst nightmare come true. He's gone without a trace, and that's how it must always remain. Never under any circumstances should you reveal this to anyone. I've only told you because you needed to know and move forward.'

'Did Uncle Aubrey have anything to do with it? The murder of my dad and Mrs. McBride?'

'Not likely. He's been compromised by your father's death. He wouldn't have gotten involved knowing what would happen to him. He may be venal in his duty to dark agendas—they all are, but he's weak and doesn't have the acumen of others. Whatever you do, keep this to yourself.'

'My mom told me that Uncle Aubrey cried. Aunt Honey told her.'

'Well, there may be hope for him yet. Listen, up ahead there's a little park that's relatively unvisited. What do you say we stretch our legs a little, and watch the river?'

'Sure, that'd be great. I love the river.'

'Right, I recall your family has property up near Harper's Ferry: Swan Cottage. I certainly remember meeting you there a few years ago. You were still a boy then. Now you're a young man.'

'I remember you too. I wasn't really looking. You were with someone, a woman.'

'Yes, my wife now.'

'Is she a spy too?'

'No, not now, she's a working mom; she works at the embassy in Paris.'

'Cool. Are you going there too?'

'As soon as I finish my work here.'

'How many kids do you have?'

Greenfield smiled at this precocious young fellow.

'Just one.'

Crossing a bridge over the Chesapeake and Ohio towpath and canal, they parked in the shade of trees parallel to the canal. Walking along the path beside the bank of the Potomac they found a secluded spot with a bench. The river was close and water flowed by in its soothing, serene silken way. The little rocky Three Sisters Islands stood resolutely in the river's course up a little to the west.

After they had sat for a time, Nevin asked out of the blue: 'Why can't you tell me your real name, Mr. Hardin? I won't tell anybody.'

Greenfield smiled. He liked Nevin, but he wasn't prepared to reveal his personal information, other than what he had already said.

'Let's not go there just yet. It's not that I don't trust you, Nevin; your father wouldn't want me to put you in any kind of danger.'

'Why would I be a threat? And to whom?'

'The situation could be potentially compromising for me. A lot of people aren't too happy with my work, because they think I'm making mountains out of molehills.'

'But my dad was killed because he was working on something.'

'No one will admit he was murdered.'

'But you know. Why don't you do anything about it?'

Greenfield sighed. 'I know it's unjust, not having the truth revealed, but to reveal it would make it worse for me in a very bad way and compromise my investigation, because I'm trying to finish what your dad started.'

'What's that?'

'Root out some serious corruption in high places.'

'You'd think these murderers would have more respect for this country and its institutions.'

'Yes, you'd think so, but they'd never admit malfeasance, because they have the power to cover up their crimes and believe they are acting in the national interest.'

'Do you know the president?'

'Yes, I do.'

'What does he have to say about it?'

'He has listened, but defers to his closest advisors. The President has so many issues to contend with, he can't be held hostage to the many threats heard about the country; in Texas there are "Wanted" posters for him "Dead or Alive" tacked about in public. I'm the guy who's trying to connect the dots to the elite back chambers of power.'

'Dad was a Ghost, a member of a secretive group, sort of like the Masons, or modern day Templars.'

'I gathered that. Did he ever speak to you about them?' asked Greenfield, fishing for any information.

'I know they used to meet at Mr. Sulla's house.'

'I've heard that too.'

'I asked dad once if it was legal, or rather if what they did was legal.'

'And?'

'He said, of course, they're legal; the Founding Fathers were Masons. But one time he mentioned that the problem with secret societies is that their allegiances are sometimes more closely bound to their own sense of honor than to law. I thought about it and figured he meant they were too proud to admit that because they felt responsible for the well-being of this country—many of them are powerful people—they would break the law if they felt it would help their cause, or if they had a problem with it. In other words, their sense of loyalty to the country overrode any observance of morality, and when I see them flout their fidelity to the country, I see total hypocrites. Mollie and I used to talk about it.'

That memory seemed to make Nevin sad again. Greenfield quickly responded.

'That's the nature of entitlement: hidden codes of conduct—*un bête noire*—anathema to moral imperatives. Did your father ever mention anything, things or people in general?'

'Sure. Lots of people we all know about.'

'How about the other kind: things we don't know about?'

'No, he never mentioned anything.'

'Mel told me you used to go into your dad's study and snoop around.'

Nevin nodded. 'Yeah, I thought I was Sherlock Holmes and would solve all the terrible problems in this country. I think it was all about trying to impress Mollie.'

'Nothing wrong with that.'

'I do remember something now,' said Nevin, more brightly. 'Before he died we were talking about sending messages to Diva because he was being watched—I tried to convince him that most of my messages were questions about aliens and my friendship with Mel revealed nothing very incriminating other than the nature of the correspondence itself. Anyway, dad had a brown manilla envelope that he said contained some updated sensitive information he wanted to pass to Diva, but wouldn't because of me, I suppose.'

'What happened to it?'

'He waved it at me like he wanted me to see it. I didn't think anything of it; it was just his way of using his hands like a figure of speech.'

'And when did all this happen?'

'Just before he died.'

'What do you think he did with it?'

'I assume he put it in his locked drawer, though I never had a chance to find it; the FBI cleared out everything in his desk.'

'When was this?'

'Just after he was killed.'

'Is it possible he hid it somewhere else?'

'I suppose it's possible, but I don't know where.'

Greenfield pondered this new information. James likely would have given him this envelope, at least it appeared he meant to, but died before he could.

'Is his desk still there?' asked Greenfield.

'Yes, I use it now. Mom and my sister seem to be alright with it.'

'There could be another hidden compartment.'

'There was no hidden compartment, just the locked bottom right drawer.'

'A perfect decoy.'

'But I know that desk; there's nothing.'

'It's a hunch. He must've put it somewhere unless he had it at his office in which case it's been taken.'

'That may be the case, Mr. Hardin.'

'Look again, Nevin. Some desks have a false bottom drawer, a sheath of some kind just big enough to fit papers.'

'Okay, I'll look.'

'If you find anything, mail it immediately to this post box address. Just make absolutely sure nobody has followed you. Then destroy the card.' Greenfield wrote down the address on a small plain card and gave it to him.

35. Lone Star

By the time Greenfield had decided what to do in a final effort to derail what he perceived to be an inevitable attempt on the life of President Kennedy, he knew only a miracle would save him. The machinery once set in motion was impossible to stop. With an ever more foreboding sense of doom and a sinking feeling in his heart, he knew that all the sinister forces now gathering momentum were in effect a phalanx of shadowy plots so layered and impervious they left nothing to chance. This had to be, he determined, a byzantine labyrinth so intricate and yet so plainly evident there could be but one outcome: Kennedy could not come out of Texas alive.

Greenfield had arrived at this conclusion in the past six weeks after his meeting with Nevin James. And so, he stared into his beer as he sat in the City Hall Bar of the Adolphus Hotel in Dallas. Dressed in a gray suit with brown cowboy boots and gray Stetson, he looked like a typical Texas businessman. His intention was to blend in like a native. Dave Washington accompanied him but he was not completely welcome in the hotel as it had been, until recently, enforcing segregation; however, when he showed his Secret Service credentials—albeit as a trainee—and with Greenfield's gruff insistence as a White House staffer, the concierge was all smiles, knowing that President Kennedy was on his way to Texas, and coming to Dallas.

In its early years, the hotel had been a well-known watering hole for the Klu Klux Klan. Washington took some pleasure in being there now, even as he was given a wide berth by a few patrons. He and Greenfield were waiting for a newsman, Bob Hume, from the *Dallas Morning News*. For Greenfield, the journey to that place had been quite a saga beginning with Nevin's discovery of a secret sheaf of papers concealed in the center drawer of his father's desk.

One week after that meeting with Nevin on the banks of the Potomac River, Greenfield had received in his post-box an envelope like the one described by

Nevin that his father had flourished before him prior to his death. Nevin had, as Greenfield suggested, taken out the center drawer, emptied its sundry contents, and shaken the drawer for any noise of papers moving, but to no avail. The bottom of the drawer was solid and thin, so it appeared normal in every sense. Ready to move on to other drawers and panels in the desk, he was just about to slip it back in on its tracks when he noticed the frame at the back of the drawer was slightly loose.

Upon closer inspection, he pried the piece of wood with a Yale letter opener, and the end piece snapped out, revealing an eighth of an inch gap between the floor of the drawer and bottom. Inside, he discovered an envelope, which he shook out and laid on the desk; then he put back the end piece and returned the drawer to the desk. The contents of the envelope revealed a few pages of notes about certain people including David Ferrie, Clay Shaw, Guy Banister, Lee Harvey Oswald, an ex-marine, and others he knew nothing about, such as Joe Campisi, Chuckie Nicoletti, and Maurice Bishop with a question mark and "CIA", which likely meant an alias.

Also revealed were interesting remarks by Madame Nhu, whose husband, Ngô Đinh Nhu, had been eventually assassinated with his brother President Ngô Đinh Diệm of Vietnam that very month in early November. The CIA and administration had wanted to replace the brothers for some time because of their mishandling of internal affairs, which had created terrible enmities within the Buddhist communities. President Điệm, and his ruthless brother had wanted to strong-arm the people into submission to a modern Western society as the most effective way to fight Communism and as a way to hold on to their power. As Catholics, and a minority, they lost the support of the majority—who by and large felt a greater affinity to Hồ Chi Minh—had a strong base among the ruling class of society, those who benefited from the French Colonial system.

When Greenfield asked Cayton about this, his response was that it was true, but Kennedy didn't want them assassinated and took it very personally that his wishes had been ignored. It couldn't be helped, said Cayton, because the rebels in the military knew that if they hadn't been killed, there would be no end of intrigues by the Ngô brothers to retain power, just as they had done to take power originally by stuffing the ballots back in the fifties. But what worried Greenfield was the vitriol that came out of the wife of Ngô Đinh Nhu after her husband's assassination, by publicly denouncing Kennedy and

America, saying that "those who indulge in it will have to pay for it".

Known widely as the "dragon lady" and the key person who kept their control of the country together, she was utterly merciless and was said to have been willing to supply the match for any Buddhist who wanted to ignite himself. She had been in America drumming up support for her family and country, and would have been back in Vietnam had she not stayed a little longer in Los Angeles to have a cyst removed from her eye. From James' notes, written long before recent events, Greenfield recalled that the Nhu family had had strong links to the drug trade, which by their demise, had effectively cut out the Corsican mafia.

Through her connections, Madame Nhu could easily have hired assassins, but Greenfield figured with all the other workings, the homegrown conspiracy had already been long hatched; however, Madame Nhu's warning and threat would in any event serve the general obfuscation of it perpetrators.

Taking a good haul of his beer, Greenfield outlined in his mind a mental picture of the winding road to Dallas. He had spent a weekend near Charlottesville, Virginia, with his friend, Dick Sinclair, at the modest estate of his wife, Alecia. The rolling green hills and forests were lush even in late October. It was a much needed rest for Greenfield, who had been feeling more and more isolated in his position at the White House. He missed terribly Hannah and Lizbet, who were living a seemingly charmed life in Paris.

On the telephone, Prinzenthal had tried to convince him to quit on numerous occasions, yet he held on with the hope of a breakthrough, which perhaps was in the cards with Sinclair's connections. Sinclair had been diagnosed with throat cancer, and told by a doctor he had only a year to live. Shocking, as it was to all, he took it almost cavalierly, saying, 'Life's been good to me, why complain now?' The two men reminisced on the porch, looking out at the Jeffersonian landscape, threw back bourbon and smoked cigars like there was no tomorrow, Sinclair refusing to give up on his comforts.

'Call Garfield Moreau,' he had said. 'He's a know-it-all with the *Times-Picayune* in New Orleans. He used to work in Washington after the war then moved back about the same time I went to New York. He's a local boy, a bit of the old South—came from a family with French ancestors.'

Greenfield later called Moreau and asked him about the men in question. Moreau explained that there was a known group of mobsters and rightwing sympathizers of which Banister was the de facto leader, although Clay

Bertrand—aka Clay Shaw, a well-known New Orleans businessman, as William James had discovered—seemed to be "the money" behind Banister, because he had been seen with Banister on occasion at the 500 Club and Banister "cowed" in his presence, according to one of Moreau's informants, a cocktail waitress. Banister had a sidekick, Oswald, who used to ply the streets downtown with pamphlets proselytizing "Free Play For Cuba", a pro-Communist movement, which, ironically, was printed and organized by Guy Banister, a seriously bent fascist, a situation all the more stunning because Oswald was an avowed anti-fascist.

Oswald had obviously allowed himself to be used rather maliciously for some as yet undiscovered ulterior motive. Greenfield presumed that if he had been with Central Intelligence, there could be but one explanation: he was involved in an operation doing what he was told, all the while informing on them, which seemed to justify the occupational hypocrisy. The question was: Why would Banister manage such an event? Was it all an elaborate scheme to implicate Oswald as the sacrificial goat?

Greenfield thought it hard to believe; yet, like his colleagues in Washington, he knew the extreme right were a well-known entity in "nut country", a reference to Texas and the South, and did things that defied reason. Someone was initiating what felt like a perfect storm converging with no apparent forecast in sight. When asked if Oswald could be found, Moreau had to get back to Greenfield; this he did the next day, saying that as far as he knew Oswald hadn't been around, and he offered the likely reason that he had gone back to Dallas, where his wife and kid lived.

Moreau provided Greenfield with the name of Bob Hume as a contact and newsman, who worked with *The Dallas Morning News.* For days now, Greenfield had waited for Hume's call, having already met him once when he first arrived and treated him to an expensive meal in the French Room, a rococo dining room in the Adolphus Hotel. Tanned and fit, as Greenfield recalled, he was a decent-looking man of medium height, wearing a bolo tie, shiny cream-colored cowboy boots and a gray suit, and sporting a modest handlebar moustache and less than cropped hair. He was the epitome of a Texas gentleman who, had he been wearing the Confederate butternut jacket and trousers, would be a dead-ringer for a civil war archetype with the drawl of a native son.

Hume was a social monkey who ingratiated himself with the cream of

Texas society, but he also knew its underbelly and, according to him, the two went hand in hand, as the wealthy needed the skills of working people to carry out their agendas, which varied from buying votes to illegal chicanery. He took to Greenfield like a lizard sunning on a rock; he marveled at Greenfield's exploits during the war, and told his own version of events as an army reporter in the Pacific theater, having witnessed firsthand the devasting results of numerous battles of the marines, from Guadalcanal to Saipan, Iwo Jima and Okinawa, and finally Japan.

After several whiskeys, two bottles of Beaujolais, huge sixteen-ounce entrées of boneless Prime Rib with fixings, then peach cobbler and pecan pie for dessert, and coffee, Hume was eating out of Greenfield's hands. He went on about the oil barons, the "feudal lords" of whom H.L. Hunt and Clint Murchison were the most prominent at the time. Both were arch-enemies of Kennedy and used their influence to peddle their anti-Kennedy diatribes. They desperately wanted Johnson in power so that they could control him and the presidency for their own purposes. Hume didn't have much to offer in the way of proof, and Greenfield put it to him plainly: find me a guy named Oswald.

James had made a note that a European fellow by the name of Jerzy Sergius von Mohrenschildt was like a mentor to Oswald, and Marina, his wife, and James suggested he was Oswald's handler. Changing his name to George de Mohrenschildt once he had emigrated from Europe to the States in 1938, he was a staunch anti-Communist who made connections easily with the elite, including the young Jacqueline Bouvier, her aunt and family on Long Island.

Having pro-Nazi sympathies, he had hoped that the Nazis would destroy Stalinist Russia, and with the help of the French secure oil for the Germans before the Americans were forced into the war. A geologist by trade, he attempted to find a position in the oil business; however, Greenfield found out from James' notes that Mohrenschildt had business interests in Haiti as well, and moved there in June. Greenfield realized that Oswald seemed to have some affinity with these rightwing people, at least how he was positioned in his strange world. What was he doing with these people? he kept asking himself.

Hume had said he would get back to Greenfield. Now three long days later, Greenfield awaited his appearance in the City Hall bar.

By this time, Dave Washington had returned from the men's room, complaining he had to show his credentials to some racist patron of the hotel.

'It's hard to fathom, a well-dressed and dapper fellow like you, being asked for ID,' said Greenfield, with a twinkle in his eye.

'Wear my skin for a day and see how it goes,' retorted Washington testily. 'Though, I appreciate the compliment in there.'

'Hey, someday everything's going to be different; that's why we're here to make a difference.'

'Texas may be a fine state, land and all—the oil and cattle—but it doesn't measure up in my eyes when people are sticking up posters of Kennedy as a wanted criminal.'

Greenfield chuckled. 'Dave, you gotta admit, they're good for jokes.'

'What jokes?'

'Somebody said, "All lawyers are assholes." A Texan spoke up and said, "I take offense!" The other guy said, "Are you a lawyer?" The Texan replied, "No, I'm an asshole."

Washington sat there quietly, but a smile emerged and he began to laugh. 'That's the stupidest joke I've ever heard!'

'Precisely. How about this: Texas occupies all the continent of North America except for a small part set aside for the United States, Canada and Mexico.'

'That's about the size of it.' Washington laughed.

'Here's another: a Texan in the panhandle was struck by lightning, and his wife demanded double indemnity claiming his death was an act of God. The insurance company said it wasn't and the case went all the way to the Supreme Court, which ruled in favor of the insurance company, saying, "Getting hit by lightning is an act of God, but an act of God that happens in Texas is pure accident."

Washington shook his head and finished his beer, as did Greenfield, who kept an eye on the crowd of people gathered in the hotel lobby; probably due to the President's visit. In his gut he felt a foreboding sense of urgency. This Oswald character, for all his peculiar activity was like the eye of a storm. He knew too much for Greenfield to think it was a coincidence, yet, from what he could gather, there was a certain naivety about him—a gun-happy tough-guy who the fixers had exploited, knowing full well how inept he was. Greenfield prayed he was wrong about the whole situation, and it would all disappear like smoke in trees, so that he could go to Paris to be with his family.

Though Washington hadn't met Hume, he knew what he looked like from having observed him from a distance when Greenfield first met him; he recognized him now in the lobby, glad-handing some gentlemen.

'Harley.' Washington indicated, turning his head in Hume's direction.

Greenfield noticed that tan Serratelli cowboy hat, and the way he tipped it up when he engaged in conversation as if he was making a point. Hume barely glanced over and saw Greenfield and Washington, though with a side-grin kept up his banter. Five minutes went by before he finally pushed his way through the crowd, his gait almost pigeon-toed, a bit like John Wayne.

'Well, I'll be: Tom Jones. Fancy meeting you here.' They shook hands, then he looked at Washington who he hadn't met, and seeing he was obviously with Greenfield, without hesitation extended his hand. 'Bob Hume.'

'Dave Washington,' he said, taking his hand.

Hume smiled. 'Now don't take this the wrong way, Mr. Washington, but with a name like that and you being black in here—this is hallowed ol' Texas turf—I could make you front page news!' He broke out laughing spreading his hands. 'Headline: *Washington Comes to Texas.*'

Washington and Greenfield laughed with him.

'You could kickstart my political career, Bob. I'd quit the service and run for Governor!' replied Washington, grinning.

'Jesus, now don't start getting ideas: this is still Texas. They'd scalp me alive like the Comanche. But you're welcome anyhow.'

'Can we take this to the French Room bar?' suggested Greenfield. 'I reserved a table.'

'Sure thing.'

They removed themselves to the more formal, dark paneled bar, and settled in at a corner table. Greenfield ordered some vintage Martell cognac, two doubles, a soda and lime for Washington, and a cheese plate.

'That's what I like about you, Tom, you know how to get down to business,' remarked Hume.

'I figured it out soon enough in this territory; a man must put his best boot forward.'

'We Texans pride ourselves on straight shootin'.'

'That's why I'm counting on you, Bob. Your reputation precedes you as true Texas blue.'

'Texas has always been blue. But some of the fellas are none too happy about Kennedy, and may look to Republican red; the only thing stopping 'em is just that: red. Makes 'em nervous like its Communist or somethin'.

'That's a laugh. With more guns per capita here, there's no need for an army.'

'You got that right!' exclaimed Hume.

The waiter placed their drinks and cheese plate on the table.

'Thanks, Homer,' said Hume to the waiter.

'You're welcome, sir.'

They all took a good sip of their drinks, and ate some cheese.

'Gotta hand it to the French,' commented Hume. 'When it comes to grapes and milk, no one comes close to their sophistication.'

'I think that's why Caesar conquered Gaul,' said Greenfield, 'he just couldn't get enough of it.'

'Even back then?'

'The Greeks were the best winemakers and introduced the Gauls to it well before the Romans. No doubt someone in the Cognac region tried to make some wine with sour white grapes—the local wild grapes—and the wine was atrocious, so they distilled it and discovered cognac, or so the story goes.'

'Well, whoever he was, here's to you.' Hume raised his glass and downed the remainder of his drink. 'Two more,' he said to the waiter.

'What did you find out?' asked Greenfield.

'Not much,' replied Hume. 'The guy's temperamental; claims to be a Marxist. You told me before when they let him back in the country after defecting to Russia. All I have to say is that he's one audacious son-of-a-bitch coming back to Texas. But he is Texan, 'cause he grew up here, though I hate to admit it. I think Amber said he came from New Orleans. She used to talk to him, and said he was nice to her and told her he was related to Robert E. Lee; that's why he was named Lee; ain't that a fact?'

'What did you find out, Bob?' asked Greenfield again.

'I don't get it, Tom; why are you so interested in this loser?'

'He knows people who are a threat to the United States is all I can say, and, like I said before, it's imperative that I find this guy and speak with him as soon as possible.'

'Yeah, yeah, listen, it's a bit sensitive; I need to be able to trust you and have you swear you'll keep this confidence between us here.' He looked at Washington, and back to Greenfield. 'It's personal.'

Both Greenfield and Washington agreed.

'Okay, I know this girl, Amber; she's a hooker, and works for a club owner named Jack Ruby. We're kinda close, you know. Anyway, she tells me all kinds of stuff that goes on, such as who sleeps with who; Ruby's connections to the mob, Chicago and New Orleans, you know. She told me just yesterday—I had tried to see her sooner, but she was on the rag, and wouldn't see me—she told me Oswald had been in the club before and knew Ruby. Finally, she asked Ruby where Oswald worked. Ruby looked at her and said, "Lee? Who wants to know?" She said to him "Lee" owed her some money when she lap-danced for him, but didn't push it as she knew Ruby was his friend.

'It was all bullshit, but Ruby bought it and said, "How much?" "Five dollars," she said. Then he gave her five bucks. But she asked again: "Where does he work?" "Who wants to know?" he repeated. "Jewels," she said—a girl who no longer worked there because she was pregnant—"Jewels? So what?" he exclaimed. Well, I tell you, Amber's a damned good liar and told him, "She's broke and needs the money." He shook his head. "Aw, fuck it," and finally said, "Texas Book Depository. But tell her to leave him alone. He's not worth the trouble. Besides, he's married and has two kids. Now don't bug me; back to work." She went back to work and finished her shift, and we met later. So there you have it.'

'Where's this place?' asked Greenfield.

'Elm and North Houston, near Dealey Plaza.'

'Good. Thank you, Bob,' said Greenfield. 'Now I have another favor to ask of you.'

'Shoot.'

Homer the waiter brought two cognacs, and they consumed more cheese.

When the waiter left, Greenfield continued, 'Don't write or say anything about this, Bob. Keep it to yourself, or you'll find yourself in a shitload of trouble; there're some real bastards out there who *would* scalp you like the Comanche, or worse. Needless to say, if you do, we might have a memory lapse and forget the promise we made to you.'

'Jesus, Tom, that's how I've survived for so long in this business: keeping my mouth shut. News as I see it is mostly a pile of crap that the public gets second-hand, unless it's some sensational event such as Kennedy coming to town. Does this have anything to do with Kennedy?'

'Like I said it's about national security.'

'It seems Dallas is crawling with people of every character; it's like the circus is in town!'

'Well, that's a safe bet that you could write about.'

'I'll think about it.'

'We gotta go,' said Greenfield, knocking back his drink.

He and Washington stood up.

'Help yourself to more French cheese, Bob,' said Washington, smiling.

'I think I will. Nice to meet you fellas; and glad to be of service to Uncle Sam.'

'Take care.'

'You need to buy a hat, Dave,' added Hume. You'd fit in better.'

'When I'm nominated for Guvnor, Bob.'

They had a laugh, shook hands and left Hume with the remaining cheese.

*

Just after three in the afternoon, Greenfield stepped out of his rental car near the corner of Elm on North Houston. He looked across the street at the imposing reddish Romanesque block of a building which housed the Texas Book Depository. The plan was to find Oswald, and if he proved cooperative, take him to a pub for a beer then entice him to open up about what he knew of the odd assortment of characters he had been known to be associated with; and whether there was a plot to kill Kennedy.

Washington would watch the street from the car as a backup in case they needed to bundle Oswald into it, and Greenfield would wait by the building, preferably without being noticed; though, because he didn't know what Oswald looked like, Greenfield would have to have him pointed out. He decided to make a phone call to the Texas Book Depository office from a pay phone down the street.

A woman answered to whom Greenfield posed as George de Mohrenschildt and using an accent asked for Lee Oswald to come outside to see his wife, who was supposedly waiting with their kids. Almost five minutes later, a scrawny, cagey-looking fellow about five foot seven came out of the building, stood on the top of the steps at the entrance, and looked around. Pedestrians walked by and Oswald turned to a man standing near him.

'Mister, did you see a mother with kids here?'

'*Net u menya net,*' replied Greenfield in Russian. No I haven't.

Oswald's eyes bore into him.

'*Chto ty s nimi sdelal?*' What have you done with them?

'*Ne volnuysya; oni v poryadke.*' Don't worry, they're fine.

'*Gde oni?*' Where are they?

Oswald then put his face three inches away from Greenfield's who was amused at this strange fellow, but looked away and signaled for Washington to drive over. Oswald looked as well, but turned back. The car pulled up to the curb.

'*Kto ty?*' Who are you?

'*Tom Dhzons.*' Tom Jones.

'*Konskoye der'mo!*' Horse shit!

Greenfield pulled out his White House identification card. Oswald barely looking at it, spat off the side of the stairs, and was about to go back inside the building. Greenfield anticipating this quickly put him in a headlock and while Oswald tried to extricate himself, he marched him down the stairs to the now waiting car. Washington, already at the back door of the car, opened it, grabbed Oswald by the arms, and shoved him inside with himself after him.

Oswald put up a fight and began punching Washington, while Greenfield shut the door then hopped into the driver's seat and sped off down the street. Oswald was no match for Washington, who blocked the glancing blows with one arm, then punched him once in the solar plexus so hard that Oswald buckled over winded, gasping for air, twisting his head this way and that in a grimace.

'Mr. Oswald,' said Washington calmly, 'we're your friends here. Don't make it so difficult for yourself. We just need to talk.'

'Fuck you!'

Greenfield was smiling into the rearview mirror. He drove around the block and turned into the rail yards where a gravel parking lot extended back to a shaded stockade-type fence just above Elm St. and Dealey Plaza. He shut off the ignition and turned around to face Oswald.

'Lee,' he began, 'are you going to be civil? We don't want to hurt you or anything. We wouldn't have bothered you if it wasn't so urgent.'

Oswald couldn't answer for half a minute. Greenfield waited patiently.

'How did you find me?' he finally wheezed.

'Don't worry about that. I'd be more worried about some of the bad company you keep.'

'I quit all that.'

'What makes you so sure that they've quit you?'

'Are you with them?'

'No, we're on the other side, the good side, and we're trying to avoid a catastrophe. We need to know who your bad friends are and what they've planned here in regards to Kennedy.'

'Well, if you're so smart why don't you figure it out? I did my part.'

'Which was?'

Oswald sat up and with a cynical expression said, 'Worked with those assholes, and pretended like I was one of them. They all hate Kennedy. It's no secret.'

'Do you?'

'No. Kennedy made some mistakes, but I don't hate him. I'm not like them. I'm Marxist. I hate fascists. Who do you work for?'

'Kennedy ... the National Security Adviser.'

'And the monkey beside me?'

'People have treated you badly in life, Lee; I can understand your hate for authority, but you are also responsible for it by your lack of restraint. Dave here's no monkey. He's with the Secret Service.'

'They hire niggers?'

Washington rolled his eyes.

'Dave's a good man,' said Greenfield evenly. 'There's no need for derogatory language here.'

Oswald smiled for a change. 'Well, if you say so.'

'Just tell us what you know, Lee.'

'I know nothin'.'

'After all the time you spent with Banister, Ferrie and this Clay Shaw?'

'Ferrie and Shaw are faggots. There were others pulling strings.'

'I need names.'

'There was one guy, Sam something; he met with Ferrie on a number of occasions.'

'Sam Hollinger?'

'Yeah, that's it. Do you know him?'

'That's an alias. He works with the agency and the military on special assignments.'

'Well, I was never in on his business with Ferrie. I know Shaw knows people in high circles, and could never figure what he wanted with the likes of

Ferrie, other than their appetite for boys.'

'What's going to happen in Dallas, Lee?'

'You mean when Kennedy gets here? How should I know? They never said anything about it, though I knew they were up to something.'

'What?'

'They talked about Marcello and Giancana and how they wanted to take out Kennedy, and how they'd do it.'

'Yes, go on.'

'They'd shoot him. Hire assassins who don't miss.'

'Where?'

'Here in Dallas obviously, though I thought it was crazy because the security would be so tight.'

'Come on, Lee; I need more than that.'

'How would I know more than that? You'd think they'd tell me?'

'Why did they keep you around, then?'

'The company saw to it, and they paid me to do stupid jobs like handing out pamphlets, or moving contraband, show people the town. I worked for a bookie too. You name it.'

'What's your alias?'

'Alek Hidell. They use me like a ghost, putting me here and there. They said it was to protect me and my family.'

'Did you handle guns? Rifles?'

'Yeah, sometimes, but that was a while ago. I own a rifle, but don't use it much. Marina doesn't like it.'

'Your Russian wife.'

'You seem to know all about me.'

'I knew your contact in the FBI.'

'Knew?'

'He was killed.'

'What? My contact isn't dead. I get paid $200 a month; it's been going on since I got back from Russia.'

'Who's your contact?'

'He doesn't tell me his name. I use a post box.'

'How do you know he's FBI? And not the CIA?'

'Does it matter?'

Greenfield had to think about that. If James had been receiving reports from some cut-out who was Oswald's actual contact, it could have been the CIA, which meant they knew all along what James knew. Therefore, if that was true, Oswald was likely a good candidate for a scapegoat. But he had no proof.

'What do you know about Maurice Bishop?'

'Bishop? Never heard of him.'

Greenfield sensed some surprise when he mentioned that name, and thought to trick him.

'I know Bishop. He's CIA. He's your handler, right?'

'Fuck you.'

'Listen, I'm on your side, Lee. Bishop is a liaison with the mob. I'm talking Joe Campisi, Chuckie Nicoletti of the Giancana mafia.'

'You don't know shit.'

'Enlighten me, or I'm taking you in.'

Oswald appeared anxious, with his mouth puckered and head down turning back and forth.

'I don't want trouble; I've got family. Okay, I know Bishop, but that's not his real name; it's Phelps, I think. He's Texan, I know that. He told me to show this guy around town; even out of town so he could do some target practice. I figured he was another gun for hire, "Jimmy", who said Chuckie put him up to it-'

'Chuckie Nicoletti,' interrupted Greenfield. 'Put him up to what?'

'Shoot somebody, obviously. These gangster assholes are always whacking somebody.'

'But why did Bishop have you show this "Jimmy" around?'

'Because I'm their fuckin' gofer, what else?'

'What does "Jimmy" look like?'

'White male, young, about twenty-one.'

'Is Kennedy the target, Lee?' asked Greenfield.

'I told you; I don't know anything about that.'

'I think you do know something about that. Everyone seems to have an axe to grind with the president, and you're in the thick of it.'

'You're not listening, Tom Jones, or whatever your name is; Kennedy has a target on his back. It's no secret. Anyway, these people have to be psycho to do that; still, the agency has to be behind it. Don't you see? The mob's like play-school compared to the CIA. You don't mess with them.'

'Where can we find "Jimmy"?'

'Hell if I know. He moves around. You know how it is.'

'No I don't, Lee. You're the best lead we have.'

'If you say so, but not by choice.'

'I do know this: they're using you, Lee, and you know it. They're setting you up to be their goat, a patsy. My advice to you is to get out of town with your family and go somewhere, anywhere but here. I have a bad feeling about this. I've spent most of my life in the intelligence business, before, during, and after the war, and my instincts were almost always right. Don't go to work tomorrow. I'm serious.'

'You're crazy. From what you say, if I leave town they'll suspect me anyway. The best thing is always to do what you're supposed to do. I work with people there in the book factory. They know me. I'm not running; I've nothing to hide. Besides, it's gotta be a hoax. Why would anyone want to kill Kennedy except maybe a few disgruntled Cubans, Giancana, Marcello and that faggot Ferrie, or Shaw, or Banister for that matter? They wouldn't dare.'

'There've been two plots foiled already: one in Chicago and the other, Miami.'

'What did he expect? Taking on the agency; they own the presidency.'

'It's not that simple: there're different allegiances.'

'Still, they'd never get away with it.'

'Certainly not without powerful people who are untouchable; and they have their own brand of national security concerns and *can* get away with it; believe me.'

'You sound paranoid. If you're so worried tell Kennedy to cancel.'

'I have. Nobody's listening.'

'What does that tell you? Can I go now?'

Greenfield opened his door and got out to open Oswald's door. Washington exited the car as well.

'One more thing,' insisted Greenfield, standing in Oswald's way.

'Make it quick; they'll be missing me at work.'

Greenfield beckoned to Oswald as he walked to the fence. Oswald followed him. They stood there a few moments looking over the fence, watching the cars drive by on Elm Street hidden intermittently by the trees on the grassy knoll.

'Why did you leave Russia?' asked Greenfield.

'I couldn't stand that god-forsaken country.'

'You don't strike me as the religious type.'

'I'm not. There was nothing to do there, no fun at all. The people have been so traumatized by Stalinist Communism, the system can't help itself. They're in perpetual lock-down; I was constantly monitored. Besides, they had no use for me. After I married Marina I wanted to show her freedom.'

'Isn't that anti-thetical to your Marxist ideology?'

'Hell no, with the advent of unionism in the West, we're closer to Marxist socialism than the Soviets. Stalin and Lenin fucked the revolution by murdering everyone including the czar and his family. They're way worse than the czars, and that's saying something. I know Russia—it's a fuckin' tragedy. Read Dr. Zhivago.'

'Pasternak.'

'Yeah, Pasternak, right. Where'd you learn Russian?' asked Oswald.

'I spent a number of years in Russia working out of our embassy.'

'Is that so? Doing what?'

'I handled assets.'

'I wanted to be a spy like that.'

'Aren't you a spy?'

'I get no respect.'

'You need to prove yourself. In order to do that you have to be in control of yourself—don't let them or your emotions control you.'

'I did prove myself. I'm here, right?'

'I'll take your word for it.'

'I like to think of myself as the Rasputin of America.'

'How's that? Rasputin was a corrupt Russian monk, or claimed to be a monk.'

'I read something that struck me in a big way: without sin we have no redemption, and without redemption we can't find salvation. That's why Rasputin fucked a lot of women including the ladies-in-waiting of the Romanov court of St. Petersburg. He saved them and himself at the same time.'

Greenfield smiled at Oswald's simple thinking, or was it an excuse for bad behavior?

'And got himself killed brutally for his efforts.'

'They couldn't kill him. He was poisoned, shot, beaten and lived.'

'Well, I think they threw him dead or half dead into the Nevka River, in

447

winter.'

'Whatever. He made his mark.'

'Take my advice, Lee: leave Dallas after work. Report sick tomorrow, and the next day. Just stay away from here.'

Oswald walked away towards the Texas Book Depository just east of them. Turning around after ten yards, he said, *'V sleduyushchiy raz, kogda vy uvidite Kennedi, peredayte yemu moi nailuchshiye pozhelaniya!'* Next time you see Kennedy, give him my regards! Then he disappeared past the little parkette where a concrete pergola was situated on the Elm Street extension. Washington approached Greenfield.

'What do you think of him, Harley?'

'He's not stupid; he just has no sense whatsoever, a wannabe. We're at a dead end.'

'What can we do? Do you believe him?'

Greenfield looked over the fence through a gap in the trees down the grassy knoll at the road.

'I suppose I do; this Bishop and Jimmy have to be CIA. With multiple plots nothing's been left to chance. All we can do is alert the service and see. I just hope Kennedy rides in the limo with a roof. Places like this are perfect for a sharpshooter.'

'The service will surely have it covered.'

'I don't know; there'll be crowds and a thousand places to cover, buildings and locations like this.'

'According to the paper the other day, the motorcade route comes through here.'

Greenfield sighed. 'This is enemy territory for Kennedy, and I have no doubt someone will be pulling strings with local forces some of which would cover the majority of the route.'

'Are you saying there'll be purposeful lapses of coverage?'

'For its audacity, a conspiracy like this would have had some multilateral interaction, even if different factions don't necessarily know what the others are doing. That's old school black ops. That's not to say a cop on the street knows anything; he just does what he's told from a plan implemented by the mayor and others above him with relative federal services. We're out of the loop here, Dave. Technically, local loyal military assets would be brought in, knowing the risks. But who knows in this case?'

'We've got to caution Kennedy!'

'I've been doing that all along. But we can try again.'

36. Ghosts

He could visualize it all in his mind before it happened: the expectant crowds waving, the police holding traffic, all lined up along the streets, the motorcade approaching the Texas School Book Depository building, turning right onto North Houston from Main Street, then a sharp left turn onto Elm. From all the well-wishers in the crowd one wouldn't know that there was another side to Texas that felt Kennedy was bad for their state and bad for America; certainly the oil barons and many others thought so. In Greenfield's mind a kind of numbness set in.

The day before, after Greenfield and Washington found Oswald, Washington contacted the service; and instead of following through with greater security, such as a limo with a top, they reprimanded him because he was a trainee, telling him to toe the line. The people in charge obviously felt that security was more than adequate, but misjudged the potential threat by a Texas mile. Greenfield made his case as well once again by phoning Marty Cayton that very morning, but had to leave a message with his secretary as neither he nor anyone one else was around.

Everything else seemed to be held in a state of suspension—a disconnection—while events were playing out. Washington reported that Oswald had shown up at work on time, and hadn't seemed the least bit concerned, and he even had a spring to his step. He must have been the cagiest person he had ever met, or the most oblivious.

By all indications, both Greenfield and Washington thought perhaps there was nothing to worry about. They both blended in with the crowds, Washington at the corner of Main and North Houston, and Greenfield at the corner of Elm and North Houston by the Book Depository building. From here Greenfield walked down Elm to have a look at the plaza and fence where he and Oswald had talked the day before. Numerous people were waiting—some with children, others with cameras—on both sides of the street.

One fellow was perched on the pergola holding a small home movie projector ready to roll. Up towards the fence a few people were standing on the grassy knoll: one man in military dress—perhaps a soldier on leave—in the shadows between the trees, another man with a child, and a few others. And behind those people on the knoll on the other side of the fence near the corner of it, Greenfield saw a hatless policeman, at least from the chest up his uniform and badge, standing with another man in civilian clothes, and another with a yellow hard hat. Along the fence quite away farther down stood another individual as well.

Greenfield was somewhat relieved that that place was covered. He then looked up at the sky, a faded blue with slight wispy clouds. Walking back towards the Book Depository, he noticed a few windows opened on the fourth and sixth floors, and immediately he realized that the secret service had been negligent by allowing that; someone was smoking a cigarette on the fourth floor. It worried Greenfield enough that he walked back to the building and was about to enter it, but he stopped when the crowd became louder down the street.

The motorcade of cars, limos and motorbikes had arrived and made the ninety-degree right turn onto North Houston. Anybody in the crowd could have fired a gun at close range and hit Kennedy because the first cars and bikes slowed down to a crawl before the president's limo made the turn. Greenfield looked up that side of the Book Depository building and saw a few more windows being opened by excited employees waiting for the motorcade to pass. Swearing under his breath, Greenfield could see that if someone wanted to kill Kennedy, that location offered an easy shot for a rifleman as the motorcade approached.

Half-expecting a gunshot, he held his breath, but none came, so he walked quickly back towards Dealey Plaza across the Elm Street extension which led to the railyard parking lot, in order to get a closer look at Kennedy, and perhaps exchange greetings with him. Greenfield thought he could still speak to Kennedy at the Dallas Trade Mart luncheon, his next stop. He had made no attempt that morning as Kennedy, with his wife Jackie, surrounded by a phalanx of people, made a short speech on Love field soon after they had landed.

Greenfield had then driven back to the Depository building where Washington was positioned and parked beside it on the Elm Street extension.

By then, the motorcade whisked away the president from the airport and his huge entourage of security, press, mayoral contingent and others. The Kennedys were driven in a limo with Governor Connally and his wife, and Vice-President Johnson travelled in another limo behind more security and police on motorbikes following the president's vehicle.

The advance car, the pilot car and lead car, full of security details, were followed by numerous motorcycles, and made the extreme one hundred and ten degree left turn onto Elm Street. Kennedy's limo, next in line, made the painstakingly slow turn, its length and turning radius cumbersome. Finally, it sped up and Greenfield standing close to the curb just west of the Book Depository, put his hand up, smiling and waving to Kennedy like everyone else there. Kennedy looked at him briefly, but, in the excitement, didn't seem to acknowledge him and quickly looked away at others. Greenfield, unfazed, felt relieved again as the motorcade moved past more quickly and headed towards the railway overpass in the distance and then the entrance ramp onto Stemmons Parkway.

The first shot seemed to echo around the buildings, which was followed by numerous echoes. In those split seconds, Greenfield was stunned as though someone had zapped him with a cattle prod. He saw Kennedy hunch forward with his elbows like wings sticking out, the president appearing to grasp his throat. As the sickening shock of what transpired in that instant seized Greenfield, an eerie moment of intense helplessness shut out all the crowd as if there was a collective hush, an involuntary cry of silence which was then punctuated by another shot louder than the rest, dead-eyed in its power.

Greenfield watched in horror as the side of the president's head snapped back and seemed to split off from his ear, the spray of blood and brains vaporizing in the air, except for some matter missing from her husband's brain which Jackie instinctively turned towards and, on her knees, climbed on the trunk to collect.

Greenfield, in a manic freeze-frame, saw in his field of view people ducking down to avoid the bullets. On the grassy knoll people jumped away from the line of fire and fell to the ground. Traces of gun smoke quickly evaporated from the stockade fence area. The soldier on the ground prostrate, furtively looked behind him. A woman was screaming and pointing towards the fence. A policeman got off his bike and ran up the knoll. The man with the home movie camera still stood on the pergola, his device in hand but lowered.

Greenfield sprinted along the row of trees across from the Elm Street extension, along the sidewalk that led through the pergola to the parking lot. He saw the policeman who had been behind the fence get in a four-door beige Plymouth sedan with a civilian and driver. The car sped down the Elm extension towards Greenfield; and as it passed, the dark-haired policeman stared at Greenfield with intense hard eyes. Greenfield detected the look of a foreigner about him; likely, he thought, one of Garvey's Sicilians. He pulled his gun out, but the car was gone, leaving him in the dust.

Then as he turned back toward the rail yard parking lot, a group of men appeared, holding out identification badges to brave civilians who now converged there from the grassy knoll and Dealey Plaza. The man wearing the yellow hard hat walked in the distance across the parking lot carrying a toolbox towards the tracks. Another man, perhaps the same one he saw farther down the stockade fence, carried something in his long bulky jacket, but got into a burgundy car and drove away. A mantra kept repeating in Greenfield's baffled mind: *They killed him! The bastards killed him right in front of me!* The first of two men approached him, holding his identification in front of him.

'We've got it covered, sir! This is a restricted area!'

'Like hell you have!' Greenfield pointed his gun at the man. 'You just let the shooters go! I saw one in that car!'

'No, sir! Easy now.'

The other man approached. A woman could be heard screaming and being manhandled away by two policemen, who were showing up en masse. Others hesitated as these men brandished their obviously fake security cards. Greenfield prayed that Washington was nearby.

'I'm with National Security,' exclaimed Greenfield. 'Now lay down your weapons or I'll kill every one of you fucking traitors!'

'No need for that. Give us a chance to explain,' the man said.

Before Greenfield could reply he felt a deep searing pain in his right side. He spun around and saw standing there Earl Bunting with a stiletto blade dripping with blood. Immediately Greenfield's legs buckled, he knew the wound had penetrated his liver.

'Bunting. You evil coward of a man.' Greenfield aimed his gun, but the men he had confronted were all over him and easily wrested his gun away from him.

'Told you I owed you one, Harley. And I'm afraid you're going the way of our mutual friend, Johnny Goodnight. Call it poetic justice. Any last words?' Bunting nodded at the two men, who then dragged Greenfield to another car and shoved him in the backseat, where he lay, unable to sit up, his life ebbing away, and his thoughts defaulting to Hannah and Lizbet, looking at him unaware, with innocent smiling faces.

'*Hannah,*' he gasped, before darkness enveloped him.

*

Dave Washington was watching the Texas Book building, where he'd been told by Greenfield to keep an eye on the door to determine whether Oswald remained at work. The motorcade had just passed by and turned onto Elm Street. He was looking at the procession and recognized the president's car as it entered the near hairpin turn onto Elm. Then after an open car of service officers, the vice-president's limo rolled by. Johnson was nowhere to be seen. Then, Washington noticed that he appeared to peep up from a crouching position then drop down again, almost as if he feared for his life from a shooter.

What the hell! Washington murmured to himself. *What does he know?* At that moment, he heard the first shots down in Dealey Plaza, and looking up at the south side of the Texas Book building, saw clearly a gun protruding from the fourth floor window disappear. More shots rang out from down Elm in the Dealey Plaza area.

Outraged, pulling out his gun, Washington ran across the street and hesitated at the front steps of the Texas Book building. Seeing a car come quickly towards him from the Elm Street extension and exiting the rail yard and parking lot, Washington pointed his gun, but the car didn't stop and he jumped out of the way as it turned, and ripped up North Houston. Then looking back towards the parking lot, he recognized Greenfield in the distance and began to run towards him just as someone stepped out of the trees by the pergola and from behind appeared to attack Greenfield, who stumbled and was accosted by two others, before being dragged to a car and pushed in.

Washington's mind raced. Greenfield was now his prime concern. What ever happened to Kennedy was beyond their control. The people who had just abducted Greenfield were no doubt complicit in the conspiracy, so he knew what he had to do.

He turned around and ran to their blue rental sedan parked up the same street. Thankfully, thought Washington, Greenfield had insisted on two sets of keys. He jumped in, started the car and raced after the off-white colored car he had seen leave with Greenfield inside. He knew there was another exit by the rail yard signals office. When he reached North Houston he noticed the car speeding north far away so he followed it, trying not to be conspicuous.

In a matter of seconds, the world had shifted. Greenfield had been right about everything. At times Washington had doubted Greenfield, but he had deferred to his experience and plain decency. Now it was up to him to save his life, if he was still alive. The thought of Greenfield dying on his watch cut him to the core; tears welled in his eyes. Harley was someone he had absolute respect for. What could he do? Ram the car and have it out in a gunfight? He had to be smart.

What would Greenfield do? he wondered. Take them head on fast and efficiently, using any stealth possible. When the car, an Impala, turned into an industrial district area, there was little traffic, so he kept farther back. Washington figured they must have pulled into an industrial lot, which he now drove past; he turned into the next lot, where a derelict one story building stood between the two lots.

Parking the car, he got out, swiftly ran to the building, and tried the door. It was locked, so, with gun in hand he carefully walked the perimeter to a point from where peering around the last corner he could see the Impala. No one was around. Without hesitation, he scrambled in a crouch to the car and looked inside. *Greenfield!* There he was, lying inert in a pool of blood. *God!* He looked dead. Washington looked about and seeing no one, opened the door, reached inside with both hands, and pulled Greenfield outside. Then quietly closed the door and with superhuman effort, hauled him up over his shoulders, double-timed it out of there, around the corner and around the building to his car. *Please stay alive!* he murmured under his breath.

He laid Greenfield out on the backseat, then got in the driver's seat, and drove away in the same direction he had come as not to be seen by the abductors. When the road turned back to the main road, he sped along it towards downtown. *Where's a hospital?* Pulling into the first gas station, he opened his window and yelled at the attendant: '*Where's the nearest hospital*?' The attendant, pointing downtown, said to get off at Harry Hines Boulevard, go west, and he would find it. Washington sped off again.

'Hold on, Harley!' he said out loud.

Leaving the main road at Harry Hines Boulevard, Washington drove in a panic northwest until he finally saw the hospital, and navigated a few streets to get there. But what greeted him was total pandemonium. Crowds of civilians, police, numerous secret service personnel and the press all milled around the ER in a lugubrious choreography; one could almost see the atmosphere of trepidation rising above the commotion. Washington realized that Harley would be held up in the crowd and if his boss's life was in the balance, he'd have to get him in elsewhere. He drove around to the front entrance and pulled Harley out of the car, once again slinging him over his shoulders like a wounded soldier on a battlefield. Somebody opened the door for him; there were crowds of people about but no police.

Inside, he called out urgently: *'Doctor, please!'*

Everyone just seemed to stare at this negro carrying on his back a white man. Finally, a young man in civilian clothes came forward and said, 'I'm an intern, follow me!' and he helped Washington carry Greenfield.

'The emergency room's jammed. The president was shot. What happened?'

'My friend here was stabbed.'

'I can see that on his right side. Looks like in the liver.'

'Where can we take him?'

'There's an intensive care unit on the second floor.'

They took him up on the elevator and rushed down a hall to a room in which a couple of nurses understood immediately what was going on. They prepared the empty ICU room as soon as they had laid him on the bed; the intern then checked for a pulse with his stethoscope.

'There's barely a pulse. He needs blood now. Prepare the IV.'

A nurse set up the IV, and the other nurse and the intern removed Greenfield's jacket and shirt to put immediate pressure on the wound.

'He'd be gone if a main artery had been cut. But I can't promise anything. Get some blood,' he instructed the nurse, who left immediately.

They had hooked Greenfield up to the IV by the time she had returned with two bags of universal O type blood, and quickly connected a bag of blood to the IV.

'How deep is the wound? Did you see the knife?' asked the intern.

'No, I was in the distance. I saw him fall when three guys attacked him.' Washington had to be careful what he said next. There was obviously a complex plot to assassinate Kennedy, and Washington didn't want any of the conspirators to know that he and Greenfield were there in case he was putting Greenfield in further danger.

'Where did this happen?' asked the intern.

'In North Dallas. I don't know exactly. I think he was being robbed.'

'Do you know the victim?' He turned to the nurse. 'Find his wallet; we'll have to report this.'

'No. I was just in the area.'

'Who are you?'

Washington thought fast. 'Jim, Jim Vernon.'

'Thomas Jones,' said the nurse, holding up Greenfield's driver's license.

'Okay.'

The intern kept his stethoscope to Harley's chest. 'He's still alive, barely. Come on, Thomas, I want you to live, so we can hear your story.'

'Can you stop the bleeding?' asked Washington.

'The liver is an incredible organ; it can repair itself rather quickly as the blood coagulates. For now, I'll clean the wound and suture it. With anti-biotics, he'll have a fighting chance. He's lucky to have lived this long.'

'He seems like a tough old guy,' remarked Washington, holding back his emotions.

'He's lucky you found him.'

'I'd like to stay with him if I could.'

'Alright, there's no one else available for now.' The doctor listened again. 'I think his pulse is improving slightly. This guy wants to live.'

'Thank, God,' whispered Washington.

'If you don't mind me asking, Jim, what is a well-dressed negro who doesn't sound like he's from Texas, doing in Texas?'

Washington half expected some further scrutiny of his presence.

'You're right. I'm a pastor from Virginia.'

'Ah, Virginia.'

One of the nurses at this moment returned to the room with tears in her eyes. 'The president is dead,' she cried.

'Oh, my God,' uttered the intern, shocked. 'Who would do such a thing?'

'Evil men,' replied Washington.

'To what purpose? I'm a Texan who thinks he was good for this country.'

'Maybe someone wanted a Texan as President.'

'Johnson?'

'Well, he's president now, or will soon be.'

'Damn, I never liked that man.'

'Well, whoever killed JFK just made a martyr of him.'

'The governor will live,' said the nurse.

'Thank heavens for that,' replied the intern.

'Thank heavens, for you,' added Washington. 'What's your name?'

'Elmer Givens.'

Elmer Givens stitched up Greenfield, who had miraculously stabilized. Washington, still wearing his suit covered in dried blood, stayed for a while longer and told Givens that he would cover all 'Mr. Jones' expenses as they sat motionless saying little, both traumatized by the events of the day. Givens had just been relieved of duty when the arrival of Kennedy turned the hospital upside down. All the senior doctors on duty were involved with Kennedy and Governor Connally, so he had stayed just in case he was needed.

The ICU they now occupied was fortunately well out of the way of the chaos which erupted below, when, apparently Kennedy's body was 'stolen' by security personnel in contravention of Texas law. But nobody was too upset other than the coroner, who'd been shoved aside. The immensity of the crime seemed to have been the ruling factor by which federal authorities took precedence; this was the initial mistake of a botched investigation, or one of them, rather, that superseded proper procedure, thus spawning a cover-up that was endorsed by Supreme Court Justice Warren and Johnson's infamous commission.

'I'm gonna move my car and maybe go and get some fresh clothes, Dr. Givens. I'll be back as soon as I can.'

Washington drove to the hotel and quickly slipped in the hotel's side entrance. He showered and put on a fresh shirt and spare identical suit; then stuffed the bloodied suit in a bag and buried it in the dumpster outside, before cleaning his car of blood and rushing back to the hospital.

*

Early that evening, a faint recollection began to coalesce in his mind. At first he could see it all as if coming through a haze: the expectant crowds calling out *"Mr. President!"* and waving; the police blocking traffic; the sky

458

an opaque blue; the motorcade crawling around the hairpin turn … then numerous shots like echoes, some on top of each other—simultaneous shots from different locations—a triangulation of fire. And he was right there! Anger arose within him. He tried to move but couldn't. A pain came from his side. Then Greenfield remembered.

Washington noticed him stirring. He was alone with him in the ICU. Elmer Givens, the intern, had left for the day and another doctor had taken over patient Thomas Jones of a post box from New York. The local police had been informed of the assault on Jones but were nowhere to be seen, having their hands full no doubt with the assassination.

'Bunting,' mumbled Greenfield, in anguish.

'Harley!' whispered Washington loudly. 'Thank God!'

Greenfield opened his eyes and saw Washington, but he took a moment to focus.

'Dave. You're a sight for sore eyes.'

Washington took Greenfield's hand. 'You're going to be okay. You're Tom Jones here; we're in Parkland Hospital. And I'm a random pastor, Jim Vernon, from Virginia—a Good Samaritan who found you after you were mugged in North Dallas. I thought it best to lie considering the circumstances.'

'You saved my life. I was a goner. That bastard Bunting blind-sided me.'

'Yeah, I saw it from down the street by the Tex Book building. Everything happened in seconds. I followed them to an industrial lot in North Dallas, where they left you for dead in the car. *I* thought you were dead. I carried you to my car unseen while they were still inside the building. I brought you straight here. It was quite the scene. You almost …' Washington shook his head sadly.

'I can imagine. And the president?'

'Dead. Head shot, right temple; another through the neck in front and one in the back; or so I was told by an intern, who heard it from one of the doctors in the ER. It was a kill zone, Harley. No escape. The governor was hit too, but survived, here in this hospital. Kennedy's body's gone, taken by the Secret Service back to Washington.'

'Of course they'd do that.'

'You were right about everything, Boss.'

'And Oswald?'

'He was picked up in a theater, from what I understand, by almost the entire

Dallas police force. Apparently he shot a policeman somewhere—Oakcliff I believe—and the President. On live news Oswald claimed he's "just a patsy" and didn't kill anyone. I bet the poor bastard wished he'd listened to you.'

'Yeah. We were so close, Dave. The bastards were all around us. I saw one of the assassins dressed as a cop by that fence where we stood yesterday. I even saw the gun smoke. I saw Kennedy's head explode. God, the irony. There we were: ground zero, with Oswald, forecasting what would happen. But I doubt he'll live to tell the tale.'

'He's in police custody.'

'They'll get to him.'

'I saw a gunman in the Tex building, south face, fourth floor. That's who probably shot him in the back.'

'It's no use.'

'We could testify.'

'It's a done deal, Dave. Johnson and his ilk will make sure all evidence will be fabricated to implicate Oswald. They'll suppress, ignore or kill all other relevant testimony.'

Greenfield winced as a nurse came in.

'Mr. Jones, glad to see you're back with us. How are you feeling?'

'Not bad, considering. I'm very thankful to Mr. Vernon here. He saved my life.'

'Yes, he must be your savior alright.'

'I could use a little painkiller if possible. My right side feels like a crocodile took a bite out of me.'

'I'll see to it, Mr. Jones. Doctor Forbes is on duty.'

'Dave,' said Greenfield when the nurse had left. 'I need to call Hannah; she'll be very worried, not only because of Kennedy's murder; but because of my trying to prevent a coup d'état.'

Washington looked for a phone in the ICU but there was none, so he went out and spoke to a nurse who said if the doctor permitted it, he could be moved to a room with a phone tomorrow.

'Then you must call for me,' said Greenfield, after Washington returned and explained the situation. 'Find a pen and some paper; I'll write down the number.'

'What should I say about you?' asked Washington.

'Tell her I love her, and miss her and Lizzy badly.'

'And?'

'Tell her … tell her I'm fine but I was attacked and have been admitted to the Parkland Hospital for observation. Tell her I'm sorry I couldn't come to the phone. I'll call tomorrow.'

'She'll ask what's wrong.'

'I don't want her coming here. Tell her that. Say I was knifed, but its non-life-threatening. Don't forget to tell her you saved my life.'

'You would've done the same for me, Boss.'

'Thanks, Dave. I'll never forget it. I really thought I was gone.'

37. The Farm

Prinzenthal was reading in bed when she received the call from the embassy at about ten o'clock that night. When she put the phone down minutes later, she just lay there stunned. All she could see in her mind was Jack Kennedy approaching her in Berlin, daring, gentlemanly, and almost doe-eyed all at once. In reflection, she remembered him as a smart, eloquent, though reckless man, which had been his appeal. Then the image shattered by the recollection that Harley had warned him repeatedly, to no avail.

She got up and turned on the television in the study. News coverage showed no current footage yet, just announcements: Johnson sworn in as president, and a lone gunman—Lee Harvey Oswald—was being held as the alleged assassin. Sickened, she turned it off and went to the window. The streets glistened with rain.

As she opened the window of their apartment and breathed in the damp Parisian air, *Harley*, she thought, *why haven't you called?* It wasn't like him. Suddenly, a sharp wave of nausea swept through her. *Something had happened!* She knew it. *Harley!* Back in bed, she couldn't sleep a wink; her mind was embroiled in fear, her nerves toxic with trepidation. She lay there for hours, until the phone jarred her out of her stupor just after four a.m.

'Yes,' she said, cautiously.

Her heart stopped for an agonizing moment.

'Dave! What happened? Where's Harley?'

Tears came to her eyes.

'Thank God.'

She listened.

'I know. The embassy called; a real tragedy that could've been averted. But Harley's okay, right?' she asked, almost pleading.

Nodding her head, she relaxed a little.

A half minute later she replied, 'I had a terrible premonition. Thank you,

Dave, you're an angel.'

She nodded again.

'I will. Tomorrow evening. Tell him I want him here in Paris as soon as he's fit enough to travel. And you will put him on that plane! Will you do that for me, Dave?'

She listened and then continued.

'You saved his life, Dave. Don't downplay it. I know Harley. I know it was close. Just get him here.'

Silence.

'Thanks, Dave. Tell Harley I love him. And that Lizbet is always asking for her daddy. Thanks ever so much.'

Prinzenthal went back to bed and lay there as if in a waking nightmare. The dark forces had triumphed, but her husband had survived, barely. It seemed there was to be no respite from these forces, no change now that Kennedy was gone. It meant more murder, more war while evil men were running the country.

For some reason, as she was not particularly religious, she began to question her old Judaic gods of prehistory; Enlil and Enki, who, as progenitors in Sumerian mythology engendered the beliefs of the tribe of Abraham—the first Jews; and the supremacy of Yahweh the vengeful God. It's all meaningless, she finally resolved. What lay in store for humanity? What was the cure? Her troubled mind soon descended into the oblivion of sleep.

*

That same day in Montreal, Melbo sat at his desk. About three p.m. in the afternoon, a colleague rushed into the office excitedly exclaiming, 'President Kennedy's been shot in Dallas!' People looked around in disbelief, saying, 'What?' But when the news reels began rolling in, their incredulity turned to utter shock, outrage and a feeling of terrible sadness that the president had indeed been killed, assassinated. 'How can it be?' Then the name of Oswald appeared as if he'd already been tried and convicted.

Melbo watched the pandemonium in the office with cautious dismay. Never the type to get overly excited, he internalized any traumatic event, such as when he'd been told as a boy that his father had been killed in the war. He needed time to process the news and find out exactly what had happened. The first thing he did was go to his boss's office. At the door, he waited a few minutes until his boss, Michel Hartman—called Mike—finished a phone call and waved him in.

'Helluva thing, eh Will?' he asked, putting his feet up on his desk, and invited Melbo to sit in the wooden chair facing his desk.

'Damn it, Mike, a real tragedy; there's only one sure thing I can see from this.'

'What's that?'

'It was a coup d'état.'

'In broad fucking daylight? With Jackie sitting right there! Blood and brains all over her! The bastard who did this has gotta pay!'

'Make that plural, boss, this was no lone gunman one-off. They've already got Oswald at the scene of the apparent shooting; they say he fired three bullets as if it was written in stone; a whole biography ready-made of him as a lone nut, a perfect patsy, just like he said publicly. It smacks of a black ops hit: brazen, shameless, preposterous! The same people that chased me out of the country are involved. I know these people, but I also know the people that were trying to hunt them down.

'Believe it or not, elements of the government, including the CIA, FBI, and military were all involved in this hit. You have to let me go to Washington and cover this: the funeral, the alleged assassin in Dallas, witnesses to the tragedy. This is my turf; I have close contacts who'll know what really happened. Trust me on this.'

'Will, I know, but that's what worries me. Also that the government could be so audacious as to carry this off.'

'The mainstream government is oblivious, but certain people in the government use the government as their cover. The actual people who conspired and carried out the shooting are in no way connected to the government, unless as contractors, but no one will ever know except those on the inside.'

'Still seems far-fetched.'

'The more far-fetched, the better the cover. Don't you see? Believe me, they'll have the mafia, a hundred conspiracy theories; people in law enforcement suppressing important testimony, and witnesses, all competing for attention.'

'My best friend is ex-CIA,' continued Melbo. 'He's the one who advised

Sadie and me to leave the country. People were dying, and we were on the hit list. He and his family are on twenty-four hour watch. His wife and child moved to Paris. I *have* to go to Washington.'

'My mother has an expression she uses in a situation like this,' replied Hartman, lighting a cigarette. '*Ça a pas d'allure!* Ridiculous! What can you possibly do against such an evil, deep-rooted network?'

'We can make a difference. Let it be known there's another side to this: the truth!'

'The truth? An oxymoron is all I've learned to be the 'truth'!'

'At least let me try, Mike. I'll report whatever has to be reported. Just let me go.'

'You told me you met him once, Kennedy.'

'I did in Cape Cod, sailing.'

'Socially?'

'My friend Harley set it up 'accidently'. His wife knew Kennedy from Berlin, 1945.'

'Is this your 'best' friend?'

'I like to think so. We took holidays together, my wife and I with him and his family.'

'He's the ex-CIA guy?'

'Yep, and worked under Kennedy in the White House for national security. I suppose he'll be out of a job now.'

'It might take some time for things to settle down.'

'Likely. But I don't think Johnson would want him around if he was Kennedy's man.'

'Why not?' asked Hartman.

'I think he was planning to quit at the end of the year. Besides Johnson hated Kennedy and all who fell in with him'

'Alright. Just watch your back, Will. If what you say is right about Kennedy's death, Johnson from the sounds of it had everything to gain from it. There were some serious allegations against Johnson according to our Washington correspondent, and he was subpoenaed to testify in congressional hearings.'

'On Monday. Well, that will all be neatly brushed aside now, won't it?'

'Could it really be that bad down there?'

'Yes, I think it runs deeper than anyone imagines,' said Melbo.

'Even Eisenhower felt threatened by the CIA. I remember that final parting speech: the words haunt me still. *'The potential for the disastrous rise of misplaced power exists and will persist.'*

Melbo pondered that before commenting.

'I think one has to look at the big picture,' he said, 'the unprecedented power of America, and the threat of Soviet imperialism, the cold war, as well as the whole alien phenomenon, which they keep from the public as a fanatical priority, a preserve of entitlement to power and control. Kennedy wanted to change the way America does business, and he went up against a brick wall— the deep state right wing elite.

'What we've seen now is that whoever killed Kennedy felt it was in their best interests to get rid of this huge threat to their agenda. He had the people on his side; he was winning the hearts and minds of America. And Kennedy was going to win the election next year, hands down, with Johnson off the ticket. There's no doubt in my mind that they didn't need Johnson anymore to win the South. With Kennedy winning a second term he would've taken back control of the intelligence community tooth and nail, and set the country on a far different course.'

Hartman considered Melbo's analysis, then answered: 'Be careful, Will.'

*

In Washington, Melbo felt that the government was in a state of paralysis. No one had any idea what to do. Most of the cabinet had been away, but they now immediately returned. Johnson, though privately thrilled at his sudden elevation, presented a solemn front to the nation and gave a promise to find out what had happened in Dallas. Later, he set up the Warren Commission, which included even Allen Sulla, but in effect it was an official whitewash shepherded by the FBI and presented to a gullible public. Melbo believed that the insiders of the conspiracy, once they were satisfied with the commission's findings, had adamantly endorsed the inane conclusion of Oswald's guilt, and supported the theory of a 'magic' bullet that had zigged and zagged through Kennedy and Governor Connally, at one point even going backwards.

Oswald, unfortunately, escorted by a phalanx of police and reporters, was subsequently shot in the basement of the Dallas Police Department, by his 'friend' Jack Ruby in an act of 'revenge' just two days after his 'killing' of the president. Oswald had been formally charged under state law with Kennedy's murder and that of Dallas police officer J.D. Tippit. Witnesses later said the killer of Tippit was someone else, as did others in regard to the shot that killed the president from the grassy knoll. Oswald emphatically denied having anything to do with either killings, but he never had a chance to defend himself. His death in Parkland Hospital signaled a *fait accompli,* Oswald being exploited as the most convenient scapegoat.

Melbo was having a difficult time in Washington, because no one knew what was really going on, except for what they gleaned from topical news and announcements such as Johnson proclaiming that the Monday following the assassination was to be a day of national mourning. The funeral procession was to be organized quickly by the military. Melbo reported the proceedings dutifully, though he needed to speak with Greenfield, who was nowhere to be found. He went to his house on Olive Street, but no one was at home.

Undeterred, he decided to call on Nevin James, thinking that the young man might offer some clue about Greenfield's whereabouts. He knew Hannah and Lizbet were in Paris, because there had been an exchange of letters between her and DeCourt via a post box, but he thought he would call her only as a last resort, fearing any surveillance of her might create more problems. However, in correspondence with DeCourt, Hannah made little reference to Greenfield, as his work was classified; she indicated only that he would be joining them before Christmas.

Nevin was at school when the news blared across the nation that the president had been shot and killed. School was dismissed early and everyone rushed home. A massive wave of panic ensued as families huddled before their television sets, crying and thinking that war was imminent; the world was coming to an end. Nevin knew now that his father had likely been a casualty of the same conspiracy—he believed it was a conspiracy—just as the mysterious Mr. Hardin, who had taken over his father's investigation, had hinted.

On Sunday, Muriel, his mom, had gone to church, while Nevin remained at home with Carolyn, who had come home the previous Thursday for the Thanksgiving long weekend. They were watching television and listening to the endless commentary on the assassination, with Nevin getting more and more agitated, when the doorbell rang.

He didn't even move from the sofa, so Carolyn got up to answer it. She came back into the living room to tell him.

'Nevin, there's a William Kane at the door. He says he's a reporter and wonders if you can speak with him.'

Nevin turned gloomily to his sister. 'A reporter for me? Why? I don't want to talk with anyone.'

'He says he knows you.'

'I don't know anybody named Kane.'

'Well, then *you* tell him to go away.'

Carolyn went upstairs. Nevin, with a sigh, pulled himself off the sofa and went to the door. The visitor stood there smiling.

'Mr. Melbo!' exclaimed Nevin. 'Why didn't you say so? Come on in!'

Melbo put his finger to his lips for quiet. 'Call me Will now, Nevin. Will Kane. Good to see you.'

'Will? Okay.'

Once they were comfortably seated at the kitchen table, Melbo explained all that had happened; they spoke of the Kennedy assassination, and the death of his father, and of the intervening years since they had last met. When Carolyn came downstairs she mentioned to Kane that he looked like George Melbo, as she had remembered him delivering his speech at the school years before.

'I do look like George Melbo,' said Melbo. 'I get that all the time.'

'You're joking, right?'

'Well, yes. Just don't tell anyone.'

'Is it because of what our father was working on?' she asked, seriously.

'It's all connected, yes.'

'That means Dad was innocent.'

'Yes he was. One hundred percent.'

'I just had to hear it from someone else.'

'I can tell you this much: the man who did it is dead.'

'How do you know that?'

'I'm not at liberty to say. I have a source and there's an ongoing investigation.'

'So will our father's name be cleared?'

'That I don't know, now that our president's dead, and the bad guys have taken over.'

'The people behind it,' she stated.

'Yes,' said Melbo. 'The same people who, I'm convinced, killed Kennedy.'

'What's happening to this country?' she wondered aloud.

'The short answer is that a few powerful people think they know better than the rest of the people.'

'What's the long answer?'

'It begins with the deception of the people by an insidious power elite, who rationalize this deception by appealing to national security concerns in order to keep us uninformed about their true agenda.'

'Which is?'

'The separation of power: the power of the legitimate government and that of the secret government—a government that doesn't govern per se, just maintains control of the secret, and will do anything to keep that control, including the murdering of the president.'

'What secret?'

'The whole alien phenomenon and its perceived threat to our right to self-determination; as well, there's a huge program to develop the alien's technology and by doing so to preserve our technological superiority on Earth; and to catalogue various alien species, cultures, and our relationship to them.'

'Unlike Nevin, I was always skeptical, until Dad died.'

Their conversation concluded when Melbo suggested to Nevin that they take a drive to see if 'Mr. Hardin' had returned home. Leaving Carolyn, who had work to do, they drove the relatively short distance to Greenfield's rented house and parked down the street. Then they walked up the steps of the house and rang the doorbell. No answer. Discouraged, they were walking back to the car when, suddenly a car came screaming towards them and Nevin and Kane had to leap out of the way to avoid being hit as they crossed the street. The man behind the wheel appeared to be laughing as he sped off.

'Bastard!' exclaimed Nevin. 'Did you see that guy?'

'No. *Asshole!*' Melbo yelled way too late.

'He was laughing!'

'Must've been a drunk,' said Melbo.

'I don't think so. That was intentional. I could tell by his expression. He was evil.'

'Could he have recognized us?'

'Maybe he was waiting for Mr. Hardin too and saw us go up to his house.'

'Could be. I need to make a call. Let's find a payphone.'

At a nearby store Melbo used a payphone to call Ken Helmsley, but there was no answer. Then he tried Dave Washington. No answer. Finally he called Jimbo, who thankfully at home told Melbo to wait for him there at the house. Twenty minutes later he arrived, slowly checking, as he passed, all the cars on the street. When he was satisfied the street was safe, he got out of his car and walking casually by Melbo's rental car, spoke into the open window.

'Stay here, Mel, until I check the house.'

Then, he unlocked the door and went inside the house. About five minutes later, he beckoned to them from the front door.

*

Near colonial Williamsburg, Virginia, the day Kennedy was assassinated, a car drove up to the gates of Camp Peary, a special facility operated by the military which hosted for the CIA a top-secret area known as 'The Farm'. The guard at the gate knew the driver, who showed his identification. In the front passenger seat was Brayden Farnes; the sole occupant of the back seat was an older man wearing glasses. The guard quickly let them pass, recognizing the older man as Allen Sulla, who, stone-faced, looked straight ahead. Sulla didn't emerge from the Farm for a couple of days, and one can only assume what he was doing there, as he was no longer the director, but obviously no one had either the guts or inclination to challenge him, he was so feared by the rank and file of the organization.

Insiders presumed he would be monitoring the situation in Dallas to shut the hatch on any agency involvement in the assassination, and especially to distance the agency from Oswald, who had for a number of years been a bit player in various operations. In fact, what worried them most had been Oswald's attempt to call his contact in Virginia, in order to communicate with his case officer, Maurice Bishop, an action that would tie him to the agency.

Mid-morning that Sunday, Sulla was about to leave The Farm.

'Still no word about Oswald,' declared Farnes, lighting a cigarette.

'I thought you had dealt with that, Brayden,' said Sulla, eyeing Farnes.

'I have, but the problem is that there's the phone record of his call to CI and of what he's been telling the Dallas Police.'

'I'm not concerned about what he says to the police or FBI; we can control that. It's the press we have to worry about. You know what I mean. The agency can't in any way be implicated.'

'Don't worry, sir. It's been taken care of, according to Garvey.'

A phone rang in the office, which had been cleared of unnecessary staff. Farnes picked it up.

'Yeah.'

He listened for a while responding with a 'Yeah' here and there before hanging up.

'Bunting says he thought he saw that Melbo guy snooping around Greenfield's house in Georgetown. He was with a kid.'

'A kid? What kid?'

'A teenager. I'd hazard a guess it was the James boy. Melbo and he became friends apparently according to Woods.'

'And Greenfield?'

'No Greenfield.'

'Where is he?'

'This is the problem.'

'What problem?'

'Apparently, Greenfield saw everything in Dallas and confronted some of the boys with his gun. Bunting came up behind him, stabbed him, then they took him somewhere on the outskirts of town. They thought he was dead—they couldn't feel a pulse—and they went in the building for a few minutes to ease their frayed nerves and get refreshment. Shortly after, they went back to the car planning to get rid of the body, but to their surprise the back seat of the car was empty and Greenfield was nowhere in sight.'

Sulla shook his head. 'Harley was in the wrong place at the wrong time and truthfully he was someone I wish hadn't been hurt.'

'He knows too much, sir; he saw Sarti shoot Kennedy.'

'Sarti?'

'One of the Sicilians.'

'Any others?'

'I don't know.'

'Hands off Greenfield. I'll deal with him. And leave the kid alone.'

'And Melbo?'

'Not now. We have to deal with leaks from the inside, through law enforcement, and media control. Melbo's a wild card, but he's up against

471

Johnson and Hoover now. Let it run its course. No one believes him anyway. We can thank Aubrey for that. Once we have Oswald under control, the rest is easy.'

'I'll tell Garvey to back off.'

'And no sign of Greenfield?'

'None, sir.'

'If they thought he was dead, he must've had help to get away.'

'Either that or he crawled off somewhere to die.'

'If I know Harley, he's alive and I'll be expecting to see him sooner or later. He was one of the best, and so was that wife of his.'

'I understand she's working in the embassy in Paris,' said Farnes.

'Good for her. That's where she ought to be, away from all this madness.'

When the phone rang again, Farnes picked it up, listened and then, smiling, put the receiver back down.

'Oswald's been shot. Looks bad.' Farnes couldn't hide his delight.

'By who?'

'Jack Ruby.'

'Ruby?'

'Born Jacob Rubenstein.'

'What about him?'

'A small-time pimp who owns a club; one of Sam Giancana's people, and Joe Campisi, the local boss, but he has connections to Marcello as well. He's surely covered his ass by shooting Oswald, no doubt about it. No choice; Oswald knew them all and would have talked.'

'Well, thank you, Jacob,' said Sulla, calmly puffing his pipe.

'Indeed. Oswald's handler, David Phelps, had originally arranged for Oswald's demise, but Oswald, the cagey bastard, went to the theater like he'd been tipped off by someone—Greenfield likely. The hitman who was supposed to take him down panicked and shot the cop when he was stopped on a residential street—apparently he resembled Oswald—a total fuck up.'

'It'll all wash if Oswald dies.'

Shortly later, they received news that Oswald had died on the operating table at Parkland Hospital. Sulla was then driven back to Washington.

*

'What were you thinking, Mel?' asked Jimbo, his deep-set, sad eyes staring at him. The three of them were standing in the hallway of Greenfield's house.

'It's Will Kane, now.'

'You still look like Mel to them.'

'I'm sorry, Jimbo,' he said. 'My boss wanted me here. *I* needed to be here.'

'They're looking for Mr. Hardin,' said Nevin. 'Not us.'

Jimbo looked at him sympathetically. 'I assume you're Bill James' son.'

'Yes, sir.'

'It's best we get you home. There's no telling what they're going to do now that they know you're here.'

'Where's Mr. Hardin?' asked Nevin, again.

'His name is Harley Greenfield,' declared Melbo. 'I think we can trust him; don't you?' he added, turning to Jimbo.

'I suppose. I'm real sorry about your dad.'

Nevin nodded. 'Thanks. So where is Mr. Greenfield?

Jimbo smiled at the determination of the lad.

'Harley's in the hospital in Dallas. He was stabbed in a fight just after the assassination. That's all I know about what happened.'

'But he's going to make it?' asked Melbo, concerned.

'Yes, Dave Washington's with him. He found him and took him to the hospital.'

'Must've have been quite a fight,' said Nevin, alarmed. 'I mean, he seemed so tough and wise.'

'No doubt.'

'When will he be coming back?' asked Melbo.

'As soon as he can.'

'Does Hannah know?'

'Yes.'

'Did Dave say anything about the assassination?'

'Just that Harley saw something that's not being reported in the news.'

'Like what?' asked Melbo, uncharacteristically impatient for any information.

'I don't know,' said Jimbo, shaking his head.

Since there was little more to say about the situation, they decided that Jimbo would drive Nevin home, and Melbo, given the circumstances, would remain at the house to wait for Greenfield. The following day, he would attend the funeral with the many thousands of mourners for the late President John F. Kennedy.

38. The House on Q Street

It would be a week before Greenfield made it back to Washington. Melbo was still staying at his house when he arrived home one evening accompanied with Dave Washington. Jimbo came around to help out. Greenfield was in good spirits, though he knew he'd been defeated by the darkness that killed Kennedy. He'd left messages with numerous people including Marty Cayton, explaining that he'd been in an accident but was recovering nicely, and not to worry. He had a bittersweet reunion with Melbo, and they stayed up until midnight talking of the traumatic events in Dallas and those since the Melbos had moved to Canada almost six months ago.

Greenfield asked Melbo to stay on another couple of days, because he felt there might be more information from work that he wanted Melbo to know before he returned to his home in Montreal. Melbo was only too happy to oblige, and called DeCourt from a payphone to explain what he was doing; he had been calling her every day, as she had been worried sick, and she was relieved to hear that Greenfield was recovering well and was returning to his usual good-natured self.

After another day of rest, Greenfield felt well enough to go to the office near the White House. Marty Cayton was happy to see him, but said he was no longer employed there as of the first of December.

'What did Mac say?' asked Greenfield.

'Nothing really. Only that under Johnson, your services were no longer required.'

'Because I'd been proved right,' professed Greenfield. 'No one wants the messenger back after that. Besides, Mac wants to keep his job.'

'Sorry, Harley.'

'Sorry? For me or America? I saw what happened in Dealey Plaza. I was knifed by that rogue agent, Earl Bunting, when I confronted some of his goons who were using fake ID to keep people away when they bravely came around to the place from where the President was shot. Kennedy was shot in the head from behind a stockade fence on that grassy knoll by a guy who looked to be dressed as a cop.'

'That's not what the FBI are saying.'

'Of course it isn't. Hoover is covering it up for Johnson. They're all a bunch of liars, Marty—accessories to murder after the fact. Johnson knew what was coming down and likely so did Hoover. Johnson was seen cowering with his head down between his legs even *before* a shot was fired! When are you going to get that?'

Cayton squirmed a little in his chair behind his desk.

'I don't know how to say this; there's a bigger picture. We must preserve the image of our government. Look, the mob was involved; Oswald was a nutcase; sure there were rogue elements in the CIA because they were working with the mob. We can't let that out. This is a national security issue.'

'You're all wearing blinders. And I'm going to testify to what I saw, and what happened to me.'

'I'd seriously advise against that, Harley. The whole government up to the Supreme Court is behind Oswald's guilt. It's a matter of national honor to bury this thing, this tragedy. Don't you see that?'

'Numerous others saw what happened in Dealey Plaza. We will all testify.'

'Harley, you're not listening! They won't be testifying! You won't be testifying!'

'You really disappoint me, Marty. I thought you were young and bright; one of Kennedy's chosen—you and Bundy. What happened? When did you decide to turn your back on the truth?'

'I'm not turning my back. I'm doing what is best for this country, even if all the facts don't fit together in this terrible event. It's a mess! And we need to fix it! Johnson did just that by establishing the Warren Commission last Friday! What more can we do?'

'You could listen and learn from the people who actually saw what happened.'

'Let the Commission be the judge of that. They will weigh in on all the evidence. Oh, by the way, I almost forgot; there was a message for you to call Brayden Farnes at CI.'

Cayton shuffled through his papers and found the note and number.

'Here.'

Greenfield took it and almost laughed. 'Farnes. The guy's up to here'—Greenfield raised his hand above his head—'in the conspiracy to take out Kennedy.'

'Harley, for your sake, just retire gracefully. Let it go. I'm sure Hannah would wish it.'

'Hannah has fought corrupt regimes most of her life. She's American by choice to escape her past. Do you really think she'd agree with you if a fascist element of our government just murdered its president?'

Greenfield walked out on Cayton and went to clear out his office. After a while he sat down and made the call to Farnes. An assistant answered and told Greenfield to call another number, which he did. The suave unmistakable voice of Allen Sulla came on the line. 'Yes?'

'Greenfield here.'

One half hour later, Greenfield passed through the gate and drove up the long narrow driveway of Sulla's house on Q Street. The property was surrounded by a high redbrick wall with a concrete capstone. He walked up the steps to the entrance and, before he could ring the doorbell, the door was opened by Sulla himself, smiling with the ever-present pipe in his mouth. Without ado, Greenfield was ushered through the main hall and into the living room where a fire burned in the hearth. Sulla went to the antique sideboard that served as a bar and poured two large brandies. Once seated, he thanked Greenfield for coming and for his years of service, offering a toast to both him and Prinzenthal, his "favorite female spy".

'Call me Al, Harley. We're both retired spies with far more behind us than in front. Though, I have to hand it to you for your courage in taking on a young wife at your age. How is Hannah, and child?'

The warm setting and fireside chat was likely pure tradecraft, thought Greenfield, given what he knew about his ex-boss and the recent events. Moreover, his being invited there sent him a clear message that he had touched a nerve in the megalithic intelligence octopus.

'They're well, Al, thank you. I'm anxious to see them and excited to be living in Paris; it's been almost five months since we moved.'

'Grand, just grand.' He relit his pipe and puffed, the sweet smoke permeating the space between them while he gathered his thoughts. 'I can imagine you don't think much of me, Harley; probably as much as you may think I think of you. However, you might be surprised to know I have the highest respect for you, and have always admired your qualities and patriotism. Some of the difficult operations against the Soviet Union would never have been successful without you, and Hannah. Most of your operations managed to evade the attention of that arch-traitor Kim Philby.'

'He was a playboy, not to be trusted, and that was Angleton's folly. Fortunately, Hannah's position in the State Department gave us some immunity; kept us off his radar.'

'I didn't trust him either. As for Angleton, he insulated me, because I protected him.'

'Hannah and I used to think we were just freedom fighters, Al.'

'That you were, and I like to think that's what I am, though on an altogether different level. My job was not only to understand and outwit our enemies but to prepare this country for the future. To plant a seedbed, if you will, that will allow us to reap a great harvest someday. Great powers throughout history have come and gone because of internal chaos and political instability, or cruel and unnatural ideology, as we both experienced in the late war. We've had the fortune of being the first great power with democratically elected leaders, who for the most part have had to balance the urges of economic tyranny with a kinder and more benevolent social order, free from religious repression and political hegemony. We must never let down our guard against totalitarian impulse. We've seen the results.'

'I couldn't agree more.' Harley was in no mood to contradict Sulla.

'Harley, I know it may seem curious that I invited you here, but I have good reasons.'

'I'm glad you did.'

'Right. Jack's death is a tragedy, not just because of the loss of his life for his wife and children, but for this great country. We had no real strategic differences. I'm nowhere near the hardliner that my brother Don was, and fear that our tactics during the Eisenhower administration will be seen as unjustified or just plain wrong when in fact they sent a strong message to the appeasers of socialism. Our actions have promoted a greater opportunity for peace—the control of peace. If we don't control the peace, and let that monkey out of the bag, there will be revolution around the world.'

'So why don't you try to control the revolution?' asked Greenfield. 'Change is necessary. Do it gradually with this power we have.'

Sulla nodded, as if in agreement. 'At some point in the future, the world will be ready for that kind of change. But not now. Kennedy was pushing too hard against the very foundation of our own great experiment in revolution: America.'

'Perhaps not hard enough,' said Greenfield, knocking back his drink. 'And he should've protected himself better. I tried to tell him. He made it easy for the conspirators.' Greenfield finished his drink in one gulp. 'Al, I saw the head shot from that fence on the grassy knoll. I know it wasn't Oswald, but probably a Sicilian contract agent; likely one of Garvey's assets. Or someone named "Jimmy", handled by Maurice Bishop, who also handled Oswald. Yes, I found Oswald the day before the assassination, and he told me. I know he didn't shoot anybody.'

'Damn it, Harley, you're just too good. You know more about it than me.'

'Al, I was knifed in the back by Earl Bunting when I tried to confront the crowd control agents involved. I was left for dead in the back seat of a car, and had it not been for my diligent friend and aide, Dave, who saw what happened to me from the distance and followed them, I'd be buried in an unknown grave out on the *llanuras de Texas*. And Hannah and Lizbet would never have known what had happened to me. Al, I know why Kennedy was killed, and I know that you had a hand in at least initiating the sequence of events down the path that led to his demise. And I understand why you need to cover it up.'

'It's not so cut and dry as that, Harley. The baser elements used by the agency—men like Bunting—are a necessary evil sometimes, as you know. I didn't invite you here to argue the moral ambiguities in the field of intelligence. I invited you here to warn you that to persist down the road you've been travelling will end badly for you and your family. I don't want any harm done to you and I've said as much to your enemies—and believe me, I'm not one of them—but I can't control the murder ball when it starts rolling.

'And I know you're not innocent by any stretch of the imagination when it comes to murder. Let it rest, and all this will go away. I'm talking about the underworld, Harley. Kennedy was a sacrifice that this country will be paying for in a kind of long amortization, if not forever, a martyrdom to redeem the soul of America. The mob is under our thumb and the forces of justice will crush them. Let them take the heat. Not you.'

'All for what? To blame the gangsters?' Greenfield shifted uncomfortably in his high-backed sofa chair, his wound throbbing in his side.

'No, of course not; but to appease the people of this nation.'

'It will never stick, the Oswald cover,' remarked Greenfield.

'You're probably right, but not until long after you and I have departed this world.'

'At which time there'll be a great revelation?' Greenfield asked, grimacing in pain.

'A refill?' asked Sulla, raising his empty glass.

'No thanks, Al. I should be going. I need to pack and make arrangements to break the lease on my house.'

'We can take care of that for you if you want.'

'No, thanks, it's not a problem.'

'Well then, please consider very carefully what I've been trying to say to you.'

Greenfield stood up. Sulla, as well.

'I have already. I'd be a fool to put my family and friends at risk for the likes of Bunting, or whomever.'

'That gladdens my heart.'

'But I have one thing to ask; and if you don't answer me honestly, I could well change my mind.'

'Alright.'

'I know Jack was trying to wrest back control of the CIA. I know that he was very concerned about the hyper-secret regime in regards to the alien programs and its unaccountability to the president and chambers of government. I know that his intention to take back control by possibly revealing to the people information about the aliens was likely the ultimate threat posed against this secret regime. And, I know that had he lived and won re-election, he would have had the power and mandate to carry it off.

'Sure, I know there were other reasons as well—his position on Cuba and Vietnam, for instance. But with the windfall of technological superiority developed from the aliens' technology, you couldn't risk disclosure for fear this technology would ultimately be disseminated among our enemies, thus losing us our advantage.

'Al, I need to hear it from you that there is in place some plan to bring this information to the people; to enlighten this world about the greatest event in the history of humanity and remove it from the clutches of a few men, whose interests contravene the Constitution and the people's right to know. Can you come clean with me on this?'

Sulla's expression never changed. His pipe was in the ashtray. He nodded slightly and smiled.

'Well done, Harley. Checkmate. Does that answer your question?'

Greenfield and Sulla looked each other in the eyes. The acknowledgement was a victory for Greenfield, but a moot one, because he knew he couldn't do anything about it, Sulla being the victor too.

'Partly,' he replied. 'Are they really so advanced we cannot find some common ground?'

'Yes and no. On the yes side, some of these beings—not the ones we know, but those we've been told about—are hundreds of millions of years more advanced, though ironically they apparently don't see us that way in an existential sense, which is a relief as they're not a threat. On the no side, *we* are the threat, an extreme threat, and they will contain us until we are ready, and are no longer a threat, which, as you can guess will take a very long time.'

'Thank you, Al. Just make sure your thugs stay away from my family and friends. You have my word I won't interfere in your investigation, your commission, which, I understand—according to Marty Cayton—you've been asked by Attorney General Robert Kennedy to be a member of... a request, which in itself—you'll excuse me if I find that a little peculiar—is foolish.'

'Robert believes in my expertise apparently. I think he's hoping that he will keep his job. I advised Johnson to do just that. No doubt Robert's putting the country first. Revenge for his brother's death is no doubt part of his plan, but he knows at present he's at a disadvantage.'

Greenfield almost laughed at the highwire antics of these powerful people. Sulla walked him to the door. They shook hands and Greenfield left, but then he turned, halfway down the steps.

'Al, if they subpoena me, I will testify.'

'Of course, you will. I wouldn't lose sleep over it.'

'I won't.'

He turned again and walked to his car.

39. The Girl with the Sun in Her Eyes

The rural highway was jammed with cars, vans and pickups as far as the eye could see. Deep summer in mid-August 1969, on that Friday afternoon, the heatwave could actually be seen rising like a mirage from the road. Thousands of young people and a few older ones marched along, some having ditched their vehicles in fields and lanes along the way, all heading to Max Yasgur's farm in upstate New York, later to be known famously as the Woodstock Music and Art Fair near the village of White Lake, and the town Bethel. Young men and women carrying packs, baskets and bundles, wearing jeans, shorts, summer dresses, t-shirts, and bandanas, some bringing guitars and sundry objects, all moved in a prodigious stream which spread out like an alluvial fan into the hills upon their arrival at the farm.

Nevin James with his pal John and his longtime girlfriend Lucy, after parking their car in a makeshift carpark in a field, managed by an entrepreneurial local about three miles back, walked along in the crowd carrying their packs, and John's guitar. It turned out to be a wise decision, as the gridlock of vehicles near the farm was beyond belief. In one hay field, so many cars were jammed in that no one would be leaving until the show emptied out in three days. The entire municipality and beyond, including the New York freeway, were at a standstill. Governor Rockefeller had wanted to call in the National Guard to disperse the crowds to end the festival, but it was too big even for that and would have caused more chaos. Wisely, he let it run its course.

People were cutting into the trees along a farm lane at the edge of the field, so Nevin and his friends decided to take their chances with it, though they had no idea where it went, but presumed it led to the festival. On their way, Nevin noticed a black Buick Riviera parked in a gap in the trees in a field jammed with innumerable other cars. When the sun shone down on it for a fleeting moment, Nevin couldn't help but see the California plates. He abruptly halted, excused himself, saying he needed to check out the car.

John and Lucy looked on, as Nevin looked in the windows, and walked around it, his hand brushing along the iconic tailfins of the approximately ten-year-old model. Hanging inside from the windshield mirror was an interesting collection of *papier mâché* bobbleheads, including the Buddha, a Beatle, probably John, Jack Kennedy, what appeared to be a flower-child nun, and a scruffy black-bearded hippie with a guitar, presumably Jerry Garcia.

Returning to his friends, he said, 'You're not going to believe this. That's Mollie's car.'

'Really?' said Lucy. 'That's incredible! How can you be sure?'

'For one, it's so Mollie: the bobbleheads hanging from the inside mirror. It's the exact same car, year and model, whitewall tires, but with California plates. There's also a Stanford sticker on the rear bumper, and she went to Stanford.'

'What an amazing coincidence,' uttered John. 'The stars have lined up for you.'

'I wouldn't go that far. Coincidence, yes, but finding her in this sea of people's another thing.'

Well behind the grandstand, near a lake they found a decent location for a campsite in a copse of trees, where they pitched their tents. The music had yet to begin, so they went for a swim, naked, and most people there were of the same mind. John had brought an ounce of black hash which they shared generously with other campers; then they took a walk around the grounds. The venue was perfect: the stage was positioned in the middle of a huge field which provided a gigantic amphitheater allowing everyone to easily see the performances on the stage.

After they had eaten hotdogs and coleslaw, filled their water canteens at a communal tank, and listened to the numerous amateur musicians in the crowd, they settled in for a long night. Everyone was high, and laughing, the spirit almost surreal with excitement. Countless thousands of people dotted the hillside moving to and fro everywhere. Finally, the show began late in the afternoon, when Richie Havens took to the stage. Nevin and friends remained until two in the morning after Joan Baez's show. Then following a surprisingly good sleep, they watched Santana the next afternoon, and a number of other bands.

Nevin, though, was finding the insane crowds a bit much. He liked solitude and quiet, but went along with the extreme conviviality, as if it were some kind of spiritual awakening to a new world and because of his belief that Mollie was out there somewhere. One woman was heard yelling: 'We're taking over the world!' About that time, Nevin found himself separated from John and Lucy, so he went back to his tent and took a breather. John and Lucy showed up in the evening with a half dozen people from Colorado, and they shared what food and water they had. Nevin started a fire and boiled some water from the lake in a small pot he had brought to make tea. After cooling, it became the communal cup, which they passed around.

Later that night, when somebody said the Grateful Dead were to play soon, a bunch of them wandered off, Nevin joining John and Lucy, who were also keen to go. It was very dark as the overcast skies didn't offer any light, and the few lights set up at various stations were inadequate. Only being closer to the stage could one see much of anything. Nevin thought it total madness; but being high on hashish, he made his way nearer the stage, where the band was setting up. John and Lucy disappeared again, having found some people John had jammed with during the day.

When the Dead began their set with the California hippie rock-lullaby, *St. Stephen*, numerous people began to dance almost ecstatically their arms, heads and hair, weaving in and out of the encompassing darkness. Nevin didn't know the music that well, but he was impressed with the laid back intensity of the song. He found the lyrics sung by the band together and especially those sung by the lead guitar-playing black-bearded fellow, Jerry Garcia, most intriguing:

'*Saint Stephen with a rose,*
In and out of the garden he goes,
Country garden in the wind and the rain,
Wherever he goes the people all complain...'

He knew that they were one of the psychedelic bands from the San Francisco area. Standing by a seventy-foot high speaker tower, with which other towers amplified the sound across the hills, Nevin, on an impulse to get a better view, decided to climb up to the first level of horizontal ties about ten feet off the ground. Looking about, he stared in awe at the scene before him. The music, the masses were all as if woven into one giant fantasy fabric. He gazed towards the band and lights of the stage watching people dancing rapturously.

Then he saw her. He noticed the way she danced, the way she moved; he'd know those hips anywhere. Stunned, he could scarcely believe she was just over there, here at Woodstock, after six years of estrangement. A few letters here and there were all somehow deficient in terms of bringing closure to their intense relationship before and after the terrible event that divided them, perhaps forever. Here was a chance to resolve themselves one way or another. He watched her and a few other young men and women dance.

They seemed to know each other, but that was pure speculation given the atmosphere of love and euphoria. Inertia pervaded his being, fearful that his presence would bring back the pain of their profound loss. How different she must be. Her brown hair looked the same though longer and loose now with what appeared to be red streamers partially braided that flailed about with her exotic movements. She was thinner as well, which was surprising; tanned, visibly braless, in bare feet, she wore a natural linen summer smock dress with colorful embroidery, tied at the waist with what appeared to be a slim woven wampum belt, a true flower child. But it was her face that shone like the sun, even in the weak light.

Finding the courage to approach her from at least a hundred feet away, he cautiously climbed down the tower, stepped and worked his way through the crowd. When he was within thirty feet, as if by some strange prescience, she turned in his direction and looked straight at him through the people. Her expression didn't change and her bodily movements continued. *She doesn't recognize me*, thought Nevin.

Then she stopped and stood there without taking her eyes off him as he approached her. The sunny face went kind of sunny-sad, as if unsure who she was seeing, but suddenly she smiled contagiously, emitting a shriek, and ran to him all but hitting him with a desperate embracing hug. The music flowed around them as if together they were a boulder in a river. She held his face and looked rapturously in his eyes, as he looked in hers, noticing how dilated they were. She was really tripping on some psychedelic.

'Nevin!' Nevin!' she cried almost traumatically, her eyes like orbs of love.

He must've seemed like a ghost to her. He could feel her body, and the electric urge, so long forgotten. *'Mollie! It's a miracle!'* he exclaimed. *'I saw your car! I knew you were here!'*

With the music so loud, there was little they could say in the moment, in this sea of madness. Mollie led him back to where she had been dancing, as she was not about to leave her friends, who Nevin realized, were a group of West Coast hippies she had likely come East with. One young man in particular looked at him intently, not unfriendly, even a bit in awe, but a little anxiously; or maybe it was the drugs. When she told her friends who he was— *'It's Nevin! It's Nevin! It's Nevin!'*—she kept repeating excitedly.

They all seemed to treat him like a specter from a fabled past; and gathered around him as if he were some apostle, even touching him with a reverence that Mollie must have inspired in them from some telling of their youth. Nevin appeared to them as not just tall, unshaven, slim, handsome and dressed in jeans, sandals, a *Disraeli Gears Cream* t-shirt, but oh so cool and intelligent with an amazing aura, lustrous in his blue eyes, light skin; his long, dark brown hair reaching his shoulders.

Mollie, in fact, had talked a lot about him, perhaps to purge herself of him; yet at the same time she had endowed him with a mythical status. Nevin felt awkward, and thought he was imposing on this traveling clique from the West coast. They were all so high; and he didn't want to interrupt their magical celebration. But he had to stay. He had to know whether he and Mollie could still find a way to heal their relationship. He danced with them and relaxed a bit as she brought out his old mojo.

She introduced him to 'Pedro', the young man, who Nevin suspected was her boyfriend, though Mollie and Pedro seemed to have an understanding of their situation. Free love came to Nevin's mind, which didn't altogether sit well with him, because he realized Mollie had developed into a woman far different from the girl he had known as a teenager. She had grown up in quite different ways than him, as if she were adopting a new culture. On one hand he was happy for her and accepted her, loved her; on the other, he didn't really know her anymore.

The Grateful Dead's performance was delayed again and abruptly ended when an electrical problem manifested sparks—likely due to the rain that had fallen earlier—threatening the safety of band members. There seemed to be an obviously drug-induced discombobulation going on as band and crew attempted to fix the electrical issues putting a kibosh on the gig at least temporarily. Mollie went to Pedro, who gave her something as they parted with a hug and kiss.

Nevin stood bemused, feeling a bit frazzled under the circumstances, when

Mollie came to him smiling beatifically, taking him by the hand to lead him away. They said little as Nevin soon took the lead and they meandered through the throngs of young people who were sitting, standing, hugging, smoking, toking, even making love, some with onlookers happily cheering.

Finally, they reached Nevin's campsite which was relatively quiet and empty. Nevin fetched a battery-powered lamp hanging on John's tent nearby and placed it on the tent pole at the entrance of his tent. Mollie was strangely quiet. The intensity of her psychotropic high, together with the miraculous appearance of a ghost from her past in the live form of Nevin, had her trembling slightly. She put something in her mouth and immediately kissed Nevin, her tongue flashing in his mouth. He felt the tab released to his tongue and swallowed it. They came up for air. Feeling his erection against her through his pants, she put her hand on it and giggled just as she used to do. Nevin tried to contain his bursting emotions for her, his pent up caution giving way to her loving gesture.

'Not now,' she purred, holding him with her head on his shoulder. 'There's no rush.'

'My long deprived friend down there begs to differ.'

'In a way I feel the same, babe. I'm wet for you, but I want you to feel what I'm feeling.'

'I think I am.'

'Not quite.'

'What did you just give me?'

'A little sunshine. A helper to bring our constellations back in sync.'

'LSD.'

'Orange Sunshine, yes; have you been experienced?'

'Not yet.'

'Mmmm, my Nevin. Just like in the church basement.'

They both laughed as they undressed each other. It felt as natural as it had always been. A sprinkle of rain blessed them while they continued to kiss and hug and talk and reminisce about all those wonderful times they had had, though they deftly avoided the murder of their parents. It didn't really occur to them to think about it; the spirit of the festival and their reunion seemed to completely rout the evil in the world.

Now inside the tent, wrapped around each other, aching to make love, Mollie still resisted until Nevin began to feel a rush in his mind and body opening up what he felt to be a percipience of immaculate perception. Looking into her eyes became almost unbearable; the emotional intensity was so acute. Her eyes searched his and she knew he was almost there. And when tears welled up in both of them, she stroked gently his erect member, as he caressed her dewy plum, kissing and suckling ears, nose, nipples; each other abandoned to passion.

They would stop and gaze again into each other's eyes at once familiar and feeling a thousand loves past and present, then seeming strange like an alien from a distance solar system, but experiencing all as relative in a universal sense of consciousness. When they were eventually joined—*au faire l'amour*—a deep overwhelming penetration so suffused them that they came almost instantly like a monstrous synchronic supernova.

The lysergic acid now fully irradiating, had the effect of prolonging their orgasm, which had them trembling and twisting and holding on to each other so tightly that it seemed life itself depended on it. Even in the afterglow, it felt like a fusion reactor about to combust again at any moment while they remained still cauterized to each other, her legs wrapped about him.

They found time to speak about almost everything. Nevin had graduated from Yale with honors, and Mollie from Stanford. Nevin was to begin his second year of law school, also at Yale. Mollie had been accepted by the Stanford University School of Medicine to go eventually into forensic psychiatry, which would begin in the following weeks. She had taken a year off, working and following the Grateful Dead on tour. They talked about the recent moon landing both reciting together Neil Armstrong's famous pronouncement: *One small step for man, one giant leap for mankind!*

Mollie explained that she loved her new life on the West Coast with its free thinking spirit, and told Nevin she would never move back East, which remained dark for her. She confessed that she had had a really hard time adjusting to the idea of another relationship, but she had tried and made some great friends, including Pedro, whose real name was Hugh Morris. They'd been close for a couple of years, and though they had had sex, she admitted that they were better just as friends. She had never mentioned him in the few letters she and Nevin had exchanged, the last being well over a year ago.

Nevin had also had a few close friendships, but just couldn't commit. He spoke of an emptiness that only Mollie could fill, and Mollie felt the same. This emptiness had led to some wild experimentation for Mollie in the form of drugs and multiple sex partners and even an orgy where she made love to another girl. Nevin took it all in but realized that whatever beauty they had had as a couple and best friends, albeit distant, their lives would continue on much as they had been before this miraculous rendezvous. What was happening between them now was, more than anything, a closure, but the kind of closure that left the wounds of the past more or less healed and the path to the future open and welcoming.

They really did have a special love, and how lucky they were to have grown up together and to have *come-of-age* together. They laughed when Nevin used that phrase. And so it went for much of the night, until sleep proved a more potent medication.

Late Sunday morning, they emerged for a swim; then they had another reunion of sorts with John and Lucy, and the four of them got together with Mollie's friends and watched more music performances. Later that day, there was a terrific thunder and lightning storm which had them hiding under a tarp. Nevin and Mollie stayed outside, preferring to get drenched and witness the carnage of torrential rain on the squirming masses, sheets and sheets of it turning the already wet fields into a swamp.

Perhaps it was the thunder and lightning that triggered memories of their last time together before the tragedy; Mollie became melancholy and wanted to go back to Nevin's tent where they expiated *in extremis* any vestige of pain through another night of psychotropically obsessive lovemaking. This time closure was absolute.

Hours later, John and Lucy happened by and coaxed them out to watch a new band, Crosby, Stills, Nash and Young, that were to begin to play. Though three in the morning, Nevin and Mollie rallied for the set, and were glad they did, as the band seemed to catch perfectly the spirit of the festival and times. An hour after the end of the set, Nevin and Mollie crashed in his tent exhausted, but got up in the morning to go for a swim and refresh themselves. Not surprisingly, by early Monday morning, most of the crowd had dispersed. Finding Mollie's friends up on the hill, they all sat in on the performance of Jimi Hendrix, the last act of the Woodstock Art and Music Fair.

Maybe it was the down-side of the residual effect of all the drugs—a pervasive return to reality—or the habitual memory of their past harmony now reunited, but when Jimi played his extraordinarily psychedelic instrumental of the *Star Spangled Banner*, Nevin and Mollie, sitting with their arms wrapped about each other, were at first in awe, and then as Hendrix went surreal with the familiar notes of the anthem plummeting into war-like chaos and star-spangled destruction, tears welled up in both of them spontaneously.

They cried silently for their parents, for their country, for the war in Vietnam, for the Kennedys and Martin Luther King, and above all for themselves. They knew their love was eternal, but also inconceivably terminal. It went unsaid. The miraculous reunion, their final consummation of unimaginable ecstasy—a kind of communion with the blessing of God—was in the end their spiritual epitaph. In that moment they were liberated and united in their new personas with all the love in the world. Holding on to each other, they stayed together, saying little until they departed. Their friends, including the cuckolded Pedro, however understanding, kept their distance witnessing the couple's divine saga in a mystical choreography, yet their pain in an ineluctable farewell.

After Woodstock, Mollie and Nevin parted ways in a kind of stunned silence, having no idea whether they would ever see each other again. For weeks they resonated in each other but were hesitant to connect which otherwise might ruin what magical beauty they had salvaged from calamity. It was Mollie, however, who would carry the consequences of their reunion. She'd been off the pill for a year and within a month as she began Medical School, she knew it was her cross to bear. And bear it she did as the perfect illumination of love and rehabilitation.

40. Dénouement

Ocean spray glittered in the sun as the *Hannah Lizbet* drove through the swells of the Caribbean Sea near St. Barthélemy having almost completed the loop from St. Barthélemy around St. Martin and Anguilla and back.

Greenfield, long retired, loved to sit at the helm of their yacht, himself as much an element as the sea and sky. His expression was always the same—neither happy nor sad accepting the vicissitudes of life—a kind of self-effacement, but one infused with contentment and appreciation. Throughout his life, his struggles, his battles, were all for this. He was a gracious survivor in spite of a world gone wrong and his attempts to make a difference. At eighty-two, he was long past caring about the near-misses and regrets that he could have done better or about feeling guilty for having killed to protect his wife and family.

He had killed evil men both during and after the war and didn't give them a second thought. The last time, twenty years ago, with the help of Jimbo, he had tracked Bunting to West Palm Beach, where he then made his home. It was in the fall of 1964 that Prinzenthal's friend Penny Poirot Beyer was murdered on the Chesapeake and Ohio canal towpath where she used to walk shot in the head and heart. Had she been asked to testify at the Warren Commission, she would have blown the report to smithereens because she knew why Kennedy had been murdered, and she had confided to others that she was very scared.

Greenfield and Jimbo surprised Bunting at his place and threatened to kill him unless he confessed to his involvement in Kennedy's assassination and Penny Beyer's murder. Bunting admitted but said he had never killed anybody, as others did that. Fearing for his life, he tried to escape through the bathroom window, which gave Greenfield an excuse to kill him in a fight, stabbing him in the heart with the same knife Bunting had used with the intent to kill Greenfield in Dallas that terrible day a year earlier. There was no civic law for

Bunting, or for Greenfield. It was kill or be killed. They fought the battle that few knew about: in the shadows of the secret world.

Prinzenthal still worked in the State Department, having spent seventeen years in Paris, living for five years in a three bedroom apartment on the Place de la Madeleine, a nine minute walk from the Embassy; then, for the remaining twelve years, living in the suburb of Garches west of the Bois de Boulogne, where she and Greenfield bought a house with a garden. They sold their house in St. Croix in 1973, when they decided to buy a large vacant lot in St. Barthélemy, a French *department* in the Caribbean and relatively undeveloped; there they built a lovely house with a pool high up into the hillside offering spectacular views of the sea between Gouverneur Beach and the harbor town of Gustavia, where they moored their yacht.

Life was truly blessed. Lizbet grew into a beautiful girl with big blue-green eyes like her father's; she had thick, light auburn hair, and was slim and sensual, like her mother; and her face blended well both parent's features. Yet she clearly projected the mindful determination of her father, always taking interest in things her parents were sometimes at a loss to completely understand, and wisely using the time and space she was granted to develop her inclinations, such as astronomy—and it's appendage astrology—ancient and modern history, karate, skiing and an obsessive love of the music of her favorite chanteuse, Joni Mitchell.

Hugely intelligent, she took to linguistics as second nature: whereas her mother was a polyglot mainly because of the circumstances of her early life, Lizbet was a natural genius, keeping to herself, who like a sponge, absorbed everything around her, including her parents' mysterious past. She grew up speaking French, English, Russian, Yiddish, Polish, and Hebrew thanks to her mom, and later, she studied and mastered languages at the Sorbonne: Italian, Spanish, German, Dutch, Arabic, Turk, and even Chinese with generous smatterings of a dozen other languages, including the Nordics, even Latin and Greek.

Wise beyond her years, she had made interesting friendships through connections at the Embassy, kids from all around the world though she had few really close friends.

With the Melbos—she would always insist on speaking to Mel about aliens—she had met Nevin on a number of occasions, the first time when she was four. On one visit, while he attended law school, he announced he'd taken up skiing because a girl he dated was on the Yale ski team; this, which then impelled Lizbet, at eight, to do the same, and she immediately joined a school extracurricular ski group, which organized supervised trips to the Alps.

From an early age, Lizbet had been impressed by Nevin, even telling him in her inimitable way when she was ten that they should marry. Nevin, of course, would play along with her childish notions, to the amusement of her parents; but when she was an undergrad at the Sorbonne and Nevin brought with him on a visit a colleague, named Cheryl, a hurt Lizbet refused to speak English, only French, Yiddish and Chinese, or any other of the numerous languages in her repertoire, and played loudly from her room over and over ad nauseum, the song *Blue* by Joni Mitchell.

At the time, Nevin was a junior lawyer with the Office of the General Counsel of the CIA, as was Cheryl. But Cheryl didn't ski, or feel amity for Lizbet, or Joni Mitchell, who together made her feel inadequate and threatened by Lizbet's obvious love for Nevin. For his part, Nevin felt like he was in the doghouse; when Cheryl left him eventually, he realized why he felt so depressed: Lizbet, at twenty-one, was constantly on his mind.

She was now a graduate and working on her master's degree at her mother's alma mater, New York's Columbia University School of International and Public Affairs. Her mom was now working in a senior position at the United Nations, and the family were living off Central Park in their old apartment, which they had never sold, but leased for many years. Nevin was extremely nervous when he called Lizbet one evening from his old house in Washington; and fearing he'd ruined their friendship and expecting rejection, he had to call three times, hanging up each time before dialing the last number.

He realized she was a woman now, independent, smarter than he was, which altogether frightened him, not because of her qualities so much—she was amazing in every way—but because his past with Mollie and the memory of their intensely sexual relationship made him feel guilty and unworthy somehow, not to mention the almost fifteen year age difference between him and Lizbet. Little did he know at the time that Lizbet, after suffering because of Cheryl, was feeling inadequate and inexperienced herself.

She had lost her virginity with a French boy her age she had known at the Sorbonne, and even dated him on and off for a year, before she felt guilty about enjoying the sex more than being with him and quit the relationship, saying she would be moving to New York. And if that wasn't enough, she then let herself be seduced by a fifty-year-old divorced diplomat of Dutch-Indonesian ancestry from the Netherlands who loved her so madly he almost succumbed to drinking himself to death from alcohol poisoning and hospitalized, when she rejected outright his marriage proposals.

This had had a terrible effect on her young conscience, making herself feel that she'd used men for her pleasure, not realizing the effect she had over them, when in reality she just wanted Nevin to see her as a woman worthy of him. Nevin finally got up the nerve to call and speak to her, not Harley, whom he usually called because over the years Harley had become like a surrogate father to him. That time she answered. Tentatively, at first, then naturally as they had been good friends, both knew in their hearts they were *prêt à aimer*, if it were not already declared by virtue of the phone call itself. And deep love soon made up in a big way for any misapprehensions.

After a few visits to New York, and formally making his intentions known to Harley and Hannah, who were much relieved for their daughter's sake, Nevin took her skiing to Mont St. Anne near Quebec City on her twenty-second birthday, where it got so cold and windy one day they had only five runs then retreated back to bed in their room with a view of the St. Lawrence river in the grand Chateau Frontenac perched on the cliff of the Plains of Abraham in Quebec City.

They were married on her twenty-third birthday in St. Barthélemy officiated by a French Rabbi friend, Raymond Ben David, who Hannah had known for many years in Paris. With the Greenfields paying his fare and putting him up in a local resort, he was only too happy to go on a holiday and perform the ceremony; Hannah had sought him out after the Kennedy assassination and her husband's near death, to commiserate with her, though she lacked faith in God, more out of a fealty to her Jewish family, of whom she was the last, aside from her daughter.

Speaking Yiddish, he told her that it was enough that she had come to him, and not to dwell in guilt, because through guilt there was no salvation, and that God did not dispense judgement in a court of law, but was the force within each of us with which we made a covenant through the ideals of love and happiness. The world was cruel to Jews, he said, and others, but that just made us stronger. He even confided in her his own doubts of God's grand plan, but concluded that it wasn't made on Earth.

After that, Hannah would go faithfully with Lizbet to his *shul* about twice a year, usually at Passover, when she lit candles for her parents and family, specifically Lizbet Ephrussi, her dear cousin.

At Lizbet's wedding, extended family and friends totaling almost a hundred people congregated at their property, where the ceremony took place on the lawn among the gardens with the view of the magnificent blue sea. Lizbet even wore her mother's wedding dress, beaming in perfect happiness under the exotically floral chuppah, when Nevin raised the veil. After a ten-day skiing honeymoon in Val d'Isère after ten days in Saint Barthélemy, they settled in Washington in the old James' house. Carolyn, a doctor, had moved to White Plains, New York where her husband owned a modest investment business.

Muriel, their mother, had remarried, this time to a younger developer, and moved to Wilmington, North Carolina. Lizbet had to make some adjustment moving from Paris and New York, but made a good fit in Washington. She was a shoo-in for a position as a junior analyst with the CIA and quickly secured the respect of her superiors, some of whom had known of her mother's exploits in the bad old days of the Cold War. The company had evolved somewhat since the Kennedy years, the rogue elements, though endemic, were apparently not so predisposed to personal agendas when they were cut loose from their masters.

Now almost a year later and five and a half months pregnant, Lizbet sat beside her father at the helm. Hannah and Nevin were sitting comfortably behind them on the refitted tan-cushioned U-shaped bench seat.

'Any thoughts on a name for the baby, honey?' asked Hannah, breaking the silence above the sail and surf.

'Perhaps,' she teased. 'Should we tell them, Nevin?'

'There's nothing classified about it, Liz.'

'Are you kidding? Of course there is with old company spies as parents.'

They all had a laugh.

'We've decided that if it's a boy, Nevin will name him; if a girl, I'll name her.' Lizbet turned around to face her mother.

'William David,' said Harley. 'If it's a boy, after his dad, and Hannah's.'

'Yup,' said Nevin, with a chuckle.

'Papa!' exclaimed Lizbet, turning back to her father. '*Comment as-tu deviné?* How did you know?'

'I know these things,' he replied, smiling. 'An occupational habit.'

'Okay, then tell me what I'll name her if a girl?' asked Lizbet saucily.

'Something different.'

'That's not a name, Papa,' she said, reprovingly.

'No. But I know you will come up with a surprise.'

'Well, you're right about that.'

'I'm dying to hear it,' said Hannah.

'Tell them, Nevin.'

'No babe, that's your department.'

'They're going to think I'm crazy.'

'No dear, we know you're crazy,' joked Hannah.

'Okay, you asked for it: Marie.'

'Marie?'

'Yes, after Mary McBride, but in French.'

'Mollie?' asked Hannah, a little surprised.

'Yes. Because I think she's wonderful, and lost her mother with Nevin's dad; but mostly because I felt a need to acknowledge her huge relevance in our lives.'

'I think that's so very considerate, honey, but I'm not sure what you mean.'

'Think about it: if that terrible thing hadn't happened to Nevin's dad, and Mollie's mom, they would've probably married, and I'd never have known Nevin. Furthermore, I did an analysis of them astrologically. My God, I've never seen anything like it! No one, but me, and of course, Nevin and Mollie, could possibly understand how intense it was for them: just beautiful, tragic and crazy. I did a composite on them; the midpoints … Venus and Mars in an exact conjunction squaring Pluto in the Twelfth House! Deep, so deep!

'Oh, there's no point in explaining; you have to take my word for it, but they would never have made it long term; they would've self-combusted eventually; they didn't stand a chance. In spite of the horrible circumstances, they were given a chance to be really happy with new lives. I feel that if there's a God looking out for us, he was truly looking out for them, and I was part of *Its* arithmetic—I was sent to Nevin. The provenance here is fascinating and naming our child Marie gives me some kind of *dénouement*—a controlling of the narrative, yet being a part of it.'

'That's quite the forensic examination, honey,' said Hannah. 'Nevin, you have my sincerest praise for loving this rare seabird. Since we're talking about it, have you heard anything about Mollie?'

'Not since her letter congratulating me and Liz on getting married. Carolyn told me a while ago that she ran into her in San Francisco at a medical conference, and they actually had a wonderful dinner together. I know now that she has a fourteen-year-old daughter, Deborah, and an eleven-year-old son, Hugo—though she never married, and that she's a psychiatrist, specializing in women's issues. She's happy and living with someone, Dan, a jazz musician—not the father of her kids who apparently died whitewater rafting after the birth of their son. They live north of the city with a view of the ocean.'

'Sounds perfect. Sorry to hear about the father.'

'Yeah. But she's a survivor, an idealist, who found her niche. I'm happy for her.'

'When was the last time you saw her?'

'Woodstock, 1969, by chance after six years apart. It was like a miracle finding her in that sea of people and drugs. But I suppose in a way we had to meet. Liz is right: we needed that closure to move on and put our past behind us, like a divorce in a weird way.'

Nevin remembered what happened between them at Woodstock and felt like a bug under a microscope of his mother-in-law; he knew she knew what must've happened. But he also knew she just wanted to understand his past better, and there was no harm in it. He had never opened up about it to anyone but Lizbet, and not completely, for obvious reasons.

'I'm not trying to bring up old hurts, dear,' said Hannah, sensing his discomfort. 'For myself, I had to overcome such extreme anxiety about my past that without Harley I don't know if I could ever have been happy. I'm so very proud and delighted you're my son-in-law, and love you as a son. I lost my father violently, too, you know.'

'Yes, we are similar in that way.'

Lizbet moved back to sit with Nevin, wrapping her arms about him, kissing him.

'Just think how our destinies are all connected,' she said. 'If it hadn't been for Mel and the aliens this little babe in me would never have happened!'

Hannah leaned over and kissed Nevin too.

'I'm not so sure,' said Harley, pondering. 'I think you would've found each other somehow.'

In April that year, Lizbet gave birth to a son, William David Prinzenthal James—Billy, they called him. In 1989, Marie Rebeque Greenfield James followed, and in 1994, another girl, Hannah Lizbet Ephrussi James.

Nevin, having risen to the top of the General Counsel for the CIA—short of the political appointee in the top position—accepted a job as counsel with a multi-national corporation where he became far more financially prosperous. He and Lizbet lived extremely busy lives, both working and raising their children.

Harley passed away in 1998 in his sleep at ninety-six, and was cremated. His ashes were cast adrift to the elements at sea tearfully by his beloved family from his yacht, the *Hannah Lizbet.*

*

Although the Melbos had adjusted well to their new life in Montreal, there was always the question of 'What would have been?' had they remained in New York City. For twenty years they made a life for themselves there even though the feeling of being displaced persons never really abandoned them. They never needed reminding of why they were there. After all, life was far more preferable to death at the hands of Joe di Lucca or his ilk, which always got their attention.

For the rest of his days, Mel used Will Kane as his professional pseudonym, but when they moved to Toronto at about the time of Nevin and Lizbet's marriage, they reverted officially to George and Melissa Melbo, although their kids grew up with the Melbo name. Melissa gave birth to two boys in three years, Harley and Jim in 1965 and 1968, and a girl, Anna, ten years later, in 1978.

For many years, Mel toiled on a book about their lives and the events leading to their moving to Canada, however, some people in the publishing business deemed it too far-fetched. It was suggested he write a sci-fi novel, which demoralized him. It wasn't that they didn't believe him; it was just that they felt there was no market for the truth, but really they were shirking the truth because of the potential liabilities. Mel struggled. The fact that he had been fired from the now defunct *New York Herald Tribune* and then joined a tabloid said it all: it dogged him as someone who was not credible; the smear continued. Those years were lean for the Melbos; they had a great house but little money.

During the late eighties and the nineties up to the present, Mel was delighted that numerous whistleblowers spoke up about the vast hyper-classified alien programs, one such person was the physicist Bob Lazlo, and another, army Colonel Philip Costa, an associate of the National Security Council, who opened up about the reality of high level alien contact—the public having been for so long inured to unacknowledgement by the government—that is, the legitimate government, which was actually clueless as to what was really going on in Area 51—to the incredible implications of an illegitimate government buried within the legitimate one.

But Mel still felt stymied with the real problem—namely, the mainstream media, who wouldn't follow through with at least sensational headlines about these whistleblowers that could have read: *Secret Government Programs Have Been Working With Alien Technology For Seventy Years!* But, no, it smacked of tabloid journalism! With the conspicuous silence of the legitimate government, the media had in effect endorsed non-disclosure by defaulting to the government's position in a conspiracy of silence, promulgated by the CIA and its agents within the system.

Yet, to the many thousands who had seen extraterrestrial vehicles around the country and world, it was the biggest manifestation of important events ever in the annals of civilization—a conundrum that screamed for resolution. Furthermore, this secret government would kill to protect their control of the technology and information, hundreds of years ahead of mainstream science. No wonder they didn't want to be held accountable.

Reluctantly, Mel began to write a more comprehensive approach in the form of a novel based on fact, entitled *Kennedy's Ghosts*, which the foreword, written by Nevin James, formerly of the CIA, decried the misapprehensions of the press about the truth. As William Kane, Mel was eventually successful in finding a modest publisher, and subsequently found himself once again receiving letters, then emails from all sorts of characters claiming inside stories about aliens and the secret world hegemon. Some were ex-special forces security personnel, various air force people, including an air force weatherman named Charles Small, who in the sixties based in Indian Springs, Nevada, befriended tall white aliens while on solitary nocturnal missions into other parts of the restricted, vast empty Nevada Test Range desert, places called Area 53 and 54, where an alien stopover base was constructed in the side of a mountain to house the aliens, their families and spacecraft when visiting Earth.

And there were other important insiders such as Hillard Doty, who, after their twenty-five year oath of secrecy had expired, spoke up about various recruitments in the news media for counter-intelligence operations, to serve both the debunking and dissemination of alien reality. The secrecy was everything, yet to those in the know, it was an open secret, which effectively acted as an excellent cover. Mel was bewildered by the human propensity to bury its heads in the sand, the likely reason being its fear of extermination, as often portrayed in the movies, or its plain ignorance.

In the tens of thousands, perhaps hundreds of thousands of years, or longer, that alien species have known of the existence of Earth, never have they threatened us. That's a long time. However, Melbo discovered that once we developed the atom bomb and used it—and with its proliferation around the world—ETs had no choice but to contain our violent and xenophobic impulses as a threat to them and the substratems of space itself, of which we have little understanding.

According to numerous accounts of military personnel, they even shut down missile bases and deactivated test ballistic missiles in orbit to make their point. We were not welcome in space until our motives and consciousness became altruistically pure—the search for truth and scientific enlightenment, and not the acquisition of technology and power for terrestrial struggles. Our predisposition to ignorance, and in the estimation of the ET's far higher consciousness, we are as a whole, primitive. Neil Armstrong and Buzz Aldrin, the first men on the moon, revealed privately that they had been warned off the moon, where on the dark side, clusters of numerous buildings of all shapes and sizes had been seen, some of which were ancient.

Upon landing on the moon, they were watched by a number of alien spacecraft hovering at the edge of the crater, and they relayed this alarming sight to ground control, who using the live delay feed cut out the pre-filmed footage and the astronauts' reactions to an unassuming public. Upon returning to Earth, Armstrong and Aldrin were threatened with death, as well as their loved ones, by the secret government if they went public with their knowledge. Because of their high profile. they were deemed to be a serious threat to the covenant of secrecy.

Aldrin apparently suffered a nervous breakdown on account of it. Mel concluded that humanity had a long, long way to go before they would be welcomed into the galactic community, perhaps thousands of years. *But we know the truth!* he wrote. *We know the Big Picture! It is a starting point, an inception, from which to begin the healing of ourselves and our beautiful planet if it were widely known.*

Mel envied the experience and subsequent story by a Pulitzer Prize winning journalist, who claimed to have been abducted, or "borrowed" by aliens near San Diego. This conservative, hard-bitten fellow, who had disdained anything 'pseudo-science' or controversial without incontestable facts, had to agree with his friends' skeptical reaction when he told them of his experience, as it would have been his own; the friends then distanced themselves from him because they believed he had gone "silly in the head".

Now deceased, this journalist, Philip Kraft, had reported diligently in a couple of books a detailed account of what had happened to him 'beamed' up—a bit like in *Star Trek*—with what began from a blue light appearing in his bedroom—he had thought initially that he had left the TV on—to a massive ship parked on the dark side of the moon. He was astounded to find there were a hundred other humans that were "invited" as well, some well-known personages. The ship was a mile wide and at least thirty stories tall, inhabited by thousands of alien people, barely distinguishable as male or female.

They were an ancient species—a couple of hundred million years beyond the human timeline. The reality was beyond comprehension. Mel had met with Kraft, and felt he was the most unlikely and begrudgingly reluctant abductee. "Ignorance is bliss," Kraft had said. "But when something like that happens, you change."

A few years after Harley's death, the Melbos sold their home in Toronto which had increased tremendously in value, and bought a country place in Southern Georgian Bay by the water, where they would remain for the rest of their lives. Previously, over the years they had taken affordable trips to Europe whenever they could, to visit the Greenfields in Paris, and to take their children on driving excursions around France and neighboring countries.

Once or twice a year they visited New York City, or Washington, and of course, St. Barthélemy, where they were always welcome to stay and to sail with Harley, who liked to be on the water whenever possible, even in his last years, as long as someone could manage to help sail the boat for him. On a number of occasions they invited Harley and Hannah to their lovely lakeside home and rented a yacht to cruise the Thirty Thousand islands of Georgian

Bay, which they found absolutely fantastic, sailing the archipelago of pink and gray granite, pine and water, so clear one could see fifty feet down. Nevin, Lizbet and kids even accompanied them a few times.

In New York on that fateful morning in 2001, they all sat stunned in Hannah's apartment in front of the television set, watching the news of the horrific 9/11 terrorist attacks on the World Trade Center, the Pentagon in Washington, and the crashed plane in Pennsylvania. The Melbos were visiting, and Lizbet was there on an assignment; she was at the door ready to leave, when Nevin called her immediately from Washington after the first jet had reportedly crashed into the North Tower. He then rushed straightaway to pick up the kids, who were already at school.

'What would Harley have thought about this?' asked Melissa, in a kind of rhetorical stupefaction. 'It's an obvious terrorist attack.'

'Squash them,' replied Hannah, in her singular way. 'Just another ideological totalitarian barbarism not worthy of diplomatic elaboration.'

More coverage of the massive hit on the Pentagon showed first responders and military personnel scrambling to save lives; and shocking footage of desperate people climbing out of the towers and hanging on for dear life only to fall to their deaths. And there was mention of the other hijacked plane.

'Alqatalat alqatalat mithl hdha la yastahiquwn alrahma, inshallah—murderous killers like that deserve no mercy, God willing,' said Lizbet, in Arabic.

'The insanely evil behavior of these terrorists will curtail indefinitely any hope of welcoming contact with the aliens,' remarked Mel, at sixty-seven, disillusioned about the human condition.

'More war,' said Hannah, sadly. 'But they'll have to be careful how they go about finding the terrorists, or innocents will be caught in the middle; and these kinds of people have no qualms about using them as human shields by hiding in their midst.'

The first tower suddenly collapsed in a heap of twisted steel, dust and rubble.

'Oh my God!' uttered Melissa.

'All those people!' cried Lizbet. 'And I was supposed to be downtown!'

'If Nevin hadn't called you, you would've gone,' said Melissa. 'We hadn't a clue.'

Melissa DeCourt Melbo, at sixty-three years of age, had turned out to be a rather obdurate and implacable spirit from long years of exile from her native New York; and from her conviction that there could be little change in the human condition. Her husband, ever the optimist, inspired her to think bigger, as his work had led them to early success with his articles about politics and the government cover-up concerning aliens. But when everything went sideways because Mel knew too much about the dark forces commensurate with the entrenchments of the Cold War, they had targets on their backs. This brought home the brutal reality of evil and the helplessness of decent citizens even in the most supposedly progressive of democracies long ago established by the Founding Fathers.

For many years in Montreal, she became depressed and even embittered, but for her overriding sense of humor. This and raising a family saved her, and Mel's undying love. She once dreamed of attaining wealth and prestige in the world of arts and society. New York was its lodestone, and she was an aspiring diva of the new generation with acquaintances like Marilyn Monroe, Jake Whitmore and a host of connections to the rich and powerful, including Jackie Kennedy herself. She was even an insider to the secret world, all to be abandoned for a life of obscurity. She cherished her lifelong friends the Greenfields, and, later, Nevin and Lizbet, and other friends she made in Canada, knowing most of them had suffered relative challenges.

Harley and Hannah were lucky to have survived at all, given the dangers and near-death experiences in their extraordinary past. Even Lizbet suffered on her parents' account, having absorbed their stories and troubles over time, even though she had been well-insulated from them. This may have inspired her interest in karate and self-defense, leading her to achieving a black belt by the age of twenty-one and winning a few awards on the way. And Nevin, of course, had lost his father to a most insidious crime.

But Melissa felt she had lost out in life. She was still beautiful, and as she grayed, she dyed her hair the luscious brunette it had always been, though she kept it shorter to her shoulders. But the blue eyes, damask lips and lovely skin withstood the test of time. She worked out constantly biking and swimming, even taking up tennis, all of which kept her fit. Professionally, she became a dedicated administrator in successive magazine companies; but, with the decline of readership in recent years, and the passing of her parents, who left her two hundred and forty thousand American dollars, she began to invest shrewdly.

For instance, she caught the Apple Inc. resurgence by buying in June 1997 two hundred thousand shares at fifty-one cents a share and selling them fifteen years later at ninety-five dollars a share. While Mel continued to write and make a pittance, she became a multi-millionaire. But they were older and the money didn't seem to have much of an effect on their general way of life after so many years of living frugally, because happiness had been hard-won that way and it didn't occur to them to change.

'You're right, Mel,' said Lizbet, at forty, looking at her with those formidable Greenfield eyes, now red from emotion and anger. 'But we do now have a clue. I will find them!'

'Darling,' said Hannah, knowing her daughter's mind, 'Please be careful. You'll have your chance to help get these horrid people who planned this attack. The agency will need you because of your skills, but today and for the next few days let the authorities get a grip on the situation before you go home. No one knows what's going on yet. There could be more attacks.'

'Your mom's right,' said Melissa.

They continued to watch the reports of destruction on television, stunned in mournful silence. Then the second tower collapsed in a sickening thunderous repeat of the first, the dust spreading across lower Manhattan, and people emerging covered and choking as if from a war zone.

*

When the Berlin Wall came down on 9 November 1989, the Greenfields were in Washington, having been present, over three weeks prior on 17 October at the birth of their granddaughter, Marie. Hannah had been invited by the State Department to speak to the new recruits from human resources, beginning both internships and fellowships, about her experiences during and since the war. She captivated her audience with Cold War tales of intrigue, barely disguising her role in the CIA, which gave her a unique perspective.

With the infamous Wall being broken and lying in pieces, there was great celebration among the warriors who were still alive almost thirty years after the dark days of its building. One evening at the James' residence with Lizbet nursing the baby, Hannah made a solemn promise to visit *Oświęcim* in Poland, universally known as Auschwitz, the unspeakable industrial-sized Nazi deathcamp and massive factory complex, where Lizbet Ephrussi and her family were sent and met their frightful deaths.

It was planned that the entire family would go including a nanny for the youngest children, but because of Nevin's and Lizbet's incredibly busy lives, and the birth of another baby, Hannah, in 1994, it wasn't until late spring 1996 that they all embarked on their family trip to Europe. Their old furnished house in the Paris suburb of Garches had until recently been leased for about fifteen years, when after the tenants vacated the house, it was put up for sale, but not before the owners had the use of it one last time while they were on holiday.

An eleven seat minibus was reserved, and the very back seats were removed to make space for their luggage. Nevin drove with Harley up front, where he found it easier getting in and out, using his hand on the support handle above the door to help pull himself up into the seat. He used a cane for a bad knee; on good days, depending on the weather, he could make do without it, but he was slow and would tell everybody in his gruff way not to wait, as he would catch up. Nobody listened, though in deference to his seniority they would wait far enough ahead to let him have his way.

Clara, the sweet, buxom nanny, and actually one of Dave Washington's nieces, had recently graduated from high school. Hired to help out on the trip, because she had babysat the kids for a number of years, she was utterly devoted to the family, and they loved and trusted her.

After a week in Paris, they drove south to Fontainebleau, the region in which Harley had been undercover during the last three years of the war. He operated in the upper Loire east from Nevers to Saumer in the west and Fontainebleau to the north, and even as far as Bourges and the *Régime de Vichy* to the south. Little known stories had emerged in his last decade of life about his war years; various operations to sabotage Nazi supply lines and help the escape of airmen, who had survived after being shot down.

The killing of Nazi SS officers was always a priority, but a delicate operation because of the Nazi propensity for extreme revenge on the innocent inhabitants of the villages, towns and communities, the most infamous being the massacre of the entire population of *Oradure-sur-Glane* just south of Harley's turf, when some six hundred-forty-two men, women and children were killed shortly after D-Day. He directed his family to a village and old church cemetery, where he laid flowers on a gravestone inscribed with *Hélène Laframboise et bébé à naître ---- 28 Avril 1916 ---- 8 Mai 1944 ---- Elle est morte pour la France*; Harley said she had been *une femme de très courageuse de la résistance.*

Tears came to his eyes as Hannah held him, for she knew that the baby had been his. Hélène had been executed with two other resistance fighters, both males, by the SS after being betrayed by a fascist Vichy army intelligence officer, who himself was later killed by Harley and members of the resistance during the *libération*. Nevin, standing behind them in that old haunted graveyard with Lizbet, Clara and the kids, considered how fate could be so twisted, and how all their lives could so easily have been different but for random tragic events over a half a century ago.

They continued east, first through Burgundy, then Switzerland and Germany, Austria, Czech Republic and finally Poland. There was no hurry; they enjoyed the sights and stopped frequently to visit places of interest, staying in rural hotels and eating well. The children were given opportunities to play and attend fêtes and visit castles wherever possible; they even spent time on lakes and rivers to cool off during a heatwave.

In Poland, they stayed in Kraków in the Old Town district, which offered a relief from their all-day visit to Auschwitz-Birkenau about fifty kilometers to the west. Hannah had spent some time in Kraków when she was living in Warsaw undercover in the early 1950s courting a Polish military attaché with the Soviet command who had grown up in the city.

Under cloudy skies, their tour of Birkenau was as expected, a very solemn affair; only little Hannah seemed oblivious, though Billy, at eleven, and Marie, in her seventh year, had been told what happened, and they kept asking questions, all of which Nevin attempted to answer, while Hannah and Lizbet walked ahead. What little remained of the massive gas chambers, and vast area of barracks of the inmates had little effect on the haunting magnitude of human genocide that had taken place there during the war.

Hannah kept feeling a sense of static in her mind; a cacophony of torment from legions of individuals whose voices or spirits cried out in terror. Then the whispering silence of the fields where the ashes of over a million men, women, and children had been spread, counteracted the noise in a kind of sonic hush.

Over the years, Hannah had made numerous enquiries about the fate of Lizbet Ephrussi and her family, but had come up empty-handed, until a journal written by a now deceased survivor was published by an Israeli Holocaust organization. In this journal a young woman was mentioned "Lizzi", who defied a Nazi officer and guards, when she was separated from her parents and younger siblings upon arrival at Birkenau. A guard beat her with a club, and yet stubbornly she kept standing up, bleeding profusely from her head, telling him calmly in Yiddish: "*Ir zent ale zayer krank mentshn.*" *You are all very sick men.*

Finally, while tottering slightly with a smile on her face, she managed to say in German: "*Ich hoffe das passiert deiner Tochter nicht.*" *I hope this doesn't happen to your daughter*, before falling down and then being summarily shot in the head. Hannah had stood for half an hour in the area where the prisoners were known to have been disgorged, filthy and half-dead, from the cattle cars to be separated; later, she went to the ruins of the gas chambers and crematoriums, and stood there for another half hour; and finally she walked out to the forest and fields beyond near a pond. '*Ick visn ez iz geven ir, Lizzi,*' she said in Yiddish. *I know it was you, Lizzy.* Her tears welled up and flowed down her cheeks. '*Ikh gebrakht meyn mshpkhh tsu bazukhn ir.*' *I brought my family to visit you.*

At that moment, a glorious ray of sunshine broke through the overcast sky, inviting them all to look up and smile. Harley moved toward Hannah, saying: 'Look, dear.' He pointed his cane, not at the sky, but at some shrubs by the pond, where a little blue bird sang joyfully. Hannah saw it too.

'Blue was Lizzy's favorite color,' she said, now beaming. 'Is that you, Lizzy?'

They found out later that bluebirds were not native to Europe, but to North America, and they were astounded by the anomaly. They could only presume that the bluebird had escaped from an aviary. While that may have been true, Hannah begged to differ, citing a miracle and that Lizbet had actually appeared to them on a need-to-know from God.

Sequel to follow: *Tamara's Gift*